THE CROSSING POINT

TALES OF THE NEPHILIM BROTHERHOOD

AUGUST ARREA

VII
PUBLISHING

Printed in the United States of America
First Printing 2021
First Edition 2021

ISBN: 978-1-7371661-3-9
Library of Congress Control Number: 2021908982

10 9 8 7 6 5 4 3 2 1

To request permissions, contact the publisher at:

VII Publishing
P. O. Box 1272
Clovis, CA 93613
www.viipublishing.com

Book Cover Design by: Diana Chituleska

For my Mom and Dad,
whose unwavering love and support has guided me to this,
and many other pivotal crossing points in my life.

TABLE OF CONTENTS

CHAPTER ONE

In The Beginning

There were four things Max Kelly had drummed into his head by his father from the day he could understand such things:

First, he was told, there exists in the world a true darkness; a darkness far more minacious than a night whose blackness even a sea of stars would fail to pierce with their collective brightness. One light, and one light only, is effective in burning back this murky brume. Veer even slightly from the guide of this beacon and you may find yourself swallowed up by the gloom.

Secondly, stay vigilant to the shadows belonging to those who cross your path, as they have an unfailing tendency to reveal much more than meets the eye about the persons who cast them.

Thirdly, never, under any circumstance, remove your shirt and expose your naked back in public, no matter if prodded by the sweat from a sweltering summer heat, or the inviting whim of running into the waves of an ocean. Do so and you might discover far too late that you've positioned yourself in the crosshairs of those set out into the world to hunt your kind and, before you know it, the unfortunate position that can visit a turtle when it finds itself wobbling helplessly on its back with its tender underbelly exposed to the sharpened beak of a hungry heron is suddenly yours. The father paused suddenly, and the young boy, after hearing the first three of the ominous edicts, prodded somewhat reluctantly, "And the fourth?"

Imagine, the father continued while looking deeply into his son's face, what strained, hoarse sounds would escape one whose throat had been severed from ear to ear. If such a horrible sound were ever to prick up your ears, and such breath were to instantly turn the air around you as frigid as the most frozen corner of the world, know the moment is at hand to gather your wits about you, for danger has already set its sights upon you and, like a coiled cobra, is poised to strike.

These were not, as Max was told, just random words of wisdom a father decides to pass on to his son. Then again Max's father was no ordinary father; he was an angel. Not the kind a person of exemplary virtue and conduct is deemed by others with less-than-stellar scruples, but a living, breathing winged entity of the biblical order. Which, by definition, meant Max was no ordinary boy but the son of an angel. Or, to be more precise, a Nephilim. And the words Max's father made a point to sow deep into his young son's impressionable mind were not casual parental directives to follow or not follow as he so chose, but the four commandments vital to survival—Max's survival, and the survival of all Nephilim who looked forward to reaching adulthood.

As is the nature of young minds, however, staying focused on such things, even those as important as life and death, can prove to be fleeting. And so, it happened late one night when the Australian teenager emerged with his friends from inside a packed theater where the excitement of the latest action-packed superhero movie had rendered him deaf and blind to any of the "warnings" his father had tried desperately to instill in him.

"Ow'bout the park for a smoke?" William (but Billy Goat to his circle of friends) suggested with a sly grin, patting the pocket over his chest of his jacket, as the group of friends huddled near the concessions stand and bandied about what to do next.

"I'm pretty knackered," said Max. "Probably just head on home."

"Home? It's not even midnight." balked Tyler, looking genuinely offended at the idea of turning in at such an early hour.

"Seriously...what's the rush Cinderfella?" Max's best friend Liam chimed in.

"Nick off," muttered Max under his breath. "You know how my father is; doesn't like me trolling around late."

"And mine doesn't like it when I do steamship impersonations out my backside at the breakfast table," said Tyler. "What's your point?"

"Son of the year, you are," Liam commented with repugnance as if imagining the unpleasant, dirty fog hanging over the family meals in the Kingston household.

"How much trouble can you get into anyway? I mean, your 'ol man's already packing you off to…what prep school did you say you're being shipped to?" James asked Max.

"You got gum in yer ears? I already told you a hundred times, it's not a prep school," answered Max. "Besides, you wouldn't have heard of it anyways if I told you the name. And they're not shipping me off."

"What would you call it, then?"

"They're sending me…and not against my will either, I might add."

"Shipping, sending…it's all the same thing for getting yer grubby arse out of their hair," snickered Tyler.

As was the case whenever the subject of his leaving was brought up—especially the new school that seemed to be a growing curiosity amongst his friends—Max was eager to shift the discussion elsewhere, and so he excused himself to go to the restroom where nature was urgently calling on him to "strain the potatoes," as he put it.

"Wait up, I'll go with," said Liam, following after Max.

Walking into the men's room, the two teens found it to be as busy as Sydney's Central railway station, and just as noisy. Only instead of trains, the ruckus came from a continuous cacophony of flushing urinals and toilets struggling to keep up with the urgent emptying of straining bladders and other more involved bodily functions. Maneuvering their way through a steady stream of comings and goings, they happily found themselves lucky enough to sidle up to a pair of vacancies at one of the porcelain troughs without having to wait.

Then it began; the humming. Liam had a most annoying habit of humming incessantly whenever he lifted his leg, so to speak. Focusing straight ahead on the maroon and ivory-colored pattern of the tile wall, Max did his best to go about his business while trying to drown out the one-man symphony playing out next to him. Not that it proved too difficult to ignore; his packing up and leaving, even if it was still a few weeks away, had been foremost on his mind as of late. Sure, he'd had all of his young life to prepare for this long-awaited moment he'd eagerly been anticipating since he was five years old when the day came his father sat him down and explained—along with the first mention of the golden rules of survival—how his life would unfold. Until now, it had always been something hovering way out in the far-distant future, like a big red circle marking the date on a calendar longingly eyed by a prison inmate who feels as if the sands of time were passing through the hourglass one grain at a time. Now that the date was suddenly closing in on him, Max found it difficult, if not impossible, to think about or focus his attention on much of anything else, so much so he didn't at first even notice the sudden flickering of the lights. Then the fluttering became more pronounced with the restroom falling dark for a second or two before the faltering lights recovered again. Whatever happened to cause it also managed, thankfully, to pull the plug on Liam's humming.

"Looks like someone forgot to pay the power bill," said Liam with a soft chuckle.

Max gave up a weak grin in return while tilting back his head and looking to the ceiling where one of the fluorescent lighting fixtures was mounted directly above him. The sound of the power wavering came in a struggling hum followed by a loud crackle, like dry kindling burning in a fireplace, as the lights proceeded to gently flicker several more times. His smile, however, was quick to fade when another voice suddenly came to tug at his ear lobe. It approached him from somewhere behind, in a low drawn-out whisper, yet loud enough to cut through and drown out the rest of the echoing clamor in the busy restroom.

"Nephilim…"

The word let loose a cold chill to run the length of Max's spine. With a slow turn of his head, he peered over his shoulder with heightened caution. His sights immediately came to rest on a closed door to one of the dozen or so toilet stalls lining the far wall several feet directly behind him.

"Neeeephilimmmmm…"

Max's gaze wandered downward to the open space at the bottom of the door where a pair of sensible brown shoes peeking out from khaki pants pushed down around the ankles were clearly visible; hardly a nefarious sight, or one to cause suspicion. Then a rather curious, if not startling, thing happened; to Max's surprise, the shadow of the faceless person sitting on the porcelain throne inside, formed by the light shining down from above and resting puddle-like at the feet of its owner, began to stir. Slowly it began to stretch itself forward in a most unusual and unnatural way. The shadow proceeded to crawl out of the stall beneath the locked door, even as its owner remained motionless inside; at least that Max could see through the small sliver of space made where the door was hinged. Again, Liam's humming went abruptly silent when he looked over and noticed right away the strange look fixed on Max's face.

"What is it, mate…or are you scouting the place for a date?"

Max said nothing. The fact Liam looked to see what had grabbed his friend's attention in such a way and saw nothing out of the ordinary that would interfere with him cracking wise only raised the willies he felt squirming in the pit of his stomach. He then proceeded to give a quick glance to the other people who were forming a constant traffic in and out of the restroom, and not a one seemed to take notice of the shadow, even as they passed right by it. And for a split-second Max questioned if somehow he was imagining it. Perhaps, he wondered, he had suffered a special effects overdose caused by the movie he had just seen that was causing him to hallucinate, in the same way a barrage of flashing lights can trigger seizures in people suffering from epilepsy.

Still, hallucination or not, he didn't once dare to blink as he eyed the shadow, appearing as human-shaped as he assumed its owner to be, when it seemed to suddenly look directly at him, even though its black faceless shape of a head was devoid of any eyes. And again, he heard the menacing hiss of a voice.

"Neeeephilimmmmm..."

This was no mirage, no matter if no one else was privy to what he was seeing. Nor was there any doubt they were feeling what he was feeling, as he noticed several faces suddenly take on stricken looks of discomfort and cursing glances turned to the air vents above when a sharp, icy coldness settled itself inside the restroom. No, this was real. And suddenly all the countless warnings his father had made it a point to drill into his consciousness about light and shadows and sounds began ringing inside his ear in an overlapping swirl of words yet delivered a succinct and direct message: Get out of there!

"Max, what is it?" Liam's voice took on a sudden lower register of concern. Max's eyes remained squarely on the shadow.

"You don't see it, do you?"

It wasn't so much a question as an unsettling observation.

"Afraid of a little power surge, are you?" needled Liam still oblivious to what had stricken his friend. "Don't worry, I'll save you from the scary drop bears if the lights go out."

Drop bears. If only it was as simple as something as trivial and juvenile as some old Australian childhood myth about giant carnivorous koalas with sharp teeth and razor-like claws leaping out of trees onto the heads of unsuspecting victims wandering below in the dark and devouring them alive, Max thought to himself. There was nothing irrational, however, about what made his blood go suddenly ice-cold in his veins. And for a moment, brief as it was, Max found himself almost envying Liam's complete obliviousness to what was creeping just a few steps away. However, being that he was denied the luxury afforded his friend, Max quickly zipped himself up, and without saying another word pushed his way through the flow entering and leaving the restroom.

He managed to make it out of the theater and down the tree-lined walkway of the mall leading to the parking garage before, to his dismay, he heard the sound of pounding feet running after him accompanied by Liam's cries to stop. Cursing under his breath, Max picked up speed and raced on into the garage where he tried to throw Liam off his trail by winding his way through the rows of cars parked inside, but it did no good. Liam remained fast behind him like a bloodhound in pursuit of a prisoner making a break for freedom until Max finally gave up trying to shake him off his tail.

"What's the matter with you...your ears need hosing out?" snarled Liam in between heaving gasps as he struggled to catch his breath from his labored chase. "Didn't you hear me calling you?"

"Sorry I have to bail on you like this mate, but I got get home," said Max.

"So you decide to just ditch me in the dunny with only me dragon in hand?"

Before Max could open his mouth to answer his alert attention was drawn to one the large florescent lights at the opposite end of the garage as it began to flicker noticeably, just as it occurred inside the theater restroom. Max swallowed nervously as he watched the light struggle to remain lit before going out. A moment later, the rest of the large lighting fixtures lining the length of the concrete parking structure began following suit.

CLAM...

CLAM...

CLAM...

One by one the lights began shutting off with a loud, echoing bang, much like a switch being thrown over and over, paving a path of darkness directly toward where the boys were standing until the entire floor of the structure was doused in night.

"You gotta blow through, mate," Max urged Liam in as calm a whisper as he could muster.

"Blow through?" said Liam half smiling and half swamped in confusion.

"I mean it...get out of here now!"

"You get bit by a mad dingo or something? What d'ya mean go?" asked Liam. "You forget you're my ride?"

Max wasn't listening. He turned his head this way and that, trying to catch sight of something he sure was there lurking in the nighttime darkness amid the field of parked cars inside the garage.

"Ahhhh, I get it now." Liam's voice suddenly sang out. "Decided to try and lead 'ol Liam here up the garden path and give me a fright, did ya?"

Max's gaze shifted to Liam, and even in the darkness he could make out a grin on his friend's mug. "What the blazes you talking about?"

"Give it away, mate. In all me years knowing you, I've never seen you turn yellow for anything or anyone. Now all of a sudden it's 'Get out of here Liam...the drop bears are coming!' " said Liam mocking what sounded like a little ankle-biter on the verge of wetting his nappy.

What Liam said was true; Max had never been one to show fright of much of anything in life, be it bullying boys bigger than himself or the slithering, creepy creatures one sometimes crossed paths with in the outback. The menacing shadow in the restroom was an altogether different thing. And even as it offered up a heaping helping of fear Max rarely tasted, what sent him scurrying out of the restroom and away from the theater had more to do with wanting to protect his friend than seeking safety. Now, here was Liam without the slightest clue of what he was mocking.

"So where are they?" asked Liam.

"Where's who?"

"Me so-called cobbers," said Liam, looking around the garage for a glimpse of the rest of their friends he was certain were crouched out of sight behind one of the cars sniggering over the attempts to give him a good-natured fright. "My guess is they're responsible for playing with the lights."

"Liam..." It was all Max could do to keep what calm he had intact and not crack Liam on the side of his head.

"Tyler...Billy Goat...James...I know you're out there hiding somewhere giggling like a bunch of little kindies," Liam called out. "Nice try, but pretty weak if you ask me you amateur dags."

The sound of Liam's voice echoing loudly throughout the cavernous garage made Max grit his teeth until he couldn't take it anymore.

"Can ya shut your gob already?" he barked under his breath while grabbing hold of Liam roughly by the collar of his shirt. "This isn't a joke. Can'ya get that through that thick melon of a'ed you've got?"

By the look in Liam's eyes, Max had managed to take hold of his full attention.

"Now for the last time, can you for once do what I ask and go. I'll explain later...but for now just move your arse and get the hell out of here!"

"Your breath," remarked Liam oddly.

Max cocked his head and gave Liam a look of utter disbelief. Really, we're going to comment on the state of my breath at a time like this? he thought to himself. That is until he, too, took notice of the small plumes of vapor escaping from his mouth with every breath he took. It was then both boys became alert that something remarkably freakish was happening. The warm, sultry evening suddenly gave way to a sharp, biting cold, as if winter itself had arrived full tilt and gave the last lingering nights of summer a bullying shove aside. The abrupt uncomfortable change moved through the boys' thin cotton clothing like hundreds of sharp needles pricking the suddenly goose-fleshed skin of their stiffening bodies.

"Bloody 'ell...there 'tis again," Liam mumbled through chattering teeth as his body shuddered. "Good trick, I'll give ya that."

A sudden jolt of dread moved through Max as he let go of Liam and again turned his attention back to the darkened garage.

"I told you it's not a trick," he muttered under his breath as his ears caught a most unnerving sound.

Something was there, of that there was no doubt. He could sense it. Worse, he could hear it. Strained, long-drawn, mucous-filled breaths, like someone at the receiving end of a brutal strangling struggling for breath. It was all just as his father had warned him so persistently. As was his nature, Max refused to give in to his veins fighting to reverse the flow of his blood and allow himself to go pale, and instead bravely took several steps out into the open, and importantly away from Liam, to face the thing that had chosen to stalk him.

"So, here I am," he called out. "You want to take me on, then let's give it a burl. But leave my friend out of it."

"Who the 'ell are you talking to?" asked Liam as he stood shivering.

"You 'ear me?" shouted Max, paying no mind to Liam.

He waited, and at first there was no answer; not a sound of any kind. Only the persistent coldness of what felt like the inside of a meat locker turned on to full arctic blast. Then, from somewhere amid the shadows, there came a noticeable scurrying, like the patter of feet—rodent feet—only larger.

Much larger.

"I'm not falling for it," Liam announced in as brave a voice as he could muster, even as it was clear in the way his feet started to slowly retreat that he was no longer certain he was the victim of a friendly prank.

"Stand still," ordered Max in a way that made Liam freeze in his tracks.

The scurrying continued. More unsettling was the fact that whoever—or whatever—was causing it seemed to be darting to and fro with a dizzying swiftness to all corners of the garage that was far too quick for any human—or animal, for that matter—to move. And then suddenly it stopped. The silence only heightened Max's angst, especially when he suddenly felt something lightly, yet most definitely, tap against his left shoulder. His eyes slowly shifted with a guarded hesitancy to look to see what it was, and found what appeared to be the sheen of something wet soaking itself into the fabric of his shirt.

"What is it?" whispered Liam, taking notice of Max's diverted attention.

The two boys could almost see the other's heart rise up into their throats as they witnessed more of the mysterious wetness drool down onto Max in thick, stringy drops. Whatever "it" was, it was coming from directly above them. And it was breathing, horrible hoarse breaths, like a diseased smoker gasping for air through a hole puncturing the trachea. Max was visibly trembling now, though he was certain it wasn't prodded by the intense cold. And even though there was absolutely nothing the world as a whole could present at that precise moment that would prove itself as more challenging and unpleasant than the simple task of having to look and see what had positioned itself over them, Max took a steadying breath and forced his eyes to roll themselves upward. And when he did no amount of courage salvaged from deep within could have prepared him for the terrible sight awaiting him.

~ ~ ~

At the same exact moment Max's cry of horror pierced the Australian night, Jacob Parrish awoke on the opposite side of the world to the drumming of rain pelting his window, his hand still clutching the rosary that hung around his neck and rested on his chest. Before turning in for the night and finally dozing off, he had managed to make his way through more than half the beaded strand.

Outside, the thunder and whistling winds that had raged through the night had finally receded and dissipated with the inky blackness of night giving way to the early morning downpour that fell with the almost peaceful, soothing patter of a tropical waterfall.

Struggling to open his eyes that remained weighted with the sands of sleep, Jacob managed to direct his gaze at the clock on the night stand a few inches away next to his bed. When he saw the time, he bolted upright, leapt to his feet and like a gazelle fleeing a lion on the hunt he made a mad dash for the bathroom.

He couldn't remember the last time he needed to set the alarm on his clock to wake him for school. His grandmother had performed the role quite well ever since she came to stay, jolting him awake every morning an hour before the start of school with three sharp knocks on his door that grew increasing louder every ten minutes that followed the longer he stayed in bed. Before that, it was his mother who took on the role of human reveille. Why he had not been graced with a wake-up call this morning, he had no idea, and with just ten minutes before the start of school he had no time to find out.

Jacob squeezed a dollop of toothpaste across his toothbrush sending half over the edge of the bristles to splatter on the sink in his rush. With one hand he quickly gave his teeth an abbreviated brushing while wetting his other hand under the faucet and running his fingers through his thick, bed-matted hair in a frenzied effort to smooth out the wayward strands. Not his best look, but it would have to do today. Tossing his toothbrush into the sink, he quickly spit out the mouthful of the frothy paste and rushed back into his bedroom. No time for rinsing.

Luckily for him he was already dressed with the jeans and T-shirt he had worn the day before and fallen asleep wearing. He raised his arms and gave his underarms a quick sniff. He was good to go, but fumbled through a pile of clothes on a nearby chair for a zip-up hoodie he could slip on to cover up his fashion faux pas of repeated wear. He then retrieved his book he attempted to read the night before from the floor next to the bed and shoved it into his backpack that he flung over his right shoulder while shuffling his feet dressed in hole-eaten socks into his sneakers. Five minutes left. He wanted to look in on his mother before he left, as did every morning before heading off to school, but there was no time. Throwing open his door, he rushed out into the hall. He was just about to tear down the stairs when he glanced toward his mother's room and stopped dead in his tracks. His grandmother was there, sitting on the needlepoint-covered chair outside the closed bedroom door.

"You didn't wake me this morning. I overslept."

She remained silent, sitting quietly with her hands folded in her lap and her head bowed.

"Grandma?"

"I thought it best to leave you sleep."

"On a school day?"

Jacob sensed something was wrong, the way she kept her face turned away from him and dabbing at her eyes in as inconspicuous a manner as possible.

"What's going on? You okay?"

When she finally looked toward him, his heart quickened in his chest at the sight of her face. She had been crying. Tears had left shiny streaks across her cheeks forming droplets along the edge of her jaw. Her eyes were red and glassy and fixed with an unmistakable look of resigned sorrow.

"What—?" Jacob began before quickly swallowing down the rest of his question. He already knew.

"I'm sorry, Jacob."

His grandmother stretched out her hand clutching a balled-up tissue.

No! It wasn't possible. Not after last night. Not after all his pleading and praying.

Jacob shrugged off his backpack which fell onto the floor with a loud thud and made a rush toward his mother's bedroom, but his grandmother rose up from the chair and blocked his way.

"It's too late, Jacob."

"The hell it is!" snapped Jacob.

He could have easily shoved her aside, but to his surprise she demonstrated an unexpected strength that managed to keep him at bay.

"You don't understand...I CAN FIX THIS...!" cried Jacob.

"You don't understand...It's not in your hands to fix," she replied in a restrained voice, yet just as passionately.

With his frustration raging and uncontrollable anguish coming in fiery bursts like a volcano erupting inside him, Jacob turned his unbridled distress onto the nearby wall with a hole-making punch. Then as the lava filled every inch of him with its painful burning, Jacob slowly receded down the hall toward the stairs as though backing away from an approaching bear whose path he'd stumbled upon in the woods.

"We have to let her go," his grandmother said softly. "She's in a good place now, healthy and free of pain. It's what God wanted."

"What God wanted?" A flash of anger and hatred came together and merged to shape a look that had never before revealed itself on Jacob's face. "WHAT GOD WANTED?"

He turned and darted down the stairs as fast as his feet could carry him before the bear he was fleeing from had a chance to pounce on him, tearing out the front door and into the torrential downpour being wrung from the shroud of black clouds that canvassed the sky. Parked in the street in front of the house, his friend Wray was already patiently waiting to give Jacob a ride to school. Upon catching sight of him, she cracked open her window.

"About time Sleeping Beauty," she ribbed jokingly.

Jacob paid her no attention, and Wray's fresh-faced smile quickly disintegrated as she watched him purposefully cut across the lawn—a path his mother had regularly scolded him for taking—and race away from the house as fast as his legs could carry him.

He'd always been a fast runner. Had he not acquired a fondness for wrestling, he might very well have flourished on the high school racing track. His feet pounded along the slick asphalt and cemented sidewalks, splashing through the pooling puddles as he raced down one street before veering down another, cutting through neighboring yards and leaping over shrubs and picketed fences framing picturesque homes that lined his path like hurdles in a marathon. He was like a wild stallion, heading for nowhere and galloping like mad to get to there.

His mad zig-zagging took him to a creek bed that bordered the northern end of the neighborhood that was now running loudly with the rainwater stirring it. Without even the slightest break in his stride, Jacob bounded over the stream and continued forward disappearing into the blanket of woods beyond. Still, no matter where his feet carried him, or how swiftly, he couldn't manage to outrun the sound of his mother's voice playing over and over again in his head.

"There is nothing else that can be done."

It was a tormenting chorus coming at him in heart-stabbing swells. For a while it looked as if finally, she was getting the upper hand on the merciless disease that had ravaged her well-being for such a long time. Such hope was dashed when Isabeth Parrish shared with her son the news from her doctor that things had taken an unexpected turn for the worse: her latest test results revealed the sickness had spread. With a vengeance. She was dying, and yet Isabeth revealed the crushing news to Jacob as calmly as if she was letting him in on her plans for a summer vacation. Only from this vacation she had no plans of returning, and the thought terrified Jacob. He could say he had already lost his father. Yet to lose something requires one to have had it in the first place. He had never known his father. The only explanation he was given was that he had simply disappeared long before Jacob was born, and the subject was never spoken about again. And although Jacob would now and then wonder about the man who had given him life and where he was in the world, he had come to accept the absence of not having a father. Now the one remaining pillar besides his grandmother he had left in his life was about to be snatched from him, and that was something with which Jacob found himself unable to make peace.

"It's okay, Jacob…"

The sound of Isabeth's voice continued to ring in Jacob's ears. The towering trees he weaved his way through offered little respite from the chill of the unrelenting shower falling from above, while those whose time had long ended lying broken and decaying across the sopping ground presented a checkered obstacle course of twisted and gnarled branches that Jacob cleared with the graceful ease of a bounding buck. A strong, sweet smell of wet forest earth filled the air, but it was the fetid scent of death which met Jacob's nose; the same ever-present bouquet of decay he had come to know inside his mother's bedroom, which even the lavender candle when lit on the dresser couldn't keep at bay. Witnessing his mother's physical beauty slowly come under attack was hard enough, with her long thick dark tresses first falling out in strands, and then shaming clumps, until she was left with a dome of baby-smooth skin; wondering silently whether her entire insides were somehow becoming an empty hull, hollowed out by the poison being pumped into her body and slowly deflating her in the process until she was nothing but skin and bones was even worse.

But the smell…

It was a constant reminder of death itself, as though its presence had somehow wormed its way inside the house and accompanied his mother up the stairs and into her bedroom as she grew weaker, hovering silently in the corner like an unwelcome guest waiting with festive patience for her to close her eyes one last time so it could move in and collect its grim reward. Yet no matter how desperate Jacob's bid to outrun both the sickening stench and his mother's voice, they kept fast to him—tormenting him.

"I knew the day the dove showed up on the ledge of my window that my days were drawing to a close, and that my Beacon had come to see me home," she had told him just the night before, when the sounds coming from the thrashing storm outside—and the distinct whispering of voices—drew him out of bed and down the darkened hall to his mother's bedroom, where he found her kneeling on the floor beside the opened window framed by delicate linen curtains being whipped about her by the wind like angry ghosts.

"What are you talking about...what Beacon?" asked Jacob, still trying to come to terms with the news of death Isabeth had only moments before dropped on her son like a head-crushing anvil, no matter how comforting she made her voice to deliver it.

"Each soul of every person born is assigned a Beacon," explained Isabeth while gently stroking the head of a dove that was huddled in its usual spot on the windowsill ever since the day several weeks back when it first appeared and refused to leave. "They take the shape of the birds you see gathered in the trees and flying through the air. Their sole purpose is to shadow the one soul they've been given the duty to keep a vigilant watch over during its time on Earth from the moment it cries out at birth to taking its final breath upon death, when it then accompanies the soul to its afterlife, much like a lighthouse guides a ship on a fog-choked ocean."

Jacob gave a skeptical glance at the dove cocooned in his mother's hands bobbing its head skittishly as the thunder rumbled loudly in the distance. He had long learned to quietly tolerate his mother's deeply rooted religious beliefs, but he found himself having to bite his tongue over her latest revelation.

"Or perhaps," he offered trying to mute somewhat the unmistakable sarcasm heard in his voice, "it's just some free-loading bird looking for the handout of birdseed you feed him every day, and not your soul."

Isabeth smiled slightly. It was just the sort the response she would expect from her pragmatic son.

"And who exactly told you all this business about birds being Beacons?" asked Jacob.

Isabeth breathed a somber sigh. "You wouldn't believe me if I told you."

Jacob was suddenly jolted free from the haze of the memory encircling him when his foot snagged against a stray tree root or rock along the sloping, uneven muddied terrain causing him to stumble forward before falling headlong into a hard tumble that sent his body head over heels downhill. Painful grunts were squeezed from him with every thudding thump his body made each time it hit the ground in what seemed to be a never-ending somersaulting fall from which he could not slow or stop. Then, as his rage became more red-colored and he wrestled with all his might to break himself free from whatever invisible hand gripped him and sent him spiraling like a bowling ball down a polished wooden lane toward a neatly arranged grouping of pins, there came a sudden, instantaneous brief moment when it seemed as if time stalled noticeably and gravity had come to a nonexistent end. Jacob felt the rolling of his body slow considerably and he managed to twist himself upright and regain his footing on the ground in a way no living thing had ever before been known to move. And not a moment too soon, as Jacob discovered the second gravity returned as he came to an instant motionless halt and found himself staring at the pointed end of a branch only a few jarring inches away from his torso, which would have most assuredly impaled him had he continued in his downhill plummet.

For a moment all was still and quiet, except for the patter of the rain. The pounding of Jacob's heart, which made itself heard in his ears, kept time with his jagged breathing as he stood wondering how he had managed such an incredible acrobatic feat while staring wide-eyed at the deadly looking branch aimed menacingly at him. His attention was then suddenly drawn to a fluttering movement he felt and heard pass by overheard. The tops of the towering trees surrounding him swayed in unison like blades of grass hit by a strong gust of wind before snapping back into place. Still slightly dazed and spinning from his fall, Jacob scoured the vacant treetops. It was there again, that familiar feeling which had been dogging him for the past few weeks, as though someone was following him, watching him.

His feet ignited again, and he was once more in full gallop, snaking his way through the cluster of trees that surrounded him like a wooded coven. Jacob soon spied a break where the woods were suddenly interrupted by a small clearing and he began running even faster. He oftentimes escaped to this peaceful nook as a young boy to search for frogs and lizards and watch the deer come to graze on the field of knee-high grass. Emerging from the dark thicket of trees, Jacob continued toward the center of the clearing before exhaustion finally forced him to a halt. The meadow was alive with the chorus of frogs chirping loudly from within the carpet of thick grass as they basked in the welcoming shower and frolicked in the pooling water. The deer, however, were nowhere to be seen, favoring dry shelter deep within the woods over a tempting meal of sweet, rain-washed grass.

With nowhere else to run, Jacob began pacing in an agitated circle in the center of the clearing, his hands cupping the back of his head as he fought to catch his breath. He was soaked through, his shirt, pants and shoes all caked in mud and pieces of dead leaves he had picked up from his tumbles on the ground. His chest heaved deeply straining both for air and attempting to stifle the great dueling waves of sorrow and anger welling in ever strengthening swells from deep inside where the pit of his being dwelled.

"Who are you crying for?" his mother's voice cooed gently in his ears.

Even the rain dribbling down Jacob's face couldn't camouflage the tears streaming from his reddening eyes. Jacob could feel the heat of his anger in them as they drooled their way down across his cheeks, and he tasted the salty bile they carried to the corners of his mouth.

"If your tears are for me, then you are wasting them. An end of one's time is not one to be mourned, but celebrated. For it means a door leading to our ultimate destiny is finally being opened to us, where not the grim figure of death awaits, but life."

The more his mother's voice rang inside his ears, the more briskly Jacob paced.

"Listen to me Jacob…what words have I made you take to heart to hold before you like a shield of armor when it seemed like all the rest of the world was lost to you?" she had asked him the night before while staring deeply into her son's eyes, even as his did their best to avoid hers. "The Lord is my shepherd; I shall not want. He maketh me to lie down in green pastures: he leadeth me beside the still waters."

Jacob knew the words even before his mother began reciting them. They had been instilled into him by his mother and committed to his memory from the earliest moment he could remember the pedals of his consciousness unfolding. And while Jacob had always been leery of the lighted path of faith his mother had blindly steered herself down, these righteous words, whether he liked it or not, had somehow taken root inside him and could be recalled without so much as a straining thought, the same way he inherently knew the fact that his hair was brown, or that his eyes were opposing hues of blue and green.

"Say it with me," Isabeth had sweetly urged her son, whose lips began to move along with his mother's voice even before her request as their last moments together quietly played themselves out. "He restoreth my soul: he leadeth me in the paths of righteousness for his name's sake. Yea, though I walk through the valley of the shadow of death, I will fear no evil: for thou art with me; thy rod and thy staff they comfort me."

However, the echoes he heard within the ghostly memory brought Jacob no comfort. If anything, it only served to further stir his rage and he suddenly became conscious of the rosary still hanging around his neck, and he reached for it. And as he did, he was reminded of the fear he was left with of losing his mother when he finally left her room. It was a bludgeoning fear that guided him back to his own room and lured him to the bottom drawer of his dresser where he quickly rifled through his balled-up clothes flinging several T-shirts over his shoulder onto the floor behind him until he uncovered buried at the bottom a holy hoard of a couple dozen rosaries of all shapes and colors his mother had given to him over the years in her failed attempts to pass her enlightenment onto him. He would always take them because it made her happy and then discard them in the drawer until his collection began taking on the appearance of an interwoven nest of beaded snakes.

Standing in the middle of the meadow, Jacob recalled reaching for the rosary which now hung around his neck from the top of the viper pile and studying the beauty of the rope of beads, a beauty he had failed to recognize when his mother first gave it to him. It was made of fine polished wood, and each bead had been delicately hand-carved into blossoming roses. Holding it also brought a strange feeling to him; a queasiness of sorts. It had been a long while since he last said the rosary, on his own, that is, without the guilt-filled urging to placate his mother. Yet say it he did, that night, while stretched out across his bed. And as he stumbled along trying to remember the order and words to the various prayers, he could hear the echo of his mother's voice reciting along with him, guiding him through the verses in that soothing supportive tone she had when she first taught him.

"Hail Mary, full of grace, the Lord is with thee..."

While making his way through the recitation, Jacob kneaded each bead between his thumb and forefinger as though he were rolling mini meatballs. And through it he felt a quiet awkwardness, as though he had been locked in a room with a friend he had just been in a fistfight with and told not to come out until hands had been shook, apologies had been made, and the friendship mended. The problem was his fight was with God—all of Heaven, actually—for what was happening to his mother, and his anger remained a festering wound which refused to heal. The rosary felt to Jacob like a strand of apologies he was being forced to make for a fight he had not provoked. Yet he had finally been pushed to the point where he was willing to try and let go of the grudge that sat in his core like a hardened peach pit, to shake that hand, to mend that friendship. If anything, for the sake of his mother. It was for her that he clutched those beads like a drowning man clings to a life preserver, mouthing the prayers over and over in a desperate mantra, hoping that the words would somehow come together like a secret password that would unleash a genie from within the magical rope and grant him a wish. Not three, but just one.

Only there was no genie. There was no magic, and certainly no granting of a wish. There was only the waking up to the news that his mother had been taken from him. Heaven had turned a deaf ear to Jacob, perhaps even laughingly so, despite his olive branch, despite his pleas. And for that, he had only three words left for the one with whom he had attempted to make amends.

"I hate you," he muttered quietly to himself before directing his gaze upward in the direction of the dark clouds which could be seen moving fast across the sky and appearing more like the smoke from a forest fire. Yet the true fire was in Jacob's eyes. For all the sorrow leaking from them, there was a glint of intense rage that was fixed and dilated on the sky above, yet directed beyond the cover gray blanketing it.

"Do you hear me?" Jacob called out louder. "I hate you!"

His grip on the rosary around his neck tightened, and with a sharp hateful tug he ripped it off and threw it as hard and as far away across the field as he could.

"I HATE YOU!"

A flash of lightning illuminated the black sky followed by a thundering boom.

"I hate you," Jacob whimpered falling to his knees.

~ ~ ~

At the same time Jacob became a broken pile, surrendering to the tidal wave of emotions he was unable to hold back any longer that finally engulfed him, leaving him wracked with sobbing, a figure loomed unseen at the edge of the clearing. He slowly made his way a short distance across the sopping field, stopping when the edge of his boot found the spot where the discarded rosary had come to land in a fit of rage. The figure reached down and picked it up, studying briefly the broken strand of beads in his hand. Then placing the rosary in the pocket of his long overcoat, the figure turned and retreated from the clearing as quietly as he came, leaving Jacob to suffer through his grief.

CHAPTER TWO

Three days after Isabeth Parrish was laid to rest at the small, park-like St. Michael's Cemetery, a figure wearing a dark, heavy overcoat stood at the front door of the Parrish home. Closing his eyes, he drew a deep breath and rapped the door with his knuckles, lightly at first, and then with a louder impatience.

"I'm coming, I'm coming," he heard a voice call out from inside.

Through the etched pane of glass in the center of the door, he caught the blurred movement of a figure approaching accompanied by the clicking of footsteps. And, even though the figure growing nearer looked warped and distorted in appearance as if moving inside the prism of a kaleidoscope, he knew instantly it was her. He managed to remain steadfast in his boots and gather back his stony impenetrable resolve that for a brief moment abandoned him when he heard the hand on the other side of the door take hold of the doorknob. Then, like a curtain parting, the door opened and there she stood.

"Yes, may I hel—"

Her greeting was bluntly snuffed by an audible gasp reserved for the rare moment when the heart stalls mid-beat and the lungs are inexplicably squeezed empty of air the moment she saw the face of the man standing on the side of the door, and the antique ivory teacup she was in the midst of drying slipped from her hand. It took a split second for the cup to fall and hit the ground. Yet, in the spheric pools that were his eyes, it seemed to float in the air, slowly rotating top over bottom in its downward descent, allowing him to capture every last detail of the delicate hand-painted green vine entwined around the cup just beneath the gold rim along with a pair of imprints on the bottom reading

"Haviland, France" and "Haviland Co. Limoges," stamped in red before shattering upon the floor.

"Gotham."

It had been so long since she uttered his name, it felt almost like taking a stab at speaking in a foreign tongue.

"Hello, Ava."

She appeared visibly stunned, staring in silent, yet overwhelming disbelief at the unexpected visitor standing in the doorway. How long, she wondered, had it been since she had last laid eyes on him, even as she knew it had been fifty long years that had passed since then. Now, here he suddenly was, looking exactly as he did the moment such images had long ago seared themselves into her memory.

Ava's hands began to nervously ring the dish towel she clutched tightly as she struggled to fight the urge she had to reach out and touch his face. To ensure he was real. And yet she couldn't bring herself to it, fearful to discover that it was only a cruel figment of her imagination brought on by the demented pleasures of old age.

Gotham could feel her distress in the shade of his shadow and he gave her time to grow accustomed to his presence until it seemed she couldn't take the sight before her anymore and quickly diverted her attention to the broken remains of the cup at her feet. He followed her down onto one knee, feeling bad that his unexpected arrival would cause her to lose such a beautiful piece of China that had meant so much to her.

"I'm sorry to have startled you."

"Not to worry. It's an old cup," she replied in as calm a manner as she could muster, averting his gaze that remained firmly on her as she hurriedly picked up the jagged pieces and placed them into the dish towel she laid haphazardly out across the floor. He reached out and gently placed his forefinger under her chin and lifted her head so he could look once more into her eyes that were now brimming with tears. Age may have made its unwelcome presence apparent in the delicate creases lining her face and the almost snow-white hair which was immaculately coiffed, but to him she remained a vision if ever there was one and yet, most certainly, one he had never come accustomed to witnessing.

"None of that." He was well acquainted with the overwhelming fog of emotion in which Ava had suddenly found herself swamped.

Fighting to regain what composure she could, Ava turned her head away from his soothing touch and quickly balled up the broken pieces of China in the towel.

"I was just making some tea," she offered pleasantly, rising to her feet. "Please, come in and make yourself at home."

She turned abruptly, even before the last words left her mouth, and hurried off down the hall where she disappeared into the kitchen, leaving Gotham standing alone in the doorway to question whether he had committed a serious error by venturing up the steps to the front porch and making his presence known. He stepped inside and closed the door behind him. His eyes immediately shifted to the sitting room off the small foyer from where music that had captured his attention as he approached the house could be heard coming and he made his way there, shrugging off the overcoat he was wearing and draping it over the railing of the wooden bannister of the stairway he passed.

Stepping into the sun-filled room, his eyes looked past the immaculate, yet homey furnishings, to a giant wooden bookcase that stretched the length of the far wall where, holed in the center, surrounded by rows of books, was an antiquated turntable, from which came the legato of a most beautiful soprano aria. It moved him, almost hypnotically, across the room to the phonograph until he stood watching the yellow label in the center of the record spin beneath the arm of the needle which mined, with just the faintest crackle of age, the glorious notes residing within the grooves etched into the vinyl.

"Mon coeur s'ouvre a ta voix." The song had long ago ingrained itself into Gotham's very core. Yet beautiful as it was, the song's true power rested in the voice singing it, like the swirling euphoria residing with deceptive stealth in the sweet bouquet of a fine wine.

Resting beside the turntable was the album's empty cardboard sleeve emblazoned with composer Camille Saint-Saens' name in white lettering across the top followed underneath by the title of his opera in a much larger orange banner, "Samson et Delila." It was the striking portrait of the beautiful woman, however, that made Gotham pick up the cover. He instantly became transfixed by the image staring back at him as he continued to listen to the music. His fingers followed the direction of the woman's upswept auburn hair that fell in ringlets around her face. The delicate features of beauty staring back were almost too much for Gotham to lay eyes upon and not feel a deep anguish well up within him: the piercing green eyes, of which the real Delilah, herself, would have gouged to possess; the scarlet mouth poised with the ability to conquer the greatest of empires and bring the most hardened of souls to their knees with a single note. Gotham found himself cursing the glossy surface beneath his touch that denied him the smoothness of the porcelain skin forever embedded in his fingertips that continued their way across the bare feminine shoulders peering out from beneath a thin, silk turquoise dress before coming to rest at the top of another name also stretched in orange across the bottom of the album cover like a marquee: Ava Delacroux.

Gotham placed the album cover back on the shelf face down, hoping that by denying his eyes the sight of such loveliness he might manage to exorcize the ghosts inside his head that were beginning to awaken from their long sleep and unravel the tapestries in their guarded possession which held the dusty remnants of memories he had long struggled to forget. Yet what may have been easy to put out of sight, proved an impossible challenge to cast out of mind, not so long as the voice spilling from the turntable continued to ring in his ears.

That voice…

Like some ethereal embodiment, it seemed to move about Gotham, circling him, in sweeping, swirling movements of resurrected life, as if the surrounding four walls were the construct of some grand ballroom raised up for the sole purpose of accommodating its haunting waltz. It taunted Gotham, this unrelenting spirit of the past, keeping its distance with flirty flourishes before rushing him straight on, attempting to take him prisoner with nothing but a heart-binding sound that continued to soar radiantly with untrammeled longing.

> *Ainsi qu'on des bles*
>
> *les epis onduler*
>
> *sous la brise legere,*
>
> *ainsi fremit mon coeur,*
>
> *pret a se consoler,*
>
> *a ta voix qui m'est chere!*

Gotham remembered when he first heard it as if it were yesterday and, in more ways than one, to him, it was. The stirring song managed to find him in the grasp of a snowy gray day and guide him down a narrow, cold German street to an ice-frosted window where the source of the lovely sound was found to be coming from a girl not a day older than ten, whose voice conspired with the flickering fire coming from the hearth to warm the small gathering of family and friends seated around her quietly listening. And then, in the dim of darkness brought by the second world war, he would hear it again. Only this time, it would call out for him in a weakened murmur, as withered, and nearly devoid of life, as the numerous corpses whose decaying stench fought to smother this last gasp of hope in a place where all hope had long been methodically incinerated. He would never forget the sight of her, unrecognizable, and yet instantly recognizable, struggling to exist as would a flower attempting to grow from the muck of an unspeakable cesspool of sewage and filth.

He chose, instead, to remember her the way he found her shortly after her deliverance from such a hell, when the darkness of war was no more, and her voice once more filled with the embers of life and passion would ring out and fill the War Memorial Opera House in San Francisco. Closing his eyes, Gotham could still see her in all her radiant beauty. She was a young woman then, all of nineteen, but a woman, nonetheless, appearing so diminished on such a great stage until she opened her mouth and let loose her mesmerizing gift that instantly and wholly transfixed the audience.

~ ~ ~

"Ironic, isn't it?"

The sound of Ava's voice ripped him from his bliss. Seemingly forgetting momentarily where he was, Gotham glanced over his shoulder to find her standing quietly behind him. So lost in the music, he hadn't even heard her return.

"I was looking for something to lift my spirits and lo and behold I happened upon this," she said moving to stand beside Gotham where she picked up the album cover he had set down. "I can't even remember the last time I played it. Strange I would choose today of all days to do so."

She began to study the image on the cover, but in a much different way than Gotham had. It seemed to bring to her a sadness that slowly filled her eyes with its weight until she, too, returned it to the shelf, face down.

"No, please—" said Gotham when Ava then reached to take the needle off the record and silence the music. "Leave it."

Ordinarily, such an earnest request would have served to flatter Ava. Only there was nothing ordinary about this moment suddenly visited upon her. And it was maybe because of that reason, or perhaps in spite of it, that Ava slowly retracted her hand and allowed the recording of her younger self to continue playing uninterrupted.

"I was just remembering when I first heard you sing it," said Gotham.

"February 5, 1946." The date rolled off Ava's tongue with ease.

She felt his gaze bend her way.

"Old age may have robbed me of my youth and beauty but I'll be damned if it steals my memories," Ava remarked with a defiant chuckle yet unaware of the day nearly ten years prior when Gotham spied her through the window of her childhood home performing as a young girl.

"In my eyes, you have been fleeced of nothing. Certainly not beauty."

His voice, while strong, had a soothing tenderness to it Ava had never gotten used to fully.

"It seems a lifetime ago." There was faint tremble in her sigh, as though suddenly caught in an incoming surge of memories washing in from the past that lifted her momentarily off her feet.

"To you maybe. For me, it's but a brief moment passed," said Gotham.

She turned to him, daring her eyes to slowly move upward to meet his. And when they met she was greeted with the familiar rush that moved through her and made her knees feel as though they might buckle at any moment.

His eyes.

It was both terrifying and pleasurable to gaze directly into the piercing pupils, more golden than the most precious ore mined from deep inside the earth. Terrifying because they seemed to possess the ability to look right through one's soul and illuminate its darkest, hidden corners. Yet they seemed to harness an almost hypnotizing power that bathed the object they were fixed upon with an inescapable warmth emanating from within. These twin orbs seemed to burn like torches inside his skull and Ava long ago found she could never hold his gaze for too long. It was just too intense, like attempting to look directly into the sun.

His chestnut brown hair was still shoulder-length, smoothed away from the face and tethered into a ponytail, except for a few loose strands that had slipped free and fell across his forehead partially obscuring his left eye that glowed like a tiger's in the night. She remembered when, as a young woman, she had tried to get him to cut his beautiful locks, like Delilah did Samson.

This time, she allowed her hand to gravitate to his face. Better now for her to know he was only an apparition of the past than to endure further this merciless joke brought on by her imaginings. She delicately brushed the tuft of hair away from his face, happy he had refused her request to undergo the snip of a barber's scissors as she felt the silky smoothness between her fingers while sweeping it back along the side of his head and draping it behind his left ear. She smiled. He was real. Solid to the touch. All flesh and bone. And yet the feel of his skin beneath her fingertips offered more pain than comfort than had she reached out and felt only empty air. As her once youthfully beautiful face had captivated him, so did the beauty of his captivate her. It was as though he were a living statue; a classical work of art, sculpted to perfection by the most skilled of the Old-World artisans and untouched by time.

Literally, untouched by time.

There wasn't a mark on him that would betray his true age. Not a line. Not a wrinkle, nor a blemish. He looked exactly as he did the day she first met him. Exactly as the image she had seared into memory and fought to hold onto with every last ounce of her strength.

Unbeknownst to Ava, the feel of her hand on Gotham's skin seemed to be as painful to him as it was for her. Closing his eyes, he couldn't help but surrender to the touch he had spent decades keeping himself far outside its reach. She traced the outside of his square jaw and slowly circled around placing the tip of her forefinger against the cleft of his chin. It was a sign he was special, she had told him once. God had left the mark of his fingertip on him like a child leaving his hand print in wet cement.

As the last note coming from the speakers lingered before slowly fading to a painful silence, the smile brought on by the memory that had momentarily lightened Ava's face slowly dissolved when she became conscious of her hand placed against his face. Wrinkled. Withered. Spotted with age. She pulled back abruptly, turning away in shame, and pulled the needle from the record.

"Why did you come back?" she asked tersely as she spun away from him.

"Trust me, Ava, I wouldn't have, had I known my presence would upset you so," answered Gotham while offering Ava some needed distance by retreating to the other end of the room. The overpowering silence that followed was pricked by the staccato ticking of a mahogany and brass clock on the fireplace mantle counting out each passing second. Gotham made busy casually perusing the numerous framed photographs adorning a long table top stretching the front of a large bay window while Ava, once more composed, found herself a seat on a large olive-green sofa next to a coffee table where right before that fateful knock on the door she had set down a tray carrying her afternoon tea. She was just about to pour herself a cup when she took notice of the empty saucer that had held the cup before she dropped and shattered it at the sight of Gotham and realized she had unknowingly arranged a tea set-up for two.

"Silly old woman," she quietly scolded herself as her eyes once again welled with tears.

"Something the matter?" asked Gotham upon hearing her mumbling. Again, Ava quickly composed herself.

"Old habits," she said. "I'm finding some of them difficult to break. This was the time-of-day Isabeth and I enjoyed ourselves our afternoon tea. That is, when she had the stomach for it."

Gotham's eyes gravitated back to the framed photo of mother and daughter he held in his hand, and he was overcome with a solemn look.

"I know she had been suffering for quite some time."

Ava remained silent; her attention fixed on the tea she continued to pour.

"If it offers any comfort," said Gotham, "I can assure you she is at peace in a wondrous place free of any pain."

"No, it does not offer any me any comfort," she snapped angrily. "Did any such assurances soothe you when David died?"

Gotham remained stone-faced, but the unexpected question pierced him painfully.

"Comfort," breathed Ava with a quiet hint of disdain. "If God is so hungry for souls, why doesn't he just come and take mine? Goodness knows I've been ready for some time now."

Ava closed her eyes and took a deep breath as she tried wrestling to the ground the brief outburst she regretted displaying. For her, it was an unfortunate characteristic. She did not like losing control in any aspect of her life, especially her emotions, which over the long years of her life she had managed to hone and keep tethered to the same leash she attached to her voice, to be made to heel or unleashed under her command.

"A mother should not have to bury her child," she continued, her voice once more, composed and gentle, as she returned to preparing her tea. "And yet I've been gifted the displeasure of having to bury both of mine. So, you would like to know if I find any comfort in that, and I can tell you very clearly that no, I do not."

Gotham's notable silence drew a guarded glance from Ava who, for a moment, feared he may have vanished back into the thin air from which he just as quickly had appeared.

"It's an odd thing, isn't it, how the happy moments of one's life can suddenly take the shape of a memorial one would rather not cast eyes upon for fear of being reduced to a puddle of tears?" said Ava, watching Gotham continue browsing through her collection of framed memories.

"Death seems to have taken a cruel enjoyment in seeing me in black, always reappearing whenever I decide to retire my funeral dress to the back of my closet. First, it was my family during the war. Then my son David, followed now by Isabeth. And, of course, my husband Silas seven winters ago," said Ava, mournfully noting the photo Gotham held in his hands and studied intently of her younger self in the loving embrace of a handsome graying man with whom she had shared the last forty years of her life before death came calling.

"He was a good man," remarked Gotham.

"Yes...he was," Ava agreed quietly. "Much too good to have settled for me."

"I doubt highly he ever once considered sharing his life with you as settling," said Gotham. "He loved you."

Such a simple phrase, and yet he struggled to release it from his tongue. Almost as much as Ava struggled with herself to hear it.

"I know," was all she replied.

~ ~ ~

Gotham returned the framed picture to its spot amongst the many others carefully arranged upon the long table.

"You understand there was nothing I could have done to have changed things...with Isabeth, I mean," he said after a few quiet moments had passed.

Ava paused, then simply nodded while stirring her tea. Despite the solemn topic of death hanging heavy in the air, a sweet, pleasant scent gradually made its way through the room, as if the wisps of steam rising from Ava's cup in swirling ribbons had somehow seeded the ceiling to rain down fragrant white citrus blossoms.

"Isabeth knew her time here was quickly drawing to an end, and she accepted it. Being as strong in her faith as she was, I doubt she would have allowed you to come between her and her fate," said Ava. "Whatever fight she showed during her sickness to keep her soul anchored to her body was solely on behalf of—"

"The boy," uttered Gotham.

"She loved him so, as any mother loves her son. Perhaps more. And with that love came tremendous worry—worry about leaving him alone with no one to guide him when the time arrived to finally reveal to him…well, you know."

"Yes, she shared with me her concerns," said Gotham. "And I did my best to put such worries at ease."

The revelation wrung from Ava a slow blossoming look of surprise. "You...you spoke with her?"

"The night of her passing," answered Gotham. "She called for me, and—"

"And you came," said Ava.

She was quick to look away, not wanting him to see how visibly moved she had become as she set down her tea and reached for a nearby napkin.

"Then it wasn't a dream," she muttered quietly to herself. "Dream?"

"I dreamt you had passed through my room…or so I believed it to be a dream." Ava dabbed at her eyes as inconspicuously as she could before abruptly shifting the direction of conversation. "He's not home, you know?"

"Yes, I know. I waited until I saw him leave," said Gotham. "And then I waited a couple more hours to gather what courage I could muster that would give me the strength to knock on your door."

"Yes…we all know how deficient you are in that department," Ava remarked facetiously. For anyone who laid eyes upon Gotham would never believe the towering, strapping figure had ever experienced a moment where he would find himself lacking courage.

"Truth be told, despite the unexpected shock of seeing you after all these years, it would be remiss of me if I didn't confess being somewhat thankful to finally have this moment with you," said Ava after taking a long sip from her tea. "That is, I never had the chance to express to you my gratitude for everything you did for my daughter by bringing her here where she and Jacob could have a safe life."

Gotham stood quiet, staring out the giant bay window framing a view of the front of the house and the surrounding neighborhood.

"It's a beautiful place. Quiet. Peaceful." There was a noticeable longing, almost sadness, in his voice. As though the beauty he spoke of was one that was unobtainable to him—like a scene captured within the confines of a painting.

"I knew when I found it that it would be the perfect place for your daughter, tucked out of sight from the ugliness of the world. A place she could have her child and raise him, and not have to worry about any lurking...shadows," he said. "And for the last sixteen years as I continued to walk this world for what seemed like the millionth time, until I have come to know by heart every putrid dark corner it holds, my footsteps would always bring me back here now and then to look in from a distance and see how they were doing. To ensure this womb was protecting them. Protecting him."

Ava felt a rush of shame come over her for the quiet anger that had been festering inside her for some time toward him.

"I didn't realize you had been watching over them all these years. Once you left I assumed—"

"That I'd abandoned them? Left them alone to fend for themselves against the wolves?"

"That's not what I meant," replied Ava with an exasperated sigh. "Only that it couldn't have been an easy thing for you...considering."

"No more difficult than it has been for you, I'm sure."

"He's my grandson, my flesh and blood," said Ava steadfastly without so much as a moment's pause. "It makes no mind to me how he came into this world. I love him wholeheartedly."

She didn't have to say it. Gotham could hear it in her voice, the same way he observed from an unseen distance her unwavering devotion to the boy over the years. Yet despite the words being spoken, Gotham knew it had been a difficult sixteen years, with each day hinged on a future clouded with uncertainty.

~　~　~

He continued to stare out the window, his eyes following a group of neighborhood children laughing as they passed in front of the house along the sidewalk. "I've watched him. He's slowly coming to realize there is something oddly different about him he can't seem to make sense of. Something that sets him apart from the other kids around him, especially these last couple years."

"Even longer than that," said Ava. "When he was a small child, there were moments I could see him struggling with this normal life his mother tried to provide for him."

"Only he's not normal—at least not in the way normal exists here in Cain's Corner, or anywhere else, as you well know," said Gotham. "Unfortunately, that false sense of normalcy has begun to create a real feeling of isolation and confusion for the boy, which I'm afraid to say will only grow more burdensome with each passing day."

"I know," Ava agreed with a sigh. "I realized that when I found out recently he had secretly been going to Dr. Gilkey in search for answers."

"Dr. Gilkey?"

"Nothing sets a teenage boy on edge more than the threat of a physical, uh...imperfection. It's really no surprise, is it, that the eventual changes to his back would send him running to the nearest doctor's office?

"Modern medicine cannot cure him of what he is," Gotham grumbled sourly.

He retreated from the view of the window and slowly began circling around the room, his every step watched by Ava.

"You haven't answered me. Why are you here?" asked Ava again, but without the emotion that had earlier choked her voice. "What is it Isabeth wished to speak with you about?

Gotham, at first, seemed hesitant in answering as he subtly shifted about on his feet.

"She told me, as she wavered closer toward her final breath, how she tried to tell the boy the truth she had kept from him all these years," said Gotham finally. "Understandably, he thought he was witnessing the delusions brought on by her sickness, and she, considerably weakened, found herself unable to gather the strength necessary to attempt to prove to him otherwise."

"So, she wanted you to tell Jacob finally what he has long been in need of hearing."

Ava clearly could see there was more.

"She wished to remind me of a promise she made me make her the night I brought her here to Cain's Corner," said Gotham.

"Promise?"

"That when the time came—when the boy reached this age of uncertainty—I would make myself known to him—take him under my wing, so to speak—and see him to the place where he can be prepared for the life he faces ahead of him," Gotham explained.

It took a moment, maybe two, before Ava came to realize what "place" Gotham was referring. Of course, there was only one place in existence where a boy like Jacob could find the answers—and believe those answers—to the questions he had not yet come to realize needed answering. More importantly, it was a place where others, like Jacob, were brought, from around the world; a place where Jacob could discover he was not alone in his uniqueness.

"Havenhid." The name escaped Ava's lips like a breath unto itself.

"I had hoped she had forgotten all about that promise she had secured from me that night so long ago, but she hadn't," said Gotham.

"What did you tell her?" asked Ava.

"What you would have expected me to," answered Gotham. "That I would make good on my vow to ensure her boy was looked after."

Ava absent-mindedly rubbed her knees with a nervous fidgetiness, as if she was suddenly overcome by the unexpected turn in the conversation.

"You'll forgive me...you've caught me a bit off-guard with this, even though I should have known this moment might possibly come at some point," she said. "When Isabeth was a little girl, I used to tell her stories about it when I tucked her in to bed at night. She'd lie there under the covers, her big brown eyes fixed on me, listening to her mother spin tales of some wonderful, fantasy place—much like Neverland. Never once did they put her to sleep. It was only when she was preparing for Jacob's arrival that she mentioned off-handedly how when he was old enough she planned to send him there, to this place I always assumed she thought was make believe."

A stony, sobering look suddenly settled itself on Ava.

"I suppose allowing you to take Jacob there would be the logical thing to do," she said. "After all, where else can a boy like him go to find himself? His inner world grows more and more confusing with each day that passes. He needs answers I'm not equipped to give him. Certainly, Cain's Corner doesn't have the means to offer him much clarity. Not that I can pretend to be over the moon by this news. Then again, I only want what's best for Jacob. He's very dear to me, and the thought of his leaving already is bringing a pang of emptiness to my heart. But if Isabeth had the foresight to believe this path is what's best for her son, then who am I to stand in the way of her wishes?"

She began to wring her hands with a growing nervousness while continuing to mull over the idea more in her head.

"Whether or not Jacob chooses to go along, however, is another matter altogether," Ava pondered aloud. "It has to be his decision, and his alone, not mine and not yours."

And the more she thought about it, the more anxious she became. It wasn't like when Jacob was a young boy and surprising him with an outing to the countryside or the beach, or a weekend excursion to an amusement park. This was his mother's last dying request. It would involve uprooting Jacob from everything and everyone he knew. What could prove to be more difficult than leaving behind one's home, school, friends—even to honor a mother's wishes? What's more, there was Gotham. How, Ava wondered, would she even broach trying to explain to Jacob who this stranger was, much less convince her grandson to accept him as his chaperone, for lack of a better word, on this journey? None of these things Ava turned over repeatedly in her mind, however, compared to the enormity of the task of finally being forced to reveal to Jacob the one secret which had been kept from him for far too long—a secret that would forever change the reflection he saw whenever he glanced into a mirror.

How would she manage to approach Jacob with any of this and somehow convince him the time had not finally arrived to commit her into the supervised care of the local twilight home for the elderly?

~ ~ ~

"When were you wanting to leave with him?" Ava finally asked.

No answer came from Gotham. In fact, he suddenly took on a look of discomfort, as though the walls of the room were slowly beginning to come together to smother him, and the feeling quickly transferred itself to Ava.

"You have no intention of taking him, do you?" she said. Gotham answered by focusing his brilliant golden eyes on her.

"I don't understand," said Ava looking confused. "You just said—"

"You inquired why Isabeth had called for me," Gotham curtly cut through Ava's voice with his own like a knife slicing through a tomato, "and I have told you."

Ava looked visibly taken aback.

"She died believing that you would look after her son. To help guide through this…this…"

"I have every intention of looking after the boy as I promised," argued Gotham.

"The boy, the boy—" Ava snapped in frustration. "He has a name: Jacob."

Gotham didn't need a reminder. "I can teach him everything he needs to know right here, without taking him from his home."

"You know that's not good enough," Ava balked loudly, abandoning her tea on the table, and with a quickness that belied her age she was on her feet and pacing about the room. "He needs to be with others who are like him, to see and know firsthand all of the things existing just out of sight that, unless he experiences it himself, he will never truly understand much less entertain belief in, even coming from your mouth."

"Be reasonable, Ava!" implored Gotham in an effort to suppress the growing angst rising in her. "Somehow, someway this place, for all these years, has proven a safe harbor for the b—…for Jacob. Do you really want to threaten that? Because that is the risk we will be taking if I were to take him. Here, at least, he has a chance at living a normal life, as his mother wanted."

"DON'T!" scolded Ava under her breath. "Don't you dare twist what Isabeth wished for her son in order to justify your actions when you know exactly what her intentions were."

Ava's hands were once again wringing one another as she made her way to the window. Standing there looking outside with the sunlight streaming inside warming her face, she was immediately taken by the faint high-pitched shrill of screaming laughter which turned her gaze further up the street to the sight of a group of small children running about as they played in a neighboring front yard.

"A normal life? Do you have any idea what the last sixteen years have been like living here? Always on edge whenever someone walked by the house or a salesman came to the front door, ever vigilant of the shadows following along the ground, never sure if they were just harmless, dark empty shapes, or hid a strange, frightening movement we were always hopeful never to see that would immediately deliver to us the unsettling news that they'd finally found us," said Ava, her eyes betraying a fear she had done well in concealing longer than she could remember.

"By God's grace, this place has been an untold blessing all these years," she continued. "But you more than anyone else know that even Cain's Corner can't shield Jacob forever, for the exact same reason he was brought here in the first place. Then what?"

"We will deal with that when the day comes."

"That's your answer?"

"It's the only one I've got."

Ava couldn't believe her ears, nor that she was having this argument with Gotham. Here. Now.

"I don't understand you," she remarked in the most heartbreaking of whispers. "We're not talking about his life, but his soul. How you can refuse to provide him with the things he will need to help protect and keep him safe is beyond comprehension."

"Do I really need to spell it out for you?" bellowed Gotham.

The tenor of his voice made the house shudder and took Ava aback momentarily, instantly neutering her anger.

"This has nothing to do with Jacob," she said, finally understanding. "This is about David...isn't it?"

Gotham turned away from her to hide the rare but distinctly wounded look he felt creep across his face at the mention of the one good thing he and Ava had managed to create together: their son.

"There's not a day that goes by that I don't think about him...mourn him," said Ava. "It's taken a long time; more time than I thought life would ever afford me. But eventually—somehow—I found a way to let go of the anger before it had a chance to consume me. Because I know that's what he would have wanted. But even more important, because I know we did what was best for him, which was to allow him to be fully that which he was."

"I did not come here to discuss this," barked Gotham.

Ava had every intention to continue. "We both knew the risks and dangers that existed where David was concerned and we accepted them. What happened to him was unfortunate—heartbreakingly so—but it was not in vain, but only because we made the conscious decision to help prepare him against such risks. Jacob is entitled the same consideration, if not more."

"This conversation is over! I've made my decision," announced Gotham as he briskly brushed past Ava.

"You know I can take him myself, if I have to," she blurted out defiantly. "I may not have the ability to see him the whole way, but thanks to you I know where to go to find the one person who can. Don't think I won't."

Of course, Gotham knew immediately to whom Ava was referring, but instead of arguing the asininity of what she was threatening, as was his first inclination, he bit his tongue and simply nodded.

"Pity I don't have my camera within reach for this moment," remarked Ava as she watched Gotham make his way toward the front door. "The sight of you once again exiting my life is definitely an image worthy of a frame. I imagine it would add just the touch of cheer needed amongst my other photographs."

Such words, especially coming from her, stung Gotham, but he did his best to allow them to wash off his back without so much as a grimace.

"Goodbye Ava," he said pausing at the door. He found himself wanting to take a last look at her but was unable to bring himself to do so. "Be well."

He closed the door behind him, and like that he was gone. Ava held her stoic stance, and surrounded by an almost unbearable silence interrupted only by the heartbeat ticking of the clock on the mantle she stared through the thinly veiled white drapes that framed the sides of the window and watched Gotham make his way across the lawn to the sidewalk and disappear up the street. Only when he was out of sight did Ava slowly wilt into a nearby chair, bow her head to her chest and begin to sob.

CHAPTER THREE

At Harpus High School, Jacob Parrish's existence was that of a Ghost. Ghost was the term used to refer to students who, for whatever reason, never managed to find a welcoming place in any of the established cliques at the school. As such, they largely drifted through their four years at the campus in much the same way a spirit lingers in a house that becomes its haunt after death; existing, yet not seeming to exist to the outside world; a transparent presence in which all eyes are largely prone to look through and thus ignore. Jacob may very much have been made of flesh and bone, but one would unlikely take notice of him unless, like an unseen spook, he made you aware he was there.

As it happened so many times before, he rounded the corner of one of the school's gray buildings without garnering so much as a look from the throngs of other students he passed while making his way toward The Pit. An amphitheater of sorts in the center of campus shaped by sculpted slopes of concrete and numerous stairways, The Pit served as a crossing point for students making their way from one of the four corners of campus to the other. To the Skaters, it was a concrete-paved nirvana serving as a sacred church where they could practice their religion of surfing land, as well as the handrails of the stairways descending down into The Pit while ear-piercing music blasted from an ancient, beat-up boom box nearby.

With a backpack weighted with bulky text books slung across his shoulder and his attention buried along with his nose inside the book he grasped in his hand, Jacob made his way blindly down the steps of The Pit oblivious to the shaggy-haired concrete surfers whipping past him as they were of him, including one in mid-kickflip who was forced to abandoned his board when Jacob strolled directly into his path.

"Yo—watch where you're goin' bro," balked the tall, lanky Skater once he had managed to regain his balance and save himself from an embarrassing face- plant.

Jacob spun around, never breaking his stride, and looked up from his book. "Sorry about that," he offered good-naturedly before spinning forward, burying his face back in his book and continuing on his way.

"Douche!" the Skater muttered under his breathe with irritable disdain, brushing back his seventies-inspired mop of locks hanging in his face with a hair-flip motion as down pat and perfected as his skating moves.

~   ~   ~

To be fair, Jacob wasn't averse to his invisible existence; in fact, he quite preferred it. One might even say his relegation to the land of Ghostdom was not so much a banishment by his peers at school as it was a self-imposed exile. After all, it's hard trying to fit in where one feels he doesn't belong. And no one felt more like a square in a world surrounded by circles than Jacob, even when on the outside he appeared as anything but.

At first look, one might mistake him as one of the Gets. Gets were the popular kids at the top of the food chain who appeared to have everything in life handed to them on a silver platter. They were the good-looking crop of students: the jocks, the cheerleaders, the spawn of the wealthy, clean-cut, primped and pressed in the latest designer fashions and trends at the moment. Jacob certainly didn't consider himself a jock, despite a short stint on the school wrestling team. That is, before the condition with his back forced him to an abrupt time out. And while he may have had a "cute" shine to him, it was in an awkward, teenaged way that came packaged in a tall, loose-limbed body with plenty of room to grow. Nor did his preferred uniform of T-shirt, jeans and well-traveled Converse sneakers do much to lower the upturned noses of the label-conscious Gets.

And despite having his face buried in a book outside of a classroom, Jacob had even less in common with those on the other end of the social spectrum: the Nerd Herd. What appeared to be a dweebish thirst for knowledge was actually nothing more than a last-minute attempt to cram into his brain as much assigned reading as possible that he had put off before his English class later in the day.

When Jacob reached the top of the steps on the other side of The Pit, he was greeted by a hand that grabbed hold of his book and snatched it out of his grasp. At first he expected to look up and see it was one of the illiterate Burnouts—the school's grungy metal heads—who every now and then enjoyed injecting a little bit of misery into an otherwise tolerable day for certain walks of life who passed through their claimed western corner boundary of their precious Pit and decided to swipe the book for a spirited game of Keep-Away. Instead, Jacob quickly discovered he had run into something far worse than an annoying Burnout when he saw the face of his best friend Ty Wrenwood staring back at him with an expression of abject horror.

"Why don't you just wear a sandwich board with the words 'Warning: Dork Crossing' painted in red across the front and 'Kick Me' on the back?" questioned Ty.

So much for the peaceful cramming session, Jacob thought to himself while sighing with exacerbation.

"So wha'cha reading there pal that's obviously made you not care about what little reputation you have left?" Ty hummed with amusement while eyeing the cover of Jacob's book. "Hmm, 'Paradise Lost'...sounds like one of those magazines at the liquor store that come sealed in a plastic bag."

"You would know," Jacob cracked dryly while making a grab for his book only to catch a handful of air as Ty took a jump backward.

"Th' infernal serpent," Ty began to mockingly recite from the book in a deep, Old World-accented voice one would associate with a stuffy English professor in need of dusting when he suddenly stopped.

" 'Th'? What the hell is 'Th'? This written by Sylvester the Cat? TTTHHHuffering TTTHHHuccotash!"

Jacob grimaced with disgust as he wiped away the spray of spittle that hit his face courtesy of Ty's impeccable, yet very wet, impression of the Bugs Bunny cartoon character.

"Come on, give it here—I've got a test next period I need to get ready for," Jacob demanded as he pursued Ty through the stream of passing students while now and then making a grab for the book that always managed to be kept a hair out of his reach. Clearing his throat, his brow furrowing, Ty resumed his theatrical reading.

"Th' infernal serpent, he it was whose guile stirred up with envy and revenge deceived the mother of mankind, what time his pride had cast him out from Heaven, with all his host of rebel angels, by whose aid, aspiring to set himself in glory above his peers, he trusted to have equaled the Most High"

"Not funny doofus," Jacob grumbled sourly.

Clearly amused whenever he could get his best friend riled up, Ty continued to make his way blindly through the crowd, walking backward just fast enough to stay just out of reach from the hand that made a grab for him now and then while remaining oblivious to the strange looks he continued to receive from other students over his obnoxious recitation.

"If he opposed, and with ambitious aim against the throne and monarchy of God raised impious war in heav'n and battle proud with vain attempt. Him the Almighty Power hurled headlong flaming from th' ethereal sky with hideous ruin and combustion down to bottomless perdition, there to dwell in adamantine chains and penal fire."

Ty suddenly stopped and turned a bewildered look onto Jacob.

"Okay, seriously, my first born in exchange for a hit of whatever this, uh, Mr. John Mitton was smoking," he said, giving the cover of the book a quick glance in search of the author's name.

"It's Milton, bonehead. And thanks for losing my place," Jacob groused while quickly reclaiming ownership of his book from Ty's clutches before disappearing into the flow of students.

"Bonehead, is it now? Well, at least I know 'the' comes with an 'e'," Ty called after him. "Your smart guy Mr. *Millllton* should have called his book 'Any Possible Comprehension in Understanding What the Hell I'm Writing Lost'."

It was then Ty became aware of the handful of his peers who had stopped to take curious notice of his outburst. They stood staring strangely at him, as if unbeknownst to himself he had shown up to school completely naked, especially when Ty proceeded to bow low at the waist to them while miming the removal of some invisible hat from atop his head.

"A penny to keep our little theater company thriving," he said, imitating a cockney accent while holding out his imaginary cap like some English street urchin brought to life from the pages of a Charles Dickens story begging passersby for a spare shilling. When all he got was a confused shaking of heads and quick dispersal of the circle of onlookers as though he had shown himself to be a carrier of plague, Ty returned the snub with a disgruntled look, fixed his invisible cap back atop his head and made off after Jacob.

~　~　~

After a visit to the food court, where they waded through a long line of other hungry students snaking around the large, concrete and brick lunch kiosk, the two boys bypassed the spread of nearby tables which, as usual, were occupied by the Gets, and circled back around toward The Knoll.

"So're you going to tell me why you were M.I.A. the first two periods of school this morning?" Ty asked Jacob as the two found a patch of lawn underneath the warming sun to enjoy their lunch—a nutritious serving of a slice of pizza to be washed down with a box of milk.

"What are you, my mother?" muttered Jacob, his nose buried once again back inside the book that from the look on his face was proving to be taxing on his concentration.

"Uh, no, but until two seconds ago I thought I was your best friend."

"That mean I have to report back to you where I am and what I do every single minute of every day?"

That's fine," Ty remarked dismissively, taking on a look that resided somewhere between wounded and offended. "I've got secrets of my own, you know...but plenty."

"That I have no doubt," Jacob mumbled under his breath as he struggled with the ever-growing difficult task of reading.

"Yeah, well, see if I share any of them with you from now on," threatened Ty.

"I will do my best to navigate my way through these suddenly stormy waters of our relationship," Jacob remarked dryly while obviously not really paying attention to the mindless back and forth taking place.

It was then that his eyes left the pages of the book he was trying to concentrate on and focused on something far more distracting than Ty's constant babbling.

"Do you have to always do that?" asked Jacob as he watched with annoyance as his friend went through his more than familiar ritual of picking off the bits of pepperoni sprinkled across the top of his pizza and flinging them out across the lawn to be swooped down upon and grabbed by the waiting birds gathered in the nearby trees.

"Do what?" asked Ty.

"That!" stressed Jacob, pointing to the pizza Ty was picking at like it was some crusty acne scab. "I don't get it. Why not just buy a cheese pizza instead?"

"Because," Ty replied with an annoyed huff and eye roll, "I happen to like the taste of whatever this topping gives the pizza. Is that some crime?"

"I think it's called pepperoni."

"Last I checked, pepperoni came in slices."

"So then what do you think you're picking off your pizza?" asked Jacob with not much interest for a response.

"For all I know, it could be rabbit raisins," answered Ty, tossing one of the greasy, pebble-sized nuggets in Jacob's direction.

Jacob managed to dodge the incoming lob and divert the chunk of meat with a swat of his hand.

"What's wrong with you?" said Jacob surly. "Can't you see I'm trying to finish reading this chapter?"

Ty didn't care. Anything to get his friend's nose out from behind that stuffy book.

"Why are you studying now anyways? It's lunchtime. What'r you pledging to join the Nerd Herd fraternity?" Ty inquired as he scouted out the other so-called bookworms scattered around The Knoll looking far more academic than it was comfortable for him to observe. "Frankly, I don't think it's all that smart for us to be sitting so close to the geek masses. It could seriously damage my reputation."

"You don't have a reputation, at least one you can be proud of," said Jacob. "Besides, I told you I have a test next period that I'm not interested in failing, and all your yakking isn't helping."

"It's literature," said Ty.

"Very good T. What gave it away...the book?"

"I mean, I don't get why it is you're putting so much totally unnecessary effort into studying when there's really no need to," explained Ty, to which Jacob could only take a soothing breath in preparation for another enlightening and worldly lesson from the school of Tyology of which now and then he found himself to be the sole student.

"Literature," continued Ty, before Jacob could tune him out, as if it were possible, " is no different than when Mr. Hanson asks us during art class to explain the meaning of some hideous so-called masterpiece that really, let's be honest, is nothing more than finger-painting by adults who then deem their work 'genius.' It's all subjective, open to the interpretation of the art form, in this case the written word. Now, you can sit there and waste what precious hours the day has given you pouring over page after page of blah, blah, blah. Or you can do what I do."

"Which is?" inquired Jacob in a tone noting his hesitation of the answer.

"Wing it, of course. B.S. your way through the B.S.," answered Ty, flashing a proud smile as though he had cracked the final missing link in the Theory of Everything.

"Wing it," echoed Jacob nonplussed.

"I see you're not a convert, so I'll prove it," challenged Ty. "I haven't read your 'Paradise Lost' there—and I pray to God I'm never forced to. But ten bucks says I can take some small excerpt of your choosing and whittle it into a viable, compelling answer if I were let's say asked to stand up in class and explain what it means. Go ahead...anything."

Jacob wasn't in the mood, but he knew he'd have no peace until he allowed "Ty the Amazing" the opportunity to show off his powers of willful ignorance. And frankly, he couldn't deny being the tiniest bit curious as to how his friend would B.S. his way—as it were so scholarly put—through such thick and tongue-unfriendly prose that he himself was struggling to comprehend. So, turning back to his book, Jacob quickly scanned the page and began to read out loud:

Thus Satan talking to his neerest Mate

With Head up-lift above the wave, and Eyes

That sparkling blaz'd, his other Parts besides

Prone on the Flood, extended long and large

Lay floating many a rood, in bulk as huge

As whom the Fables name of monstrous size,

Titanian, or Earth-born, that warr'd on Jove,

Briareos or Typhon, whom the Den

By ancient Tarsus held, or that Sea-beast

Leviathan, which God of all his works

Created hugest that swim th' Ocean stream.

When he had finished, Jacob looked to Ty, who couldn't have looked more glazed over by what he had just heard than if he'd been clobbered over the head with a two-by-four.

"Well, genius?"

"Alright, I got it," said Ty clearing his throat. The hamster-occupied wheel inside his head could almost be heard to crank feverishly into motion.

"So we all know this Milton guy was a staunch pacifist," he began.

"Wait a minute," interrupted Jacob. "And just how exactly do you know Milton was a pacifist?"

"I don't. And ten to one odds say neither does the teacher," explained Ty. "By stating something as fact, you've already won half the battle. The teacher likely won't have any idea whether some made up bit of trivia is true or not and won't want to risk being made to look like an idiot by challenging you on it on the off-hand chance he, or she, could be proven wrong."

"Is that how it works?" asked Jacob dryly while quietly debating to himself whether he was in the company of an idiot of the purest form, or a genius mastermind in the making who would someday manage to use his heightened powers of deduction to earn himself a prime spot on the FBI's most wanted list.

~ ~ ~

"Shall I continue?" asked Ty.

"Oh, please," answered Jacob.

Suddenly intrigue to hear what his friend's feverish mind would concoct next, Jacob looked on with numbing awe as Ty embarked on a bombastic, yet smartly sounding bloviation arguing impossibly—and strangely possible at the same time—that Milton's words held a dual, deeper meaning in describing the military might of the United States—"that Sea-beast Leviathan"—who with the help of its "neerest Mate"—England—gained domination across the globe as the world's super power, and slowly came to be looked upon, by some, as the great "Satan."

While Jacob continued to listen to what was arguably the most creative, yet undeniably the biggest steaming pile of nonsense he'd heard, and would likely ever hear for the remainder of his life, a strange feeling suddenly came over him. It drew his attention upward into the nearby trees where the lively chatter of birds continued to ring out and tug at his ears. That he heard voices speaking distinctive words he could understand coming from within the choruses of whistling tweets and chirps wasn't unusual, at least to him. He had always had the inexplicable ability of deciphering the noises made by the feathered creatures (not to mention dogs and cats) for as long as he could remember. What was unusual was the excitement he heard in their incessant noise.

Jacob's gaze then drifted beyond the trees and settled on the clock tower on the other end of The Knoll. It was from there he felt a strong, almost indescribable feeling he was being watched. A feeling he had felt on and off before on more than a few occasions as a young boy growing up, only now it had returned in recent weeks and carried with it a certain noticeable weight. So much so he half expected to see some strange figure staring back at him as he searched first the top of the out-of-commission tower right above the giant clock face, its iron hands long frozen and taking on the decaying reddish crust of a slow rust, before giving the empty blue sky above a quick, fleeting glance. Not surprisingly, there was no one there, just like all the previous times he found himself looking over his shoulder; but while the phantom eyes Jacob sought remained just that, so did the feeling they remained fixed on him.

"Earth to Jacob," Ty finally called out, diverting Jacob's attention away from the clock. "Here I am trying to enlighten you and save you from possible nerddom and you're willfully tuning me out."

"Oh, I heard you," said Jacob.

"And?"

"And that may just be the stupidest thing I've ever been forced to listen to in my life."

"Stupid?" mused Ty thoughtfully. "Or pretty darn brilliant?"

"No, I'm pretty sure stupid is the correct word here," said Jacob. "First of all Milton wrote 'Paradise Lost' more than a hundred years before America was even founded."

"Seriously?" said Ty with a surprised cock of his head. "So then one could argue he was the Nostradamus of his time. Even better, it brings in a whole philosophical angle to it."

Jacob could only stare at his friend with utter bafflement.

"This explains so much your solid C grade-point average."

"AHHHH…," said Ty with a triumphant pointing of a finger skyward, "as opposed to failing. A perfectly acceptable and passable grade-point average built on the golden rule of B.S., or what I like to refer to as 'The Three C's— Creative Cognitive Crap.'"

Shaking his head, Jacob let out a sigh of defeat. "You exhaust me! You know that, don't you?"

"As long as it puts a smile on your face, my friend." It was the rare moment Ty offered a fully sincere response, devoid of all sarcasm or wisecracks, and Jacob recognized and appreciated it for what it was.

It had been nearly two weeks since his mother had died, and still Jacob found himself wrestling with the pain as if it were yesterday. No matter how hard he tried, he couldn't shirk the anger that continued to roil his insides. As a result, he seemed to exist under a perpetual black cloud—moody and quiet, and always simmering, like a smoldering volcano inching its way closer towards the moment of eruption, even as his friend did his best to cool the lava with his antics.

"Speaking of smiles," said Ty. "What say next weekend the two of us head up to Penuel Point for a little sky kissing?"

Penuel Point was a two-hour winding drive to the highest peak of the nearby mountain range offering a breath-taking view of Cain's Corner and the valley which it resided nestled at its feet. It was also the place Jacob and Ty went to whenever they felt the need to get high nature's way with nothing but a parachute strapped to their backs and nerve laced to their feet as they willingly ran full-speed toward a waiting sheer cliff and catapulted themselves into the arms of nothingness to kiss the sky Jimi Hendrix-style in exchange for a mind- numbing jolt of adrenaline. Some of the duo's best times had been spent up at Penuel Point and Ty knew if there was one thing that could raise his friend's spirits it was a day of dare-devilry. Except Jacob didn't react to the suggestion with the gusto Ty expected. In fact, Jacob didn't seem to even be paying any attention to his friend.

"Uh, hello…did you hear me or did I lose you again?" asked Ty.

"Yeah…Penuel Point next weekend. Sounds like a plan," answered Jacob.

Only there was absent any twinkle of excitement previous proposed outings brought to his eyes which instead seemed to latch themselves to something off in the distance that made his jaw visibly tighten while instantly erasing what was left his smile. The grimace didn't escape Ty, who followed Jacob's glare fixed past his shoulder to see what had made his friend's face go sour. When his gaze instantly landed on the familiar sight of Wray Bliss standing near the library, it didn't surprise him one bit. Not that Wray alone could ever darken Jacob's expression the way it had. In fact, she had an effortless way of doing quite the opposite. However, she was not alone, and the person she was seen cavorting with was an entirely different matter altogether.

Yul Dane.

If ever there was one individual who managed to get under Jacob's skin like some Lyme disease-carrying tick, it was Yul Dane. He was the epitome of a Harpus High "Get": Blond, statuesque build, perfectly chiseled good looks, and the school's star athlete. He was also a contemptible jerk to those he saw as beneath him—which was pretty much everyone, especially Ghosts—and was notorious for using them as stepping stones whenever he could so the bottoms of his designer shoes wouldn't be dirtied by the ground. Which made the sight of seeing him and Wray together all the more mind-numbing. Like Jacob and Ty, she, too, was a fellow Ghost. Only she possessed an odd beauty that refused to allow her to fully disappear from sight into the hordes of other invisible castaways. What made matters worse was the fact that she was holding hands with the enemy and canoodling with him in a giggly, innocent way, yet canoodling all the same, a sight which all but made vapors of steam escape from Jacob's ears.

"I don't get it," said Ty to Jacob who had returned to his book and was furiously scanning the words inside even though nothing was sticking.

"You'll have to be more specific," said Jacob.

"Why you haven't put a stop to that."

"A stop to what?"

"THAT!" said Ty, framing the sight of Wray and Yul between his outstretched hands.

"What am I, her father?" said Jacob irritably.

"No, but she is your girlfriend," said Ty.

Jacob shot Ty a look over the top of his book as though it were a pair of bifocals pinching the end of his nose. "I'm sorry? Girlfriend?"

"Yeah...you know..." Ty proceeded to bring his hands together in front of him to form the shape of a heart before taking note of the completely humorless glare Jacob returned his way. "Am I lying?"

"If by girlfriend you mean she's a girl who also happens to be a friend of mine, then no, you're not."

"Please," said Ty rolling his eyes. "The two of you are about as much friends as Batman and Robin."

Jacob straightened his back while staring at Ty as though he were a head-scratching calculus problem he'd been called upon to solve.

"We've gone through this before. There's nothing romantic between Batman and Robin. Never was, never has been," said Jacob. "And even it were true, your comparison makes absolutely no sense whatsoever. "

"Of course it does," argued Ty. "Love is love. And please…the only thing that isn't a wonder about the Boy Wonder is that he is as straight as cooked spaghetti. I mean he rocks a green Speedo and pixie boots for crying out loud."

Jacob could only close his eyes and take a calming breath upon hearing such an argument.

"All I'm saying is I can't believe you're sitting here reading some crusty old book while your sworn enemy is moving in on your girlfriend—sorry, I mean *friiiieeend*," said Ty while dramatically etching invisible quote marks into the air.

"For the last time, Wray is not my girlfriend, nor do I desire her to be my girlfriend," Jacob explained in the calm voice one uses when reasoning with a stubborn toddler.

Ty's mouth immediately cocked itself but Jacob quickly hushed him before he could get the first syllable of his retort out.

"Now, can we just end this already? Please?" implored Jacob.

"Fine," Ty huffed in agreement. "If you tell me where you were this morning."

Blackmail. Subtle and backhanded, but blackmail just the same. It was so in keeping with Ty's character.

"There's still my theory about Samwise Gamgee and Frodo you still haven't allowed me to share with you yet," Ty sang threateningly when he noticed Jacob wavering on the fence as he considered his options.

"Alright, fine...you win," grumbled Jacob as he quickly reached deep into his pocket.

No way could he take another of Ty's gay revelations. Somewhere along the line Ty had become the self-imposed designated outer of fictional characters. It didn't matter who they were—Batman and Robin, Sherlock Holmes and Watson, The Lone Ranger and Tonto, even Bert and Ernie—no one was off target from his warped and, oftentimes, obviously malfunctioning gay radar. But Frodo and Sam— and how the One Ring was really the subtext about the first same-sex marriage in literature—was where Jacob drew the line. More importantly, Jacob wanted to put the kibosh on any more speculative talk regarding his friendship with Wray.

"Here," Jacob snapped sharply while thrusting a twice-folded crumbled piece of paper Ty's way.

"What's this?" asked Ty before even unfolding the paper and reading the scribbled handwriting inside.

"A note from my doctor clearing me to rejoin the wrestling team." Ty's eyes lit up from the news.

"You're kidding? That's great! But why would you keep it a secret from me?"

"I wasn't keeping it a secret," said Jacob. "I just hadn't told you...yet."

Ty's gaze shifted to Jacob's shoulders, first the right, then the left.

"So that means your, uh...you know, your...that is, it's..." Ty stammered while gesturing over his own shoulder with a point of his extended thumb to his back.

"It's improving. In fact, I'm pretty much good as new," Jacob lied.

Ty may have been his best friend with whom he shared pretty much everything, but this was one thing he had difficulty being open and truthful about. It wasn't an easy thing having something which made you different from everyone else around you, even your best friend. And how could he be completely honest with the one person he knew wouldn't judge him when he himself had trouble not judging himself.

"You know the best part of this?" said Ty. "You might finally get your chance to knock Yul Dane off that pedestal of his."

"You're not going to be happy until Yul and I are thrown into a gladiator arena and forced to fight to the death, are you?" asked Jacob.

"Not death…just a little maiming," answered Ty, his eyes gleaming with a glint of mischief at the thought. "I just can't wait to see the look on his face when he finds out about this."

~ ~ ~

"When who finds out about what?"

The sound of Wray's voice caught both Ty and Jacob off guard. Slowly, both boys looked up to see she had made her way over unbeknownst to them while they were caught up in their conversation and was now standing looking down at them. And she wasn't alone. Yul was hitched right beside her, his arm snaked loosely yet possessively around her middle, looking as smug in his blond smugness as could be.

"Uh nothing," said Jacob. "Ty here was just explaining how his dad's head's gonna explode when he finds out Captain Kirk and Spock had boldy gone where few men knew they had gone before."

"S'up, Wray?" said Ty, before giving Yul a nonchalantly friendly nod. "Kong."

Jacob had to bite his lip to choke down his chuckle, especially at the sight of the vacant expression on Yul's face at the mention of the classic cinematic damsel in distress Faye Wray and her giant ape captor that had apparently sailed way over the tops of his head.

"Still raiding imaginary closets, Ty?" inquired Wray with a cocked eyebrow.

"You know what they say about guys who are overly preoccupied about other guys who graze on the other side of the fence?" said Yul.

"Get warned about that a lot, do you, Yul?" Ty replied without missing beat and instantly erasing the snarky grin etched on the jock's face.

"So, where you two heading off to?" Jacob chimed in quickly as a courtesy to Ty to hopefully prevent the meeting of his friend's face with Yul's oversized fist, which he spied clenching itself into a knobby ball of knuckles.

"Yul's walking me to class," said Wray. "I just wanted to stop by and say hi, and to see if you needed a ride home after school."

"Uh, yeah...if it's no trouble."

"I wouldn't have asked if it was."

"Great. That'll give you a chance to tell her the good news," Ty piped in. Jacob shot Ty a look shaped with the points of a dozen razor-sharp daggers.

"What news?" asked Wray.

Ty was oblivious to the potency of the look of death trained on him.

"Just that our boy Jacob here just got green-lighted to rejoin the wrestling team," he said flashing the doctor's note still in his possession before Jacob lunged forward and angrily snatched it back.

"You've got such a big mouth," Jacob hissed under his breath.

"What's the big deal?"

The answer came when Yul's voice followed as expected.

"Well, whattaya know about that? I guess congrats are in order," Yul said through a crooked grin of overly white teeth, though he looked none too pleased by the news. "I guess that means that weird training bra you've been strapped into finally did its job and you finally get to step out...a woman."

"Knock it off, Yul," Wray muttered disapprovingly under her breath as Yul bellowed with laughter.

"Ah, he knows I'm just playing with him, babe. Don't you, Parrish?"

Jacob feigned as close a smile as he could muster, though it was more a gritting of teeth to keep back the bile wanting to spew forth, mostly from the cringing sound of the word "babe" coming from the meathead's mouth.

"Seriously, have you looked in the mirror?" mumbled Ty, drawing a lancing glare from Yul.

"What's that, mouth?" snarled Yul.

"I'm just stating an obvious, yet non-confrontational observation that if there's anyone here amongst us who should be rumored to have benefitted from wearing a training bra, it would be, well, you," said Ty, before quickly adding: "No offense, Wray."

What was clearly intended as a slam, however, was immediately realized to be the ultimate compliment when heard out loud, especially to a jock like Yul, who mugged cockily and popped with pride his impressive, muscle-swollen pecs which were on noticeable display beneath the tight polo shirt he wore that Ty had failed in deflating.

"You know what I meant," Ty mumbled with frustration.

Jacob just stared in disbelief at his friend while shaking his head wondering when the sewage rupture would be turned off and uttered the simple plea, "No!" As in "For the love of God, super glue your lips together."

The sound of the school bell, when it finally came, never had a more welcome ring to it.

"Well, I better get to class," said Wray, looking somewhat like a mother whose child had just embarrassed her by throwing a tantrum in the store. "I'll meet you after school in the parking lot?"

"See you then," said Jacob, smiling weakly.

"Guess I'll be seeing you on the wrestling mat, champ," said Yul, giving Jacob a friendly yet unmistakably challenging slap on the back.

He could be heard chuckling softly to himself as he followed along after Wray, as though he were privy to some secret joke. If there was one thing Jacob detested more than anything, it was to be laughed at in his face. Worse, still, was the sound of a lingering giggle coming from the muscle-headed jock at his expense being savored and sucked upon with enjoyment as if it were an after dinner hard candy mint.

"*Awwwk-ward!*" Ty sang as he sidled up closer to Jacob oblivious to the slow burn taking place with his friend.

As the two watched Wray and the Neanderthal towering beside her make their way across the grassy knoll, Jacob could hear the beating of his heart in his ears carried by the boiling flow of blood being pumped through his veins. And for the first time he wasn't sure who he had the desire to kill first if given the opportunity: Yul, or his best friend.

CHAPTER FOUR

WHAT ARE FRIENDS FOR?

Suffice to say, Jacob committed no acts of homicide that day. The fact he somehow managed to not bomb his quiz in literature class despite Ty's chatty efforts to the contrary during lunch may have had a hand in calming his murderous impulses. Yet the sulky mood which stalked Jacob the remainder of the day followed him out to the parking lot when school ended where he found Wray waiting for him in her white and tan Jeep.

The ride home was unusually quiet except for the drumming sound of Fleetwood Mac's "Dreams" blaring from the stereo. Any other time, Jacob likely would have cracked wise about the song choice. Wray was a Fleetwood Mac fanatic. Actually, her obsession lied with the band's bewitching songstress, Stevie Nicks. Behind the wheel mouthing along to the classic melody, Wray even bore a striking resemblance to the gold dust woman in her heyday, with her mane of gold-gleaming hair streaking carefree about her sun-kissed face while wearing a gypsy-inspired outfit of billowing chiffon and suede platform boots. On anyone else, such a look would have drawn snickering stares, like a Halloween costume donned in February; on Wray it was a look that breathed natural. Alluring, even, in the same way the song coming from the stereo retained a classic timelessness.

In many ways, it was the perfect soundtrack accompaniment. Slouched in his seat, Jacob watched through brooding eyes the people going about their business in a manner not rushed and seemingly without a care in the world. "Welcome to Cain's Corner, Population 57,643" a large wooden sign painted white with dark green lettering announced as they drove through the main thoroughfare of town. It always seemed to Jacob as though Cain's Corner was much smaller than the number boasted by the sign of people who had come to call it home.

Cain's Corner.

It was not by accident nor happenstance that Jacob had come to grow up in such an idyllic, homespun corner of the world, where grocery chains had not yet displaced the corner market and the barber's pole with its helical red, white and blue stripes still spun with life. And yet Jacob couldn't imagine anyone coming to Cain's Corner except by accident, and then, for whatever reason, deciding to call it home. Not that Jacob had any dislike for Cain's Corner. It was a perfectly fine place, as far as small towns go. In many ways, it reminded him of every town in every movie serving as a perfect picturesque backdrop for a coming attack by space aliens, or Ground Zero for an outbreak of some deadly, fast-spreading contagion. There was an unexplainable feeling about Cain's Corner, as if it existed in a secluded pocket detached from the reality that governed the rest of the world—a tiny town walled in behind the thick glass of a snow globe and untouched by time.

Yet even a relaxed and seemingly peaceful place as Cain's Corner was not without its blemishes.

Whatever thoughts Jacob found himself momentarily lost in dissipated when he noticed the Jeep had stalled at a stop sign longer than what was necessary. He saw Wray had stopped singing along with Stevie about the thunder and the rain and was instead staring straight ahead glaring at a huge billboard on the other side of the road crossing in front of them.

"Not to state the obvious, but it's not a stoplight," said Jacob, motioning to the stop sign posted off to the side of where they were stopped.

"One day I'm going to find a way to pull that sign down," said Wray, clearly upset.

Here we go again, thought Jacob as he sighed deeply and sank deeper into his seat. It was the same thing every time they drove past that certain intersection. A small atheist group in town had put up the billboard a month or so earlier. "IN THE BEGINNING, MAN CREATED GOD" it blared in giant red letters, while underneath in smaller type read, "Let go of the imaginary, choose reality!"

"I can't believe this town would allow something like that to be posted," Wray fumed.

"As opposed to what, denying someone their right to free speech?" questioned Jacob.

"Please…that is not free speech!" argued Wray. "It's just another blatant attempt to mock others who choose to believe in something they do not."

"Like it or not, that's the reason why we have the First Amendment."

"I don't like it," replied Wray through gritted teeth.

She then jammed her foot against the gas pedal sending her Jeep forward with a high-pitched squeal of the tires. Even as she sped away, she did not leave her irritation behind her.

"I just don't get it. If you don't believe in God, then don't. Why pay the money and go through the effort of putting up a sign to put down those who think differently?" Wray continued with her rant. "I mean, why do you give two hoots about what I believe? Does it really affect your life that much? Are you really that empty inside that you can't get a good night's sleep until everyone is as angry and miserable as you are?"

Jacob had heard it all before and he closed his eyes to shield the painful expression fixed in them knowing he had a stretch of road ahead to travel before Wray got it all out of her system.

"Do I care what the Jewish people believe, or the Indians, or Buddhists, or how about the people who dance around with poisonous snakes? No, I do not! And why don't I? Because I'm me and they're them," continued Wray. "I don't understand why everyone can't focus on their own stuff and let everyone else be. If I were to choose to believe in a dancing bear dressed in a tutu made out of daisies as the supreme being of the universe, whose business is it to tell me otherwise?"

Now there was some food for thought. After all, if the Hindus could worship an elephant god with numerous arms and hands, why would a tutu-wearing bear raise any eyebrows? And salty as Jacob was, he couldn't keep the corner of his mouth from curling upward ever so slightly imagining such a deity.

"What's so funny?" snapped Wray, catching sight of Jacob's subtle amusement.

"Nothing," Jacob, growing instantly serious once more, replied. "I was just wondering about the prayers one would say to this holy bear of yours. Would it go something like 'Our Bear, who art the cuddliest in heaven'—"

"You're missing the point! All I'm saying is live and let live."

At that very moment, as Wray continued in her rant, Jacob caught a glimpse of something suddenly darting out across the street straight into their path.

"LOOK OUT!" he yelled.

Wray slammed her foot on the brake and the Jeep came to a skidding, screeching halt; but not before there was felt a heart-stopping, thudding bump beneath the tires accompanied by a high-pitched yelp. The look in Wray's face was one of instant horror.

"Please tell me that wasn't what I think it was." she implored in what was more a whispered prayer than a question.

"Stay put and I'll go see," said Jacob while sharing in Wray's hopes.

Wray's eyes stayed glued to him as he slowly made his way around to the front of the Jeep with cautious, hesitant steps. When Jacob finally glanced back at her, Wray knew by the sympathetic look in his eyes the discovery wasn't a good one. With tears already beginning to form, she managed to force herself out of her seat and maneuver her way to the front of the vehicle where her horrified look instantly collapsed into one of anguish at the sight of a mid-sized brown and white dog lying with an unmistakable stillness on its side on the pavement.

"Oh no, no, no…" Wray began to whimper from behind the hand she brought to her mouth. "Look what I've done."

"It was an accident," said Jacob. "He just darted into the street from nowhere."

Wray, who once spent ten terrifying minutes herding a giant spider that had gotten into her house back outside into nature instead of simply squashing the hideous creature, couldn't be consoled.

"Look what I've done," she repeated sobbing, as if she had purposefully gunned her Jeep and ran the poor dog down for her own sick amusement.

Jacob knelt down on the ground to closer examine the dog. Maybe, he thought—hoped, even—it had just been knocked out and needed a little nudge to come to again.

"I'll grab a blanket," said Wray.

Before Jacob could stop her, she had already rushed off toward the back of the Jeep. He knew a blanket wouldn't do any good, except serve as a death shroud. The moment he touched the pooch, he could tell the life had been knocked free from the dog the instant the Jeep struck it. He checked for a collar and found attached to it a silver tag engraved with a name: Jasper. Poor little guy, Jacob thought to himself as he stared down at the mutt who looked only to be taking a peaceful afternoon nap. Probably was on his way home after enjoying an exciting afternoon of exploring the neighborhood before meeting his cruel fate beneath the tires of the Jeep. And as he continued to gently stroke the animal's soft fur with his fingers, Jacob found himself wishing there was some way he could somehow awaken Jasper and send him along on his way. If nothing else, to relieve Wray of the punishing weight of guilt he knew would settle itself upon her shoulders like a sack of bricks for some time to come.

That's when Jacob observed something most peculiar; the veins on the inside of his arm beginning at his wrist were slowly and prominently becoming visible through his skin. It was as if he was undergoing a transfusion of some unknown, dark fluid that was being pumped somehow into his bloodstream and gradually revealing the branch-like tendrils of his veins webbing their way like miniature river channels higher and higher through the tissues of his arm. It startled Jacob at first, and may very well have caused him to have a public freak-out session had his attention not been wrenched away to the fact that Jasper was now stirring with movements of life. To his utter shock, Jacob watched open-mouthed the dog rise up onto his paws and brush off his moment of rest with a good, hearty shake.

"You're alive!" Jacob gasped with disbelief.

As if to prove he wasn't a hallucination, Jasper sidled up to Jacob and offered up a friendly, if not slobbery, lick on the cheek before bolting off down the street, continuing with the run from which he had been briefly detained. When Wray finally returned with a red and white plaid wool blanket in her arms, she found Jacob still kneeling in front of her Jeep and, more noticeably, the spot on the asphalt where the dog was last seen lying now vacant.

"Where did he go?" she asked, looking around with alarm.

"Don't know. He just got up and ran off," said Jacob, staring off in the direction where he had watched Jasper run off, disappearing around a nearby corner. "Guess he was just knocked out for a moment."

Even more of a relief to Jacob than knowing they had not snuffed the life out of some helpless pup was when he glanced back down at his arms and saw the pronounced state his veins had revealed themselves through his skin had dissipated and faded back to invisible normalcy. Whatever freak thing had caused it, whatever momentary hallucination, he was just glad it was gone.

~ ~ ~

Wray and Jacob got back in the Jeep and continued along the street lined with poplar and maple trees towering high above with their tentacle-like branches intertwining to form a kind of protective canopy around the quaint quiet neighborhood. Turning the corner onto Tudor Drive, Wray quietly mouthed along to Stevie as she drove halfway down the narrow block before pulling over across the street from a cozy-looking, lived-in two-story home with pale yellow wood siding and charcoal color trim. She shut off the engine, turned down the volume on her stereo which continued to play and sat back into her seat.

"Do you think he's really alright?" she asked.

"Who?" said Jacob.

"What do you mean who? The dog, of course. What if he's wandering around hurt and in need of care?"

"Believe me, he's fine. He didn't have so much as a limp when he took off," said Jacob.

Wray could tell something far weightier than the dog's near-death experience was occupying Jacob's thoughts and she knew what it was.

"So...are you going to sulk about it now for the rest of the night?" she asked.

"Any objections if I do?" Jacob muttered with a quiet surliness. His eyes remained fixed looking straight ahead as they had for most of the drive home.

The "it" being the details of Jacob's visit to Dr. Gilkey's office that morning, which he decided to share with Wray along with an order of chili cheese fries at a nearby fast-food joint when school let out before the drive home. He needed someone to talk to about it, and while he felt bad he hadn't been completely honest with Ty about his examination, he had good reason, namely his best friend's unmalicious tendency for letting his loose lips flutter. That and, frankly, he wasn't in the mood for whatever off-the-wall diagnosis would surely come if he had confided in his friend. Wray, however, was different.

"I know it's frustrating." Her voice had a way, when necessary, of feeling like a cozy blanket being wrapped around the shoulders on a chilly day. "Just remember the doctor did say you're not the only one who's had to deal with this uh...um——"

"Scapula dysrhythmia," Jacob muttered under his breath while at the same time cringing inside at the sound of the word.

Dr. Gilkey's diagnosis was more dire-sounding than it actually was. Jacob much more preferred the less threatening, more commonly known name used for the malady he suffered: Winging scapula. Jacob didn't even know anything was wrong with himself until one day he was changing in the locker room after wrestling practice when he noticed one of his teammates down the row looking at him strangely. "You in an accident or something?" the boy asked. It wasn't until Jacob got home, stripped off his shirt and with the help of a hand mirror while standing in front of the larger mirror in his bathroom did he see what the boy was talking about. Two rounded oblong-shaped lumps were visibly beginning to balloon from his upper back region where his shoulder blades were located. He slowly leaned forward while twisting his body slightly to the right to try and get a better look, and as he did, his flexing made the anomaly more pronounced. To his horror, it appeared as if two stems or stumps were trying to push their way through his skin. He reached over his shoulder with his free hand to examine one of the lumps. It was definitely his shoulder blade. He could feel the hardness of bone pushing back beneath the surface of his flesh. He straightened back up and as he did the two protruding masses diminished in appearance.

"We usually see this sort of thing in athletes and people whose jobs involve the lifting of heavy objects such as furniture movers where the shoulder blade of the person afflicted is abnormally positioned giving a wing-like appearance," Dr. Gilkey explained to Jacob during his first examination. "The cause is usually the result of blunt trauma or paralysis of the long thoracic nerve in the shoulder and weakening of the serratus anterior muscles which leads to the winging."

Jacob's first thought was he had somehow injured himself during one of his wrestling matches. He was used to taking hard body slams, but he couldn't recall any particular moment when he had been consciously hurt, at least not so much as to cause what was happening to his back. The good news, Jacob learned much to his relief, was that the condition was caught in its beginning stages and treatable. Dr. Gilkey prescribed a rehabilitation regimen that included strength training and other physical therapy exercises, along with strapping Jacob's body into a specially designed brace, an unwelcome and frankly embarrassing contraption which only served to freshen the jibs and jabs that came his way when Yul and his cronies caught sight of it in the locker room and immediately branded it the "man bra." Jacob chose to suffer in silence. After all, Dr. Gilkey had touted great success treating others with the same condition, and if wearing the embarrassing gizmo and suffering a few taunts in the process was the price he had to pay to successfully alleviate and diminish, if not completely cure, what was ailing his back, then so be it.

Six months later, however, Jacob could tell by the knotty look of puzzlement on the doctor's face when he went to see him that day that the results were not what he was expecting. Not that it was of any surprise to Jacob. His own bathroom mirror, which he found himself standing in front of for hours staring at his back since his deformity was first brought to his attention, was a constant, day-to-day update that his freak-like condition was not improving. If anything, it was getting worse.

~ ~ ~

"I don't understand, I thought you said earlier the doctor told you he could still fix your back," said Wray.

Might be able to. Might!" snapped Jacob with an irritable edge to his tone.

"Alright might. It's certainly better than not being able to at all. So why get yourself all worked up over something when you don't even know the outcome yet?" said Wray.

"Oh sure, why get myself worked up? It's not like we're talking about my only option left at this point is surgery, except that it is."

"You see, this is where I end up confused," said Wray. "Your back is not improving—in fact, it's getting worse—and yet your doctor signs a permission slip for you saying it's okay for you to rejoin the wrestling team. Why would he do that?"

"Because I asked him to," answered Jacob matter-of-factly. "I mean, what difference does it make? Either way, I'm going to have to go under the knife."

"Oh, well, that makes a ton of sense," Wray remarked snidely. "Here you are whining over the possibility of your back not getting fixed, yet you want to risk possibly injuring yourself and making it even worse by wrestling. I mean, are you really that—"

"Stupid?"

"I was going to say reckless," corrected Wray.

"What's so reckless about not quitting?" Jacob spat. "Maybe I'm not ready to let life sideline me this early in the game. Maybe I refuse to allow this...condition to force me to surrender doing the things I enjoy doing like it has the last year."

"And maybe by doing so you could end up making matters worse," said Wray.

The gentle look in her eyes reflected not an intent to fight, but a genuine concern. Jacob didn't see it, or he refused to as he leaned forward and began hurriedly grabbing his things tucked between his feet on the floor board.

"Look, I don't want to talk about this anymore, alright?" he grumbled angrily. "How can you possibly understand having your back twisted into some deformity that has even your own doctor baffled, who has no idea what is even causing it or if it can be corrected, and even if it can be corrected you have to A) wait until you turn eighteen to have the necessary surgery, or B) find the guts to tell your grandmother to get the permission needed, which you're not too keen on doing while she's still in mourning over losing her daughter, and in exchange you get to live out your vital teenage years existing as some sort of side-show freak in a backwoods circus? But for you I will definitely try to chill out and turn my frown upside down."

Wray sank heavily back into her seat with a sigh of exasperation, her arms folded tightly across her chest. Fine...if that's the way he was going to be, she wouldn't say another word. If he was looking for sympathy from her with that attitude, he was in the wrong Jeep.

"I guess it's lucky for you then that there's a bell tower downtown," she muttered instead under her breath.

The comment stopped Jacob cold before he slowly turned and fixed the disbelieving look in his eyes on her.

"I'm sorry, was that...did you just infer I was Quasimodo?"

"If the hump fits," she mumbled sourly. "Or in your case two."

She gave him a sideways glance that raised doubt on whether the remark was meant to be funny or a painful jab. When she saw, however, the smile beginning to take shape from behind Jacob's glum expression, her own scowl eventually softened and the corners of her tightly lipped mouth couldn't refrain from turning upward ever so slightly. Jacob was the first to break out in laughter. If there was anything that could crack a foul mood that had taken hold of him, it was inappropriate humor, especially when he was the butt of it. And Wray had acquired a knack of shattering many of his moody dispositions with such a technique, helping to tighten the bond the two had shared for so long.

Despite his friend Ty's inference earlier in the day during lunch that Wray and Jacob were an undeclared item, Jacob had no designs on her. They were good friends, nothing more. At least, that's what he had convinced himself. Still, in that moment in the Jeep as the two shared a light-hearted laugh, Jacob found himself suddenly struck by Wray's smile. There was an infectious way about her, subtle and intangible, that every now and then seemed to draw him in like a honeybee to the powdery pollen of a blossoming flower. And just like all the times before, when he suddenly became aware of the changing rhythm to the steady beating happening inside his chest, he was quick to turn his focus elsewhere. This time it was to the stereo where the warbling of Stevie Nicks' voice continued to leak. "Sanctuary"—he recognized the song. It was Wray's favorite. In fact, Jacob couldn't remember a time riding as a passenger in Wray's Jeep that the song didn't materialize without fail at some point along the drive.

"Seriously, don't you ever get tired of this song?" asked Jacob.

Wray responded by joining in and bellowing forth a verse along with her rock goddess in a pitchy tone worthy of an "American Idol" reject.

"Forget I asked," Jacob interjected with a pained look usually reserved for moments when fingernails and blackboards meet.

"Come on, you can't deny it's a great song. It's one of the music world's great travesties she's never officially released it, and I will forever be thankful to the Internet gods that this bootleg demo exists," said Wray.

In fact, thanks to Wray's constant loop of the song playing in her Jeep, Jacob had come to like the tune quite a bit; even catching himself singing a few bars of it every now and then when he was alone. Although, not nearly as marring as Wray's rendition.

"You know, the homecoming dance is right around the corner," Wray remarked out of the blue.

Jacob gave an indifferent shrug. "And? Does anyone really go to those things anymore? Seems kinda cheesy."

"Of course it is. That's what makes it fun, like prom, or the winter formal," said Wray with a giggle. "It gives everyone the chance to get dressed up and have their picture taken in front of some god-awful backdrop so one day twenty years from now when you're feeling all nostalgic you have something to look back upon that will most likely horrify you and leave you wondering what possessed you to wear such a hideous-looking dress."

"See, this is precisely why I'm not a big fan. I don't want to be reminded when I'm old how horrible the dress I chose to wear to some dance actually was," said Jacob with a dry seriousness. "Besides, there's a monster movie marathon that's going to be on. They're going to be showing all the classics: 'Frankenstein,' 'The Invisible Man,' and you're favorite 'The Creature from the Black Lagoon.' I thought the two of us could watch it together."

Ordinarily, such a proposal would have brought a twinkle of excitement to Wray's eye. Afterall, the two first forged their friendship over their mutual love of the classic horror movie genre. Instead, Jacob's invitation caused Wray's smile to slowly deflate.

"I don't think I'll be able to," she said with quiet remorse.

"What do you mean? We always watch these kinds of marathons together. It's like a tradition." Yet he suddenly understood without Wray having to offer any explanation. "Oh, I get it…the dance. So, uh…I guess you'll be going with Yul."

"I don't know. I haven't really decided yet," Wray replied with a sigh.

"What do you mean you haven't decided? Isn't it pretty much a foregone conclusion that two people seeing each other would go together to the dance?" asked Jacob. "Or are you worried one day twenty years from now when you're all tingly with nostalgia you'll end up looking back and wondering what possessed you pick the douchiest douche for a boyfriend?"

"Yul is not a…what you called him," snapped Wray unable to bring herself to utter the "D" word, not because she was so prim and proper, but because she refused to take something associated with the feminine and support its being reshaped as a putdown. "And who said anything about him being my boyfriend?"

"Oh, please—" Jacob chuckled out loud. "It's pretty obvious by how cozy the two of you look at school."

"I don't care how it looks, we're just friends."

"Friends…" snickered Jacob.

"That's right, friends," stated Wray emphatically. "I don't know why you have such a problem with Yul unless it's because you're jealous of him. Or do you just automatically develop a dislike for anyone who is a Get?"

"No, I'm pretty much one hundred percent sure it's because he's simply a douche," said Jacob.

Frustrated—and bristling once more at that use of that term—Wray launched into a wordy defense of Yul attempting to convince Jacob there existed a nice guy once one got past the rough edges. Yet she knew her attempt to shorten the fangs Jacob had doodled on the mental image he carried around in his head of the jock had fallen on deaf ears, especially when her suggestion that the two boys could wind up friends if given the chance was met with an immediate sneer of "when hell freezes over" mockery.

Grabbing his backpack resting between his feet with one hand while pushing open the passenger door with the other, Jacob had one foot out of the Jeep when he turned suddenly, leaned toward Wray and gave her a quick parting peck on the cheek. Wray inhaled deeply, feeling her chest swell as though she were about to submerge herself inside a swimming pool, and closed her eyes savoring the friendly gesture for all it was worth. Smiling nervously, she tried to retain her composure when he pulled away and brushed her cheek with his hand. She was certain he had felt her tremble.

"Thanks for listening...you know, earlier," said Jacob.

"What are friends for?"

"Oh, and by the way...the day me and Yul become friends is the day I sprout wings and can fly," Jacob added with a sarcastic smile while quickly closing the door behind him before Wray had a chance to respond.

Wray watched as he made his way around the front of the Jeep and across the street toward his house.

"I'll call you later," she called out after him.

Giving a wave over his shoulder, Jacob smiled as the sound of Stevie Nicks' voice turned up and wailing from the Jeep faded in the distance as Wray drove away.

CHAPTER FIVE

On the day wrestling tryouts finally rolled around, Coach Mercer stoodwith his hands on his hips looking over the two dozen or so prospects who were huddled together on the bottom rungs of the bleachers inside the gym and asked, "So, which one of you's wants to go first today?"

It wasn't a question so much as it was a dare. One didn't just try out for the Harpus High wrestling team; one had to prove himself worthy of the honor of being part of such an exclusive group. Coach Mercer was not a subscriber to the belief of inclusion—that every kid be afforded the right to participate in the name of school spirit. He only cared about one thing—winning—and every boy who had assembled inside the gymnasium knew the coach was far from easy to impress and had no patience for what he deemed "weak links."

No one felt like more of a weak link than Jacob. He had already quietly scouted out the competition and placed bets with himself on who he thought would be quickly sent on their way. But it was a short list. There were a lot of hearty contenders, many of whom he had already seen in action on the mat from when he first managed to be part of the team. Sure he had gone up against many of them during practice, and come out the victor more than not. He had also committed the most unforgivable sin; he'd quit the team. In Coach Mercer's eyes, there only one thing worse than a loser, and that was a quitter. It didn't matter whether or not Jacob's reason was medical. If anything, it only made it that much worse; the coach now knew one of his once promising wrestlers was flawed, and that made Jacob a dreaded weak link.

So when Coach Mercer put the challenge out to see which of the boys had the chutzpah to be the first to step up to the mat and forcibly grab their spot on the team, Jacob knew it was his do or die moment.

"Right here."

The coach, with a pair of cheap spectacles that he never seemed to use perched on top his head, looked up from the clipboard on which he was busily scribbling notes. When he saw the volunteer was Jacob, he let out an exasperated sigh as if he were the bouncer at some club Jacob had been tirelessly attempting to gain entrance to with a slew of phony IDs. Lowering his clipboard, he beckoned Jacob forward with two fingers.

"Look son, I appreciate your spirit, but unless I hear from your doctor—"

Before the coach could finish, Jacob fished the crumpled note from Dr. Gilkey from inside his pocket. The coach gave the note a quick read before turning a skeptical look back onto the boy.

"The number's there in case you want to verify," said Jacob without pause.

The coach continued to study Jacob's face for any sign of willful deception given away by a tell-tale blink of an eye, but Jacob didn't so much as let an eyelash flutter.

"Alright, Parrish, choose your partner," said the coach finally.

Jacob's mouth widened with a grin of victory. Only now came the hard part. Spinning around, he faced the bleachers. The first face he saw belonged to Ty, who proceeded to signal as subtly as he could with a hand across the throat for Jacob not choose him. Jacob quickly looked past Ty, as well as the other boys, toward the center of the grouping where he found his target. All heads turned in the direction of where Jacob's finger eventually pointed and a noticeable hush descended on the gym when everyone saw it was aimed straight at Yul Dane. No one was more taken aback than Yul himself.

"You're actually calling me out?" questioned Yul with a chuckle of disbelief, until he saw from the serious look fixed on Jacob's face that it was no joke.

"No offense, Parrish, but maybe you better get yourself checked out again by your doctor. Only this time have him examine that head of yours because you're obviously not thinking too clearly," said Yul, rousing some snickering from the other boys.

Even Coach Mercer, who had always enjoyed watching an underdog go up against a bigger fish, seemed to have reservations about what was shaping up to be a face-off between a modern-day David and Goliath.

"I admire your spunk, Parrish, but I think you might want to reconsider your choice here and pick someone from your own weight class," he advised. "I mean, no sense risking getting hurt your first time back on the mat."

"Better listen to coach, Parrish," Yul's voice came from the bleachers. "I thought you were looking to make it back on the team, not embarrass yourself in front of everybody."

Jacob refused to budge. "If I thought there was any chance for that, I certainly wouldn't have picked you now, would I have, Yul?"

There was a hushed groan of doom from the other boys and the pompous smile spread wide on Yul's face slowly faded. Never had anyone even entertained the thought of challenging the burly jock unless they had a suicide pact. And no one certainly dared to call him by his real name. To everyone at school, he was known as Dane. Period. To call him by any other name, especially his given name, of which he hated, was to ensure a personal and painful correction.

Yul stood up, his muscles already flexed and fists clenched. His menacing gaze locked on Jacob, he began pushing heads and bodies aside to clear a path for himself as he made his way down the bleachers, the wooden slats groaning and cracking under his weight. He sauntered up to Jacob until only a hairline of daylight separated their bodies. Jacob refused to shrink in the shadow of his rival's threatening size that noticeably eclipsed his own or look away from the squinted glare locked on him. There was a brooding sullenness that had settled in Jacob's eyes, absent of fear and offering a glint of the anger that had been simmering ever since the death of his mother darkened his once happy-go-lucky personality.

"Alright boys, keep it clean," Coach Mercer instructed after directing the two teens to the blue rubber mat spread out across the gymnasium floor. Yet even he couldn't hide the same sick excitement he shared with the other boys who watched from the sidelines in growing anticipation for what promised to be a pay-per-view-caliber event.

The two boys took their neutral positions facing one another at the center of the mat.

"When you go home crying, don't say I didn't try to warn you," taunted Yul.

~ ~ ~

It wasn't that Jacob thought he had a clear-cut victory in going up against Yul. In fact, it was just the opposite. Dr. Gilkey's note may have given him a pass to try out, but it in no way secured him a spot on the team. For that, Jacob knew he had one chance in which to demonstrate to the coach in no uncertain terms he still had the makings of being a winner, despite the time-out his condition had briefly forced upon him. And, in Jacob's head, there was only one way in which he would be able to do that; and that was by calling out the biggest and strongest wrestler on the team to go up against.

If, however, Jacob entertained any notion he had a chance of coming out victorious in this match-up, he soon found himself second-guessing his bright idea once the two were grappling on the mat. It was there Jacob got an up-close introduction of just how strong a brute Yul was. Not to say Jacob didn't show off more than a few impressive moments. Sure, he was smaller and couldn't bench a small moving van the same way Yul could, but he was also wiry and quick as a cockroach caught in the light. Wrestling with Jacob was like wrestling with a greased pig at the fair, and more than once did he manage to slither his way out Yul's frustrated attempts to pin his opponent. One such time, Yul maneuvered his way in to bring Jacob down on the mat with a double leg takedown. Yet before Yul could secure a pin Jacob was able to rotate his body out from under Yul and, with remarkable swiftness, swung himself up and around the muscled beast hovering over him.

"How the heck did you do that?" Yul huffed with temporary bafflement in suddenly finding himself in the grip of a half nelson that had somehow been slipped on him like a hangman's noose.

The shouting from the bleachers grew louder eliciting a mighty groan from Yul as he fought for freedom. No way would he be taken down like this. Not this quickly. And certainly not by Jacob Parrish. He reached behind his head and grabbed hold of the hand clamped down on his neck. As he struggled to pry the arm away, he sidled forward working a knee up under himself until he was able to swing his hips around into a sitting position. Then with a loud feverish cry of exertion Yul pushed off with all the strength his legs could muster knocking Jacob off balance and sending the two of them backward onto the mat where he quickly regained his freedom.

"Not as easy as you thought, huh?" Jacob huffed heavily as the two boys quickly got to their feet and again faced one another.

Yet Jacob knew better than to pump himself up too much with a false sense of inflated ego. Yul was a good wrestler. He was also a dirty wrestler, especially when he was angry, and it was pretty clear he was simmering at this point.

Yul lifted the bottom of his damp shirt to wipe away the sweat that dripped from his face. His cocky smirk had long disappeared and he shot looks of annoyance toward the bleachers where the cheers seemed to gradually grow louder in favor of Jacob. Again the two boys circled, and again they clashed. Hands clinched necks, and the sides of their faces pressed against each other as they struggled against one another like sumo wrestlers. Yul suddenly lowered himself while snaking his arm around Jacob's neck and lifted the boy up off the ground like a firefighter carrying a victim out of a burning building. With a huge grim stretched across his face, Yul began to pirouette around the mat in showboat fashion bringing a wave of laughter from the other boys. Around and around he twirled, spinning himself to the center of the mat. Then, in a move more suitable for a cage match, he knowingly and purposefully body-slammed Jacob against the floor with his brawny weight behind it.

Jacob gasped from the flash of pain that detonated itself from somewhere in vicinity of the center of his spine. If that wasn't enough, a deliberate and dirty jab of Yul's fist to the solar plexus sent a burning flash of pain to explode in Jacob's chest. If Jacob had cried out in pain, he didn't hear it; the ringing in his ears was too loud, though not loud enough to drown out the chirping of Coach Mercer's whistle which was frantically being blown.

"You know better than to pull dirty stunts like that, Dane," the coach barked. "Hit the showers!"

Jacob managed to catch enough of a breath to voice a loud and defiant "No!" As in no way was he going to win on a technicality of dirty play. With sweat now pouring out of him and his face blazing red like a beet, Jacob struggled with all his might to keep Yul from his goal of pinning his back flat to the floor. Eyes squeezed tight, Jacob could feel every muscle in his body being straining to the breaking point. He could feel the veins in his neck popping out from beneath his skin sending more pressure to his head until he was sure it would explode and splatter his brains across the mat.

"Ready to say uncle?" taunted Yul like an older bully of a brother tormenting his younger, weaker sibling.

"In your dreams," Jacob hissed back.

Somehow he managed to slither his way onto his belly, but he gained little except maybe time before Yul inevitably would manage to wrangle him back over and claim his victory with a deflating pinning to the floor. Panting heavily as though he'd just collapsed at the finish line of a 15-mile marathon, Jacob struggled to catch his breath. His strength was spent, his arms felt like limp noodles attached to his body. There was nothing worse than the feeling of imminent defeat, especially at the hands of this meathead jock; nothing, that is, until Jacob managed to look up and spy the faces of the other boys watching from the bleachers witnessing his defeat, including Ty.

Perhaps that was all it took—seeing such looks of pity fixed on him—that Jacob came to feel a second breath collect itself inside him. Whatever it was, he found to his surprise the floor suddenly dropping out from beneath him when he gave a last desperate push to lift himself up off it. Only it wasn't the floor that fell away but himself rising up in the air. And in that open space, Jacob found himself rolling his way out from underneath the body crushing him from above and somehow maneuvering his way in a twisting motion and positioning himself on top the dumbfounded jock before riding him like a cowboy saddled to a bucking bull back down hard onto the floor which reared back up to meet them where he quickly pinned his noticeably stunned opponent.

It was a moment that appeared lightning-quick to everyone watching but played out in surreal slowness in Jacob's eyes.

If there was any cheering of his victory that followed, Jacob didn't hear it. He was far too stunned to notice anything except the heap of muscle lying defeated on the mat beneath him. He had won—he had actually won. It was how he won, however, that left him baffled, and like everyone else who had witnessed the great taking down of Yul Dane, Jacob could only stand there looking like he'd taken a hit to the side of the head with a brick and wonder to himself, What the heck just happened?

"What in the name of Jesus, Mary and Joseph was that, Parrish?" barked Coach Mercer, looking like a man in need of the glasses sitting on top his head.

"I…I don't know," stammered Jacob. "I was just trying to win."

"Well, thanks to that stunt, you did." The coach sounded as angry as he looked. Until he smiled, that is. "You also made the team. Good job!"

It took a moment for the words to sink in, but when they finally did Jacob was filled with a warm sense of elation. Looking down at Yul, who still had a cloudy haze over what had just happened alighting his eyes, Jacob extended his hand to the beaten jock both in a gesture of good sportsmanship and to help him to his feet. Yul wanted neither.

"Keep away from me, Parrish!" he barked while angrily slapping away the hand held out for him to take.

He slowly pulled himself up, his hulking body swaying unsteadily back and forth. There was a dazed look in his eyes. And an unmistakable contempt.

"What the hell kind of freak are you?" hissed Yul while giving Jacob a look as though he was infected with some plague-like disease.

The charge stung. And yet, as Jacob watched the jock retreat to the bleachers to lick his wounds, it was a question that rang out over and over inside his head.

What kind of freak are you?

~ ~ ~

The question repeated itself inside Jacob's head long after the wresting tryouts ended and the other boys disappeared into the locker room. Alone in the darkened gym, Jacob circled the now vacant blue mat while replaying the match between Yul and himself in his mind, revisiting each move. Moment by moment.

Stepping inside the gold-colored circle in the center of the mat, he stared down into the sea of blue envisioning himself sprawled out on his belly struggling with all his might against Yul's attempt to twist him over onto his back like a crocodile hunter grappling with an uncooperative swamp beast. The smell of dried sweat and rubber met Jacob as he sank to his knees and positioned himself face-down in the exact same spot on the mat. A lingering burn in the muscles in his arms served as a reminder of the exertion he spent trying to escape Yul's strong, vice-like grasp as Jacob placed his hands palms down against the mat just outside his chest to mirror the moment playing out inside his head when gravity somehow reached down, grabbed hold of him and pulled him—and Yul—off the floor.

How had he managed to pull off such an acrobatic feat? Jacob questioned himself for the umpteenth time. There wasn't even a name for such a wrestling move because, as far as Jacob knew, such a wrestling move didn't even exist. All he could remember was an intense need to get out from underneath the crushing weight of muscle pressing down on him from above. And so he did what had to be done then; he pressed his hands firmly against the mat and pushed off with all his might. The floor left him, but only for a split second, and then just by only a foot or two before his body fell flat against the mat with a sounding splat. Again he attempted to recreate the winning move that had stunned all who had seen it, not least of all himself, and again he failed. Over and over he tried, accomplishing nothing but repeated reps of what appeared to be a spastic demonstration of a most awkward concept of an extreme pushup until a mixture of fatigue and frustration caused him to falter before the laws of physics drove him face-first into the mat. A familiar metallic taste was quick to greet his tongue. Sitting up, Jacob brought his fingers to his bottom lip to reveal the stain of blood which he wiped away on his shorts.

"You really are a freak, aren't you, Parrish?" Jacob muttered to himself.

"You're trying too hard," a voice suddenly echoed from somewhere behind him.

Thinking he was alone in the now vacant gym, Jacob was startled at first. He turned his head and glanced over his shoulder toward the wall of bleachers behind him. Scanning the seats, he didn't see anybody, at first.

"Who's there?" he asked.

Then, under the dim lights, he caught sight of the lone shadowy figure of a man near the top. He was stretched out casually, lying on his back across one of the wooden slats, eyes closed with one leg crossing the other and hands folded on top his chest looking as though he were enjoying a nice afternoon of sunning himself in the park.

"You're focusing all your energy on the muscles in your limbs, when the problem you're having rests solely in your mind. It's not yet in sync with what the rest of your body already knows," continued the man.

Jacob's first instinct was to not engage the stranger, but he couldn't help himself. "And just what exactly is it the rest of my body knows that my mind doesn't?" he asked.

"My guess would be not so much in how you managed to take down someone like Yul Dane, but the manner in which you did. That is why I find you here, is it not, beating your head against a rock, so to speak, trying to make some semblance of sense in how it's possible for you to sometimes not be constrained by the laws of motion that govern other boys your age? Therein lies the disconnect between mind and body, and why you now find yourself frustrated and struggling to try and replicate the movements you managed to perform earlier without so much as a thought," said the man. "But fret not, most boys like you find it to be a bit awkward at first, even those who grow up with the knowledge of knowing from which tree they've sprouted. All you are in need of is some training, from the right teachers, to mend the disconnect you're feeling."

The words coming from the man's mouth met Jacob's ears like some indecipherable riddle. Not only was he nowhere closer to understanding this "disconnect" of which the man spoke, but talk of training and sprouting from trees only complicated the confusion. And what exactly did the man mean by "most boys like you?"

"Alright then...thanks a lot for the tip," said Jacob with a friendly nod of the head and half a smile thinking better than to engage the man any further.

Most likely some crazy street person who found his way into the gymnasium to make use of the bleachers to sleep off the alcoholic haze brought on from whatever cheap bottle of booze he'd managed to save up for from a morning of panhandling, Jacob thought to himself as he was about to start for the locker room.

"No need to hurry off, Jacob," the man called out after him. "I can assure you I'm quite sane. And quite sober. Though I guess I'll have to rethink my choice of wardrobe if my fashion sense is giving off a transient vibe."

"I'm sorry, do I know you?" asked Jacob at hearing his name while straining his eyes to get a better look at the figure lying supine on the bleachers.

"From a distance, one could say," said the man sitting himself upright and slowly getting to his feet. "But I guess I've gotten a little ahead of myself, haven't I?"

Jacob kept a fixed eye on the man who proceeded to make his way down the bleachers, slowly emerging from the shadows with each step and into the reach of the few lights left on inside the gymnasium. When the man's face finally came into view, Jacob could see right away he did not recognize the stranger, and yet there was something strangely familiar about him.

"Your grandmother has a unique and strident way of harnessing one's guilt. It was she who, shall we say, stressed somewhat vigorously that I make myself formally known to you," said the man.

"You know my grandmother?" asked Jacob somewhat disbelievingly, as the man looked nothing like the sort of person his grandmother would be acquainted with, except perhaps in passing, like a cashier at the local grocery store.

"For some time now," said the man when he reached the last wooden plank at the foot of the bleachers. "My name is Gotham."

"Gotham. As in Gotham City from Batman?" questioned Jacob, his slight grin revealing his bemusement at the name. And yet Jacob found the name oddly fitting for this inscrutable figure who, in just a short reveal under the lights, had an intense aura of mystery surrounding him beyond any fictional character found in some silly comic book.

"It's short for Gothamel," said the man who, from the serious look on his face, found nothing amusing about his name. "As for the rest of the formalities, I'm afraid it won't be quite as simple. I've found over time there is never an easy way to do this except to just come right out and say it so that we may get on with the business at hand."

"Say what exactly?" inquired Jacob, who once again found himself struggling to follow what the man was saying.

"I'm an angel," answered Gotham as simply as if revealing the zodiac sign under which he was born.

~ ~ ~

Naturally, the man could have stripped off his long wool overcoat and revealed himself to be wearing a Catholic schoolgirl's uniform underneath and Jacob wouldn't have been caught any more off guard.

"Angel, you say. Is that a fact?" he said.

Only this time he couldn't keep his growing grin from surfacing. "That's right," said Gotham.

"As in with wings?"

"You might say they've been clipped some, but I still manage to sail the skies. I am what mankind has so often depicted in its literature and art as an angel of the fallen variety."

"Uh-huh...of course...a fallen angel," said Jacob who was now snickering openly even as Gotham fixed a firm gaze on him from the other side of the gymnasium. "Look, I've really gotta go, but the next time you do a fly-by of heaven, be sure to give a shout out from me."

Gotham bowed his head and patiently endured the lingering chortle while clenching his jaw. It was, after all, par for the course. Then as Jacob turned on his heel to head to the locker room he was stopped dead in his tracks by the sight of the man now suddenly standing in his path. Nearly leaping out of his own skin, Jacob whipped his head around to look back toward the bleachers to the spot where the man had been standing just seconds earlier only to find it vacant and then back to the sight of the figure standing before him, and the color instantly drained from his face.

"Wh–what the—? How did you do that?" There was a noticeable tremble in his voice, though not necessarily caused by fear.

"The same as anyone with two working legs—by simply putting one foot in front of the other to get from one point to another, only in a manner far quicker than the human eye is able to observe," explained the stranger in an off-handed manner.

Even as he felt his own body urging him to retreat, Jacob remained fast where he stood as the towering figure of a man slowly stepped his way closer toward him like the dark shadow of a great mountain stretching itself across the landscape as the sun sinks into the horizon. Despite the bulky dark overcoat draped over the stranger's body, Jacob could see the man possessed a powerful build underneath, the weight of which could be heard in the heavy footsteps of the loosely laced boots that carried the beat-up, scuffed scarring of never being retired to the back of a closet treading their way across the slick, polished wood of the gymnasium floor. When the man stopped in front of him, Jacob could only tilt back his head to better examine the face staring down at him. The man was quite tall—much taller than he appeared from across the gymnasium—but the imposing height was momentarily forgotten when Jacob looked into what seemed like two vats of swirling molten gold that formed two piercing and penetrating eyes bringing life to a stone, expressionless face which cracked momentarily with a slight smile while staring down into the perplexed look fixed in the boy's own eyes.

"Who am I, you're asking yourself. And so I shall tell you again, as I did a few moments ago to your scoff, that indeed I am an angel, though you still will not believe me. That, as they say, will come in time," Gotham began. "It's what I've been tasked to tell you about your own self that you will have difficulty in accepting far more than the idea of an angel standing before you at this moment. Yet that, too, will come in time."

"Wh–what about me?" asked Jacob with noted trepidation.

"That you are a Nephilim," answered Gotham.

The declaration made Jacob tilt his head slightly in confusion like that of dog trying to decipher words coming from human lips.

"What the blazes is a Neph…Nephol—"

At first Jacob wasn't sure whether or not he'd just been insulted by some foreign word he found himself tripping over his tongue trying to pronounce.

"Nephilim," repeated Gotham. "A Nephilim is a halfling of sorts—in this case, someone who is born to a mortal woman, but fathered by an angel."

An intensely troubled look slowly darkened its way across Jacob's face. Not that he believed any of the nonsense the man was concocting, but the elaborateness of crazy the man was conjuring had suddenly taken an unfunny turn. It was one thing for someone to proclaim themselves to be an angel. Mrs. Cossmeyer, the local eccentric who spent her days in the downtown park surrounded by a flock of loyal pigeons, believed herself to be Mother Nature. It was a harmless, not to mention amusingly entertaining detachment from reality. But this—this had a completely different feel to it. There was nothing amusing about being painted inside another person's delusions. It made Jacob recall a spat of tragic, unfortunate stories that had made their way across the news in recent years about instances of normal-looking yet deranged persons opening fire on unsuspecting innocents at numerous school campuses, malls and movie theaters, and suddenly he found himself eyeing the man's overcoat a little more suspiciously.

"Look, uh, it was great meeting you and all, uh—" Jacob began awkwardly.

"Gotham," the man helped out quietly noting the boy's nervousness.

"Right…Gotham," said Jacob. "But, uh, Mr. O'Brien's going to be showing up any moment now to lock up so—"

"Not for another few minutes," said Gotham. "We've still got a little time left."

Another shiver made its way up the middle of Jacob's back.

"You're not afraid of me, are you, Jacob?" asked Gotham.

"Why should I be afraid of you? I mean…you're an angel, right?" answered Jacob not too convincingly. "But like I told you earlier, I really have to get going."

He spun himself on the ball of his foot before even finishing the sentence, wanting nothing more at that moment than to slink out of the gymnasium as quickly as possible and let Mr. O'Brien, the school security guard, know about the looney tunes inside.

"Your mother warned me you'd be a difficult one to convince regarding this revelation," Gotham called after Jacob. "I see now she was quite right."

It was the only thing at the moment that would have been able to bring Jacob's feet to a standstill.

"My mother's dead," replied Jacob, glancing back at Gotham with an angry glare.

"Yes, I know. I visited her the night she passed," said Gotham. "She told me she had tried to explain to you that night when you went to sit with her in her room what I have now revealed to you, only she was far too weak and overcome by her illness to continue before you ushered her to the confines of her bed. Not that it would have mattered much had she found the strength, as you most likely would have brushed off what she had to say as the delusional ravings of a severely sick woman."

Jacob struggled to choke down the emotion rising up inside himself as he listened to the man eerily describe the last moments he remembered spending with his mother that remained etched in his memory. Yet the tears brewing in his eyes were quickly vaporized by the heat of anger he felt surge through him.

"Who the hell are you?" Jacob hissed at the man.

"I've already told you twice. I doubt the third time will prove to be the charm," answered Gotham.

"Alright, fine, have it your way, Gotham the angel. Just...what do you want with me?" Jacob implored with a frustrated sigh.

"It's not my wants at play here, but your mother's—and, to a larger extent, your grandmother's. See me, if you will, only as a reluctant messenger sent to shed light on the truth they struggled to bring out of the shadows and reveal to you who and what you truly are," said Gotham. "And yet I suspect what I've told you, incomprehensible as you may at this very moment find it to be, isn't as surprising or shocking as you might lead one to believe."

Jacob wanted nothing more in the world for this man and this conversation to no longer exist, and still he couldn't help but ask, albeit warily, "What do you mean?"

"Discovering one is different—in your case, markedly—than other boys can be off-putting, to say the least," said Gotham. "Subtle as they may have been at first, those differences—whether it was the speed with which you could run, or distance your legs could carry you in a single leap—were likely happily embraced in the beginning, in the same way a young athlete recognizes a shining ability that will one day carry him to Olympic greatness. But it wasn't long before you began to take notice of other unnatural abilities beginning to blossom within yourself. Like suddenly being surrounded by the sounds of nature, and instead of the overlapping drone of birds and dogs and cats and other creatures that fills the ears of others, you hear individual voices speaking words you can decipher and understand as if spoken by any other person. Or the day in Mrs. Lopez's Spanish class when your tongue got away from you and, to your surprise, began speaking the language you had been struggling to comprehend. Understandably, you found it easiest to explain away the unexplainable by convincing yourself it was all some kind of ruse: that the voices of animals you now made sense of like some modern-day Dr. Doolittle was concocted by an imagination having a bit of fun with you, and the overnight fluency of a foreign language nothing more than the fruits of labor that come from focusing harder on your studies finally kicking in. Yet all the while a crawling realization begins to congregate in the back of your mind that there is something innately different about you, something you can't quite pin-point, and a slow-brewing fear sets in. It undoubtedly leads you to do your best to turn a blind eye to your abilities. For what young boy wants to reveal himself as anything more or less than what has been sketched out by others as normal and risk the loneliness of being branded an outcast?"

Jacob stood listening without uttering one syllable of a rebuttal because, for the first time since he rose up out of the bleachers, the man was speaking sense Jacob not only understood, but couldn't deny. And in a brief moment that rarely visited itself upon him, Jacob no longer felt unseen while mirrored in the golden gleam of Gotham's gaze—he no longer felt like a Ghost. If anything, he was suddenly overcome by an uncomfortably vulnerable feeling; the same kind of feeling one gets when caught in the realm of a dream where the dreamer finds himself naked in a grocery store or standing before an auditorium filled with people with all eyes fixed on him.

"But now other things have surfaced you can't ignore, or bury, haven't they?" continued Gotham. "Now your physical body is revealing your truth, and no matter how hard you might try you cannot turn a blind eye to it."

Jacob knew immediately to what Gotham was referring.

"The doctor said it was a condition called winging scapula," said Jacob, instinctively bringing his hand to nervously rub the space between his neck and shoulder.

"The good doctor is only half correct," said Gotham.

He took a step toward the boy, and as he did Jacob automatically took an equal one back to ensure the distance between them.

"Are you that close-minded as to readily accept the conclusion you are suffering a cruel betrayal by your body rather than consider, if be for a moment, the possibility you've been given a divine gift?" asked Gotham.

"You're kidding me, right?" answered Jacob. "You're asking me to believe I'm half human and half angel."

He almost couldn't get the words to flow from his lips.

"The sooner you do, the easier it will be for you to embrace the next stage of your...awakening," said Gotham.

Next stage? What did he mean by that? Jacob wondered. Before he could ask, the sound of the door to the gym opening broke through the silence with a loud drawn-out squeal. Jacob turned to see Mr. O'Brien, a short, pear-shaped man squeezed into a gray security guard's uniform, making his rounds at just about the time Gotham said he would.

"You ready to call it a day, Jacob? I'm about to lock everything up," the security guard announced.

"Yeah...no problem. We were just getting ready to leave," said Jacob, bringing a curious look to the security guard's face.

"We?" asked Mr. O'Brien, casting a puzzled glance to the four corners of the gym.

Jacob turned to look where Gotham had stood just moments before and saw he was nowhere to be found, and strangely he found his sudden disappearance oddly fitting.

"When you're ready to speak again," the mysterious man's voice suddenly made itself heard inside Jacob's head, *"I'll come to you."*

Jacob's eyes darted from one side of the gym to the other and all points in between and the noticeable emptiness sent a strange tremble through him.

"Me," he mumbled to himself under his breath as if to soothe the sudden fear that he might be losing a good portion of his functioning mind. "It's just me."

CHAPTER SIX

The Buried Secret

"I'm home!" Jacob's announcement echoed through the house when he walked in through the front door. "Hello?"

Silence.

He headed upstairs. His long-limbed legs effortlessly took the stairs two at a time as he bounded his way toward his room. When he reached the top, he called out for his grandmother. There was no answer. The house was empty. Even markedly so. Then again, these days the house seemed to have acquired a permanent hollow, vacant feel to it. It was a bothersome, shiftless feeling Jacob did his best to try and ignore. This time he couldn't—or wouldn't—and he found himself allowing his gaze to drift toward the one area of the house he consciously forced himself to avert his eyes whenever he went upstairs where the emptiness seemed to emanate with the greatest strength: the door leading to his mother's bedroom at the end of the darkened hallway straight ahead of him.

Now, strangely, after kicking off his sneakers at the doorway of his own bedroom, his feet walked him to the end of that hallway he had consciously ignored. How long he stood staring at the closed door while struggling with the decision of whether to go inside or not he did not know. It had remained closed tight ever since the day his mother...you know. It had been almost as if a wall had been erected to end that part of the house from existing. It was an eerie feeling, one which nudged Jacob's feet to turn direction and walk themselves back down the hall. Instead, he slowly took hold of the doorknob, turned it and the door swung open with a yawning squeal of his hinges.

Jacob took a tentative step inside the room and immediately the familiar scent of his mother swirled about him to greet him. Lilacs and jasmine with a hint of gardenia. It was strong enough that if he closed his eyes he could almost imagine her still in the room, before the added stench of sickness took up residence with its unwelcome presence. For a minute or two, Jacob stood in the middle of the room and just breathed in the remnants of his mother and for the first few inhales it proved to be comforting, but only the first few. Then suddenly it wasn't comforting any longer, and an overwhelming sense of missing her made him rush to the window which he hurriedly flung open. The breeze from outside came to his aide and helped to steady him as he breathed deeply the tangy wood fragrance coming off the nearby eucalyptus trees.

His grandmother had left her mark on the room. Jacob could see it in every corner. It was spotless. Everything was in its place. Even the bed where his mother had been shackled like some prisoner was meticulously made with the pillows arranged just so. No one would ever guess death had paid a visit and made itself a guest there only a short time ago, and that, strangely enough, was an unsettling thing to Jacob. Moments before he had been gripped with an uncomfortable fear of confronting the ghosts which lurked behind the closed bedroom door only to discover an impeccable cleanliness had managed to give the appearance the room had never before been occupied. Except for the familiar strand of rosary beads resting atop a small Bible on the night table next to the bed and the few personal items carefully arranged on a nearby dresser, all signs that his mother had lived there had been scrubbed away. In many ways, it was as if she had never been there. For Jacob, that proved far more unsettling than any memory of her long-lived suffering.

As he looked about, Jacob suddenly found himself thinking about the strange man with shimmering gold eyes who had approached him at school. He went to his mother's dresser and with some hesitation began nosing through the drawers, careful not to mess up the neatly folded blouses inside. What he was looking for he didn't know, yet he moved at a faster more determined pace with each drawer he searched. Drawer after drawer, however, failed to offer up whatever it was for which he was searching. When he had finished, he was quick to leave and closed the door behind returning the bedroom to the sealed tomb it had become without a body resting inside.

Jacob stood for some time in the hallway with his mind blank and yet wrestling with a flood of thoughts at the same time. He then came to notice a warmth of light resting on the right side of his face. Turning his head, he saw he was standing in front of his grandmother's bedroom. The door was open and sunlight was streaming in through the window inviting him inside. And most likely he would have had he not heard the opening and closing of the front door downstairs.

~ ~ ~

Rushing downstairs in his stocking feet, he found his grandmother hanging up her coat in the entry closet.

"I was wondering where you went off to," he said.

"What you mean to say is you were beginning to worry I might have become like one of those old persons you hear about in the news who go out for a walk and suddenly can't remember their way home." said Ava. "Well, fear not. I needed a couple things at the market and somehow I managed the survive the treacherous journey."

She went to pick up the bag of groceries she had set down but Jacob rushed over and beat her to it.

"Thank you, dear," she said, giving her grandson a grateful pat before leading the way to the kitchen.

"I wish you would let me know when you need a grocery run. I could have picked these things up for you on my way home from school," said Jacob while peering down into the grocery bag to see what goodies might be inside.

"What am I, suffering from infirmity?" scolded Ava, "You'll notice I'm still able to depend on two able legs to get around and not some mechanical scooter of which everyone seems in a rush to get behind the wheel."

"Yes, but—"

"But nothing," said Ava, motioning with her finger to a place on the counter for Jacob to set the bag. "Besides, I'm going to trust you to know how to pick out porcinis?"

"Porcinis? That's cheese, right? How hard can that be?"

A knowing look of judgment came to Ava's face.

"I rest my case," she said, retrieving the bag of fresh mushrooms from her bundle of groceries.

When she turned to make her way to the refrigerator, Jacob instantly began to rummage through the rest of the groceries. Potatoes, carrots, celery—it was clear his grandmother was preparing to make a batch of her vegetable soup.

"All I'm saying is the grocery store is a good half mile away."

"I enjoy the walk, especially at this time of the year," said Ava. "Perhaps you'd rather I stayed cooped up in this house twenty-four hours and get my allowance of exercise through a pair of knitting needles."

"I'm not saying that," said Jacob, with a sigh of frustration. "I'm just not sure being out alone carrying groceries for such a long way is a good idea for someone so—"

Jacob stopped himself, but not soon enough. Ava leveled on him a piercing glare from across the counter with those steely blue eyes of hers. She grabbed from Jacob's hands the bunch of red grapes he had found knowing he could devour the entire bunch faster than a swarm of locusts to a corn crop and leave nothing behind but the dried-up vine as evidence.

"So what? Old?" She allowed the last word to be cast from lips with a noted infliction of disdain.

"Delicate, as all beautiful, grand women are," Jacob brown-nosed with a matching smirk which only made Ava's left eyebrow arch itself even higher.

"Do yourself a favor while you remain one step ahead of being disinherited and grab me the soup pot and get it ready for the stove while I finish putting away the rest of the groceries. That is if my delicate arms can muster enough strength for such labor," she said, plucking free a small bunch from the grapes she held for Jacob to nibble.

She couldn't help faintly smiling while watching him go about the task she had given him. She found him to be a good and kind-hearted young man, even when his kind-heartedness reminded her of her advanced years. All ninety-four of them, of which she held more and more in contempt. Not because of any vanity she possessed, but from the added worry each passing year brought with it; worry that the limited time she had left would take her from him too soon. Especially now when she was all he had left.

"How is school?" she inquired suddenly in an attempt to clear her mind of such unsettling thoughts. "I trust you are keeping up with your studies."

"Sure," replied Jacob as he waited at the sink for the pot to fill with water.

"I hope so. Beautiful, grand woman as I may be," she gave a sarcastic glance over her shoulder as she continued to put food away in the refrigerator, "I'm not so much that I've forgotten what it's like to be a teenager."

Discussing his studies, or the generation of teenagers long passed was the last thing Jacob was interested in doing. Placing the pot on the stove, he turned on the burner igniting a flowering blue flame beneath it. He then leaned himself against the counter and watched his grandmother grab the last remaining items from the grocery bag. His mind, however, was clearly elsewhere—miles elsewhere—which Ava was quick to notice.

"You okay?" she asked.

"Perfect," replied Jacob through a not-so-convincing half-smile.

He nervously started drumming his fingers against the edge of the counter while continuing to compete in the ongoing tug-of-war taking place with his thoughts.

"Speaking of school," he finally forced himself to say rather tentatively. "I had a visitor today."

"That's nice, dear, " replied Ava, who remained busy with her groceries.

"Yeah. In fact, he said he knew you."

"That so? Who was it?"

Jacob hesitated at first.

"He said his name was Gotham."

Ava came to an abrupt halt just short of the refrigerator, as if she ran straight into some invisible wall, and lost hold of the carton of eggs in her grip.

"Grandma?"

She remained stock-still, not even moving to clean up the omelette of broken egg shells and running yolk pooling at her feet.

"You've seen him? Gotham?" she finally inquired in a faint voice as if fearful to even pose the question. "What did he want?"

"Maybe you better sit down—" said Jacob, gesturing to the kitchen table, but Ava was in no mood for his convalescent handling of her with kid gloves.

"What did he want?" she repeated with noted impatience.

"I'm not really sure. He didn't really seem to be playing with a full deck."

"What do you mean?"

"Well, for starters, he told me he was an angel," Jacob answered with a forced chuckle while closely watching his grandmother's reaction. Yet his words didn't seem to faze her in the slightest. Not even a questionable flinch. If anything, what looked to be a wave of relief swept its way visibly across the profile of Ava's face serving to only confuse Jacob all the more.

"He changed his mind," he heard her mutter in a comforting whisper to herself while closing her eyes and bringing her clenched hands to her bosom. "He changed his mind."

"Did you hear what I said?"

"He told you he was an angel. Alas, my hearing is one of the few things not yet diminished by age." She then took a few steps forward to close the door to the refrigerator she had left open and asked simply, "Was that all?"

Was that all? Jacob thought to himself. Wasn't claiming to be some kind of winged myth enough?

"Hmmm, well, let me think here for a minute," Jacob hemmed sarcastically. "Oh yeah, there was one other thing he brought up. He said he wanted to inform me I was a neph—a nephol—"

For some reason Jacob's tongue couldn't find the word, and in his growing frustration he found himself stammering even more until Ava, with a heavy sigh, put silent her grandson's continued hiccupping search for the word by interjecting clearly and calmly, "Nephilim."

The kitchen once more grew quiet. Ava didn't need to glance over at her grandson to know he was staring at her with dazed disbelief.

"Perhaps the pronunciation of the word got itself tangled up in all that sarcasm," she remarked.

Ava didn't need to worry about any further mockery passing through Jacob's lips. He was too busy trying to dull the unpleasant shiver he felt beginning to make a slow crawl up his back.

His back...

"What's going on?" Jacob managed to ask with great hesitation.

It was then she finally turned her gaze on him, and at first Jacob wasn't sure which to focus on first, the faint smile curving his grandmother's lips, or the glistening of tears in her eyes she struggled to choke back, which made it all the more difficult to decipher whether it was good news or bad she seemed to be preparing herself to unload upon him.

"What's going on, indeed. I guess you've waited long enough to finally have that question answered, yes?" asked Ava, her smile overcoming the diminishing tears, and yet offering little comfort to Jacob.

"Why don't you turn off the burner and let us go up to my room, hmm?" said Ava. "What I have to tell you may take some time."

~ ~ ~

There comes a moment in each person's lives when Destiny chooses to reveal itself to us, Ava told Jacob as they climbed the stairs to her bedroom.

How it ultimately chooses to unveil itself is as different for each person as there are stars in the heavens. For some, it could be as jarring as the most numbing of tragedies or profound good fortune, while for others it chooses to be as subtle as a leaf surrendering itself to an autumn breeze as it takes leave of a tree. More often than not, however, it comes and goes with as much fanfare as two strangers crossing paths on the street offering little more than a polite exchange of nods in passing.

The endgame of Fate's presence, however brief its visit, is always the same, to be certain; to forever alter the course of the life held in its sights, in the same manner trade winds change the trajectory of a boat set adrift upon an uncharted sea.

For Jacob, such a moment presented itself in the simple opening of an aged cigar box unburied from the bottom of an old cedar chest where it lay concealed beneath the weight and clutter of a lifetime of memories basted in the musky scent of mothballs and time. The unbelievable truth the contents of the box would spell out in front of him when they finally were carefully unpacked would prove far beyond anything Jacob had already come to conclude concerning his supposed destiny in life, if he in fact believed in such things, which he did not. Not by a long shot.

~   ~   ~

Lingering in the doorway of his grandmother's bedroom, Jacob watched as she made her way to the sturdy chest resting at the foot of her bed. Not surprisingly, his grandmother's room was as tidy as could be. Unlike his mother's room, his grandmother's presence could be seen in every corner; from the photographs capturing frozen moments of her youth displayed in frames lining the top of her dresser, to the walls decorated with the surprisingly beautiful oil landscapes she painted over the years; a past-time hobby she acquired to help keep her arthritic hands limber.

Ava knelt down in front of the chest and pulled away the cream-colored crocheted blanket which was carefully folded and draped over the top of it. The chest let out a creak as she opened it and a pungent scent of locked-away age wrapped in mothballs rose up and met her nose. Inside held a cargo of relics from a time long passed into memory: some linen, a few hats from when women wore such things, and what looked to be several finely made costumes tailored for the stage.

"It never ceases to amaze me how a life garnering as many years as mine has can be reduced to fit within the confines of a simple cedar chest," Ava remarked as she busily dug her way deeper into the folded artifacts.

It wasn't long before she found what she was looking for and brought into light the large cigar humidor she had long ago secreted at the bottom of the trunk. The sight of the box seemed to drape a veil of sadness over Ava, and Jacob could tell instantly his grandmother held an untold reverence for whatever resided inside it. The way she held it was unmistakably guarded, like someone holding an urn containing the ashes of their most beloved, and for a few moments she sat quietly with it until she turned to Jacob and held the box out for him to take.

"There's something inside here you should see," she said.

With some hesitation, Jacob forced his feet to step across the room to where his grandmother remained kneeling beside the trunk and take the box from her before taking a seat on the edge of the nearby bed. There he looked over the mysterious wooden box, nondescript in appearance except for a faded but decorative carving etched across the top. There was a keyhole in front but when Jacob attempted to open the lid he found it was not locked.

Inside more mementos of the past lay hidden, but Jacob knew right away before even looking through them that these items were far more personal in nature than anything else residing in the trunk, beginning with the small bundle of letters resting on top. They were tied together with a wilted white linen ribbon slightly discolored with age which also held in place a large, grayish-colored feather. Only it wasn't like any feather Jacob had ever before seen. At least not from any of the birds who made their home in their nearby woods where he frequently walked. Nor did it feel like an ordinary feather when he went to touch it. There was an armored hardness to it which would make one think twice before stuffing a pillow with it.

When Jacob went to slide the feather out to get a closer look, the plume's edge severed the ribbon as easily as if it had been cut by a knife or a pair of scissors. The unbound letters fell across his lap and onto the floor. Jacob saw each envelope was addressed simply to "Ava." On the back of each envelope where the carefully opened flap had once been sealed was imprinted a mysterious symbol, not by ink but what somehow looked to be burned into the paper itself as if by a tiny branding iron. Jacob had never before seen the symbol. Yet it seemed to register with some part of his brain, in the same way the Spanish words scrawled on the blackboard in Mrs. Lopez' class suddenly unscrambled themselves just like any word written in English. Whatever this symbol was, he knew it stood for the letter "G."

"G"?

Jacob then scoured through the rest of the articles inside the box. A small clear bottle filled with what looked to be water rested beside a worn, brown leather-bound book. There was also a brightly colored flower so fresh and alive it looked as if it had been picked no more than a few minutes earlier. And like the feather it was oddly unlike any other flower Jacob had ever before seen. It gave off the most wonderful of scents, and its soft pedals appeared to subtly change hue right before his very eyes. Yet as strangely magnificent as the flower was, Jacob soon found himself looking past it to the upside-down face staring out from a black and white photograph half-covered beneath the book.

He pulled the photograph out for a closer look, and an uncomfortable feeling slunk its way over him. In the photo was a man— a man whose face he recognized instantly.

"This is the man I saw in gym after wrestling practice today," said Jacob.

He then took notice of a woman with a small, light-haired boy also in the photograph standing beside the man, and he grew even more puzzled. The woman was his grandmother. Only she appeared not as she did now, but how she was then, in her youth—the way she looked in many of the numerous photos scattered in frames around her bedroom and downstairs.

"That can't be right. That's you in the picture, isn't it?" asked Jacob, pointing at the Ava who had yet to be touched by the finger of age and stood frozen in the prime of her youthful beauty, while looking to his grandmother for an explanation.

"So, what...you knew this Gotham guy's father?"

Ava could help but smile slightly.

"I doubt I'd be sitting here with you now had I been granted the privilege of such a face-to-face meeting," she answered cryptically. "No, that would be the man you met today. That is Gotham."

Jacob felt his chest tighten. It couldn't be possible. The man beside her in the photograph looked exactly the same as the one he saw in the school gymnasium, as if he had somehow managed to step out of the photograph into the color of the modern world like Dorothy walking through the front door of her drab farmhouse into the technicolor of Oz. But how? Unless, maybe, he had one of those rare aging diseases. You know, the kind which makes a person who has it look older than they really are, only in reverse. Yet even then—the photo itself was taken a good sixty years ago—even the idea of such a preposterous notion was—

"Inconceivable, I know," Ava's voice echoed his own thoughts. "I had a hard time accepting it at first myself, despite everything I was taught to believe in growing up. Then again, I was just as cynical and head-strong as you are now when I was your age."

She came and sat on the bed beside Jacob with what looked to be a large green scrapbook with gold trim on her lap which she proceeded to open.

"Where to even begin," she muttered to herself after turning the first couple pages. "If only I could unfold the memories I carry inside me as easily as opening this scrapbook, as many I wish to share with you are far more vivid than anything I can offer your inquisitive eyes."

Jacob glanced down as Ava continued to thumb through the scrapbook and saw the pages inside held numerous newspaper clippings and articles cut from magazines which told the story of Ava's short yet illustrious career as one of the most renown soprano singer's ever to bend the world's ear.

~ ~ ~

In a time long removed from the present, Ava Delacroux was known as the "Living Aphrodite of the operatic stage"—at least that seemed to be the consensus according to the clippings Jacob scanned. Of course there was little question why when one glanced at the numerous accompanying photos of Ava in her youth. Her's was a classic beauty; subtle enough to quicken a man's heart while powerful enough to bring an army of men to its knees if she had ever so desired. Her captivating presence, however, went far beyond just the beauty of her living portrait. It was her voice: soft when she spoke, infinite when she sang. A voice which was laced with a hidden spell to take all who heard it to profound, sublime places and turn oceans into molten mercury into which anyone whose ears had been blessed to take in such sounds would willingly cast themselves to drown, and die so quite happily.

"There was a time I was certain my destiny had revealed itself to me the first time I stepped out on a stage and wrung roaring applause from the audience with the notes I sang," recalled Ava. "It was only later I came to realize my voice was simply a means to uncover my true fate."

The idea his grandmother could think, even for a second, her singing was anything less than destiny's calling was flummoxing to

Jacob. He himself had grown up listening to his grandmother's singing, and while opera wasn't particularly the kind of music his ears gravitated toward in general, he secretly found it to be a rare treat whenever Ava would decide, for one reason or other, to put a record of one of her performances on her old phonograph in the living room. Soon her magical voice would fill the house and no matter what he might be doing at the time, he found himself stopping and listening.

Just listening.

If angels did indeed exist, Jacob would have been the first to argue it would have only taken his grandmother singing but a few notes to draw one of the otherworldly beings out from whatever invisible ether they might dwell. Of course the key word was "if," though Jacob couldn't deny his intense curiosity in what his grandmother had to say to try and prove to himself otherwise.

"I wasn't any older than you are now, when my family packed up the life they knew here and moved it across the ocean to Germany," Ava began. "This was during the good times, when the nightmare of what would become World War II was something no one could foresee coming, even in nightmares. My father was a research scientist whose work with a consortium of other scientists around the world promised to open the door behind which resided an important, life-altering discovery that would benefit all mankind. And so it was in hopeful further search for the key to open this elusive door that my father brought his wife and three children across the Atlantic. There we settled in a home in the countryside just outside Berlin. It was a beautiful home, large and stately, yet not obnoxiously so. In fact, more ostentatious than the house were the vast, lush gardens surrounding it. In my eyes, it was as if we had been transported to a magical castle in some make-believe storybook, but even more so I remember how happy and proud I was knowing others in the world had finally recognized, as I had long ago, how very important and special a man my father was.

"Unfortunately, the excitement of being in a foreign country was not all sunshine and roses as it was in the beginning, and I would quickly discover our new home was not as welcoming as it first appeared. Nowhere was that more apparent than at the school I was enrolled in where the other kids I had hoped to forge new friendships with were anything but friendly, especially the girls. I don't know whether their hostility toward me was because I was American, or simply jealousy of how I looked. Thankfully, my remedial understanding of the German language helped blunt their taunts and snide remarks. Still, hatred is very recognizable no matter the language it takes and I quickly found Germany a lonely place to be. What little joy I managed to find came from singing, which my mother encouraged by hiring a renowned voice coach to provide me lessons every day at home after school. But once the lesson was over the emptiness of the house was swift in its return. My twin brothers were just four at the time—hardly suitable playmates—and they took up most of whatever free time my mother might find to spend with me. And beautiful as the country was where we lived, it had a way of making the aloneness I was experiencing all the more pronounced, and I quickly found myself homesick for the neighborhood we had left behind in the States where the constant drone of children playing in the streets served only as a distant echo against the quiet now surrounding me. So it happened, as I began spending more and more time wandering the gardens like some inmate pacing the yard in what had become a prison of solitude, that I came to meet Gotham."

Jacob had been listening so intently to his grandmother's reminiscing about her youth that he almost forgot the point of her telling the story.

"Don't tell me, let me guess; he was your gardener," Jacob remarked flippantly.

"In a manner of speaking," said Ava. "He was one of the caretakers on the property who dealt with the menial maintenance problems that would pop up from time to time. Mostly, his time was spent tending to the gardens on the grounds."

"Must have been some garden having an angel gardener and all," Jacob muttered under his breath with a chuckle.

"Naturally, I hadn't any idea at first he was an angel," said Ava.

"So, he kept his wings hidden from you as well?"

Ava, who knew the moment she led her grandson up the stairs to her room and revealed what rested at the bottom of her trunk that she was in for a good amount of fleering, simply ignored the boy and continued on with her story.

"As I was saying," she said, shooting Jacob a look to quiet him, which it did. "I began spending more and more time in the garden shadowing Gotham while he worked. To tell the truth, I'm quite sure my company was more a nuisance to him than anything else. Not that he was short or unkind to my uninvited presence. He was a quiet man who kept very much to himself and seemed to almost try to hide himself away from the world in his work. I suppose it was his quiet nature that intrigued me so and made me want to crack through the hard veneer he had around him, and eventually my persistence wore him down. He slowly began to warm to me. One might even say he began to look forward to my daily visits."

"And is that when he told you he was an angel?" asked Jacob not attempting to be funny or sarcastic in his question.

"No...that would come later. Much later," answered Ava. "Even before that I knew there was something strange about Gotham—not strange in a bad way, but rather unusual. I can't explain it. He had a way about him. One could almost see the flowers break open from their buds and bloom right before your eyes as he tended them. And yet you were never really sure if your eyes were playing tricks on you because you were so entranced listening to the stories he told. He seemed to know so much about the world and the people living in it to be just an ordinary gardener. There was a vastness of knowledge he held about life, and it reflected itself in his eyes in a way from which I never could seem to look away. Like staring into the setting sun without the light hurting your eyes, his eyes were."

Her voice trailed off, as if she had suddenly found herself looking into the twin pools of gold upon which she reflected. Jacob himself knew something of what she meant. It was the one thing that had so vividly stuck with him since meeting the man inside the gym—those piercing eyes that were altogether fierce and kind at the same time, and had an uncomfortable way of burrowing straight through the flesh and bone of the person upon whom they were fixed.

"Then when exactly did you find out?" asked Jacob. "About him being an angel, that is?"

His grandmother sat quiet for a moment or two and a bereaved look, better suited for loved ones gathered around an open casket inside a funeral parlor, slowly crept across her face.

"When the incoming tide of war finally visited itself upon us," she finally answered.

~   ~   ~

Closing the scrapbook and setting it aside, Ava got up and made her way to the window where she stood for some time staring out into the sunlit afternoon. Jacob instinctively knew not to say another word whenever the subject of the war came up, knowing his grandmother would continue with her story when she could muster the words to tell it.

"The first Nazi I ever saw up close was from the stage of a small theater where I began performing," continued Ava. "He was an SS officer seated in the fifth row right in my sightline. I didn't need to look any further than the cold lifeless eyes and cruel mouth to know I could never have enough distance from him to feel at ease. After the show, he came back stage to introduce himself and express his enjoyment of my singing. It soon became clear his appreciation for my talents extended far beyond my voice when he returned the next night and then the next, always to the same fifth-row seat where he sat holding me captive in the confines of his most unnerving and uncomfortable gaze. Each night he came backstage after the show and sang to me praises every girl would love to hear, and so would I have, but not from this…man. Then came the night he made his nightly visit backstage after the performance, only this time he declared his true intentions concerning me in the same way an uncouth man belches after swallowing down a plate of food, and just as crudely. Fortunately for me my father was nearby to observe his advances and made it clear it would be over his dead body that his daughter would ever come to be seen in such cretinous company as a Nazi, and that proved to be very unfortunate."

"How do you mean?" asked Jacob.

"My father had misgivings even before we moved about the political shift that had taken root in Germany, but he was assured what was happening was a good thing for the country and its people. It was only after we had been living there for a while that my father's initial gut feelings were realized about the Third Reich, and what had been promised as a good thing eventually showed its true face and began its slow destructive spread like a deadly cancer. But by then it was too late. Two days after the confrontation backstage between my father and the SS officer, the Gestapo made an unannounced visit at our home. Before any of us knew what was happening to us, my brothers and I along with our mother and father were shipped off to Treblinka."

"What's Treblinka?" asked Jacob, though he knew by the tone in his grandmother's voice it was not a good place.

"At the time Treblinka was touted as a labor camp," said Ava. "We quickly came to know it as it truly was—a death camp."

Jacob felt a lump rise up in his throat.

"A concentration camp? That doesn't even make sense. Why would you be sent there? You're not even Jewish."

He thought he heard a faint chuckle escape his grandmother.

"One did not need to be Jewish to be sent to such places—only breathing," said Ava. "Countless men, women...children...shipped off like cattle in endless miles of packed boxcars to these waiting factories whose assembly lines churned out the most unimaginable horrors that turned the blue skies gray with an around-the-clock feeding of billowing ash from smokestacks carrying the stench of burning flesh—and all because some had committed the audacious crime of taking a breath of life."

Jacob had learned about the dark stain of the Holocaust in his history class. Still, he found it difficult to conceive how anyone could be subjected to such atrocities for simply existing. And yet he could hear in his grandmother's voice as she spoke the weight of guilt she carried for the fate she and especially her family came to all for the simple sin of refusing the unwanted advances of a Nazi ogler.

"One could not walk through the gates of such places and witness what took place behind the barbed wire perimeter and not be convinced beyond question the existence of Satan. The Nazis, however, gave the devil a run for his money when it came to dispensing their version of Hell on earth." As he listened, Jacob took notice of his grandmother nervously kneading the inside of her left wrist as she spoke. "They came for my mother first, sending her off with a group of other women all sharing the same terrified look and clutching one another for dear life as they were herded off to the showers that we all knew were not showers at all. They staggered each of our demises, the Nazis did, coming for us when we least expected it, even though every minute of every day was spent waiting in terror for it to arrive. My brothers were next. Such heartless, cold-blooded monsters the Nazis were, they refused even to allow the boys the company of the other as a tiniest strand of comfort as they were marched off to their death. It was far more gratifying to the bastards to induce the greatest amount of terror into each boy, who had no idea what was happening to them as they were pried apart. To this day I cannot rid myself of the sight of each of them kicking and clawing for one another or their terrified screams as they were carried away. How I prayed each would pass from fright before meeting their ultimate end."

Ava took a steadying breath, as did Jacob. He had learned growing up from his mother about the hard times his grandmother had faced during the war, but only in the vaguest of mentions. It was, as his mother said, something better left unspoken and forgotten. And now Jacob understood why.

"By the time my father was finally led away, a sort of numbness had set in. The tears had long gone dry and I eagerly awaited the moment the Nazi guards would finally come and end my suffering. That day, much to my dismay, would never come," said Ava. "Whatever the reason, my sentence was to be not death, but life, if you would call such an existence that. I was left to languish amongst the other rotting souls for God knows how long with only the cursed sounds of our own breathing to mark the passing of time, like the slow ticking of a clock. Not one of us held faith our bodies would hold out to see the day the reign of this Hell on earth would finally come to an end, but the day eventually arrived.

"Even then, with the encroaching Allied forces closing in, we were certain the coming of freedom was sure to be denied us as a chorus of gunfire rang out through the camp. We didn't have to see to know it was the sound of our Nazi keepers going from barracks to barracks to wring out the last vestiges of their cruelty. Many of the prisoners ran in desperate search for a place to hide, but there was no such place at

Treblinka. Myself…I just remember sitting on the ground in the sun continuing to sing in what ravaged voice I had—'Mon coeur s'ouvre a ta voix.' It was a hauntingly beautiful song my mother used to play around the house that had a way of feeding the delirium of a happy moment as well as lend comfort in the doldrums of unhappiness, and it was while I sung and hummed in an attempt to soothe a young girl that the commotion began. I hugged the poor frightened child close to me even as the gunshots grew louder and closer and waited for the moment that had long been denied me, and just as I heard lives being lost around me and could feel death make its way closer I saw it. Cast upon the ground by the sun above came a shadow from behind me. It was in the shape of a man—my executioner, I had no doubt. But it was instantly clear it was no Nazi, nor an Allied soldier. No, this shadow had wings—great, huge wings outstretched like that of an eagle soaring across the sky, and for a moment I began to wonder if death had already managed to snatch me without my knowing and taken me up to Heaven's edge. I was almost too terrified to turn around, and when I managed to I couldn't believe my eyes. It was Gotham."

Jacob remained quiet for some time, even though there was so much he wanted to ask his grandmother about the story she had just shared. Like whether or not she ever considered the fact she might have been imagining what she believed she saw. After all, she was in a state. And if in indeed Gotham was an angel, why did it take so long for him to come to her rescue?

"Even if what you are saying is true—" Jacob began instead.

"If?" Ava shot her grandson a look while sounding a touch offended.

"You were in a concentration camp," said Jacob, as if his grandmother needed reminding. "What you must have went through, at that age, I doubt few people could have survived—starvation, disease, the unimaginable loss of your entire family and living every day thinking your end was coming. Don't you think it's the tiniest bit probable when the American soldiers finally arrived to free you from the camp your mind, in your frail state, made you see one of the soldiers as an angel? They were, after all, at that moment your saviors."

"Thank you very much doctor for your insightful analysis," Ava remarked with a raising of an eyebrow. "But I assure you, whatever doubts I may have had were put to rest long after Treblinka and I parted ways, and in ways you can't even begin to imagine."

Fair enough, thought Jacob to himself knowing it was a losing battle to engage in arguing the point any further with his grandmother, who was obviously unbudging on the point.

"I'm just trying to make sense out of what any of this has to with me," he said with growing impatience. "I mean, if you want to believe in angels and all that, great, have at it. But what in the world could possibly make you think even for a second that I'm one of these..."

"Nephilim?"

"Yes, that," said Jacob, touching the end of his nose as though the two were having a spirited game of charades.

"It's not that difficult a notion to wrap one's head around," said Ava. "Especially considering the fact you're not the first Nephilim to be born into this family."

~ ~ ~

She could almost hear Jacob's jaw come unhinged.

"What do you mean not the first?" he asked in a most cautious manner.

Ava turned to face her grandson and took in a breath. Now came the difficult part.

"The boy in the photo I showed you earlier, his name is David. He was my first child," she said, before quickly noting, "He was my and Gotham's child."

Her and Gotham's? Nothing coming from her mouth could have shocked Jacob more, even the horrific details he had moments earlier endured about Ava's experience at Treblinka. He quickly grabbed up the old photo again and went in for a closer look. Sure enough, he couldn't deny the fact there was a noticeable enough resemblance shared between the young boy in the photo and the more youthful Ava seated beside him that couldn't be ignored, and an even more striking resemblance between child and supposed angel.

"He was a beautiful and very special child," said Ava. "The apple of my eye, and the sun that rose and set in his father's. In many ways, you remind me quite a bit of him. Headstrong and—"

"This is ridiculous," Jacob interrupted. "You do know that, don't you?"

"What's so ridiculous about it?" inquired Ava. "A woman bears a child fathered by an angel, naturally the child is going to inherit traits from his father as all children do."

Jacob couldn't believe his ears.

"Where is he then?" he asked. "If this half-angel son of your really exists, why haven't I ever seen or met him before?"

A noticeable darkness immediately cast itself upon Ava and a sad, mournful look Jacob hadn't seen since his mother's funeral settled itself like a widow's black veil across her face.

"Once understanding that the light of angels do indeed color this world of ours, one doesn't need to look very far to realize equal yet much darker forces lurk about as well," said Ava. "Unfortunately, when David was about the age you are now, he found himself in the crosshairs of one of these evil entities. Sadly, he did not survive the encounter."

Any doubt Jacob may have continued to harbor instantly dissipated as he noted the intense look of sadness that welled up in his grandmother's face, and even greater sorrow heard in her voice.

"Why haven't I ever heard this story before?" he asked.

"There are many stories you haven't heard," replied his grandmother as she turned away from Jacob to hide her moment of grief.

As the room fell silence, Jacob glanced again at the photograph still clutched in his hands studying first the image of the young boy and then that of Gotham, and in his pensiveness a most inconceivable notion slowly dawned on him.

"This man...he isn't my father, is he?" spouted Jacob.

"Your fa—?"

The question caught Ava by surprise at first, though it shouldn't have. The subject of Jacob's father had always been one of deep mystery to the boy. There were no photos. Jacob didn't even know his name. It was as if he had never existed. All Jacob was ever told by his mother was that his father had disappeared long before he was born, and she explained it in such a way that Jacob knew it was a topic better left not breached, and so he didn't though it would always fester in the back of his mind like some unanswered riddle. Now, with all the talk of angels and the incredulous assertion that he himself was some half angel, half human creation, it suddenly seemed to Jacob a logical question to ask.

At first Ava's hesitation offered a glimmer of hope that the question of who his father would finally be answered, but she quickly dashed such hope with a simple shake of her head.

"No, he's not."

"Then...do you know who is?" Jacob pressed. "I mean now that we've supposedly narrowed the potential candidates down to those with wings, it shouldn't be that difficult to figure out right?"

Despite the flippant way Jacob addressed the issue, Ava could hear the serious yearning in her grandson's voice to finally know the answer which had evaded him his whole life.

"I wish I could answer that question for you," said Ava when she finally answered, "but I can't."

"So then what does this Gotham want with me?" asked Jacob. "When we were at the gym he said something to the effect of once I believed and accepted what it is you two are trying to convince me I am that we could then move to the next stage. What's the next stage?"

"There's a place—a very special place few have ever seen with their own eyes—where boys, like yourself, eventually go to learn and develop all the many pertinent skills needed to live life as a Nephilim in a world where such things are considered nothing but a myth," Ava explained in a way that made it all seem as natural as summer camp.

"You mean like a Hogwarts? Only instead of wizards the student body is made up of the children of angels?"

Ava couldn't fault the boy for his mocking jokes and did her best to ignore the snickers that slipped past her grandson's crooked grin.

"Every Nephilim, once they reach a certain age, is brought there. My own son was as well," she said. "When Gotham showed up here at the house several weeks ago the discussion about him taking you there as well was brought up. He declined, which is why I appeared so flustered when you first told me he came to see you and revealed to you who he is. I can only assume he has had a change of heart."

"You're serious about this, aren't you?" asked Jacob as the look of levity faded from his face.

"I've never been more," answered Ava.

"You're actually suggesting I go off with some strange man—I'm sorry, angel—and allow him to take me to some secret place that just happens to be some kind of school for mythical beings? Do I have it all correct or am I missing something?"

"It's what your mother wanted for you when the time was right," said Ava.

"And where exactly is this place you're looking to send me off to?" asked Jacob.

Ava turned her sights to a nearby wall of her bedroom where a dozen or so more of her paintings hung. They were all different in size but each equal in framing a beautiful arrangement of color on the canvas to capture breathtaking still-shots of scenic landscapes it seemed impossible for nature to replicate. One painting, however, seemed to hold Ava's attention more so than the others; it was a view from high above looking out over a vast expanse of forests and open land disturbed only by a mighty river snaking through the lushness lit beneath a brilliant sky.

"You wouldn't believe me if I were to tell you," she said.

~ ~ ~

To Jacob's ears, the conversation had passed the point of ridiculous and began stretching itself into the realm of the insane. All the talk of angels and Nephilim and now a secret place where the two converged was becoming too much for Jacob to take in and not feel as if he had fallen into the same rabbit hole Alice had once ventured. If this was all an elaborate joke, no one seemed ready to yell out "April Fools," and it was that realization which sent an unease of discomfort through Jacob and made him begin a slow retreat out of his grandmother's bedroom and across the hallway to his own.

There in the doorway he found a saving moment to take in a breath or two, but the more he mulled over the ridiculousness of what he had just heard, the more unwound he became until the need to get out of the house proved too great. He quickly located his sneakers on the floor nearby and as he hastily worked his feet back into them he happened to glance toward his open closet and spy the corner of a duffel bag peeking out from beneath a heap of dirty clothes piled on top and an idea shot to the forefront of his mind. He grabbed it up, bolted from his room and was halfway down the stairs in his race for the front door when his grandmother's voice brought him to a halt.

"Where are you going?" she asked, looking unusually concerned as she peered down from the top of the stairs.

"To prove to myself whether or not what you've just told me is really true or not," answered Jacob.

And before Ava could say anything more he was gone with the slamming of the front door.

CHAPTER SEVEN

The Bridge

Jacob rose to his feet and as he stood along the edge at the center of the Darren's Creek Bridge he took in a deep breath and slowly exhaled. Gone was the sun, and the last lingering embers of its light coloring the sky had almost completely faded leaving nothing but a far-reaching arm of darkness in front of him. Even the early hours of the arriving night was unable to blot the view of the surrounding woods that had long ingrained itself in Jacob's mind from all the countless afternoons he spent staring out from the same exact spot on the bridge with his legs dangling over the side and the sun beaming down basking everything in its golden warmth.

The Darren's Creek Bridge was an old iron truss crossing stretching across a gorge at the edge of town. In its heyday it served as a welcome mat for the countless freight and passenger trains passing through Cain's Corner on their winding journey through the vast forests of the northwest. However, faster more convenient routes would eventually steer the steel engines and their cargo in different directions, and the echo of train whistles last heard to come from the steep, narrow ravine quickly faded into memory. In its place came the piercing screams of young thrill-seekers who saw the abandoned bridge as the perfect platform from which to willingly leap off of with nothing but empty air to catch their free fall and an elastic Bungee cord tethered to their ankles to yank them back from the jaws of death.

It was here Jacob first forged his friendship with Ty and, long before graduating to the heights of Penuel Point, where after a lot of prodding and much reluctance he eventually added his own virginal cry of terror to the many screams that had echoed through the gorge before his, not thinking it possible his voice could reach such high girlish octaves. Nor was he prepared that one frightening fall could be able to lift someone to such extreme heights by the intense rush that followed, a frisson of adrenaline Jacob could still feel clutching his insides in a twisting death grip even now as he stood there on the bridge recalling that first jump.

If ever there was one place suited to prove the existence of a so-called angel, this was the place.

~   ~   ~

When darkness finally came, his eyes rolled upward to a bare lightbulb burning brightly above him from an old, rusted fixture, and he knew that wouldn't do. Not tonight. He pulled from his pocket a couple rocks he picked up from the ground near where the bridge began and took aim. The first rock he hurled overshot the light by a couple inches, but the second hit its target and shattered the bulb with a loud pop.

What light remained was a dim silvery blue glow from the fingernail clipping of a crescent moon cradled in the sky of black velvet. Some three hundred feet beneath him, Jacob could hear the dark waters of Darren's Creek churning loudly and sounding more like the rushing river it was than creek.

"So now what?" Jacob murmured to himself.

This Gotham character had said he'd come when Jacob was ready to further talk, or at least that's what the voice he was sure he'd imagined hearing inside his head said. How would this man even know he was there on the bridge wanting a second face-to-face? Then again, if he was truly angel he should know—right? Well, now Jacob was ready. Or, at least, he thought he was. He glanced down at his feet to make sure they were hidden by the shadows of the night, but the longer he waited with only the sound of the creek flowing furiously below, and the *thump-thump-thump* of his heart growing increasingly louder in his chest to keep him company, the more Jacob questioned what he was doing there on the bridge. He couldn't keep from replaying over and over in his head everything his grandmother had revealed to him earlier. And the more time he had to sit with it all, the more he heard it being repeated inside his head, the more uneasy it made him.

"This is crazy," Jacob finally blurted. He no longer wanted to be on that bridge and was ready to leave. Not because he found the whole idea about angels and their Nephilim offspring beyond ridiculous, which he did, but rather because he found himself suddenly facing an uncomfortable prospect that filled him with an unwanted anxiety. The prospect of what if.

What if it was all true?

"What do you find to be crazy?"

Even though he had heard it only one time before, Jacob recognized instantly the voice that suddenly made itself heard behind him. He gave a reluctant glance over his shoulder and saw a darkened figure standing a few feet away.

"Is it the fact that you find yourself here on this bridge waiting for someone you don't believe to exist?" asked the figure. "Or is it the idea you may very well be—"

"A freak?" said Jacob, unwilling to let the man finish.

"More than what you thought yourself to be when you woke up this morning, is what I was going to say," corrected the man.

"I don't believe it," said Jacob.

"Which? That I'm an angel? Or that you're a Nephilim?" The figure stepped forward sweeping the veil of shadows from his face and, sure enough, revealing it was the man who called himself Gotham, looking the same as when Jacob first saw him in the school gymnasium wearing a long dark overcoat with his long hair pulled back and his eyes looking like two caldrons simmering with molten sunlight.

"Both," Jacob brusquely replied. "I don't believe either thing you just said.

"He answered quickly and so definitively," muttered Gotham as if reciting the narrative to some story.

He stepped to the edge of the bridge and gazed out at the night-cloaked view. "Tell me Jacob, why would I, a complete stranger whom you've seemingly never met, come to you out of the blue and tell you such an outlandish thing, if in fact it weren't true?"

Of course such a thought was among the hundreds Jacob had already entertained.

"There's a homeless man outside the movie theater who's been swearing for the past two years that a huge asteroid is going to smash into the earth any day," said Jacob, giving a glance of disbelief toward the sky. "Have yet to see any cataclysmic boulder headed this way."

"I see. And what about your grandmother?" asked Gotham.

"What about her?"

"You undoubtedly mentioned to her our meeting, offhandedly of course," said Gotham. "What purpose would she have in sitting you down and sharing with her beloved grandchild an untold history of her life secreted away inside a box at the bottom of a trunk only to fill your ears with nonsense and untruths?"

Another thought Jacob had mulled over more than once, only this one didn't bring about as quick a retort.

"She's...old," Jacob managed to mutter after a long pause.

"She may show wear from a long path traveled, but you know as well as I her mind holds the same clarity as a freshly washed window," said Gotham. "Besides, I doubt highly I would have found you waiting here on this bridge at this precise moment if you thought anything your grandmother confided to you was the ramblings of an old woman's fantasies shaped by senility."

Perhaps it was because Gotham revealed himself to know more than Jacob felt comfortable with that Jacob found himself slowly growing irritated.

"Alright then, how about I ask you a question?" he challenged. "If you're an angel as you claim you are, then where are your wings?"

"Again with the wings," Gotham uttered with annoyance under his breath as if it were a question he was hounded with daily ad nauseam.

"That's right, wings. You know, to fly. You do have them, right?" Gotham slowly shifted his gaze to the boy.

"I do," he answered simply.

"Show me, then," demanded Jacob.

Now he knew he had this charlatan right where he wanted him. Even the overcoat this so-called angel was wearing wouldn't be enough to cover a pair of wings a man his size would need to even remotely raise him off the ground. There wasn't even any sign of bulging coming from the man's back.

"That's what would convince you that I am what I say I am...a glimpse of my wings?" asked Gotham, with a curious tilt of his head. "Is the fabric of your faith so thin it relies only on what your eyes can see to keep it from completely unraveling?"

Jacob shrugged pompously. "You know the old saying: seeing is believing."

It appeared as if Gotham was about to meet Jacob's dare when he visibly drew back.

"I don't perform tricks like some circus animal," said Gotham. "I guess you will just have to go on believing that angels are as real as Santa Clause."

"Not good enough," said Jacob. "Either you show me a pair of wings, or admit to me right here, right now that you're a fraud and somehow managed to convince my grandmother to buy into this bogus story. It's your choice, but pick one of the other or I'll—"

"Or you'll what?" Gotham pressed as if daring the boy to see through whatever threat was poised on the end of his tongue.

Jacob hesitated under the glare of the bright eyes trained unnervingly on him, but only briefly. "I'll jump."

The ultimatum appeared to tickle Gotham. "It's a long way down just to prove a point."

"I swear, I'll do it," said Jacob, inching his way closer to the edge of the bridge.

"And what if I'm a—what did you call me? A fraud?"

"Then you'll stop me by admitting it. I doubt you'd want my blood on your conscience over a stupid prank," said Jacob.

"You've got a point there," said Gotham, pondering the boy's logic.

"And if you're an angel you'd have to save me and I will know everything you and my grandma have told me is true. Although if it is, I'd rather you just let me perish into the water."

A dark seriousness passed visibly across Gotham's face. "Now, you're speaking nonsense."

He stretched a hand toward Jacob, but Jacob stepped out of its reach. "Last chance," Jacob threatened.

The two fiercely locked eyes.

"I'm not lying to you, boy. And I refuse to entertain any more of your childish games," said Gotham, without a chink to reveal even the slightest glimmer of deception.

Jacob felt his stomach turn. He had betted surely with himself this game of chicken would have long since finished in his favor. Staring at Gotham he felt his jaw tighten and he took in a deep breath.

"Wrong answer," he exclaimed. And with that he pushed himself free from the footing he had on the bridge. The last thing he saw as he went over the edge and into the arms of the night was a look of unexpected surprise reflected in Gotham's face.

~ ~ ~

The sensation which came from the inevitable fall that followed made Jacob's stomach roll over. Yet it was not the tremor of excitement which greeted Jacob in past jumps that caused the immediate release of adrenaline to course through his veins. Rather it was the not knowing what was—or was not—about to happen as he plummeted through the smothering darkness.

It was almost impossible to keep his eyes trained on anything around him, especially the black shape of the bridge which was fast getting further and further away. Then, just when Jacob was certain the answer he sought had been given to him, his ears caught a distinct fluttering sound, even through the wail of air he was rapidly passing through whistling in his ears. In that instant, he managed a glimpse of a blurred figure fast approaching him from above. Jacob felt his heart skip a beat, or two, when he saw movement come from the diving figure which looked to be mimicking a pair of giant, outstretched *WINGS!*

The figure was just about in his reach when suddenly Jacob felt a familiar tightening grip his ankles followed by a gradual tug slowing his fall. It was the Bungee rope he had discreetly tethered himself to before Gotham's arrival at the bridge—an idea that popped into his mind when he caught sight of the duffel bag in which the cord was packed away on the floor of his closet before he bolted from his house. He braced himself and just as the winged figure was about to grab hold of him, Jacob's body was suddenly yanked upward in the opposite direction leaving the pursuing figure to continue its downward dive right past him.

As he bobbed and swung about wildly in the air beneath the bridge like a flailing fish dangling from the end of a fisherman's hook, Jacob desperately searched the darkness around him. Despite growing dizzy he finally spotted him: Gotham. Coatless and levitating in the air by a pair of massive wings. And from the look in his eyes which had become two pilot lights of rage, he appeared none too happy. For a moment, Jacob wished there was a way he could cut himself free from the Bungee cord and let the raging waters beneath him swallow him up, especially when Gotham came at him full speed and he felt the crushing grip that grabbed hold of him.

"You should know I don't find the games mortals play to be amusing," Gotham bellowed angrily once they returned to the bridge.

With an effortless heave, he sent Jacob skidding painfully across the wooden planks where the abandoned iron rails ran. Jacob, too filled with fear to find his tongue, or his legs, desperately scampered backwards across the rails trying to keep his distance from the winged man slowly making his way toward him with heavy determined steps. The Bungee rope to which Jacob was still anchored allowed him to go only so far; like a dog tugging uselessly to free itself from its own leash. Not that there was any place for him to escape.

"You seek proof of angels?" seethed Gotham. "Then look long and look hard at the one before you and try to deny what your own eyes witness."

Indeed, Jacob's eyes looked as if they might not ever blink again as they stared wide and fixed on what he couldn't deny was an angel standing over him. Only this was unlike any angel he had ever envisioned, even as an imaginary myth. Between the bare torso which looked like a breastplate of impenetrable armor and glowing eyes that made one question if they could shoot flames of fire to incinerate the enemy caught in their glare, Gotham appeared nothing less than terrifying.

But the wings...

Nothing Jacob had ever before laid eyes on were as awesome as the massive pair of feathered appendages attached to Gotham's back. Grayish in color, they were bird-like in every way, and yet like nothing ever seen to carry a bird across the sky. Fantastic as they were to behold, the one thought that somehow managed to push its way to the front of Jacob's mind was the puzzlement of how Gotham had been able to conceal such sizable things beneath his overcoat. It was a pondering short-lived when Gotham suddenly began to furiously beat his wings, and in demonstrating their great power they produced a strong unrelenting gust of wind. It felt and sounded like a furious tornado, stirring up years of dust and dirt that had settled on the bridge to swirl around Gotham and Jacob. So strong was the wind brought about by the flapping wings that Jacob was glad to still be tethered to the Bungee cord for fear he might be swept off the bridge.

"Now do you see?" Gotham yelled.

The rusted light fixtures lining the bridge creaked and clanked as they swung about wildly. And then the lights themselves, both the bulbs that had long ago gone dead and those still pulsating with life before Jacob disabled them permanently with well-aimed rocks, suddenly began to flicker. Little by little they grew brighter until they were glowing with an intenseness far beyond what the filaments of any modern lightbulb were capable of producing. Jacob tried to shield his eyes with his hands from both the dust swirling around and the retina-searing brightness blazing down on him.

"DO YOU SEE?" Gotham cried out again louder.

"Yes...," Jacob screamed back. "YES!"

There came a loud explosion when all at once the blinding lights suddenly extinguished themselves in a shower of sparks. The wind began to subside as Gotham gradually stilled his wings. And then there was a pronounced silence.

"Yes," Jacob repeated quietly to himself.

Eventually he lowered his hands from his face and saw the darkness of night had been returned and the dust was settling once again like a dirty snowfall around him. And then there was Gotham, still standing over him. His wings had retreated from sight, as did the anger that had so darkened his face. Yet there remained an ever-present cool sternness in his eyes, which no longer burned with fire but still gleamed ever so subtly with a golden hue that surprisingly was warming—comforting even—to look into.

"Now that that's out of the way, the two of us can talk," said Gotham before he held out his hand for the boy to take.

~   ~   ~

Later that same night found Jacob locked away at home in his bedroom. His mind was still sopped by a fog as it turned its way through everything that happened earlier at the bridge to pay any attention to the black-and-white image of the Creature from "The Creature from the Black Lagoon" slowly and menacingly making his way toward the camera flickering on a small television screen behind him. Instead, he was furiously combing the one thing he could think of in his search for answers: his computer. After all, when it came to UFOs, the paranormal, or in Jacob's case angels, what better authority existed than a world-wide database made accessible with the click of button to help explain away events witnessed through one's own eyes?

What he soon came to learn the more he read, however, was that the online accounts concerning Nephilim did not come close to matching what had been told to him by his grandmother, or Gotham, for that matter. In fact, the narrative which had been stitched together through a trail of dozens of web sites to tell the legend of Nephilim was something quite shocking. They were not described as normal teenaged boys afflicted with a few muted traits passed down through their angelic parentage. Instead, the reigning consensus was that Nephilim were monstrous, oversized beings. Creatures, really, like the Gill-man discovered in the Black Lagoon. Towering abnormalities of forbidden breeding gone hopelessly wrong marked by six fingers on each hand and six toes on each foot. As he read this, Jacob couldn't keep his eyes from drifting downward to give his own hands a quick glance even though he knew his hands—not to mention his feet—had the appropriate number of digits.

"Jacob, I think you're beginning to lose your mind," he muttered to himself balling up both hands into fists and clenching them tightly.

Such things were easy to shake off. Then there were the photos, which were not as easily dismissed. They showed archeologists uncovering skeletons at various excavation sites around the world: Greece, Peru, Saudi Arabia and even Pennsylvania. Only the bones discovered in the dirt didn't belong to dinosaurs but humans. Giant humans. Some measuring more than thirty feet in height.

Jacob leaned in to his computer screen to give the photos a closer look with his skeptical, unblinking eyes. He didn't believe it. They had to be fake. After all, these would be world-changing discoveries. How had they not make the front page of every newspaper in the world at the time of being found?

It reminded Jacob of the time as a young boy when he was spellbound by a television show purporting to show the discovery and autopsy of an alien. For a long time afterward, he found himself unable to look up at the night sky without seeing the grainy image of that eerie, dark-eyed being squat and long-limbed stretched out motionless across a stainless-steel table as his own eyes searched the starry blackness. Then, years later, it was revealed to be all a hoax. The alien, nothing more than the result of an elaborate con to dupe gullible TV viewers, had never existed. And, immediately after, Jacob never felt the need to gaze up at the sky, and when he did it was never again with a glimmer of wonderment.

If the photos of the Nephilim skeletons were indeed faked, Jacob found them to be damn good fakes. Then again, he was well aware it was a Photoshop world in which he lived. Skeptically, his eyes studied the archeologists posing next to their unbelievable finds. The sheer difference in size between the flesh and blood men and the skeletal remains stretched out in their dirt beds was boggling to the mind. One photo showed an archeologist crouched down in a shallow pit carefully excavating around the exposed mammoth skull of an intact skeleton curled up in a fetal position, and it was clear the Nephilim when alive would have had the ability to swallow the man whole had he wanted. The skulls themselves were frightening to look at with their black, hallowed out eye sockets and large, gaping oversized mouths. The thought of what they may have looked like wrapped in skin blinking and breathing proved a far more unsettling thought to Jacob.

"They're not real," Jacob stated aloud in as convincing a manner as he could to himself. "They just can't be."

Yet mindful as he was that the photos could be nothing more than an enterprising use of photo-enhancing software and an imaginative mind, Jacob couldn't help but keep a small seed planted in the back of his head forcing him to ask himself, "What if?" After all, it wasn't too long ago he was certain angels were about as real as leprechauns and pixies. Even he couldn't cast away what he saw just a short while ago at the bridge, and that's what made the photos that much more disturbing.

~ ~ ~

Just then he heard the hinge of his door give out its familiar creak whenever it swung open and he knew his grandmother had come into his room.

"I thought I heard noises coming from up here," she remarked softly.

Jacob had found her dozed off in front of the television downstairs when he finally returned home and left her to sleep while he went to his room to sort through his jumbled thoughts.

"So are we all supposed to be hideous giants? Or am I one of the slow- growing variety of Nephilim?" asked Jacob.

"Giants?" Ava's shoes clicked across the floor as she came up close behind Jacob and peered down over his shoulder at the computer on the desk in front of him. She immediately let out a gasp of disgust and quickly lowered the screen dousing from Jacob's face the white light which had radiated brightly the monstrous images from the laptop.

"You would do yourself well to ignore such made-up nonsense?" she warned sharply.

"Is it? Made-up nonsense, I mean?" asked Jacob. "Cause I'm finding it a little difficult to tell what's real anymore and what's not."

The heavy sigh that came from Ava as she sat herself on the edge of Jacob's unmade bed seemed to share the same exasperation heard in her grandson's voice.

"I take it you've seen Gotham."

"That would be the understatement of the year," said Jacob, getting up from his seat and shutting off his TV as he crossed the room to stare out from the window into the waiting darkness of the night. "I went to Darren's Creek Bridge."

"And?"

"You were right," said Jacob, staring blankly through one of the small panes of glass. "He's an angel And how!"

Ava could hear the struggle it took for Jacob to make such a statement out loud.

"He showed you."

Jacob shook his head. "Not at first. He said it was my problem not his if I needed to see proof in order to believe in the existence of something. But I forced him."

Ava cocked her head slightly and her brow furrowed with curiosity. "Forced him?"

"I threatened to kill myself by jumping off the bridge."

Ava's eyes widened in alarm and she clutched her chest. "You did what?"

"I don't believe he thought I was serious, that is until I actually jumped."

The look on Ava's face grew more horrified at the thought of Jacob's body tumbling from such a high structure.

"And of course he saved you," she said. And as she imagined the rescue a glow came to her face. "Then it stands to reason some part of you must have believed he was who I said he was and that he would save you, otherwise you never would have risked your life in such a careless manner."

"I didn't risk anything," Jacob replied. "I was tethered to my Bungee cord to break my fall."

Knowing Gotham as only she did, her look once more darkened when she imagined how such a prank would stoke his wrath and she buried her face in her hands knowingly.

"Oh Jacob, tell me you didn't." Yet she knew he had, Of course he did. It was exactly the sort of thing Jacob would do to prove something true or false, no matter how outlandish. And maybe, just maybe, it was for the better that he did.

"Well...I suspect now that it's over you must feel somewhat relieved," she said.

Jacob turned away abruptly from the window. "Relieved? What makes you think any of this is a relief to me?" he spat.

Never before had he raised his voice to his grandmother. It took her aback.

"Now you know the truth."

"I didn't want this to be the truth, don't you see that?" argued Jacob angrily. "I wanted to prove this to be nothing but a dirty lie. A big April Fool's joke."

"I would think knowing the existence of angels would be a comforting thing," said Ava. "It certainly was for me growing up."

"Well, it isn't comforting. Not by a long shot," barked Jacob, his increased frustration becoming more apparent. "Don't you see? If everything about Gotham is true, then it means everything you've said about me is true as well."

He was barely able to finish the last few words he uttered when the anger with which he spoke quickly dissolved and an almost childlike uncertainty could be readily seen sweeping over him, so much so that he turned away again toward the window in hopes of hiding from his grandmother the embarrassment of revealing such vulnerability he felt beginning to well up in his eyes. It was then Ava understood the fear that had suddenly gripped her grandson, a fear she had no idea how to assuage.

"Why didn't she tell me?" asked Jacob, after a moment, in a quiet breath which matched the silence that had settled itself upon the room.

Ava knew rightly Jacob was referring to his mother, but he could well have been wondering aloud the same thing about herself.

"Oh, Jacob, if you only knew how much she struggled to do just that," answered Ava with an exhaustive sigh. "But I ask you, how does one decide when the appropriate time is to reveal to a child such a thing? And would you ever have believed her if she had managed to tell you?"

Jacob didn't answer, but his thoughts at that moment drifted to the night his mother passed away when he came into her room in the wee hours. She had tried that night to tell him then but he shrugged off her words as nothing more than the delirious ramblings stirred by her illness, just as Gotham described in the school gymnasium. And instead of listening to her, he tucked her into bed not knowing the moment she would close her eyes and drift off to sleep they would never again open.

"I know all of this is a shock to you," said Ava, trying to lend some comfort to the boy. "In less time that it took for the sun to rise and set you have been given a life-changing jolt. But you must see what a glorious, special gift it is you've been given."

Jacob's eyes turned to his grandmother but instead of being aflame with anger they mirrored a lingering sadness.

"Gift? How can you say this is a gift? I'm a freak!"

An almost offended look came over Ava.

"I don't ever want to hear you refer to yourself in such a way again," she scolded him in a sharp yet loving voice. "You are not a freak. But you are different, different in a good way. Different in a way that only being touched by something so incredibly special can make someone like you."

When he looked away in disregard she knew it would take more than just her words to convince him otherwise. That and time.

Lots of time.

"He...he wants to take me away," Jacob said hesitantly. "Just like you said."

The sudden change in subject made Ava sit up a little straighter.

"The place I told you about earlier...Gotham told you this?"

Jacob nodded his head and Ava closed her eyes in silent gratitude while at the same time exhaling a breath of relief.

"When?"

"Tomorrow."

Ava's eyes opened wide revealing the unexpected surprise of the answer.

Tomorrow?

"So soon."

"He said we would already be pushing against time to make it there in time, whatever that means," said Jacob. "It's just...I'm just not exactly sure I want go."

"Not go," Ava replied with alarm. "But why? I would think a school for Nephilim, not to mention meeting others like you, would be an exciting prospect to you."

"I already go to school," argued Jacob. "In a few more years I'll be graduating. Not to mention all my friends are here."

"You'll not be gone forever. You'll be back here, and living more comfortably in your skin because you'll know better who you are. How can you even think of denying yourself that?"

"I understand that, but..."

"But..." Ava's attention honed itself to the way her grandson's voice wavered, and as her steely blue eyes narrowed themselves as they carefully searched her grandson's face, a light of clarity was illuminated inside them. "But you're afraid of going off and leaving me behind, is that it?"

When Jacob didn't answer, her back straightened and she folded her arms across her chest defiantly.

"You think I can't manage being on my own without you watching out for me?"

She pointed a finger, made slightly crooked by arthritis, and motioned for him to come sit beside her. Once he did, she proceeded to do something she rarely did before—she pulled back her dress sleeve to reveal a part of her forearm she always kept covered.

"Do I need to explain to you what this is and what it means?" she asked pointedly. After hearing Ava's telling of her childhood earlier that night, Jacob shook his head while cringing slightly at the sight of the six grayish numbers crudely tattooed into her alabaster white skin—a lasting reminder of the horror his grandmother was forced to visit in a Nazi concentration camp during the war.

"Then you know I am quite capable of surviving far worse things than being separated from my grandson for a little while."

"I know you're strong, grandma, and I'm not trying to start an argument with you," Jacob said as kindly as possible. "But you're also a lot older."

Ava rolled down her sleeve and with a look most disconcerting aimed at Jacob she simply exclaimed, "Phooey!"

Jacob sat silent for a moment while staring at his grandmother with a barrage of thoughts swirling inside his head. "It means a lot to you that I go, doesn't it?"

"It only matters what it means to you, Jacob," answered Ava. "But by no means allow your decision to be hinged on some sense of servitude you feel you owe me. When my time comes, and indeed one day it will, your presence whether it be at my side as you are now or on the other end of the globe will not impede that moment. Just as you were unable to stand between your mother and the journey which awaited her."

Jacob jumped to his feet and began pacing the floor about his room.

"I would be lying if I said I haven't been thinking about going to this place, wherever it is." There was an air of excitement in his voice.

"There's a part of me that feels it's the only way I might ever feel...I don't know...normal. It's just..."

He hesitated to go on, until he glanced over and saw the understanding look radiating from his grandmother's eyes.

"I'm scared." He felt shame for even admitting it but Ava gave him a comforting smile.

"Of course you are," she said. "What life would be worth living if untouched by fear?"

"Then you think I should go?"

"Are you not the polestar of your own destiny, dear boy?" answered Ava. "It's the foolish person who makes his way through life being guided by someone else's sails. Keep to your own compass."

With that she got up, but before she left Jacob to his thoughts she pulled out something hidden within the folds of the shawl she had wrapped around her. It was the brown, leather-bound book Jacob saw hidden away in the box buried at the bottom of his grandmother's trunk.

"I gave this journal to my son a long time ago on the eve of the day when he was set to leave with Gotham on the same trip."

Jacob took the book from his grandmother and carefully opened it. There was nothing written inside. In fact, a third of the pages at the beginning of the journal strangely were missing, torn free from the binding.

"It was returned to me like that. Whatever thoughts they may have held are long lost." There was a marked sadness in Ava's voice which she struggled to keep steady. "I would like you to have it now. And should you decide to go tomorrow, it would comfort me to know your journey picked up where his ended."

The two hugged, but only briefly before Ava pulled away. For they both knew in the moment they embraced that the decision concerning Jacob's quest had already been made, and that he'd be leaving for an untold length of time in a few short hours. Maybe then, with the warmth of the morning sun on her face to help dry her tears as her eyes threatened to shed them, she would be better able to manage her goodbyes. But not now.

"Isn't the school dance tonight?" she asked, pausing in the doorway while glancing off as if thinking out loud.

"What about it?" Jacob replied.

"Oh, no reason really. It just dawned on me earlier when you were lamenting over leaving your friends what a shame it is you didn't go."

She had a way of saying something without ever uttering the words. And so she did again before disappearing into the hallway.

CHAPTER EIGHT

The homecoming dance was already in full swing when Jacob finally arrived on foot at Harpus High. He could hear the dull, drumming pulse of music pumping away inside the gymnasium, even from where he stood at the far corner of the school where the football and track fields sat eerily vacant in the darkness of the chilly night.

In a flash, he scaled the chain-link fence separating himself from the school grounds on the other side. He then sprinted across the width of the open grassy field he had been forced to run in circles around countless times during gym class toward the large tan and maroon-colored building from which the music spilled. That was the easy part. Getting inside the gymnasium where the dance was taking place, however, would be a completely different matter altogether.

The entrance to the gym was made completely of glass, which offered a birds-eye view of everything going on inside. It also made slipping inside nonchalantly virtually impossible, mostly because of Mrs. Braukoff's unmistakable presence, which Jacob spied almost immediately. She was standing alone off to the side looking permanently pinched as she usually did in a dowdy, drab floral print dress which hung sad and lifeless on her formless frame with a strand of pearls dangling from around her thin cranelike neck. Her gaze managed to be on everything and everyone at once, like that of a prison guard watching over the inmates from the gun tower.

Not only was Elvira Braukoff the student counselor at the high school, she also served as a Bible teacher at the nearby neighborhood church. Which meant she was well-positioned to ensure a wide-swath of teenagers were steered from falling into the Devil's waiting clutches. And if there was anyone evenly matched to go up against the Devil it was Mrs. Braukoff, saccharine-voiced though she was. While her unassuming presence was more ice than fire, the manner in which she doled out reprimands to students for any act she deemed an unholy or sinful indiscretion was pure brimstone. Exactly what was considered unholy or sinful in Mrs. Braukoff's eyes, however, seemed to change like the weather and usually extended much further than the school's own rules of conduct. An outfit one chose to wear to school or the overheard punch line to a questionable joke could bring a disapproving frown to Mrs. Braukoff's face as easily as bullying or cheating. One thing was certain, one knew instantly they had committed an infraction when they felt an ear suddenly and most painfully being taken hold of by the vice that was Mrs. Braufoff's sausage-like thumb and forefinger.

Even the town's name wasn't safe from Mrs. Braukoff's righteous ire. Cain's Corner, she argued to anyone who would listen, was an evil and unclean name for any community to label itself, and she proceeded to spearhead an unrelenting campaign over the years to force the city council to have it changed. It didn't matter that the town's namesake came not from the biblical Cain who slaughtered his brother Abel but Cain Crawford, an ambitious entrepreneur who migrated to the Pacific Northwest in the mid-1800s to make a killing during the Gold Rush only to find his fortune in the slaughtering of trees by starting up Crawford Lumber Co., the first landmark of the town he founded.

"Mark my words," Mrs. Braukoff was fond of saying, "by branding our fair and wholesome town with such an unholy moniker is to extend an invitation addressed to an evil most unwelcome."

Naturally, it proved to be an uncomfortable coincidence when Mrs. Braukoff's marriage of nearly thirty years to the well-liked and respected Reverend Horace Braukoff came to an abrupt end one day two winters earlier as he was driving home after performing the last rites on one of his parishioners when his car suddenly, without any foreseen cause, veered off the road and slammed head-on into a tree and exploded into a fireball of flames. The shocking tragedy made some in the community rethink the validity of the crusade to change the town's name. The students of Harpus High contended—quietly, of course—that Mrs. Braukoff's manner of Bible thumping was too much to take in daily doses, even for the poor departed reverend, who saw the tree as a merciful and permanent escape from the righteous bleating he had been forced to endure.

Still, parents loved Mrs. Braukoff because she was more than willing to do that with which they preferred not to be bothered: keeping their children on a tight leash when out of their sights and, when the situation called for it, meting out the proper discipline. Even Jacob didn't share his classmates immense disdain for Mrs. Braukoff, nor did he take part in their constant mockery of her behind her back. True he didn't care much for her, but he felt more sympathy than dislike for the woman and found it best for him, and his ears, to take an abrupt detour whenever he saw her heading his way down the same hallway at school. Unfortunately, there weren't many detour options Jacob could see around her or her ear-pinching claws this night at the dance.

~   ~   ~

For some time Jacob stood just outside the reach of the lights illuminating the entrance into the gym watching the happenings of the dance through the fleece portal formed around his face by the dark gray hoodie pulled up over his head.

"Where are you?" he muttered to himself as his eyes scanned the clamor of bodies gyrating to the incessant beat pounding away loudly from the other side of the large bank of windows. It didn't take long before he was drawn to the disturbingly familiar moves belonging to his friend Ty, whose bizarre repertoire of dance moves were uniquely spastic, if not seizure-like in their execution. Jacob found it to be like watching a musical exorcism taking place in the middle of the dance floor.

With Ty in his sights, Jacob dug into his pocket for his phone. The bright light from its screen lit up his face as his fingers quickly tapped out a message: "Oh. My. God. For the love of everything that is good and pure, PLEASE LEAVE THE DANCE FLOOR! I'm outside the gym with no way of getting around the battle- axe watchdog. Need to speak to you. Code: Urgent!"

Between the loud, pulsing music and Ty's continuing best efforts to match his wild writhing convulsions to the beat, Jacob knew it could take a while for his sent text to be noticed. All he could do was wait. And watch. Which was equally hard as it was entertaining. Try as he might, Jacob was unable to stifle the toothy grin fighting for release behind his pursed mouth as he debated which was more comical, the absolute seriousness his best friend committed himself to his performance, or those dancing next to him bearing the unsure expressions of whether or not an ambulance needed to be called.

Jacob's smile was short-lasting when his gaze shifted somewhat closer toward the center of the dance floor. There he saw Wray and Yul oblivious to the show Ty was putting on for the rest of the crowd. They were dancing close together slowly, even though the beat—and everyone else around them—was moving light years faster than their feet. Immediately Jacob felt those gut-eating pangs of jealousy that had recently made themselves familiar to him stir themselves awake as he stood glowering in the darkness. Intensely focused, his eyes held watch on Yul's hands positioned on Wray's back as if in prayer. Then they gradually made their way downward to the small of her back and then—

The couple circled around, and as they did Jacob, to his great relief, managed to catch a glimpse of angst in Wray's face. Her body tightened visibly with discomfort as she made an attempt to pull back from the hands groping her and allow some much-needed light between herself and Yul. Jacob knew Wray was a tough girl who could take care of herself, as he witnessed first-hand on more than a few occasions when hormone-raging boys had attempted to cross the line with her. Yul, however, was different. Being caught in the blonde meathead's muscle-banded arms was like finding oneself face to face with an octopus. And even Jacob could see Wray was having trouble prying herself away from the tentacles holding her.

Before he even realized what his feet were doing, Jacob was marching straight toward the gymnasium. All thoughts of Mrs. Braukoff had vanished. Obviously she wasn't the all-seeing oracle everyone feared with Yul openly pawing Wray in the middle of the dance floor like he was. His gaze burning with hatred was locked on its target like a sniper's scope. The perverted grin on Yul's mouth as he attempted to relax Wray with cooing whispers to the ear was enough to make Jacob see an instant curtain of red. Blood red.

Blood.

It would most definitely be spilled tonight on the gymnasium floor, Jacob assured himself while clenching tighter his fists with every advancing step. Even if it ended up being his own, at least it would free Wray of the vulgarian's dirty paws. Jacob, however, envisioned a very different outcome. One which involved personally yanking Yul's arms straight from their—

"Is there something I may help you with, Mr. Parrish?"

Mrs. Braukoff. She was suddenly there, blocking the way into the gym like a police barricade just as Jacob pulled open the door and incinerating instantly the image he enjoyed ever so briefly of seeing Yul Dane standing helpless in the middle of the gym armless and spurting copious amount of blood from his shoulder sockets as his peers surrounded him and laughed at his just punishment.

"Mrs. Braukoff!" Jacob exclaimed in as polite a manner as he could muster while screaming at himself "Why didn't you stay where you were moron?"

"Pardon me for saying so, but you look exceptionally, uh, nice tonight." His fast-thinking but obvious attempt at softening her with flattery failed as she seemed to become even more pinched than she usually appeared.

"I asked if there was something I may help you with," she repeated as her right eyebrow slowly arched itself like the back of a black cat.

"If it's alright with you, I just need to slip inside for a quick second," said Jacob while attempting to look past Mrs. Braukoff and her sad floral-print dress. It was amazing to him how one woman could manage to block such a large portion of the dance floor behind her.

"Do you know what this is, Mr. Parrish?" Mrs. Braukoff coolly inquired while thrusting her handy clipboard in Jacob's face before immediately proceeding to answer her own question. "This is a list of names of students who signed up as instructed to say they would be attending the homecoming dance. And why do we have such a list you may ask yourself? To help prevent strays from neighboring schools and other outside riffraff up to no good from sneaking their way into this gymnasium and soiling what should be a respectable function for the students of Harpus High."

"But I'm not a stray from another school or outside riffraff. I'm a student here," said Jacob.

"Yes, you are," Mrs. Braukoff concurred in her high-pitched saccharine voice that was anything but sweet. "But I think you know me well enough to know that I have not needed to refer once to this list all evening, and that is because I have committed to memory every single last name on this piece of paper. And you know as well I that your name—is not—on—the list!"

Jacob had to bite his tongue to keep from telling Mrs. Braukoff what she could do with her blasted list.

"Maybe, you might make an exception?" he said instead, forcing his mouth to form a pleasant smile.

"Should God have made an exception when he turned Lot's wife into a pillar of salt for turning around to watch the destruction of Sodom and Gomorrah after she was told not to?" replied Mrs. Braukoff, who had a refined talent of finding an opportunity to reference scripture in almost every conversation she had.

"No, Mr. Parrish, rules are just that, rules. And I will tell you what I told the four other students who showed up here before you did tonight: If you wanted to attend this function, you should have had the foresight to make sure your name found its way onto the list," said Mrs. Braukoff, dangling the clipboard clenched in her hand in front of Jacob's face as though it were the last golden ticket to get into the Wonka chocolate factory. "Although, to be quite frank, even if your name was on the list I can most assure you the way you're dressed alone would keep you from passing through these doors."

Jacob glanced down and gave himself a slow once-over. It was true the T-shirt and jeans he was wearing along with a pair of Converse sneakers, which had seen better days, was a noticeable downgrade compared to the semi-formal spit and shine seen parading around inside the gymnasium. It hardly deserved the snobbish glare focused down the end of Mrs. Braukoff's upturned nose as though Jacob was some replicant of the Peanuts character Pigpen come to life.

"We do have a dress code, as I'm sure you're aware," Mrs. Braukoff sang with odd glee.

"Look, Mrs. Braukoff, I'm not dressed to go to the dance because I'm not here to crash the dance," Jacob tried to explain. "I just need to find someone inside and—"

"Need I remind you, young man," Mrs. Braukoff cut him off sharply, "that this is a school dance and not a place to socialize."

The absurdity of the words that met Jacob's ears was enough to make his head spin like a top joined to his neck.

"Now then," Mrs. Braukoff continued, "what I wish to see is the back of your head getting smaller and smaller as you walk yourself away from this doorway, and may I suggest to you that you contact the party inside responsible for the ants in your pants by texting them, or Tweeting them, or whatever new way you younger generation have discovered to communicate to one another without loosening your tongue."

Speaking of tongues, there was nothing else Jacob wanted more at that moment than to reach into the miserable spinster's mouth, grab her's by its forked end and bring her to a strangled silence by wrapping it several times around her neck. As he stood glaring his contempt for her, a feel-good thought suddenly came to him, aside from the beautiful image of seeing her tongue finally put to good use. He could easily just bowl past the woman and accomplish two feats at once: get inside the dance to Ty and Wray, and earn the eternal gratitude of his classmates who would get the choice experience of seeing Mrs. Braukoff knocked flat on her backside. Sure it would likely mean spending the rest of the year in detention and whatever else Mrs. Braukoff could think of as punishment. Then again, Jacob wasn't planning on being back at school the coming Monday.

~   ~   ~

Thankfully for Mrs. Braukoff and her derriere, the gleam in Jacob's eye was doused by the sudden roar of music escaping the gym through an opening door a further ways down and the sight of Ty coming to his aid.

"It's okay Mrs. Braukoff, you can call off the hounds. He's with me," Ty announced as he swaggered his way over to where they stood. It was only while grinning self-assuredly at both Mrs. Braukoff and Jacob that Ty suddenly clued in to the fixed expressions on both faces—one unamused, the other perplexed, yet amused—and realizing the double entendre of his words that a look of swelling anxiety swept over him.

"Not to mean Jacob's with me, with me," Ty quickly attempted to explain before Mrs. Braukoff had the opportunity to aim a verse from the Book of Leviticus at him with both barrels. "That is, he's not my date. What I mean is we're not—you know. Which I'm sure is probably obvious—I hope. But in this day who's to know for sure who's dating who. And how great is it that our society is becoming more tolerant of one another and who they choose to want to be with? Not that there's a need for tolerance right now at this exact moment because I can tell you truthfully Jacob and I have not chosen to be together. At least not in a tolerating sort of way—"

"Ty," Jacob whispered calmly in an attempt to halt the snowballing vomit of his friend's words. However, it was as if Ty had lost all control over his mouth.

"Not to say I wouldn't take Jacob to a dance. If he were my type—which he isn't—but if he were—I mean, what guy wouldn't consider himself lucky to be able to go out with someone like my man Jacob? Not that he's my man. Even though as close as we are as friends it could almost seem as if we're dating—"

"TY!" barked Jacob. Finally he managed to break through his friend's rambling trance before adding calmly, "We get it."

Mrs. Braukoff stood staring at both boys with a wilting look. It was one of the rare moments she had been struck speechless.

"I will give you five minutes, Mr. Parrish," she eventually conceded much to Jacob's relief. "Make sure you stay in my sight in the light, or you needn't bother trying to come back inside, understand Mr. Wrenwood?"

"Make sure you stay in my sight in the light," mimicked Ty in a dead-on, pitchy impersonation of Mrs. Braukoff, once she had retreated safely from out of earshot back inside the gymnasium, that is. "Handled that pretty brilliantly, wouldn't you agree?"

Jacob nodded. "If by brilliant you mean you managed to convince her you're a closet case in desperate need of the spiritual cure to get back on the straight and narrow, with emphasis on the word 'straight,' then yes, I agree," he remarked sarcastically. "Although, the jacket you're wearing alone was enough to do that."

It wasn't every day Jacob got to see his friend dressed in anything other than what had become a regulation uniform of jeans, T-shirt and sneakers. To suddenly see him dressed to the nines, or at least sevens, with a pressed shirt and dress pants (and was that the shine of polished shoes laced to his feet?)—it was just weird. The pièce de résistance, however, was the jacket. For starters it was plaid. And it was orange. Bright, glow in the dark orange that Jacob surmised could quite possibly be visible from as far away as space itself.

"What's wrong with the jacket?" asked Ty with genuine perplexity.

"Nothing," answered Jacob. "If you're sharing a wardrobe with Elton John."

Ty stood patiently with his eyes fixed skyward for the expected ribbing to come as Jacob leaned in closer with his squinted eyes focused on Ty's usually untamed shag of hair which he now noticed was swept back from his face and coiffed neatly into place in what looked to be a hard, shellacked helmet.

"Is that gel you have in your hair?" asked Jacob.

"Yes it's gel if you must know, thank you very much." Ty replied with annoyance while trying to bat away the insistent finger coming at him trying desperately to give his noggin an investigative poke. "And I'd appreciate not having my head thumped like a cantaloupe. Took me an hour to get it all to stay in place, and I don't need you turning me into a troll doll for my date."

Carefully he tapped lightly the top of his head making sure the sculpted strands of his hair were still frozen in place.

"What are you doing here anyway?" he asked. "Last I heard you had planned a very festive evening alone at home."

Jacob turned his attention back to the dance to look for Wray and to his surprise found her standing in the doorway listening. More importantly, she looked like some ethereal vision of loveliness encompassing everything and all that was good in the world that, for a single blessing-filled moment, fulfilled every last wish and desire Jacob could ever want from life if he were to never draw another breath again.

~   ~   ~

"What's going on?" she quietly asked looking quite puzzled at seeing Jacob there.

Jacob opened his mouth to answer when he noticed Yul lurking right behind her and his mood instantly darkened once more. In that moment, all he could see in undulating shades of red was Wray being groped by the blonde jock and a familiar hatred inside him began to rapidly percolate. The same hatred that had him ready to storm the dance floor until Mrs. Braukoff placed herself squarely in his war path and quashed his attack.

"That's quite the outfit you're sporting there, Parrish," Yul remarked snidely. "You have that tailored especially for the dance tonight?"

Again with the clothes, Jacob thought to himself. Wray was quick to hush Yul and pushed back his smug face which craned itself over her left shoulder.

"Even your boyfriend here had the good sense to put on a tie, though good taste is a whole other matter," continued Yul, who couldn't keep himself from getting in one more dig.

Thankfully Ty didn't launch into an encore performance of "I'm not gay, but if I was." Jacob, too, held his tongue, hard as it was to do so.

"I need to speak to you," Jacob said to Wray in a cool collected voice. And when Wray complied, stepping out into the night with Yul still close to her heels, Jacob was quick to add in a most unyielding tone, "Alone."

"It's a free country, Parrish," said Yul. "Besides, Wray and I have no secrets. What you say to her you can say in front of me."

He was knowingly goading Jacob; even Ty could see in the subtle way Jacob's eyes narrowed while fixed on Yul that his friend was close to exhausting the last bit of patience he was grasping.

"Here's an idea," Ty suggested. "What say you two wrestle over it, you know, like you did earlier today during tryouts?"

Yul's toothy grin vanished in an instant. It was apparent Yul hadn't shared with Wray, who looked quite confused by the suggestion, his humiliating defeat on the wrestling mat at the hands of her best friend.

"Why don't you go have your talk with—him," Yul said as calmly as possible while his eyes aimed fire at Jacob. "I'm just going to go back inside and get myself some punch—or something."

"What was that all about?" asked Wray once Yul disappeared back inside, but not before giving Ty one last threatening scowl.

"Just a little inside joke between the three of us," answered Jacob.

"And boy does it have one hell of a hilarious punch line," Ty added with a chuckle.

~ ~ ~

Once Jacob had finally managed to find himself alone with his two friends, he was suddenly struck by a halting thought. It came at him like some shadowy assailant lurching from behind a cloaking hedge to pounce upon an unsuspecting victim. What would he tell them? What could he tell them? Certainly not the truth. How could he, when he himself wasn't one hundred percent convinced of what the truth was, despite the barrage of things he had been told; not to mention seen with his own eyes in such a short amount of time.

"What's the matter?" Wray eventually asked in the nurturing way she had whenever she noticed something was weighing heavily on Jacob despite his attempts to hide it.

"N-nothing," Jacob replied unconvincingly. "Let's go sit down over here."

He walked Wray and Ty over to a concrete bench a short distance away, ever mindful of Mrs. Braukoff's occasional glances coming from inside the dance to make sure they remained in sight within the reach of light where she could keep tabs on them.

"So, what exactly is so urgent?" asked Ty.

Oh, nothing really, except I just found out I'm a Nephilim, that's all, Jacob's voice echoed sarcastically inside his head. Or how about '*You know those humps coming out of my back? Funny thing…they're wings.*'

"You're starting to scare me Jacob. What is it?" prodded Wray.

Jacob did his best not to look at either of his friends in the face. The weight of their anxious stares fixed on him made it all the more difficult to try and come up with some explanation of why they wouldn't be seeing him for some time. Yet no matter how hard he tried he just couldn't seem to come up with a viable alternative to the truth—that is, a believable version of it.

"I'm—I just wanted to make you aware of the fact that I'm…" he began awkwardly. At the same time Ty and Wray leaned in closer as if to aid him in helping drag out the words which seemed caught in his throat. "That is…I wanted the two of you to know…"

I'm leaving. LEAVING…

The words repeated themselves loudly in Jacob's head, but he just couldn't bring himself to spit them out. Because to do so would mean explaining why he was leaving, and that was just something he didn't have an answer for—at least one he could share with them and expect them to understand, much less believe.

"Um, okay,…Mr. Sajak's, I'd like to buy a vowel for my friend here, " Ty remarked impatiently. "Know what?"

"Just how much I've appreciated how the two of you have been there for me the past couple months," Jacob eventually said with as much sincerity as he could muster.

"Seriously? That's why you dragged us out here?" replied Ty completely unaffected. "What exactly were you doing tonight at home, binge-watching the Hallmark Channel?"

His insensitive remark quickly earned him a slap to the shoulder by Wray. "Don't be a jerk," she scolded.

"It's just…it's been a hard time ever since my mom…you know," said Jacob. It may not have been the original intent he went to the dance in such a fiery way in search for his two closest friends, but nor was it any less truthful. "I just realized I never made it a point of thanking the two of you for being there for me. I don't think I could have made it through it all if it wasn't for you. That's all."

"Hey, it's no problem. That's what best friends are for, after all, right?" said Ty, giving his friend a warm squeeze of his arm now that he understood the depth of Jacob's gesture.

At that moment, a screeching cry rang out for Ty. It was his date Stacey Ballard, looking so much more lovelier than the ear-splitting voice she used to beckon him from the entrance to the gym.

"Well, well, well…you lucky dog, you!" remarked Jacob, giving Ty a friendly jab with his finger.

"Oh, lucky isn't quite the word I'd use," said Ty. By the look on his friend's face, Jacob guessed the discomfort of having to get all gussied up for the girl Ty couldn't seem to stop talking about in the days leading up to the dance hadn't been quite worth it.

"Trouble in paradise?"

"Paradise?" said Ty. "From the second we got here she's had me on the dance floor. You try dancing two hours nonstop in these shoes and talk to me about paradise. This has been the first moment my feet have been able to rest."

The shrill call echoed again even louder into the night, and with great reluctance Ty started back toward the dance, but not before Jacob called out to him one last time.

"If it's any consolation," he said, "you look like a regular Tony Manero out there."

The puzzled look on Ty's face when the "Saturday Night Fever" reference skidded completely over his head only tickled Jacob more.

"Hey, we're still on for tomorrow? Penuel Point?" Ty yelled back.

Penuel Point. Jacob had forgotten all about the plans he had made with Ty to head up to their favorite spot high in the mountains for a little cliff jumping.

"You think you're going to be up to it?" Jacob answered jokingly and feeling every bit the heel knowing full well he would be flaking big time on his friend.

"You kidding me? I've been looking forward to it all week," said Ty with a renewed boost of energy.

Jacob waved in return and chuckled to himself as he continued to watch as Ty, walking with noticeable discomfort, was pulled back into the dance by the unwelcome enthusiasm waiting for him from his date. His smile then slipped away when he turned to Wray and found her solemn expression staring back at him.

"What is it?" he asked.

"Nothing," she said. "I just thought…I mean, it seems as though something else might be bugging you."

"No," said Jacob with a simple shake of his head. How he hated lying to Wray, even when the lies were harmless little untruths. Only tonight he had not really told her a lie, little or otherwise. He'd just purposefully kept the truth from her, and that somehow felt much worse.

~   ~   ~

As he sat there next to her, Jacob couldn't stop noticing how beautiful she looked that evening. Yes, she was the kind of girl from whom beauty never strayed too far. This night it looked as though it had been given a little extra polish. The curl of her hair, for instance, usually a tousle of summer gold left to dance carefree in the breeze hung in perfectly poised ringlets down across her shoulders. What little makeup she wore served only to accentuate the loveliness already there, like the emerald stones glistening in her eyes. They alone were enough to keep any admiring gaze from wandering further and completely overlook the beautiful dress she wore. Not Jacob. Wray's eyes may have held his gaze in their spell, but he noticed plenty the graceful cut of the elegant gown and how the black velvet fit seamlessly her lithe figure and contrasted sharply against the glow of her white skin.

"What's wrong?" she asked when she noticed the intense look fixed her way.

"Nothing," Jacob was quick to reply. "It's just…you look so different…than usual, I mean. You look beautiful."

Even before he saw Wray's eyebrows rise up on her forehead, Jacob's expression dropped like a stone the moment he heard the words leave his mouth.

"I mean…uh…oh boy, that didn't come out right did it?" he stammered. "Not saying you're not always beautiful, cause you are…it's just tonight—dressed like that—you're…you're…"

"Even more beautiful?" offered Wray.

"Stunning," Jacob one-upped.

They both turned away at the exact same time to watch the dance through the towering wall of glass for different reasons: for Wray it was to hide her delight at witnessing Jacob's appreciation through his boyish awkwardness, and for Jacob it was to shield from sight the sudden reddening he felt begin to burn his face and ears and leave him awash in nervous sweat.

"I'm glad to see at least your mood has changed," said Wray after a long pause of silence.

"What do you mean?" asked Jacob.

"I saw you earlier, right before Mrs. Braukoff stopped you at the door. You looked furious, like you were going to kill someone."

"Oh that," Jacob replied, slightly embarrassed she had caught a glimpse of him consumed by the green-eyed monster. "I wouldn't really say kill. More like dismember. Your boyfriend, actually."

"Yul?" Wray sounded more surprised that amused. "I told you before he's not my boyfriend."

"It's not the way it looked from out here watching the two of you dance."

Even now, Jacob could feel the familiar stirring rising up from the pit of his stomach as he recalled the sight of Wray and Yul on the dance floor.

"How can you let that meathead paw you like that—"

"Let him?" Wray was fast to question Jacob's choice of words.

"You know what I mean," said Jacob, trying to temper his cool by squeezing his molars together tightly. "God, how I can't stand that guy. And to see the two of you together like that just…"

He stopped himself from going further, realizing he was beginning to sound as jealous as he felt, but he had said more than enough.

"Well, you only have yourself to blame, you know?" Wray retorted.

Jacob gave her a baffled sideways glance. "Me?"

"Do you think all of this was originally for Yul?" answered Wray, gesturing to her gown with a sweep of her hands.

"I'm sorry…I don't know what you mean," said Jacob, looking every bit the clueless boy he was at that moment.

"Of course you don't," said Wray with a sigh of tired disappointment. "Goodness knows I dropped you enough hints. I did everything but ask you to the dance myself, and you can call me an old-fashioned snob, but…well, frankly I'm too pretty to have to resort to asking a guy for a date."

While she giggled at her unintentional narcissism, Jacob felt his face grow flush with a renewed shade of red.

"I'm sorry. I really had no idea," he said, feeling like a brain-dead chump. "I guess I've just had other things on my mind lately."

"Why do I have a feeling something is going on with you that you've been keeping from me," Wray remarked suddenly from out the blue.

There came a marked quiet. Even the music coming from inside the gym paused. Jacob continued to stare off straight ahead, not saying anything in return. What could he say? He had always in the past shared his most personal secrets with her. And the times he didn't, she seemed to have an almost clairvoyant way of figuring them out; but this secret— even she wasn't able to unlock the box which held it. And even if he wanted to, how could he even begin to explain what he himself found inexplicable?

~   ~   ~

Just when the silence was becoming unbearable, it passed and a familiar melody suddenly spilled its way from inside the gymnasium and grabbed Jacob's attention by both ears. He gave Wray a sideways glance out of the corner of his eye.

"You've got to be kidding me."

The brief moment of seriousness that had gathered like some dark storm cloud over the couple's head instantly dissipated. Wray, who was seated tight- lipped looking like a devious cat who had just swallowed a canary, gave a breezy shrug. Even she couldn't hide her own surprise of hearing the song—that song—suddenly being played. And then a moment later the cooing vibrato of Stevie Nicks' unmistakable voice swept out into the still night like a gentle breeze.

Jacob sat staring at Wray, a knowing smirk growing wider across his face.

"There's no way this is some weird coincidence," he said with a slight chuckle as the familiar words of "Sanctuary" came out and found the couple like it always had the habit of doing.

"What can I say? I happen to be friends with the DJ who just happens to share the same impeccable taste in music as I have," said Wray. "That said, I had no idea you'd show up here tonight like you did. So the fact that this song is playing right now at this moment is not a coincidence."

He couldn't argue with her. Nor did he when she reached over, took his hand into her's and, despite her rule regarding pretty girls, asked quietly in that warm, honey-sweet voice of hers, "Dance with me?"

"You don't want to dance with me, trust me," answered Jacob with a shy smile. "I would make Ty look like Fred Astaire."

"Please?" Wray insisted.

"What about Yul? I doubt he'd like that too much."

"Would I have asked if I cared?" answered Wray.

And in that moment neither did Jacob as he slowly got to his feet and followed her as she led the way to the gymnasium, her hand still clutching his. The instant they stepped through the glass doors, the song that had so subtly beckoned them inside guided them like a living chaperone through the crush of young teenagers swaying slowly in the dimly lit darkness to a spot near the center of the dance floor. There they turned to face one another and in a manner that was both noticeably self-conscious and bashful they paused before stiffly embracing.

Jacob's feet were immediately clumsy in their first steps to move with the music, stepping squarely on Wray's delicate toes more than once. It was enough to make him want to flee and disappear into the cover of the crowd. Wray prevented such an escape by tightening her hold on him.

"Just follow me," she instructed with a reassuring softness.

Jacob hesitantly surrendered to her lead and slowly Wray felt his body begin to relax against her own. What had felt so awkward one minute, quickly became comfortable, and soon the two were moving together in an easy sway as if they had spent a lifetime spinning their way across an endless ballroom. The embarrassment Jacob felt over standing out from his classmates in his grubby street clothes evaporated and the only awareness he was left with was the inviting flowery scent that drew his nose closer to Wray's soft golden hair.

Wray suddenly became conscious of Jacob's hands moving downward across her back. She felt her breath catch in her chest as she waited for the inevitable to spoil what had been a pleasant moment. To her surprise, as well as hopeful expectation, Jacob's hands traveled no further than her waist and came to a respectable and gentle rest at the small of her back.

"What is it?" asked Jacob when he felt her release a deep breath.

She shook her head and smiled. "Nothing. Absolutely nothing."

~ ~ ~

As they continued to dance, Jacob took a quick look around the darkened gymnasium. Nearby he spied Ty slow-dancing with his date, his eyes closed and a completely blissful look pasted on his face. Perhaps he had fallen asleep, Jacob thought while smiling to himself. His smile, though, quickly faded when he caught sight of Yul standing off by himself in the corner with two eyes blazing straight in his direction and looking none too happy at seeing Jacob and his date together as they were.

What rooftop is he fantasizing about throwing me off now? Jacob thought to himself.

He turned the focus of his gaze elsewhere, first to several teachers gathered together near a table lined with refreshments, then to a group of girls giggling secretly to themselves as they returned from a trip to the restroom. That's when he caught sight of him, and the eyes reflecting flashes of gold from a dark corner where the silhouette of his body huddled unnoticed by anyone.

Jacob caught sharply his breath.

Gotham?

"What is it?"

He found Wray looking questionably at him.

"Nothing…," Jacob replied dismissively.

He looked again in the direction of the figure, but to his surprise— or maybe not—it had vanished. Perhaps, he thought, he imagined it. After all, with everything that had happened that day—then again, what reason would Gotham have to be at a high school dance?

"It's nothing," he repeated again. Only this time when he looked down into Wray's face there was nothing capable of pulling his eyes away from her glowing face, even an angel. "I guess I didn't realize how much I love this song."

Had she always been this beautiful, Jacob found himself wondering. And before either one knew what had happened, they kissed. A sweet, brief kiss, but one which felt fused by eternity.

The song seemed to come up around them and cradle them in the quiet eye of some invisible storm; this melody that somehow found a way to make itself heard whenever Jacob and Wray were together; one which seemed destined to haunt them to their last breath. It was so that Jacob almost found it difficult not to believe Stevie Nicks herself wasn't in the gym solely to sing her song about the sanctuary of fated love to the couple who didn't even realize—or at least admit to one another before this night—the sanctuary of their own coupling. They kissed again, this time longer, all the while swaying together to the voice lulling them into a tighter embrace. And in that instant, Jacob found himself questioning the decision he made to leave the next day.

There was never a more perfect moment; but a brief moment it was when suddenly the right side of Jacob's head exploded with a burning, stabbing pain. His face instantly screwed itself up in a frozen look of agony. He knew even before he heard her voice that Mrs. Braukoff's claw had latched itself onto his ear.

"Not on my watch, Mr. Parrish!" he heard her say in her sugary-sweet voice while cruelly testing how pliable the cartilage in his ear was.

The blinding pain pulled him out of the sanctuary that was Wray's arms and guided him in stumbling steps backward across the gymnasium floor. Little did Jacob know it would be some time before he would ever see Wray Bliss' face again.

CHAPTER NINE

Saturday, Oct. 23

So here goes my first entry.

I've never kept a journal before, and I guess the only reason I'm starting now is because grandma gave this to me before I left and I know its importance to her. Or maybe it's because my mind is on overload from so many thoughts that I'm hoping writing them down will help me sort through them and make sense of everything that is happening. I'm also bored out of my head, which is odd considering the fact we've arrived in Budapest of all places. Then again I'm tired. Exhausted actually. So much so I can barely keep my eyes open. One would think a trip like this would be an exciting adventure to a boy my age, but so far it has been anything but. I still haven't the faintest clue as to where we're going and the further we get from home the more anxious I find myself becoming.

Despite not knowing exactly where we're headed, I know enough of where we've been to realize our trip is taking far longer than it needs to. For whatever reason, we seem to be traveling by way of side roads and small towns, bypassing major cities and metropolitan areas unless it proves necessary. And only then it's to dart quickly through an airport to catch a flight at the very last minute possible. If I didn't know better, I would think I've been placed in the care of an escaped fugitive on the run from the law. This man Gotham—if I may even call him a man—proves to be more mysterious to me the longer I am with him.

Before leaving the U.S., we found ourselves in a small town—a real rural, backwoods place that I would have normally insisted we push through without stopping had it not been for the fact that I was starving (Usually I have to chow down on something at least every three hours and it had been nearly twice that long, and I could hear my stomach growling with hunger). We found a small diner and stopped to eat. Well, I ate, at least. Since leaving Cain's Corner I have yet to see Gotham eat anything. When I inquired about it, I was told simply angels don't have a need for food.

He's not much for talking, but what he does say I find intriguing. We sat there in the booth in silence, like we had so far for most of the trip. And as I ate my burger I found myself looking at this "angel" (I use quotes because despite what I've seen I'm still not completely sure what to make of him). I found myself studying him, his clothes, his hair, his face. Especially his face. I could see how grandma could have fallen for him in her day. Aside from his obvious good looks, he has a certain inexplicable charm that seems almost spellbinding to women, including our waitress at the diner who couldn't seem take her eyes off him and was reduced to speaking almost gibberish every time she came to the table. And yet at the same time I've noticed even the burliest of guys we've crossed paths with who happen to glance his way are quick to divert their eyes elsewhere as if intimidated. There's a hardness to Gotham—a fierce coldness, actually—particularly in his eyes, despite their unusual gold color. I find myself wondering if it's because I know he is fallen (at least, that's what he refers to himself as), or if it's always been there. Whatever the answer, I know instinctively he is not someone to be messed with by anyone. Maybe it's because of that I find myself unable to see him as this thing—this "angel"—he claims to be.

Anyways, as I was sitting there in the diner gorging myself on a greasy burger and fries while carefully studying him as he continued to stare quietly out the window next to our booth, he suddenly asked me, "And what exactly did you expect an angel to look like?" I was somewhat taken aback because at that moment I had found myself thinking just how unangelic he seemed to me. If anything, he's what I would imagine a gladiator plucked from the Coliseum and dropped into present times in present-day clothes would look like. Or better yet, an actor to follow in the footsteps of Adrian Paul in a television reboot of "Highlander." I shrugged, not knowing exactly how to answer while trying to swallow down the mouthful of food ballooning my mouth. I told him I'd always imagined angels in white robes with halos poised above their heads and playing harps. Well, I noted the lack of any sign of a halo positioned over his head, and I definitely couldn't picture him strumming a harp, I told him.

Tell me Jacob, he said, if you were the big man upstairs forming a celestial army, would it be one dressed in robes and armed with harps as you imagine? Or would you, instead, make sure to create the fiercest, most powerful warriors the heavens had ever bore witness to, a legion of merciless killers capable of protecting your throne from any enemy that dared to rise up against it?

His query at once seemed to make perfect sense though I felt myself tremble slightly while imagining more like him—an army's worth, in fact, of Gothams. Or perhaps it was due to that cold fierceness I described earlier of which I caught a fleeting glint in his eyes as he spoke. Whatever it was, I found myself during this rare moment of conversation between the two of us wanting to spew forth a flood of questions I had desperately wanted to ask him since we left Cain's Corner. Like, what was God like? And what about Heaven? Was my mom there? What horrible thing did you do to cause your fall? But Gotham appeared distracted and I noticed his attention kept veering toward the window beside us that carried the greasy ketchup-smeared fingerprints of small children who had sat at our booth before us. I followed his icy gaze past the few cars filling the small parking lot outside and out toward the gas pumps located right off the two-lane highway we had been driving for such a long time. Parked nearby was a large truck—a total hick mobile, if there ever was one. Its bright yellow paint was splattered with dried mud that had been kicked up from the oversized tires, also caked thick with brown muck. Two middle-aged looking men were standing near the back of the truck talking. Gotham's eyes were fixed on the two of them with an intense look I'm not sure I even have the word to even describe.

He dug some money from his coat, tossed it on the table and asked me if I was through eating, and before I could answer he was already up and *heading towards the door. He was halfway across the parking lot heading in the direction of the two men when I finally caught up to him. His manner of walking appeared easy and casual and yet somehow my legs were struggling to keep up with his pace without being forced to break into an easy jog. I tried to ask him what the matter was, but he didn't answer. He just continued forward with his eyes fixed and his jaw tight. As we grew near, I noticed what looked to be a pair of hoofed legs sticking up from behind the tailgate of the truck along with what appeared to be the smooth, bare branches of a tree. As the men continued talking, Gotham brushed right past them without a word or glance and peered inside the bed of the truck.*

"Beautiful ain't it?" the younger of the two men asked when he finally took notice of us. Gotham didn't say a word at first. He just stood there, silent and still. Out of curiosity, I moved in closer and snuck a look at what had drawn Gotham out of the diner and across the parking lot in such a brisk fashion. It was the body of a big, healthy buck of a deer sprawled out lifeless in the back of the truck, its size so impressively large the truck bed was almost too small to contain it. What I thought had been the branches of a tree were in fact a spectacular set of giant antlers.

"I said beautiful ain't it," the man asked again with the backwoods' twang you'd expect to hear in this part of the country, and in movies marked by an eery chorus of notes plucked from a banjo. He was a good 'ol boy from the dirt- stained trucker hat on his head and worn-out boots on his feet to the soggy wad of tobacco ballooning his bottom lip. His proud smile revealed an eagerness to hear the praise he expected to come from his prize. From the conversation I partially overheard him having with the other man, I assumed at first he was referring to the truck, which looked fairly new, or close to despite the splatter of caked-on mud, and was clearly the man's pride and joy. But it soon became clear he was referring to the limp carcass lying in the back.

Gotham remained silent and then with a very solemn tone that was barely above a whisper I heard him reply, "Yes. It was." There was a deep, noticeable sadness to his voice, and if I wasn't able to glance into his face I would think he might shed a tear and possibly sob over this animal. But I was able to glance into his face, and what I saw made me want to warn the two men to take off running as quickly as their legs could carry them.

The other man, who had stopped to fill up on gas and wandered over to admire the hunter's kill, commented on how good eating the deer looked, which made the hunter chuckle arrogantly. "You don't shoot a stag like this for eating," he said.

I noticed Gotham grow even darker, as if a shadow had passed over and settled itself above him. Why shoot it then? the man asked the hunter.

The hunter brushed up beside Gotham and reaching inside the Jeep, grabbed an antler and lifted the limp deer's head up off the floor for all to see.

"You tell me how impressive this is going to look mounted above my fireplace," the hunter replied. I looked into Gotham's face and the growing contempt I saw past his flaming eyes was almost palpable.

"And God wonders why his edict that we bow down before such creatures as man filled our mouths with the bile of contempt," I heard him mutter to himself. He looked to the arsenal of guns laid piled beside the deer and reached for one. It wasn't a hunting rifle, but a full on assault rifle—the kind you'd expect to see in the hands of an elite sniper in the military. Gotham asked the man if it was the gun he had used and the man released his hold of the deer's head and took the gun in his hand. With the excitement of a child with a new toy, the man began reciting everything there was to know about the gun, from its fire power to the pin-point accuracy of its scope that allowed him drop an animal from a great distance without ever being seen, or even having his scent detected. And as he spoke, his pasty, tobacco-stuffed face lit up with an almost sick ecstasy from the inflated sense of pride and bravado which seemed to surge through the fingers gripping tight and caressing the body of the rifle. It was then, as the hunter went to show off another one of his numerous guns, that Gotham asked him pointedly if he *had ever before engaged himself in a fair fight. It wasn't so much a question as a snide assessment and one not lost on the hunter.*

"Excuse me?" asked the man as the smug smile he had been wearing slowly faded from his face.

"As I suspected, even the premise is completely lost to someone like you," Gotham said. "You stand here armed to the teeth with weapons no animal has any hope of fighting against, let alone outrunning, and you call it sport. What sport, I ask, pits two opponents against one another on unequal playing fields?"

The hunter traded a dumbstruck look with his friend, as if to confirm his ears had actually heard the dressing down he'd just received from this stranger.

"Are you for real?" asked the man turning back to Gotham. I nearly found myself breaking up at the irony of the question. "And just who do you think you're talkin' to, huh?"

"A coward," replied Gotham without missing a beat. "For only a truly weak, putrid excuse of a man would stand here and tell the outcome between a fly and flyswatter and then, in the same breath, crow that some great act of skill and strength had taken place. You, who hides behind a scope and camouflage, robbing from his unsuspecting opponent even the smallest dignity of seeing who would steal its last breath, only you would claim with such pride a trophy as this for your pitiful mantle in an attempt to depict your manhood."

The hunter at first was at a loss for words, but it was clear he was becoming more and more incensed. I could tell by the way the gooey, brown tobacco juice he had been spitting intermittently onto the asphalt was coming in more frequent spurts.

"I see what you are," he finally growled. "You're one of those liberal sissies from Hollyweird? A limp-wristed, tree-hugging—"

His face became hate-filled as he unleashed a verbal assault on Gotham that was more a laundry list of all the profanity he had added to his vocabulary over his lifetime. I probably would have found it more humorous than I did had it not been for all those guns being within reach of the enraged hunter. "Fair fight. Did you ever hear of such a thing, Harvey?" the man said to his friend with an angry chuckle. Then as he settled a fuming glare on Gotham, I knew instantly what was coming next when he suddenly cried out, "I'll give you a fair fight."

I didn't have the time to warn Gotham, who was looking away from the man, when the hunter suddenly lunged toward him while drawing back his fist. He swung at Gotham with all his might aimed at the side of his turned head. But the assault came to a dead stop when Gotham, without so much as looking, caught the man's fist in his hand. An immediate look of intense pain swept over the hunter's face as the sound of bones cracking could be heard.

"Trust me when I tell you, you're a fly going up against a flyswatter," Gotham warned the man. "And as much as I'd love to engage you, it wouldn't be a fair fight."

Gotham then turned back to the deer, leaving the whimpering hunter to nurse the pain of his broken hand. I watched as Gotham placed his hand gently on the buck's side and closed his eyes as though to block out the man's continued ranting. A moment later he opened his eyes and looked to me and said it was time to leave. I gave the deer one final glance as I turned to follow, and as I did I could have sworn I saw its dark dead eyes blink. Obviously I was seeing things I told myself and went to follow Gotham. Then, just as we were about halfway across the parking lot, a terrible ruckus erupted behind us. The hunter's threats which had trailed us suddenly went silent, and as I turned I saw the hunter and his friend standing motionless with their mouths hanging open and staring wide-eyed at the truck that was lurching violently upon its wheels. And within moments I held the same look.

There, in the back of the truck, the deer that had been lying dead was up on its feet bucking about like mad and thrashing its head wildly while baying loudly. It came bounding out of the truck and began butting and ramming all sides of the hunter's precious truck. Its antlers punched through doors and sliced huge gouges out of the metal exterior as easily as a can opener working through a lid of Campbell's Soup. Windows exploded in shards of glass and the chrome grill in front of the truck was laid to waste in a matter of seconds. And then the buck took aim at the oversized tires.

The man with the hunter was the first to find his voice, and screamed to his friend to shoot the deer. The frozen hunter was shaking like crazy and nearly in tears as he attempted to remove the safety from his gun with his wounded hand and take aim. Before he was able, the angry buck set its sights on him and bounded toward him. Both men let out the high-pitched shrieks more suitable for housewives crossing paths with a mouse scurrying across the kitchen floor as they were sent sprawling across the ground by painful butts from the buck who then quickly ran off toward the nearby hills leaving behind two scared men clinging to one another and a completely demolished truck looking like so many that have collided with deer on the highway. Only it was the deer who walked away and the truck that lay dead on the side of the road.

Still shocked by what I had just witnessed, I looked to Gotham and saw a satisfied smirk on his face. "Thou shall not kill," I heard him remark. "You will not find a footnote of exceptions etched in the stone upon which that commandment was written."

Later, when we had resumed our travel, with the altercation still stuck in his craw, he told me the history of the battle man has waged on animals. It stemmed, he said, from a deep-seated resentment held by man that God had created the animals first, and knowing full-well the immense pride and love God had for these creatures. And it was shortly after man was created and instructed to look after the animals that man turned on them, enslaving them under his dominance and violence in a jealous attempt to gain primary favor with God. It was, Gotham said, a similar jealousy angels would soon feel toward man that would result in the Great War in Heaven.

"To kill an animal and disrespect the beauty of the creatures that roam this world is to spit in the face of God," he said to me. No doubt this is the first of many important lessons awaiting me.

It looks like our train is ready to be boarded. We're now off to Tatvan— wherever that is.

~ ~ ~

The first thing to grab Jacob's attention when he climbed aboard the Van Gölü Ekspresi and navigated his way down the aisle of one of the passenger cars filled with excited but tired tourists looking forward to a good night's rest were all the different voices. Polish, Armenian, German, Dutch, Hungarian—the cacophony of languages circulated through the air in a dull drone of chatter, and strangely Jacob found he could understand every single foreign word to find his ears, even Uzbek coming from a young couple sitting towards the front of the car. Was this really happening? Or were his ears—and head—playing tricks on him? he wondered. As he found himself looking to the mouths of those talking, he saw the various lips truly were enunciating what he was hearing. It spooked him somewhat and made his feet move just a bit quicker to catch up with Gotham, who was leading the way at a brisk pace to the adjoining private sleeping car.

As they proceeded down the car's narrow corridor, various eyes stole curious glances from inside the neighboring compartments they passed. An elderly woman, with a head of cotton candy white hair that carried a subtle tint of mauve, glanced up from her magazine and over the top of a pair of rectangular-shaped reading glasses perched on the end of her nose. A small boy tapped incessantly against the window of another compartment with a plastic toy dinosaur gripped tightly in his hand while his mother sat slumped in her seat fast asleep from exhaustion. Further down, a heavy-set businessman wearing a rumpled cheap brown tweed suit with a striped tie pulled loose from its strangling hug around his thick neck momentarily ceased his agitated pacing back and forth within the small confines and barking into a cell phone to fix his dark, beady eyes on Jacob before yanking down the shade over the window of his door.

Once inside their own compartment, Jacob immediately shrugged from his aching shoulder the weight of his duffel bag he had been lugging around for what had seemed like an eternity and collapsed with an exhausted sigh onto one of the waiting seats. Never had his feet been more grateful to be issued a reprieve from taking another single step. The day had been a non-stop blur of planes, trains and taxis punctuated by tedious waiting inside countless stations stretching from London to Budapest and Jacob was never more thankful to leave it behind when he felt the train beneath him finally lurch forward as it slowly pulled out of the station. Outside the window of the compartment, through tired eyes, Jacob caught the last glimmer of the grand cultural mosaic of Istanbul, lit up brightly like a sparkling jewel, growing smaller and fainter until its light was eventually snuffed out like the flame of a candle by the pitch-black darkness of night.

The train lumbered along the tracks, creeping along at a painfully slow pace, its wheels seemingly timid to pick up a faster speed. The bright lights fixed upon the nose of the engine fought to cut through the thick, almost impregnable inky blackness that swallowed whole the vast, open Turkish landscape with a spooky hunger. Jacob's eyes quickly grew heavier and heavier, and within moments he surrendered without resistance to the staccato grinding of the train making its way along the tracks which lulled him to sleep.

~   ~   ~

He dreamed a dream of flying.

It began with him rushing toward a cliff's edge at Penuel Point as he had done many times before with his friend Ty and leaping into the vast openness of the waiting beauty. Only there was no chute strapped to his back. He did not need one. For he was suddenly fixed with a pair of majestic wings. They took him soaring high along the slopes of the mountain peaks, allowing him to share the sky with the birds circling about him. He had become one of them, darting and diving with ease upon the wind that seemed to hold him up with gentle fingers, and he was filled with a freedom he had never before experienced, as well as a feeling of immense power.

Then a great dark shadow suddenly materializing above him, spreading across the sky like a tide of spilled black ink slowly dribbling its way across the top of a wooden desk sending the birds scattering in a frightful flurry to all directions of the wind. An intense wave of fear overtook Jacob as he tried to move himself faster through the emptiness that surrounded him, desperate to escape the ominous cloud bearing down on him while slowly saturating the sky and suffocating everything around him in a charred blackness.

Suddenly from within the darkness emerged a deep rumbling growl driving a horrifying chill deep into his being. And from within the billowing blackness a monstrous face emerged with two red orbs for eyes, brightly illuminated like two coals consumed in the burning flames of fire.

"Destiny." The voice came from within in a terrifying roar.

Jacob fought with all his might to escape the horrifying presence, yet nothing but blackness surrounded him. Everywhere blackness, reeking with the putrid, acrid stench of sulphur. And then there was a great pain, the searing pain of fire across his back and digging its way deep into his shoulder blades. Jacob gave a glance over his shoulder and saw his great wings suddenly ablaze and in a fiery instant the flames had eaten through his brilliant plumage and scattered the disintegrated cinders to the wind.

The world seemed to suddenly be pulled out from beneath him and he began to fall. Down...down...down.... Deeper into the blackness, and then past it to where the beauty of the green valley below resurfaced, but only for a moment, and then the lush scenery was seen to wilt away in a matter of seconds and transform into a brown, desolate wasteland. It was coming up fast to meet Jacob in a most unpleasant way leaving him to claw at the air whistling loudly past him in a useless attempt to slow his fall. He managed a hopeless wail right before slamming into the ground.

To his surprise the fall had not obliterated him, but left him sprawled face- down upon the hard, hot ground. With his back still smoldering, Jacob got to his feet and was struck immediately by the unforgiving heat bearing down upon him from the blazing sun. It was suffocating, strangling. Where was he? A desert of some kind, it looked to him. Miles and miles of it. And not a sign of another living thing in sight. And then he heard the voice again, only not as monstrous as it sounded before, but human.

"Destiny."

~ ~ ~

Jacob awoke with a start, wide-eyed and damp with sweat. His face was pressed up against the cold window where he was greeted with nothing but the dark void of night. For a moment he had forgotten where he was, forgotten about the train he had boarded only a few hours before.

Destiny.

Destiny.

Destiny.

Destiny.

The voice echoing its haunting refrain in a far-off distance gradually faded and merged with the rhythmic clamor of the train's wheels grinding against the rails.

Dream. It was just a dream.

And yet so real.

But a dream nonetheless. One Jacob wished to never revisit again, and yet one he found himself being stalked by beginning a couple nights earlier.

He righted himself in his seat, tilted back his head and took several deep breaths, trying to calm his heart which was pounding wildly in his chest when he became aware he wasn't alone.

His eyes flew open and shot to the seat directly across from him where he found Gotham quietly sitting. The angel's hawkish eyes, as though lit from within by a candle placed strategically in his skull, burned through the dark pall seeping inside from the night outside and were leveled firmly on the boy.

"Bad dream?"

Jacob didn't want to talk about it.

"What time is it?" he asked with a yawn.

"I rarely have use in keeping track of the hour of any given day," Gotham replied. "But if I had to guess…," his gaze rolled to the right to sneak a glance at the night through the window, "I would say just a hair past three in the morning."

Jacob reached for his phone which momentarily pierced the darkness with its light. "Three after three. Not bad," said Jacob, to which Gotham nodded in a mocking manner to acknowledge his brilliant feat.

"So how come you're sitting here in the dark wide awake?" asked Jacob. "I figured you'd be just as dead tired as I was after such a long day of traveling."

Before Gotham could answer, Jacob quickly cut him off before he could speak. "I know, you don't have a need for food or clocks so I'm guessing sleep is out of the question for you angels as well?"

"What can I say?" said Gotham. "We just have no use for the creature comforts required by civilians."

"Civilians?"

"Just a term we've come to use when speaking of mortals."

"No sleep either, huh?" pondered Jacob aloud while staring inquisitively at Gotham. "It must get, among other things, boring for you at times. I mean, what do you do in the middle of the night when everyone around you has fallen asleep?"

"Strange as you might find it, I quite enjoy these hours, brief as they are, when the world falls away and I am left alone in the stillness and quiet left behind. It gives me time to think and reflect."

Jacob didn't find it strange at all. In fact, he understood quite well the quiet moments Gotham spoke of with a sort of cherished fondness. He, himself, often times found relaxing solace in his own aloneness. There were also times such stillness brought with it a loudness that sent him in search of random clamor to drown out such silence.

"Aren't there others around who you could hang with who are…you know… um, like you?" Jacob inquired somewhat clumsily.

Gotham appeared subtly amused by the way the boy tiptoed his tongue around using certain words.

"You mean Fallen?" he asked. "It's alright, you can say the word without fear of being struck by some proverbial bolt of lightning. And yes, there are many of us roaming this world, Fallen and unfallen alike. But, as it is, shame keeps me from one, intense hatred from the other.

Unfortunately, that is the best uncomplicated answer I can give to your very complicated question in explaining my self-imposed solitary existence."

"Sounds lonely," said Jacob.

"I will admit, loneliness has been an unwanted companion to me on more occasions than I have wished it to be." Gotham took a noticeable pause. At first Jacob thought the angel had suddenly found himself reflecting on the loneliness he had described. Then he saw Gotham's eyes were fixed hard on something else entirely. Jacob followed the gaze and saw it had fallen upon the brown leather-bound journal, which rested on the seat beside him.

"It's one of the very few things angels and civilians share in common, loneliness," continued Gotham while his eyes remained firmly fixed on the journal. "Where did you get that book?"

There was cold accusatory tone in his voice.

"My grandmother gave it to me the night before we left," answered Jacob. "She thought it was important that I remember all my experiences on this trip by writing them down."

While it never left Jacob's mind the boy the journal once belonged to was his grandmother's son, it suddenly dawned on him the boy was also the angel's son as well. And the glimpse of sorrow spied in Gotham's face as he stared at the journal quickly made sense. Not knowing how to respond, Jacob took the journal in his hand and offered it to Gotham.

"Maybe it would be better if you were to have it."

Gotham didn't respond to the gesture at first, but eventually rejected it. "Your grandmother wouldn't have given it to you if she didn't feel it the right thing to do," he said.

Reluctantly, Jacob kept the journal, though he felt funny about doing so, and quickly tucked it away out of sight in his bag.

~ ~ ~

The sound of the train winding its way along the steel tracks was the only thing standing in the way of complete silence engulfing the compartment where Jacob and Gotham sat motionless in their seats across from one another. Gotham had urged Jacob to close his eyes and get some rest. Sleep, however, was the last thing Jacob wanted, for sleep required him to return to the dark canopy of his subconscious where the dream that had been terrorizing him seemed to be patiently lying in wait for him to close his eyes ready to pounce.

Instead, he rifled through his bag and retrieved from it another book he had tucked away: "Paradise Lost." Why he decided to pack it away at the last minute before leaving home and bring it along was beyond him. For weeks, he had laboriously been trying to work his way through the tedious read assigned to him by his literature teacher, Mrs. Kretch. Now, reading the book no longer felt like the chore of homework. Instead, it was something tangible which he looked to for some answers to explain this strange turn his life had suddenly taken, despite the unnaturalness of the words that made him feel at times like a first- grader attempting to read for the first time.

During one of his small victories of finishing one page and turning to the next, he came to one of the many illustrations inside the book and he stopped reading any further. It showed a flock of angels tumbling down from the heavens. They were being driven downward by another group of angels wielding swords. Those falling were shielding their faces from streaks of bright light raining down upon them like lightning bolts.

Jacob found himself captivated by the picture, and continued to study it for a long time. As he did, he glanced over at Gotham who was quietly occupying his time lost in his own thoughts as he said he usually did when the dead of night had settled upon him.

"Why?" Jacob heard himself asking out loud without meaning to pose the question.

It was the question burning most inside him since they had left Cain's Corner: Why would an angel, who knows without question the existence of everything humans—or civilians, as Gotham was fond of calling them—struggled to believe in, turn against it? Yet it was one he had been most afraid to ask, perhaps out of trepidation of how the angel would react to being asked.

Jacob watched as Gotham's eyes closed, not because of rest or sleep he did not need, but as though he had long anticipated the inquiry.

"There is not enough track beneath this train required to properly answer your question," answered the angel.

Gotham's brow then furrowed, and it appeared to Jacob in that moment the question had somewhat wounded the angel and he was suddenly filled with regret for asking it. He turned his eyes back to the battle frozen in the page of his book and he knew he would not be greeted with the answer he sought.

~ ~ ~

The forty-hour train ride to Tatvan wasn't the most pleasant of journeys. And it didn't take long before one felt the wear of every single mile traveled as night gave way to day before at long last being consumed by night once again.

In sunlight, the Turkish countryside, spread out in endless vast open spaces of mostly dry flatness framed in bland, uninviting colors, served as a constant unchanging backdrop rolling slowly past the car windows as the train limped its way along. It was almost a welcome relief when the skies would begin to darken and the sun would slowly be wrestled to the horizon by the return of night to blot out the monotony.

When the walls enclosing the small compartment seemed to move in tighter and he could no longer stave off the always present cabin fever, Jacob would venture out and walk the train's narrow passageways. He would go from car to car peering through the windows of the couchettes and scouring the rows of seats in the economy section investigating ways the other travelers staved off the boredom of the long, tedious ride. Many had their attention buried in books they had smartly stuffed into their carry-on bag. Those without books tiredly stared bleary-eyed into the small bright window of whatever high-tech gadget they clutched in their hands, their dour faces basking in a bluish glow of light that only served to illuminate more prominently the weariness of the long trip seen in their vacant, checked-out looks. Still others chose to surrender to the long hibernation a blanket and a pillow brought. And for a select few, hibernation chose them.

Such was the case for a small group of Turkish soldiers. From the moment the train left the station in Istanbul, the passengers in the car had suffered the drunken presence of the five men who were returning home from their holiday leave in Bangladesh. Now it was with a sense of long-hoped-for relief that the passengers were able to bask in the quiet when the effects of the soldiers' weekend of debauchery finally caught up with them and left them passed out in their seats. As Jacob made his way slowly past the men, his nose caught the strong stench of stale alcohol and cigarettes that hung in an unsavory pall over the soldiers' snoring, unconscious corpses corroborating the tales they shamelessly boasted of earlier at obnoxious decibels.

It was always with a sense of dread when eventually Jacob would reach the end of the last passenger car. It meant turning around and retracing his steps leading back to the compartment and the window next to his seat looking out onto the sleep-inducing view. Sometimes if his stomach demanded—which most times it did—he would stop at the dining car and find himself a table. The same Turkish waiter would always be there to greet him. He was tall and lean and his face seemed to always come dressed with a pleasant smile. Each visit would begin with the same question asked in heavily accented English, "There will be only one for you?"

The answer was always the same.

Quietly, Jacob would sit and eat, with the rhythmic hum of the train's wheels grinding along the rails serenading him as he filled himself with a variety of delicious foods depending on the hour of day: eggs, bread, jam, cheese and olives for breakfast; grilled meats, kababs, salads and meze for lunch and dinner. Oftentimes, when his appetite had been satiated and the empty plates had been cleared away, the thought of returning to the stagnant confines of the compartment, whose walls he'd come to memorize down to the smallest nick in the paint and where the remaining hours had a tendency to stretch themselves even longer, proved too torturous for Jacob to bear. Instead, he'd quietly sit staring out the window focusing once more on the familiar scenery floating past. His mind remained elsewhere, replaying over and over the events of the past few days, and pondering what the days ahead might have in store for him. Frequently, he would find himself inconspicuously reaching over his shoulder and allowing his hand to roam across his upper back and caress the hard mass of bone protruding from beneath his skin that seemed to be growing more pronounced with each passing day. While it no longer felt to him as the horrid disfigurement he had for so long sought to rid himself of, the idea of a pair of wings waiting to sprout from his back didn't offer much comfort either.

Wings…

How was this possible? Was this some kind of cruel cosmic joke being perpetrated upon him? Sure the idea of flying was a requisite fantasy every kid in the world entertained at one point or another growing up. Yet there was a major difference between staring into a cloud and day-dreaming the impossible and looking into a mirror and having reality reflected back in crystal clear clarity. After all, this wasn't just some cape he could put on and shed at will like some comic book superhero; his body was literally evolving physically before his very eyes and conforming to some unreal image that was, well, very comic book-like. What kind of life awaited a boy with wings that didn't involve a circus sideshow or a residency on the Las Vegas strip? He could almost hear the familiar tune of an organ grinder accompanying a baritone announcer wearing a black felt top hat and flaming red coat with tails enticing a wide-eyed crowd gathered in front of a stage on the midway of a traveling carnival: Step right up folks, and see a most fantastical and bizarre sight—Jacob, the Winged Wonder of the World.

~ ~ ~

The Turkish soldiers could be heard even before Jacob reached the train car that housed them on one of his walks back towards the front of the train from the dining car. Much to the displeasure of the other passengers, the group of disheveled soldiers had finally risen from their alcohol-induced comas putting an end to the short-lived peace that had briefly settled inside the car. A round of fresh beers was quickly served up and ribbons of smoke from an ashtray shared by four smoldering cigars rose to form an obnoxious-smelling haze of gray above where four of the soldiers sat lazily slumped in their seats engaged in a game of cards. With their greasy, black, uncombed hair, unshaven faces and heavy, bloodshot eyes, the men looked more like a band of mercenaries than officers of an elite army.

As he slowly walked past the group of men, Jacob couldn't help but shoot a passing glance at the lone soldier sitting across the aisle appearing quite bored as he looked on at the card game while a coin spun like a top upon the table between the man's drumming fingers. When it finally tired and toppled motionless upon its side, it was instantly picked up by the soldier and spun back into motion with a flick of a finger.

Just ahead of where the soldiers were leisurely spread out, Jacob spied a couple seats left vacant by its occupants who were likely taking advantage of the length of the train to stretch their legs, and escape the noisy nuisance of the card game taking place right behind them. Still not ready to return to the compartment where Gotham no doubt was beginning to wonder what was keeping him, Jacob slid himself into one of the empty seats before scoping out the rest of the passenger car. The other travelers were all doing their best to divert their attention from what was taking place in the rear of the car. The only one who seemed not the slightest bit intimidated by the annoying group of soldiers was a young Armenian boy, who looked to be no older than seven or eight with straight dark hair and eyes to match, sitting with his mother a couple seats ahead across the aisle from Jacob. The boy had a coin in his hand and was watching intently the Turkish soldier who was sitting off by himself slouched down in his seat and absent-mindedly spinning his own coin. Jacob looked on with amusement as the boy clumsily tried to mimic the soldier, attempting over and over again to set the coin spinning on its edge like a top and failing each time.

Watching as the boy grew more and more frustrated, Jacob reached into his own front pocket and pulled out a handful of change from which he picked out a quarter. He then pulled out the makeshift table which unfolded from the back of the seat in front of him upon which he placed the rest of his loose change and made a grab for the boy's attention. The boy looked on curiously from his seat as Jacob proceeded to demonstrate the art of the coin spin by taking the quarter and sending it pirouetting across the top of the plastic table. It took several tries until finally, with a look of great satisfaction, the boy managed to spin some life out of his coin. The boy seemed dazzled by his accomplishment, watching without blinking his eyes once as his coin wobbled awkwardly on its edge, but spun nonetheless, before finally tipping over and sputtering to a stop. Jacob then picked out another quarter from his pile of change and held up both silver coins for the boy to see as if he were a magician preparing to perform a trick. Placing the two quarters side by side against one another, Jacob grasped them tightly between his forefinger and middle finger and his thumb. Then, with the young boy's eyes fixed firmly on him, Jacob released the quarters with a subtle flick of his wrist as if he were snapping his fingers, only there was no Snap. There came a sound similar to that made when dice are rolled when the quarters hit the table in spinning fashion, not independently of each other, mind you, but together. That is, the two coins were spinning as close to one another as possible without hitting, and as they spun, they rotated together in a clockwise fashion like a couple waltzing gracefully across a dance floor.

The gleeful reaction from the Armenian kid, who giggled quietly as he watched, brought a satisfied grin to Jacob until, almost immediately, he was struck by a strange and overwhelming sense of Déjà vu. Suddenly, he found himself visited by a memory long lost to the deep recesses of his mind. It came rushing forward, like light pushing its way through a door being opened, and it took the familiar shape of his bedroom back home in Cain's Corner. Jacob found himself in the room, only now he was much younger, like the Armenian boy he was watching. He was sitting at a small desk with a pair of scissors in one hand and carefully cutting his way through a folded piece of white paper clutched in the other.

"What is that you're making?" a familiar voice was suddenly heard to ask.

"A snowflake," the young Jacob replied without so much as a glance at the shape of a man suddenly found to be seated next to him but whose face was obscured by the bright sunlight filtering into the room.

"Do you know the one thing snowflakes and people have in common?" Jacob was asked.

"No two are alike," answered Jacob without hesitation.

"No, they are not," agreed the man.

The young Jacob continued with his cutting before commenting offhandedly, "The kids at school tease me for being different."

"Yes, I know," the man replied with a lilt of sympathy in his voice. "It's an unfortunate price to be paid when others recognize how unlike themselves another is."

"How different am I?"

The man was quiet at first, as if carefully considering his words. "There was a time once not so long ago when you were no more than a folded piece of paper, like that which you're holding. The great pair of hands above which cut forth your image did so with impeccable precision and meticulous design, and what was sent to float down into this world was the rare snowflake so different it manages to catch the eye even when set adrift in a snow flurry, and capable of extraordinary things.

"But," the man was quick to stress, "in this world which strives to celebrate and embrace all that is different, yet fails miserably to do just that, you must always be vigilante to keep hidden all that which makes you so uniquely unlike other boys. Do you understand what I'm saying to you?"

Jacob set down his scissors and proceeded to unfold the paper he had been carefully cutting random shapes and patterns into to reveal his snowflake, and while it was as beautiful as a newly knitted doily, it failed to bring a smile to his face.

"What if I don't want to be different?" asked Jacob.

"Maybe the trick is not to see yourself as different," said the man, recognizing the heavy look in the boy's face, "but as something more than what first meets the eye."

With that, the man revealed the castaway paper trimmings in the shapes of triangles, diamond and half-moons he had scooped up from the top of the desk which he now held in the palm of his hand before leaning in and blowing them like dust into the air. Only what came floating back down was not bits of paper but, much to the young Jacob's astonishment and joy, actual snow—not just a few flakes of ice but a constant stream falling like glittering diamonds as if the bedroom had suddenly been encased inside a shaken snow globe. However, it wasn't the sight of snow falling indoors that stayed with Jacob as the memory slowly began to fade, but the revelation of who the snowmaker was when the man leaned in and blew into his hand giving Jacob an unobscured look of his face.

It was Gotham.

~ ~ ~

"Do you mind?"

The sudden voice in Jacob's ear tore away the memory like a bandage being quickly ripped off a scabbed-over cut. Jacob turned his head and saw it came from one of the Turkish soldiers wearing a very noticeable gold ring with a black onyx stone upon his finger.

"It's most annoying," said the soldier, still engrossed in his card game.

At first, Jacob wasn't sure the soldier was speaking to him until he caught the quiet yet noticeable scratchy humming being emitted from his quarters as they spun on the table, and he quickly silenced them.

"Sorry 'bout that. Just trying to kill some time by entertaining the kid with a little trick," said Jacob, flashing a friendly if not awkward smile.

"Some trick," the soldier with the coin seated off to the side mumbled under his breath with a snide snicker.

Not the friendliest group, that was for sure.

"Yeah, well…I was kinda building up to something much more showier," said Jacob. "You see, there's this little trick I do where I spin two quarters—"

"Yes…I saw," said the soldier curtly.

"No, not that. There's another one where I spin them together, but in a different way."

It was obvious the soldier was no longer paying the boy any mind.

"One on top of the other," Jacob threw in under his breath. He began to turn back around in his seat when the soldier's gaze was once more on him.

"You said one on top of the other?" questioned the soldier, mimicking with his hands the placement of two coins joined as described while repeating back the words carefully as though to make sure he not misheard the boy. "Two coins?"

"Sometimes three."

The soldier turned to his card-playing comrades and wrangled their attention by speaking to them in their native tongue. A quiet hush fell upon the back of the car for a brief moment. And then laughter. Loud, raucous laughter that erupted first from the soldier with the coin whose hardened face proved finally it could be malleable to lighter moments, and then the other men.

"Did I say something funny?" asked Jacob when it became more than a little obvious the laughter was being directed his way.

The only one who showed no signs of amusement was the soldier with the ring who slowly got to his feet and brushed his way past the roaring soldiers to the seat where Jacob was sitting. He was a tall man, lean and unimposing in his stature. Yet what he lacked in brawn, he made up for with an unseen aura of intimidation that moved alongside him like a ghost companion instantly quieting the other men.

"Perhaps you will understand when I politely explain how your presence is interfering with me enjoying a nice game of cards." His voice, thickly accented like the other soldiers, was thin and kind, but in an uncomfortably deceptive way. "So may I express, politely, for you to turn around in your seat and indulge yourself with silence, before you make Enes here angry with your blatant falsehoods and then we have unpleasantness that maybe could have been well avoided."

"Fine," said Jacob. "But for the record I wasn't lying."

"It's impossible!" insisted Enes. "If you were able to do what you say then your name like mine would be in the Guinness Book of World Records stating such a feat could be done, and I know it is not."

"You're in the Guinness Book of World Records?" asked Jacob. "For what?"

"Enes here has broken the world record three times now for the longest spinning coin," another of the soldiers playing cards declared in boisterous spirit while raising his half-empty bottle in congratulatory fashion to his comrade and inciting a cheer from the other men.

"Really? I didn't even know there was such a thing," Jacob said to Enes whose serious expression remained unbroken by the sudden burst of praise. "And what exactly is the record, if I may ask?"

"Thirty nine point thirteen seconds," answered Enes.

"And he has held that record now for more than three years," added a voice from the card table.

"Thirty nine seconds," Jacob repeated softly.

"Thirty nine point thirteen," corrected Enes quickly and pointedly.

"Of course, thirty nine point thirteen," Jacob repeated apologetically while pondering the feat silently in his head. "Is that it?"

He had not meant to demean the accomplishment held in obvious high regard, but it instantly incited a roar of offense from the other soldiers, a roar which was quickly silenced when Enes slammed his fist down on the table giving bounce to the still-spinning coin in front of him and causing it to falter and abruptly fall motionless on the table.

"Is that it?" he seethed while glaring at the boy.

"It just seems…to me, at least…such a short amount of time, you know," Jacob stammered. "Not that I'm any kind of an expert."

"I suppose you can do better," Enes all but challenged the boy.

Jacob chuckled nervously and gave a shrug as he was fond of doing whenever situations became uncomfortable.

"It's hard to say. I've never really timed myself before," he replied.

"Then we shall find out," said the soldier motioning to the vacant seat across the table from him.

With some hesitation, Jacob stepped cautiously around the soldier with the ring who shadowed him to the table. In a friendly attempt to deflect the intense discomfort of being in direct line of the soldier's gaze that never shifted away from him, Jacob introduced himself while reaching across the table and offering the man his hand.

"Mehmet," the soldier answered begrudgingly though he refused to shake the boy's hand.

"Okay, so what do we do?" asked Jacob.

Enes picked his coin up from the table. "We spin together."

Jacob dug into the front of his jeans and retrieved a quarter from his pocket of change and a hand instantly came slamming down on the table.

"NO!" barked Mehmet. "Not with American coin."

"It's all I have with me."

Enes reached into his pocket and pulled out several silver and copper Turkish coins, one of which he tossed Jacob's way before depositing the rest onto the table. He then motioned to one of his comrades to time the contest on his watch.

"Ready?" he then asked the boy preparing to set his coin into motion.

Jacob nodded, and at the go the two coins were released. The soldiers, who stood forming a scrum around the table began cheering loudly over the spinning silver pieces, all except Mehmet who remained quiet, his eyes coldly watching the coins engaged in their duel.

Jacob glanced over at Enes whose face was tense with concentration. And only when the soldier saw the momentum of the challenging coin begin to wobble while his continued to keep its form did a smile of victory emerge from his face. When Jacob's coin finally sputtered in defeat, the men loudly cheered Enes.

~ ~ ~

"What can I say? You have shamefully proven to me that thirty nine seconds is no small feat in trying to beat," said Jacob humbly to his competition.

"Point thirteen," Enes replied pointedly.

"Point thirteen, yes."

"And just to prove I am not heartless, I will not force you any further humiliation with that ridiculous claim you boasted of earlier."

"You still don't believe I can do what I say?"

"Please, two coins, one on top of the other…it's impossible," said Enes with a dismissive wave.

Jacob reached once more into his jeans and retrieved a crumpled wad of paper money from which he pulled a crinkled bill. "Twenty bucks says I can."

The challenge brought a questionable look to Enes' face and instantly sparked chuckles from the other men who quickly began searching their own pants for money. Twenty. Forty. They began calling out bets in denominations of their homeland's currency.

"One hundred," Mehmet offered coolly, holding in his hand several rumpled lira banknotes he had retrieved from his pocket.

He set his bet on the pile of money that had formed on the table and smiled like a tabby cat that had just cornered a mouse.

Jacob reached across the table for another of Enes' coins. All eyes watched closely as he took the two silver and copper intricately engraved pieces and fit them in his hand—the middle and forefinger on one side and the thumb pressed firmly on the other. Jacob rubbed the two coins against each other in a circular motion then tightened his hold. Bringing back his arm slightly he made a snapping motion and the coins were released. There was a hushed silenced and then a collective gasp as they hit the table spinning in unison, one balanced on the edge of the other just as Jacob had boasted.

"I don't believe it," Enes uttered with awe. His eyes were wide with disbelief and together with the other men he leaned in closer to the table in an attempt to see more clearly that which appeared to defy any known law. That is until Mehmet suddenly reached out and slammed his hand down upon the dazzling display as though he were swatting an annoying fly.

"What is this?" he hissed angrily at Jacob. "What kind of trick are you attempting to pull?"

He swept the coins up from the table and began to examine them up close from all sides and angles.

"They're coins from your own country. You saw Enes pull them from his own pocket," Jacob retorted.

When Mehmet saw nothing unusual or fixed with the coins, he handed them off to the other outstretched hands eager to examine them. Yet the look aimed at Jacob that remained on his face was one of distrust.

"Choose a new set of coins, and I will do it again," said Jacob defiantly as he slowly began to grow tired of the soldier's demeaning attitude. "Only this time I will do it with three."

Eager to see a repeat of the trick, the men frantically went for their pockets to fish out some coins but were quickly motioned by Mehmet to stop. He then retrieved from his own pants three coins and held them up for everyone to see before handing them over to Jacob. Quiet again descended, and every move Jacob made was carefully followed by the many eyes fixed upon him. After methodically fitting the coins between his fingers, just as he had before, Jacob snapped them into motion and again an audible gasp rose at the sight of all three coins brought to life on the table, one upon the other, reflecting flashes of silver and gold. And as the men marveled at them, Jacob reached across the table to the pile of coins at Enes' side and quickly set into motion another set. Then another. And another. And before long the small tabletop had been turned into a ballroom floor for the dancing coins.

"It is not possible what my eyes are seeing," remarked Mehmet, the anger in his voice finally surrendering to suspended doubt. "How is it you are to do this trick?"

Jacob sat silent, his eyes marveling at the coins dancing before him with the same wonderment fixed upon the faces of the other soldiers gathered about the table. How did he do it? Indeed, it was a question he himself longed for an answer since before he left Cain's Corner, an answer that suddenly, for the first time came in a one-word whisper echoing in his head: Nephilim. And in that very moment when the desire for clarity which had proven so elusive was finally recognized, Jacob basked in the response he drew from the befuddled men about him watching hypnotically as he continued playing maestro to the spinning objects.

"They don't stop," Enes muttered almost too softly to be heard. "They just keep going and going and going…" The bewilderment at what he was witnessing was clear in his voice, but also a hint of disappointment in seeing his record, if not officially, diminished in such an astonishing display.

"Can you do more than three?" one of the men suddenly asked.

Before Jacob could open his mouth to answer, he grimaced from a sudden flash of pain that burst from the side of his head. Something had taken a sharp hold of his ear and was cruelly twisting, lifting him from out of his seat. If he were anywhere else, his first thought would have been that Mrs. Braukoff had found him, but he knew without so much as a glance that it was Gotham. He cried out as the pain yanked his concentration from the table, and as it did, the spinning coins came to a simultaneous abrupt halt and, with a loud clamor, came crashing down.

Jacob's feet struggled clumsily in their attempt to help him retain his balance as well as keep pace with the brisk speed in which he was being dragged away from the table and down the aisle of the passenger car away from the soldiers.

"Wait—my money!" he cried out.

CHAPTER TEN

"**I**DIOT!"

Jacob tripped over his feet as he was given a forceful shove through the doorway of the train compartment causing him to stumble forward onto his knees upon the floor. He immediately reached for his ear, which had finally been granted a merciful reprieve from the pinching hold that had dragged him with unwavering swiftness through four passenger cars. It throbbed and pounded against the side of his head as though it were his heart dislodged from its place inside his chest, and it burned hotly against his caressing touch. Yet the pain was quickly put out of mind when Jacob turned and saw Gotham suddenly upon him.

"Dunderheaded fool of a boy!" the angel seethed with an anger he struggled to keep at bay. "I should snatch both your ears for they obviously serve you no useful purpose."

"It was just a silly trick. What are you getting yourself so worked up over?" grumbled Jacob.

"Did you see the look on the faces of the men watching you perform your silly trick?" drilled Gotham. "The world is scoured from corner to corner in search of those those performing such tricks, only such discoveries are not met with fawning cheers of amazement but by a cold damnation once saved for Salem witches. And here you are calling out to it like a lighthouse shining its beacon through a shroud of fog."

He began pacing the floor, the tiny compartment providing his long-legged stride only a couple steps before having to quickly switch direction.

"You will remain in this compartment for the remainder of time we have left until we reach Tatvan," instructed Gotham. "No more wandering about the train. Whatever meals you may require, you will have delivered here."

Jacob became suddenly incensed at the definitive tone being leveled toward him and he quickly jumped to his feet.

"You don't have the authority to tell me what to do."

"That is where you are mistaken. The moment your grandmother placed you in my care gave me every authority and more," Gotham snapped back. "Stamp, cry and pout over how I choose to exercise that authority, as long as it keeps you safe so be it."

Jacob was having none of it. "Let's just get something straight. My grandmother may have talked me into going on this excursion with you, or whatever you want to call it, but I will not be taking any orders from you or anyone else for that matter. Who do you think you are anyway? You're not my father. You're not even a true angel. You're a castaway— a…what do like to call yourself?—a Fallen. You're nobody."

There was suddenly a great rumbling like that of an earth-shifting tremor with the force to break loose pieces of mountain and set into motion an avalanche of rolling boulders to come tumbling down and crush into dust everything standing in its path. Jacob was certain at that moment the train had hit something and was about to careen off its tracks until he saw a look cross Gotham's face which spooked him more than the prospect of some massive catastrophic railway accident. It made him slowly back away until the confines of the compartment pressed itself against his back preventing him from retreating any further. He then took notice of a darkness beginning to seep from within the walls, threatening to consume and snuff out with its emerging shadows the last vestiges of light the remaining hours of day had to offer.

"Do not attempt to engage me in your petulant mortal baiting, boy," the angel's voice echoed with a great terrifying roar. "Or I will reveal to you the stupidity of stirring the wrath of an angel, sitting or castaway."

When he had finished speaking, the darkness retreated back into the walls from which it came, and the rumbling fell silent to the returning sound of the train.

"As for not being your father," Gotham continued in a much calmer, yet equally stern voice, "you are correct. But I'm the closest thing you've got, for the time being at least."

Jacob felt his heart beating fast and waited for the expected ruckus of jilted passengers and stewards to quickly fill the hallway outside the door to investigate the terrible sounds they surely heard come from the compartment, but no one stirred. Then as Gotham collapsed heavy in his seat, Jacob, as quietly as he could, followed suit. It didn't require much insight to see the angel was troubled.

"You're bothered by something, and I don't think it has anything to do with my coin-spinning abilities," said Jacob, braving whatever response his words might provoke. "It seems the further we travel, the more troubled you become."

Gotham didn't respond. Instead, he directed his focus on the day which was beginning to darken with the slow-approaching night on the other side of the window.

"I have no idea where we're headed, but wherever it is, I have a gut feeling it's a place you wish you were heading in the opposite direction from," said Jacob. "I'm right about that, aren't I?"

The angel shifted his eyes to Jacob, and the marked heaviness seen lingering within his gaze retreated somewhat behind a subtle smile which crept its way upon his face.

"It seems I was mistaken. You might be a boy who does foolish things from time to time, but a fool you are not. In fact, you are quite perceptive and observant. A very promising sign for a young Nephilim," said Gotham, but he could see his words offered the boy no comfort and attempted to further assuage him. "I made a promise long ago to your mother to guide you on this journey when the time was right. I am here to fulfill that promise made. But you are right, my apprehension grows greater with each mile of track we pass."

The angel's words only confused Jacob more. "But why if this place is as wonderful as you and my grandmother have promised?"

"For you it will be wonderful," answered Gotham assuredly, "but that wonder was lost to me long ago."

He paused again and shifted his gaze once more to the window and the passing scenery that had become a darkened silhouette cast against the setting sun. Whoever the thief was who had stolen this wonder, Gotham refused to name it.

"It has been quite some time since I last stepped foot there, almost a life-time in human years," he pondered aloud. "I find myself questioning if I am ready to return to it. More importantly, I wonder if it's ready for my return."

Jacob opened his mouth to question Gotham further, but he thought better of pushing for those answers he itched to know. At least for the time being. Instead, they rode in quiet for some time, each silently left to their own thoughts.

"I remembered you," blurted Jacob suddenly.

Gotham turned a curious eye onto the boy.

"When I was back in the passenger car, you know, right before I was…showing off. And you were right. I was, and it was a stupid thing for me to do." How Jacob hated to apologize, especially when he knew he was in the wrong.

"There was a little kid trying to mimic one of the soldiers he was watching spinning a coin," continued Jacob. "I dunno, something about it caught my attention. That's when this memory came up out of nowhere of when I was about his same age sitting in my room cutting out paper snowflakes. You were there, suddenly, at the window."

If Jacob held any doubt his memory was some false image conjured up inside his mind, Gotham cast it away.

"You knew even then at such a young age that you were unique," said Gotham.

"I understand why my mom didn't tell me, but why didn't you tell me?" asked Jacob.

Gotham was silent for a moment, as though mulling carefully the words to his answer.

"Despite the many special gifts you possess, being a Nephilim is not an easy existence. Nor is it a particularly safe one," explained Gotham. "I may not have agreed with your mother's decision to keep this life-changing secret from you, but I understood her selfless desire in wanting for you a piece of normalcy, however brief in passing it might be. I also knew the only way for you to have a normal childhood—or as normal as humanly possible—was to first and foremost ensure your safety and keep you out of harm's reach. And the only true defense I knew was in making sure you remained blind and oblivious to who and what you really are."

Jacob was having a difficult time following. After all, what possible harm would a small boy, Nephilim or not, need protecting from growing up in Cain's Corner, aside from taking a possible spill off the swing set in the nearby park or the traumatic experience of a first haircut by old Harvey Floyd, who owned the local barbershop?

"You said earlier—and I quote—'The world is scoured from corner to corner in search of those those performing such tricks, and such discoveries are not met with fawning cheers of amazement but by a cold damnation once saved for Salem witches,' " recalled Jacob from the screaming match moments before between himself and the angel.

"You are as sharp in your recollections as you are perceptive," noted Gotham.

"But what did you mean?"

"I think it best if we leave that for a later discussion."

"Why does everything I ask get the same response: later, later, later?" asked Jacob irritably. "You said being a Nephilim isn't a particularly safe existence. Am I in some kind of danger? If so, I think I deserve to know what it is."

For once, Gotham couldn't argue with the boy. "There are many dark forces which roam this world," he said finally with a breath heavy with apprehension. "But there is one in particular which poses an especially grave threat to you. The closer we get to Tatvan, the more they can sense your presence growing nearer. They don't know who you are, of that you have in your favor…for the time being. But they have come to know the scent of the marked soul of a Nephilim, and possess an uncanny ability of sniffing them out from amongst ordinary civilians."

"Do—do I want to know who they are?" asked Jacob, though the question was as much for himself as it was for Gotham.

The angel released a deep sigh that carried with it a tinge of despair. He turned his gaze to the window and stared out into the dark void beyond.

"Not who, but rather what. Unfortunately, you will eventually come to know them first hand," said the angel ominously. "In fact, I fear they may already be blindly stalking you based on the way I've watched you toss and turn while sleeping."

Jacob most certainly didn't like the sound of that.

"You think the bad dreams I've been having are because of—them?"

"I don't know of your dreams except that they seem to be visiting you with ever-growing restlessness the further into our journey we wade, and a Nephilim who has not learned how to guard and control his thoughts is extremely vulnerable," said Gotham. "The mind is as weak as it is strong, but never is it quite as defenseless as when it surrenders to sleep and dwells into the ethers of awaiting dreamscapes. It is then a gaping opening is left for these unwanted forces to enter and invade unsuspecting thoughts. The Furies know this. They use these moments to learn all they can about each quarry they hunt; their fears, their weaknesses, and of course where they can be tracked. Now you know why it is I keep you naive of many things you long to know, especially where we are headed."

The Furies.

Jacob became suddenly aware of a creeping fear beginning to chill him and he did his best to try and conceal it, even as he sank deeper into his seat with unease trying to imagine these faceless beings, these creatures of darkness. "So…what exactly do these Furies want?"

"To turn you," answered Gotham with an unsettling coolness. "To keep me from taking you to the water."

"Water? What water?" asked Jacob as his brain tried feverishly to make some sense of the growing riddle put before him.

Gotham could see the boy was growing increasingly frustrated to the information being fed to him in piecemeal like breadcrumbs scattered for a flock of pigeons, and he smiled knowingly.

"I know you are tired of hearing me say so, but the less you know, the safer you will be. Trust me." And when Jacob opened his mouth, the angel held up his hand to keep the first syllable from being uttered. "The last thing I want to cause you is more angst. All will be revealed to you soon, I promise. The important thing at this moment is for us to get to where we're going. For now, try and sleep. We have still a long journey ahead of us for which you will need your rest."

Sleep? How could I possibly think about closing my eyes now, Jacob thought to himself. Especially after the revelation of the Furies, whatever they were, possibly laying in wait for him to drift off in defenseless sleep so they could tinker with the insides of his skull. Eventually, as the hour grew later and the night longer, the heaviness of his eyes forced him to lie himself down across the seats. Just for comfort, he assured himself, but not for sleep.

"I'm sorry by the way," he mumbled to Gotham drowsily.

"What about?" asked Gotham.

"The crack I made earlier. You know, about you not being my father and not a true angel. It wasn't cool."

The apology, fleeting as it was, left Gotham silent for a moment as he sat in his seat and watched the boy slowly surrender to the coming slumber he struggled to keep at bay.

"Forgiven," he replied softly.

Jacob was already asleep.

~ ~ ~

DESSSSSTINYYYYYY...

~ ~ ~

Jacob awoke with a breathless jolt. Even though a few hours had passed since he drifted off, it felt to him like he had only closed his eyes for a brief second. And just as he feared, the dream—or rather nightmare—reared itself more vivid and terrifying than the last time it showed itself.

It took a moment or two for him to realize he was still on the train, safe in the private compartment. He felt hot, and he was sweaty. When he moved to sit upright, his body ached with a dull discomfort courtesy of the thinly cushioned seats, and the stiffness in his neck from using the armrest for a pillow made him grimace slightly. As he attempted to massage away the kinks, he glanced over and caught Gotham slumped in a relaxed position across the two joining seats on his side of the compartment beneath the yellowish glow of an incandescent light burning above him. His foot fitted in a large, heavy, worn boot looking as though it had walked a path countless times around the globe was perched on the edge of his seat and Jacob was surprised to find his face buried behind a book. His book.

"I hope you don't mind. I happened to see it lying on the seat next to you," came Gotham's voice from behind the cover.

There was something Jacob found weirdly ironic about waking up to the sight of a fallen angel with his nose buried inside a book telling the quintessential tale about fallen angels that made him wonder if maybe he might still be dreaming.

"I'm surprised to see a boy your age engaged by a classic such as this."

"I don't think 'engaged' is quite the right word I'd use," said Jacob. "First time I've needed Cliff Notes to understand the Cliff Notes to a book."

"And yet you're still reading it thousands of miles away from your classroom," said Gotham.

"It's starting to grow on me, I guess," Jacob replied. "I mean, once you get past the weird English, it's not really that bad for being a..."

He stopped himself from finishing causing Gotham to peer over at him from behind the pages of the book.

"Yes? Go on," he said in low, coaxing voice. "For being a fairy tale?"

"I don't know if I'd necessarily use the phrase fairy tale, but…well, yeah," said Jacob, careful in not wanting to anger again the man sitting across from him. "Look, I can accept that you are who you say you are."

"The word is angel," said Gotham as if introducing the first letter of the alphabet to a first-grader.

"Fine then, angel," said Jacob with a slight roll of the eyes. "But even you have to admit the whole battle of good angels versus bad angels fighting for control of Heaven and Satan being cast down into the Garden of Eden where he becomes a snake and tempts Eve with a forbidden apple is all a bit much. Like Snow White."

Jacob winced slightly at his choice of literary comparison and braced himself for a not-so-pleasant response to his critique but, instead, was surprised to see a grin flash across Gotham's face.

"It is a fantastical story, that I'll give you. Especially for those who resist the fantastical so strongly," said Gotham, sounding not a bit offended. "Which is why I searched long and far for just the right author who could put down into words the story exactly the way it occurred."

Jacob blinked once or twice while sitting silently, as though the words spoken somehow prevented his brain from filtering their meaning. Then, after a moment when it appeared his brain had jump-started back to life, a smile came to him and he let forth a chuckle.

"You're joking, right?"

There was no sign of leg-pulling on Gotham's face.

"You're telling me you knew John Milton?" asked the boy, his head cocked halfway between curiosity and disbelief.

"I believe it was 1652 when I came to him," answered Gotham, turning his gaze toward the ceiling in thought. "Correction, it was 1653. He had gone blind by then, but he could see more in his shroud of darkness than most men with two good eyes. An impressively smart man. One of the few civilians I've come across during my time here for whom I found a genuine liking."

"And you expect me to believe the story of 'Paradise Lost' is one that you told to him? Personally?" pressed Jacob, making no effort to conceal his disbelief.

"Like most of mankind, I've only come to expect from you the skepticism you've so completely walled yourself behind. But trust when I say your disbelief does not change the facts as I tell them to you," noted Gotham with a scolding tone before continuing on.

"Milton had originally planned to create an opus based on the life of a Saxon king, but I managed to convince him that there was a greater tale to be told, one more epic in its telling filled with the political and social theater he himself had been so passionate about. Once agreed, he took me on in the role of his amanuensis to transcribe the words he tirelessly wove so beautifully into the poetic masterpiece I hold now. Then a couple hundred years later I extended the same help to a man by the name of Paul Gustave Louis Christophe Dorè who would bring to life Milton's words in his illustrations."

Jacob sprang upright in his seat with a growing look of exasperation and held out his hand to stop the angel from speaking further.

"Wait a minute," he said with an incredulous look. "You're saying you were not only acquainted with Milton, but you also knew whatever his name is..."

"You wander the planet for as long as I have, you end up crossing countless paths. Gustave's, like John's, just happened to be one of the countless," said Gotham.

"So, the drawings in the book are—"

"I revealed to him what he needed to see in order to bring into being what he ended up creating," explained Gotham. As he spoke, he turned the book he held to reveal to Jacob one of the illustrations inside. It showed the fallen angels being cast down from Heaven—the same drawing that had captured Jacob's attention the night before

"And how did you do that? Show him, I mean?" inquired Jacob somewhat warily.

Gotham closed the book and tossed it in the boy's direction. Only instead of flying heavily across the compartment, it took lightly to the air, moving soft and weightlessly as though it were a feather loosened from a bird and set adrift upon a calm breeze where it slowly came to a gentle rest on the seat beside Jacob. Then planting his booted feet firmly on the floor before him, the angel shifted to the very edge of his seat, leaned forward and instructed Jacob to do the same until their knees and toes were lined up just short of touching.

"Look into my eyes," instructed Gotham. And Jacob did, straight into the twin orbs which began to bubble with life like fiery eruptions exploding from within two dazzling suns and growing ever brighter. Instantly, Jacob found himself hypnotically captured in their brilliance and the ability to look away, even if he wanted to, was no longer in his possession. "Now take hold of my hands, and you shall see what very few other men have."

Jacob cautiously reached forward and, in the instant his fingers grazed Gotham's, there came a horrific grinding clamor as the walls of the compartment surrounding them first began to buckle and then tear away in large jagged pieces until, in one terrifying moment, the train split apart and disintegrated from existence.

Jacob gasped at the horror of suddenly finding himself suspended in open sky with no sign of earth anywhere beneath him. Neither was Gotham anywhere to be seen, though Jacob could still feel the angels' hands clutched in his grasp. And before he could attempt to decipher what was happening—or how—he caught the sound of a great disturbance fast approaching in the distance. It began as a rumbling of thunder coming from within the quickly-darkening clouds suddenly taking the shape of great beasts in all directions around him, and it was accompanied by what sounded like a herd of galloping horses. Then from within the clouds was suddenly belched forth an unimaginable chaos. The vast sky instantly became filled with hundreds—then quickly thousands—of men.

Winged men.

Angels.

And yet not angels, at least no longer. Rage and hate distorted their faces, and their threatening cries of violence and rebuke which filled the air in a chilling chorus was answered by angry claps of thunder. They looked to be in retreat, being driven downward from the higher plains of the heavens in a growing multitude. The pounding cadence of horse hooves grew louder, and an unseen trumpet blew loudly. Then suddenly a cavalry of more angels appeared, charging through the billowing clouds wielding swords which carried a blinding light in their blades. The steeds they rode upon looked to be almost ghostlike, as though they themselves were created from the wisps of the clouds.

Yet in all the chaos that quickly ensued, Jacob's attention was instantly drawn with enamored amazement to the angel leading the charge. It was Gotham, eyes ablaze and body gleaming with the rippling power it possessed, leading the other angels with an unbridled fierceness that cut down and swept aside everything in his path. Behind him and the rest of the cavalry following, a brilliant whiteness began parting the skies, and from it the skeletal fingers of lightning shot forth in wicked flashes of blinding light forever marking the angels in retreat with its scarring, scorching heat aimed at their foreheads with vengeful precision.

Jacob's unblinking eyes watched in shock and awe at what was happening all around him, flinching now and then as angels brushed dangerously close past him in their free-fall toward a fiery plain that slowly opened itself beneath him. He found himself continuously squeezing desperately the hands he still felt in his, even as his eyes watched Gotham tearing across the sky like a warrior stamping his mark on some ancient battleground.

~ ~ ~

Then it was gone, the halting vision vanishing as quickly as it had appeared. And the train compartment that had fallen away reappeared intact, and Jacob found himself sitting exactly where he had been before across from Gotham. He yanked free his hands from the angel's grasp exhaling deeply as he fell back deep into his seat.

"Do I read from the stunned look on your face that you have reconsidered The Great War being the concoction of the Brothers Grimm?" asked Gotham somewhat facetiously.

"You were leading the charge," blurted Jacob still swimming in a haze of disbelief at what he had witnessed.

"That I was."

"You were leading the charge against the rebellion."

There was a perplexed look in Jacob's eyes and Gotham quickly came to recognize it.

"I see," was all he remarked in his moment of understanding.

Gotham paused, then rose from his seat. He stood silent for a moment peering out from the window of the cabin partially obscured by translucent pebbly looking water drops from a soft rain which had earlier begun to fall.

"In Revelation, the apostle John writes of seven angels who stand before God," he said finally. "They are known as the seven Archangels: Michael, Gabriel, Raphael, Uriel, Barachiel, Sealtiel and Jehudiel. The truth is, there were originally nine angels who were chosen to form this celestial order, two of which would eventually suffer separate and great falls. The first, whose name has long since been purged from Heaven, has come to be known by many identities. You perhaps know him best as Satan. To those of us who knew him as one of our brethren he is known by another name: the Dragon. And it is that name I shall use to refer to him since his true name has never breathed its way past my lips since the moment of his deception.

"At one time he was not only a great angel and mighty warrior, but the most beautifully created of all the angels under Heaven's reign. There was a way about him…a brilliance, some would argue that made him all the more beautiful. However, lurking within that brilliance stirred a darkness; a darkness of arrogance, cunningness and guile that proved to be much stronger, and slowly the light began to grow dim within him before it was eventually snuffed out altogether like the smoldering wick of a candle. He came to embrace the idea of self-greatness conjured up by his own mind, and it wasn't long before he came to the belief that his greatness overshadowed that of his Maker. Angels, he argued wrongly, are self-begot and as such he deemed himself as equal to God, and it wasn't long before he put to use his cunningness in devising a scheme to overthrow the rule of his Creator and place himself upon Heaven's throne. There was only one small hurdle standing in his way: the eight other Archangels who remained steadfast in their loyalty to God. And of those eight one, in particular, would prove to be his downfall."

Gotham paused, turned his gaze away from his transparent reflection captured in the window darkened by the rainy night and glanced over his shoulder in the direction of Jacob who was sitting quietly listening to his story. "Yes, in case you have already rendered a guess, I was the other who was once counted amongst those nine, and I was held by the others with great esteem and rank. More importantly, I held great favor with the One who made me, even more so than any of the others angels, for whatever reason of which had never been made known to me. And because of that, I was never outside the illuminated realm of my Maker's presence. It was a position I humbly embraced, as well as guarded fervently.

"Naturally, there were whispers. Jealousy, like a seductive mistress, has never tired in her attempts to bring my brothers under her spell, and their rumblings of malcontent and resentment against me did not escape my ears. Nowhere, however, was that jealousy more evident than with the one who fell before me. Every time he looked my way, his eyes mirrored a deep loathing, and I could see his intense hatred was working to hatch a feverish plotting inside his head. It was only when the clandestine chattering took a venomous shift away from me and toward my Maker that my anger gave rise. I began to hear the echoes of rebellion carried like an infectious fever spread by the forked-tongue of the Dragon amongst factions of angels and I readied my hand near my sword."

It was then Jacob was startled by the sudden movement of the book resting on the seat beside him as it flew open and the pages inside began to rustle and quickly turn on their own accord. When they finally stopped, the book had fallen open to an illustration titled "Abdiel strikes Satan."

"Has your reading of the book reached this point yet?" asked Gotham.

Jacob gave a quick nod. "It's right before the war," he said. "An angel named Abdiel learns of Satan's plan and tells God of the coming rebellion and he is rewarded for his loyalty. This basically pisses off Satan, and as the two sides prepare for battle, Satan and Abdiel face off against one another. Abdiel tells Satan his fight is in vain, and that pride and vanity had blinded him to the reality that the legions of angels still loyal to God were ready to throw down and kick some tail. But Satan argues spitefully that there was no freedom in Heaven and basically called the loyal angels slaves. Then, being the bad ass he is, Abdiel strikes Satan with a powerful blow which brings him to his knee."

Gotham's brow slowly rose with growing intrigue as he sat listening to the choice of words the boy used in the blunt narrative to summarize a portion of a classic work of literature as only a modern-day teenager could.

"And Satan said, 'Take heed, for I shall make it my personal vow to see the righteousness with which you stand before me in the name of God turn on you like a striking serpent and into you sink its fangs to sicken you with its venom,'" uttered Gotham in a quiet reflective whisper.

Jacob studied more closely the illustration showing Abdiel raising his sword to Satan while reflecting on the story he had just recited as well as the vision of the rebellion he had witnessed earlier when his gaze suddenly shifted to Gotham.

"It's you, isn't it?" asked Jacob. "Abdiel is you."

Gotham only needed to look at the boy for Jacob to know he was correct in his suspicions.

"But I still don't understand," said Jacob. "You remained loyal and helped defeat the rebellion by casting Satan and his army out of Heaven. You showed me so. So how is it you still became Fallen?"

Gotham sighed heavily in his hesitation to answer the boy, yet knew it was a question that demanded an answer.

~ ~ ~

In the hours of night that remained, Gotham spoke of a time long after The Great War, and even further past when the paradise depicted by Milton had been lost; when man and woman were cast into the wilderness of the world burdened with the weight of God's curse heavy on their backs.

Eden may have been lost to the two marked souls, explained Gotham, but mercy was not, and one day it came down to them in the form of angels called Watchers, who were sent to help those who had become lost, pitiful beings, navigate their way through the harshness of the new world they now found surrounding them. Very quickly many of these Watchers became lost, pitiful beings themselves. They were lured to sinful ways by some of the Fallen they had helped cast from Heaven's skirt and who now took great pleasure in poisoning the minds of men and women as an act of revenge on the Almighty. And they used the women to tempt the Watchers into committing sins of the flesh until one day, as Gotham told it, he was called upon by a deafening clap of thunder.

"I was summoned before my father, and he sharpened my blade with his wrath," said Gotham, "and I was commanded to go down and exact punishment for the sins they birthed.

He suddenly fell quiet and bowed his head low, and it was as though a storm cloud from outside had somehow drifted inside the compartment and unleashed a downpour upon him.

"Never once had I refused my Maker, nor any command he might ask of me. But this—" His words became strained and choked in his throat. Jacob shifted to the edge of his seat afraid of what was to come, and daring not ask when it didn't.

Eventually Gotham continued. "It took less than twenty minutes, though it felt like twenty days. Through it all I wept; tears of sorrow, tears of rage. The sounds made by the women were unimaginable, as though every swipe of my sword pierced them. The men cursed me as they cursed God, shaking their fists angrily at the sky. And the Fallen— putrid souls that they now were—looked on with serpent-like smiles on their faces. They began to taunt me, latching tight to the first signs of weakness I had ever shown as it was roused awake inside me through my growing rage. 'Look what your God has you do in his name?' they mocked with merciless glee. 'Look at the sin he so easily has you commit, though a sin he dares not call it when it comes at his hand.' Their words came at me in a hissing chorus, unrelenting and worming its way inside my head. Yet more troubling was that for the first time such blasphemous insults against the one I so loved did not incite me to turn my blood-coated blade on them and run it deep through their insolent existence. And for a brief moment, when time seemed to come to a deafening halt and all around me was red—red with blood, and red with rage—I surrendered to the Darkness chiding me and, with an uncontrollable hatred I could not stem, I silently rebuked my creator."

A deafening hush engulfed the cabin, and Jacob, taken aback by what he had heard, found himself afraid to even breathe for the sound it might make. What horrible task had Gotham been forced to do, Jacob desperately wanted to ask, and yet he couldn't find the nerve when he saw the anguish it brought Gotham reliving it in his mind.

"Sometimes one's stumble from Heaven's graces comes in a moment so fleeting and quiet, he doesn't even know he has fallen. And by the time he realizes it, it is too late," Gotham uttered mournfully.

He turned again from the window and returned to his seat.

"Once I had carried out fully the task handed me, the skies broke open and water poured down in a deluge to drown out the cries and screams I had left in my wake. But on my return to Heaven I was stopped halfway by the Archangel Michael, and with a pained and solemn look on his face he told me I was no longer allowed to enter my home. Why? I implored of him. Had I not done what had been asked of me? Was the blood that caked my blade and stained my hands not evidence of my obedience? But it was in vain, for I already knew where I had erred and what sin I had committed. Yet instead of remorse I once again felt anger rise up within me. And I looked past Michael and cast my eyes ablaze with contempt toward the heavens and unleashed a hateful curse from my tongue, for nothing else had been left to me at that moment. And from it a streak of lightning, vengeful as it was blinding, flashed forth and struck my forehead marking the beginning of my banishment. I was sent spiraling back down to the earth below taking with me only my name which, like the Dragon's before me, was vanquished from ever being spoken again. In Heaven, at least."

Jacob's gaze slowly turned to Gotham's forehead. There, near the temple over his left eye which the angel, lost momentarily in the memory he revisited, absentmindedly rubbed, was a scar. It reminded Jacob of the vein-like fingers found etched on the back of a sand dollar, only seared deep into the flesh as though by a branding iron.

"Is that it, where you were struck?" asked Jacob, his voice hoarse with emotion, while motioning to the spot above the angel's temple.

"Attractive, isn't it?" Gotham replied removing his hand and offering his profile so the boy could see more clearly the scarring. "The mark of the Fallen."

Jacob didn't agree or disagree. He didn't say anything, at first. It was all, to say the least, a bit much to digest in one sitting. The only thing he was certain of was suddenly finding himself filled with deep sympathy for Gotham, though he knew such feelings would be met with disdain by the proud angel if it were made known.

"I can understand how you lost your faith after hearing all of that," he finally remarked, which for whatever reason that remained unclear to him brought a slight smile to Gotham's sober face.

"To the contrary. The loss of my faith wouldn't come until much later," said Gotham. "You see, I would come to find my father had not quite finished meting out his punishment to me yet."

"Why…what happened?" he asked with a gnawing reluctance.

An air of angst seemed to come and congregate itself around the angel, and Jacob knew whatever words were beginning to form on Gotham's lips, they would be tragic, but the words never came.

"Strangely, I could ask the same of you," Gotham, drawing a puzzled look from the boy, remarked. "You held a faith as strong as your mother's at one time. I know this to be true. How did it come to be lost to you?"

The question caught Jacob by surprise.

"I believe in God," he answered, even as the words themselves were notably flimsy as he spoke them.

"That is not what I asked," said Gotham. "Do not be mistaken in thinking belief and faith are the same thing. I believe in the human race because I witness their existence. But I have little hope or trust in it."

Jacob's first inclination was to argue against what he knew was being insinuated. Then again he knew the angel would see such an answer for what it truly was—a lie.

"I don't know," said Jacob with a shrug. "I suppose it disappeared when my mom died."

"No, no," the angel replied shaking his head. "Your mother's death may have hardened your resolve, but it had disappeared long before she took leave of this world."

The boy began to fidget uncomfortably in his seat while fingering mindlessly the big toe of his foot trying to poke its way out of the hole eating its way through his sock.

"I haven't got a clue," he mumbled.

"Of course you do," insisted Gotham. "Anyone who has ever truly possessed faith remembers the precise moment they willingly released it."

And Jacob did remember, the moment the question was asked him. Saying the answer out loud, however, was not something he wished to do, though, he knew it was the least he owed the angel after his own revelation. Gotham saw this and refrained from pressing the boy further. Instead he looked to the window and the coming morning which was ever so faintly beginning to reveal its approach in the distance.

"It shouldn't be too much longer," the angel muttered.

~   ~   ~

After a short stop in Elazig, the train continued slowly on its journey, leaving behind nearly all remnants of civilization as it entered into the most isolated parts of Turkey. And from that isolation slowly emerged the stunning scenery that had largely been absent from the long trip. Soon passengers' faces were pressed up against the windows, until now mostly ignored, and peered out with gratitude as the train made its way through a wild gorge carved out by the Murat River.

A gaggle of excitement and fingers tapping against the glass of the windows rang out from car to car as a small village seemingly undeterred by the remoteness surrounding it or the congregation of storks that had seemed to overtake the small hamlet came into view. Hundreds of the white, long-necked birds could be seen perched in nests dotting the rooftops, power poles and any available high spot like Russian fur hats, watching curiously with tilted heads as the train passed through. Suddenly the river valley began to retreat and the train ascended high into the approaching mountains passing through dozens of long tunnels eating a passageway through miles of rock until finally the mighty Van Gölü lake appeared. And nestled quaintly on its western shore came the first glimpse of Tatvan.

They had finally made it, Jacob thought as he stared out of the window, but the sense of relief that greeted him was quickly dulled by a jolt of uncertainty.

What now?

What was waiting for him down there in that small diminutive town and the waters beyond?

There came a nagging feeling inside that his journey was only just beginning.

CHAPTER ELEVEN

Tatvan existed quietly behind a promenade of beach hugging a massive lake. A sprawl of small houses, local shops and businesses, muted in both architecture and color, dotted the foot of mountains surrounding the town. Lording over the town, Mount Nemrut Dagi, a long-extinguished volcano, stretched high toward the skies.

Never a destination point, Tatvan served as a stop-over point for wayward travelers and businessmen in search of a meal or a bed before pushing on with their journey to more spectacular sights, usually to the far shores across the lake which were rich with the remnants of ancient history. For Gotham and other angels, the seemingly benign hamlet had long ago revealed itself to be anything but. It was there, and all along the shores where the lake water lapped, that an unseen darkness lurked, patiently lying in wait for the eventual arrival of the winged beings forced to cross its threshold in order to reach their ultimate destination. More importantly, it waited for the unsuspecting Nephilim the angels kept close guard over, guiding them closer toward the water of the Van Gölü. It was an unavoidable danger Gotham had come to know only too well, a danger which could not be sidestepped but charged head-on in a full run, and as the train pulled into the station he readied himself for what awaited them.

~ ~ ~

A cluster of storm clouds hung ominously over the lakeside town like a giant beast ready to pounce before finally releasing the deluge it carried in its belly just as Gotham and Jacob stepped off the train. A large group of small children waiting nearby for the train's arrival quickly broke up into small packs and descended upon the fresh batch of passengers disembarking the cars.

"Moony, moony, moony," they began to chant in a prayer-like mantra, their hands stretched outward pleading to be filled with something. Anything.

"We must hurry," instructed Gotham as he took hold of Jacob's arm and ushered the boy toward the exit of the station. At the same time, he quickly discharged a few dollar bills from his pocket and blindly tossed them over his shoulder to rain down on the ground behind him where they were voraciously pounced upon as if by a school of feeding piranha. They proceeded to hurry outside and, with a torrent of water raining down on them, they ran through the slick streets with a throng of half a dozen or so kids hot on their trail.

"Moony, moony, moony..."

The chanting rang out in cadence to the footsteps splashing their way through the growing puddles and followed Gotham and Jacob into the heart of the town's downtown hub. There they found a respite from the rain in the doorway of a restaurant.

"We need to catch a ferry on the far side of the beach as soon as possible," said Gotham loudly, trying to keep his voice from being drowned out by the clamoring of water spilling in sheets from off the rooftops.

"In this weather?" asked Jacob.

"We cannot stay here. It's too dangerous." Gotham then noticed Jacob was shivering slightly inside the damp cotton hoodie he wore. Winter had arrived ahead of them, and the slushy cold rain falling was just short of adding more white to the streets already powdered with remnants of snow.

"You're shivering. Don't you have a heavier coat with you?" Gotham asked the boy.

"I'm fine," said Jacob even as his bottom lip trembled slightly.

Gotham wiped away the water trickling down his face and glanced around the streets and sidewalks that were abandoned of any people except for the children who had followed them from the station huddling nearby, waiting silently in the pouring rain, their grubby faces getting a much-needed washing.

"Wait here," Gotham told Jacob.

"Where are you going?"

"Just stay here. I'll only be gone a few minutes. Do not talk to anybody, and do not move from this spot. Understand?" instructed the angel in an emphatic tone as though speaking to dog he had just let off its leash.

Jacob nodded and, after giving a last cautious glance around, Gotham reluctantly backed away from the doorway. When he finally turned and sprinted off into the downpour, the familiar "munny" chorus erupted once more following after him and disappearing around a corner.

Left alone, Jacob folded his arms tightly across his chest in an attempt to ward off the chill. It was his feet, however, which he now found himself growing more conscious of as they were beginning to feel like blocks of ice inside the soaked canvas Converse sneakers he wore. To make matters worse, he was hungry. Famished, actually. Cupping a hand to the window of the restaurant, he peered inside. The tables were half-filled with people looking dry and content waiting out the storm over warming cups of steaming coffee and plates of food filled with a scrumptious looking variety of Turkish cuisine. A waft of thyme, chubritza, oregano and paprika permeated from inside the restaurant beckoning a grumble from Jacob's stomach. And when his mouth took on the drooling of a St. Bernard he turned away looking to focus his attention on something less torturous.

It was then he discovered he was not alone.

~ ~ ~

Standing quietly and motionless in the rain a few feet away from Jacob was a boy who looked to be about the same age, if not slightly younger than himself. His clothes, hole-eaten and spotted with stains, were soaked through. One of the beggars from the station who remained behind, Jacob thought, though he didn't remember seeing this particular face when getting off the train.

"Hello," said Jacob, offering a nod and a friendly smile..

The boy remained silent, his face expressionless, like a flesh-colored statue, staring coldly past the drops of water that dribbled steadily from the tips of his wet, tangled black hair. No plea for "munny," no outstretched hands. Still, Jacob dug into his damp jeans and fished out the few remaining dollars he had. Not much, he thought, but enough at least to buy something to eat. He stretched out his hand toward the boy, but the boy made no move to accept the charitable gesture.

"Really, it's okay," said Jacob, thrusting the offering toward the boy. Then remembering where he was he repeated himself, this time in perfect Kurdish. He wasn't even phased that the words he spoke were of a language that had never before passed across his tongue.

The boy, not even glancing at the wadded-up money, kept his gaze frozen on Jacob, who slowly felt a chilly unease creep up upon him that could not be blamed on the cold rain.

"Alright. Just trying to be friendly," muttered Jacob under his breath.

He proceeded to smooth out the damp, wrinkled bills before folding them neatly together and shoving them back into his pocket.

Maybe the kid was shy, Jacob thought to himself. Or perhaps he wasn't fond of foreigners. It was understandable. Americans, after all, weren't exactly the cat's meow in some parts of the world. The Turkish soldiers back on the train made him acutely aware of that.

Hoping the boy would eventually move along on his way, Jacob turned his attention once again to the customers inside the restaurant. Yet watching people shoveling food into their mouths was the last thing he wanted to see, as it only incited his stomach to grumble once more reminding him how hungry he was. He pulled his phone out from his pocket to check the time, and as he did he could see out of the corner of his eye that the boy remained standing in his spot nearby, still watching him.

What was taking Gotham so long?

Jacob looked to the end of the street impatiently waiting for the familiar dark overcoat figure to reappear around the corner. Wherever it was they were headed to next, he wished they would soon be on their way. He then snuck a look upward hoping to spy some sign of a break in the gray gloom hanging overhead from which the rain was being wrung like a sponge. It was then at that moment of distraction when the boy loitering nearby in the open street caught Jacob by surprise when he suddenly lurched in his direction, swept something from off the ground near his feet and quickly took off running down the street. For a moment, Jacob was relieved to finally be free of him and his unsettling presence. Then he noticed his blue nylon bag he had set on the ground in the corner of the doorway was gone and looked to see the boy had it tucked tightly under his arm as he tore down the sidewalk.

Jacob yelled out loudly for him stop but the boy quickly vanished around the corner. Without missing a beat, Jacob took off after him, leaving the echo of Gotham's implicit demand that he stay put until his return to fade silent in the cold wet doorway. Rounding the corner Jacob caught sight of the fleeing figure now a good block ahead and quickened his pace. His wet, dingy white Converse sneakers splashed their way loudly through the puddles of water pooling along the sidewalk. The freezing rain pelted his face painfully, blurring his vision and making it difficult to keep his focus on the boy ahead. The faster he ran, the harder the rain seemed to fall, and there was no doubt he was moving with impressive swiftness—faster than any normal boy, any normal man, any normal human—until it felt to him as though he was moving through the streets like some phantom blur, and yet despite the unnatural speed being pumped from his legs he still found himself unable to gain ground on the fleeing target he struggled to keep in his sights.

How was the boy managing to stay out of his reach?

After snaking through several blocks, the boy quickly veered to the left and disappeared down an alleyway between two large buildings. Jacob slowed himself as he approached the entrance to the alley before stopping to catch his breath while peering down the long dark and narrow corridor. There was no sign of the boy. Just an old rusted dumpster, some broken up wooden slats and the remnants of paper litter pulverized by the rain and left in rotting clumps along the sidewalk. For a passing moment, Jacob entertained the thought of turning back, not so much out of trepidation but from being winded by the long, taxing chase, when there came from somewhere unseen the faint sound of laughter. Or so Jacob thought.

Cautiously, he entered the alley where he was immediately met by a foul stench of cat urine mixed with the sweet scent of ozone. He made sure to keep to one side of the dank passageway and out of the path of runoff from the rain coming off the roof of the buildings in sheets to form a rushing stream down the center of the alley which spilled its way into a large circular sewer grate. A black cat with white markings leapt with a high-pitched screech from amongst the garbage spoils filling the dumpster as Jacob passed, tripping the heavy metal lid propped open to come slamming closed with a thundering crash that made the startled teen jump. Through gritted teeth, Jacob silently cursed the rain-matted feline as it scampered away down the alley in a desperate search for a dry refuge.

Again the sound of laughter was heard. It was not Jacob's imagination playing tricks on him. When he reached the end of the alley, Jacob found a weathered iron gate ajar leading to what appeared to be a large, enclosed storage area filled with piles of old crates in one corner and rusted scraps of metal and pipe in another. A large, steel roll down door leading into the back of the building was closed and secured with a padlock. More noticeable, however, was the fact there was no sign of the boy. Aside from the locked metal door and the alleyway, there was no way in or out, except to scale the walls straight up to the roof above, which clearly was an impossible feat—unless one was a spider, or Spiderman.

"Alright, so where'd you go?" Jacob muttered to himself, too focused on trying to figure out the magic disappearing trick that had obviously occurred to notice the stark cold which had suddenly chilled the damp air and shaped his breath into a visible cloud of vapor as he spoke.

~ ~ ~

He was about ready to resign himself to the fact the boy, and his things, had somehow vanished without a trace and was about to turn back when there came from the steady drumming of the rain the quick-moving patter of footsteps. Not in front of him or behind, but oddly from above. Circling. Jacob looked up, shielding his eyes from the falling rain while spinning around to dizzying effect to try and get a focus on the sound rapidly shifting in direction.

Then the footsteps stopped, and suddenly Jacob felt something behind him and quickly spun around. It was the boy. He was standing on the far side of the enclosure, like an apparition suddenly reappearing out of nowhere but with the same dead look once again fixed on Jacob.

"You know, you would have come out further ahead if you'd just taken the money I offered you," Jacob noted, nodding to the nylon bag the boy still gripped in his hand. "I'm afraid all you're going to find in there is some T-shirts, a couple pair of jeans that have seen better days, some dirty socks and a toothbrush."

The boy didn't respond and Jacob suddenly found himself wondering if maybe the kid was deaf. Or mute. Or both.

"Look, kid, I didn't chase after you all this way to get into it with you, honestly. If you want my bag so badly, take it. I'll even throw in the money I offered you earlier," said Jacob. "The only thing I ask is that you hand over the journal packed inside. It's just a book. It's not worth anything, but it's important to me. Whattaya say, fair enough deal?"

The boy raised the bag in a gesture that appeared as though he was preparing to return it to Jacob along with an apology only to toss is aside where it landed with a splash in a puddle on the ground. Jacob immediately felt the friendly nature he was trying hard to retain drain from him.

"What's your problem, kid?" he questioned with a scowl.

"Do you really think I'm interested in your bag or money, Nephilim?" The boy finally spoke, but the words he spoke sent an uncomfortable shudder through Jacob. Or at least one word did.

"What did you call me?" asked Jacob softly, his voice trembling slightly but no longer from the cold.

"Nephilim. N-E-P-H-I-L-I-M, Nephilim," the boy replied jovially as though he had just taken the lead at the school spelling bee. A smile then appeared on the boy's face revealing a row of teeth that had grown crooked and discolored from years of neglect.

"Nephilim? What the hell's that?" Jacob answered, feigning ignorance. Even with his face dripping with rain, he felt the distinct beginnings of a cold sweat form across his forehead.

"Nephilim? What the hell's that?" echoed the boy mockingly. Only it was Jacob's voice that came out of his mouth, leaving Jacob to think for a split second he had suddenly discovered in this most inopportune of times that he had the gift of ventriloquism.

"Who better to know what a Nephilim is, than a Nephilim. Right, Nephilim?" continued the boy in his own voice.

The word Jacob had grown to despise now terrified him coming from the mouth of the grubby street urchin who slowly moved toward him. Instinctively, he felt his feet clench inside his soggy shoes. They were ready to bolt, to carry him as swiftly from the alley and back to his dry spot in the nook in front of the eatery as they had brought him here to this dark dead end. When Jacob spun quickly around and prepared to break for his escape, he found the way blocked by the boy. His eyes widened with shock. He opened his mouth to question how the boy had managed to move from one side of the enclosure to the other in a blink of an eye, but stopped himself.

He already knew.

He couldn't be another angel. The boy was too young, too small, too unGotham-like to be a member of God's mighty winged legion. Perhaps he was another half breed such as himself. A fellow Nephilim. Still, there was an unexplainable fear Jacob felt that made him back away out of reach from the boy who continued to move toward him.

"Monstrous offspring born to the Sons of God by the daughters of men. An abomination set forth in the eyes of God. That is what you are, isn't it Nephilim?" There was noted disdain in the boy's voice as he spoke, an almost palpable hatred dripping from every syllable uttered.

"Look kid, I don't know what you're talking about," said Jacob as naively as he could. "But I've got to get back—"

"To your guardian angel?" The boy was grinning hideously.

Angel? He knew?

"Remove your shirt," the boy demanded.

"What?"

"Your shirt. Remove it," the order came more curtly.

Jacob hesitated, clenching and unclenching his fists. His eyes darted about wildly in search of a path to freedom, but there was none. Only the entrance leading to the alleyway that was now blocked by the figure standing in front of him upon whom his gaze settled and began to slowly look over up and down. He had certainly taken on bigger and stronger boys on the wrestling mat and emerged victorious. Yul Dane, to name one. Why, he wondered, did he not just steam roll over the boy and be done with this?

"That would be a stupid move. I guarantee you, he is much stronger than he looks," the boy replied, taking Jacob aback. Another mind-reader. He must be an angel, he thought to himself, but why was he referring to himself in the third person?

"Now remove your shirt," the boy demanded once more. "Or shall I remove it myself?"

It was one threat too many from someone so unthreatening, and a sly grin slowly emerged on Jacob's face. "You really think you're capable?"

The two boys' eyes narrowed tightly on one another.

"Why don't you tell me?" the boy replied.

Jacob's keen hearing picked up the pinging of drops hitting water, even over the roaring patter of the rain. His eyes moved downward toward the boy's feet where they caught sight of droplets of blood hitting the ground and spreading out across the wet cement in thin ribbons of bright red. He followed the drops to the boy's right hand where he saw to his own amazement the fingernails growing rapidly, thickening as they emerged from the fingertips while at the same time curving their shape until they appeared as razor-sharp talons. His mouth opened but no words came, swiftly extinguished from the fear he felt welling inside his chest.

No…this was no angel.

Without further hesitation, or the desire to see what else might poke its way out of the flesh and blood figure standing before him, Jacob did as the boy demanded by first taking off his sweatshirt followed by the rain-soaked shirt that clung tightly to his torso making it feel as though he were stripping off a second skin.

"There," barked Jacob irritably. "Satisfy your thrill?"

"Now turn around."

"Look, I've had about enough of this."

"I SAID TURN AROUND!" the boy hissed venomously in a deep guttural voice that was a species removed from anything human.

When Jacob continued to hesitate the boy took a step forward, his eyes becoming more fierce. "I won't ask you again."

The rain was beginning to fall harder, and Jacob knew even if he were to yell out for help it would be swallowed up in the deafening drum roll of the deluge. It could not, however, drown out the sound inside Jacob's ears of his own heart pounding wildly against the wall of his chest as though it was attempting to break its way out. Slowly he began to turn away from the boy all the while straining to keep in the furthest corner of his eye the flexing fingers that formed the sharp claws, watching as the clinging drops of rain trickled across the smooth talons and clung quivering to the razor-sharp tips. He could hear them, mimicking the sound of a knife blade being sharpened as they scraped against one another. It made his throat tighten.

Once his naked back was revealed, Jacob heard a deep grumbling sigh exhale itself from the boy. He waited, bracing himself for what would come next. His lip was trembling. From the cold of the rain pelting his naked torso or from fright, he wasn't sure. Then finally, with a voice made meek from his hesitance to hear the answer, he forced out the question that had been struggling inside himself to be heard.

"Who are you?"

~ ~ ~

Instantly the boy was upon Jacob. A hand clasped tightly the back of Jacob's neck and his body was jettisoned forward by a tremendous force. Jacob's feet began to kick wildly at the open air desperately searching for the ground that had vanished instantly beneath him. He saw the wall of the building ahead coming toward him at a great speed and he struggled harder to free himself of the hold firmly locked on him. The only thing he managed to release was a loud wail that was quickly snuffed into silence when he was slammed face-first against the hard, wet cement. The pain was tremendous. Shooting to every corner of his body before exploding inside his head in a gigantic inferno of a million tiny blinding white flashes.

"Do you still want to deny your Nephilim blood, Nephilim?" the voice hissed from behind into Jacob's ear. "You show the markings of an impressive set of a wings I've yet to see on a half breed."

"Well, you know what they say about a Nephilim with big wings?" Jacob couldn't help in flinging forth the sarcastic quip despite being winded.

He then felt the gnarled claws against his skin, and his body tensed sharply. The tips held the sharp prickliness of needles as they traced their way slowly across his upper back. And he felt his body fight to cringe away from the uncomfortable sensation, but he was pinned fast against the side of the building and unable to move.

"And yet I could easily reach inside you and snap your spine like a branch from a termite-infested tree," the boy hissed.

Jacob's teeth clenched tightly as the claws dug deeper into the skin.

"Listen to me, I don't know who or what you think I am. I'm just here on vacation," he said, wincing with pain while struggling to piece together some believable string from the jumble of words swirling around his head that would somehow appease and call off the menacing figure pinned across his back.

"There's only one reason a boy like you comes to Tatvan." The voice growling in Jacob's ear let loose an ominous chuckle. "So close you were to your destination. Just a hop, skip and a jump left to go before reaching the Gate. Unfortunately for you, yet fortunately for us, you will never get the chance to step through it."

"Gate? What are you talking about? What gate?" The panic grew in Jacob's voice. His feet continued to kick freely in the air, his toes barely able to graze the surface of the ground above which the boy dangled him. He glanced about him wildly and then to the ground below littered with various objects that had been tossed and left forgotten into the back alley. His eyes spied a small pile of cement cinder blocks near his flailing feet that were impossibly out of his reach.

"RELEASE YOUR HOLD ON HIM, DEMON!"

Jacob felt his breath give slightly with relief at the familiar voice ringing out from somewhere behind. His attacker looked over his shoulder and scowled with rage at the sight of Gotham standing drenched at the far side of the dead-end enclosure. He let loose an angry chilling hiss that sounded like a combination between a snake revealing its venomous fangs and a cornered cat with its back arched ready to pounce on the dog it stood facing. And the whole of the boy's eyes rolled back into his head like that of a feeding shark until only the vacant whiteness remained showing.

"Stand back, angel! You've lost him."

Jacob cried out again in pain as the claws pressed harder against his skin. Gritting his teeth, he tried to calm and steady himself. He turned his gaze once more to the pile of cinder blocks on the ground. There was no earthly reason to suggest he could even come close at making a grab for one of the blocks. Yet he knew, somehow, instinctively, what appeared futile wasn't necessarily impossible, and he focused his concentration with all the strength he could muster into the five fingertips of his outstretched hand until—miraculously—one of the blocks shuddered with movement.

"RELEASE HIM!" Gotham's voice once more thundered loudly.

The hold on Jacob only tightened more painfully. Jacob focused harder his gaze and pushed forward everything he had onto the cement block. Then, suddenly, to his amazement, it sprang forward from the ground and was in his hand. Without a moment's hesitation, he swung his arm up and over his shoulder with all the force he had and the cinder block exploded against the side of his attacker's head.

The blow knocked the boy aside leaving him momentarily stunned and howling with a demonic growl. Jacob, free of the painful hold on him, was left sprawled across the hard, wet ground. He would have sprung to his feet and run as fast as his feet could carry him, but when the boy turned back on him with a face that was becoming more distorted from the growing rage and the menacing void in the whiteness that was now his eyes, Jacob froze with terror. The boy came at him again with a fury and Jacob quickly attempted to scurry away backwards across the ground like a crab desperate to keep out of reach from the clawed hand looking to find residence in his flesh once more.

In a flash of movement, Gotham swept forward and grabbed hold of the monstrous boy, lifting him off from the ground as though he were a bag of dirty laundry, and threw him hard against the building where Jacob moments earlier had been slammed up against.

"Go Jacob. Run. NOW!" barked Gotham with a fiery urgency before pouncing once again on the boy.

Jacob hesitated a moment, watching with wide-eyed horror the boy who attacked him thrashing and hissing wildly like something possessed against the captive hold Gotham once more had on him. When Jacob finally jumped to his feet to do as the angel had instructed, the boy's pupil-erased eyes focused themselves on him with an unmistakable viciousness, and with a point of the boy's clawed finger Jacob felt a breath-stealing, unseen force suddenly take hold of him and snatch him from his footing. Backward across the alley, Jacob was sent sailing through the air to slam hard against the wall of the neighboring building. An explosion of pain tore through his writhing, limp body, and when he finally managed to pry open his eyes he found much to his surprise that he had not been reduced to pile of busted body parts lying in a battered heap upon the ground. Whatever unseen force had tossed him about so effortlessly continued to hold him several feet off the ground and pinned tight to the side of the building, and as it did it also nudged one of the many steel rebar rods left rusting on the ground and sent it hurling toward Jacob. It struck the building grazing the outside of Jacob's right arm and impaled itself into the hard cement wall like the prong of a fork into a soft slab of butter.

Another iron rod was stirred from the ground, followed by another and another. They came at Jacob from all directions with a blinding speed burrowing themselves into the wall to form a perfect outline around his body. And then, as if they were living things, they began to move, twisting and slithering across Jacob's body and binding themselves tightly around his limbs and across his neck until he was securely imprisoned in a strangling reinforced web of steel. Jacob struggled with all his might to pull himself free, but it was a futile use of his strength.

A chilling cackle came from the boy still flailing wildly about in Gotham's clutches, and he began to taunt and mock the angel.

"Oh, how you long to kill me, don't you, angel? I can see it flaming in your eyes," said the boy in a wickedly hissing voice. "It would be so easy, just to end me and be done with it, wouldn't it? But you won't dare, will you? For to do so would mean killing this precious, young boy."

Gotham held the boy tightly by the neck in one hand while the other kept immobile the razor-sharp clawed hand that fought to slash to ribbons the angel and everything in its path. He leaned forward until his face was inches from the boy's and stared deep into the lifeless white void that were his eyes.

"Do not dare test my constitution at this moment, demon," warned Gotham in a withering whisper. "You better than anyone should know I've drawn the blood of those far more innocent."

The mocking laughter continued and grew louder. The angel's eyes blazed brighter from behind his darkening face and his fingers began to slowly tighten themselves around the boy's neck. Quickly, the laughter was replaced with the gasping and choking that comes with a straining struggle to breathe when life is slowly choked away.

"No...DON'T!" Jacob cried out. Despite whatever monstrous thing had attacked him, Jacob couldn't see past the sight of a young boy fighting for his life in Gotham's unyielding grip.

The boy's body began to contort in the most unnatural of ways. His legs were kicking all about in a desperate attempt for freedom, sending an onslaught of powerful blows from his free hand to Gotham's torso, none of which seemed to faze the angel in the slightest. Gotham's grip grew tighter on the slender neck fighting for air until finally a deep guttural growl filled with defeated rage left the boy and swept through the back alley. The boy's rabid movements began to quell and go limp. With a look of shock still residing upon his face, Jacob caught sight of what looked like the movement of shadow emerge from the boy's feet that had now ceased their vengeful kicking, only there was no sun to allow the existence of such a shape, and even if there was, this shadow moved independently from the body casting it. The black formless shape slipped to the ground like a plume of oil and quickly retreated to a corner of the alley where it disappeared into the darkness it found residing there.

CHAPTER TWELVE

THE HEART OF AKDAMAR

"What the hell was that?" Jacob bellowed once Gotham had pried him loose from the iron rods holding him captive. His body pulsated with the dull, painful throbbing being slammed into the side of a building can bring.

"What part of stay in this doorway and don't move didn't you understand?" barked Gotham. It was more a statement than a question and it was spoken in a voice still laced with anger.

Jacob's attention, however, had already turned to the boy who had attacked him slumped on the ground against the side of the building. Despite what had occurred moments earlier, a sense of dread came over Jacob as he looked down at the lifeless, limp body. The youthful face, no longer distorted by the mysterious shadow that had consumed it, looked calm and peaceful. And innocent.

"Is he…dead?" asked Jacob hesitantly.

"Don't worry, he'll be fine," assured Gotham. "He will awaken bewildered and confused—somewhat sore, I might add—but he will not carry any recollection of how he ended up in this alley or what took place here."

"What about his hand?" asked Jacob, motioning to the one that lay by the boy's side bleeding from the puncture wounds at the fingertips made by the sharp claws that were no longer visible.

Gotham knelt by the boy and took the hand in his own. He then dipped his other into a nearby rain puddle and carefully drizzled the water across the bleeding fingertips, and Jacob's eyes widened with amazement. As the blood was washed away, so too had any sign of the wounds.

"Get your things, we must go," instructed the angel, rising to his feet. "Now that they know you are here, they will quickly return. And in greater numbers."

Jacob hurriedly retrieved his shirt from the ground and wrung the rainwater from it before slipping it back over his damp torso. There would be time to change into drier clothes later, away from this alley.

"Who?" asked Jacob with his stolen bag once more in his possession. "Who are 'they'?"

Instead of answering the boy, Gotham tossed him a shopping bag he left sitting on a steel drum in the corner of the alley with a surly, "Here, take it!"

"What's this?" asked Jacob.

Opening the bag, he looked and found inside a heavy, warm coat.

"You'll thank me later. It gets cold at night in these parts this time of year," said Gotham.

Jacob found it to be an oddly thoughtful gesture from someone who didn't so much as crack a smile when he presented it. He knew then there was much more to the angel beyond the steely armored shell he had come to know.

"Had I known you would have pulled such a stupid stunt like you did, I would have sooner let you freeze, instead," Gotham was quick to add gruffly once Jacob had wrapped himself in the warmth of his new jacket and gave the angel a smile of gratitude. "Now we must hurry, and let us hope this diversion hasn't cost us our boat ride."

They hurried out of the alley and ran nonstop in the direction of the lake where they managed to board the last ferry as it was about to pull away from the dock. As the charter boat slowly began making its way out across the Van Gölü, Jacob sighed heavily as he stood watching and making sure Tatvan, and the darkness that lurked in its corners, was left behind in the ferry's wake. Had he made it? Was he finally safe?

Gotham had told him while aboard the train about the Furies and, for whatever reason, their desire to keep him from the water. Now he was cruising across the lake watching Tatvan grow smaller in the distance, and yet he couldn't shake the deep-seated sense of dread that danger continued to stalk them. The only sign of brightness came when Jacob noticed the drenching rain had stopped, vanishing as abruptly as it arrived when they exited the train in Tatvan, and he turned a squinting eye skyward where he felt the warmth of the sun begin to penetrate its way through the dark storm clouds.

"It was a Fury, wasn't it?" Jacob asked the angel once they were a safe distance from the shore, even though the feeling of being safe never quite managed to settle in around him.

"Had it have been, it is highly doubtful you'd be sitting here able to ask the question," said Gotham. "Furies aren't in the habit of toying with their prey. They are more vicious than anything you will likely ever encounter, and when they choose to strike, their target almost never knows what hit them."

"Then what was it?"

"An evil entity known as an Infector, but evil nonetheless. And like their name they favor moving amongst civilians, like a deadly virus, infecting as many as they can with their foul, unclean ways and turning otherwise good souls in the same way milk left to curdle goes sour," Gotham explained. "Be glad their attempt was made through the guise of a boy. Their true physical form is much more deadly and dangerous. I fear had you looked upon one as they truly exist, unready and untrained as you are now, the great terror they likely would have provoked from you would have overtaken your ability to fight it off as well as you were able."

Jacob couldn't imagine anything much more terrifying than what he had just witnessed, still unable to shirk from his mind the image of the knife-like talons emerging from the boy's fingers, or the white eyes filled with so much evil and rage. Or the hissing voice.

Gotham could readily see how troubled the incident had left the boy. A Nephilim's first encounter with an Infector, a Fury or any of the soulless souls that inhabited the Darkness was never not jarring, and almost always left some sort of scar, physical or otherwise. He offered Jacob a rare smile of encouragement. "You did well, considering. The makings of a strong Nephilim, you have shown."

Strong was the last thing Jacob was feeling, however.

"Some Nephilim. I actually thought he was an angel at first," remarked Jacob sourly. "I heard you call it a demon."

"I called it what it is," said Gotham.

"It spoke about some kind of gate," recalled Jacob. "It said I would never reach it."

Gotham stood silent, his gaze lost in the distance of the open water, and Jacob didn't bother to question him about the what or where of any such gate figuring the angel would reply with the same answer he'd received since leaving Cain's Corner—wait and see. And frankly, he was resigned to do just that.

"It said I was an abomination," Jacob muttered warily under his breath, but quiet enough that Gotham did not hear. He felt himself growing somewhat nauseous, only not the kind of churning sickness commonly visited upon unsuspecting stomachs out in the middle of open water.

~   ~   ~

The sun began to eat its way through the dark black clouds that soon disintegrated like a thin shroud of moth-chewed silk as the bright warmth pierced its way through and sent thick bands of sunlight to descend from the heavens and illuminate the surface of the lake. The gray brackish waters were suddenly transformed to brilliant shades of blue upon which the ferry cut a frothy path to a small shoreline landing at the foot of an island residing in the middle of the lake. There a member of the crew, wearing white linen trousers slightly dirt-smudged and fraying at the ankles and brown leather sandals that were a size or two too big for his feet, jumped off the boat holding the end of a thick woven rope which he secured to a wooden bollard.

"Welcome to Akdamar Island," he announced jovially in a thick Turkish accent to each of the passengers he helped onto the platform as they filed off the ferry one by one.

Jacob and Gotham followed the other excited tourists up a narrow flight of concrete steps snaking its way along the grey, limestone landscape. When they reached the end of their ascension, they were met by the impressive ruins of a great church that immediately elicited a collective cooing from its visitors. Built with various shades of red and pink volcanic tufa, the four-lobed, clover-shaped church with its massive pyramidal dome was striking in contrast against its barren, dry rocky surroundings. The lilies and hyacinths, euphorbias, wild onions and other various species of flowering plants that usually blanketed the island with the colors of life had withered and dried, retreating back into the rocky soil from the approaching cold of winter. The almond trees that grew in cloisters nearby and usually perfumed the air surrounding the church with the sweet fragrance from their blooming flowers now stood skeletal as they slipped into dormancy. One look at the ruins, however, and it was clear it needed none of nature's ornaments to procure immediate adoration from the island visitors as they disembarked the ferry.

"What is this place?" asked Jacob.

"It depends to whom you're referring when asking the question," answered Gotham.

Great, thought Jacob with a roll of his eyes, *another riddle.*

Despite the number of tourists wandering about, the island felt empty and ghostly to Jacob. Together, he and Gotham walked with the crowd along a narrow dirt path past what was left of a low, crumbling stone wall bordering much of the church. The dusty, rocky ground crunched loudly beneath the soles of their feet as they passed through pockets of visitors who had arrived at the island earlier in the day and mulled about the foot of the ancient structure where one-worded gasps of wonder spoken in different languages could be heard being traded amongst them. Dark sunglasses shielding eyes from the blinding light of the sun were all focused upward while digital cameras and cell phones trained on the wall of the church's great conical dome clicked away in unison. Jacob looked up to see what grabbed the attention of the throngs, rustling them with so much excitement. There he found ornamental reliefs of striking figures adorning the wall's faceted surface that had been cut like crystals to resemble a great stone jewel. Four circular carvings containing the portraits of what looked to be holy men floated above a much larger relief of a boat and a man falling prey to a great fish.

"Isn't it amazing?" remarked a woman as she came up from behind Jacob, an iPhone capturing the church from numerous angles gripped tightly in her hand. She looked every bit the part of a typical middle-aged tourist from the one-size-too-small sparkly, blinged-out jeans she had squeezed herself into, to the fanny pack cinched tight around her middle. Her freshly frosted blonde hair was pulled back in a tight ponytail and covered beneath a pink duck-billed cap trimmed with sequined daisies that danced with brilliant flashes of light beneath the sun. Taking note of the blank confused look fixed on Jacob's face, she ceased snapping pictures of the carvings and blurted loudly, "It's Jonah!"

She waited a moment for a look of clarity to cross the boy's face. When she failed to see it, her body slumped with disbelief.

"You know…Jonah. From the Bible. He was swallowed up by a whale."

Her words came slow and succinctly, as though she were speaking to a two year old, or a foreigner she believed could pick up the English language instantaneously if only she spoke slowly enough, not to mention loudly enough.

"Of course—Jonah," replied Jacob, flashing her a half-smile and nodding politely. The woman shrugged and went about taking her pictures leaving Jacob to turn his attention back to the relief. Now that he knew, he could make out more clearly the fabled story.

"Impressive," came Gotham's voice from over the boy's shoulder. "Don't you think?"

"Looks more like a fish than a whale," muttered Jacob with a nod to the oddly scaled figures etched into the pale red rock.

Yet despite the seemingly lack of enthusiasm emanating from the boy, the angel could see the beginnings of wonderment in the teen's eyes. For rarely could anyone who treaded in the presence of the stone church look upon its hollowed remains and not be somewhat enamored by the weathered markings.

"One hundred and fifty three figures are carved onto these walls. Same as the number of fish said to have been miraculously pulled from the sea by the apostles in the New Testament," said Gotham. "Together they tell the history of mankind, beginning with his creation."

The angel guided the boy along the walls making up the perimeter of the church, describing to the boy the various figures, some of which seemed to erupt from the surface of the stone facade like living, breathing sculptures aided by the shadows being cast from the chiseled edges by the shifting sun. The biblical David was seen overpowering the giant Goliath. Samson stood victorious from battle and Daniel was flanked by two lions licking his feet, their tails hanging submissively between their hind legs, while the saints George, Sergius and Theodore did battle against evil forces that surrounded them in the form of dragons and ferocious cats. And elsewhere, there was the presence of angels.

Always the presence of angels.

Only when they came to a sculptural relief showing Abraham, his dagger at the ready, wrestling with the decision to sacrifice his son to God did Gotham suddenly grow quiet. Noticeably so. And Jacob saw the angel's face had darkened as he stood staring at the image; mournfully or brewing with anger he could not tell. Nor did he ask. When they reached the eastern facade of the church, they were greeted with images of St. John the Baptist, St. Thaddeus and the prophet Elijah. It was the lone figure surrounded by numerous animals, however, that kept it hold of Jacob's attention. And for once, the boy needed no explanation of who the solitary carving was meant to depict.

"And Adam gave names to the animals," he translated aloud from a cryptic inscription chiseled nearby into the wall.

Further down, the story of humanity was begun with a rendering of Adam and Eve coupled with the Tree of Life and a forked-tongue serpent with four legs. And as Jacob followed the story around another corner of the church, the adjoining north wall revealed the ultimate fall and expulsion of the first man and woman from the Bible's sacred garden—the Garden of Eden. Gotham remained silent as he stood beside the boy. His eyes roamed across the figures that somehow held the long history of the ancient world in full upon the small canvas of stone. His mouth parted, and he spoke in a gently, hushed tone.

"Amidst the rush and roar of life,

Oh, beauty, carved in stone, you stand mute and still, alone and aloof.

Great Time sits enamored at your feet, and murmurs:

'Speak, speak to me, my love, speak, my bride!"

But your speech is shut up in stone,

O Immovable Beauty!"

Once he had finished, a familiar voice rang out from behind, "That was one of the most beautiful things I've ever heard."

Gotham and Jacob peered in unison over their shoulders to find the woman with the sequined daisy cap. She had made her way around the opposite side of the church and intersected with their path.

"The Bengali poet Rabindranath Tagore would have been pleased to know his words moved you so, " said Gotham with a friendly crook of his mouth.

"I couldn't help but hear you earlier explaining the various images," the woman remarked rather giddily. "You seem to know so much about the church. May I ask, are you a professor or something?"

The question brought a smile to Gotham's face, but only briefly when he then glanced over at Jacob and found the boy looking a little too tickled at such an idea.

"No, I'm not a professor," answered Gotham. "Just a great follower of history."

"You can say that again," quipped Jacob under his breath with a chuckle, drawing a narrowing glare from Gotham.

"Do you think if I left you here a little while you can manage to keep out of trouble?" asked the angel once the lady had returned to her picture-taking.

"We're on an island in the middle of a lake," answered Jacob, offering little reassurance to Gotham.

"I'll be back in a moment. There's someone here I wish you to meet," said Gotham.

He did not need to second-guess leaving the boy alone. Unlike Tatvan, or anywhere else one might draw breath in the world, he knew the island was one of the few places whose threshold the agents of the Darkness would think twice to cross. As Gotham disappeared around the corner of the church, Jacob turned to find the woman's gaze fixed curiously on him.

"Adam," he said with a confident grin, pointing to the relief depicting the father of all mankind. "You know, as in Adam and Eve."

~   ~   ~

Gotham had to duck somewhat and bend himself forward to fit himself through the low, square doorway set within a rounded archway of multi-colored stone blocks to enter the zhamatun of the church. Inside he came to a sudden pause. He looked curiously about the large, empty oblong hall pierced by a minimal amount of sunlight that followed him from behind through the doorway and streamed in through the half a dozen or so small, rectangular windows lining the walls. It looked the same as when he last stepped foot inside the sacred vestibule, perfectly preserved in its hapless ruins. Yet something was different. It had changed. Or rather it had been changed.

The inside of the great room was as dark and black as he remembered, looking like a charred, burnt-out hull. The pink hue of the tufa stone walls was permanently scarred by fire damage as were the numerous stone pillars supporting the massive archways lining the hall. The air carried a faint acrid stench, the lingering remnants of the fires that once burned freely inside the zhamatun and church by vagrants looking to beat back the chill of the night air and the looters who used the firelight to aid in their work. There was another smell, a new one: the dank scent of fresh mortar and cement.

He glanced about the room and then to the ceiling above. Immediately he noticed the earthen roof that had covered the top of the zhamatun since it was constructed had been replaced by a thick layer of cement. And he felt a tinge of sorrow recalling the beauty the roof had once provided the church in the spring when the island was alive and in full bloom, appearing like a giant emerald block of green plants decorated with brilliantly colored flowers. As he made his way slowly cross the hall, the echo of his heavy footsteps caught his ears. They sounded strangely odd in the tomb-like surroundings. He glanced downward to the floor which felt noticeably different beneath his feet and he saw that the mishmash of round, irregularly shaped stones that had once paved the ground had been removed and replaced with more cement and modern-cut rock.

What had happened here? he wondered to himself.

When he reached the entrance leading into the cathedral, he felt a sense of tension move through him. What was awaiting him on the other side of the doorway? What other changes? What further desecrations? He took a calming breath and again ducked through another low opening. Inside he found the cathedral empty except for the presence of two Turkish guards relaxing against a far wall joking with one another while enjoying a smoke. When they saw they were no longer alone, their smiles quickly vanished and they reluctantly straightened themselves. Gotham watched as they each took a final drag from their cigarettes and his cold, icy glare followed the remains that were discarded with an unconcerned flick of their fingers and left to smolder on the floor.

Turning his back on the two men, he sighed with disgust and slowly took in the cathedral's cavernous innards. Time and man had not been kind to this holy place, that much was certain, but at least they had not been so outwardly venomous or malicious to its soul. The frescoes, for instance, that had once dressed every inch of the stone walls, pillared archways, and numerous niches in brilliant details and colors still managed to cling to life, though many were close to being sandblasted out of existence by the elements and left in tattered patches by the looters and vandals over the centuries. High above, the faded and chipped remnants of images detailing the life of Jesus from the nativity to the crucifixion still clung to the walls in ghostly hues of blues and browns. And, inside the drum of the cathedral's great dome, vestiges of the story of Genesis could still be seen.

The sun coming through a ring of eight small, rectangular openings illuminated the inside of the dome and was reflected downward to the floor below in a circular burst of brilliant white light where Gotham stood. With his golden eyes gleaming brightly, he stared upward studying the fragmentary scenes that told of the birth of Adam and Eve, their seduction into sin and finally the tragic fall from their terrestrial paradise. A faint whisper of voices coming from the rafters pricked his ears; voices that had long been extinguished, yet continued to linger within the church's walls. Gotham closed his eyes and listened to them as they circled about him, carried on the wings of a gentle breeze that came from outside and moved within the stone structure like an invisible phantom. Then he heard the echo of another voice coming from elsewhere inside the church. And the whispers vanished.

He opened his eyes and directed them to the movement he spied inside an apse on the other side of the cathedral. Casually, he slunk away from the circle of light surrounding him and retreated from sight into the darkness lurking in an inconspicuous nearby corner where he quietly waited. Within moments, a group of a dozen or so tourists emerged from within the niche. They trailed behind an elderly man with white hair that hung in long frizzy strands to just above his shoulders dressed in khaki pants and a long-sleeved, blue button- down shirt, both of which appeared to be a size or two too large for the somewhat frail body they loosely covered.

"There are many ancient churches rooted to the shores surrounding the Van Gölü: Surb Hovhannes, Surb Echmiadzin in Soradir, Yedi Kilise, also known as the Seven Churches, Surb Bartolomeos, Surb Tikin in the village of Elmac and so on. But this church here at Akdamar is unique even residing in a chest containing so many jewels," said the old man to the group that gathered around him in the light beneath the dome. "The generations of Armenians who long established themselves here in this part of the world have an old saying: 'Van in this world, paradise in the next.' "

The adage elicited a murmur of approval from the group.

"Unfortunately, that about concludes our time together," said the old man. "But if anyone has any more questions, I will do my best to answer them."

His offer was quickly accepted by a round-face woman whose homeland revealed itself in the German accent that phrased each and every syllable. "Is it true the island is named after a horrible drowning?" she asked.

"I take it you are referring to the legend of a tragic love story between a peasant boy and an Armenian princess," replied the old man, nodding knowingly as though he had been asked the question—not to mention recited the answer—countless times before.

"As the tale goes," he began, "a beautiful Armenian princess named Tamar once lived on the island and she fell in love with a commoner who came across the lake to Akdamar each day to tend to the fruit trees. Her father the king, however, soon learned of the relationship and was none too pleased about it and he forbad his daughter to ever lay eyes on the boy again. Tamar and the boy, however, were too much in love and the thought of never being together, even for one day, was too painful to endure. So they came up with a way to deceive the king. In order for the two to see each other, the boy would secretly cross from the mainland to the island each night, guided by a beacon Tamar would light so he could make his way safely through the dense darkness. When her father learned of the clandestine visits, he became enraged and vowed to keep the young lovers apart once and for all. So, one particularly stormy night, as Tamar awaited her beloved's arrival, her father found the light she had dutifully lit and snuffed it out. As the boy crossed the lake, his boat became overwhelmed by a sudden storm and capsized, throwing him into the cold, churning waters. He tried to swim, but without the light to guide him he became lost in the blinding darkness and soon succumbed to exhaustion and the overwhelming waves which eventually swallowed him."

The old man studied each face staring back at him, wholly transfixed to the story. "It is said the boy's drowning cries of 'Akh Tamar, Akh Tamar—Oh Tamar'—can be heard to this day coming across the water at night."

A coo of appreciation for the tale came from crowd. All except the woman who had inquired about the legend and was clumsily fumbling through her purse in search of a tissue to dab the tears now streaming down her cheeks.

"I've also heard that there's a creature that lives in Lake Van. Like the Loch Ness monster," another tourist chimed in, eliciting giggles from within the group.

The old man's heavily craggy face lightened with a smile.

"Ah, yes, of course," he replied with a chuckle, running a hand over the top of his frizzy hair that glowed an almost blinding white beneath the light coming down from the dome above. "I don't think I've yet conducted a tour where I haven't been asked about the famous monster of Van Gölü."

"Have you seen it?" another prodded jokingly.

"Well, I guess that all depends on what you deem to be a monster," answered the old man. "At one time there were stories of great reptilian-like monsters said to roam the Indonesian Islands that explorers later discovered to be Komodo dragons. Dangerous, yes. Monsters…?"

He turned his face to the light streaming down from above. And his gaze framed with the deep creases of time widened pushing back the tired, sagging folds of his eyelids to reveal a glint of gold that flashed from his pupils as they came to rest on the images looking down from within the dome.

"And the Lord God said to the serpent: 'Because you have done this, cursed are you among all animals and among all beasts of the field; on your belly you shall crawl, dust shall you eat, all the days of your life.' " he muttered. And his recitation seemed to confuse somewhat the tourists patiently waiting to hear if the lake indeed was home to some unseen, legendary creature.

"The word 'monster' derives from the Latin word monstrum, meaning an aberrant occurrence rising up from within the natural order," continued the old man as he turned back toward the tourists and recognized the puzzled look on their faces.

"You ask if the existence of a monster lurks within these waters." He gave a carefree unknowing shrug and smiled. "Then again my reality of the natural order of things most likely differs from yours."

~ ~ ~

"The island of Akdamar is a very special place. It is said this spot bore witness to the creation of mankind, and also its destruction by the Great Flood as told in the Book of Genesis," the old man continued. "There is reason why Akdamar has become marked by so much legend and folklore and continues to bring hordes of visitors to her shores. Whether it be the echoes of a tragic lost love heard rising in the night, or some kind of dark, unknown entity swimming beneath the tides. Or that Van Gölü itself, as legend also holds, is enchanted and frequented by angels seen coming in and out of its—"

The old man's voice trailed off abruptly as he glanced past the crowd before him to the entrance of the church at the far end of the zhamatun revealing the blue waters of the lake on the other side of the stoned archway. His eyes, however, shifted sharply about the church until they found Gotham's presence cloaked within the shadows of a far wall.

"Waters," the old man finally uttered in a quiet exhale of breath.

He quickly announced the end of the tour to the group of tourists thanking them for their time and attention with a pleasant smile before inviting them to continue on with their exploration of the church and the island grounds outside. Patiently he took time to shake hands with several members of the group, and humbly accepted their gracious thanks for the entertaining knowledge he had provided them. And once the last of the crowd had dispersed to the far corners of the cathedral to examine more closely the visual relics on its walls, the old man looked again in the direction of the entrance and found Gotham still at his spot.

Slowly, with a worn, tired shuffle he made his way to him.

"Do my eyes dare deceive me?" asked the old man.

Gotham reached out and grasped the man's upper arm and gave the delicate limb a reassuring squeeze.

"It's good to see you again, Johiel," said Gotham.

The old man's frail, slightly stooped frame appeared even more diminutive standing before the angel's towering presence.

"How long has it been?" asked the old man.

"Long enough."

"I wasn't sure you'd ever grace these shores again."

Gotham nodded and forced forth a smile. "Neither did I, dear friend. Did the thrush I send ahead deliver my message to you?"

"Night before last," said Johiel, drawing Gotham's gaze upward to where the small brown bird whose white chest adorned with a collage of black spots could be seen perched on the rim of the dome cleaning the plumage of its wings. "And a most peculiar message it was. I could not help but be certain the thrush had grossly misunderstood you."

Gotham's answer came in the silence that followed and they both succumbed to the peacefulness surrounding them. Johiel fixed his gaze on Gotham's eyes and, as he searched deeply the golden orbs, a troubled look slowly surfaced in his face.

"You're not alone."

Gotham opened his mouth to answer, but before he could form a word the man looked away toward the entrance to the church. Pulling away from the angel's grasp, he made his way as fast as his age could carry him to the open doorway where a breeze sweeping up the gray limestone cliffs from the lake below greeted him. His eyes darted about the few tourists seen wandering the church grounds. Not finding what they were looking for, he moved swiftly along the perimeter of the stone wall. When he reached the corner, he was met with more crowds milling about. Again he searched the sea of colored T-shirts paying particular attention to the handful of teenaged children in the tow of their parents when finally he caught sight of Jacob wandering nearby. In that moment, it was as though he were stricken by some unseen hand that had reached into his chest and gripped tightly his beating heart.

"That would be him, wouldn't it? The boy you sent word to me about?" asked the old man while carefully studying the teen still engrossed in the biblical hieroglyphics embossed upon the outside walls of the church. Yet it was a question to which he already knew the answer.

"Then it's true. You expect to be granted passage through the Gate," said Johiel with an air of disbelief to Gotham, who stood silently behind him.

"I expect—" Gotham began before catching his tongue. "I would hope you would do for him what you would do for any other Nephilim. If anything, out of respect for our close bond that has withstood far greater challenges."

"This goes far beyond any bond you and I might share, Gothamel. Just as this boy is unlike any Nephilim who has ever set foot on Akdamar," argued Johiel with a tone of growing anger that he quickly wrestled to restrain to ensure his words wouldn't reach nearby wandering ears. "How can you expect me to act in accordance to your wishes, Gothamel? I have a duty. To conspire with you on such an act would be an ultimate act of betrayal on my part. Worse, it would be a high crime of treason against the heavens themselves."

Gotham was prepared that his visit to Akdamar would be challenging. And perhaps even fruitless.

"Would it not be a worse crime to not get down in the mud and wrestle fate when you and I both know the unfortunate path left should we not?" asked Gotham. And the angel's words seemed to take hold of the old man. "I am Fallen, and because of that such things shouldn't heed a moment of my concern. But it does. And I knew you of all would understand it's not who plants the seed, but who tends to it in the growing years that determines the beauty and strength of a tree."

Johiel stood quietly watching the boy in the distance while listening to Gotham with the weight of conflict clearly visible in his haggard face.

"You have to know the steadfast anger such a brazen act would draw from the other side," the old man remarked.

"Most certainly, at first," said Gotham. "But it would also be quickly dulled when it is realized the decision to allow the boy through came from someone as highly regarded as yourself."

The old man's weathered face cracked a smile. "Do not attempt to win me over with such a cheap ploy as flattery."

"All I ask is that you meet the boy," said Gotham. "If he doesn't manage to win you over himself then we will leave the same way we came. No hard feelings."

The old man stood quietly mulling the request while staring deeply into Gotham's eyes.

"The tourists will be leaving the island in about another hour or so. Take cover further inland until they leave and then we will have our introductions," said Johiel.

Gotham sighed a hint of relief. The hard part was over; Johiel was at least willing to consider his appeal. Johiel, however, was quick to add with a firm grip to Gotham's arm, "Understand, I make you no promises."

He gave a last lingering look Jacob's way before turning and making his way back into the sanctuary of the church.

CHAPTER THIRTEEN

There were only a few hours of daylight left. The sun was beginning to soften and the shadows along Akdamar's rocky landscape slowly began to stretch and lengthen in their reach. The deep, baritone horn from the last ferry docked at the water's edge sounded in the distance signaling to the remaining tourists that it was time to depart. For the two Turkish officers, it meant their day-long shift of standing watch over the grounds would come to an end with the final task of accompanying the last visitors onto the waiting boat, and they began rounding up the stragglers and hurrying them along like sheep dogs nudging their herd.

Johiel accompanied the small group the short distance to where the island began to bow down to the water below. There he offered each of the tourists his hand and a kind goodbye. Watching from the foot of the stairway, Johiel chuckled to himself and returned waves to the tourists as the ferry slowly pulled away from the makeshift dock and began its trek back toward the mainland. When the boat had sailed far enough into the distance, leaving in its wake a trail of frothy rolling waves that gradually widened and receded back into the calm of the deep blue lake waters, Johiel turned to face the deserted island. Pursing his lips together, he let loose a blaring whistle that sounded like a large bird swooping down from the skies. His eyes grazed the terrain farther inland that ascended to the island's higher ground until they came to a cluster of large boulders where Gotham emerged from behind with Jacob in tow. Johiel motioned to them with a wave of his hand that it was safe to come out and the two started back toward the church.

"We're alone now. The last have headed back to the mainland. So now we have a chance of getting better acquainted." The old man turned to Jacob and extended his hand. "I am Johiel, Guardian of the Gate."

Jacob reached out and gently took the old man's hand. Yet the grip that greeted his was not that of a frail old man. It was strong and unyielding. And there was an immense warmth cupped within the palm. It moved up his arm like an incoming tidal surge and flooded to every corner of his body an intense sensation of comfort like none he had ever before experienced. And he knew instantly this was no ordinary old man standing before him.

"I'm Jacob…very confused teen," the boy replied with an awkward laugh.

The old man smiled. It was a kind smile, and mirrored the kindness that filled his drawn and ancient, yet surprisingly youthful eyes.

"As the many who have come before you, I have no doubt," he said.

~　~　~

"So, young Jacob, tell me, what do you think of the Surb Khach," asked Johiel.

Jacob at first appeared to ponder the old man's question.

"Surb Kha—Church of the Holy Cross," he answered transcribing the church's Armenian name. "It's pretty spectacular. I don't think I've ever seen a church that color before."

"Pumice stone and red volcanic rock," said Johiel. "King Gagik Ardzrouni, who had this Palatine Cathedral of the Holy Cross built in 915 A.D., had vast amounts transported to the island and assigned an architect monk by the name of Trdat Mendet the enormous task of overseeing the construction of not only the church, but also the Palace of Aght'amar which the king had built right up there."

Jacob looked in the direction of where Johiel's finger pointed to find empty gray cliffs rising in the far distance.

"Before long," the old man continued, "the island became a fortified city paved with streets, lush gardens and terraced parks spread throughout the royal complex that included an armory, court, stores, school, prison, and of course the church. But for King Gagik, like the Roman emperors and Egyptian pharaohs before him who sought immortality in the monuments built in their name, it was the palace he had constructed that was the crowning jewel, rising up out of the center of the island like some grand monolith desperate to catch the eye of Heaven with its gilded cupolas gleaming with a golden brightness that could be seen for miles around. And with the arrival of each passing night, the music and laughter from the nightly festivities at the palace spilled out into the darkness and swept across the water to the far shores of the Van Gölü and beyond."

There was a far-off look fixed in the old man's eyes as he spoke while staring off into the distance. One could almost see a glint of the once glorious city reflected in his aged gaze.

"Like all things in this vast but short-lived mortal realm, it eventually fell victim to the scythe of time. Today, as you can well see, the roots of only a few trees from the fragrant orchards hold to the ground, but the beautiful gardens have vanished along with the buildings. And, should you care to investigate, the crumbled foundation is all you'll find left beyond those rocks of the once grand palace," said Johiel.

"Strange that the church still stands," noted Jacob. "And in such good condition."

Johiel turned his gaze to the walls of the red-sandstone wonder that rose high like a beacon overlooking the vast carpet of blue surrounding Akdamar like some roped-off partition in a museum served to protect a priceless artifact from the reaches of outside hands.

"The church has dulled greatly over the centuries." Johiel's voice was heavy with lament. "Its once brilliantly painted colors have faded. The precious gems, pearls and encrusted gold that made it sparkle and shine like a star-filled night sky have long been picked clean like the bones of some carrion carcass and replaced with bullet holes by vandals who've reduced this once spectacular holy site to nothing but a bullseye for their target practice.

"That must be why they look so angry," remarked Jacob.

The old man gave the boy a quizzical look. "Of whom might you be speaking?"

Jacob gave a nod to the faces of the numerous reliefs staring back from the walls of the church where the eyes of every saint, every angel, every animal contained hollowed out holes burrowed deep into the stone where priceless jewels had long been pried loose by thieving hands. Even Christ himself was fixed with a wild, wide-eyed look of pupils robbed of the sparkling life that once filled the darkened crevices.

"I know it sounds strange," continued Jacob in his observation, "but the longer I look at them, the more they seem to be alive.

He quickly felt a sense of embarrassment when he realized what he had just muttered aloud was more fitting a child ten years his junior.

"Stupid, huh?" he said almost apologetically.

The almost childlike observation seemed to momentarily lighten Johiel's mood somewhat.

"Hardly. You manage to see what most who come here cannot," said Johiel. "The heart of Akdamar beats strong within the walls of this church. It has seen much in its time, forced through many changes. Becoming part of a monastery in the centuries following the glory days of King Gagik, a home to the Armenian Catholicosate, a cemetery for the monks of Aght'amar whose blood would come to feed the fruit trees and stain the church walls as they were massacred during the genocide, and ultimately a victim of vulturous vandals until, finally, by the end of the first world war, it was left abandoned and forgotten. An empty shell. Its once grand cathedral looted. The monastic buildings destroyed. All left to rot. And crumble."

As Jacob listened to Johiel, his eyes continued to roam the stone reliefs adorning the church walls.

"That's him, isn't it? King Gagik?" asked Jacob, pointing out one of the reliefs among the biblical friezes.

"You're quite astute," said Johiel.

Jacob studied the image depicting a man with a halo surrounding his head offering what looked to be a model of the church to Jesus while two seraphim angels look on.

"He sure had a high opinion of himself, didn't he?" mumbled Jacob under his breath as he took notice of how significantly larger the king was next to the much smaller Messiah. It was a simple, off-the-cuff observation, yet one which drew Johiel to look upon the boy with increased curiosity.

"Yes," said the old man quietly as he studied the boy. "Well, then, there's much more you've yet to see, and little light left to do so properly. Come, let's go inside, shall we?"

Gotham, who was quietly standing nearby, knew right then by the invitation Johiel extended that Jacob had unknowingly managed to move himself one step closer to the destination they'd traveled so long a way to reach.

~ ~ ~

Johiel led Jacob and Gotham through long-forgotten gardens surrounding the church where a small grove of almond trees remained standing. Scattered across the craggy ground beneath the gnarled outstretched limbs were the fractured remnants of numerous weathered khachtars jutting up from the ground like old tree stumps.

"Tombstones?" asked Jacob while noting the Christian markings framed within patterns of vines, grapes and pomegranates elaborately inscribed upon the stone faces.

"Markers," corrected Johiel. "Erected for the salvation of the soul. And protection."

The cry of a saker falcon soaring high above the island echoed loudly in the distance, drawing a glance from Johiel as he ushered Gotham and Jacob through the arched entrance of the gavit leading to the church. The weakening sunlight spilling through the tomblike doorway and small rectangular openings cut along the wall guided the way past the blackened pillared arches lining the oblong room. There was a noticeable chill in the air.

"The earthen roof," noted Gotham, pointing to the ceiling. "It's been altered since the last time I've been here."

Johiel nodded and sighed a heavy breath.

"They came several years ago, the Turkish workers. A mission of mercy for this old relic, they called it. And a glimmer of hope for reconciliation between Turks and Armenians," said Johiel. "For two years I watched from a distance as they sealed off the church from visitors, barricading it behind wire fencing and encasing its fragile walls in steel scaffolding. And then they went to work, shearing off the roof of this zhamatun and replacing it with the concrete and modern stone you now see. How long these walls will be able to carry the added weight before finally buckling, I do not know."

Jacob's eyes followed the old man's to the ceiling above them, and he felt a shiver move through his body imaging the walls surrounding them suddenly crumbling and bringing the heavy stone slab crashing down upon them.

"The floor was replaced soon after," continued Johiel. "I wish I could say that was all that was changed."

Even in the faint light, Jacob could see the pained look that suddenly settled itself upon the old man's face.

"Funny, man is," said Johiel. "Constructing their monuments in a desperate attempt to fend off what time inevitably steals from them, only to destroy that which gave temporary immortality to their mortal lives.

~   ~   ~

When they reached the end of the hall, Johiel motioned Gotham and Jacob to the cathedral entrance telling them he would rejoin them shortly before disappearing through an adjacent darkened doorway. As the two entered the great dwelling that was the cathedral, Jacob's stride slowed. The air inside was thick and carried a strong, dank smell to it like that of cement that had been saturated with the first rain of the season, but it was not the air that gave his feet pause but rather the time-gnawed frescoes adorning the tall, vertical stone walls like torn pieces of parchment.

Jacob found it to be as though he had stepped into a larger than life picture book of the Bible. Everywhere he turned read like a page torn from the Good Book offering still frames of scenes and characters in fading colors desecrated by the ravages of time desperate to scour them clean from the walls and out of existence. Slowly, Jacob circled the cathedral, his eyes moving from image to image that seemed to unfold before him like chapters shuffled out of order and displayed in a random pattern that attempted to meld the Old Testament and the New Testament into one giant, unified tapestry. He suddenly paused when he came to a detailed scene depicting a large enthroned King Herod giving his orders for the massacre of newborns. His gaze then shifted to the figures of six bereaved mothers looking on from an adjoining pillar, and he was drawn to the sorrow brimming in their dark eyes. They seemed to reach out and grab him. Not just the weeping women, but the rising Lazarus, wrapped in linen and surrounded by his sisters as he is seen emerging from his tomb. And six of the apostles, survivors of the ravages of age and man that had consumed the other half of their brethren. They loomed large and stoic, as though appointed guardians of this stone-encased sanctuary, clutching protectively the gospels from which some of the surrounding figures were plucked. They all had the same eyes, large and black. Expressionless, yet full of expression. And feeling. And life. Most importantly, life. While all were gazing with glances turned slightly upward toward the heavens, Jacob couldn't shake the feeling he was being watched. However, it was much more than just a feeling when, to the boy's utter shock, he gradually began to notice the many images on the walls slowly started to shift their focus subtly downward onto him as if drawn to his presence.

"What is it?" Gotham asked, when he noticed the boy slowly backing away from the walls toward the center of the cathedral.

"Call me crazy, but I think they're moving…the images," answered Jacob, sounding somewhat spooked.

"It's only the stirrings of curiosity," said Gotham.

"I think they're watching me."

A faint, knowing smile crossed the angel's face. "It's just your eyes readjusting themselves."

"What do you mean readjusting? I have twenty-twenty vision," said Jacob with a slight panic in his voice.

"It's nothing more than the ongoing changes all Nephilim experience, like a second puberty, if you will, that has a habit of accelerating somewhat the closer we get to where we're going. As far as your eyes are concerned, soon you will see things as the angels do, and not as mortal man."

"And how is that exactly? First paintings that come to life. What next? X-ray vision like Superman?"

The corners of Gotham's mouth turned upward slightly. Embracing the changes was always a bit unnerving in the beginning. "You've been given a special gift, Jacob, discombobulating as it may feel at first. But fear not, you will soon see the world in a completely differently light."

Yet fear was the one thing Jacob was not feeling. Impatience, confusion, an overwhelming sense of not having control over what was happening to him, yes. But not fear, even as his eyes darted from wall to wall keeping close watch on the fabled biblical images that continued to show signs of life. As he backed his way across the floor of the cathedral, he stepped into the ring of light cast down from the great dome above, and he felt himself become fully engulfed in a great warmth. A faint chorus of whispers sounding like silk draperies rustled by a gentle breeze coming through the open windows suddenly pricked Jacob's ears. It called his attention upward to the dome illuminated with the orange-red glow of sunlight spilling through the circle of small openings ringing the upper portion which suddenly grew brighter—much brighter, and whiter, and more brilliant a light than he had ever before seen. Yet it did not hurt his eyes or cause him to squint or shield himself from the intense brightness. And he stared unblinking straight into the white gauze and gazed upon the constellation of weathered biblical images depicting the creation of man looming high above him. Adam and Eve. Jacob recognized them instantly, even though Eve's face had been eaten away to a blank void framed by long stringy hair, and he followed the couple's tragic story that unfolded within the dome wall detailing their great fall at the roots of the Tree of the Life in the shadow of an evil, fork-tongued serpent. And a great, inexplicable sadness overcame Jacob while staring into the doomed pair's large, black painted eyes filled with so much sorrow and regret as they were shown being escorted by an angel out of paradise. The whispered voices grew louder and seemed to descend from the inside of the dome and move freely, circling and darting about like sparrows. Yet Jacob's attention stayed firmly fixed on the mythic image of the banishment above. His eyes narrowed with curiosity, and they fixed themselves firmly on the figure of the angel escorting the sinners out of the Garden of Eden. Closer he focused on the face, young and fair, and framed with long locks of light-colored hair. There was something strangely familiar about it. Something recognizable within the fading, cracking paint.

"It's him," Jacob muttered to himself, and then to Gotham, "He's an angel as well, isn't he?"

Gotham glanced upward at the Genesis scene scrolled within the dome and the haloed figure upon which the boy's attention had become transfixed and he knew of whom the question was being asked. He opened his mouth to answer when a voice from behind interrupted him.

"I thought you might be hungry."

It was Johiel, standing in a darkened doorway at the far end of the cathedral holding a beat-up silver pitcher filled with water and a chipped porcelain mug in one hand and a plate of sliced vegetables and fruit, a helping of almonds and a couple slices of bread in the other. Carefully balancing the offerings in his trembling hands he crossed the cathedral to where Jacob was standing.

"The guards make it a habit to make sure there's some food here to tide them over when they come to the island." he said. "It isn't much. But enough to keep your strength."

Jacob took a long, quenching swig from the mug of water he poured himself and with gusto began sampling from the plate of food. So much had happened over the course of the day that he had completely ignored the growing grumbling coming from his empty stomach.

"So will I eventually lose a need for food altogether, and for that matter sleep?" he asked.

"Unfortunately—or perhaps fortunately, depending on how you look at it—no," answered Johiel, his craggy face as soft and inviting as the smile he seemed to always have fixed in his eyes and the corners of his mouth. "Unlike Gothamel and myself, you are still very much mortal, and as such will continue to require their creature comforts."

"Then, I'm right," said Jacob, "you are an angel."

"You sound surprised," answered Johiel.

"Not really," said Jacob, his cheeks ballooned with grapes. "I kinda suspected it when you were telling the history of this place. I mean, the way you speak of it—the church, the island, palaces that are no longer here—it's not like anything you would hear from a regular tour guide, you know? I dunno…it's like you've been here through it all. Lived its history."

The boy's assessment only seemed to intrigue the old man more. "There's always been one of us here. Before the palace. And after the palace. A great dark wing will always cast its shadow across the face of this island," he stated quietly. "And yet I can see a flicker of doubt remaining still in your eyes."

"No, not really. That is…well…it's just…," Jacob stammered. "I just didn't realize that you were able to…you know…*grow so old.*"

He winced as he muttered the last few words as if he were throwing forth some unforgivable insult, and the old man appeared momentarily taken aback by the comment. He glanced down at his hands, bringing them up into the light to examine more closely the dark sunspots that freckled his skin and the slightly arthritic fingers which he wriggled stiffly. Suddenly, he began to chuckle, lightly at first, and then with an increased vigor.

"Ah yes, I tend to forget this withered cloak I wear," he said. "A fitting skin to match the weariness that has aged and bored its way into the depths of my soul after these countless lifetimes to which I've served as witness. I found long ago it provided a nonthreatening—invisible, if you will—means which allowed for my continuing existence on Akdamar during an ever-changing occupancy through the centuries. Surprisingly, I've grown quite comfortable in it despite how uncomfortable it may appear from the outside."

Johiel turned and in his slow, aged gait he made his way to a corner of the cathedral where a large stone bowl, filled with water for tourists to dip their fingers into and bless themselves while visiting the church, rested upon a pedestal. With his back facing Jacob, Johiel immersed his cupped hands into the bowl and brought a splash of the water across his face, then swept his wet hands slowly over his forehead and back across the covering of white sprouting from his head. And as he did, the fizzy hair began to change instantly, growing thicker and stronger beneath the passing of his fingers, and becoming chameleon-like with its color from the roots outward until the white became a long, silky mane of dark blonde.

Jacob watched with open-mouthed amazement as the stooped, hunched body before him straightened and grew in stature before him. The baggy clothes that had once hung loose on the frail form now strained tight against a fit, muscular body. And when Johiel finally turned back around, the face weathered and aged had somehow vanquished the lines and creases time had set deeply into place and now appeared youthfully handsome and beaming with a confident strength.

"Behold," exclaimed Johiel with a youthful timber sending the deep tenure of his voice to echo powerfully through the cathedral chamber, "and look upon me as I truly am. Then turn your ear to what I am about to speak, and let us see if we can't quiet the chorus of questions ringing in your head."

~ ~ ~

Jacob sank to the cold, hard concrete of the cathedral floor just inside the circle that held the warm orange glow of the waning day outside streaming down from the church's dome. Anxious was he to hear what was about to be told him, like a child curled up warm in his bed awaiting a story to be recited from his favorite book. His dusty, loosely laced sneakered feet were crossed at the ankles and knees pulled close to his chest, and his eyes were quietly fixed on Johiel, moving pensively about in front of him. They still held a look of awe after witnessing the angel's cocoon-like transformation only moments earlier. After what seemed to be a never-ending silence that might never be pricked again by sound, Johiel cleared his throat and began to speak.

And, like all good stories worth listening to, he began at the beginning with the creation. Not that of man, but of the angels. He told of their numbers, and he spoke their names. Some Jacob had heard of before: Gabriel, Raphael, Uriel, Michael. Many he had not, such as Haniel, Anahel, Uzziel and Zerachiel. And as Johiel recited the names, he motioned to the numerous, almost countless images of angels peering down from the columns and walls and ceiling, some bold and impressive in size, and others less so.

"They are your bloodline, the roots to the great tree of which you are but a limb just beginning to sprout," said Johiel.

His voice held an echoing command within the church walls as it retold the events that gave way to the creation of the world—Jacob's world, the world in which mankind would come to dwell—and mankind itself. Johiel spoke with great authority, like a biblical scholar. And, in fact, Johiel's version of events were much like those Jacob remembered being read to him from the Bible countless times by his mother when he was a child, and yet it was as though he was hearing it all for the very first time. Jacob found himself spellbound by the words that seemed to unfold like the great tapestries painted on the walls and ceiling around him. His attention strayed for only a moment when Johiel began to talk of the Great War in Heaven in much the same way Gotham had on the train, and he looked for Gotham who was listening silently from a nearby corner to which he had receded. Despite the gathering darkness, Jacob could see a trace of unease in the angel's face with the retelling of stories he appeared to silently wish would be erased from his memory.

Johiel suddenly became silent and drew his gaze upward to the small openings encircling the cathedral dome where the last remaining moments of day could be seen in the thin rose-colored light that was fast growing dimmer.

"I see the night is almost upon us," he said, and he crossed the floor to where an extinguished torch was fixed in the wall. He leaned his face to the charred head and blew his breath upon it and it instantly ignited with a flame.

"I've never cared much for the darkness," he remarked. Then turning his head and cupping a hand to the side of his mouth he blew forth another breath, only much deeper, and one by one in quick succession numerous other torches throughout the church came to life filling the cavernous space with their flickering light.

"Even in the brightest of lights, darkness looms on its periphery," said Johiel to Jacob with an arched brow. "Always remember that."

Jacob looked to the walls, and the walls looked to be alive from the movements made within them by the images. And while he continued to find it unnerving, he was slowly becoming more and more used to what shouldn't be.

"So, why is it the angels came to despise man?" It wasn't until Jacob heard his own voice that he realized he had spoken out loud the thought which crept up suddenly out of nowhere from the dark recesses of his brain.

Johiel swung back around to face Jacob, and a curious smile crept across his face. "You are, if anything, direct with your questions, young one."

"Sorry," said Jacob, hoping his question wasn't met with offense. "It's just something I remembered my teacher Mrs. Braukoff saying in Bible class once when I was little. It always struck me as odd."

Johiel slowly made his way back toward the dome, not in movements he made when disguised with age, but as a strong man caught in the tight grip of deep reflection.

"Despise." He muttered the word several times to himself under his breath, as if it came from new language with which he was unfamiliar and was pining for its meaning.

"The relationship between angel and mortal man has always been a complex one," said Johiel finally. "Angels have always seen themselves as far superior to man. We find contempt with man's inability to fight the slide into temptation. We see him as weak and undeserving of the special devotion God has placed upon him. Yet the truth is the creation of man ultimately revealed the same weaknesses in ourselves. For we saw the making of man as our unmaking, something that had been created to take our place as God's favorite."

"So you're saying then it's a jealousy thing?" asked Jacob.

"Jealousy," echoed Johiel with a sigh. "Envy. Arrogance. Vanity. It took hold of all of us in some form or another, some more than others. And in those few it found particular fertile ground to take root. Their light became pregnant with a darkness which would fester and metastasize within them. And when man was finally presented before us by our Creator and we were commanded to bow down and serve him, the Darkness reared in defiance. The call to war rang out and it would come to pass that a third of my brothers would fall from the Heavens like stars shaken free and collapsing from the skies. And soon after, what had been a turn to jealousy became a great resentment—resentment over the fact that when the time came when man, himself, eventual fell into sin, God would extend to him the ultimate act of mercy he refused the angels he banished: forgiveness.”

As Jacob listened intently, he cast a glance at the angel's forehead in search of the telltale scar that marked Gotham.

“You don't carry the mark,” he noted with a sense of puzzlement.

“I would hope not, seeing as I am not Fallen,” said Johiel. “But that does not shield me from feeling for my brothers who are and lamenting the sentence imposed upon them.”

“Then why are you here, alone on this island, living in this run-down church?” asked Jacob.

Johiel at once appeared offended at the characterization of what had long been his home many mortal lifetimes over. “I grant you this church is but a shell of its former glory, but I would take umbrage in referring to it as run-down.”

“What I meant was why are you here on an island in the middle of a lake when you could be…you know?” said Jacob, making an upward pointing gesture with his finger.

Johiel grinned and turned his attention toward the inside of the cathedral dome where the light from the flickering torches brought mysterious movements to shadowy shapes, knowing it was the heavens beyond to which the boy referred.

“Those of us who roam about this world do so for different reasons, both the Fallen and those who have not,” he said. “It would take yet another Fall to set my feet upon this earth, not that of angels, but the one who had been held before us like some precious unearthed gem. It was orchestrated with teething glee by the Dark Dragon, who after being cast down from the heavens took chase after man with a burning hatred, fed by an even more burning hatred for the One who made him. For he knew all too well the only way to wound his vanquisher was through his most beloved creation. So it came to be he led man to commit the Great Sin against God and forever secured the punishment upon all of mankind forever after in the form of a much different mark."

"You can't mean Adam and Eve," said Jacob.

The remark made Johiel's left eyebrow rise defensively. "I take it by the dubious tone in your voice the truthfulness of what I have spoken has aroused your doubt. But hear me when I tell you it was I who was sent down to deliver God's rebuke upon them, and as they stood before me, made of the same flesh and blood as are you I most certainly assure you, it was I who cast them from Eden's lair out into the unsettled world naked and pitiful in their shame."

And, strangely, the conviction with which the angel spoke seemed to immediately silence the doubt Jacob had expressed, and his eyes followed Johiel's as they returned to the painted image within the dome of Adam and Eve being led out of Eden.

"You have been the first to recognize that it is me who is painted upon that wall. Even the artist I oversaw during the construction of this church failed to see the image he shaped with the tip of his brush and the man before him, not yet taken to an aged form, were one and the same."

"But why have you remained here after all this time?" pressed Jacob.

"As I told you when we first met, I am Guardian of the Gate. As long as the Gate exists, so too does my presence here."

Jacob was becoming more visibly dumbfounded by Johiel's words. "That doesn't make any sense. If the Gate still exists as you say and the reason you are here is to serve as guardian to it, that would mean Eden—"

He stopped himself, as if realizing the words coming from his mouth, even posed as hypothetical, were the most ridiculous ever to be spoken by another person.

"Is it that difficult a thing to fathom?" answered Johiel, sounding equally as perplexed.

Difficult to fathom?

"You're joking right?" asked Jacob, looking like someone who was experiencing having his leg pulled and trying to figure out who was doing the tugging as he glanced over at Gotham, who also showed no signs of foolery. "You're talking about Eden. As in The Garden of Eden."

"Angels are many things," said Johiel. "Pranksters, we are not."

Jacob felt his head begin to swim. "Alright…for now let's say I believe you. Where is it then, and how is it the rest of the world isn't aware of its existence?"

"That is something you would have to see for yourself, for I am certain your belief—what little of it there is—would quickly wane even more-so if I were to tell you," said Johiel.

Jacob could hear echoes of his grandmother's voice in the angel's words. It was almost exactly the same answer she gave him when he asked her where it was Gotham was planning to take him. Hearing it come from the angel suddenly brought a jarring sense of reality to everything he had so far experienced.

"Yes, Eden exists," said Johiel as if to put a final stamp of fact on the revelation revealed to the boy. "But the Gate remains sealed, as it has since the day man was exiled from the Garden. The ones allowed through are angels and their offspring and it is through me, and me alone, that such passage is granted. But you should know it is not an easy voyage getting there. And despite my efforts to provide safe passage, it does not come without the risk of danger, especially from an unsavory presence which infests these lands in growing numbers."

"You must mean the Furies," said Jacob, taking an uneducated guess.

"Ah, then you know of them?" inquired Johiel.

"Not officially, thankfully," said Jacob. "I was sort of introduced to other members of the family in the form of a midget panhandler."

Johiel turned to Gotham with a quizzical look.

"We had a run-in with an Infector on our way here," explained Gotham.

"I see," said Johiel with a nod. "A truly nasty and vicious parasite set upon mankind, Infectors are. Goodness knows I've had more than my fair share of run-ins with them, so it bodes well for you that you show nary a mark on your skin from your first encounter. Furies, I regret to say, are an entirely different breed of malignancy."

"I remember learning something about Furies in my history class last year," recalled Jacob. "If I remember right, they were nasty spirits who went after people who murdered family members and punished them by driving them mad."

"Erinyes, as they were better known," said Johiel. "Female deities of justice and vengeance also referred to as the infernal goddesses."

"But they're a part of Greek mythology," said Jacob, bringing a smile to Johiel.

"All myths and legends conjured by mortals sprout from some seedling of truth. Unfortunately, when it comes to the Furies, the myth pales to the reality."

It was not an answer that proved especially comforting to Jacob by any means.

"What I don't understand is," he contemplated aloud, "what beef do these… things…especially the Furies…have with me?"

An ominous look suddenly shadowed Johiel's face in the firelight of the burning torches and he looked once more to Gotham.

"You haven't told him?"

The only answer to come from Gotham was the continuing look of resignation that had kept a silent vigil in the angel's eyes as he sat silently listening to Johiel explain to Jacob the history which led to the boy being brought to Akdamar.

~　~　~

"Gotham said they were part of the Darkness—demons," answered Jacob hesitantly when Gotham didn't. The sudden palpable tension between Johiel and Gotham told Jacob there was more to these creatures than he had been told.

"Okay, you two are kinda starting to freak me out a little here," said Jacob with a nervous chuckle. "Is there something you're not telling me about these Furies? I mean, who exactly are they?"

"Not who, but rather what," Johiel was quick to correct the boy. "Always remember that."

"That makes it a lot less ominous," said Jacob. And for a moment he thought maybe it might be better not to know. Still, he couldn't refrain from asking, "Alright, *what* are they then?"

Johiel's gaze came back to rest upon Jacob, and a dire foreshadowing retained itself within the golden orbs that were his eyes reflecting the still- burning torches.

"They were once what you are now," came the answer.

"What do you mean…what I am—" began Jacob before the answer lit up inside him like a lightbulb. "Wait…you mean—"

"The poor wretched souls of the early Nephilim, cut down by a flaming sword and washed out of existence by flood waters carrying God's wrath," said Johiel.

Nephilim?

Jacob watched stunned as the angel before him turned and began slowly making his way around the perimeter of the church dome.

"After the angel's Fall from Heaven and man's Fall from Grace, came a third great fall," Johiel began. "And it was this Fall that would come to hurt God the most. For shortly after man's Fall and expulsion from Eden, God saw the hardship and pain that had befallen upon his beloved creations. And so, in an act of mercy, he sent down a band of eleven angels known as the Watchers to give man aid and guidance in his survival. Each angel possessed a unique, special skill, and together they gave man instruction to the signs of the earth, and the science of the constellations. They taught root-cutting and how to grow plants for food, and for a brief moment, man and angel for the first time came together in a way that pleased God."

The look on Johiel's face offered warning that the story he told was deprived of a happy ending. "As would always be the case, the Dark Dragon remained near, watching and scheming," continued Johiel. "Despite leading man to their downfall through sin, he still carried a thirst for revenge. And with the Watchers he saw an opportunity to deal another stinging blow to the heavens. He turned to a Watcher named Azazel, and Azazel began teaching the men how to make swords and shields, and through them war. To the women, Azazel taught how to beautify their faces with coloring tinctures and adorn themselves with ornaments. He began seducing the women, and when he had finished, he sent the women off to seduce the other Watchers. Mind you, not all the Watchers fell prey to their charms and remained loyal to their Maker. But many chose different. They became known as the Grigori, and in that name they swiftly abandoned their allegiance to Heaven to become what they had once so despised in men. As for the men, they watched helplessly with a growing fury as their wives gravitated without shame to the company of the Grigori and the Fallen, and they began growing large with the fruits of their sin. Before long the first cries from the offspring of these forbidden unions rang out and reached God's ears. And a great darkness fell upon the face of the earth."

The church grew uncomfortably still and silent, and Jacob noticed even the images on the walls no longer moved as though they, too, were engrossed in the story Johiel was in the midst of telling.

"God called upon his most trusted and loved of all angels and whispered to him his judgment," continued Johiel. "And when those who were so flagrant in their sinning ways looked to the skies and saw an angel of vengeance coming with the fury of God gripped in his hand, the fear in their eyes was immediate. They recoiled in terror, desperate to escape the angel's drawn sword whose blade burned as if forged by a mighty and searing flame. Their pleas and screams fell deaf to the one whose ears they beckoned, and all they could do was shield their own ears from the young Nephilim whose cries succumbed to abrupt silence in the grips of their eradication."

As Jacob sat listening, the story met his ears with a growing familiarity. Soon he remembered it was first told to him in the middle of the night aboard the train on the way to Tatvan by Gotham. Only Gotham had failed to make mention of one very important detail: that the horrible task he had been instructed to carry out which led to his eventual Fall was the slaughtering of Nephilim. When he finally realized the story Gotham and the angel Johiel told were one and the same, Jacob looked over to where Gotham sat, and when their eyes met the angel slowly leaned his body toward a pocket of shadow out of reach of the torch light to cloak the profound shame that had settled upon his face.

"They were just children," whispered Jacob.

"Children yes, but in Heaven's eyes they were an abhorrence of a sin that had so flagrantly been committed," answered Johiel in way that was both direct and choked with genuine sympathy. "Once the judgment had been carried out, the heavens unleashed the Great Flood to wash away the blood and remnants of the great sin and drown into silence the cries of sorrow that rose in a deafening chorus of anguish. And the Dark Dragon watched it all with a smug contentment. Not only had he hoped the act of carnage would bring forth a divide between God and his remaining legions of angels that could never be mended, but as he looked to the heavens he was gifted with an unexpected sight which filled him with victorious glee, and that was witnessing the angel who had helped bring about his own Fall become at that moment himself marked in a familiar branding of lightning and sent tumbling down to earth."

Jacob was quiet for some time as he imagined what was undoubtedly, in every way, an unimaginable horror.

"Why are they called the Furies?" he asked when he finally managed to find his tongue.

"Though still angry, God eventually took mercy on the souls of the slain Nephilim and opened the gates of Heaven to them. But it was too late. The Darkness had already moved in and poisoned and perverted the young minds against God and the race of man, and it shepherded them into the deep pit of damnation that had been opened for the Dark Dragon and the Fallen who followed him. And they helped nurture and strengthen the hatred raging inside these youthful souls before unleashing them upon the world above to seek their vengeance against God."

"Just like the Furies in Greek mythology," muttered Jacob before turning back to Johiel. "You said they hunt other Nephilim. Why would they seek out and harm their own kind?"

"The reason lies in your question," answered Johiel. "You are not their kind. You were given a choice they never were: life. And they hate you for it. They want you to succumb to the Darkness as they have, and if you choose not to, then death is the only alternative."

"And to ensure the one long promised to come and pave the way to the Darkness' ultimate defeat never comes to be." Johiel and Jacob turned their heads in unison at the sound of Gotham's voice, and they saw the angel had emerged from the darkened corner of the church where he had sought his temporary refuge. And as he came toward them, they could see his face was once again filled with the beaming strength and untethered resolve momentarily lost to him.

"If you're going to tell him, you may as well tell everything," he grumbled as he brushed past Johiel.

~ ~ ~

They watched him cross to the far side of the church and stand before a large swath of wall deeply scarred by what appeared to have been a long-ago fire that left it encrusted in a shroud of pitch and blackness.

"You heard Johiel speak of three great Falls. Well, this wall once told of yet another—the beginnings of a final battle to be waged between the Light and the Darkness which would lead to the eventual banishment of the Dark Dragon from this world, just as he had fallen from Heaven," explained Gotham as Jacob and Johiel flanked him on each side. His eyes were transfixed on the wall in front of him as if remembering the images desecrated by the blackness but still remained seared in his memory.

"What happened to it?" asked Jacob. "It looks like someone took a blowtorch to it."

"The Furies," answered Johiel. "The one and only time they dared to set foot on Akdamar, when the Infectors used their dark influences over man to incite the Medzegherm against the Armenian people here."

"Medzegherm—" repeated Jacob, before his tongue found the English translation of the word. "The Great Slaughter."

"Genocide," Gotham voiced more bluntly.

"While the Ottoman military unleashed its horror, the Infectors brought their own here to Akdamar, with a band of Furies in tow, and with great relish they took to slaughtering the monks," Johiel began, before a wave of emotion seemed to overcome him. First sorrow, and then an even greater anger. "I wish I could say I protected them. The first screams of the Medzegherm drew me to the mainland to witness the nightmare that had suddenly reared up, just as it was intended, and it was then I heard the cries being carried across the water from Akdamar in a terrifying breath of wind. When I returned, not one had been spared. Their blood fed the earth in pools of it, and the church was left scorched and smoldering."

"What is lost in the telling of this savage event, at least to the civilian world," Gotham broke in when Johiel refused to continue on, "was there were also fourteen Nephilim here at this church waiting to make the journey through the Gate when the Furies attacked. They, too, were cut down."

Jacob stared blankly at the wall in front of him, imagining the unimaginable while trying to block it from his consciousness at the same time. How he came to notice it was quite by accident, but his eyes came to spy hidden in a nook and veiled almost completely by the shadows of the night a fragment of an image left unmarred by the vandals' hands. He moved in for a closer look and saw what appeared to be a rendering of an angel and a man facing one another. The blackness scarring the wall had consumed the bottom portion of their bodies, but stopped mysteriously at their waists. In between the two images stood another figure holding in one hand a sword and in the other an olive branch. The surface of wall where his face once graced had been chipped away, and from behind the left side of his shoulder was seen a large wing, like that of a bird.

"Was this supposed to be part of the painting?" asked Jacob.

"Somehow, it was the only piece to survive, and ironically the most important," answered Gotham before adding with a rather bitter spit of breath, "At least, at one time."

"What's so important about it?"

"It speaks to an Apocrypha."

"Apocrypha," mumbled Jacob with intrigue and yet the strange, unknown word he had never before heard failed to translate its meaning like other foreign languages or animal calls that met his ear.

"Apocrypha are writings absent from the known canon of Scripture. They contain secret teachings, and in some cases, hidden prophesies," explained Johiel. "One such prophesy foretells the last final Fall. It speaks of a Nephilim who will come from the shadow of a mighty angel's wing and rise up like a newborn lamb attempting its first steps. Yet beneath his foot will come the first step in a march of war against the Dragon. He would be known as the Light Bearer, and in the world's darkest moment he will bring angel and man together to forge an impregnable army that eventually will vanquish the Darkness."

Jacob listened as Johiel spoke while trying to picture the images showing man and angel fighting side by side on some unimaginable battlefield once contained in the great mural now obliterated within the blackened wall.

"Do you believe it…the prophesy?" Jacob asked both angels.

"I wouldn't hold my breath if I were you," grumbled Gotham under his breath with an unmistakable dismissiveness. Jacob couldn't help but notice a cloak of gloom which seemed to have wrapped itself around the angel. Yet it was hard to tell from his fire-lit profile if it was anger or sadness that weighed so visibly upon him as he continued to stare at the chipped-away face of the one- winged figure. And before Jacob could ask what he meant, Gotham turned his back to the wall and removed himself once more to a far corner of the church.

"What's wrong with him?" Jacob asked Johiel.

"Oh…nothing that need concern you," answered the angel. "These hollowed grounds have a way of stirring memories long past, both good and bad."

Jacob noticed Johiel's expression, as well, held a weight of despair similar to Gotham's, and he found himself wondering if the words of the so-called Apocrypha were not the good news it sounded to be—at least to the two angels. And maybe to all angels in general. Perhaps, Jacob thought, they didn't care for the idea of a Nephilim—or anyone for that matter—bringing angels and mortals together, even to bind their strengths against the Darkness.

"Light Bearer," echoed Jacob as he returned his gaze once again to the small revelation he somehow found so intriguing the more he pondered it. "I don't mean to sound flippant, but what you told me sounds pretty fantastic."

"Perhaps," replied Johiel softly. "But the Darkness believes it to be true, which is why the Furies and Infectors hunt Nephilim such as yourself with such a fiery and savage hunger. And to ensure you do not make it past the Gate into Eden. Only then can they be certain the future is never illuminated by the promise of a Light Bearer."

Jacob glanced back over his shoulder and his attention gravitated to the section of wall where the weeping women convened and he was suddenly met with an uncomfortable feeling.

"Like Herod having all the newborn males slaughtered," he said quietly.

"Precisely, child," noted Johiel with a solemn smile. "Just like Herod."

CHAPTER FOURTEEN

GOD'S THUMB PRINT

Jacob found his mother in her bedroom, sitting by the window, clothed in her favorite robe, feeding her dove from the palm of her hand like some fairytale princess. She looked to be healthy and joyous. The stench of disease no longer surrounded her. Instead, a pleasant bouquet of lavender and gardenia filled the air.

"My angel," she said softly, looking to her son with a smile shaped by genuine happiness, and not forced to disguise the pain and sadness Jacob had come to recognize. She stretched her hand out toward Jacob and he moved to take hold of it when a darkness suddenly descended upon the room, churning wildly like a tornado of smoky ash. It swirled about Jacob, keeping him from moving, and more importantly reaching out for his mother. A deep, demonic roar came from deep within it encircling Jacob, and it ignited a chill deep inside of him.

"The water!" his mother cried out suddenly to him over the thunderous roar that seemed to grow angrier. "You must get to the water!"

Jacob wailed for his mother as he became overcome by a deep-seated anguish of losing her again. And then she was gone, suddenly and immediate, wholly consumed and snuffed out of existence by the overpowering swirling blackness. He opened his mouth to set loose a scream when he suddenly was yanked free of the chaos with a jolt.

~ ~ ~

He found himself sitting on the hard, stone floor, slumped against a wall in a corner of the church. His hand still clutched a pen which remained pressed against a page of his journal where he had desperately worked to scribble down everything he had seen and heard while on Akdamar as it remained fresh in his mind before the sound of the waters of the Van Gölü lapping against the island's shores lulled him to sleep. Not that he could possibly forget anything he had so far witnessed.

As he tucked the journal away in his bag, Jacob looked about the church for Johiel and Gotham, but there was no sign of either, and he wondered, as he often found himself, what these winged beings did during these long stretches when the world fell dark and they found themselves with nothing but the silence to keep them company.

Climbing to his feet, Jacob crossed the dimly lit cathedral, glancing briefly at the towering walls while trying to step gently to keep his footsteps against the stone floor from puncturing the blanket of quiet that cloaked the polygon- shaped room in an eerily soothing fashion. Or to wake the frescoes on the walls that seemed to be asleep, no longer moving or showing signs that they were aware of his presence as they had before. He made his way through the darkened hall of the zhamatun guided by the whistling of wind moving along the corridor and the scampering feet of an unseen rodent, or some other island creature, scurrying quickly upon the stone slabs as he approached.

Stepping outside into the crisp chill of the night, Jacob was met by a cool, brisk breeze, and a full moon hanging low in the black sky like a giant precious pearl. All around him was bathed in its ethereal glow making the surroundings of the islands appear almost dreamlike. Otherworldly. And for a moment he wondered if in fact he was dreaming. It was only by the absence of the smoky blackness that had been stalking him each time he closed his eyes and drawing a cold sweat from his body that he knew he was, in fact, wide awake.

Something brushed up against his lower leg that made him jump slightly. He looked down and smiled with surprise—and relief—to find a harmless white cat slinking leisurely in a figure eight fashion between his feet.

"And who might you be?" asked Jacob.

He knelt down and stroked his fingers through the feline's thick coat of hair. It was soft, unusually soft, reminding him of a rabbit's foot key chain he once carried around in his pocket as a child. The cat meowed with appreciation and arched its back sharply to welcome the friendly caress. Jacob found it to be the most unusual looking cat he'd ever seen. For starters, its eyes were large and of different colors—one an icy turquoise blue, the other a deep golden amber, much like his own opposing-colored eyes. Its feet were quite large and wide, as though it had not quite yet grown completely into them. Yet it stood a bit bigger than most cats he'd seen. Equally as odd was its puffy red ring-patterned bottlebrush tail which looked to be more suited for a fox than a cat.

"Looks like you got yourself into a bit of a scrap," Jacob commented while noticing the purring cat was missing its left ear as he scratched it along the top of its head.

Straightening back up, Jacob strolled into the night toward the water. The cat followed close at his heels. When he reached the neck of the island where the stone walkway led down to the dock, he took a seat on one of the steps, and the cat was quickly back between his feet pacing back and forth while brushing his body up against Jacob's legs until the scratching fingers once again dug themselves into the snow-white fur. The purring resumed.

"You've met Van Gogh, I see."

The unexpected voice startled Jacob, who swung his head around to find Johiel standing behind him, youthful and ageless in the moonlight.

"Van Gogh…I get it…because of the ear," noted Jacob amusingly. "So I take it he belongs to you?"

"Belong? One can never truly hold ownership over any earthly creature," the angel replied. "No, he appeared on the island a few years ago and has been a faithful companion to me ever since."

Johiel took a seat on the narrow slab next to the boy. The cat meowed in recognition of the angel's presence and moved from pacing back and forth between Jacob's feet to take its loyal position at Johiel's. The angel smiled and reached down to scoop the feline up in his hands.

"The Turkish Van, or Van Kedisi as they are called in these parts, is a very rare, very ancient breed. They are also considered to be very lucky," said Johiel.

"I dunno about that. I'm not sure I would consider missing an ear all that lucky," said Jacob jokingly.

"There's an old Persian proverb: 'The lion sneezed, and the cat appeared,' " said Johiel. "According to legend, during the time of the Great Flood when Noah was set adrift, he became aware of several rats on board that were trying to gnaw a hole through the bottom of the ark. Unable to stop them and fearing the demise of his family not to mention all the animals on board should these devilish rodents succeed in their undertaking and send the ark into the waters that had swallowed the earth, Noah pleaded for God's help. God in turn sent him to the lion, and from the lion's nose came a pair of cats who went and dealt with the destructive rats and, thus, keeping the ark afloat until it came to rest on Mount Arafat."

Jacob followed the direction of Johiel's gaze northward across the water to the far end of the lake where, unbeknownst him, the biblical snow-capped mountain of which the angel spoke resided unseen in the dark beyond the shore at the opposite end of the lake.

"As the cats were leaving the ark along with the other animals, God blessed them with a touch of his hand and left behind this mark." As he spoke, the angel turned the cat's back to Jacob and smoothed the fur along its neck to reveal a dark discolored mark in the snow-white coat between the shoulder blades similar to the red-ringed patterns found on the tail. "The Kurds say it's God's thumb print."

The cat purred loudly in Johiel's arms, its large dual-colored eyes mirroring Jacob's contrasting blue and green-colored irises fixed themselves firmly on the boy while continuing to enjoy the fingers stroking its thick, soft hair. Sure enough, Jacob could see as he stroked the cat the blemish marking its hide did indeed look like a thumb print, though much larger than the shape of his own thumb.

"I sense maybe you've become bored with my telling of church ruins, battles between good and evil and cats carrying divine markings," Johiel, noticing an occupied look in the boy's face, said.

"No, not at all. In fact, I could sit here all day long and listen to your stories," said Jacob. And he was telling the truth. "It's just…"

"Go on," prodded Johiel curiously.

"I can't keep from thinking about what you said about the Furies. You know, how they came to be what they are now," said Jacob. "They were killed because they were Nephilim."

The frown fixed on Johiel's forehead gradually receded. "And naturally you wonder why a similar judgment hasn't been cast down upon yourself and the other Nephilim roaming the world."

"You said yourself Nephilim were a sin which angered God the most."

"It was not the Nephilim who were the sin, but the manner in which they came to be," explained Johiel.

"Um, I know I didn't pass biology with perfect marks," said Jacob, "but I'm pretty sure the manner everyone walking the planet came to be is universally the same."

The boy's reply forced a mirthful chuckle from Johiel. "Quite true, young Jacob," the angel said. "But what truly shapes sin is not so much the transgression itself but the intent behind which it is committed. The union of angel and woman was not what angered God but the fact it was stirred by the Darkness. And as is everything which the Darkness has served as architect, it was a sin designed to pierce the heart of our Creator and tear asunder the loyalty and devotion the remaining angels had with Heaven."

The words Johiel spoke appeared to only add weight to the troubled look fixed on Jacob's face as he listened. "The boy who attacked me in Tatvan—or, rather the Infector—it said I was an abomination."

"And it would be correct," noted Johiel, drawing an even more unsettled look from the boy. "You are an abomination…to it, and most especially the Furies whose path you might cross. Because you are unlike them. You exist in the Light, while they dwell in the Dark. The only way for you to cease being an abomination in their eyes and thus end their torment of your existence is for you to willingly follow them into the shadows."

"That will never happen!" Jacob exclaimed adamantly, and Johiel was pleased to hear the cemented defiance in his voice.

Lifting the cat from his lap, the angel brought his mouth to the feline's one ear and whispered into it. He then set the cat back down upon the steps and Jacob watched as it quickly scurried off along the walkway. When it reached the dock serving to greet the daily arrival of ferry's carrying visitors to the island, the cat maneuvered its way across the jagged rocks lining the shore and waded out into the water.

"Now that's a first for me; witnessing a cat willingly go into water like that," remarked Jacob. "Where's he going?"

"To ensure your passage through the Gate."

The answer appeared to catch Jacob by surprise. "Gotham made it sound earlier like you might not be too keen on letting us through."

Johiel grew quiet for a moment. "In many ways Eden is like an exclusive club. One has to be very careful who is allowed inside something so protected," he finally said thoughtfully. "These hours I've had to spend and talk with you have proven very insightful. Surprisingly so."

"And?" pressed Jacob, unsure if what the angel was saying was a slight or a compliment.

"And," answered Johiel, "Eden would be well off to have you."

Jacob smiled and turned back to the lake where he looked for Van Gogh who could be seen paddling further out into the depths, its white head bobbing along the smooth silvery surface like the periscope of a submarine.

~　~　~

"What's it like?" asked Jacob.

"Even if I attempted to describe it to you, I doubt you would find my words very believable," said Johiel. "Eden is something which must actually be seen with one's own eyes in order to exist as something beyond the trappings of some aged fable."

"When I was a little kid growing up, my grandmother used to tell me stories about a place like this—like Eden," said Jacob, his eyes remaining fixed on the water long after Van Gogh had swam out of sight and faded into the darkness. "I would sit and listen to her with wonder imagining this wondrous, beautiful place she described. It sounded like something out of a fantasy or fairy tale. Like Neverland come to life. And I wanted so badly to go there, to see it for myself. Now, here I am, standing at the doorstep, and suddenly—"

"You fear it," injected the angel, finishing the boy's sentence with words he knew wouldn't be uttered. "Because even now you don't truly believe."

Jacob didn't answer, because Johiel had managed to put into words exactly what he was feeling.

"So, tell me, young Jacob," inquired the angel in his soothing tone. "How was it your faith became lost to you?"

It was the same question Gotham had asked of him on the train ride to Tatvan. The same one Jacob had refused to answer. And still now he hesitated.

"You had a childhood friend named Christopher. I'm guessing he had a lot to do with it, didn't he?" asked Johiel.

The mention of his friend caught Jacob sharply off guard.

"How do you know about him?" he asked almost defensively.

Yet, as he looked into the piercing gold orbs fixed firmly on him, Jacob already knew the answer. And he suddenly found himself feeling as though he were naked to the eyes seemingly boring into him.

"He was the first best friend I ever had," Jacob remarked quietly.

"Was," Johniel echoed as his gaze fixed themselves ever more intently upon the boy.

"We had planned a campout in his backyard," Jacob began with a notable hesitation in his voice as though fearful to revisit the memory he had fought to forget yet couldn't. "I remember the two of us bouncing in our seats with excitement in the back of the car when his mother picked me up. Christopher's family lived on the outskirts of town, and the drive along a two-lane narrow road that swept past acres and acres of open grass fields and woods leading to his house seemed to take longer than it actually did. We must have been about halfway to his house when Christopher noticed something in the middle of the road up ahead. As we got closer we could see it was duck. Somehow it had hurt its wing and was fluttering helplessly about in the opposite lane. Christopher argued for his mother to stop the car and she pulled over, with all of us staring out of the windows at the poor struggling bird. When he opened the car door to get out, his mom stopped him, but he was insistent. We can't just leave it there and let it get run over, he said. Saint Francis of Cain's Corner—that's what I used to call him, because he was the Florence Nightingale of injured animals. I don't think there was ever a time I went to his house where he wasn't tending to some wounded critter. Birds, lizards, squirrels, you name it—his room looked like a rehabilitation center at an animal hospital. But the last thing Mrs. Whitling wanted was to bring home another patient. Christopher argued all he wanted to do was get the injured duck off the road and even pointed out a patch of tall grass nearby where he knew it would be safe. Finally, Mrs. Whitling relented, and as he darted out of the car I watched her cautiously scout the long stretch of road behind her that she had just driven and then ahead where the road snaked to the left, vanished for a short distance down an incline before reappearing at the bottom of the hill. I, too, looked as did Christopher. There wasn't a car in sight.

"I watched as Christopher slowly stepped his way toward the duck while speaking gently to it in order to calm the agitated bird flapping about helplessly on the asphalt. He had a way with animals and was quickly able to scoop it up into his arms and the duck instantly settled down as though it knew Christopher's intentions to help it."

Jacob's gaze became even more mournful and distant. It was as though the darkness of the night surrounding him and Johiel had opened a portal before him revealing the long-ago scene.

"It happened so quick. I don't think either one of us, Mrs. Whitling or myself, knew what was actually happening, even as we were witnessing it. Suddenly, there was a truck. It was just there, appearing as if out of thin air and barreling over the top of the incline. I can still hear the sound of the horn blaring and the ear-piercing screeching of tires desperately grabbing at the pavement. And then that thud—that horrendous thud as Christopher was violently cleared from my sight. Just like that. He was gone. I never knew another living person could create the kind of sound that left Mrs. Whitling at that moment. It was as though she herself had been struck down and left dying in the road. Thinking about it now I guess she had." Jacob let loose a choked sigh.

"I don't remember much after that. It all seemed to go silent and everything was in slow motion—like in a dream. I remember getting out of the car and slowly making my way toward the wreckage. I'm not sure why. I just knew at that moment I needed to see Christopher. I knew I could help him. I walked past Mrs. Whitling, oblivious to her cursing at the truck driver who was holding her back while trying to calm her as she screamed at the top of her lungs for Christopher. No one seemed to notice me at first, though under the circumstances, why would they? I remember mumbling 'I can save him,' even when I reached the truck and peered past the front that was crushed and bent. I never would have imagined the impact of a fragile nine-year-old boy's body could do so much damage. And then I saw him, lying still on the asphalt, more still than I think I've even seen a fallen tree lay stretched across the ground in the woods. He was still clutching tight the duck, or what was left of it. Feathers blew about everywhere. I remember looking at the socks hanging off his feet and wondering where his shoes had gone. That's when someone grabbed me and pulled me away, but I fought to get to Christopher, screaming almost hysterically 'I can save him'…"

Jacob stopped abruptly, suddenly remembering the presence of the angel seated beside him who he had momentarily forgotten. His eyes had grown misty at the long-ago memory, and he fought to quell the wall of water threatening to spill over the brim and streak down his cheeks. If there was one thing he did not want, it was to show this kind of weakness to an angel.

"I never said another prayer from that day on," continued Jacob, once he had managed to regain his composure. "Sure I would pretend when I was in the presence of my mother, or mouth a rosary just to make her happy. But not the way one should. Not until the night before she died, what little good that did."

~ ~ ~

"Of all things, death has always been the most difficult and trying for mortals to grasp," said Johiel softly when finally he spoke. "You veil it in shrouds, adorn it in black and cure it with endless tears or sorrow."

"You're saying it should be opposite, that death is a happy thing? Something we should cheer and perhaps dance a drunken jig to?" said Jacob though not meaning the words which left his tongue to sound as hostilely sarcastic as they did.

"In a manner of speaking, yes," answered Johiel who took no offense to the boy's mocking quip. "It has never failed to astound me how man looks upon the inevitability of death's arrival with fear. Oh sure, for a man who has lived a wicked and selfish life such fear is well warranted. But, for others, death should be a welcome celebration, for life in this world is not the true gift that has been given you, but what awaits on other side of the Gate, which death serves only to usher you through, no matter how tragic the circumstances it may come to do so."

"In other words, getting run down by a big rig while trying to do a kind and selfless deed is actually a gift mortals are just too blind and dumb to see?" said Jacob.

"What I'm saying, young Jacob, is even in the grimmest of tragedies, Light, if you choose to see it, glimmers," answered Johiel. "In your eyes, Christopher coming to the aid of a creature in need was met by a horrific punishment in which God stood idly by and did nothing. Yet is it so hard to cast your gaze on that memory that has so embittered you and see, maybe, the kind and selfless act, as you deemed it to be, and rightly so, was instead met not by punishment but instant reward? The same reward your mother would later come to receive—the reward of paradise?"

The mention of his mother grabbed Jacob, but only for a moment.

"No offense, but it's easy for you to say," said Jacob. "You have the advantage of seeing and knowing without a doubt everything we don't."

"Don't be so quick and sure in your assessment," said Johiel as he gazed out over the waters of the Van Gölü. "God has a tendency to navigate through this existence he has created in mysterious ways; ways so mysterious even angels are left to feel our way through darkness. In the end, as it is with mortals, all we really have left to us is faith."

Jacob seemed to mull carefully the angel's words and as he did he shook his head ever so subtly as though he held a private disagreement with some voice only he himself could hear.

"It sounds so easy coming from you, but I don't know if I can believe in anything I can't clearly see," he said quietly as though shamefully confessing his sins to a priest positioned on the other side of a screen partition inside a church confessional. "Even sitting here listening to you speak about Eden I find it hard to believe its true. Despite everything I've already seen and experienced, I'm not sure I believe a hundred percent. It's as though it's all been a dream. A long, drawn-out dream that I'm waiting to awaken from."

Once the words had left his lips, he regretted speaking them. And he braced himself for Johiel's reaction. Anger, disappointment, pity, he had no idea. Certainly a banishment from the island, and the chance to never venture past its shores to have his disbelief proven or otherwise about the mythic Gate and the promised land said to reside beyond it. Instead, Johiel placed a comforting hand on Jacob's shoulder and smiled; a smile that held the same unique kindness upon the youthful face as it did the one disguised with age.

"And that dear boy, you will come to discover, is the unfortunate chink in your armor," said Johiel. "For true faith resides in not what one can see, but what one can't. Which is what makes it such a difficult thing to truly possess, and why so few do. Believing in Eden and angels is not the challenge at hand for you. You will very soon find out that all this is far from a dream, and Neverland, as you so call it, will reveal itself to you in ways your imagination could never before comprehend. It is what comes later—that is where your true test lies. And then, mark my words, you will believe."

The angel's words brought both comfort and angst to Jacob at the same time. Then the golden eyes that held him firmly in their gaze quickly narrowed with a seriousness that made his body tighten.

"But be mindful, child," continued Johiel, his soothing voice suddenly taking a grave tone. "True faith, as it is known, is a rare and very powerful weapon, but easily perverted and twisted to the ways of the Darkness. Trust me when I tell you many much stronger than you have succumbed to the enchantments of the Shadows. Once you have been visited by faith—and I hold hope you will—grab hold of it. Tightly. And don't let go. For a day will come when you will be brought face to face with the Darkness and it will serve as your salvation, or your total undoing."

There was no smile of comfort to help soften the warning. And for the first time since leaving home for this ancient corner of civilization, Jacob felt a chilling shiver of fear move through him far more than any Infector could stir. The fleeting thought of getting on the next ferry back to the mainland and catching the quickest passage home passed as quickly as it came when he heard Gotham's voice. Jacob turned to find the angel standing nearby and the first thing to spring into his mind was to wonder how long Gotham had been standing there, and had he been listening the entire time?

"The day is only a few more hours from being upon us," Gotham announced.

Jacob felt the hand on his shoulder tighten and looked back at Johiel whose smile had once again returned.

"And so, the moment of truth is at hand," said the angel.

~ ~ ~

Gotham and Jacob followed Johiel down the path leading to the water. Moored to the far side of the dock was a small rowboat.

"It will take you a bit longer to cross, but it's the best way to make the journey as quietly and undetectable as possible," said Johiel.

Jacob eyed the small rickety boat, and then out across the vast expanse of open water that stretched as far as the eye could see and he felt a subtle queasiness stir in his stomach.

"I've sent word ahead alerting to your arrival. So you should have no trouble passing through," continued Johiel.

Gotham took Johiel's hand in his own. "Thank you for your trust. I know it was not an easy decision for you."

"To the contrary," replied Johiel, looking kindly upon Jacob whose attention was still held by the lake. "These few hours spent talking with the boy made it surprisingly less difficult."

When Gotham turned to board the small boat, Johiel grabbed him tightly at the wrist and held him firmly in his place. His face darkened with a seriousness.

"Be wary!" he said, leaning in closer and speaking with a low, hushed whisper so the boy would not hear. "It has been quite some time since you last passed. In that time, we've managed to eradicate the Furies from these shores. The Infectors, however, are an entirely different matter altogether; they have become a plague in these parts. I am certain your presence has not gone unnoticed."

Gotham gave a quiet nod of understanding to the words of caution offered him. Their final parting was quick and without words. Just a brief glance into one another's eyes and a friendly clasp of one another's shoulder. The boat rocked uneasily back and forth from the sudden weight when Gotham stepped down into it causing the water to splash loudly against its sides.

"Wish me luck," said Jacob when Johiel turned to him to bid his farewell.

"You have more than luck watching over you," said Johiel with a smile.

"I'm glad to have met you."

"And I you, young Jacob. But lament not, this is not goodbye." The angel held out his hand for the boy to take, not only as a handshake, but a guiding support to step down into the boat.

"Remember what I told you," said Johiel before releasing his hold. His gaze then shifted to Gotham. "Both of you."

"We'll be okay," said Jacob with a smile and carefully maneuvered his way to his seat on the plank opposite Gotham.

Once Johiel untied the thick woven rope tethering the boat to the dock, Gotham dipped the oars into the water and began guiding the boat away from the shore. Shivering, Jacob took hold of the hood of the sweatshirt he wore beneath the coat gifted to him by Gotham and brought it up over his head to help ward off the brisk chill blowing across the water. He then turned and gazed over his shoulder for one last look of the island they were leaving behind. Remaining at the edge of the landing was Johiel, though no longer the strong, youthful presence who saw them off, but instead the wilted and weathered figure who first greeted them upon their arrival.

CHAPTER FIFTEEN

Not a word was spoken between Gotham and Jacob as the small rowboat winded its way around Akdamar Island in a northerly direction. The screeching from a pair of water birds frolicking in the far-off distance was the only noise to penetrate the almost unnatural stillness surrounding them. That and the oars stirring the silvery waters stroke after stroke.

Jacob hugged his arms tighter against his body in an effort to stave off the growing chill. His thoughts remained not on the cold but on the island they had left behind, and he found himself replaying Johiel's words over and over again in his head as he was told of the Furies and how they came to be. And he found himself imagining Gotham with his sword drawn and bloodied standing over the small Nephilim boys, and he was moved with a strong desire to say something to the angel. What, he did not know. Something, though, anything to break the weighted silence they now found accompanying them.

"I'm sorry," he finally muttered softly.

"For what have you to be sorry?" asked Gotham.

"You know, about the story Johiel told of the Furies," answered Jacob. "I'm sorry you had to do such a horrible thing."

"That's just it, isn't it? I had a choice not to do it."

"How can you say that?" asked Jacob. "You were ordered to do it. If you hadn't, you would have become Fallen."

"And yet I became Fallen anyway," said Gotham in an answer weighted with the finality of coming to terms with what Jacob struggled to find escape out of a no-win situation.

They drifted on in silence for a dozen or so more strokes of the oars before Gotham took a turn at stirring conversation.

"I'm sorry, too," he said. "For the pain of losing your friend."

So the angel had overheard the conversation he had with Johiel, Jacob realized.

"I wish you would have felt comfortable enough to share your story with me when I asked," said Gotham. And in that moment Jacob wished he had done so as well.

"Tell me, though, what made you think you could save him?" Gotham then asked out of the blue.

Jacob gave a glance over his shoulder to where the angel was sitting with a confused look as though he didn't understand the question.

"You told Johiel you kept repeating 'I can save him, I can save him,' even screaming it at one point," Gotham pointed out. "What did you mean by that?"

Jacob turned away from the angel, a blank look on his face, and simply shrugged his shoulders. "I don't know."

A strange and uneasy feeling befell Gotham with those three words he knew weren't spoken with one hundred percent truth, but he did not press any further.

~ ~ ~

The cadence of Gotham's rowing was easy, almost leisurely. Yet the boat traveled swiftly across the water as though it were being guided by a crew of a dozen oarsmen. After a while, a seagull swooped across the water and hovered low over the boat eyeing its occupants. It was soon joined a short while later by another gull. Then another. And soon, what sounded like the squawking of hundreds of gulls could be heard echoing in the distance. Jacob leaned forward on the hard wooden plank upon which he sat and squinted his eyes against the darkness which occupied the waning hours of night. He focused hard in the direction of the noise and caught sight of what appeared to be a dark hump breaching the surface of the water far ahead.

"I think I see something," he announced to Gotham.

"Carpanak Island. We're almost there," noted Gotham without even a hint of breathlessness stemming from the great distance he had rowed.

The silvery darkness of night was beginning to recede and gave way to a soft lavender of the slow-approaching morning emerging from behind the eastern range of mountains when they finally reached the shallow waters surrounding the island and dragged the boat up on the flat rocky shore. It was a small island, much smaller than Akdamar. From what Jacob could see as he scouted the terrain before him in a few quick glances, it was a dry and desolate place. Dead, actually, it seemed at first look. Existing like the remnant of an old fingernail clipping snipped from the mainland and left to float forgotten upon the lake.

Jacob grabbed his pack from the boat and as he flung it across his shoulder he looked to the sky where the squawking from a large flock of gulls just awakening offered the only sign of life coming from the island and yet offering no clue as to what attracted them to congregate at such an uninviting place. And then he saw it. Just below the circling birds, there stood a large structure of some kind several yards from the water's edge.

"What is it?" Jacob asked Gotham.

"At one time, it was a monastery," came the reply.

"They sure love their churches around here, don't they?" Jacob mumbled to himself before quickly taking after Gotham along a narrow path of beach pocked with clumps of sage which quickly gave way to rocky ground.

Their steps treaded over the dry, brittle remains of overgrown vegetation covering the interior of the island in a patchwork of colors patterned in hues of gold, copper and gray. As they walked, Jacob's attention stayed fixed on the mediaeval monastery which, in many ways, reminded him of the one they had left on Akdamar Island. And yet it was completely different. The large rectangular-shaped structure with its yellow cut stone facade and earthen roof covered with more of the same withered, dead plants that sprouted from the ground appeared almost invisible, blending into the surrounding landscape like some giant chameleon.

Jacob hurried to keep up with Gotham's ever-quickening pace. He wondered to himself what the sudden rush was, but he did not ask, keeping his focus instead on the obstacle of rock lay strewn across his path. And as he did he soon came to realize the square-shaped rocky berms were not the island itself, but man-made footprints; ruins that served as foundations to numerous other buildings that had long ago vanished. What had they once been? Jacob wondered silently. And who once chose to live in this dead secluded spot surrounded by a dead lake? Had Gotham been in closer reach, Jacob would have posed the questions to him, but the angel had moved far ahead of him forcing Jacob to walk even faster in an attempt to catch up.

"Can we look inside?" asked Jacob when he managed to find himself once again at the angel's side and nearing the monastery.

"Trust me, there's nothing of interest in there," Gotham replied curtly.

And at first glance Jacob was inclined to agree. For where time had been unkind to the church on Akdamar, it seemed to have taken a pointed vengeance against this particular monastery. Sections of the walls, plain and void of any biblical carvings or storytelling that had so intrigued the boy at Akdamar, were in various stages of crumbling, as though gnawed upon by some stone-loving rats. The roof of the monastery dome—or what was left of it—was not only much smaller and less grand in scale than that of the church on Akdamar, but it was riddled with gaping holes from where more dead plants sprouted, providing nesting for many of the gulls that appeared to have settled in. Yet there was something about it. Somewhere within such a dead place there was an unmistakable beat of life which somehow seemed to tug at Jacob as they passed in the shadow of the decrepit shell of stone. It pulled at him. Fought to draw him closer.

Then suddenly, from out of the corner of his eye, Jacob caught a glimpse of movement coming from one of the open windows cut into the wall of the monastery. He stopped walking and stared into the hollow blackness framed within the arched opening and was stricken to spy a figure on the other side staring down at him. The dark deep blue from the blanketing shroud of the early morning revealed only the sinewy build of a shirtless torso. The face, however, was hidden except for the stark gleaming of two golden orbs peering out from the darkness, like light shining through the openings of two keyholes, and Jacob's heart instantly quickened. Then, from an adjacent window, Jacob caught the silhouette of a second naked torso. And still a third from another.

"There's someone here," whispered Jacob in a voice much too hushed to have reached Gotham's ears. He then suddenly remembered the alley in Tatvan and a pronounced coldness descended upon him. The feel of a phantom claw pressed threateningly against his back made his skin crawl and his muscles tightened, and he was left with only one thought.

Infectors!

Or perhaps Furies. Then again, maybe some other type of demon he had yet to learn about. One thing was certain, Jacob had no interest in another introduction. Before panic could set in, something very odd happened. From out of nowhere a white cat suddenly leapt into view from inside the monastery onto the ledge of the window framing the first ominous figure and Jacob recognized instantly from its solitary ear and fox-like tail that it was Van Gogh. The cat, who Jacob had last seen swimming out across the lake, paced back and forth along the ledge before finally taking a seat, and the hand of the figure standing in the window behind reached out and began stroking the feline.

Slowly, Jacob backed away from the monastery. His eyes darted back and forth among the numerous windows looking for other shadowy figure, but all he could see were the three, all marked by a set of glowing eyes piercing through the darkness like those of jungle cats laying in wait in tall grass. They followed Jacob in unison as he finally took off in a sprint in Gotham's direction.

"There's someone inside. Watching from the windows," he gasped breathlessly, nipping once more at the angel's heels.

"Pay them no mind and just keep walking," answered Gotham calmly without so much as a glance toward the monastery.

"I thought at first they might be Infectors?"

"They're not Infectors."

"Then maybe they're the Furies Johiel warned us about."

"They're not Furies."

"Then who?" pressed Jacob while stepping clumsily along the rocky, uneven ground.

"They're Powers."

Powers?

"What's that…another sort of demon?" asked Jacob.

"Powers are a hierarchy of angels," explained Gotham with a growing irritability in his voice. "They're protectors. And right now we're treading upon what they protect."

"Now it makes sense," said Jacob with a huff of relief. "That explains Van Gogh. He swam here to deliver Johiel's message to these…Powers."

"Had he not, we would not be strolling across this island now. In one piece, at least."

"Aren't you exaggerating just a tad?" asked Jacob with a light chuckle.

"You find it hard to believe, I take," said Gotham without the faintest hint of amusement.

"Just a little. I mean, we're talking about angels after all. Who better to know than you?"

Jacob barely finished speaking when his foot hit a ragged rock protruding from the ground sending him stumbling forward. Gotham quickly grabbed hold of his arm and steadied him from seeing through what would have been painful face plant.

"You're right, I am an angel. Which means I know of what I speak," Gotham growled sternly while keeping his grip tightly on Jacob. There was an icy steeliness in the intense burning of his eyes which brought an immediate seriousness to Jacob's face. "You still quite don't understand, do you? 'Never take your own revenge, beloved, but leave room for the wrath of God, for it is written, "Vengeance is Mine, I will repay," saith the Lord.' Are you familiar with the scripture?"

It took every ounce of strength Jacob had just to nod his head.

"Who do you think is tasked with carrying out the repayment of such vengeance? It is us, the angels, who serve as the messengers, and you'd be wise to take to heart there exists amongst us many who relish in cleaving both the sin and the sinner," spoke Gotham through gritted teeth. "The images dressed in halos and harps you choose to entertain in your mind do not exist. Angels, yes, but the Powers are unmerciful slayers when called upon and they are as cold as the vengeance they serve.

And heed my words, they are as dangerous as that which hunts you, if not more so."

When he had finished, the brightness in Gotham's eyes slowly receded and a somewhat sympathetic look softened his brow as he searched for understanding in the boy's unblinking eyes. He then looked to the sky, not directly upward, but to the east.

"We must hurry," he said. "It will be light soon, and the Van Gölü will soon awake with ferries carrying travelers."

He released his hold on Jacob with a reassuring, almost apologetic pat and continued on leaving the boy to quietly contemplate following him further. Jacob glanced back toward the monastery, and had it not been in the path of any possible exit he may have turned and retraced his steps in a quick retreat. Instead he chose to follow Gotham. After all, at this point, where else was there to go?

They circled around the monastery and were met by a mass of rock which rose steeply in two terraced shapes from the rest of the island's flat surface. Gotham swiftly scaled the gray, jagged monolith with the graceful ease of a mountain goat, leaving Jacob struggling to keep up. When he finally reached the top, the teen collapsed in a breathless, sweaty heap, his hands bleeding here and there with the nicks and scrapes he suffered from the rock's sharp edges. Once he caught his breath he rose to his feet and circled around surveying the expanse of blue water surrounding them.

"So now what?" he asked the angel, sounding at a loss.

"We go through the Gate," answered Gotham, shrugging off his heavy overcoat and proceeding to unbutton his shirt.

Again Jacob scoured the surroundings, focusing first on the dragon-shaped claw of the mainland stretching out toward the island. Nowhere, for as far as the eye could see, was there any sign of a gate, much less a garden of paradise, fabled or otherwise. The confused look on Jacob's sweat-shined face grew even more pronounced when a sudden faint whispering of voices came up from behind him like gasps from within the gentle breeze. He slowly swung his head around and looked over his shoulder with disbelief across the main body of the lake that seemed to stretch without end from which the familiar chatter rose and sailed its way across the dark waters. And suddenly he knew.

"Right over there, in the center of the lake," came Gotham's voice from behind. "Sealed off from the world long ago by the remnants of the mighty flood that swallowed this earth."

Jacob turned his baffled gaze from the sea of water to the angel. "You mean…?"

Gotham stripped off his shirt, picked up his coat that lay at his feet upon the rock and tossed his belongings to the boy.

"And now you must listen very carefully to what I am about to say," he said stepping toward Jacob once the boy had packed the clothing away in his pack. "We now come to the most dangerous part of our journey. I will need you to hold tight to me. And when I tell you to do so, you will need to fill your lungs with the deepest breath you've ever been forced to hold."

Jacob listened carefully to the instructions given him, all the while feeling his heart pounding harder inside his chest. Whether from fear or anticipation of the unknown he had no real inkling.

"And whatever you do," Gotham enunciated with a dire urgency. *"Do not! Let! Go!"*

The words came in three, separate, direct commands that reverberated in a continuous echo in Jacob's head. He turned and looked back over his shoulder again at the water, vast and seemingly endless. It may have been a lake, but the reality was it appeared more like an ocean to the eyes. And then he heard a loud fluttering behind him, and Jacob's eyes caught sight of a majestic image captured in the faint shadow cast by the fast-approaching dawn down upon the rocky ground at his feet. When he swung back around his mouth fell slack at the awesome sight of Gotham standing before him, his mighty gray wings unfurled in all their paramount grandeur and power. It was a vision Jacob had only been privy to witnessing one other time in his life and yet it met him as though it was the first, and in that instant any fear or trepidation he felt instantly vanished and instead became replaced with an incited eagerness to spring off the rocky landing they were standing upon.

"So then, are you ready?" asked Gotham, the corners of his mouth rising before the answer met his ears.

~   ~   ~

The water reflected back to Jacob a crystal-clear mirror image of himself being carried in Gotham's arms as the two skimmed across the lake's surface. So close were they to the water that Jacob was able to reach out and trawl his fingers across its surface. The sound of the angel's wings beat with a rhythmic cadence when suddenly Jacob felt an abrupt stomach-churning pull upward and the water and the world below abruptly fell away from them as they sailed straight up into the soft, pre-dawn lit sky.

"You okay?" asked Gotham grinning, his wings flapping with an ease of Spanish fans in the clutches of two elderly Señoritas gently shooing from their face the heat of a summer's day.

Jacob gave a nod he was more than okay and glanced down. For the first time, he could see almost in its entirety the ocean-sized Van Gölü from shore to shore. It was a tremendously beautiful sight, and yet nerve-rattling. Never before in all his experiences jumping off bridges or high mountain cliffs had he ever experienced a fear or timidity of heights. Now, suddenly, he felt an unexpected twist to his insides that made him tighten his hold on Gotham. As he did, he noticed immediately a look of concern cross the angel's face that was most prominent in the crease that met the middle of his furrowed brow. His eyes had narrowed and were slowly and carefully searching all around.

"Something wrong?" asked Jacob.

"Remember I told you we were approaching the most dangerous point of our journey?" said Gotham. "I sense such danger is close, and its eyes are at this moment upon us."

The words brought a sense of alarm to Jacob, and like the angel he began to look all about them. All he could see, however, was sky and water and ranges of mountain surrounding them.

The angel again repeated to Jacob his earlier instructions to hold tight to him and to capture a deep breath upon his command, and again Jacob nodded his understanding, then proceeded to open his mouth to speak. Before he could utter even a syllable, it was as though an invisible trap door of air upon which they were standing suddenly gave way sending them hurtling in free fall head- first downward back toward the waiting waters. It was beyond any drop the most stomach-stealing of roller coasters in existence could serve to a car full of screaming thrill-seekers. Jacob managed a shrieking scream, his eyes widely fixed on the lake that was fast approaching. The fear was short-lived and quickly replaced with an indescribable rush that surged through his body unlike any other he had felt before, and his scream quickly morphed to an ecstatic yelp.

The air whistled loudly past his ears and blew through his hair. He had to consciously remember to hang tight to Gotham, but his arms longed to release their hold of the angel and stretch themselves out into the open air like they themselves were wings. The water grew closer, a mass of blue that looked to be rising up in a growing swell from the earth's floor to greet them. Jacob felt like he could reach out and touch it.

"Get ready!" instructed Gotham.

Jacob's body tightened with anticipation as he prepared to take that final, deep breath of air when, suddenly, a tremendous force slammed into them, and instead of inhaling, Jacob felt the wind knocked painfully from his body. It felt like a car collision. The jolt nearly pried him free from Gotham, but he felt the angel's hand retain its tight grip on him. Gotham quickly regained control of the air through which the two were sent spinning, but dizzying stars continued to flash before Jacob's eyes which he fought desperately to look past. Then he felt it— a sudden biting cold he first experienced in the dank back alley in Tatvan. And Jacob didn't need clear vision to know instantly what had blocked their way.

~ ~ ~

At first they were nowhere to be seen. The sky appeared an empty void except for the voluminous clouds gathered in billowy clusters all around. Yet it was from the clouds they revealed themselves, their shapes camouflaged in the darker shades of the marbled cumuli like so many insects gifted with the ability to hide in plain sight upon the bark of a tree trunk or among the leaves of a plant. They swooped in like patches of night. There appeared to be a half dozen, at least, flying all about. Winged creatures, just as Gotham was. Though there was nothing angelic about them in the least.

"Infectors?" asked Jacob in a voice holding hope his guess was off the mark.

"Remember when I told you back in Tatvan how you had been lucky to have been spared witnessing their true form?" answered Gotham. "It now appears your luck, unfortunately, has just ran out."

Jacob watched with growing unease the circling figures. They were shrouded all in black, phantom faceless beings wrapped in flowing garbs of darkness that made them appear more like wispy shadows that had been cut loose from the physical form which had once cast them upon the ground. The wings they possessed were enormous and threatening, not shaped with the smooth, sleek quills like that of a bird, but the vein-etched, crepey skin reminiscent of a bat. Or dragon. And when the wings flapped, they sliced through the air with a loud, wicked sound. Gotham was fast to his sword, its blade singing as it was drawn with lightning speed from a concealed sheath of skin hidden within the feathered plumes of his wings.

"Take heed this warning demons, for I will only offer it once," Gotham called out to the shadowy figures hovering about them. "Clear yourselves from our path, or be sure my blade will! Or has the black rot that has long befouled you cast such a long pall over your memory that you've forgotten the fate of your brethren that came between an angel and the waters below?"

A growling, ominous laughter echoed through the skies as though coming up from the bowels of a cavern carved deep in a mountain side.

"Your stinging sword may be swift, angel," came a deep, menacing voice from one of the figures, slithering through the air with a hiss reminiscent of a snake, "but it's wielded by one hand, while the other is hobbled by that which cowers in its noble but futile protection."

Before the last word had finished being uttered, one of the Infectors suddenly rushed forward with a great terrifying speed while sounding loudly a metal-grating scream. Gotham drew back his sword and just when the phantom demon was within its reach the gleaming blade was swung forth. The black shape exploded like gunpowder as the angel's sword ripped through it. The piercing scream abruptly fell silent and a ball of ashy soot that had once been the slain Infector drifted momentarily in the air before dissipating into nothingness.

"The approaching sun has yet to greet the Toros Taglari and already you are one fewer," Gotham called out to the remaining dark figures with a steely confidence.

"Cast aside the baggage that weights you, angel, and you are free to pass," a hissing voice replied.

Jacob turned and saw the angel's face darken behind the golden eyes that were now blazing bright with flames of contempt narrowed and fixed on the Infectors hovering before them in the distance. His mouth parted and when he spoke it was with an icy, restrained tone.

"Make haste to the unholy domicile whose halls you have chosen to dwell, or shall the waters below be fed with another helping of heads severed from your smote carcasses?"

The Infectors let out a collective endless scream and began to suddenly circle. Moving at a frightening pace, they came at Gotham and Jacob, swooping in and darting through the sky like a flock of angry ravens, yet staying out of reach of the sword poised to strike the one who ventured too close. Following their movements proved dizzying to Jacob's eyes, and the chorus of high- pitched cries filling the air even more painful to his ears. Yet he dared to not slacken the hold he had on Gotham in order to cover them with his hands.

"The waters are about to savor a new delicacy," came the serpent-like voice of one of the grim figures passing dangerously close.

Gotham watched with a fiery coldness the black shapes soaring past when suddenly he was struck hard from behind. The firm stance he had held was momentarily lost to him, and it was all the Infectors needed. They came at him two of them from different directions, striking him repeatedly with an unrelenting viciousness. Gotham struggled to regain his lost footing, but the barrage of pounding blows and stinging rips of the Infectors' knife-like claws slicing into his skin became too overwhelming. The Infector' words proved correct—holding onto the boy had unintentionally hobbled Gotham at a moment where he needed both his hands free to fight back the overpowering malefic swarm. The blows intensified, coming in rapid, merciless order, and Gotham knew it would not cease until the boy had been knocked free from his clutches.

Still, Gotham held tight with all the strength he could muster while swinging blindly with his sword to no avail. The pounding from the winged figures and blinding pain of exertion throbbing in the striating muscles bulging in his weakening arm holding Jacob protectively to his side was taking its toll. He could feel his hold giving way and he cried out with a growing anguish.

"Remember what I told you," Gotham managed to sputter painfully to the boy.

One of the black figures swooped down upon Gotham from directly above and delivered him a powerful, glancing blow. The angel's arm finally ceded for mercy and he felt Jacob slip from his protective grasp yet managed in the midst of his fall to grab hold of Gotham's ankle. The suffering blows relented somewhat as several of the figures fell away, and Gotham knew their attentions had turned to the boy who was dangling precariously in the open air like ripe grapes being eyed by a passing hungry fox. Immediately, he began kicking his leg in an attempt to shake free the weight clutching his ankle. Jacob cried out for him to stop while struggling to hold firm to the angel's leg. He looked to the water below and knew his safety lurked within its tides. Yet despite the steep cliffs he had cast himself freely from in the past, Jacob found the long drop beneath his dangling feet too daunting to succumb. He then heard the flapping of the beastly wings of the Infectors who had taken leave of abusing Gotham, and Jacob looked to see two of the screeching phantoms heading toward him, and his heart quickened.

There was then heard another rustling stir the wind, and he turned his wide eyes upward to see two other black shapes who had returned to resume their torturous beating of Gotham suddenly explode in a puff of billowy blackness. And when the soot-filled air cleared two angels with mighty wings and swords drawn could be seen against the soft dawn-colored sky. Jacob knew immediately that the winged warriors who had flown to their rescue were the Powers whose flaming tiger eyes lurking within mysterious silhouettes he had spied peering out from behind the walls of the monastery on Carpanak Island. And in that moment he not only came to understand the reason for the cabalistic vigil they held there amid the isolated ruins, but he realized in the instant he witnessed the fierce look they carried in their face that everything Gotham had said of them, and more, was true.

In short order, the remaining Infectors quickly attempted to disperse amid the sudden presence of the Powers, but their retreat came too late and the sky was soon filled with the ashen snowfall of their demise. Jacob released a victorious cry, but his sense of relief was brief when the spine-shivering cry of an Infector once more rang painfully in his ears.

~   ~   ~

Jacob turned and saw the blackness suddenly upon him. He was given not a chance to yell out or reexamine his fear of the stomach-pulling distance that remained between himself and the water below and instinctively released his hold of Gotham's ankle. The fall seemed eternal before he was immersed in the icy coldness of the Van Gölü, and the piercing cries of the Infector momentarily snuffed into silence was replaced with the peaceful bubbling of the water. Jacob looked all around him desperately seeking the Gate Gotham told him was within the waters. All he could see, however, was nothing but a dark blue emptiness surrounding him, and that, too, was okay with him. Because for a fleeting moment he felt safe treading in this underwater world out of reach of the danger lurking above from the Infectors, who had not given chase past the water's surface. His refuge was short-lived and his straining lungs soon had him paddling toward air.

When he reached the surface he came face to face with the black shape with its white lifeless eyes waiting for him, and it let out a loud, angry wail that sent a rolling ring of ripples across the water. Jacob attempted to retreat back into the waves but the Infector snatched hold of him, preventing him from escaping.

"Unfortunately, Nephilim, this is as close to Eden as you'll ever get," hissed forth a voice from within the phantom shape. Jacob attempted to put forth a mask of bravery, but his fear was thick as he looked into the deep black emptiness that offered not a glimpse of the demon's cloaked face except two empty sockets of white blazing bright with a hatred burning from within. He then heard what sounded like the scrapping of dagger blades running against one another and he caught sight of the razor-sharp clawed hand the Infector slowly raised. And as the creature drew back its hand, Jacob clenched his jaw and tried to steel himself for the inevitable.

Gotham was suddenly upon the Infector's back, and the demon let loose a horrific cry. It quaked and shook violently to and fro in a desperate attempt to shake loose the angel, but Gotham's hold was strong and fast, like a rodeo cowboy riding a raging, snorting and violently bucking bull. With his sword clutched in one hand, he grabbed hold of the Infector's head and, as he did, the creature's face—gray-skinned, scaled and too monstrous to behold— lurched forward from within the shroud covering it. Jacob cried out with a momentary terror then drew back a fist and sent a debilitating blow straight into the snarling ugliness.

The Infector roared with anger, a murderous look the only thing alive in its otherwise empty dead eyes, and as it prepared to strike with its clawed hand, Gotham, backed by a look of vengeance cast upon his battered face, drew back his sword and swung. The Infector burst into a cloud of black ashen specks that were sent adrift upon the wind, and all that remained was its shrouded head clutched in Gotham's hand that was tossed aside into the water like a discarded head of cabbage.

It was not the last of the Infectors, and almost immediately another black figure sounding an angry cry was racing toward them low across the water. Gotham quickly pulled Jacob from the lake and as he took flight upward he gestured to the water with a sweep of his hand. The water instantly began to churn and bubble. And, as the Infector gave chase with a growing fierceness, a column of water shot upward, and from within it the liquid shape of some mythic leviathan took form. The Infector saw it and cried out, but it was too late. The watery beast took hold of it with its crushing jaws and dragged the demon, shrieking all the way, down into the murky depths.

Gotham soared upward past the Powers who continued to lay waste to the remaining Infectors.

"Go quickly, or there will surely be more to come," one of the Powers called out to Gotham from behind the clouded remains of the slaughter that filled the sky.

Gotham nodded his gratitude to the angel then turned to the sound of yet another Infector fast-approaching them at a terrifying speed.

"Take your breath, as deep as you can," Gotham instructed Jacob, and the sky once again released its support of them and they plummeted toward the water.

Like pelicans dive-bombing their way into a school of fish to fill their gullets with a fresh feast, they broke through the water's surface and disappeared from the world above. For a brief moment, Jacob felt a need to breathe a sigh of relief when it looked as though they had finally made it out of reach of the hideous creatures. With nothing except what seemed to be an eternal pit of water ahead of them, he dared not allow one single air bubble escape from his nostrils.

~ ~ ~

Guided by the morning light penetrating the underwater realm from above in streaming, glistening bands, Gotham took them further into the foreign depths with a great speed. They quickly came upon the peaks of a cluster of massive stromatolites emerging from deep within the lake's bowels like gnarled fossilized fingers of rock formed from the invisible grains of salt and sediment churning in the ever-growing icy currents. The further they descended, the more stromatolites appeared, rising up from the unseen lake floor like a kelp bed in a colony of tree-like trunks that grew more monstrous in size the deeper they went.

It wasn't long before the first skull appeared, resting on its side upon a shelf jutting from the main body of one of the stromatolites. At first glance Jacob thought it to be an odd deformity of the encrusted surface. Then he noticed the teeth. Not human teeth, but the sharp, fang-like choppers like that of a wild dog. And his mind instantly flashed to the image of the creatures that attacked above the lake waters, the gnashing teeth lining their cruel mouths, and the heads that were severed from the grotesquely winged bodies and tossed into the water where they plummeted from sight.

Further on, another head. Then another. And soon numerous heads lay littered among the pylons, all in various states of decomposition. While some had obviously been there for unknown ages, others were still encased in the gray, reptilian-like skin that was slowly flaking and breaking away in torn bits of decay to be carried away by the icy currents. Jacob was almost thankful that the rays of sunlight illuminating their path grew dimmer and dimmer until they were finally blocked by the towering pillars. The water grew murkier and more frigid. Jacob felt his body growing numb. He began to tremble, though from the cold, he was not certain. There was an ominous, unsettling feeling deep within the thicket of the neptunian, petrified forest. Nothing stirred. Not even a trace of the pearl mullet fish, the lone life force that had somehow managed to acclimate and survive in the lifeless, liquid void of the Van Gölü could be seen. The building pressure began to squeeze down on Jacob's head. His ears began to throb with pain, as though offering a warning that swimming any deeper would threaten an implosion of his skull. He felt his lungs beginning to betray him, and quickly burn inside his chest with a growing need for air. And with no sign of a gate, or light, or an end to what appeared to be a seemingly endless watery tomb before them, a panic began its rise up inside him.

Despite the swift speed with which the angel propelled the two of them forward, it suddenly felt to Jacob to take on the pace of a snail. He began to kick his legs with a flailing urgency, and as he did he felt the angel's hand pressed against the center of his chest take hold of him tighter and pull him in closer as though sensing the boy was bracing to bolt. And from the angel's touch a familiar warmth moved through Jacob, working to soothe him, but it was not enough to ease the increasing pressure crushing down on his skull the deeper they descended, or the screaming that was erupting from his lungs. So intense were both, he could not decipher which was causing him the greatest crisis.

What he did know was he needed air, and he needed it now. Or surely within another moment or two he would slip away and come to rest among the litter of skulls in their wake—not just his head, but his entire body left to drift in an eternal slumber in this underwater graveyard. Jacob's struggles increased. No longer did he care about the Gate. No longer did he care to lay witness to and set foot inside the biblical paradise promised on the other side; all of it, as elusive as its legend, and now proving to be just as dangerous.

He began thrashing about wildly, flailing and punching until he felt his body free itself from the angel's hold. His legs kicked with all their might desperate to force himself upward away from Gotham and toward the surface that appeared to be floating a hundred miles above, but a hand grabbed him by the ankle halting his ascent and yanked him back down. And as it did his mouth opened and the last gasp of air held inside his lungs escaped him in a precious burst of bubbles.

Face to face with the angel, Jacob's eyes were wide as saucers and fixed with a knowing terror. He tried to exhale, but there was nothing left inside him. The last bit of life squeezed from his chest. And then he heard a voice.

"Relax, Jacob!"

It belonged to Gotham, but Gotham's mouth did not move to speak. Gotham reached out and grabbed Jacob by the back of the neck and pulled him toward him. In an instant his mouth clamped down over the boy's nose. Jacob's eyes widened even larger and he struggled to pull away. The angel's hold was firm. And Jacob felt a breath move past through his nostrils and journey down into his chest to fully inflate his withered lungs.

The panic quickly subsided, and so, too, did Jacob's struggles. Gotham held the boy's head in his hands, and in the watery stillness Jacob heard the angel's voice echo from within his head.

"We're almost there. Just a ways longer. You trust me?"

The eyes staring back at Jacob appeared like swirling spheres of molten gold and a great calm came over him. He nodded in agreement and the angel took hold of him once again and led him through the murky unknown. They soon reached what appeared to be the lake floor. There the stromatolites grew thicker, extending in every direction like prehistoric tree roots twisting and curving and jutting upward suddenly, creating a vast mountainous underwater sculpture pocked with arches and cave openings. It was a mesmerizing sight. So amazing was it, in fact, it seemed to take Jacob's attention away from the skull-splitting pain that continued to hold him in its grip. Never had Jacob seen, or imagined anything like it. And yet there was a strange familiarity to it all.

They made their way through a maze of arches and tight, narrow passageways that eventually led to the mouth of a giant cave-like opening. As they approached it, Jacob's heart quickened.

He began to feel his lungs start to strain once again, and the blackness which lurked inside offered no sign they were closing in on the end of their trek. Still, the panic that had previously engulfed Jacob remained at bay, for he now knew the angel would see him through safely. And yet he was unable to keep his body from tightening when they passed through the cave entrance and into the pitch darkness waiting inside.

CHAPTER SIXTEEN

There is darkness.

And then there is a darkness beyond the reaches even the deepest of blacks are able to color. A darkness which manages to swallow from memory anything and everything that ever existed outside its realm. An infinite void of nothingness. An utter, and inescapable grip of absolute emptiness.

Such was the darkness Jacob found filling the inside of the underwater cave into which Gotham led him.

Solid.

Thick.

A wall of black impenetrable by even the brightest of lights. For here, light had long ago been vanquished, if it ever existed. Any glint permanently extinguished by this living breathing entity unto itself, consuming everything in its path. And it was in that instant Jacob knew there was no gate, at least not as he had imagined in his mind. A gleaming ornamental barrier welded of steel bars chained and padlocked shut did not exist. No, this—this blackness—this was the Gate. For what made for a more impregnable passage than this unwelcoming darkness? Or the merciless Powers posted as guards at its entrance? And to anyone who doubted a breach was possible, a pile of skulls strewn along the threshold offered a final, definitive warning.

Jacob fought to keep his hands at his sides and not hold them out in front of him to feel for any unseen obstacles lurking ahead. From the feel of the icy currents flowing against his face, he knew they were still maintaining a great speed through the never-ending emptiness and it unnerved him to be going as fast as they were and not be able to see anything in their path. That and feeling Gotham's breath which filled his lungs start to give way made his heart begin pounding wildly inside his chest. And Gotham, feeling the manic drumming beneath where his hand clutched the boy by the chest, offered a comforting squeeze while tightening his hold.

"Just a ways further," the angel's voice once again reverberated reassuringly inside his head.

And just when the blackness smothering them vowed to stretch on for all eternity, Jacob felt an inexplicable shift within the bottomless pit. He couldn't see anything, but there was definitely a change in the direction they swam. They were moving upward. And the pain from the crushing grip that had taken hold of his head began to slowly recede. Then, suddenly, in the far distance, a flicker, piercing the void. A pin-prick of light, like a distant star in the night sky. Dim at first, it slowly grew brighter the closer they swam toward it. And larger. For a moment, it was a comforting sight. Then a jarring thought came to Jacob. From out of nowhere his brain regurgitated the memory of a TV show he once saw on near-death experiences and the people who had them. They each shared the same story of traveling toward a light at the end of a dark tunnel. Was he now passing through some tunnel of death to "The Light"? Had he, unbeknownst himself, succumbed to drowning he wondered as he clenched his hands into fists to ensure he was still a physical form of flesh and blood while staring cautiously at the brightening light ahead.

Gradually eating away at the surrounding shroud of blackness, the light beckoned Jacob and Gotham through a gaping breach punctured through the ceiling of the cave shaped like the giant blowhole of some ancient sea creature lumbering in the ocean depths. Bands of illumination spilled through the mouth and streamed toward them like phantom arms of salvation out-stretched to greet them. The fraying blackness began to retreat, recoiling in the presence of this undesirable intruder, this glorious light, into its lightless den. And with the light came sight from the temporary blindness that had enveloped Jacob; and what a sight it was.

~ ~ ~

Coming up from the belly of the abyss, Jacob found himself ascending through an underwater cavern immense in size housing a colony of stalactites jutting down in all shapes and sizes from the jagged rocky skin inside the cave like massive fangs lining the jaws of a beast. It was both breathtaking and yet baleful in its beauty. And had his lungs not been engulfed once more in a burning strain to breathe, Jacob found he would have lingered there, mesmerized in the fact that neither he nor Gotham had met their demise impaled at the end of one of the twisted skewers of rock while shooting forward blindly through the blackness.

Once they had emerged from the intestines of the cave, they were met by a vast, open sea and Jacob immediately felt the noticeable change. The water carried the color of an almost dreamlike swirl of blue and green-tinted turquoise. It flowed with a crystal-clear clarity, and unlike the waters of the lake they had left behind, it was teeming with life. Schools of fish of every kind and size swam in great numbers all around, and a rainbow of coral and sea plants formed an underwater paradise for as far as the eye could see. Jacob wriggled his way free of Gotham's grasp, and this time his squirming for freedom wasn't hampered by an overpowering hand to keep him clutched to the angel's side. Instead, Jacob was given a forceful push that sent him streaming upward toward the glistening ripple of sunlight that danced on the water's surface above. He paddled and kicked furiously towards it until he crashed through, mouth agape to inhale deeply the first gulp of the life-giving salty sea air awaiting him. With the first few breaths came a sharp pain that shot through his chest. It felt as if the air itself was infested with razor blades slicing through his starved lungs. And as he convulsed in a drawn-out fit of coughing and sputtering, he noticed Gotham bobbing upon the water nearby, exerting not so much as a gasp from their near-suffocating trek and calmly waiting for the boy to regain his composure.

"Tell me again what the upside is to this Nephilim thing?" Jacob spat angrily, his voice laced with an envious resentment. "I can't fly. I can barely hold my breath. I just now nearly drowned. All I seem to have been given from this deal is two humps on my back, the ability to understand some birds and a few fancy moves. Hardly selling points."

Gotham remained silent recognizing the boy's growing frustration that soon subsided with the labored hacking and gasps of breath as his attention was drawn to the sea depths beneath him.

"The water, it tingles," noted Jacob. He lifted his arm out of the blue ocean upon which he treaded, his eyes following the liquid beads trickling across his skin as though he was expecting to see something clinging to his arm. What, he had no idea.

"The Dilmun Sea," said Gotham. "Filled with the waters that flow from the heart of Eden from which all life came to be."

"Eden? You're saying we're here?" asked Jacob. Yet there remained a guarded doubt in his voice.

His eyes began searching feverishly the surrounding horizon. Yet all he could see was an endless expanse of water stretching every which way he attempted to look and coming toward him in a parade of gently rolling swells. The only other thing in existence besides the water was a bank of dense fog in the distance resting upon the surface of sea appearing like some impregnable fortress wall.

"I see nothing," Jacob exclaimed with a resigned disappointment.

Gotham smiled. Not with amusement, but with a disappointment for which he seemed prepared.

"Unfortunately, that remains your greatest obstacle," said the angel.

Before Jacob could press Gotham further about Eden's location, the angel closed his eyes and retreated into a moment of silence. His mouth then parted as though to take a breath, and from his lips came a litany of whispers. They were spoken as words, but they met the ear as foreign sounds that Jacob had never before heard. And yet they were as familiar as the English he spoke. Repeated over and over in a string of hushed tones, they spilled out into the air, swirling about before dispersing its echoed calling into the silence of the water itself. Jacob waited but nothing seemed to happen. Then, there was a splashing sound and Jacob turned to find in the distance a dolphin leaping from the water high into the air before disappearing back into the depths. A moment later it leapt again, followed by a second dolphin. Soon a third could be seen, then a fourth. Within moments, what looked like a herd numbering at more than fifty could be seen stampeding across the ocean toward them like wild stallions galloping across the open plains.

Jacob stared wide-eyed at the spectacle. Never had he seen anything so fantastic as this pod of dolphins ripping through the water with such aquatic grace and prowess. And for an instant he felt his heart begin to race when they were suddenly upon him and Gotham, cutting through the water a hand's reach away and leaping overhead through the air in synchronized, balletic arches, their sleek gray bodies glistening brightly in the sun. When he realized there was no fear of being trampled, he turned to Gotham, who was smiling as widely as he was.

"Take hold, and enjoy the ride!" Gotham cried out over the churning splashes with a mischievous wink. And with that he latched onto the dorsal fin of one of the passing dolphins and was swiftly whisked away.

"Wait!" Jacob called out excitedly.

He turned back to the approaching pod. The sheer number coming at him and leaping above was unnerving. His attempts to follow them all with his eyes while trying to decipher which one to grab ahold of made him grow dizzy and disoriented until, finally, he blindly reached out and managed to find a passing fin to latch onto and was jerked into motion.

Jacob felt the adrenaline pumping wildly through his veins. If flying through the air while holding fast to an angel proved to be the biggest rush he felt in all of his extreme sport adventures, racing at high-speed on the back of a dolphin across the ocean's surface with the cool, refreshing spray of water across his face was a very close second. Jacob let out a series of loud whoops. It was like riding an underwater bronco without the fear of being bucked off. The other dolphins followed along for a bit, continuing their stampede before they began to fall away one by one and disappear from sight into the depths of the ocean. The sea once again fell still and the two remaining dolphins with their passengers holding tight continued to skim across the tide toward the fog bank that loomed ahead. When Jacob saw where they were heading, his exuberant laughter and smile faded. Gotham looked back over his shoulder at the boy.

"I'll see you on the other side," he called out before being swallowed up by the dense cloud-like vapor.

For a split second, Jacob felt an urge to let go of the dolphin beneath him and fall free to the open water. Instead, his hold on the smooth fleshy rudder in his grasp tightened. The dolphin sped forward. The billowy barrier that became more massive in height the closer they approached it was coming fast at him, like a concrete wall in which he was about to smash into face first. His stomach tightened. He took a deep breath, even though he remained above water, and at the very last second shut his eyes tightly.

~ ~ ~

Cold.

It enveloped Jacob instantly and wholly with a biting chill that penetrated its way to his very bones. With some reluctance, Jacob opened his eyes and still found himself blinded, but instead of being thrown into another pit of blackness, he instead was immersed in a grayish white haze which, in an instant, obliterated the rest of the world. Even with the water spraying up from across the dolphin's back, Jacob could feel the heavy mist hanging in the air and the dampness of a million tiny drops of wetness raining down on him.

The fog seemed to stretch on endlessly, and what was only a few minutes within its clutches seemed to Jacob to last hours. He found himself trying to shrug off a growing chill that didn't come from the cold of the water but an unsettling apprehension rising up inside him. What awaited him on the other side of this ocean barrier? Was there an other side? Or was this it?

He called out for Gotham. Then again, louder.

"I can't see you!"

At first, there was nothing. No reply. No sound. Just the sloshing of water. Then there came laughter. It was faint at first—a muffled, far off laughter tickling the nothingness before him and barely pricked his ears. He knew it belonged to Gotham, despite never before having recalled witnessing the angel laugh. It seemed to move toward him, growing louder and more robust, and moving dizzily about him like the swirling of wind before falling abruptly silent within the suffocating denseness.

The dolphin beneath him surged forth showing not even the slightest hesitation inside the blank slate of gray. Its movements were confident and focused, as though it knew precisely where it was headed, and that somehow offered Jacob some ease. Still, he held on tightly to his escort's fin, not wanting to chance somehow slipping free and finding himself left behind treading the cold waters lost and alone inside this phantom purgatory. Finally, the cloud mass began to separate and reveal gaping holes within the thick billowing innards much like a cotton shirt that falls victim to a closet full of moths. Glimpses of blue sky and sunlight from the blotted out world came into view and the apprehension which had crept up on Jacob and latched onto his shirt collar with its icy fingers fell away and disappeared into the wake waters churned by the dolphin's tail. And then a short way ahead he spied Gotham, careening across the water like the most perfect stone being skipped along the surface of a lake.

"Is that the fastest you can go?" yelled the angel over his shoulder with a baiting cockiness. His gray wings were folded tight across his broad back and chunky strands of his shoulder-length hair had managed to slip free from the confines of its ponytail to dance with wild abandon about his head and face. The smile of relief that had returned to Jacob's water-beaded face narrowed in concert with his eyes into one of caginess. Instinctively, he laid a hand upon the head of his aquatic steed near its eye and leaned forward.

"Are you going to let your friend leave you in the dust like this?"

He didn't speak the words. Instead, he somehow felt an innate ability within himself to communicate with the animal silently and transmit his thoughts through his fingertips.

"Come on, and let's show them what we're made of!"

There was no logical expectation to Jacob that the dolphin would respond to his voice, much less his unheard thoughts. He may have had angel blood running through his veins, but the power to prod a dolphin to follow his whim, much less beckon a platoon of the magnificent sea creatures from the ocean depths as he had witnessed Gotham do, was beyond even contemplating with any hint of seriousness. Yet the dolphin did hear, and seemingly understood. And with a mighty jolt, it bucked beneath Jacob and lurched forward. Jacob let loose a yelp of startled exhilaration while holding onto the dolphin's fin for dear life struggling to keep from being ripped away by the increase drag from the water that he found himself flying across at an incredible speed.

"That's it, go. *Go!*" he cried out with a fervor of excitement.

Veering sharply toward Gotham and his ride, the dolphin darted through the rolling currents with an astonishing swiftness, and before long the distance between Jacob and the angel quickly vanished.

"Look out, you're about to get whooped by a Nephilim!" Jacob called out, flashing a smug smile when he finally sailed past Gotham.

"Hasn't happened before," Gotham retorted. His golden eyes sparkled with a devious competitive glint. "It certainly isn't going to happen now."

They were soon racing across the water like two cowboys hammering their way fast and furious over an open prairie. Their laughter and howls boomed loudly through the air, and the barrier of fog along with its frigid bite quickly dissipated leaving only wispy fingers of mist trailing after trying to recapture them and drag them back into the brumous realm they had punctured and escaped. The blotted out world soon returned in all its crystal-clear clarity and almost immediately the look on Jacob's face was overtaken by one of immense awe. There before him stood a mammoth pillar of sea-gnawed rock jutting high out of the water. The first of three, it loomed large and ominous like a great arm or some submerged beast rising from the ocean depths flanked on either side by two other titanic columns.

Jacob cupped a hand over his brow to shield his squinting eyes from the brilliance of the sun shining down brightly from the deep blue sky and followed the rocks to their peaks. There he saw the figures of three men perched atop each pillar that seemed to serve as watchtowers to some mighty fortress. They stood in almost militant fashion with their booted feet planted firmly upon the rock. Their bare sinewy torsos gleamed against the sunlight with an intimidating power and strength. At first sight, they reminded Jacob of the sword-wielding winged Powers who had swept down from the sky and aided to cut down the terror which rained down on him and Gotham before their plunge into the waters of the Van Gölü. And immediately he knew he was again in the company of angels.

From their posts the three figures watched silently with fierce golden eyes that shone through stern, expressionless faces as Jacob and Gotham passed through the shadow of the giant pillars on the backs of their dolphin chaperones. And as they made their way through the massive stalks of rock, Jacob saw the angel standing upon the furthest pillar lift a great golden trumpet gripped in his hand and bring it to his mouth. A dark, single-note crescendo was released and it filled the air and moved across the sea like a flock of angry birds. Once the dolphins had carried Jacob and Gotham past the rock columns, Jacob turned and looked in the direction of where they were headed. And his mouth fell open, and he gasped.

Land.

The promised land.

Eden.

~ ~ ~

The dolphins carried their human cargo to the point where the rolling sea suddenly began to pitch and froth, collapsing in thunderous somersaults at the foot of a beach rising from its waters. Gotham thanked the creatures with an appreciative stroke across their shiny, sleek hides as their heads bobbed out of the water. An enthusiastic series of loud clicks punctuating their high-pitched squeals came from the perpetual smiles frozen on their bottle-nose-shaped faces. What Jacob heard from the dolphin speak was as clear as if spoken by a human.

Welcome home winged prince. We are always at your service.

Then with a splash from their tails slapping against the ocean's surface, they quickly vanished, disappearing back into the blue fathoms from which they had appeared. Gotham then turned his gaze toward the shore and Jacob could see clearly a look of apprehension deep-set in the angel's hawk-like eyes. He almost expected Gotham to release a second whispered call that would retrieve the dolphins from the ocean's pit to carry him back from which he came.

"You alright?" asked Jacob somewhat hesitantly as the two treaded upon the water.

At first it seemed as though Gotham had not heard him. Then he turned and looked at the boy. And when he did, whatever had given him momentary pause had left him without a trace, and the familiar cocksure fiery glint emerged once more and repositioned itself in his eyes.

"Come, sanctuary awaits," said Gotham.

And with that he swam off and Jacob followed after him. When they were in reach of the pulling current from the breakers ahead, Jacob and Gotham surrendered themselves to the mighty force of the roaring water as it carried the two of them swiftly upon its foaming, churning tides to be deposited on the waiting shore. Looking like something of a drowned rodent emerging from the ocean's clutches with his soaked clothes heavy with water and clinging to his body, Jacob sighed with gratifying relief when the solid feel of land met his steps. The beach's dry, salt-white sand was unusually soft, almost powder-like against the soles of his feet and between his toes. Relieving himself of his water-logged pack which hung heavy across his torso, Jacob collapsed to his knees in a heap, his shoulders rising and falling with his heavy breaths. Eventually his body slackened further from the exhaustion he felt and rolled itself over, and while sprawled out on his back upon the sand, which felt like the softest of feather-stuffed mattresses ever created, his eyes immediately became transfixed by the vast sky hanging above him. It was like no sky he had ever seen before, the color unlike any he had ever known: blue, but rich and more vibrant than even the bluest of blues he could recall ever seeing. And for a brief moment Jacob felt a confusing doubt whether it was actually sky he was seeing.

And the sun.

It appeared as a giant disc of blinding white light yet, strangely, it did not hurt Jacob's eyes, even as he lay staring directly into it. Instead, it slowly began to lull his eyes closed and his drenched, pruning skin succumbed to its great soothing warmth. And as Jacob basked lazily in the pleasure that had completely enveloped himself, a grin of contentment spread across his face. The moment of perfect leisure, however, was quickly interrupted by a loud rustling and Jacob felt himself being pelted by cold water suddenly raining down upon him. His eyes cracked open irritably and he found Gotham standing over him looking like a giant silhouette against the brightness of the sun above, his massive wings outstretched flapping and shaking briskly in the air to rid themselves of the wetness coating its feathers. Jacob raised his hands in front of his face to shield himself from what felt to be a hundred freshly bathed dogs released from their tubs and lined up around him to shake at will.

"Oh…I'm so sorry. Did I get you?" Gotham remarked with a mischievous grin that betrayed the fakery of his sincerity. With the threat of Infectors or any other looming danger seemingly a world away, he looked to be for the first time—momentarily, at least—free of the tension that had accompanied him over the many long miles of their journey.

"You know, there's something I've wanted to do for quite some time," said Jacob while drawn to the chance of testing the angel's playful side, which until arriving at the beach he was certain didn't exist.

"What's that?" asked Gotham, his attention now occupied by the task of shaking out the tangled mane of his hair.

And with that Jacob swept his leg with all his strength at the angel's powerful legs planted tantalizingly close, clipping them right above the Achilles heel. The blow caught Gotham off guard, knocking his feet out from under him and sending him tumbling down onto the beach. The stunned look on Gotham's face was beyond priceless to Jacob and worth any amount of retribution that might follow.

"Oh…I'm so sorry," Jacob mimicked an apology in his best Gotham imitation from behind a goading grin. "It must have been a spasm in my leg."

"So, you want to play that way, do you?" said Gotham with a sneer while spitting away the grains of sand dotting his lips.

They became engaged in a friendly wrestling match, and the once quiet beach came alive with the sound of their laughter, the first of which they had shared together since beginning their journey, until exhaustion once again overtook Jacob in a surrendering moment of finding himself pinned fast beneath Gotham.

"So, this is it? This is the famous biblical Eden?" Jacob wondered aloud once he had managed to catch his breath as he lay supine on the sand searching with his eyes the landscape surrounding them. Rising to his feet, he appeared almost ghostlike with his body and clothes dusted with the white sand.

"Consider this its welcome mat. Eden lies still a ways inland just beyond there," answered Gotham, nodding toward the towering gray, craggy cliffs of a giant crescent-shaped mountain cradling the small, narrow beach. He then turned his gaze to the boy whose eyes were fixed on the mountain but whose thoughts were clearly elsewhere.

"Nervous?"

"No," Jacob shot back in an almost defensive manner that gave way to a meeker tone almost as quickly as his response. "Maybe a little. It's just very confusing. Where exactly are we?"

"You're right, it is confusing. And I'm not sure my explanation will make it any less so," said Gotham. But try he did.

"This," he began, circling as he gestured to all that surrounded them: the beach, the ocean, the mountains. "This is what's called Sagun, or what is better known as one of the Seven Heavens."

"Heaven?" echoed Jacob somewhat alarmed. "You're saying we're in Heaven?"

"The Third Heaven, to be more precise," said Gotham.

Jacob suddenly found himself thinking about the Gate they had just passed through. More specifically the light at the end of the dark tunnel scenario, and his face began to whiten.

"This might be a stupid question, but, um…don't you have to, you know…die to get to Heaven?" he asked.

"In most cases. But not here," answered Gotham. "The Heavens are just other worlds, as the mortal realm is to you. Some are further away. Others border one another with nothing but a simple doorway separating them. You just have to know where the doorway lies."

As strange and foreign as it sounded, Jacob found the concept not so difficult to understand, especially with an angel explaining it.

"And the Gate we just passed through beneath the lake is the doorway to this one—Sagun."

"Now you're grasping it," Gotham replied with a smile.

There was an urge to shrug off everything Jacob was hearing as complete nonsense, if not for one thing—it was there in front of him. He was standing in the midst of it, surrounded by it in living, breathing, indisputable color. He could see it. Smell it. More importantly, he could touch it. It was real. That he could not deny no matter how much he may have wanted to, only he didn't want to. Not by a long shot.

"I don't want you to take this the wrong way or anything," said Jacob, "but I'm surprised Fallen angels would be allowed inside Eden."

"They're not," replied Gotham matter-of-factly. "In fact, I'm the only one who's ever been granted passage through the Gate."

"How's that?"

"That, you'd have to ask my brothers," answered Gotham. "But if I were to guess, I would venture they have taken into account the true nature of my unforgivable crime."

"That, despite everything, your loyalty still lies with the Light," Jacob offered.

"That I remain resolute in my allegiance *against* the Darkness," corrected Gotham in a notably cold manner, and in that brief moment the angel's playful levity seemed to take leave of him and Jacob regretted breaching the subject.

Again, there came a loud rustling and again Jacob felt himself being pelted, only this time it was by the powdery sand which caked Gotham's wings courtesy of the wrestling match he had engaged in earlier with the boy. The mischievous grin quickly returned to Gotham's face.

"Okay, that I could say I'm sorry about, but truthfully I would be lying," he offered with a growing chuckle brought about by the displeased look on Jacob's face.

~ ~ ~

"Now, we should be going if we want to make it there before nightfall," suggested Gotham.

Jacob went and fetched his bag leaving Gotham to continue flapping and beating his wings in an effort to clean the sandy, gray feathers. The first thing Jacob did was rummage through his things to check on his journal, phone and other valuable belongings Gotham had instructed him back on Akdamar to secure in plastic bags for protection before the dive into the Van Gölü. Once he was relieved to see they remained safe and dry, he fished out his sneakers. While he sat lacing his shoes to his feet, his attention was drawn once again to the skies. This time it wasn't the vibrant color or the brilliance of the sun that drew it, but something he could not see. A strange stirring. He felt it. A movement of a breeze where there was none.

He rose to his feet and slowly positioned his knapsack over his head and across his chest, all the while cautiously searching the sky, when in a flash something swooped down from out of nowhere and buzzed past him with a cyclone-like force knocking him off his feet. He quickly swung his head around to try and see what had sent him reeling to the ground as it raced past. Whatever it was, its movements were so fast it appeared as nothing more than a blur. It headed toward Gotham, who remained caught up in the cleaning of his plumage and oblivious to the object coming at him with great speed. Jacob opened his mouth to shout a warning to the angel but it came too late. Gotham looked up just as the blur hit him with a crushing force that lifted him off his feet and sent him airborne halfway down the beach before his body skidded across the sand while kicking up a white powdery cloud in his path. Jacob jumped to his feet and began racing across the beach to where Gotham lay. He stopped abruptly when from within the cloud of dissipating sand emerged the shocking sight of another winged being standing over Gotham.

"I'm surprised you would have the audacity to show your face around here again," the figure hissed in a venomous tone.

"From the looks of things around here, I figured my face was exactly the thing this place could use to elevate it back to being the fabled beauty it once was," retorted Gotham.

He attempted to rise up, but the angel above him placed a foot against his chest and held him firmly to the ground. Then reaching to his wing, he retrieved from within the charcoal-colored plumage a sword gilded with blinding flares of sunlight it reflected off its silver mirrored blade as it cut through the air with a deadly whooshing sound before coming to a threatening rest against Gotham's neck.

"Give me two good reasons why I shouldn't clip you of your wings?"

Jacob stood frozen, a lump frozen in the middle of his throat. His wide eyes remained fixed on Gotham's face. If the angel was feeling any fear, he sure didn't show it.

"I have only one to offer you that matters, brother," answered Gotham. "You're not strong enough to do the job."

And with that Gotham took hold of the foot that held him pinned to the ground, and with a grit of his teeth and flare of the thick sinewy muscle within his arms he lifted his oppressor from off his feet and sent him flying backward through the air to tumble hard across the sandy beach. In a flash, both men were back on their feet, coming toward one another with threatening steps, muscles tensed and bunched and brows furrowed.

"I should have cut you down when I had the chance," the mysterious winged presence spit menacingly, slicing the air in front of him with the blade that remained firmly in his grip.

"A wasted opportunity you shall never have within your grasp for the rest of your days, angel," said Gotham with equal malice.

They continued toward each other, a fevered gleam to fight alive in their eyes. Jacob held his breath in his chest afraid to breathe as he wondered to himself why Gotham had yet to draw his own sword to fight against the menace coming at him. They were nearly upon one another, nose to nose, the sun-illuminated sword poised to cut down

Gotham when suddenly they ceased their advancement. Their warring faces cracked giving way to grins followed by full smiles as they lunged forward and embraced one another tightly. With their laughter ringing out loudly, they appeared as long-lost friends reunited after years of separation.

"My thanks to you; I just finished brushing these clean," complained Gotham when they finally parted and turned his attention back to his wings colored with a fresh dusting of sand.

"I see you have not lost that narcissistic charm of yours which has left you little endearment with the heavens," the angel with the sword remarked.

"It was not always so," Gotham muttered begrudgingly while glancing ever so slightly skyward as he spoke.

The stranger chuckled, giving the side of Gotham's face a sharp but friendly slap, and as he did he noticed several nasty wounds marking the otherwise flawless skin.

"I see someone got to you first," remarked the strange figure. "The Furies are showing an increasing bravery to match their viciousness these days. There was a time one wouldn't come within striking distance of that face you hold in such high regard. But I can see the temptation in risking a vengeful swipe at it, especially when it belongs to their executioner."

The words drew an unamused glare from Gotham. "Infectors were responsible for this," he said dryly. "Not to worry, they paid the price for their trouble—again."

"That I have no doubt," said the stranger with a knowing chuckle and, with a flap of his great wings, he cast off the sand coating his own feathers from his scrimmage on the beach and sent the debris onto a grimacing Gotham before turning his attention to Jacob.

Slipping his sword back into the confines of the plumes, he folded his wings across his back in the same fashion long-deceased members of the French elite with a penchant for top hats and thin cigarettes would sweep back the silk-lined capes draped across their shoulders, and he made his way toward the boy. He was large, standing as tall as Gotham and exhibiting the same arsenal of strength beneath a hide of smooth golden skin stretched taut across his naked torso. Sandy brown hair framed a kind, yet fierce face in loose ringlets of curls that fell to his shoulders and blew freely across his forehead.

"And I take it you must be the reason for this unexpected return after such a long absence," he said in a friendly, yet inquisitive manner. "I'm Damiel, Angel of the Sword."

With slight timidity, Jacob took hold of the hand extended his way and the warmth that greeted his palm and spread through him was no longer strange and surprising, but familiar. Yet as soothing as the angel's embrace was, Jacob noticed a look slowly make its way across the angel's face. It was the same look he had seen on Johiel's face when the old man first laid eyes on him—a startled look. One that brought with it a slight recoil. One Jacob thought he had imagined.

"I'm Jacob. Jacob Parrish," he said with an awkward smile.

The angel was studying him much harder now.

"Something wrong?" asked Jacob.

"It's the strangest thing," muttered Damiel with a slight cock of his head.

"What, my name?"

The angel continued to study the boy, and the more he did the more his eyes narrowed as if in an attempt to burrow their way under Jacob's skin.

"It can't be," Jacob thought he heard Damiel mumble under his breath as if arguing against some unheard voice suddenly whispering inside his head. And then as if sensing the growing discomfort which came from the piercing way his eyes were carefully studying the boy, Damiel's face softened with a friendly if not completely authentic smile.

"Jacob is it?" said Damiel. "I am pleased to make your acquaintance."

He then looked to Gotham as did Jacob, each one carrying quizzical expressions on their faces but for different reasons.

"I guess we should probably get going," suggested Gotham, doing his best to avoid the eyes of both.

"Yes, the others will be most interested to learn of your arrival," said Damiel as though awakening from a brief trance. "Your timing is perfect. The last of the new group of Fledglings arrived just yesterday."

"Fledglings?" inquired Jacob curiously.

"Young Nephilim such as yourself who have come here to train," explained Gotham.

"Yes," said Damiel, giving Jacob a strange glance out of the corner of his eye. "A special dinner to welcome the new brood is being held this evening."

Then unfurling his wings in preparation to take to the sky, Damiel said, "Shall we go?"

Gotham's wings remained tight to his back.

"I think we shall walk, at least part of the way," he replied. "I want to give the boy here a chance to fully experience this new place."

"Of course," said Damiel with an unsure smile. "It is without doubt infinitely more breath-taking in scope on foot than by wing. Perhaps I will join you, if you don't mind. It will give us a chance to catch up over these long years."

Jacob thought he caught a brief moment of hesitation in the glance Gotham exchanged with Damiel, yet he nodded approvingly.

"Lead the way, old friend," said Gotham.

The anxious feeling that had held its grip on Jacob eased somewhat, though not completely, as he was guided along the beach, an angel on each side, toward the unknown resting beyond the looming mountains.

CHAPTER SEVENTEEN

Jacob soon found his feet tracing the narrow pathway leading the way up a great rock of a mountain just beyond the beach's white sands, with two angels in tow as his guide. Below them the great Dilmun Sea glistened peacefully, and the thunderous growls from the encroaching waves breaking upon the shore was replaced with the whistling of wind moving through the caverns and crevices of the mountain. Halfway up, the path came to an abrupt end offering no means to continue on unless one was a lizard with the ability to scamper with ease up the remaining stretch of cliffs, which appeared almost like the walls of some undiscovered fortress by the sheer vertical nature in which they rose to greater heights.

"Looks like a dead end,," observed Jacob.

"The Emmaus Corridor is the only way to enter Eden by foot," answered Damiel.

Taking note of the confused look on the boy's face, Damiel placed his hand on the mountain wall and whispered a phrase of words too quiet for Jacob's ears to hear. There followed a loud rumbling and the crumbling sound of rock, and the ground beneath quivered sharply, as if the mountain was shifting itself. Then, to Jacob's amazement, he saw a fractured break reveal itself in the rock where Damiel had placed his hand. The break grew bigger, splitting the side of the cliff in two before slowly separating and widening. When the rumbling finally stopped, a dark, narrow passage leading deep into the bowels of the mighty mountain was revealed. One by one they entered with Damiel leading the way, his sword once more drawn and its blade, somehow containing the dancing light of the blazing sun even where sunlight was denied entry, cutting back the darkness that met them.

The passageway was extremely tight, claustrophobically so, allowing no more than the width of a single man to pass at a time between the smooth, cold rock that seemed to rise up indefinitely. Jacob's alert eyes darted amongst the strange silhouetted images that appeared to take shape and come to life from the flickering shadows cast upon the smothering walls of rock by the light coming from Damiel's sword. Higher above, where the blackness loomed out of reach of the beacon, the wind sweeping through the corridor howled loudly. And from within the wind and the darkness emerged a wave of deep ominous moans. It was not the wind, however, but rather it seemed to resonate from within the walls of rock, as though the mountain itself was alive.

"She is welcoming us," Gotham's whispering voice came from behind to meet Jacob's ear.

"I'd hate to hear what she sounds like if she wasn't," answered Jacob.

~ ~ ~

When they finally reached the end of the passageway, the familiar loud rumbling sounded once more and again the ground trembled, and when Jacob turned to look, the corridor from which they had passed through had vanished from sight leaving visible only an impregnable solid gray wall.

"Angels. Shadowy demons. Moving mountains. Can't wait to see what's next to challenge my sense of reality," said Jacob.

"Perhaps you might consider a different tact as you move forward from here and allow yourself to accept something other than the finite realm of the world you've left behind. Only then will you be able to see

Eden as it truly is," offered Gotham, who like Damiel appeared to find the mountain's movements nothing less than normal.

"I know it will be a difficult, if not impossible task for a bridge-jumping realist such as yourself," Gotham was quick to add dryly with a measured sigh.

Jacob shot Gotham a sideways glare, pausing to determine from the expressionless look on the angel's face whether the sarcastic quip was meant as a backhanded dig or more light-hearted joking first observed down at the beach.

"Well then? For what are you waiting? I would think you would be anxious to finally satiate that skeptical curiosity of yours and see where this journey has brought you," pressed Gotham, directing the boy's attention with a nod to an overlook jutting from the mountain's side a short distance from where they stood.

Since the moment he learned of Eden's unlikely existence on the island of Akdamar, Jacob had silently spent his time wondering what it might look like, rummaging through visions of wondrous beauty inside his head conjured up from the wildest spectrum of his imagination. Back home in Cain's Corner, Penuel Point had proven to be the most beautiful place on earth, and against which he judged everything else touched by nature's hand. Yet nothing, not even the majesty of Penuel Point, could compare to the celestial magnificence that unfolded into view when Jacob walked to the edge of the plateau. An audible gasp escaped his lips, and his eyes grew large when they gazed out upon the greenest of forests he'd ever seen stretching for countless leagues as far as the eyes could follow beneath his feet. From numerous gray mountains of rock greened with clumps of clinging trees and shrubs spilled magnificent waterfalls. And slithering peacefully along a path long laid through the center of the forest was a massive, majestic river. Its bluest of water flowed serpentine-like through the forests like a vein pumping with life-giving blood on its way to the Dilmun Sea. It felt to

Jacob as though he was watching an episode on the National Geographic Channel about some undiscovered jungle found in some remote part of the world impossibly untouched by human presence. Except high-definition television couldn't begin to do justice to what Jacob was now seeing.

"I certainly didn't expect anything like this," Jacob fawned with awe. "It's so...so..."

"Beautiful?" said Damiel, offering up a simplistic word the boy struggled to find to describe the most grandiose of things he'd ever seen.

"Big," answered Jacob.

And, yes, beautiful. Abundantly so. The colors alone were beyond the spectrum of anything Jacob knew. It was almost dreamlike. And the air. It was alive with pleasant scents gathered up in the arms of the gentle breeze from blooming flowers seen and unseen. Jacob closed his eyes and breathed deeply, and a smile of contentment stretched itself across his face. Pure heaven.

Literally.

"God's garden," came Damiel's voice from over the boy's left shoulder where the angel now stood. "It's hard to fathom its existence even when that existence stands before your very eyes. It holds a beauty that even I, myself, have not become fully accustomed to in all my many centuries spent here—this place where all life was birthed."

"As well as death."

Jacob turned toward the sound of Gotham's voice and found the angel standing nearby where he had been silently gazing down at the scenery in which they were all sharing.

"It may not catch your eye from where we stand, but it is there, trust me," said Gotham. "Even the abundance of so much beauty cannot conceal its presence entirely."

His face, almost statuesque in its profile, was barren of any expression. Yet his eyes could not fully hide a pained sadness lingering amid a brewing contempt that Jacob spied holding court deep within Gotham's smoldering golden gaze. And feeling the boy's gaze upon him, Gotham suddenly turned away from the vista.

"We should be moving. We've a long walk ahead of us," he said, avoiding eye contact with both Jacob and Damiel as he moved briskly past them.

~ ~ ~

They continued along a terrace of rock winding its way through gullies and caverns as it led a path down the side of the mountain. In short time, the path guided them down the steep cliffs and brought them to the thicket of the Forest. There they came upon two trees of centurion size standing like fortress guards at the foot of the mountain where their gnarled roots had anchored themselves to the thick hide of rock. Jacob marveled at their size which made him feel no bigger than an ant in their looming presence. And yet all the while he could not help but sense Damiel's burning gaze upon him. Constant it had been on him, during their ascent up the mountain and now back down.

"Where to now?" asked Jacob, staring into the Forest ahead while trying with a growing uncomfortableness to ignore the angel's penetrating eyes fixed on him.

"We follow the path through the Forest," answered Gotham.

"Looks to be quite a walk."

"That it is," said Damiel as if a gentle warning as they crossed the Forest's threshold. "You may begin to wonder if it has an end by the time we reach our destination."

The angel's words caused Jacob no pause. He was far too taken by his new surroundings to wonder where they were headed much less worry about the toll the path they walked threatened to take on his feet. And in his unharnessed eagerness, he wandered off ahead of his winged chaperones to explore the mysterious new place that was slowly unveiling more of itself to him with each step he took. Once immersed deep in the woods, Jacob immediately became aware of an almost sacred serenity that moved amongst the trees. It was church- like, as though the peacefulness itself was an unseen but very real presence.

Here, the slanting sunlight was thin, pushing its way through a thick canopy of branches and leaves above that all but blotted out the sky. The feathered fingers of fern bejeweled with drops of dew from the constant light drizzle in the air glistened brightly as they unfurled from their thick clusters and stretched upward toward the streaming warmth. An ever-hanging mist hovered low like a veil of silk fluttering gently in the breeze. It bathed the Forest in an almost unreal, dreamlike gauze as it moved amongst the trees like some ghostly apparition.

And then there were the trees themselves.

If Jacob had not laid eyes on them himself, he never would have believed they could grow into the colossal giants that surrounded him. It was as if he had stepped into a prehistoric world no longer in existence, and maybe never was. The trunks of the rooted giants looked as though it would take a couple dozen men holding hands to fully encircle, and they stretched to the heavens higher than the eye could follow. Stoic they were in their stature, like elder statesmen proudly poised amongst the smaller trees and saplings far too young to have witnessed the birthing of their world as they had. Their tough, gray hides, draped in the coils of leafy vines and ivy, were like that of an elephant, yet brightly greened with moss and emanating a pleasant and sweet, pungent woodsy perfume that permeated the air all around. And despite the peacefulness that reigned through the Forest, the unmistakable sounds of life lurking within the thick greenery growing all around echoed from all corners.

The calls of the wild soon had Jacob performing clumsy pirouettes while making his way along the damp dirt path that snaked its way through the Forest, as his eyes darted all about him trying to catch a glimpse of the elusive creatures. Above him, rustling about unseen high in the trees, his ears pricked to the chatter of birds. The language of some was familiar; others he had never before heard. Yet their growing curiosity as they fluttered about in their attempts at gaining closer looks at the stranger strolling through their woods was unmistakable.

Leaving Jacob unhindered to acquaint himself with the new surroundings slowly unfolding itself with every step, Damiel and Gotham lingered some distance behind, their pace easy and unhurried. The stretch of path had lent them a chance to talk alone and reacquaint themselves since they had last seen one another, which by then had seen the passing of many decades when Gotham last stepped foot inside Eden's borders before disappearing without a trace into the world beyond its Gate. Yet it wasn't long before a noticeably awkward quiet fell over the two, and for a moment that seemed to each of them much longer they walked in silence with only the tranquil sounds of the Forest accompanying them.

When Damiel finally breached the quiet to speak, his voice was quiet, yet firm. "Tell me my eyes are playing to deceive me."

Gotham didn't need to look to Damiel to know the angel's gaze, like his own, was fixed firmly on Jacob scampering far ahead of them along the path. Patiently, Gotham had awaited the inevitable question visibly eating at Damiel long before the three had journeyed up the mountain pass and through the hidden corridor, and now that they finally had a private moment out of earshot from Jacob, he dreaded it.

"I take it's the boy to whom you refer?" asked Gotham.

"You know exactly to what I am referring," snapped Damiel.

Gotham sighed with a knowing resignation. "The resemblance is striking, is it not?"

"Then it's not my imagination."

"From the look on your face when you first laid eyes on him down at the beach, I suspect you already knew the answer. And I thank you, Damiel, for holding tight your tongue until we had this moment alone to speak about it."

"You're telling me he doesn't know?"

Gotham smiled and shook his head much to Damiel's amazement. "Up until yesterday he thought of angels as harp-strumming cherubs flying in the clouds, and Eden as something out of a Peter Pan fairy tale," recounted Gotham. "The day I came into his life he was already concerting with a physician to help cure him of the mysterious deformity that had found its way onto his back. So yes, I believe it's safe to say he's very much oblivious where his heritage is concerned."

"Would it be so naive of me to ask how the son of your greatest enemy came to be your ward?" inquired Damiel.

"How, indeed," answered Gotham in a quiet way as though he himself had only just then pondered the question. "Fate seems to deride great amusement in the schizophrenic way it stalks me; clothed as a most amusing joker one minute while trying to sink its blood-stained fangs into my skin when my guard is down. The intent of its fickle ways is lost to me."

"That is your answer; that fate brought him to you?"

Gotham let free an almost resigned sigh. "I can tell you only what I myself have been able to make sense of, Damiel," said Gotham. "But it's a long story in telling and, if all the same to you, I'd rather it be heard by all ears demanding to hear it, as they most surely will, when we reach the Garden."

"As you wish. But at least answer me this much: why on earth would you dare to bring him here? To Eden, of all places?" asked Damiel.

"Because he is a Nephilim," said Gotham. "And because like the other Fledglings brought here, he is deserving of training and to learn who and what he is."

"And what is that exactly, Gotham? Have you given any thought to that question as you ponder the twisted interest fate has taken in yourself?" asked Damiel.

"He is the product of what we have been given the choice to create, like every other Fledgling who's stepped foot within this Forest," answered Gotham testily.

"Like every other Fled—? Are you hearing the words escaping your lips?" An abrupt surge of anger gave brief rise to Damiel's voice before he managed to regain his calm and keep his rumblings from being carried through the trees ahead and overheard by Jacob. "Certainly you of all people should know what his presence here will mean. For all of us."

Gotham stopped abruptly in his tracks and grabbed hold of Damiel tightly at the shoulder, his eyes narrowing its flame. "And certainly you, Damiel, of all people have not let slip from your mind that no one has made the acquaintance of the dangers which lurk just beyond these borders more intimately than I. Certainly no one carries more deeper the scars."

The words seemed to take a visible and rare hold of Damiel and made him shrink back within himself.

"Fair enough," said Damiel coolly. "But tell me…how exactly do you plan to approach the White Circle about this? I know you're not naive enough to think your unexpected calling won't be met with an outcry of protest, to put it mildly."

"I will deal with the council—and Anahel—if only to remind them of Eden's duty," replied Gotham before leveling a more earnest look on his angel friend. "And I am hoping I can count on your support."

Damiel was taken aback at such a suggestion. "You dare petition me for such a thing at the same moment I find myself questioning whether or not I'm abetting in the commission of treason by accompanying you through Eden this very moment? You ask a lot."

"I know what I ask," agreed Gotham with a subtle nod. "But, like you, I am one of great reserve and thoughtfulness, and you know I would not set forth into motion any action I thought would bring about any detriment. Especially here, to this place."

"Why then, can you tell me, do I have such an unsettling feeling gnawing away at my insides?"

"You, Damiel?" said Gotham with a grin. "You the most fearless and brazen of God's winged creatures, whose only reaction I've seen come from you in the face of Furies, Infectors and all our dark nemeses is the lending of a hearty chuckle—"

Damiel, though, quickly cut the angel off sharply. "This goes beyond the Furies and Infectors, Gothamel. In an instant, we have now suddenly found ourselves willingly arousing the burning embers of the Underneath itself." His face, at once both beautiful and strong, offered for the first time that Gotham could remember a fissure of worry.

"Trust me, my dear Damiel, all will be right," said Gotham in a calming voice while clasping the back of the angel's neck which he stroked reassuringly. "He may be of his father, but his father he is not. That you will see."

~　～　~

Again, they resumed their way along the earthen path and soon caught up with Jacob who was standing still as a stone facing away from them and looking off in the distance. As they moved toward him, he raised his hand and waved to them to be quiet and cautious in their approach.

"What is it?" whispered Gotham, suddenly at alert.

"Over there." Jacob pointed in the direction of a cluster of trees that gave way to a small clearing. There, leg-deep in a feathery sea of fern, stood a deer and her fawn.

"We have deer back home, but I've never seen one with a baby." Jacob's awe could be heard even in his whispered words.

Gotham brushed past Jacob and, as he did, the boy grabbed hold of him.

"You'll scare them off."

A smile came to Gotham's face and he looked to Damiel, who was also smiling, and winked. "You have much to learn about Eden."

They'd taken only a dozen or so steps when the sharp snap from a brittle twig from somewhere in the distance called Jacob's attention to the fact they weren't alone. Again Gotham felt a tug to his arm, and when he turned, he found the boy's eyes frozen wide with surprise.

"Forget the deer, and tell me that's not a pack of wolves I'm looking at right at this moment," said Jacob.

Gotham followed the boy's line of sight to the stretch of forest on the opposite side of the path upon which they walked and sure enough, emerging from amongst the trees, five wolves suddenly appeared trotting down the Forest slope. Two looked to be twins with their coats carrying nearly identical gray and white markings. Another was colored red and white while the fourth was as black as night with pearl white eyes shining brightly from behind the ebony pelt. The one who seemed to be leading the pack was as white as the black one was dark, and appeared as a fast-moving iceberg floating gracefully amongst the trees. They were large; larger than Jacob imagined wolves could be, and they were quickly descending the slope.

Jacob's gaze shot to the deer and her fawn, both seemingly oblivious to the pack that was quickly making their way in their direction.

"They're going to attack them!" he gasped.

The mother turned her head and looked in the direction of the approaching wolves with her large dark eyes that surprisingly mirrored no cause to take flight.

"Why don't they run?" asked Jacob with growing alarm.

"Obviously, you keep forgetting where you are, and more importantly where you are not," said Gotham who appeared unflappable in the face of the advancing wolf pack. And with that he cupped a hand to his mouth and let loose a loud bark-like cry that tore through the thick blanket of silence engulfing the Forest. Instantly, the white leader broke its gait and turned its gaze in the direction of where the angels and Jacob were standing. Seeing them, it immediately left the company of the others and made its way toward them in full sprint.

Jacob remained fast where he stood between Gotham and Damiel, secure in the comfort that came from being flanked by these two mighty winged beings he knew were armed with swords. Yet it was not enough to keep his heart from pounding harder inside his chest at the sight of a wolf tearing toward him. Then, suddenly, it was upon them, just a few feet away, when it leapt up from the ground. Jacob waited for the sounds of growling and gnashing teeth, but instead what followed was a loud panting and a friendly chorus of piercing yelps and whines. The wolf had attacked Gotham, but with the slobbering licks a house dog unleashes when greeting its owner returning home. It was truly a sight to see the wolf up on its hind legs hugging the angel who returned the greeting with a vigorous rubbing of its thick white coat.

The wolf then hopped down and repeated its affectionate show onto Damiel, and when it had finished it looked to Jacob who couldn't keep from inching backwards somewhat when the animal moved closer toward him while giving him a quick curious sniff. And when the wolf rose up on its hind legs and draped its front paws over his shoulders, Jacob's breath caught itself in his throat, for the size of the beast alone was enough to intimidate him. Then Jacob heard a faint whimper escape the canine that was anything but threatening or ferocious, and he felt a nuzzle to the side of his face, followed by the warm wetness of its tongue, and he knew there was nothing to fear from the animal.

"Check it out!" he then said to Gotham and Damiel, motioning to where the deer and her fawn, not looking the slightest bit spooked, mingled with the other wolves as though they themselves were deer as well.

The trio made their way over, and to Jacob's amazement even their own presence didn't seem to bother the deer, who without any sense of timidness came up to him nudging his hand for a pet.

"It's like I stepped into a Disney movie in a strange, spooky way," said Jacob, sliding his hand across the deer's soft chestnut brown fur.

"There's never been a reason or cause in Eden for creatures of the land or sea to fear humans nor prey on one another," said Gotham.

They stayed a short while until the wolves decided it was time to move on and disappeared into the thicket, and the deer and her

yearling soon after followed. Then, when the trio started on their way once more, Jacob felt something following close on his heels and discovered it to be the white wolf who had remained behind from its pack.

"You better get going and catch up with your friends," said Jacob, finally stopping and motioning to the direction of the Forest the other wolves had run off. The wolf responded by sitting down and letting loose a loud bark. Its translucent white eyes framed within a thin sphere of piercing blue stayed fixed on Jacob.

"Looks like you've got a new friend," said Damiel.

"What am I supposed to do? I can't keep a wolf!" replied Jacob.

"You're quite right about that. And if it's any consolation, you won't be," said Gotham. "He's chosen you."

Before Jacob could ask, Gotham continued on his way with Damiel without any further explanation.

Chosen me? Jacob thought. *As what?"*

~   ~   ~

It soon became clear that this new wondrous place known as Eden stretched much further and wider than it first appeared from the overhang outside the threshold of the Emmaus Corridor, and before long, Jacob began to ponder the words Damiel muttered to him when they stepped foot past the first tree, and wondered if the Forest would indeed ever come to an end.

To help pass the time and draw Jacob's attention away from the growing miles being clocked beneath his steps, Gotham and Damiel took turns schooling the boy about the strange new world into which he had stepped. Now and then one of the angels would cry out with strange sounds, and each sound would bring forth a new kind of animal from within the Forest. The mightiest of birds from owls and great eagles to the most delicate of sparrows and hummingbirds would swoop down from the canopy of tree branches stretching overhead and come to rest on the shoulder or arm of the angel who had called it. Then there were the beautiful exotic creatures of flight. Many looked to have been created by the strokes of a paintbrush; their plumes brightly tinted and patterned in every imaginable color, and the feathers on their heads coiffed into showy headdresses and their tails draped like the trains of elegant evening gowns. From the veil of brush, animals of the four-legged variety emerged: Hyraxes, quoll, bears, foxes, tree mice and hares, and stags with tree-like antlers. There was also an equal number of creatures to come forward which Jacob had never before seen, nor would he ever beyond the reach of the Forest where they had long been snuffed out from existence in the outside world. Like he did with the wolves who came before, Jacob was at first apprehensive of the creatures who came within petting distance, particularly when he caught sight of a Bengal tiger with its white fangs slinking its way down the Forest slope of trees toward him. Yet like the wolves, Jacob quickly found the animals to be docile and nonthreatening.

The intermingling with the woodland creatures made the hours of walking pass quickly by, and eventually the trees began to thin and, in the distance, a break in the Forest could be seen. The mist began to recede as the thin sunlight gradually grew stronger and the blue sky began to reveal itself overhead. As they drew nearer, Jacob noticed the path before them began to stir, slightly at first and then more noticeably.

"Look at the ground," he said to Gotham and Damiel, bringing the three of them to an abrupt stop. Quietly they stood, including the white wolf, their eyes fixed on the ground before them. Suddenly the faint movements gave way to a burst and the ground appeared to spring upward into the air, and what had been thought to be a dirt pathway sprouted wings and began fluttering.

"Butterflies!" gasped Jacob with surprise.

As they took to the air, more and more stirred along the Forest floor where they lay camouflaged. And as they unfurled their wings they revealed an explosion of pulsating colors: red, green, yellow, blue, orange. Soon hundreds became thousand, and thousands became tens of thousands, and still they came. They rose upward in spiraling columns of brilliant hues and Jacob followed them with eyes glad for the sight as they climbed toward the treetops. Their presence seemed to magically stir to life the leaves of the trees. Looking closer, Jacob realized what he first thought to be leaves were even more butterflies. They were covering the branches in the millions hanging in massive clusters. Then, in an instant, they sprang forth in an extravaganza of dazzling color worthy of a Fourth of July fireworks finale. They took to the air in the same skilled manner as a flock of birds, maneuvering their synchronized movements in a way to segregate themselves by color. And like parade ribbons, they delicately drifted through the air circling around the spectators below and eliciting a chorus of excited barks from the wolf. Jacob sank to his knee beside the wolf draping an arm around his new-found companion and together their mesmerized eyes followed the entrancing movements filling the air around them.

"I don't know about you," he whispered to the wolf, "but I thought it would take more than a bunch of butterflies to leave me speechless."

~   ~   ~

When they finally emerged from the Forest, they found themselves on the edge of a large swath of emerald grassland. The path they had followed for countless miles had now been replaced with miles of green rolling hills outlined by the divided Forest which continued to press on northward along its surrounding borders. As they stepped out into the knee-high grass swaying like ocean currents in the breeze, a black-chested snake eagle came soaring from behind the tree tops. Its piercing squawk of a cry rang out loudly, and as the shadow cast down by the eagle swept past across the sea of green, the white wolf reared up and tore after it in swift chase with Jacob quickly following behind.

Jacob crossed the slopes of two lazy hills with amazing speed, yet not fast enough to gain on the wind-like movements of the wolf. When they reached the top of the third hill the sight that suddenly came into view brought his feet to an abrupt halt, and the angels he had left behind were soon at his side.

"We've reached the River of Life," declared Damiel, before leading Jacob and Gotham down the slope of the hill toward the wide river slithering its way through the green Valley. All around were animals drawn to the gentle flow of water to drink and bathe and lie lazily amid the lush grass. For a moment, it seemed to Jacob as if he had suddenly been transported to a kind of African safari. Yet he still hadn't been able to fully get used to the strange disconnect of seeing animals he had known to be natural enemies mingling with one another as though they were all part of one herd, one family.

Jacob's parched throat led him down the slope of the hill to the River's bank where he knelt down next to the wolf, who was already lapping at the water. He dunked his cupped hands into the cool water and was about to drink when he stopped at the sight of a shadow coming up beside him. He looked up and saw Gotham hovering above.

"It's alright, isn't it?" asked Jacob, suddenly cautious.

The angel smiled and nodded toward the wolf. "Why don't you ask your friend?"

The wolf stopped drinking and turned her white eyes on Jacob, her muzzle dripping with the river's water, and barked.

With a smile, Jacob proceeded to drink, and despite the cool, refreshing nature of the water passing between his lips he immediately felt a warmth from it flow through his body. It began in his throat and quickly moved through his chest, stomach and finally his limbs. It was the same warmth he had come to know when he shook Gotham's hand. And Johiel's. And Damiel's.

As he continued to quench his thirst he noticed Gotham out of the corner of his eye squat down next to him and sample a palm-full of the River water.

"I thought angels didn't have to drink or eat," Jacob commented.

"To survive like civilians, no. But it doesn't mean we don't. Especially here," replied Gotham.

"What about them?" asked Jacob, motioning to the many animals seen wandering about. "They have to eat something. If not each other, then what?"

"The River supplies all they need to survive," said Gotham. "The hunt for food doesn't exist here."

As he spoke the angel cast his eyes upon the River's surface and from within the rippling, crystal-clear waters his image was reflected back with a mirror-like quality.

"Damiel was right," said Gotham, bringing a hand to where several deep scratches lined the side of his face. "The Infectors did do a bit of a number on me, didn't they?"

Jacob didn't answer, but he had noticed the deep cuts made to the angel's skin by the Infector's knife-like talons. Specifically, he noticed Gotham didn't seem to bleed from his wounds. At least not with the kind of blood he was familiar with seeing: red. Instead, it looked as though water dripped from the wounds, something Jacob had disregarded as water from the ocean trickling down across the skin. Or perhaps drops of sweat. Jacob then watched curiously as Gotham scooped some water from the River with his hand, sending his reflection rippling along the surface, and splashed it across his face. Tilting his head back, the angel closed his eyes to the sun above as the drops of water dribbling across his skin began to suddenly move of their own volition against gravity toward the battle-marred areas. Curiously, Jacob watched with some easing of disbelief, yet disbelief none the same, as the gashes began to seal themselves and recede back into the flesh, and the bruising slowly began to fade from sight.

"It's like what I saw you do to that boy's hand back in Tatvan," said Jacob. "Is it the water's doing, or yours?"

The question seemed to draw a pondering pause from Gotham. Tilting his head forward once more toward the water, he gave himself another splashing before answering. "And God said, 'Let there be a firmament in the midst of the waters, and let it divide the waters from the waters.' So it says in Genesis, and so it was."

He raised the forefinger of his right hand and Jacob, who was listening intently while studying the face that had been returned to its flawless, unblemished perfection, followed it with a curious gaze to the water. As Gotham slowly began stirring the River's surface with the tip of his finger he continued to speak: "When the waters were divided, the angels were created, and it is the reason why water is a great vessel of strength for us."

Slowly and steadily he continued to stir the water in an easy clockwise motion drawing more and more of the River's surface into a swirling motion that gradually grew faster and faster. Much faster than it was being stirred. It became hypnotic to Jacob to look upon, appearing as though the plug to some unknown giant drain along the riverbed had been pulled and the River was suddenly being sucked dry. Once the surface of the River was in motion, Gotham slowly began raising his hand. As he did, the water swirled its way out into the center of the river and formed what looked to be a sort of water spout. Jacob watched as the swirling tornado of water grew in size as it continued to rise up like some Egyptian cobra coaxed from the confines of a marketplace basket by music coming from a swami's beckoning flute. Then, before his eyes, Jacob watched as the column of water took the shape of a human figure, and from the figure's back sprouted a huge pair of watery wings. In a flash, Gotham swept his hand upward and pointed to the sky and the water-sculpted angel flapped its wings and barreled forth in flight toward the clouds until, with another sweep of Gotham's hand, the liquid angel turned direction and as it dived toward the water its liquid shape dissipated into a massive geyser that retreated back into the refuge of the River with a thunderous splash.

"What power flows through the veins of angels—and by extension all Nephilim—comes from the power which churns within this mighty

River," said Gotham. Even as he spoke, Gotham could see Jacob's attention rested elsewhere. "My tricks, as they were, don't seem to impress you as easily as they once did."

At first it didn't seem as though Jacob, who kept glancing now and then over his shoulder, had heard Gotham.

"No…it was really cool," he replied finally, though in a tone completely lacking in the usual enthusiasm Gotham had grown familiar to hearing.

"So are you going to tell me what's bothering you?" asked Gotham, who was nothing if not direct.

"It's nothing really…just…," Again Jacob snuck a peek back in the direction of where Damiel was seen resting comfortably in the shade of a tree a short distance away. "Is he okay? With me, I mean?"

"Why do you ask?"

"I'm just not sure he cares much for me being here."

"What makes you say that?" asked Gotham, though his voice and shifting glance toward the reclining angel noted no surprise.

"I don't know…just a feeling I get," said Jacob. "The way he looks at me—it's like he's suspicious of me for something."

Gotham sat quiet for a moment. "I wouldn't put much concern in it," he said. "Angels can be a curious bunch. They are very protective, especially of this place here which the Darkness managed to breach under their watch. It's likely you might be greeted with the same impersonal manner by the others. Pay it no mind; they'll come around."

There came a sudden sloshing of water, and Jacob looked to find a large elephant wading in the River nearby from where they sat. It lifted its trunk from the water, and when it did Jacob heard Gotham utter a cautious yet recognizable "Uh-oh" while attempting to back away from the water's edge. But it was too late, both in moving to a safe spot or to sound a warning, and the trunk took aim at the shore where the two sat and let loose a spray of water dousing both Gotham and Jacob in the torrent.

"Guess angels aren't the only ones who have found ways to tap into the power of water," said Gotham, succumbing to a hearty laugh, followed by Jacob. The elephant also seemed to join in, curling back its trunk and blowing loud its trumpet call. This time, however, when Gotham and Jacob saw the elephant's trunk slink its way back to the water to refill itself and caught the gleam of mischievous intent in its eyes, they quickly got to their feet and hurried themselves out of reach of a repeat attack. Beneath the shade of a nearby tree lush with pink and white blossoms, they found Damiel stretched out on his back upon the soft grass. The wolf was laying near his side watching the bees busily flying overhead from bloom to bloom.

"If you're done with your splashing about, perhaps we can push on again while we've still got sunlight in our favor," suggested Damiel as he regrettably abandoned his comfy spot and rose to his feet.

"Yes, I can see you have been quite put out by our tomfoolery," Gotham retorted.

"Tomfoolery?" echoed Jacob, shooting the angel a questionable look. "Did you just say tomfoolery."

"Yes…tomfoolery. Silliness. What of it?" inquired Gotham with a rare and weird naivety that came from not promptly recognizing the layer of dust and cobwebs time had left on his word choice which Jacob found so amusing.

"Nothing…nothing at all. It's a perfectly fine word…for someone sporting a handlebar mustache and cruising the main cobblestone strip in a horse-drawn carriage," cracked Jacob while trying to suppress a giggle or two fighting to be heard.

"And what word, may I ask, would be more to your liking: shenanigans, high jinx, monkey business?"

"Well, at least you managed to move up to the 'Leave It to Beaver' era," answered Jacob.

"Forgive me," snarked Gotham when he saw even Damiel's face crack with levity and realized his error. "When one spends as many centuries living amongst civilians such as yourself as I have, the tongue sometimes has trouble keeping the language of the day in order."

"I think maybe your tongue slid back to keep your hair company," Jacob chided with a chortle.

A look of offense took hold of Gotham. "What's wrong with my hair?"

"I didn't say there was anything wrong with it," said Jacob. "But it has made this whole experience feel as if I got sucked into an episode of 'Highlander.' "

Gotham discreetly and inconspicuously as possible ran his hand across the top of his head and over his gathered long locks tethered in a ponytail. The blank look on his face, however, revealed a complete and utter loss to the pop culture references made by the smirking teen who continued to parrot the angel's word several times in mocking fashion under his breath while in the crosshairs of Gotham's perplexed glare.

"Tomfoolery. It was tomfoolery," Gotham debated with himself under his breath as the trio prepared to resume their way northward.

"Time being as it is, perhaps we should ride the rest of the way," suggested Damiel.

"I wouldn't be opposed to such a proposition," Gotham replied with conscientious—if not awkward—phrasing of his carefully chosen string of words while glowering at the boy.

"How much further do we have to go?" asked Jacob.

"I'm afraid we're still a bit of ways out," said Damiel.

"Then I, too, wouldn't be opposed to such a proposition. In fact, I'm betting it'll be a real hootenanny," Jacob seconded with a giggle while shooting Gotham a mischievous wink.

"Just one thing…what are you suggesting we ride?" asked the boy, scouting the immediate area and the animals seen wandering about. "The elephant?"

"Not quite. There's only one way to ride through Eden," said Damiel.

"And that is?"

"The Snowdrifts, of course."

Of course, Jacob had no idea what the Snowdrifts Damiel spoke of were. For all he knew in this strange unconventional world he now found himself in, the angel could have been referring to actual snowdrifts, and it wouldn't have surprised him in the least if a cold gust of wind was beckoned to carry them the rest of their journey. Well, it may have surprised him a little. Instead of prodding Damiel with the logical question of what the Snowdrifts he spoke of were, however, Jacob waited quietly for the answer he knew would soon come when the angel closed his eyes and began whispering a quiet chant. It immediately reminded Jacob of earlier in the day when he and Gotham surfaced in the Dilmun Sea after passing through the Gate. Right before the stampede of dolphins. And, ironically, what sounded to be a stampede again caught his ears. It began faint, as if from a faraway distance, but it quickly grew louder, fast approaching unseen where they stood from behind a sloping hill they had crossed on their way to the River's edge. And it was to the top of the hill Jacob turned his gaze.

Damiel continued his hushed chant. It seemed to take flight upon the breeze which carried it over the grasslands in an echo of whispers, and the thundering sound of hoofs pounding in a drumming cadence grew louder. The neigh of a horse rang out, and suddenly the first of a majestic equine herd came leaping over the hilltop. There were six of them total, and they were each a brilliant, almost blinding white. They sped past, galloping in full gait down the backside slope of the hillside toward the River. Instead of slowing or changing direction as they drew closer to the water, they continued forth full tilt until their hooves reached the very last inch of the bank. Then with an impressive synchronized leap their powerful legs took them effortlessly—and Jacob would have guessed quite impossibly—across the wide berth of water. Once on the other side of the River, they made a wide circle back around for a repeat jump, and as Jacob stood watching the creatures, he instantly knew the reason they were called the Snowdrifts. The fine mane of hair streaming from the horses head and neck along with their tails took to the air as they ran in such a way it gave them an ethereal ghostly quality. And with their bright winter-like coats, they appeared more like large wisps of snow being blown across the Arctic tundra. From where Jacob stood watching, it was almost like spotting a freak weather anomaly sweeping across the rich green landscape.

"Beautiful!" he whispered spellbound.

~ ~ ~

All six horses remained together even though only three were needed to carry Gotham, Damiel and Jacob. Once mounted, they continued on their way at an easy pace and, with the wolf following alongside, they passed a pride of lions lying lazy in the warm grass amid a scattered herd of grazing gazelles and zebras. They allowed the River to be their guide, plodding north along its winding banks as it led the way back into more waiting forests and across still more grassy meadows and fields of flowers. The day deepened, and as the sun grew long shadows on its way westward, the River revealed rows of scale-like ripples, like the hide belonging to a reptilian, slinking their way along its surface, making the channel appear more like some living, breathing creature slithering its way alongside the travelers. Above them, the once vivid blue sky became a flaming sea of red highlighted with thin veils of fiery gold clouds and the River reflected it with brilliant clarity as though it were a giant mirror laid beneath it. And as Jacob rode along the water's edge, it gave the almost dream-like illusion he was walking amid the clouds with nothing but sky above him as well as below.

When finally they approached a pass formed by two towering mountains, the River they followed alongside from the south was joined by three other very similar rivers. They each snaked their way in different directions—one to the west, one to the east, and the third flowing somewhat parallel in a southerly direction. Further north, between where the two mountains served as a gateway, flowed the headwaters of an even more massive river in one spectacular channel of water before it splintered off in the four separate fingers which would touch every corner of Eden. No one had to tell Jacob they were close to their destination, and he felt a strange mix of excitement and apprehension as Damiel led the way through the pass.

They quickly came upon a fertile emerald green valley residing tranquilly between a wall of mountains both to the east and west whose craggy cliffs carried clinging clusters of Forest trees attempting to push forward to higher ground. The River that had flowed so peacefully through Eden's grasslands and woods reared with life the further they made their way upstream as it moved over mammoth rocks in stunning displays of waterfalls as the channel of water swept down over steep drops on its rushed journey from higher ground. When they finally came to a stop, Gotham dismounted his horse and walked to the edge of a steep embankment where he stood silent. Damiel and Jacob joined him in a view overlooking a wide-open circular oasis of lush greenery fed by the path carved through its middle by the River. It unfolded itself against a spectacular backdrop of precipitous mountains along the far northern border where magnificent falls spilled from its cliffs while more steep-climbing forests could be seen fanning out to the range of mountains shouldering the east and west.

"Behold, the Garden!" said Gotham in a hushed voice, as if cautious not to disturb the serenity surrounding them, and yet at the same time carrying a certain unhappiness.

Jacob knew at first glance, even before Gotham had said the words, they had reached their destination.

~ ~ ~

The Snowdrifts were given a last rub of their soft hides and sent on their way. When they had disappeared back into the Forest, Damiel led the way down a winding path to the green grass below. The air was cool and damp from the thin spray of mist carried from the nearby waterfalls. As they walked, Jacob couldn't help gawk at the magnificence of the falls and the cliffs from which they spilled which were almost too much to behold. Even from a distance, their towering presence left one feeling, at once, insignificant and small. And as he stared upward to the main fall, formed by three spectacular but lesser falls pouring over the highest cliffs of the mountain, he noticed two golden orbs glowing from behind the rushing veil of water. It was coming from what looked to be a formation in the rock, but the rush of water falling in front of it made it difficult to make out what it was. And at first glance the light reminded him of eyes belonging to angels, which he had first seen peering out from behind Gotham's face.

"What is that light?" he asked pointing to the waterfall.

"The Chamber," answered Damiel. "It's where the White Circle meets."

"The White Circle?"

"A council of angels tasked in overseeing Eden. Now, we must hurry. The Formal Greeting is to begin at twilight and the light in the sky tells me we are already late."

As they quickened their pace, Gotham suddenly veered in a separate direction.

"Where are you going?" asked Jacob.

"Go on ahead and take him to the Hall of Light," Gotham instructed Damiel, ignoring Jacob's inquiry.

"But Gothamel, he's your charge. You must be the one to present him to Anahel," said Damiel.

"Please, just take him. I will join you there shortly."

Damiel opened his mouth to speak, but knew there was no point as he watched Gotham walk off before disappearing behind a sloping hill.

"Where is he going?" asked Jacob again.

"My guess would be to the Tree," Damiel replied.

"Tree? What for?"

Damiel was silent for a moment.

"To see his son," he answered quietly.

CHAPTER EIGHTEEN

*S**on?*

The answer caught Jacob by surprised. For a moment he stood flummoxed staring in the direction Gotham had dropped from sight until he heard Damiel calling for him to follow.

"How many sons has he had?" asked Jacob when he was once more at Damiel's side, his feet struggling to keep up with the angel's fast-paced stride.

"Just the one," answered Damiel curtly.

"But I thought he'd died."

"You'd be right."

"Okay, I get that this is Eden and I'm still coming to grips with seeing things outside the norm, but how do you go see someone who is dead?" asked Jacob, before quickly adding, "And please don't let the answer be what I'm thinking it might."

"And what would that be? Spirits? Ghosts?" Damiel replied without even the smallest hint of humor in his voice. "When I said Gothamel's gone to see his son, I meant visit him. The boy lies where the earth is shaded by the Tree of Life."

"You mean to tell me there's an actual Tree of Life? The one that grows the forbidden fruit?"

"We are in Eden. Why would the existence of the Tree of Life be of surprise to you?"

Such a simple answer should have made sense to Jacob, but it didn't. At least, not easily. Not when he still found himself somewhat shell-shocked by the reality of his surroundings. However, with the topic breached and his curiosity newly stoked, Jacob saw a chance to quell other questions he held in the back of his mind about Gotham's mysterious child.

"So, um, how long ago did he, you know…die?"

"Who, David? Must be just passed fifty years since it happened," answered Damiel with a sudden glumness. "Gothamel has not shared this with you? Of course not, if now you're asking me. And if such is the case it is not for my lips to reveal to you the details. Even if I wished— which I do not—there is not enough time left in the waning minutes we have left. Now come!"

Damiel led Jacob to a small grove of trees growing in a tight cluster on both sides of the River's banks. Like some of the trees he had come across in the long trek through the numerous forests, they were of a kind never before seen by Jacob in the outside world. They stood strong and tall, but again not nearly as tall as some of the Forest giants. And yet their massive trunks formed by limbs of wood twisted and braided together belied an age far greater than anything born inside the thicket of the forests. The branches of the trees lush with leaves came together from both sides of the riverbank to form a wide, bridge-like canopy over the River which bubbled peacefully as it flowed out into Eden's lands. And deep within the branches Jacob spied numerous lights that glowed softly and warmly, like lights shining from the windows of a cottage draped in the foggy mist hugging an English countryside. The dense foliage and the dimming sunlight, however, made it impossible to see clearly what the lights were, or what created them. At one of the trees bearing a large hollow within its twisted trunk, they came to a halt.

"After you," Damiel, gesturing to the dark opening with a gentlemanly sweep of his hand, said invitingly.

"I thought Gotham said we were to go to a hall," said Jacob.

"That's right," answered Damiel with a nod. "Right through here." And again he motioned to the hollow.

Jacob gave the gaping hole a suspicious study. What did Damiel think he was, a squirrel? Or better yet, a Keebler elf (though he didn't voice such thoughts aloud)? Even from where he was standing he could see it would be a squeeze getting himself through such an opening. And then what? Certainly it couldn't lead to anywhere except an even tighter fit. The look on Damiel's face was insistent, and becoming more impatient. Bracing his hands against the frame of the hollow, Jacob first stuck his head inside which, as he expected, revealed nothing but a deep darkness. Then calling for the white wolf who was watching nearby to follow, Jacob took a deep breath and turned his body to allow for the passage of his shoulders. After taking another step, he found himself completely inside the tree's trunk, and to his surprise it was not the tight fit he had expected to greet him.

"Keep moving straight ahead," Damiel's voice came from behind.

"I'm trying, but it's pitch dark and I can't see where I'm going," said Jacob.

With baby steps, he carefully shuffled forward waiting for the inside of the tree to quickly come up against his face. Yet as he felt blindly about him, there was nothing but empty space that met his hands.

"There's something strange going on inside here," said Jacob.

He then caught a glimmer of light shining down from somewhere above, and the darkness gave way to reveal the first step to what appeared to be a staircase.

"Follow the stairs," Damiel, whose voice rang out right behind the boy, instructed.

Jacob found himself wondering how someone as big and brawny as the angel had managed to fit through the hollow of the tree when he, himself, found it to be a squeeze. Yet he did what Damiel instructed and began climbing the steps, and he found himself moving up a spiral staircase. Around and around it wound, and upward it rose, far higher it felt to Jacob than he remembered the tree being. Yet the bark-textured walls beneath his fingers as he felt his way through the dimly lit darkness and the deep musky scent of wood told him he was, indeed, still moving through the inside of the tree. As Jacob neared the top of the stairs, he found the wolf who had somehow slipped past him during the climb already there sitting patiently. And beyond the wolf a magnificent space came into view making Jacob suddenly take pause. For a moment, Jacob thought he had stepped into a grand foyer belonging inside the walls of a palace in some far-away country. Everything was made of wood intricately carved and polished to a rich sheen beginning with two massive pillars Jacob and Damiel had to step past to enter the large circular foyer. Two more pillars stood at the foot of a pair of grand, winding staircases also shaped from wood with ornately crafted rails. They led to a second-floor balcony framed behind a row of elegant archways. And bathing everything in a soft inviting glow of light was what at first glance looked to be a large elegant chandelier hanging in the center of the foyer. A closer look, however, revealed it to be not a physical chandelier, but delicate orbs of light carefully arranged to offer the appearance of a chandelier and somehow magically held adrift.

"Welcome to Havenhid!" said Damiel.

Havenhid.

Jacob repeated the name quietly in his head several times, and as he did he quickly came to realize no place had ever been christened with a more appropriate name. Slowly, he pivoted on his feet trying impossibly to glance at everything surrounding him all at one time. Where there should have been physical walls to enclose the fantastic structure he found himself inside, he instead saw branches and leaves, only the branches had somehow come together to form beautiful archways leading to terraces overlooking the Garden below. They were indeed up in the tree tops, and it was then Jacob realized the source of the lights he had seen coming from inside the trees when he approached them. And he felt his mouth beginning to open and form the first word to the question poised on his tongue: "How is this possible?" However, he quickly retreated from asking it when he suddenly recalled the words Gotham had offered him before he was given his first glimpse of Eden.

"Allow yourself to accept something other than the finite realm of the world we've left behind. Only then will you be able to see Eden as it truly is."

Then he heard Damiel beckon to him. "There will be plenty of time for you to explore your new surroundings, but now we really must continue to the Hall of Light."

Jacob followed Damiel through a large archway past the winding staircase. It led to a long corridor which they hurriedly made their way along. The hall stretched long and far; more so, Jacob surmised, than what could physically be contained within the tree tops. And all along the passage there were many doors, and Jacob found himself wondering what laid behind each one they passed. Then after many turns, the corridor came to an end before a towering set of doors.

"Come, quietly," instructed Damiel as he pushed one of the heavy doors ajar. A smattering of applause spilled into the corridor from within, and Jacob slipped inside with his wolf companion following close at his side. All the while Jacob tried to keep focused on Gotham's words which continued to reverberate inside his head, but there was nothing to prepare him for what came into view on the other side of the door.

~ ~ ~

The Hall of Light, as he had heard it referred to several times, was more like an Old-World cathedral, monumental in size and opulent beyond all imaginings. Like the rest of Havenhid, the large rectangular-shaped nave was made completely of wood intricately shaped and ornamented with beautiful carvings. Several large columns in the form of angels lined the way, each carved with their heads bowed and swords gripped in their hands before their chests with the blades pointing toward the floor. They stood guard along both sides of a long table stretching nearly the length of the room and divided into two halves to create an aisle in between. Seated on the outside of each table were at least four dozen boys looking to be the same age as Jacob. Above them, more chandeliers of floating light bathed the Hall with an almost magical illumination.

"This is impossible," whispered Jacob to himself, finally choosing to ignore Gotham's voice. "Eden or not, this is impossible."

The gleeful smile fixed upon his face belied his astonished declaration of doubt. He could see the construction of the angel-lined colonnade had been meticulously formed by the living branches of the surrounding trees, and sneaking a peek through one of the open arched bay windows it was clear to him from the view they were still up in the tree tops. Impossibly the cathedral-like monolith in which he stood resided in the tree tops, and hidden no less. Havenhid and the trees, he came to realize, were one and the same. Even more improbable was Jacob's growing ability—slow as it was to come—to step outside the mortal boundaries within his mind to accept such an impossibility for what it was—an unbelievable marvel. Because here, somehow, slowly, the unbelievable was becoming believable.

Recognizing the familiar dumbstruck state he had seen in the faces of other boys brought into the Hall for the first time, Damiel leaned down to whisper in Jacob's ear.

"Try not to wet yourself."

"I'm afraid it might be too late," said Jacob jokingly, and yet not. "Shhhh...Anahel is about to speak," noted Damiel motioning to the front of the Hall where all attention seemed to be held.

"Who's Anahel?" asked Jacob.

"He's one of the guards of the Gates of the West Wind, the prince of angels of the Third Heaven, and the one who presides over Eden," answered Damiel.

At the same time Damiel spoke came Anahel's introduction to the other boys seated in the great room in words closely echoing the angel's, and another wave of applause rang out through the Hall. Jacob strained his eyes to the front of the Hall anxious to catch a glimpse of the angel who held such importance. There, before a towering wall of stained glass sparkling brilliantly with color within a frame of rich wood, Anahel slowly rose from his high-back chair and came around the long table he shared with four other angels.

At first glance, Jacob expected an angel who held such esteemed authority to be older than what Anahel appeared. The memory of his time at the church on Akdamar Island, however, was quick to flash in his mind and he was reminded of Johiel and the timeless mold in which angels were cast. Which is not to say Anahel didn't appear the princely angelic figure he was. Even from the far end of the vast hall, Jacob could see Anahel possessed the magisterial great height and stature as Gotham and Damiel. And while he wore a loose tunic-like shirt, rich blue in color and specifically tailored to his back to leave free his folded wings, it was evident through the thin fabric and the way it hung open across his torso he also possessed a powerful warrior-like build. His face, ageless and beautiful, was equally as striking in the great authority and dignity it possessed; his hair fell to his shoulders and held both a wisp of curl and the color of sunlight; his golden eyes were bright and fearless; and when he stood upon the dais looking out across the gathered Nephilim and opened his mouth to speak, his voice took a commanding reign over the Hall.

"Now that you all have been sufficiently fed and have gotten to know one another a little better, I would now like to take this opportunity to formally receive all of you in what will be your home for the coming months. Welcome to Havenhid, and more importantly welcome to your place in a family whose roots reach back many millennia."

Anahel's words drew more applause of excitement from the boys.

"Tonight begins a profound moment for each of you, for it marks the start of a blessed journey. In many respects, it will be a rebirth. And as I take a quick look at all of you who have come from all walks of life and from every corner of the civilian world, I am reminded of the countless faces who have passed through Eden's Gate under my watch and have sat in the chairs you now occupy. And I dare say I believe I may be looking at what could be the strongest flock to have yet graced this sacred hall," said Anahel to again more applause, this time with swaggering cheers.

Jacob listened intently as Anahel spoke, but his eyes continued to wander about the Hall with continuing fascination. He especially found himself captivated by the vaulted ceiling looming high above him. Particularly since just a few moments earlier before Anahel began speaking Jacob recalled seeing open sky in place of the ceiling. Queerly, he noticed the many limbs of the trees beginning to stir the darker it drew outside. As the sun faded and the stars began bejeweling the night sky, the branches began to come together, like a flower closing itself inside its pedals. And as the branches formed a canopy overhead, the limbs intertwined with one another in an inexplicable way to form the intricate arch work of the vaulted ceiling. Even more impressive, as the ceiling was formed so, too, was revealed decoratively painted murals of images taken from the books of Genesis and Revelation chronicling the Creation and Fall of man and the Second Coming. They reminded Jacob of the images he had seen inside the church on Akdamar Island, only much more elaborate and detailed, and untouched by the ravages of time. And while the images didn't appear to move like those at

Akdamar—at least at the moment he was looking up at them—the many kinds of birds depicted inside the paintings did. Not only did they move, but they had the ability to fly at will in and out of the murals, and transforming back and forth between painted images and flesh and blood creatures as they did.

From the dais, Anahel continued with his speech: "I will not lie and tell you your stay here will mirror your paradise surroundings. With every birth, there is labor. And the road before each of you will at times prove challenging. Luckily, I have a team of teachers here to see you through those challenges. They are what remain of a band of angels known as Watchers, unnamed or mentioned in history except within these hallowed walls, who stood steadfast and loyal in their service in the shadow of their Fallen brethren. Long ago, they were sent to the mortal world to enlighten the fathers and mothers of mankind with the tools necessary to wade their way through the hardships of mortal life. Here, you will come to know them as your Guides, for they will guide you with the tools necessary for you to exist as Nephilim. What you end up doing with those tools will ultimately be of your own choosing."

He then turned to the long table behind him where three figures were quietly seated dressed in open tunic-like shirts of differing colors similar to that worn by Anahel. One by one, they rose to their feet with an air of gallantry as Anahel introduced them.

First, there was Zuriel. His face, while sculpted with pleasant features, held an intimidating coldness made more pronounced by a mane of long hair as black as the feathers of a raven's wing. The long shiny locks held numerous braids secured by a long vine of emerald green ivy.

"Many of you undoubtedly are already aware of the unique and special cache of abilities gifted to Nephilim upon their birth. From Zuriel, you will come to learn those things that set you apart from ordinary civilian boys, and more importantly help you tap into those talents, and strengthen those gifts."

Next was Thaniel. Rare amongst angels, his light curled tresses had been shorn short to the scalp, giving his already ageless face an even more youthful appearance. And yet a far-reaching depth of wisdom emanated from his visage giving him a distinguished maturity as well. So it was no surprise when Anahel revealed his forte.

"From Thaniel, you will learn the history from which you came, both your mortal side as well as non-mortal. As well, you will be educated in everything you need to know about the dark forces which plague our existence and seek the destruction of the Light. For without knowledge, no amount of power will provide you with a weapon sturdy enough to do battle against them," said Anahel.

Then there was Eksel. With his hands clasped behind his back, he stood proud and powerful like a warrior fresh off the battlefront. His piercing gold-lit eyes staring out from behind his fearless exterior seemingly dared just one of the Nephilim he looked down upon to conjure the courage to meet his gaze with their own.

"Without question, I'm sure it is safe to guess most of you are anxious to learn to fly," said Anahel.

The answer from the boys came in a resounding chorus of enthusiastic cheers.

Anahel nodded knowingly while motioning for a return to silence. "From Eksel, you will learn how to take the skies. But I must forewarn you, one's coming into wings is not absolute, despite how your back may appear in its physicality. It is something each one of you will discover is earned, and as such not certain."

As Eksel sank back into his seat, Anahel's eyes fell upon the empty chair beside him.

"Finally, you will be lessoned in the art of combat," he continued. "And when the time comes you will each be gifted with a special sword. Unfortunately, for reasons lost to me, the one tasked with this duty doesn't appear to be with us at the moment."

"I'm here," a voice rang out turning all heads in unison toward the back of the Hall. It came from Damiel and, as he made his way toward Anahel, all eyes turned to follow him.

"Forgive me. I've spent the day walking from the shore."

"Walking from the shore?" echoed Anahel with confusion. "Strange time to embark on such an excursion with Havenhid brimming with our newly arrived guests."

"I was escorting a late arrival."

"Oh, I see." Anahel turned his gaze toward the back of the Hall. "Well, by all means bring him forward for a proper introduction."

Damiel glanced at Jacob over his shoulder and, with visible hesitation, motioned for the boy to come forward.

~ ~ ~

Jacob could feel the weight of curious eyes upon him as he made his way between the divided table where the gathering of boys sat. Their whispers to one another could not escape his keen hearing. Ahead, the golden glare of the Guides' eyes focused hard on him, particularly Anahel's, and Jacob took comfort with the presence of his wolf companion who remained close to his side. And as Jacob drew closer, he found himself growing more and more self-conscious when he suddenly noticed the same odd look that came to Johiel and Damiel when they first laid eyes on him had continued its trend, this time with Anahel.

The whispers grew, now amongst the other three Guides, and they became louder with a growing urgency with every advancing step Jacob took causing an uncomfortable nervousness to rise up inside the boy.

Once at Damiel's side, he found settled upon Anahel's face a strange expression of recognition he somehow wished was not there.

"This would be Jacob Parrish," said Damiel as though he was braced for an unfavorable response from his introduction. It was an almost peculiar timidness Jacob never would have expected to come from such an unflinching tower of strength as one deemed Angel of the Sword.

A most awkward silence followed. Jacob gathered his wits and with a muster of confidence he pushed past the inquisitive stare boring into him and held out his hand to Anahel. At first Anahel continued to look down at the boy and kept his hand to his side. It came almost as a relief to Jacob when Eksel suddenly jumped to his feet and broke the silence by bellowing loudly: "Am I actually witnessing what is taking place before our very eyes in the light of this sacred Hall?"

"SILENCE!" Anahel's voice rumbled through the Hall like a crack of thunder. And when the instant flash of anger had swept from his face as quickly as it burst into sight, he turned a kind yet still cautiously suspicious eye back to Jacob and finally took hold of the boy's hand in a warming grasp.

"Welcome, Jacob Parrish," said Anahel in a tone which made Jacob question the sincerity of the spoken sentiment. "You must forgive Eksel's outburst. Your arrival here tonight is, shall we say…unexpected, for lack of a better word."

"It's okay," replied Jacob still somewhat nervously. "I didn't know until only a few days ago I was coming myself."

"Is that so?" Then casting upon Damiel a sterner, less welcoming look Anahel asked, "Tell me Damiel, I saw you in the Garden as late as early this morning. And I can see all too clearly that even if you had come upon some untold magic which lends to creating a full-grown child in a single afternoon, this particular one was not brought forth by you. So explain, if you will, how is it this Fledgling came to be in your charge?"

Damiel opened his mouth to answer, but it was Gotham's voice that made itself heard. "The boy is not in his charge, but mine. It is I who have brought him here."

A gasp of surprise greeted the sight of the angel standing just inside the threshold of the great Hall as the large arching doors slowly swung shut behind him. Gotham's steps echoed heavily as he made his way past the table of wide-eyed Nephilim rendered silent by the intimidating presence moving past them.

"Gothamel…" The shock in Anahel's voice mirrored the same reflected in his eyes as they watched the familiar figure approach.

"Why am I not surprised," Eksel's voice once more sounded. "And how was it you managed to sneak your way past Johiel and the Powers to get through the Gate?"

The snide accusation hurled forth made Jacob's back suddenly raise up defensively. Before he knew he had even spoken, Jacob quickly blurted out, "We didn't sneak through!"

The Watcher Eksel turned his menacing glare onto Jacob. "If that is the truth, then we are in need of a new Gatekeeper," he replied in a voice simmering with disdain.

"I will not ask again for you, Eksel, to hold your tongue," barked Anahel rebukingly before turning to Gotham who had taken a protective stance next to Jacob. "It is a rare moment that leaves me speechless. But here it is."

"My apologies for this unannounced intrusion," said Gotham in a manner somewhat coolly guarded. "I wasn't sure I'd be welcome otherwise.

"And, yes, Johiel granted us passage through the Gate, but not without considerable cajoling from myself," he added, shooting a steely look in Eksel's direction and that of the other Guides.

"As he should," said Anahel, placing a clasping hand on both Gotham's shoulders. "I'm not sure I ever expected that you would again step foot inside Eden's borders. But I am happy to see your footprints have once again marked its soil."

Anahel then wrapped his arms around Gotham in a tight embrace. Yet warm and inviting a gesture as it was, Gotham met it with a noticeable stiffness.

"It is only because of the boy that I am here," Gotham was quick to make clear and the hug embracing him suddenly grew slack.

Anahel took a step back and his gaze shifted once more to Jacob, who had enjoyed being forgotten in that brief moment, and then once more to Gotham. A silence fell over the Hall as Anahel and Gotham stared intently into one another's faces and engaged in a brief whispered exchange though the lips of neither angel moved, nor did their voices meet the ears of anyone gathered around them.

"I see," Anahel said finally. "Then we should move elsewhere to discuss the matter as expeditiously as possible."

Zuriel rose to his feet. "I shall call for the White Circle to convene at once," he announced.

"No, no, that won't be necessary. For now, at least," said Anahel with a wave of his hand. "I prefer first to discuss the matter in private—in my quarters. If that meets with your approval."

"Perfectly," answered Gotham, and as they prepared to leave with Damiel and Jacob in tow, the other Guides hurried to their feet and quickly followed. They were halfway to the Hall doors when Anahel suddenly paused abruptly and turned to the Nephilim he had momentarily forgotten still dutifully in their seats.

"Forgive me for this unseen interruption," he said to them. "Please, take advantage of the rest of this wonderful evening to eat and get to know one another better. But be mindful your training begins first thing in the morrow and plenty of rest is advantageous to your success. After all, before you realize it, Illumination will be upon us and you will each want to make your fathers proud.

"As always," he then remarked, "Eden is your home and you are free to treat it as such. But, as with any home, there are rules to be followed which were explained to you upon your arrival, the most important of which I would hasten to argue bears a need to be repeated; so listen carefully to my voice. You are free to roam and explore Eden's lands wherever you wish. There are, however, three exceptions most vital in being met with your obedience. The first being, no mortal is allowed to tread past the crimson blossoms of the Immortalis flower growing near the Tree at Life, and while you might be Nephilim, never forget civilian blood continues to pass through your veins. To commit such a trespass would call upon the Cherub and his sword of fire. I assure you it is a sight to which you will regret bearing witness. There are, also, two places which you are strictly forbidden to trespass: the Barrens, which lie in the Northern Lands opposite Broken Earth just beyond the falls which feeds the River; and the Silent Forest, whose unmistakable presence resides in the eastern-most pocket of the Garden. To break any of these rules would be met with the harshest of repercussions."

Anahel's eyes slowly made their way to each of the Nephilim sitting at the table. "It would be for the well-being of your life, not to mention your soul, that you be mindful of my words. Darkness has a tendency of lurking where you least expect to find it, and even Eden itself is not immune to its slithering presence, as history can attest."

With that he turned on his heel and led the way through the doorway of the great Hall.

CHAPTER NINETEEN

Anahel's small, but spacious-enough room opened itself to a large terrace overseeing most of the Garden. There Gotham stood staring out at the breath- stealing view of the falls in the distance that had become ribbons of liquid silver shimmering brightly in the moonlit night. Above him, a galaxy of stars sparkled against a sky of velvety blackness where the moon loomed big and full. A soothing night breeze blew across the terrace rustling to life the leaves of the trees with its passing, and Gotham closed his eyes as its gentle fingers grazed his skin.

"I'd almost forgotten how beautiful it is here," he said.

"I can hear by the night sounds echoing around us it, too, is pleased with your return," Anahel's voice came from behind.

Gotham turned to find the leader of Eden seated in a nearby chair. Elsewhere, receded in the faint warm glow of light, were Damiel and the other Guides standing, sitting and leaning in various spots around the room, anxiously awaiting to move past pleasantries and tackle the task at hand.

"Might I ask what you've been doing in these years since we've last seen you?" inquired Anahel.

Gotham drew pensive for a moment, visibly laboring to find the right word to the question before stating simply, "Drifting."

"Drifting?" repeated Anahel, raising his brow with intrigue. "Sounds more like something civilians do, not angels."

"You'd be right. Let's not forget you're speaking with a Fallen, after all," the corrective murmur of Eksel's voice made itself heard.

"When one is sent to exist amongst civilians, it's hard not to become one," said Gotham, ignoring the Watcher's slight.

"You did not need to go live beyond the Gate," said Anahel. "You know you've always had a home here in Eden."

"Home," muttered Gotham with a sigh as though such a suggestion was ridiculous, if not outright offensive. "Kind as it is, you know what you offer is an impossibility for me. Though I thank you for the gesture."

A shadow of sorrow darkened Anahel's face and sent his gaze to rest heavily upon the floor.

"There is something else I wish to thank you for that I regrettably failed to take the time to do," said Gotham. "And that is I am deeply grateful to you for allowing me to bring my son David here. Understandably, you were met with heated resistance, yet you defied a sacred rule forbidding the offspring of Fallen into Eden at the risk of your own detriment on behalf of his honor and his soul. And because of that, I will always be in your debt."

Anahel rose from his seat and approached Gotham. "Yours is a debt that has been paid many times over as far as I'm concerned," he said, placing his hand firmly on the angel's shoulder.

Gotham, feeling the excruciating welling of emotion rarely felt amongst angels, quickly turned away while spurning it with all his might.

"Have you been yet to the Tree?" asked Anahel.

Gotham nodded, knowing full well to which tree the angel was referring.

"Then you've witnessed its remarkable, and quite unexpected, transformation," said Anahel. "It's quite inspiriting to see it returned to its former glory. Since the fall of man the Tree of Life came to exist as the Tree of Death, standing withered and decimated after being struck dead by the hand of God. Then, miraculously, it was roused by the first buds of life to grace its branches soon after the body of your son was laid to rest at its rooted feet."

"I still say it was wrong," Eksel interrupted, breaking the silence from where he stood listening with a deepening aggrieved scowl.

"Please, Eksel, now's not the time," said Damiel, shooting the brooding angel a glare to hold his tongue.

"You're right, Damiel, the time's long past," sniped Eksel as his eyes attempted to burn their way through Anahel. "You had no right to defile what has always been sacred ground."

"Yes, Eksel, you have more than made clear your position on the matter," snapped Anahel.

"If you please—and I say this with no due disrespect to Gothamel or the decision you, Anahel, made in regards to the matter—but in an effort to blunt Eksel as the lone bad guy amongst us, I must ultimately agree with him," the young-faced Thaniel chimed in. "Much as I liked David personally—and you know, Gothamel, how true a statement that is coming from me—the fact remains the Tree of Life was desecrated by mortals. And as such mortals were forever forbidden from treading upon the earth where its roots dwell. To then defy this edict by allowing the final resting place of a mortal—Nephilim or not—to reside at the foot of the Tree is, for lack of better word, impious."

"I am surprised to find that out of all of us, Thaniel, your memory seems most fleeting," said Damiel. "Or have you forgotten completely the calling which earned the boy his resting place?"

"Calling? Ha! I believe it is your memory, Damiel, which has failed you," spat Eksel vehemently. "The only calling which visited itself upon that boy was that of traitor seduced by the whims of Darkness."

The Watcher's words drew Gotham's seething stare from beneath his narrowing brow, and his temples could be seen pulsating with the clenching of his jaw which he tightened to retain his calm.

"When have you ever known life where there was none to suddenly come blooming and lend the comfort of shade to the bones of one so traitorous?" retorted Damiel.

Before further argument could be voiced, Anahel signaled quiet with a raising of his hand. "Enough of this! We are not here to autopsy a decision that was mine, and mine alone, to make."

"No, we are not," Zuriel's voice rose from where he had quietly sat listening. His eyes gleamed from behind a shadow cast upon his face which remained out of reach of the fire light. "There is, however, something I would like to know; what I think we'd all like to know, before we turn our discussion to the real reason we are gathered here." Zuriel then cast a pointed look in Gotham's direction. "And that is, what occurred once you left Eden after laying to rest your son?"

"Why do you ask me?" answered Gotham warily. "Surely, Damiel provided you with an accounting, as he was at hand to witness what had taken place."

"That I did," answered Damiel with a nod.

"There you have it then. Or do you somehow question his word?"

"It is not his word we question, but after what we've all witnessed this evening in the Hall of Light I do believe the incident in question, of which the details were vague and sparse at best, deserves a retelling to all of us present in this room, and that it should come from your lips," Zuriel said with persistence. "The last any of us saw, you left here with a length of Herrinsu vine and a murderous fire emblazoned in your eyes. All we wish is to know without doubt is what happened."

"What do you think happened?" hissed Gotham, flashing at the black-haired Guide a fierce gaze now filled with a deep-set anger slowly being stoked to life by the long-ago events he had fought long to forget. Yet it was clear from the faces staring back a more substantive answer was required.

"Please, Gothamel," Anahel coaxed gently. "I know this causes you much displeasure, but it would help us to hear an actual account in your own words now that we have the chance."

And with a heavy, burdensome sigh, Gotham turned away and gazed once more out into the nighttime splendor of the Garden.

~ ~ ~

"I did not know an angel could feel the pain that weighted itself upon me when I laid David in the shadow of the Tree and cast my eyes upon him for the final time," said Gotham, when his lips finally moved to speak after a long silence. "Such anguish I thought had been a burden placed specifically on the shoulders of civilians, and civilians alone. But there it was, constantly gnawing away at my insides. And yet it was quickly overwhelmed by a rage never before made known to me. So great was it, I could not even see fully the glory of the Tree begin to awaken from its deathly slumber before my very eyes, nor did I care. I had become engulfed by the riptides of a boiling sea of red."

"I witnessed the look taken prisoner in your eyes, and it is one I hope never to see again," remarked Anahel, sullenly. "I knew God himself would not have the power to stop you in your quest for vengeance, when it finally came."

The corner of Gotham's mouth turned upward in a grin as he chuckled. His smile, however, was not one of joviality, nor was his chuckle sparked by levity. "No, God, himself, would not stop me, nor do I think he cared to," he muttered under his breath leaving the other angels in the room to trade curious looks with one another.

"I kept seeing his face," continued Gotham. "He had laughed at me. Smugly looking down at me from behind a mask of contemptuousness, he actually laughed at me as I knelt on the ground cradling the limp body of my dead boy. I saw him eyeing the sword laying on the ground between him and me, and I could see him quietly debating to himself whether he was the owner of the courage needed to risk making a grab for it. 'Go for it,' I coaxed him with a hiss of hatred. 'I beg of you.' But even with greed for what he had long coveted blazing in his eyes like a beacon burning through a dense fog, he dared not to. 'Keep the sword,' he said to me, hesitant though he was to utter the words. 'As fate would have it, it has served its purpose.' And he was gone like the reaper of a bad dream."

"You're speaking of Samael?" said Zuriel.

"Samael." Anahel breathed forth the name with a heavy and troubled-filled sigh. "I have always questioned who was truly the more dangerous, the Dark Dragon or Samael. The Dragon has gone down in legend as the great adversary of God and corrupter of man. And mind my words, that he is, and much more, as each of us have intimately come to witness. But his great sin has always been one of vanity and a refusal to see anything as being greater than himself. Samael on the other hand—I'm certain each of you share agreement with me—has always been a true serpent of darkness. More vile and repugnant than anything in creation. It is inside him true evil lies like a stagnant swamp. But I have interrupted you, Gothamel. Please, go on."

And Gotham did, though with great reluctance. "I couldn't escape the sound of his laughter ringing in my ears, or the twisted look of pleasure draped across his face, even when I shut my eyes. It fed inside me a rage I feared would lead me to an inescapable brink from which I would find myself unable to return. It was hard enough trying to come to terms with my own responsibility for David's death, but I could not let walk the one who gleefully led him like a sacrificial lamb to an altar to be slaughtered. And so I went on the hunt for him, and my hunt took me to the cruelest place on earth: the Infernum Desert."

It grew hushed for a moment except for the sounds coming from within the moon-lit night and the nearby falls.

"And what was the sword to which Samael referred?" asked Zuriel.

"There is only one sword to which a dweller of the Underneath would be drawn," answered Damiel.

"Destiny," said Thaniel, uttering under his breath the name by which the sword in question was known.

"Within its blade is forged a rare and great power, greater than anything known to mortal man and angel alike," said Anahel. "So much blood has been shed over the centuries in a rabid hunger to possess it. But nothing has craved ownership of the sword more than the Darkness. It's an endless path of countless souls laid to waste who have stood between it and its tireless search to lay claim to the most coveted of all weapons forged in the name of death."

"Which begs the question, if the sword is so coveted by the Darkness, why then would Samael, given the chance to seize it, choose to surrender the opportunity?" asked Zuriel.

"He did not surrender it willingly, I assure you," answered Gotham. "For I saw him eyeing the weapon laying upon the ground, where it had fallen the moment David was struck down, between himself and where I knelt cradling my boy. Unclaimed and so close within his reach, it was. But he wisely chose instead to take advantage of the anguish that had brought me to my knees and make a quick retreat while he was able rather than risk a futile attempt to lay claim to something so deadly within my reach."

The weight of the story showed itself when Gotham bowed low his head. "Besides," he continued, "at that moment he had secured something far more precious than any sword, even one of Destiny's calibre."

And though no one uttered it, everyone in the room who heard Gotham's words knew of what he spoke.

"If I might then ask you, Gothamel, what kept you from smiting Samael?" asked Zuriel. "He had, after all, led your son to slaughter, as you put it, and you had in your possession the one sword with the power to see through the task. No one would have found fault in your actions had you done so."

"Believe me, Zuriel, there was nothing left residing in my consciousness except that aim," said Gotham. "But as I was about to leave here to exact my vengeance I happened upon the Herrinsu vine and I realized a far greater punishment resided within its coils than the sting of my blade. So I cut myself a long stretch of it."

"But the vine, despite how deceptively thin and delicate it appears to the eye, is known to be impervious to being cut or pruned, including by our own swords. Am I not right, Thaniel?" inquired Zuriel.

"You are correct," answered Thaniel whose knowledge about all living things and otherwise inside Eden, as well as outside, knew no bounds. "The Herrinsu vine is as far as I know indestructible. An attempt to slice through its delicate stem would be like trying to run the end of one's sword into the side of mountain made of corundum."

"Unless the sword you are wielding is Destiny," Gotham interjected. "Then cutting through the vine is as easy as snipping a strand of hair from one's head."

~ ~ ~

Gotham continued as best he could with his telling of the story that, until that evening in the privacy of Anahel's domicile, had existed only as whispered lore to the small band of angels gathered in the small, fire-lit room.

"I knew Samael would not be stupid enough to show himself to me no matter how long I stood in the middle of the Infernal Desert and beckoned for him. Yet there was one bait I had which I knew he could not refuse," said Gotham.

"The Sword of Destiny," said Anahel.

"And his unquenchable hatred for me," said Gotham. "I placed the sword on a nearby rock and cried out to the ears I knew were listening. 'Come face me, and it's yours.' Finally he appeared and, when he saw the look in my eyes as I came at him with no weapon drawn but my bare fists, the grin that had seared itself in my memory was nowhere to be seen."

"For two straight days Samael and I fought, but no amount of pummeling one another seemed to exhaust the hatred and rage driving our balled fists. He knew not of the strength of the Herrinsu vine, but he eyed it suspiciously and there was a wariness in his eyes as he silently tried to figure out why I'd chosen to come armed with such a flimsy rope of a plant instead of the most powerful of swords I had long ago claimed," continued Gotham. "My countless attempts to tether him proved fruitless, but shortly after dawn on the third day he made a fatal move and I managed to snare him. Once in the clutches of the vine he quickly realized his defeat."

Occasionally, while they quietly listened, the other angels would glance Damiel's way, and the angel who had borne partial witness to the events being recited would nod agreement.

"I soon had his arms and legs securely bound," continued Gotham, "then stood over him watching as he flailed about like a fish cast from the water upon dry land. And the more he struggled the more the vine tightened its python-like hold and he quickly realized there was no escaping its painful binds. 'So now what? Is this the extent of your vengeance?' he hissed at me. As he writhed on the scorching clay-baked earth, he saw my intent was to leave him imprisoned in the wasteland surrounding him—the most desolate, uninhabitable hellish pock of desert I knew to exist in the mortal world—and he began to laugh; the same laugh he made heard as I cradled my dead boy. 'You're a fool, Gothamel. Surely you know this can't hold me forever,' he cried. And I bent down to him and I said with more glee than hate, 'You can summon to your aid all the retched souls from the depths of the Underneath, including the Dark Dragon himself, and if it pleases you to do so you can fashion Hell fire into a blowtorch and turn it on your shackles. But it will be fruitless, and you will only find the vine grow tighter in its binding. There is only one thing that can be used to cut you free, and the sword you used to lead my son to his demise now holds court over yours.' And he saw what I spoke was the truth, and as I left him to his rotting he attempted to bring sway over me with promises of riches and rule as though I were a common civilian. When he saw his words did not slow my footsteps as I continued to walk away from him he began to curse me in the vilest of ways. I found such cries to be the sweetest of sounds. For I knew I had rendered unto him something far worse than death."

"It is true," said Damiel. "I stood watching from a distance when Gotham spotted me atop a ridge of rock, as I shared with you once already. As he came toward me I could see Samael bound tight by the Herrinsu vine, and even though he appeared as a watery vapor through the searing heat I could see in his fit of rage his body beginning to morph into unnatural forms as he thrashed wildly upon the ground in a futile attempt to free himself. And his screams soon became demonic growls sent across the barren pit of desert where not even bone-picking birds dare venture."

The room fell silent once more before Anahel cleared his throat.

"Then it is true, and it explains the marked change in the air I sensed those many years ago, as if the Darkness had retreated from the shores of existence in a perpetual low tide," he said thoughtfully. "Which bring us to the boy."

All eyes followed the mighty leader's slow steps as they paced back and forth along the terrace. The breeze carried by the night gently fluttered the hem of his shirt. "While it was beyond clear to all us when we first laid eyes upon him the remarkable resemblance seen in the boy's face—particularly around the eyes— the question demands to be asked," said Anahel, before stopping and looking pointedly at Gotham. "Is he the offspring of Samael?"

Gotham gave a hesitant glance around the room to the other angels readily awaiting to hear his answer.

"Yes," said Gotham when he finally answered. "I believe him to be Samael's son."

~　~　~

When the tide of grumbling voices from the other angels greeted his answer, Gotham was not surprised. It was not every day the offspring of the enemy was brought willingly into their sanctuary. And now he braced himself for the expected backlash for being the perpetrator of such an unsanctioned breach.

"But how can this be?" inquired Eksel. "If what you have claimed tonight is true, then Samael has been left bound in some desolate desert for at least the last fifty-odd years."

"Meaning?" asked Gotham.

"Meaning," spat Eksel snidely, "how do you account for him being able to sire a son who can be no more than fifteen?"

"He is sixteen, to be exact," corrected Gotham.

"Sometimes, Eksel, I am amazed you can ask such questions and still claim yourself a Guide," said Anahel with an exasperating sigh that brought a rare smirk to Gotham's face.

"By what are you implying with that remark?"

"I believe what he's inferring to," Zuriel quickly broke in, "is the fact that while an angel, Fallen or not, can be bound as Gothamel states he did to Samael, it does not bind his power to move outside his physical presence."

Eksel looked to his fellow angels somewhat baffled. "Then what may I ask was the point in binding him with the Herrinsu vine?"

"An angel's ability to roam free of the body is similar to the way the Infectors choose to move in shadow among civilians, but in a much more diminished capacity," explained Anahel. "Samael may be able to exercise that power, but he is basically a powerless apparition, like a figure in a dream."

"Except to breed if he so desires," said Eksel. And from the look crossing Anahel's face, no further comment was needed. "So then, with all due respect, not so powerless as you attested."

"And how is it the child found its way into your charge?" Thaniel asked Gotham.

"The mother is the daughter of the woman who came to bear my child. And, no, before you inquire, I do not believe that is mere coincidence" answered Gotham. "I'm sure you're all sharing the same silent question in your mind, and that is why now? As far as any of us are aware, this is Samael's first and only child. For reasons unbeknownst us, he has refrained all these centuries from siring a son. So why now? And why choose this woman?"

Anahel's gaze fixed intently on Gotham suddenly cast itself to the floor as the growing conjecture heard in the angel's voice made its way around the room. "And why do you think that is?" he asked, but the tone in his voice indicated he was already privy to the answer.

"He knew the boy would be safe," answered Gotham. "He knew suspicion over who the father was wouldn't come until after the boy had grown some and began showing the obvious resemblances. He gambled that I would not be unable to strike down another innocent Fledgling, even one who turned out to be his own son. But more importantly that I would find it impossible to bring upon Ava the devastating pain that would come to her by committing such an act, especially after what had befallen her own child. He gambled right."

Anahel mulled the answer quietly with an understanding nod of his head. "And what of the mother?" he then asked. "What does she say of the father?"

"It was a struggle for her to understand. I came to learn he came to her on several occasions in her dreams while she slept, or so she believed at first. He was charming and kind, deceptive in form as an angel of light, not dark. To say she was devastated when she learned the true nature of the stranger visiting her would be an understatement," said Gotham. "Long ago she sought my vow to bring the boy here to ensure he would become what his father is not. It was the only way she knew to attempt to combat this terrible deceptive act heaped upon her, and the boy whom she loved dearly. She has recently passed, which is how he has come into my charge, to answer your question, Thaniel."

At that moment, Eksel suddenly pushed his way past his fellow Guides.

"You may have proved yourself too weak to sever this dangerous bloodline, but I am not," he said with a determined growl. And, as he reached behind to his left wing to retrieve a gleaming sword, Damiel stepped forward and placed a halting hand against his chest.

"You would dare draw your sword here against one of our Fledglings?"

"Maybe yours, but not mine," snarled Eksel, before pushing Damiel aside.

He took only a couple steps toward the door when in a blur of movement Gotham was suddenly standing before him blocking his path.

"It will only be over my lifeless body that you be allowed another step!" said the angel with a steely coolness.

"Don't tempt me," said Eksel.

"Enough!" barked Anahel, before ordering Eksel to return his weapon back into the plumage from which it was drawn. And with the fiery glare of Anahel's eyes narrowed on him, Eksel knew better than to challenge him.

"Now, then," Anahel, turning to Gotham after taking a calming breath, continued, "last time we were face to face, you placed before me a difficult decision, one which created an uneasy and marked division within the Garden that remains to this day. And now you return these many years later with an even more difficult situation in need of ruling by me, and already you can see here tonight the conflict it is causing. So I ask you, what do you believe would be fair?"

"A chance," Gotham offered simply. "The boy deserves as much. Despite who his father may be, he remains a Nephilim, the same as the other boys who are gathered in the Hall tonight, and as such a member of our clade. We have an obligation to provide him equal guidance. Otherwise, we willingly cast him to the Darkness to meet what we have already perceived to be his fate."

"And what of Samael?" growled Eksel. "Do you think he is going to stand by, bound or not, to his son being brought here?"

"Since when has Samael achieved success in sending a yellow stripe between your wings?" Gotham snapped back.

Before another spat could erupt between the two angels, Zuriel stepped forward between the two. "I must echo Eksel's concern. While I tend to agree with Gothamel about our duty to the Nephilim, whether they come from Fallen stock or not, this goes beyond the pale. Allowing the boy to remain will cast a dangerous pall over Eden. The Darkness with see this as a willful affront and an act of war on our part."

"A war that is destined to be waged whether the boy stays here or not," argued Damiel.

"Then you stand in support of what Gothamel has laid at our feet?" asked Zuriel.

Earlier in the day Gotham had appealed to Damiel for his support as the two walked through the Forest accompanying Jacob to the Garden. Now, Damiel found himself sharing a hesitant look with Gotham as he continued to waver over what he knew would be a divisive stance on his part amongst the other Guides.

"I do," he finally said with a finality void of question, at least none betrayed in his voice.

"Have you taken leave of your senses, Damiel?" Eksel bellowed in angst. "Was it not enough Eden and everything residing in the Light was nearly lost at the hands of Gothamel's own son? You want now to hold open the door and invite in this same messenger who now gifts us with a Trojan horse crafted by the Darkness itself."

"My senses, razor sharp should you care to test them, Eksel, remind me that the argument you continue to scream forth concerning Gothamel's son is exactly the reason why we should support his request," answered Damiel brashly. "Despite whatever personal feeling anyone in this room may have where Gothamel is concerned, you cannot deny he has paid the ultimate sacrifice to both Eden and the Light. Nor can any one of you, whether you care to admit it outright, lay forth the claim he has not been loyal and true in his service when he had no right or gain to be so."

The fervency with which Damiel voiced his words of support seemed at first to catch Gotham off guard and drew a thankful, heartfelt nod from the angel. Gotham then turned to Anahel who was carefully taking in everything being spoken. "You know I would never do anything to bring unnecessary danger to Eden, or to those of us outside its boundaries. I have weighed this decision until my head ached from the uncertainty. Be assured, however, if you deem it to be too precarious a situation beyond your comfort, I will return the boy with haste and without ill will to the outside world and provide him, to the best of my abilities, with the knowledge and training he would have gotten here."

Anahel left Gotham's side and all eyes watched as he wandered about the room. With a deeply pensive look, he looked to the night sky above where the stars appeared as glittering diamonds strewn across a fathomless black sea. And when he finally took a breath and parted his lips to speak his decision, a relieved smile came to Gotham's face.

"With all due respect, Anahel, I would offer that a decision of this magnitude should come forth from the full council of the White Circle," said Zuriel.

Anahel turned his gaze to Gotham. "No, I don't believe the White Circle need concern itself with this matter," he said, after momentarily pondering the Guide's words. "I have always trusted Gothamel's judgment. If anything, he has earned the right from us to at least entertain his request and see how it goes. For the time being at least."

"Then you will choose to honor the wishes of a Fallen over the rest of us?" spat Eksel with contempt.

"What I do is not tied to the honor of anyone's wishes, but based on the oftentimes forgotten reason why Eden's Gate was reopened in the first place, as well as the duty that has been bestowed upon us, which Gothamel has well reminded me," answered Anahel in a voice rising in growing frustration toward the Watcher. "You'd be well-served to refresh yourself on that matter."

Eksel's eyes flashed with malice at Gotham and, turning abruptly on his heel, he quickly made for the door before being stopped once more by Anahel's voice.

"One thing more, Eksel: stew if you so choose to," warned Anahel, "but I caution you now, you will treat the boy as you would any other Nephilim left in your instruction. Understood?"

Want as he might, Eksel knew better than to argue a directive coming from Anahel. So smartly holding his tongue he continued his leave from the room.

"Need I say that goes for the rest of you, as well," said Anahel to the remaining Guides who quickly followed in Eksel's steps, but with less charge and with much less anger.

~ ~ ~

"There's no love lost between him and I, is there?" Gotham remarked to Anahel when they were alone.

"Eksel is a good soul. Hot-headed and simple in his own way, but good," replied Anahel, before casting a serious look onto Gotham. "And now that he and the others have gone I must be blunt with you, Gothamel. I sided with you tonight because it was the right thing to do, but I will be honest and tell you I share many of the concerns Eksel voiced, and more. Be sure I do not come to regret the decision I have made."

Gotham nodded with understanding. "There's just one thing more."

"There always is," said Anahel with an sigh of exacerbation.

"It is with uttermost importance that what has been said here tonight in regards to Samael remains in this room."

Anahel cocked his head with curiousness. "Am I to make from the concern heard in your voice the boy doesn't know Samael's his father?"

Gotham shook his head. "For some reason he hasn't inquired yet about who his father might be, but I can sense the question on the edge of his tongue. When the time comes I would like to be the one to offer the answer. Right now, though, I'd like for him to just get his head wrapped around where he is and who he is."

"Whatever you deem best for the lad, I will comply," said Anahel.

"You will see to it then my request is honored by the others a well?"

Anahel nodded.

"I've noticed in this short amount of time tonight since your arrival that you've taken an unusually protective stance when it comes to the boy," Anahel commented as the two began making their way toward the door.

"What's so unusual about it?" asked Gotham.

"Nothing really. After all, he was put in your charge. And, considering who his mother is, it's only natural you would be cautious of his well-being. Yet I can't help but wonder."

Gotham waited for Anahel to finish the thought that for a moment drew a pregnant silence.

"What do you wonder?" he finally asked.

"If maybe you see an opportunity to steal from Samael what he first stole from you."

"Trust me, Anahel, were my aim to smite the boy I would have done so long ago and saved myself the aggravation of bringing him here."

"Who mentioned anything about smiting the boy?" questioned Anahel. "There are plenty of methods to do unto Samael that which he has done unto you without the aid of a sword, and just as insufferable."

Gotham was visibly taken back by Anahel's pointed if not perceptive suggestion. Before he could answer, Anahel opened the door to his room where sitting on the other side was Jacob, patiently waiting with his wolf at his side.

CHAPTER TWENTY

With the long, often contentious meeting ended and the fate of Jacob's stay in Eden finally decided, Gotham excused himself for the night leaving Anahel to take the boy on a tour through Havenhid. They strolled at a leisurely pace with Jacob listening intently as Anahel recited the history of when angels worked with the trees to create the deceptive-looking palatial dwelling.

"You're having a hard believing that which your eyes are doing their best to try and convince you is true," said Anahel when he glanced over at Jacob and noticed the skeptical look in the boy's eyes as they studied the towering architecture surrounding them.

"I'll admit, it's a tad much to take in all at one time," Jacob replied.

"The trick is to cast free from your mind the fact you're up in the trees," offered Anahel. "Otherwise you will wander the halls of Havenhid for as long as you're here with a spellbound look upon your face struggling to render possible what is seemingly impossible."

Jacob did his best to follow the angel's advice, but it often proved difficult as they meandered their way down many delusory long halls and turning corridors leading the way through several large fire-lit sitting rooms cozy with plush furnishings. Numerous verandas circling outside Havenhid offered places to spend a quiet moment indulging in the beauty of the surrounding Garden. Surprisingly, or perhaps not, there was even a church chapel nestled in the corner of Havenhid. It was quaint in size, and yet more exquisite than the most opulent cathedrals preserved in the old world. Even though the darkness of night had long settled itself over the Garden, the large stained-glass windows encrusting the towering walls were illuminated like sparkling jewels, as if the sun was still shining its bright light through their rainbow-colored prisms. There were no statues or other religious figures shaped from either stone or wood as found in other churches, but floating overhead in the center of the chapel were still more panes of stained glass levitating horizontally in such a way as to form what looked to be the numerous steps of a spiral staircase. Like the windows, they too glowed in a brilliance of color as they wound their way through a large circular opening formed in the center of the impressive Gothic-vaulted ceiling shaped by the tree limbs and continued endlessly upward into the blackness of sky beyond.

"Is that what I think it is?" asked Jacob.

"That all depends on what you think it is," Anahel replied coyly.

"When I was little, every night before I went to sleep my mother would come and read me a story. No matter what, it was always a story from the Bible. The one I liked best was when Jacob dreamt of a ladder with which he could see angels climbing to Heaven from Earth and back again," recounted Jacob while staring fixedly at the sparkling steps of colorful stained glass overhead. "I never believed it would be a ladder, but rather a stairway...you know like the song."

"Your mother was wise when she chose your name," said Anahel with a smile. "Now come, and let us see where you'll be staying."

~ ~ ~

Leaving the chapel, their steps found their way to the main foyer where Jacob first stepped foot from inside the hollow of the tree trunk. They proceeded up one of the winding staircases to the arched landing above. Making a couple quick turns down a last few short corridors, they came upon a hallway leading to several rooms.

"The excitement of settling into a new place," noted Anahel when they were greeted by the rowdy voices of boys heard coming from behind the row of numerous closed doors they passed.

They continued until they reached the last door situated at the end of the hall. When Anahel went to reach for the door knob Jacob stepped in front of the door to prevent him from opening it.

"Is something the matter?" asked Anahel.

"While I have a moment alone with you…I just wanted to say I appreciate you taking the time to show me around and all, and I've really enjoyed the time I've spent here so far," said Jacob.

"I'm glad to hear it," replied Anahel, though he could see by the noticeable bit of hesitation coming from the boy that there was more to be said.

"It's just…am I…that is, are you sure it's okay for me to be here?"

The question formed a frown on Anahel forehead. "I'm not sure I understand."

"What I mean is…I heard you and the other angels in your room earlier."

A grave expression surfaced in Anahel's face. "You heard our discussion?"

"Not specifically. Just a lot of arguing and raised voices," said Jacob. "I take it, it was about me."

Anahel forced forth a light smile. "Nothing to concern yourself with, I assure you. Just a brief, er, disagreement, which we managed to put to rest."

"It's just…well…I sorta feel like I've crashed a party I wasn't exactly invited to," continued Jacob clumsily. "You're like the third angel I've come in contact with who's had the same reaction when first meeting me—as though you're a bug and I'm a can of some kind of deadly repellent. And, frankly, I'm starting to get a slight complex from it."

Jacob's eyes suddenly grew round when he realized the words he had let slip from his tongue. "Not that you're some kind of insect or anything like that," he quickly added apologetically. "That wasn't—I mean, I wasn't mocking you just because you have wings or anything like that. After all who am I to talk, right?"

Anahel listened to the boy as he continued in his bumbling stammering. It had taken them two thousand eighty seven steps to walk from his own doorstep through Havenhid to where they now stood, and by that final step Anahel knew he had made the right decision in allowing the boy to stay. The long corridors had allowed him time to converse with Jacob and instead of sensing a seed of darkness one would expect to be lurking inside the offspring of Samael readying to sprout, Anahel found a genuinely kind spirit he rarely recognized even amongst other Nephilim brought to the Garden, despite the fact it resided beneath a hardened shell of skepticism. Yet there was something else, something that was unlike anything he sensed from the many offspring of his brothers who had come before to Eden. What exactly it was, however, resided far beyond anything he could recognize outright or put his finger upon. It lay cloaked behind the deep pools of Jacob's eyes, like a burst of light that comes with the birth of a star in the heavens, of which even his own angel sight was unable to spy a glimpse. Stranger still, Anahel found in the short time he had so far spent with Jacob that he had inexplicably come to understand—share in, even—the same protective fondness Gotham had for the boy.

"It would appear even us angels aren't immune to the act of rudeness, and for that I apologize," said Anahel, in the sincerest of voices. "We here at Havenhid are very protective of this place, and of those who reside here. I admit your arrival was…unexpected. But I assure you will find the rest of your stay here pleasant and enlightening."

Jacob gave a relieved smile. "There's just one more thing."

"As there always is," replied Anahel with a sigh.

He then followed Jacob's gaze downward to where the wolf, who ever since meeting Jacob in the Forest had never strayed far from the boy's shadow trailing along the floor, quietly lingered.

"For some reason, she took a liking to me when we crossed paths in the Forest," said Jacob. "And now, I have to admit, I've kinda taken a liking to her."

"I see. And you want my permission allowing her to stay; within Havenhid's halls, that is," said Anahel.

"If it's no trouble."

"We've never really had a need for a rule regarding Fledglings keeping animals in their rooms." Then speaking to the wolf, Anahel asked, "And why do I have the feeling this is more your idea than Jacob's here?"

With its piercing eyes fixed on the angel, the wolf cocked its head and gave two loud barks before sitting back obediently upon its hind legs.

"Just as I thought," said Anahel with a chuckle. "Alright, I see no reason why she may not stay, so long as the other boys don't mind."

"Why would they mind?" said Jacob. "She'll be like a guard dog."

A grin came to Anahel's face. "I doubt you'll find much use for a guard dog in Eden. Now, shall we go meet your roommates?"

When the door was opened, the four boys inside the room leapt to their feet at the sight of Anahel as though they were buck privates in the army about to undergo a surprise inspection by their commanding officer who had just entered the barracks.

"Good evening, Fledglings, I'm sorry to pop in on you unannounced like this," said Anahel. "I trust you have found the accommodations to your liking?"

The four boys expressed their approval in unison.

"Good, good! Well, then, I have with me here Jacob Parrish, who arrived here just today, as you all know. He will be staying here with you, so I'm hopeful and more than confident you will not only make room for him but make him feel welcome as well."

Jacob gave the boys a nod while quickly sizing them up as they, likewise, did him, and at first appearance they looked to be a friendly, though messy bunch.

Giving Jacob a final pat on the back, Anahel turned to leave, but before closing the door behind him he paused. "I would advise each of you to get a good night's sleep so that you will be up and ready first thing in the morning. The Guides are not ones to be kept waiting."

~ ~ ~

Once Anahel was gone, Jacob spied a bed in the corner of the room that didn't appear to be taken and carefully stepped his way around the numerous articles of clothing strewn across the floor toward it. When he reached it, he found it piled with a couple open nylon bags and more clothes.

"Sorry about that," said one of the boys who quickly hurried over and cleared them away. "We're still unpacking, as you can see by the mess."

"No problem," Jacob replied as he shrugged his own bag from off his shoulder and sat himself heavily onto the mattress. He then looked around the room. It was decent in size. Enough to fit five beds in various niches and recesses and allow for a few sparse furnishings.

"I'm Max Kelly," said the boy once he had freed his arms of the stuff he'd cleared from Jacob's bed and was able to extend a free hand to shake.

"Jacob. Jacob Parrish."

"You're a yank."

"A what?"

"Yank," Max repeated. "Y'know, American."

"Oh, right. Is that a problem?" asked Jacob, not sure whether Max was making a friendly or judgmental observation, even though his demeanor seemed inviting enough.

"Are you kidding? I love Americans," came the answer. "So where'n America are you from Jacob Parrish?"

"Cain's Corner."

"Fancy that! I'm a cane toad, myself," said Max.

"Come again?" Jacob queried with a cock of his head, thinking for a moment his hearing had picked up some kind of static.

"Cane toad," repeated Max. "Just a 'lil pet name given to those of us who hail from Queensland."

"So you're from the land down under. I thought I caught an accent."

"That noticeable, is it?" The sincerity with which the inquiry was posed in a voice thick with the twang of Max's homeland tickled Jacob's ribs.

"Only slightly," he answered with a snigger.

Max stood tall and wiry with a dark mop of hair falling thick across his forehead. His green eyes, hooded beneath a pair of pronounced eyebrows which curved near the bridge of his nose like the front of two facing skis, held an unmistakable glint of mischief-making; something which appeared to be supported by a half-inch scar freshly set in the otherwise unblemished skin of his left cheek. And despite the few moments of having just met, Jacob knew as the two shared together the light-hearted moment that he had found himself a friend.

Max then proceeded to introduce Jacob to the other three boys in the room. First there was Kairo, a lean, sinewy black boy from Lagos,

Nigeria with a clean-shaven scalp and a wardrobe of brightly colored clothes detailing his passion for soccer—or rather football, as he was quick to correct when Jacob inquired. Next, there was Leos, a tall, blue-eyed Slavic boy from Prague who sported a head of spiky, white-blonde hair. Lying on his back across his bed, he glanced away from the baseball he was absentmindedly tossing in the air to offer his welcome in an accent even thicker than Max's. Then there was Ethan, a fellow American hailing from a small town nestled in the beauty of Colorado's snow-capped mountains. Sitting motionless on the edge of his bed with his straggly head of chestnut-colored hair peeking out from beneath a thin, gray knit cap pulled down over his ears, his brown eyes were unblinkingly fixed on the snow-white canid who was sitting at Jacob's feet.

"Um…I'm sure this is a stupid question…but is that a wolf?" Ethan, holding between his molars a large wad of gum he had long-ceased chewing, inquired.

"It's alright, she's harmless," said Jacob, reaching down to give the wolf a ruffling of its fur on top of its head to prove the point.

"But…it's a wolf," pressed Ethan insistently.

"Yeah," said Jacob. "You don't mind her staying with me, do you?"

"You mean here? In this room? Where we close our eyes when the lights are turned off?"

As though sensing the boy's unease by its presence, the wolf rose to her feet and slowly approached him.

"*AHHHHHH!*" The noise escaping Ethan grew louder and more pronounced, as if he was suddenly in a doctor's office with a tongue depressor probing his mouth, and his body slowly began leaning back away from the wet nose prodding his hand for a pet.

"Don't be such a wuss," said Leos, tossing aside his baseball and kneeling next to the wolf to offer up the head scratch she failed to coax from Ethan. "Can't you see she's just trying to make friends?"

"Or checking out what's in the deli case for her next meal," Ethan muttered quietly while continuing to eye the animal suspiciously.

"So, what's her name?" asked Kairo.

Curiously, Jacob had never thought to bestow a name on his new-found friend, and for a moment or two stared at the wolf who returned his blank look as though she, too, had been patiently waiting for a moniker. As the room drew quiet with the boys waiting to know the name, Jacob's mind retreated back to the moment he first saw the wolf moving through the Forest at the head of her pack with her brilliant white pelt giving off the appearance of vapors of some fast-moving ground fog.

"Uh, Mist…her name is Mist," said Jacob finally. And it seemed as though both his new roommates—and more importantly Mist, herself—approved of the name.

"So, I hope my getting dumped on you like this isn't too much of an inconvenience," said Jacob, feeling some kind of an apology was in order to the other boys for being forced to clear some space for his late arrival.

"Well, that all depends," said Max. "Do you snore when you sleep?"

"Not that I know of," answered Jacob.

"Do you engage in other rude and inappropriate bodily noises?"

"Uh…not if I can help it," said Jacob with a grin.

"Hmm…maybe it's you then who is owed an apology for getting stuck with us," said Max before quickly adding, "especially from Ethan, here, which you'll unfortunately discover for yourself soon enough."

"I think what Max is trying to say is the more the merrier and welcome," said Kairo.

"Who says I snore? I don't snore," said Ethan defensively.

"Notice how it's only snoring he claims not to engage in," said Max, throwing Jacob a wink before dodging out of the way of an incoming pillow hurled his way by Ethan.

"It could be worse. You could have found yourself rooming with Creed," said Kairo. "Not that you would have ever been considered for such an honor."

"Who's Creed?" asked Jacob.

"Creed Maggert," answered Max with a noticeably snide tone. "He thinks just because his father is an AA that he's above all the rest of us regular Nephilim."

The reply caused Jacob's brow to furrow with bemusement. "His father's in Alcoholics Anonymous? Seriously?"

Jacob's guess drew a grin of warm approval from Max.

"Archangel."

"He's not just any Archangel, but one of the Angels of the Plague," said Ethan.

"You're joking right?" said Jacob, glancing at each of the boys for some sign of leg-pulling. "Plague? As in pestilence?"

"For starters," said Kairo. "There's also swarms of locusts, frogs falling from the sky, turning rivers to blood, fiery hail…he's got lots of tricks in his bag, that one."

"Sounds pretty old school Old Testament," said Jacob.

"Creepy is more like it. Seriously," said Ethan who looked uncomfortable with even having the subject of Creed Maggert's father brought up in conversation.

"You should have seen Creed when he arrived here at Havenhid. He thought he owned the place. Even demanded that he have his own room. But Anahel put the squash on that quick enough," said Kairo.

"Yeah, but his father still made sure he got first pick of rooms, as well as the choice of who he roomed with," Ethan was quick to note.

"You should have seen his face, though, when Jacob walked into the Hall of Light tonight," Leos piped in from his bed where he resumed in tossing his baseball. "It was like somebody went up and swiped his pedestal as top dog right out from underneath that pompous butt of his."

"I don't get it,' said Jacob with noted confusion.

"It's okay, you don't have to be modest around us," said Ethan.

"No, seriously," said Jacob, "what are you talking about? Why would this Creed Maggert kid care anything about me? He doesn't even know me."

"He doesn't need to know you, only where you come from," said Leos still offering no parting of the clouds for Jacob.

"What does Cain's Corner have to do with it?"

"We're not talking about Cain's Corner," said Ethan which only confused Jacob all the more.

"Let me break it down for you, alright?" Kairo interjected. "It's like a game of chess, follow? Creed's father is an archangel, which in most cases is like a queen."

"Better not let him hear you call his father a queen," Max warned, playfully.

"And being queen might be all well and good," continued Kairo, "but Gotham, on the other hand, is legend around here, or what most people would consider king."

Jacob traded looks with the other three boys in the room to see if they were catching what he obviously was not.

"I must have missed something in that analogy," he said turning back to Kairo. "What do chess pieces have to do with me?"

Kairo rolled his eyes and let out an exasperated groan.

"Don't you get it? Everyone knows while the queen might be the most powerful piece in a game of chess, the king is hands down the most important," he explained. "And in the eyes of most Nephilim, at least the ones I know, the son of a legend definitely trumps a Creed Maggert."

Finally, it began to make sense, but only the words.

"But...I'm not Gotham's son," Jacob managed to sputter.

Now it was the other boys' turn to share in a look of confusion.

"What d'ya mean you're not his son?" asked Max. "Earlier tonight in the Hall he said he was one who brought you here."

"That's right."

"And all Nephilim are brought here by their fathers."

All Jacob could manage was a shrug. "I don't know anything about that, only that he's not my father."

"Then...who is your father?" asked Ethan somewhat hesitantly.

The question brought a familiar embarrassment to Jacob as it had whenever the subject had found its way to him in the past.

"You're guess is as good as mine," he said with another shrug. "I've never known who he was. Sorry to disappoint you."

"Well, hey...," said Max who sensed they were breaching a topic Jacob would rather side-step as he would any land mine lying in his path, "look on the bright side. At least no one can call you a Weed."

"Weed?" asked Jacob who was beginning to ponder retrieving his journal from his bag and jotting down some of the terms being thrown at him for future reference.

"Just a name used to refer to Nephilim whose fathers are Fallen," explained Leos.

"They're called Weeds because they're outcasts—undesirables," added Max. "No one wants weeds in their garden, especially this Garden."

"Makes sense," said Jacob. "Glad to know I'm in no danger of being sprayed with weed killer."

~ ~ ~

A notable quiet came over the room and Jacob searched desperately for something—anything—to steer toward a new topic of discussion that didn't have to do with family trees or garden pests. He quickly found one in Max's face.

"So, that looked like it had to sting a bit."

Max shot him a curious look. "What's that?"

Jacob brought a finger to his own cheek just beneath his left eye which was the same spot Max sported his scar.

"Oh, that," said Max, fingering the permanent gouge to his flesh. "Yeah, well, you should see the other guy."

"Kid from school?" guessed Jacob, figuring Max might have suffered the same taunting he had in recent years, especially while noticing the familiar-looking protruding curves fixed to Max's back beneath the T-shirt he was wearing.

"Fury," replied Max.

Jacob's face instantly tightened with surprise.

"You had a run-in with a Fury?"

"Few weeks ago before I came here. I was coming out of a movie theater."

"So, what did it look like?"

"Not a pretty sight, I can tell you," answered Max. "Ugly as a box full of blowflies, in fact."

I guess that would be pretty ugly, thought Jacob to himself. Not that he would know what a blowfly looked like if it landed on him, much less a box-full.

"Luckily you had someone with you to fight it off," said Jacob.

"You got that right," Max shot back. "Me, myself and I."

Now Jacob was impressed. Even though Max looked to be the same size as himself and able to take on a garden variety bully, Jacob had been schooled firsthand by Gotham and Johiel on how wickedly strong and ravenous Furies were. And while Jacob only had the experience of being in the clawed grips of an Infector and surviving the ordeal by the skin of his teeth, it was enough to know he never wanted to endure a face-to-face with the much worse Fury. How, he suddenly wondered, did this kid manage to fend off such an attack and walk away with just a scar?

"Luckily, my father taught me from a very young age to keep my eyes and ears open for these nasty creatures, so I was prepared to fend it off," said Max.

"I wish I had been as lucky," said Jacob with a sigh.

"No kiddin', you've tangled with a Fury, too?" asked Max.

"In an alley on my way here," said Jacob. "Although, not so much a Fury as an Infector."

"Equally nasty buggers." Max narrowed his eyes on Jacob and gave him a closer once-over. "Looks like you managed alright. Not a mark on you that I can see."

"Well, you know how it is," said Jacob flexing his arms confidently before allowing his body to deflate where he sat. "To be honest, if it wasn't for Gotham coming to my rescue, I'd still be doing a pretty good impression of a shish kebab."

Jacob's way of taking a self-deprecating jab at himself over something so serious in such a humorous way made Max smile appreciatively.

"If you want know the truth," he leaned in closer to Jacob to whisper so the others wouldn't hear, "I owe my narrow squeak to nothing more than the fast pair of feet I was born with and am lucky all I've got to show from it is this scar—not to mention a soiled pair of grundies."

The two boys shared a hearty chuckle over the truthful disclosure.

"My father wanted to heal the scar and make it disappear, but I didn't want to. At least not yet," Max continued. "I see it as a kind of badge of honor. I went up against a Fury and I lived to tell about it."

"I'm not sure which I'd rather choose to go up against if I was forced to do so," Kairo pondered out loud.

"I sure as heck know the answer to that scenario: Neither!" Ethan replied emphatically.

"What if you didn't have a choice, which would be your pick?" pressed Leos. "Odds are we'll each of us be visited with that unavoidable introduction at some point in our lives."

"If I didn't have the option to avoid both, I guess I'd have to go with a Fury," Ethan answered though with great reluctance.

"Really? A Fury?" said Max.

"You said I had to pick one! Besides, even though my father warned me for as long as I can remember how vicious and monstrous Furies are, I just think Infectors are way worse. I mean, they're the actual Darkness come to life."

After experiencing a swarm of these dark demons up close and not having the unfortunate luck of witnessing a Fury in the flesh like Max, Jacob couldn't help but agree with Ethan.

"Besides," Ethan was quick to add, "it really gives me the willies that they have the ability to get inside you and control you."

"I can tell you this, whether it's another Fury or a hideous troll of an Infector, none of those buggers are going to get another opportunity to leave a mark on me," Max vowed confidently. "Especially once I find out what my Grace is."

"You're grace?" Jacob, instantly intrigued, asked. "What's that?"

Max shot him an odd glance. "You know…Grace."

Again Jacob found himself thrown by unfamiliar jargon that seemed so familiar to the others.

"I know grace before meals, and that's about it." he said.

"Grace," said Max, as though repeating the word would somehow unveil its meaning to Jacob. When it was clear the blank look in Jacob's eyes wasn't going to leave, he took a seat on the edge of his bed. "There are two things Nephilim look forward to the most in coming to Eden: the first is flying, no question, and the second is learning what one's Grace is. You see, each Nephilim has a special power passed on to him from his father. That's what's known as your Grace. But the only way to find out what that power is by coming here."

Jacob could feel a surge of excitement rise up inside himself. "What kind of power?"

"We're not told what the option of these powers are until right before our Grace is revealed to us. Hopefully we find out tomorrow when training starts," said Max. "Personally, if I had my pick I'd love to be able to make myself invisible. To be able to go anywhere in the world, and do anything without anyone having the slightest clue I was there. Not to mention make those Furies and any other creature from the Underneath think twice about messing with the stealthiest weapon they'd ever have the displeasure of tangling with."

"Reading minds." Everyone's eyes turned to Leos who was quietly lying stretched out on his bed pondering the prospect. "It's the one thing I always envied my dad of being able to do. I would love to be able to know what other people were thinking and plotting whenever I wanted. Either that or having super strength."

"You already have strength beyond what regular people have," said Kairo.

"I know…but I'm talking super, super strength," said Leos.

"I'm not sure I'd want to read people's mind," Ethan remarked with a sour look on his face. "I know a lot of stupid people who I would have no interest in knowing what's going on in their heads. Having the power to manipulate what's going on in those heads—now, that's a different story."

"Who cares about other people's thoughts?" said Kairo, dismissively.

"Alright, what would you pick if you had the choice?" asked Ethan. "And don't say become the world's greatest soccer player."

"Football!" Kairo shot back. "It's football, man!"

"Whatever…what power would you want?"

"Easy. To fly," Kairo quickly responded with a smile. "The other powers I don't care about. All I'm looking forward to is the day I get my wings and I am able to take to the sky like a bird. When that happens I don't think I will ever allow my feet to touch the ground again."

Jacob couldn't help but share Kairo's smile while catching the dreamy, far-off sparkle dancing inside his eyes.

"Well, those are all pretty good, but I've got the ultimate power wish," Ethan announced coyly.

"Oh let me guess, Obi Wan Ka-dopey. You'd want to have the power of a Jedi," Max remarked sarcastically, drawing a snicker from Leos and Kairo.

"A lot you know. Jedi Knights don't have powers," Ethan shot back. "They have The Force. Big difference!"

Max leaned toward Jacob to fill him in on the joke. "You'll find out soon enough for yourself, but our bloke Ethan here is a real dag when it comes to Star Wars, he is."

"Dag?" Ethan and Jacob asked in unison.

"You know, a member of the nerd society."

Jacob looked to Ethan and grinned. It wasn't hard to see Ethan possessed in spades that certain geeky quality shared amongst the costume-wearing Comic Con crowd, and all Jacob could think was how all this—Nephilim, Havenhid, and pondering mysterious Graces— must have been to Ethan like a Dungeons & Dragons wet dream come to life.

"So let's have it," coaxed Jacob, curious to hear what fantasy Ethan was mulling about inside his head.

Ethan glanced around the room, and only when he had everyone's full attention did he finally disclose it. "If I could choose anything…it would be the power to make any woman I so desire to fall helplessly and madly in love with me," he said, "and become the world's true Casanova."

The answer instantly sparked a muffle of suppressed giggles that eventually erupted into full-blown laughter.

"What's so funny about that?" Ethan, looking a tad wounded, asked.

"Brother, that's not just a Grace, that's a full-blown miracle," said Kairo with a chuckle.

"Yeah, I'm not even sure all the angels of Heaven could help you with that one," Leos chided.

When the laughter finally began to subside, Max looked to Jacob.

"What about you? You didn't say what power you'd like to have."

Jacob felt every eye in the room move onto him and he drew quiet with thought continuing to carefully mull over the question he first began pondering from the moment the revelation of Graces was first made known to him.

"I think it would have to be the ability to control time," came the answer when he finally spoke. "I'd like to be able to move time forward. But especially turn it back, at least for a few moments, to when my mom was alive and well."

He hadn't meant for his answer to draw the weighted silence it did, and for a moment he had wished for that time-controlling power, if only a couple seconds, so he could change his answer to something light and meaningless like shooting lasers from his eyeballs.

After a few awkwardly silent moments, Max turned to him with a forlorn look fixed upon his face.

"Well, if you were ever able to do that, may I just offer you a friendly piece of advice?" he asked, looking as though he was about to voice a heavy offering of solace. "Just make sure Ethan here is nowhere around at the time to sweep her off her feet."

His face melted instantly into unrestrained giddiness and together with Jacob they collapsed against one another in uncontrollable laughter that quickly spread to Leos and Kairo.

"Ha, ha, very funny!" Ethan muttered unamused beneath his breath.

~ ~ ~

The boys talked and laughed well into the deep hours of the night when one by one they slowly began drifting off to sleep until eventually Max and Jacob remained the only ones awake. Jacob had still yet to settle in and he grabbed his pack. Unzipping the bag, he started to pull out articles of clothing stuffed inside beginning with Gotham's thick overcoat. Tossing it aside, he continued rummaging through the bag until he found his journal and phone buried between his T-shirts and socks.

"You know that's not going to do you much good here for too long, don't you?" said Max who looked on quietly while lying comfortably stretched out across his bed.

"Why's that?"

"Look around you. This place isn't quite equipped with electricity to recharge it once it goes dead," said Max. "That is, unless someone finds out their Grace is mastering lightning like Thor."

"I guess I'll just have to be judicious with the battery life I've got left," said Jacob.

"You think that's bad, you should see a few guys down the hall already twitching at the thumbs from going through texting withdrawals…poor buggers," said Max. "You'd think the Garden of Eden in this day and age would at least be wired for wi-fi."

Jacob smiled at the idea and took a seat on the ledge of a large open arched window shaped within the wall constructed by the branches of the trees. He checked to see if the plastic bag had managed to protect his phone from the waters of the Van Gölü during his wet journey into Eden, and was happy to see when it lit up with life. A rustling of the leaves in the trees outside caught his attention and, as he peered outside, his gaze happened upon the silhouette of a figure moving across the ground below. As he took a closer look, he could see it was Gotham and he watched him cross to the far edge of the Garden grounds and disappear into the dark blanket of forest.

"Have you been to see the Tree of Life yet?" he asked to no reply. "Max?"

When Jacob received no answer he looked and found Max had finally succumbed to sleep. Jacob turned his gaze once more to the spot where he'd seen Gotham disappear into the shadow of the trees and he wondered many things. He then looked upward to the night sky and was quickly taken aback by the sight of the moon shining big and bright above the towering mountain peaks without any planetary shadow to blight the fullness of its presence. So big was it, Jacob was sure he could reach out and graze it with the tip of his fingers, and so clear, he could make out its cratered surface in startling clarity. The silvery blue light it cast down illuminated Eden in a dreamlike gauze.

Slipping the buds of his phone into his ears, he scanned a rolling list of his downloaded songs until the title he was searching for scrolled into view, and he pressed play. The familiar music began followed by the even more familiar voice of Stevie Nicks singing her song "Sanctuary," the words of which Jacob had somehow in his repeated listenings of the song managed to commit to memory. He sat there in the frame of the window and as he gazed out into the Garden he thought of the last time he had heard the song, inside the gymnasium of his school where he slow-danced with Wray. And he remembered the sweet smell of perfume on her neck as he held her close knowing it would be a long time—if ever—before he would see her again. It was then, for a brief moment, he felt the first pangs of homesickness since leaving Cain's Corner.

He abruptly turned the song off and pulled the buds from his ears. He had only wanted a moment to return to the world he had left behind, but he knew the Garden was going to be his world for the near foreseeable future, and he readily accepted it. In fact, there was no place else he wished to be at that moment, even enclosed in Wray's arms. And despite the lull of sleep beginning to settle its heavy weight upon him, Jacob wanted to spend the rest of the night sitting on the window ledge staring out at the beauty surrounding him, afraid that if he were to close his eyes to sleep he might awaken and discover it had all been a dream. A wondrous, sometimes terrifying dream, but a dream, nonetheless.

He reached for his journal and opened it. And in the moonlight he was just able to make out on the blank page he stared at the faint scratches pressed into the paper from earlier writings made by the boy who first owned the journal; Gotham's son David. Jacob knew the scratches—not legible enough to read— were all that remained of the lost pages mysteriously torn free from the journal, and he found himself wondering what secret thoughts was this journal the keeper of at one time. What untold experiences were scribbled down in these pages only to be ripped free so as to never be shared with another pair of eyes that might crack open the book? As he wondered these things with the sound of snoring from his sleeping roommates serenading him, Jacob took his pen and placed the tip against the thick paper, and for some time he sat there without writing a word as he relived in his head the events of the day.

And then—

~   ~   ~

Oct. 27
Eden—
I'm here.
It's real.

CHAPTER TWENTY-ONE

The early hours of the next morning came with the energized drumming of footsteps hurrying their way downstairs. Delicious smells filled the air and led the Nephilim by the nose—and grumbling stomachs—through the halls of Havenhid like a pack of bloodhounds in search of the mouth-watering source. The mix of aromas led them through the doors of the Hall of Light. There they found an immense breakfast buffet spread out across both halves of the long table stretching the center of the great room. Numerous dishes held piles of breads, fruit and nuts, along with eggs cooked in every variety imaginable (scrambled, poached, omelets). There were also several mystery dishes no one could quite make out, but all it took was one curious nibble to not care.

Like the other boys seated around him, Jacob was quick to dive in and pile his plate high with food before sitting down and stuffing himself with vigor. As he did, his eyes wandered upward to where he had watched with great astonishment the night before the many tree branches come together to shape the architecture of the Hall's vaulted ceiling. Now, in the light of day, the branches had once again loosened and unraveled their woven construct they had with one another, allowing the ceiling to part like the top of a convertible car and letting the sunlight slip inside and fill the Hall with its radiance. The many birds painted inside the elaborate canvas framed within the vaulted carved beams continued to stir as they had during the greeting ceremony, sweeping down from the Hall's rafters as flesh and blood creatures to accept the pieces of fruit and bread offered them by the amused Nephilim.

"Is it my imagination or does it look like we've been invited to breakfast at the United Nations?" Max leaned in to whisper to Jacob with a nudge to the ribs.

Jacob followed Max's gaze to the other Nephilim seated at the other half of the table across from them. And while it was a comment made in jest, Jacob found it nonetheless an astute observation. A simple glance at the feeding faces and it was clear no corner of the world outside Eden was not present in the Hall of Light, like Koji Sawa, a hip-looking Asian kid who, at first glance, looked to have a penchant for American rockabilly with loose-fitting trousers, leather slip- on shoes and stringy, jet-black hair styled into an early Elvis-like coif. Or Nils Christoffer, of Switzerland, who looked as if he had been birthed from the snow of the Swiss Alps with his paler than blond hair and seemingly pigment-free skin. He looked strangely like an artist's sketch on a white canvas void of any color except the eyes, and even they, in their bright blue hue, looked to have been touched by winter. Then there was the gangly, copper-headed Daelin McGinty, who hailed from Adare, Ireland and was the one boy Jacob found whose tongue carried a thicker accent from his homeland than Max's.

"So, how many are there?" Jacob asked his roommates who were seated around him concentrating on working their way through the food piled on their plates. "I don't mean here, but outside of Eden?"

"You mean other Nephilim?" Max asked before pausing to ponder the question which seemed to stump him. "Not sure. Can't say I ever really thought about it before. Never knew another Nephilim before coming here. I think they like to keep us somewhat separated from one another when we're growing up. It helps us to blend in and makes it more difficult for those bloody Furies from picking us out from regular boys, y'know?"

"My father told me once there's quite a few," said Ethan, his cheeks ballooned with scrambled eggs and apple muffin.

"What's considered 'quite a few'?" asked Leos.

"Enough to form a massive army," answered Ethan in an off-handed fashion before inhaling another mouthful of food into his already crammed face. "At least that's what my father told me."

"Wow, that's quite a bit," said Kairo.

"Which are you referring to? The number of Nephilim, or the amount food 'ol Ethan 'ere can manage to stuff into that pie hole of 'is?" said Max who watched with growing disgust at the feeding spectacle taking place next to him.

"Ha, ha, very funny!" came Ethan's reply which was muffled by his gluttonous enthusiasm. "What do you want from me? I'm a growing boy."

"Ain't that the truth. And we're watching that growth happen literally right before our eyes," said Leos.

~　~　~

As stomachs finally grew full, Anahel entered the Hall and made his way down the aisle between the two tables before coming to a halt in the center. Again he welcomed the boys warmly and extended his hope that all had a restful night's sleep. He then turned his gaze upon Jacob and in a clear voice formally introduced him as a Fledgling to the other Nephilim and, with a sudden turn of heads, Jacob found the same curious stares he himself had gazed out across the table and studied the other boys with were now fixed in his direction, only multiplied. And with his mouth slightly stained from the various fruit with which he had gorged himself, he attempted to swallow down the food bloating his cheeks in order to extend a diffident smile and wave of his hand.

"And now if you please," said Anahel, "you have a few more minutes to finish up with breakfast. Once you're through, please come down in an orderly fashion and meet me outside in the Garden where I will advise you of the day's itinerary."

He turned to leave, and before disappearing through the Hall's massive wooden doors he turned once more to the boys. "Please don't dawdle. There is much work for you to begin, and as I've noted before the Guides aren't patient with being kept waiting."

A short while later, a drumming of feet clamoring down wooden steps drew louder and louder from inside the hollow of the tree trunk serving as the entrance to Havenhid until one by one the boys came spilling out from inside. When Jacob finally emerged, it was impossible for him to not be immediately struck by the perfection of the morning that greeted him. The sun was shining warm and bright, and the air was perfumed with the scent of trees, flowers and other living things that had never before teased his nostrils. Just a stone's throw away, the River bended its way between the tree cluster, bubbling with the refreshing cool water it carried to the furthest ends of Eden from the thundering falls in the distance. Nearby, a frolicking pair of brown and white long-eared rabbits incited Mist to give playful chase after them. Quickly, they sped off across the Garden tearing past Anahel who stood waiting for the boys beneath the canopy of shade from the trees.

"Come, Fledglings, and gather about me," he called out to the boys, motioning them forward to form a semi-circle in front of him. "I sense you are all teeming with excitement this morning. As it should be, for today marks an important turn in your young lives of which there will be many as you approach the threshold into manhood. Yet unlike adulthood, becoming a Nephilim doesn't just happen as nature dictates. Sure, you have Nephilim blood coursing through your veins, and your bodies are capable of performing feats beyond mortal ability. Being a Nephilim, however, takes more than blood and strength; it takes hard work paid in sweat, pain, frustration and, yes, even tears—all of which you will get your fair dose of with each passing day. More importantly it takes perseverance and belief—belief in what you are as well as what you stand for."

As Anahel continued to speak, Jacob's eyes rolled upward with a focusing squint to the nearby tree tops stretching out over the River. There, even with the sun beaming down brightly, he could only barely make out Havenhid except in the faintest hint of a dwelling outlined in the camouflage of branches from which it was constructed deep inside the foliage of the trees. And while it was nowhere near the size needed to house all the spacious rooms and winding corridors, not to mention the library, the chapel and Hall of Light, he could see it existed. However inexplicable, Havenhid existed.

"And now, before I send you off to begin your training, you will be divided into three groups of sixteen to be known from this point forth as the Opreys, Harriers and Shrikes," Anahel continuing in his orientation. "For today, one group will be directed to the Library for educational instruction with Thaniel. A second group will head to Lions Bite where Damiel will guide you in body strengthening and combat training. And a third and final group will gather at the Crescent Scar where, with Zuriel's guidance, you will come to identify which Grace you each possess through the help of the Blackstone. Then, come tomorrow, the three groups will rotate and so on and so forth. Does everyone understand?"

Anahel was about to begin counting out the first group when the question hanging on the tip of every one of the boys' tongue was blurted.

"Haven't you forgotten something?"

Anahel turned his head and his eyes narrowed to the direction from which the question came.

"And what might that be Mr. Maggert?"

Maggert...

The name caught Jacob's attention like a pull of the hair.

Creed Maggert.

Jacob craned his neck while rising up on the tips of toes to peer over the heads of the other boys in order to get a look at this Creed Maggert whose name he quickly remembered being mentioned the night before by his roommates in glowing terms befitting a spoiled, entitled brat; or "wanker" as Max was prone to calling him. It didn't take long for Jacob to pick Creed Maggert out from the other boys. It wasn't that he was particularly taller or stronger looking than the other boys. Just the way he stood made it seem like he lorded over anyone within arm's reach—as if he was perched upon some invisible pedestal beneath his feet.

"Flying," answered Creed, in a voice weighted with testosterone while flexing his back in an anticipation. "So shouldn't there actually be four groups?"

Anahel's left brow arched itself sharply upward. "If I were you Mr. Maggert, I wouldn't be too quick to assume the skies would permit your presence with the ease in which it embraces birds," he said with a doubtful nod of his head. "Before a Nephilim is able to tread upon the wind, he must first have firm footing on the earth. No, you have much to learn first before making the journey to Broken Earth, and even then many of you will be quick to discover the wings you so eagerly covet to be elusive despite your physical appearance."

Creed's jaw tightened visibly but he refrained from saying anything further, and when Anahel saw there would be no further discussion on the matter, he quickly continued with the task at hand of counting off the number of boys needed for each group. As the angel busily tapped his way past head after head, Jacob, Leos, Kairo, Ethan and Max maneuvered themselves to the end of the line as inconspicuously as they could to ensure they be in the same group. Never one to have anything put over on him, however, Anahel flashed the boys a knowing look when he reached the cut-off for the third and final group, though he allowed them to stay put much to their relief.

When the first group—the Ospreys—was then instructed to report back inside Havenhid to the Library, there came an audible sigh of relief from the other two groups. If there was one thing no one wished, it was to be sent back indoors and forced to sit in a room full of musty smelling books after having been given a taste of the full bloom of Eden's sun-filled morning. And for a moment, Jacob felt almost sorry looking at the long, dour faces of the unfortunate Ospreys as they disappeared one by one back inside the hollow of the tree; but only for a moment.

"And now, to decide which of the remaining two groups to send where," mumbled Anahel with a ponderous tone before settling his gaze on Leos who stood with the fingers of both hands crossed behind his back. Jacob peered out of the corner of his eye and tried to suppress the grin he felt creeping across his face at Max who stood next to him quietly muttering under his breath "Crescent Scar, Crescent Scar, Crescent Scar…" in a prayer-like mantra while biting down on his bottom lip in growing anticipation as he watched Anahel move slowly back to where the other group of boys shared in the anxious wait. The anticipation soon became like a slow suffering and in a way Anahel seemed to get a tickle at looking down into all the wide, unblinking eyes firmly fixed on him. Finally, with a point of his finger he rendered his decision leaving Max to mouth a grateful thank you to the fates who had answered his plea that he and the rest of his group of Shrikes be granted the gift to go to Crescent Scar. However, not everyone was accepting at first of Anahel's decision.

"Is there yet something else I've forgotten, Mr. Maggert?" asked Anahel when he saw Creed was not going the way of the other Harriers.

"My father thought it extremely important that I go to the Crescent Scar first thing and not wait any longer than necessary to learn my Grace," answered Creed.

Anahel seemed more intrigued by the entitled if not impertinent young man than perturbed. "I assure you, Mr. Maggert, you will find every lesson you undertake in the weeks and months to come carry equal weight in importance."

"I'm sure," Creed replied snidely. "But I know you know well my father, and I assure you he was quite insistent. I'd hate to think how angry he'd become if he knew his wishes were purposefully being ignored, especially after being brought to your attention."

Anahel slowly walked over to where Creed was standing. And for a moment Jacob and the other boys wondered if maybe they were about to witness the wringing of a neck so rightly deserved.

"You're correct, Mr. Maggert, I know well your father, and the anger he is quick to express," said Anahel calmly with his hands fast at his sides without even the slightest hint they posed a threat to the choke-worthy neck within their reach. "And while I thank you for your…how should I put it…notice, I'll risk seeing you off to Lions Bite this very morn and spend the rest of what I am sure will be a rather uncomfortable day quaking in my boots for fear of the retribution my decision is sure to bring upon myself."

It took all the strength Jacob had not to laugh out loud at the drollness with which Anahel smacked down the petulant threat lobbed his way. Creed, on the other hand, was anything but amused. In fact, he looked rather beside himself. Not only had his demands not been kowtowed to in a way he found satisfactory—something he rarely, if ever, experienced—but it had been done so in front of other Nephilim, and by a Guide no less. Still, he knew well enough not to further butt heads with Anahel and backed down, though in a tight-jawed and scowling manner. As he eventually began in the direction of the other Harriers making their way across the Garden's green open spaces toward Lions Bite, a snickering from some of the boys in the remaining group, particularly Ethan and Leos, caught Creed's ear. He peered back over his shoulder, but it was Jacob his fuming eyes locked themselves on and held for several contemptuous moments.

"What'd I tell ya?" Max whispered into Jacob's ear. "A real charmer, that one."

Once Creed and the other Harriers were far enough along on their way, Anahel turned back to the remaining boys.

"That means for you Shrikes, your destination lies halfway up the mountain behind me," he said. "I would advise you make haste. You have a bit of a climb before you."

It didn't take much more to prod the group into action, and in their excitement they bolted for the cluster of mountains shouldering the western edge of the Garden..

"Oh, and Ethan," Anahel called out as the boy rushed past him bringing him to a fast halt. "To you especially, I extend a wish of luck. Or rather, shall it be said, may the force be with you…Casanova."

Ethan caught the faint sparkle of hilarity in the angel's face and a slow burn of embarrassment came over him. He then noticed Max and Jacob nearby sharing a giggle between them.

"Ha, ha, very funny…," mumbled Ethan under his breath as he balled his fist and gave chase after them.

~ ~ ~

The growing excitement bubbling inside the boys carried them swiftly along the lengthy, often steep path leading to the Crescent Scar. Snaking their way around huge boulders and between towering pillars of jagged granite spotted with course lichen, they soon came upon a large ragged semi-circle shaped outcrop of rock protruding from the side of the mountain face pocked with towering trees and colored in various greenery. At first glance, it looked to the group as if they had stumbled upon the ruins of an ancient amphitheater, though much smaller and intimate in size. Several large oblong rocks looking almost like stone-age benches were arranged in a wide semi-circle, and in the center there was a large crescent-shaped image appearing like some prehistoric cave drawing permanently scorched into the earth. It was dissected into six sections and each section contained a strange, stick-figure symbol similar to hieroglyphics found in the sealed tombs of long-ago Egyptian pharaohs. The boys eyed with a shared curiosity the strange image while mindfully stepping their way around it, careful not to tread within its borders as they muttered to one another.

"This is it— the Crescent Scar."

"It looks like it's carved into the ground."

"I don't think so. It looks like it's the actual ground itself."

"What are the symbols?"

No one seemed to have an answer, at first.

After a long silence had fallen upon the group, Max, who had been studying the strange etchings along with everyone else, answered, "It's Caelestian,"

"What's Caelestian?" asked Jacob.

"Basically, it's angelic writing. We have the English alphabet, they have theirs," explained Max. "My father tried teaching it to me when I was younger, but I really didn't put much effort into learning it."

Despite their shared abilities to understand foreign languages and writings, none of the other boys seemed able to decipher the meaning of any of the symbols. Even if one of them managed the expertise to crack the encryption of the strange code, such an effort was quickly interrupted when Ethan was suddenly heard calling out, "Over here, you gotta check this out."

The group of boys migrated their way to the very edge of the overlook where Ethan stood and they were immediately gripped in the awe of the view unveiled to them. Looking straight to the east, they could see the vast stretch of forest butting up against the foot of a wall of mountain before encroaching the higher peaks in clumps of green. To the north, dramatic falls of water spilled over the brim of higher, more precipitous cliffs rising high into the skies as if to form some magnificent crown of unknown royalty.

Jacob stood mesmerized along with his fellow Nephilim silently bearing witness to the biblical Xanadu below looking almost unrealistic in its beauty. The quaint valley of rolling green spaces and groves of shade trees appeared peaceful in the presence of the River emerging from within the ghostly ball of mist rising up at the fall's feet. The transfixed gazes gradually shifted one by one to the sight of a magnificent eagle circling weightlessly above the valley as it glided about a blanket of deep blue with its impressive wings unfurled like an archer's bow. Its sleek brown and white patterned feathers fluttered against the wind and with a screeching cry it made a sudden swoop downward and began flying directly toward where the boys stood watching. As it drew nearer, it became clear it was much larger than that of a normal eagle. Its piercing shrill of a cry sounded once more—and much louder. Slowly, the boys backed away from the ledge of the mountain as it looked more and more like the eagle, with its golden raptorial eyes fixed upon them, was coming in for an attack. And just as it reached the cliff terrace, the eagle reared its body up with its powerful wings rustling loudly as they swiped powerfully at the air, and a glint of sunlight caught one of the polished, razor sharp talons with a flash of brilliance, like a switchblade knife suddenly drawn from the confines of a pocket. Instantly, the mouths of the boys, who had ducked for cover, began to drop open at the sight of the eagle's two spindly limbs, which began to elongate into the shape of human legs. At the same time, the rest of the bird also began quickly changing its form into that of a human. And when the feet touched the ground, the eagle had vanished from sight and in its place stood Zuriel.

The transformation brought a collective "Woooooah" from the boys. Zuriel paid no attention to the frozen looks of amazement locked on him as he brushed past without so much as a look at the gawking group of boys who quickly side-stepped out of his way. He briskly made his way to the center of the mountain shelf, and with his back to the boys he gestured to the stone slabs arranged in a circle around him.

"Come, and take yourselves a seat," he gruffly instructed.

The boys scrambled to claim a spot amid the various smooth, yet time-weathered seats and waited with bated breath for the angel to speak.

"Let me begin by saying you are not here for instruction in magic tricks. There exists here no hocus-pocus. No spells, no wands, no supernatural balderdash. Nor am I here to indulge you in any juvenile fantasies some of you may have entertained that involves transforming yourself into some mortal superhero. Do I make myself clear?" There was a cool, no-nonsense tone in Zuriel's voice, one which seemingly dared anyone present to stray from the absolute attention and order it demanded.

"The skills you learn here will demand great responsibility and maturity, and even greater discipline," he continued. "What you choose to do with them once you leave Eden is not for me to dictate. Those actions, as well as their consequences you will forever after be bound by from this day forward, are yours and yours alone to make and, if need be, suffer. But while you are here, you will conduct yourselves as the learned apprentices you are. I trust you are each of you smart enough to not force me to repeat myself on this point."

His eyes, while like two golden suns, were penetrating in their iciness as they slowly grazed the faces staring back at him as if waiting to see who might be brave enough to take the opportunity presented to voice their dissension.

"I take it by your silence we understand one another," Zuriel surmised, after a pregnant pause. "Very good, then let us get started, shall we?"

Zuriel turned on his heel and several of the boys leaned forward on the stone slabs upon which they sat anxiously awaiting to learn what the strange crescent-shaped image on the ground might be. To their dismay, Zuriel was not yet done with his lecture.

"By now, you all I'm certain have discovered in varying degrees while living in the outside world certain unique abilities you share that set you apart from other mortal boys," he said. "Undoubtedly, your fathers have prepared you in realizing these abilities. Still, there is no comfort in being different. Especially when that difference comes with such a vast stroke. It's difficult enough existing in mortal skin in a mortal world with all its flaws and self-imposed hurdles. And for many of you, I'm confident it goes without saying, being a Nephilim has more often times than not felt like a curse that has brought upon you nothing but ridicule or left you feeling ostracized by those who view you as freakish in nature, for lack of better words. Am I correct?"

A grumbling of agreement rose up in response around Jacob. Even Max, sitting beside him, who had seemed to Jacob to be so comfortable and even confident in his own skin couldn't hide the recognition of what Zuriel said from passing visibly across his face. Jacob then gave the other boys seated around him a quick, perplexed passing glance. None of the boys looked particularly odd or seemed to possess any strange habits to note that he would suspect might leave them open to ridicule from other kids. In fact, they appeared much like him; average, normal teenagers who could have been plucked from any average, normal high school. Some even looked as if they could easily step into the shoes of a bully if they so chose to answer the call. Yet here they sat admitting to Zuriel's simply inquiry with a quiet unstated murmur that they had struggled with the same feelings of inferiority Jacob had. And for the first time

Jacob realized he was not—as Zuriel had put it, as well as himself on more than one occasion—as freakish in nature as he had been made to feel more often than not the past couple years. More importantly, in that brief, vulnerable moment, he began feeling, for the first time, an inexplicable kinship to these other boys, many with whom he had yet to exchange a single word.

"I wish I could tell you it gets better," continued Zuriel. "But the isolated gulf you feel between yourself and the life of regular civilians is likely only going to widen. You have now approached the age where your abilities—and soon enough your physical bodies as well—have begun to mature. My role here is to not only guide you through this state of flux, but more importantly train you in embracing and exercising your gifts to their ultimate potential. The first step in this process, however, is to identify the Grace that resides within each of you."

A hand immediately shot up into the air.

"Yes, Mr. Caph," acknowledged Zuriel, before his eyes even touched upon the boy who looked to be freshly plucked off a surfboard with his sun-kissed wiry limbs and dirty blond hair worn shaggy and bowl-shaped over the ears.

"So what kind of, uh, powers are we talking about exactly with these Graces?" the boy, unable to hide his eagerness despite his hesitancy to pose the question, asked.

Suddenly Zuriel was gone, disappearing into thin air as is he had never been there.

"Where did he go?" The question came in an echoing chorus as the group of boys looked all around, their head's swiveling wildly in every possible direction searching for some sign of the angel, but there was no one else present besides themselves. And then as quickly as he had vanished, Zuriel reappeared, standing in a completely different spot from where he had been when he fell out of sight. He was also now wearing a heavy charcoal-colored wool overcoat, the shoulders of which carried a light dusting of white snow. And as he made his way back toward the center of the circle, he tossed a rolled-up paper he held clutched in his gloved hand onto Leos's lap in passing.

"It's a newspaper," said Leos somewhat confused as he unrolled the paper. "A French newspaper."

"Will you, please, state out loud for the class the date on it?" inquired Zuriel as he shrugged off the heavy coat he was wearing and tossed it aside.

"January 26, 1924," answered Leos, as his eyes wandered further down the page grazing the bold French headlines. "It's all about the opening ceremony of the winter Olympics in Chamonix, France."

"Correct, which is from where I've just returned," announced Zuriel, drawing an even more confused murmur from the group of boys. "Now then, who can recite for me the seven heavenly virtues?"

The question drew a notable silence amongst the boys, broken only by the chattering of birds flitting about in the nearby trees.

"Am I to understand not one of you can answer what should have been the first words out of your mouths after 'mommy' and 'daddy'?" questioned Zuriel, sounding both disappointed as well as annoyed.

Jacob glanced around him as inconspicuously as he could and, when he saw no one was willing to venture an answer, he slowly, though not without some hesitation, raised his hand.

"Mr. Parrish." Zuriel narrowed a questionable gaze on Jacob while tugging at the fingers of the soft leather gloves he worked to remove from his hands. "Please…bowl me and everyone gathered here over with your elucidation."

For a moment Jacob cursed himself for volunteering.

"Well, um…there's Chastity," he began in a hoarse whisper.

"Speak up!" instructed Zuriel sharply.

"Chastity, I said," repeated Jacob louder than need be after clearing his throat. "Then there's, uh…Humility…"

"Not exactly flowing from your tongue, are they Mr. Parrish?" Zuriel remarked with a tone of judgment.

Trying not to let the angel's impatience rattle him any more than he was, Jacob paused for a moment as if carefully combing the inside of his skull for the remaining words. Then he quickly proceeded to blurt in quick succession his remaining guesses: "Liberality, Diligence, Meekness, Kindness and, um, Temperance."

For once, Jacob was grateful for the sound of Mrs. Braukoff voice ringing shrilly in his head as he named off each virtue while remembering the first time he learned of them as a child in her Bible class. The look which remained on Zuriel's face, however, made Jacob question whether he had managed to recall the list of virtues correctly. In fact, he was certain by the arch of the angel's brow he had most definitely gotten them wrong.

"Very good, Mr. Parrish," the angel finally remarked to Jacob's surprise, though the understated tone was hardly congratulatory. Jacob squirmed somewhat uncomfortably as Zuriel's gaze stayed firmly fixed on him for some time as though trying to bore its way through his flesh like a blowtorch. It was only when the penetrating eyes finally shifted from him did Jacob breathe a sigh of relief as Zuriel continued on with his lesson.

"While angels are gifted with many wondrous abilities, there is inherent in each of us seven core powers, for lack of a better word. These powers are extended to us as manifestations, if you will, of the seven heavenly virtues. They are known as the Seven Graces," explained Zuriel while strolling his way amongst the boys with easy steps. "One of these Graces, as I just demonstrated to you, is what we refer to as Drifting. It derives from the virtue of Diligence, meaning to be steadfast in your work. No matter what stands in one's way, or problems one might face, the person practicing this virtue will accomplish whatever it is he sets out to do, and what greater barrier is there than time and the physical restraints of the body? With the power of Drifting, one has the ability to wander through the dimensions of time, step outside the physical body and even occupy the physical shell belonging to another. A few moments ago I chose to venture back to 1924 Chamonix-Mont-Blanc in the Rhône-Alpes, site of the first Winter Olympics. Beautiful country. So beautiful I spent two days there, even though to all of you it appeared as a blink of an eye."

~ ~ ~

Zuriel then proceeded to begin naming the remaining powers.

"The power of Bending comes from the virtue Temperance, which calls for a constant mindfulness of others and one's surroundings. Another way to think of it is the voice you sometimes hear inside your head attempting to guide your steps when your feet attempt to lead you astray," said Zuriel. "With Bending, you become the voice, as you are given the ability to not only tap into and read the thoughts of others, but influence them as well."

"No kidding? You mean like a Jedi Knight?" Ethan blurted out with an intense seriousness as he seemed to become momentarily stunned by the revelation, bringing chuckles from the other boys.

Zuriel, however, ignored the inquiry with an exasperated roll of his eyes and moved to Gazing, which he explained came from the virtue Meekness and its call for a willingness to forgive and show mercy in the face of adversity. With the Grace of Gazing, one would be given the power to peer into the soul of another and see in intimate detail, including every dark, hidden secret, a life in full from start to finish. For what better way to accept the faults of others without prejudice than to be able to see the seed from which a rose sprouted and understand how it came to be given thorns, explained Zuriel to the sea of bewildered faces focused intently on his words.

And while Nephilim may have had the ability to understand the sounds of nature, a passing butterfly gave Zuriel the opportunity to demonstrate how the power of Whispering held the voice of the beasts, and the lone butterfly was quickly joined by a colorful swarm to follow any command the angel gave much like an army to its general. The power of such of Grace came from Kindness, or the virtue of being good towards all life.

"There's good reason the creatures of the earth have long been timid and leery of man, and that is because unprejudiced and compassionate sounds are absent from his tongue," said Zuriel. "Those gifted with the power of Whispering have harnessed the one language lost to man—the call of the wild; and a most powerful language it is."

Then there was Summoning. Derided from the virtue of Chastity—or achieving purity by being unhindered by worldly desires, as Zuriel explained—this Grace gave its holder the power to control not only the elements of earth such as water, wind and fire, but maneuver the time of day as well, because nothing was as pure as the very things from which all life sprang forth. To demonstrate this extraordinary feat, Zuriel awakened a sudden squall from thin air to breathe its wrath briefly through the peaceful outlook and knock several of the boys off their stone slabs before it dissipated into the surrounding mountain cliffs.

"I'll be stuffed!" Jacob heard Max exclaim with disbelief under his breath when the wind subsided. And under any other circumstances, Jacob would have likely offered up an appreciative snicker at his friend's unique cache of down under phrases that he had quickly come to find amusing had he, too, not been struck speechless by the demonstration. Especially when moments later Jacob watched with ever-widening eyes as Zuriel suddenly began to bend forward at the waist in an unnatural manner. And as his did, his body quickly began to change its shape, becoming slimmer and more elongated as it lowered itself onto all fours. When the hands met the ground they were no longer hands, but giant paws, and the human form that was Zuriel in an instant once again slipped from sight and in its place was a large, black panther whose fierce golden eyes peered brightly from behind an ebony pelt as black as the angel's own long locks.

Glued to the stone slabs upon which they remained seated, the group of wide-eyed Nephilim cautiously leaned as far back as they could from the intimidating creature purring loudly as it moved stealthily past them. It continued along the curved aisle of stone pedestals until it reached the end of the row where Ethan sat stiff as a board and motionless except for his rounded eyes which followed the animal as far as they could as it circled around behind him.

"And of course I've already shown you at the beginning of class the ability to mimic the form of any living creature," came Zuriel's voice again, and when Ethan managed the courage to turn his head and look to the angel his pie-shaped eyes grew even wider.

"AHHH, IT'S ME!" he cried out when he found himself staring back into a mirror image of himself kneeling on the ground beside him.

"Terrifying, isn't it? Both for me taking on this form as well as you getting a gander of it up close, I would well imagine," came Zuriel's voice from Ethan's clone, drawing a chorus of giggles from the other boys. And in a flash, Zuriel reemerged from Ethan's carbon copy wearing a satisfied grin on his face.

"Ha, ha, very funny! Ethan remarked under his breath as Zuriel rose to his feet to continue on with his oration.

"The Grace called Cloaking not only allows one to change physical shape but appear as a beacon of light, a plume of smoke, a drift of fog and, just like the virtue of Humility, from which this power is derived, it allows one to exist unseen," said Zuriel to the stone-rendered faces staring back in replicated awe at all they'd just witnessed. "So there you have the Graces: Gazing, Bending, Summoning, Drifting, Whispering and, finally, Cloaking. You will sometimes hear these powers referred to as Angel's Breath. This is because Graces are passed onto Nephilim offspring upon their birth by the angels who father them. It is only at a certain age when the Nephilim child is brought here that the Grace, which has remained unknown to himself and even the angel who fathered him, is revealed."

Zuriel had barely finished speaking when nearly every boy's hand shot up into the air in unison.

"Dare I ask the questions riding on the tip of every one of your tongues?" he muttered to himself before nodding to one of the boys who looked to be the most in desperate need of a pass to the bathroom.

"How do we find out what Grace we have?"

For as long as Zuriel had stood in this spot on the mountain terrace before endless groups of Nephilim, it was this question, the one almost inevitably voiced first, that brought a piercing silence to everything around them. The boys became as stone-like as the slabs they were perched upon, anxiously awaiting the answer .

"Inside the realm of this Crescent Scar lies the answer to what you ask," answered Zuriel, crossing to the center of the peculiar image with its strange markings on the ground. "Each section, as you can see, is marked with a symbol representing the six Graces I have just revealed to you. And this is the key to knowing which Grace you possess."

With that he held out his hand, and residing in his palm for all eyes to see was a large, round rock, smooth as glass and black as night in color.

"The Blackstone. Also known as The Marker. Taken from deep within the living, breathing rock of the Northern Mountain, at the bottom of the gash known as Broken Earth where only a handful of souls have ever set foot," said Zuriel, holding the rock up for all to gaze upon. "It, and only it, is able to reveal what Grace inhabits your being."

Then, following a pause, a faint smile formed on his lips and he asked the question that didn't need asking. "Who would like to go first?"

~ ~ ~

Every hand shot up in unison, leaving the boys noticeably straining to reach higher into the air than the person sitting near them. Zuriel found the pent-up enthusiasm amusing and for his own twisted pleasure he pretended to labor over the choice before him, and only when it appeared as though arms might begin popping from their sockets from the competitive angst did he stretch forth his hand and focus his finger on Leos. Beaming a toothy smile, Leos leapt victorious from his seat, ignoring the audible groans from some of the others, and in three long-legged lunges he was at the angel's side.

"So, what do I do?" he asked while trying to tamp down his excitement.

"Nothing. Which should make following directions uncomplicated," answered Zuriel, before guiding Leos to the center of the open space cradled by the crescent shape scarred into the ground and instructing him to remain standing still. "The Blackstone will do the rest."

When Zuriel then returned to stand outside the image, the rest of the boys leaned forward in an almost synchronized movement and they waited with their eyes focused intently on Leos, fearful to even blink for fear of missing whatever it was that was poised to happen. Leos stood quietly studying the large skirt of foreign symbols at his feet when a strange look came over his face.

"There's only six," he exclaimed suddenly.

"I applaud your mathematical prowess, Mr. Krall," Zuriel noted dryly.

"You said angels possessed seven Graces. But there are only six markings here," said Leos. His eyes then rolled upward to rest on the sky in thought. "Come to think of it, you only named six Graces."

A rumbling of whispers came from the other boys who, after reflecting back upon the angel's demonstration and taking their own mental count, realized Leos was correct and looked suspiciously to Zuriel for an explanation.

"You may retract your speculative gazes, Fledglings. Looking to me as though you've been robbed of something which two seconds ago you didn't know to even exist," Zuriel remarked coolly before turning to Leos. "You are very observant, Mr. Krall, and quite right. I did state that angels possess seven Graces of power, and quite correctly at that. What I failed to explain, however, is that the seventh Grace is one which cannot be inherited by a Nephilim."

"What is it?" asked Max with notable intrigue visibly shared equally amongst the other boys.

"The conjuring of life. To make breathe once again what death has stilled. It is the ultimate Grace brought forth by the virtue of Liberality, or Charity; it is a quality that exists only within the noblest of souls; it is Godlike in its genesis, and as such makes it the most important, and even rarer of virtues. God, himself, entrusted the Grace of Healing in small measure to his angels, and angels alone. Which is why, as you have noted, its marking is absent from the Crescent Scar," said Zuriel. "Now then, are we finally ready?"

"Since yesterday," answered Leos.

And with that Zuriel took the Blackstone he clutched and pitched it underhanded into the air toward Leos, who instinctively moved to catch it. As soon as the rock crossed the crescent-shaped boundary, however, there came a fiery flash. It was as if the rock, like an asteroid penetrating the Earth's atmosphere, had broken through some sort of invisible film, or barrier, encircling the scar, momentarily made visible in a ripple of bluish-white when struck by the rock. The Blackstone suddenly came to an abrupt halt, hovering weightlessly at eye level with Leos, whose gaze was as transfixed on the object as were the other Nephilims'.

"W-what's happening?" asked Leos in a tone at once both impatient and skittish.

"Patience," said Zuriel in a calm voice.

Suddenly, the rock began to move. At first, it circled slowly around Leos in a clockwise direction while gradually picking up speed. Around and around it spun. Then faster and faster. Soon it was nothing but a waxy blur proving impossible to the eyes attempting to follow it without being quickly hit with a nauseous wave of dizziness. Leos, who had appeared cocksure and stout when he bounded onto the Crescent Scar now looked less than certain he had made the right choice in volunteering to be the first candidate. His forehead had begun to take on a sheen from the pin prick drops of sweat beginning to bead his skin, and his body appeared to grow more and more tense the longer the Blackstone circled him with such terrific speed and force. Zuriel had referred to the rock as The Marker, after all. Why would a rock be called The Marker, after all, unless it was known to mark things? Nephilim, in particular, who stupidly chose to stand in the middle of something as strange as a Crescent Scar. It was such thoughts that made Leos open and close his fists rhythmically preparing for the possible moment the Blackstone might suddenly kick free of its hyper-speed orbit and fulfill its role as Marker by nailing him painfully in the head.

Instead, the rock quickly came to halt and Leos felt his breath catch in his chest. Slowly, he turned his head and peered out of the corner of his eye over his left shoulder where he saw the rock still floating in the air before it dropped to the ground with a deadening thud. He then turned his unblinking gaze back to Zuriel.

"Is it through?" he asked in a voice choked with anticipation.

Without answering, Zuriel circled his way around to where the rock lay motionless inside one of the marked sections of the crescent image and knelt beside it. A curious look came to his face as his gaze narrowed on the rock smoldering with faint wisps of white smoke and the symbol upon which it came to rest.

"Interesting," the angel remarked cryptically.

"What? What's interesting?" Leos cried out, looking as though he was on the verge of leaping out his own skin.

Picking up the rock, Zuriel rose to his feet. "The Blackstone has read your Grace to be Bending."

Leos' expression relaxed, and the toothy smile suddenly beaming forth from his face said more than any words could to describe his happy reaction to the outcome. With a jaunty bounce in his step, he returned to his seat high-fiving the other boys along the way.

Zuriel stood silent for a few moments tossing the rock casually in the air like a baseball. Once quiet had somewhat restored itself he called out, "Who'll be next?"

~ ~ ~

One by one, the other Nephilim took their turns inside the circle, and there came no boredom in watching each time the Blackstone was thrown to begin its revolutions at blinding speed. In fact, each toss seemed to bring a renewed burst of energy from the others watching, leaving them quietly wondering to themselves, and sometimes whispering bets to one another where the rock would fall next. And even then, more unexpected surprises revealed themselves. Such was the case when Max finally took his turn when the Blackstone seemed to spin through the air longer than usual. When the rock finally fell to the ground, it landed evenly on the border dividing two marked sections.

"What does that mean?" Max, looking anxiously to Zuriel, asked.

"While somewhat rare, though not all that uncommon, there are some Nephilim who come to possess more than one Grace," said Zuriel. "By the looks of where the Blackstone has landed, it appears as though your name has been added to this elite class."

"No bloody way!" Max replied slack-jawed.

"Bloody way," said Zuriel.

"Well, how many do I have?" asked Max, as his eyes grew with greed at the possibilities.

"Two," answered Zuriel while studying the spot where the Blackstone rested.

"You're sure it's just two?"

Not one to be second-guessed, especially by a Fledgling, Zuriel turned a cold stare onto Max. "Two, Mr. Kelly," he said. "While a Nephilim may find himself blessed with two Graces, it is the rarest of occasions when one comes to possess three. And rest assured never has a Nephilim come to inherit more than three. The Blackstone clearly shows you to carry two Graces: Cloaking and Summoning. Be grateful of the blessing."

"I'll take it!" Max quipped with glee.

Once Max had returned to his seat and received his congratulatory high-fives from those nearest him, Zuriel turned his attention to Jacob. "Well then, that leaves just you, Mr. Parrish."

Despite the crowing of support from his friends surrounding him, Jacob rose sheepishly to his feet and made his way to the Crescent Scar with a noticeable lack of enthusiasm that had guided the others.

"You appear apprehensive," noted Zuriel who had been watching the boy from the corner of his eye during the demonstrations.

"No…not really," said Jacob with a shrug, though he was not being completely truthful. While he shared the same eagerness as the other boys in learning what his Grace was, there was an uneasiness brewing inside him. What it was or why he was feeling it, he did not know. Yet it was present enough to keep him sitting quietly in his seat until the very last moment when he would be forced to take his turn. Zuriel sensed this unease and, raising an eyebrow sharply, he motioned Jacob into the cradled space of the Crescent Scar with a nod of his head. Once he had taken his place, Jacob looked to the angel while clenching his feet inside his sneakers in an attempt to somehow gain a firmer stance on the ground than he already had.

Zuriel drew back his arm and the Blackstone was thrown. There came the familiar blinding flash Jacob and the others had come to expect and the rock came to a levitated standstill. Jacob's nervous gaze remained on Zuriel who stood away with his hands clasped behind his back and settling his now hard stare uncomfortably upon the boy from behind the blurred path of the spinning rock. Suddenly, there was another explosion of bluish light—one that had not occurred with any of the other boys—and the Blackstone was cast free from its blinding orbit and sent sailing through the air across the enclave, nearly striking Zuriel before it fell to the ground mere inches from the sheer cliff of the overlook with a loud, weighted thud. The boys jumped from their seats and followed Zuriel to where the rock lay smoldering and immediately began inundating the angel with questions.

"What happened?"

"Why did it do that?"

"What does it mean?"

Picking up the Blackstone and staring hard at it, yet through it, with a pensively troubled expression, Zuriel didn't answer at first. He then peered back to the Crescent Scar where Jacob remained unmoved in his spot.

"My guess is the Blackstone doesn't sense a Grace within you," he said.

"But I thought you said all Nephilim have a Grace," said Ethan.

"Some even more, like Max here," another commented.

"That they do," answered Zuriel, his eyes not leaving Jacob.

"So what are you saying? That he's not a Nephilim?" asked Kairo.

"Of course not. It's quite possible Mr. Parrish here is just a late bloomer," the angel said before making his way back to the circle with the other boys in tow.

"How old are you, Fledgling?" he asked Jacob.

"Sixteen."

"Hmmmmm," Zuriel replied without offering any further insight to his pondering hum. He then glanced toward the other boys around him. "Let's return to your seats. Now that you have knowledge of your Grace, the next step is in learning how to use them as well as the rules binding their use."

He started behind the boys who rushed back to their slabs when he noticed Jacob remained standing inside the circle. "That means you as well, Mr. Parrish."

Before Zuriel could continue on Jacob rushed forward and blocked his way.

"Wait a minute. What about me?"

"What about you?"

"Well, does this mean I don't have a Grace?"

"For now it does," said Zuriel. "As I said, I suspect you may just be a late bloomer. Give it some time. We will try again soon, and likely by then the Blackstone will perform differently."

"Well…has it ever happened before?" asked Jacob as Zuriel moved past before the question again brought him to a halt.

Zuriel paused a moment, almost reluctantly, but his only reply was, "Your seat, Mr. Parrish."

CHAPTER TWENTY-TWO

LIONS BITE

Oct. 28

Maybe the Blackstone is fallible. Or maybe, for whatever reason, it somehow happened to miss reading or seeing (or whatever it is it does) the Grace I'm supposed to have when it was my turn to stand in the Crescent Scar today. Those are the only two possibilities I can come up with to make sense of what happened just a little while ago tonight.

As I began earlier, the five of us—Max, Leos, Kairo, Ethan and myself—were up in our room earlier than usual. All the Shrikes had been bursting with excitement and bouncing off the walls since returning from the Crescent Scar eager to begin the exercises Zuriel had given them to start tapping into their new-found powers. I wanted to share in the same excitement as my roommates, but the only thing I brought back with me from the Crescent Scar was the constant replaying in my mind of the moment the Blackstone flung itself from the ring-shaped blur it had formed around me and landed far outside the bounds of the marker containing the six Graces. Zuriel had suggested it was probably just a fluke. I'm probably just a late bloomer, as he put it. But I couldn't help pondering other possibilities. Like what if the real reason is a mistake has been made? What if Gotham and my mother and my grandmother have been wrong? What if I'm not a Nephilim at all? Maybe these two ugly protrusions on my back are just that…two ugly protrusions, like Dr. Gilkey concluded when he examined me. Maybe all I am is just a normal, regular kid with a messed up, deformed back. What really surprises me was just a few days ago I'd have been elated to learn that were the case. Now, I'm not so sure I would be. In fact, I have a feeling I would be as distraught discovering I wasn't a Nephilim as when I first learned I was. Funny how things like that happen.

Trying to empty my head of these rambling thoughts, I reclined on my bed and began writing in here what had taken place earlier in the day. It was impossible, however, to ignore the entertaining show taking place in front of me. Leos, Max, Kairo and Ethan were like a bunch of excited children on Christmas morning ready to rip their way through their pile of presents under the tree. Kairo's Grace is Drifting, but the only drifting I saw him doing was pacing about his bed. He looked to be somewhat nervous and kept mumbling quietly to himself as if to psyche himself up. Then suddenly he gave out a slight whimper and he was no longer there; he just vanished into thin air. The room became quiet. None of us spoke. We just sat there staring at the spot where he disappeared. We waited and while it felt like hours had passed it was only a few short seconds before he magically reappeared. One of his eyes, which were both squeezed tightly shut, slowly opened and only when he saw he was standing once more beside his bed did his tensed-up body relax.

"That. Was. Awwwwwesome!" he finally managed to exhale with a deep breath.

Leos was the one to ask the question we all waited to hear the answer to which was, "Where did you end up going?"

For some strange reason Kairo seemed reluctant to share. "Not far," was all he said.

We began naming places and moments in history we'd each relish in journeying to in a blink of an eye. Ancient Egypt? Woodstock? To witness the game-winning "Shot Heard 'Round the World" home run by New York Giants outfielder Bobby Thomson that won the '51 National League pennant?

Just around here, Kairo said, whatever that meant.

Now we were becoming more intrigued. "So like what, you went back to the time when Adam and Eve lived here?" Max asked.

"This morning, alright? I just went back to this morning," Kairo finally confessed when he realized we would just continue to pester him until he spilled the beans.

Everyone burst out into laughter, myself included, which only seemed to irritate Kairo more.

"Hey, it was my first try and I wanted to make sure if I had a problem getting back I'd only be a few hours behind you all. Haven't any of you heard of baby steps?" he barked at us.

He then stomped over to where Ethan was sitting, reached into his pocket and pulled out a gray and white rabbit's foot dangling from a silver key chain. Ethan had lost it sometime during the day and had been frantically searching the room for it. When he saw it, his eyes lit up.

Where'd you find it? he asked.

When I was following the five of us just now back up to Crescent Scar I saw it had fallen out of your pocket, Kairo grumbled. "You're welcome."

As Ethan gripped the fuzzy paw tight in his grip, we told him he'd better be careful none of the Guides caught sight of it. They undoubtedly wouldn't be too pleased to see a rabbit had been denied a foot to make him a precious little charm, but Ethan assured us it was fake.

Max of course couldn't help give Kairo one last ribbing. "Good going Kairo. Maybe when you manage to work your way back to 2005 you can find my favorite pair of sunglasses I misplaced. Of course I might be dead of old age by the time you work your way that far back."

But as he spoke, Max suddenly without seemingly knowing it began rubbing his stomach with one hand while doing the same to the top of his head at the same time. It was only when he noticed the snickering in the room was now turned to him did he realize what was happening. Naturally we all looked to Leos, who had been noticeably quiet on his bed with his eyes fixed on Max with an intense look of concentration. Leos' Grace is Bending and it was obvious he was getting the hang of his new-found talent. He was also tackled by Max for his humorous efforts.

Max is the only one of all the Shrikes who is lucky enough to have two Graces: Cloaking and Summoning. While I personally would have favored Cloaking, he seemed much more drawn to the other power and spent most of the night huddled over his desk trying to make the water inside a glass move and dance at his whim. With nothing but steady concentration and the subtlest of direction given by his forefinger, as Zuriel had shown him, he managed eventually to sculpt the water into a mini spout and make it rise out of the glass which was pretty impressive, though not as much as making the water shape itself into the image of an angel like Gotham demonstrated while sitting on the bank of the River on our way to Havenhid.

Easily the most entertained any of us were tonight was watching Ethan. Much to his disappointment, his Grace was also Cloaking, which was not as Jedi-like as the Grace of Bending which he had hoped for. More than once we were near tears from laughing so hard while watching him attempt to take on his first shape. Even Mist looked on somewhat baffled from where she lay on the floor. More than an hour passed with Ethan sitting in his chair and staring straight ahead looking like he was suffering from severe constipation. Actually, it was more like he had been given the role as the world's first pregnant man trying to push forth new life into the world.

With tears in his eyes from laughing so hard, Max finally asked Ethan what shape he was trying to transform into. A lion, Ethan answered, which made Max remark quite humorously, "I think you're going to have to push a whole lot harder," which made all of us laugh all the more much to Ethan's annoyance. Kairo then suggested he try something a little less ambitious and more closely tied to his character.

Like what? Ethan asked waiting for another barb to be shot his way.

A chipmunk, Leos was quick to chime in.

Despite all the funning, I could see as I quietly looked on where Ethan was getting caught up and having trouble, and very seriously I told him he was doing it all wrong. Ethan and the others looked at me in unison as if wondering how could I possibly have a clue. Fair enough. But even though

I was Graceless, according to the Blackstone, I still made it a point to pay attention to Zuriel's instruction during class in case it was true what he said that I might just be a late bloomer.

I put aside my journal and went and sat directly across from Ethan. I told him he was only concentrating on the physical appearance of the form he was trying to take. How I knew that to be true I had no idea, but I did. To make a successful transformation, I told him, he had to fixate on becoming the entire essence of the animal he wished to transform into, not just its physical shape. Ethan stared at me with a blank, confused look and I told him I would try and help him through it. Taking hold of his hands in mine, I had him focus on my eyes and the words I spoke as if I was a traveling gypsy conducting some kind of circus tent seance. Ethan had been working on changing into a lion so I began describing the animal as best as I could. First physically, and then in ways in which lions are known to move and act and be. Then I told Ethan to imagine himself a lion and what it must be like inhabiting a lion skin and peering out at the world through lion eyes. We did this for some time and before long, as I continued to talk him along, I noticed a strange look slowly make its way across Ethan's face.

"Your eyes..." he mumbled under his breath.

It was then I felt a strange churning inside me. I glanced down at my hands clutching Ethan's and I saw them begin to change in front of my eyes. My fingers began to retreat and shrink from sight and my hands grew bigger and paw-like. Then there were my arms; they began sprouting yellow-blond fur. I instantly panicked while at the same time falling to the floor. I must have blacked out after that because the next thing I knew Kairo, Leos and Max were kneeling over me helping me come to. I immediately looked myself over beginning with my hands and they appeared normal to me. My fingers were back and the fur was gone.

What the heck happened? I asked trying not to sound as panicked as I felt.

"You were turning into a lion, that's what happened," Kairo said.

Of course I didn't believe it and immediately turned a suspicious gaze to Leos. After all, he had been having quite the jolly time goofing on Max earlier by making him scratch himself and perform silly gestures without realizing it. It only made sense he decided to have some fun with me by making me hallucinate what I saw and believe I had somehow turned into a lion. But he denied it. Vigorously. And Max defended him, with equal vigor.

You turned into a lion, he said, beaming his big smile as though it was he who had performed the feat. "Not all the way, and it was only for a second until you freaked out. But it was definitely a lion."

Ethan remained in his seat looking as though he had just come face to face with a—well, lion. He said as I was coaching him on what to concentrate on he saw the image of a lion emerge from the pupils of my eyes right before I started to morph. But how? I asked my roommates, as well as myself, when the Blackstone only a few hours earlier couldn't read a Grace within me. No one seemed to have an answer, except for Max.

Maybe, he suggested, you've bloomed.

~ ~ ~

The walk to Lions Bite the next morning was far lengthier than Jacob imagined it would be. Maybe it was because it led in the direction of the falls whose immense size somehow made it seem as if the mountain cliffs from which it spilled stood much closer to Havenhid than they really did. More likely it was because of the whispering chatter coming from some of the other boys walking a close distance behind Jacob which pricked his ears.

There seemed to be an increasing curiosity about Jacob amongst a certain number of his fellow Nephilim. It had followed him—along with inquisitive stares—since the moment he first stepped foot in the Hall of Light. Jacob had hoped over the coming days it would have gradually ceased once the newness of his presence had faded. After all, what could anyone possibly find so interesting or intriguing about himself? Certainly, the pair of curving humps protruding behind his shoulders, which had become more noticeable beneath the cover of his shirt, couldn't be the source of amusement as they had to the kids in Cain's Corner. Here in Eden, they all shared the same sameness as well as the defects that came with it. Yet the more he pondered it, the more he found himself revisited by the same uncomfortable self-conscious feelings he carried when he was back at school. And while he did his best to ignore the looks he felt directed his way, the whispering was a bit more difficult. One thing about Nephilim ears; they had a tendency to hear everything.

"So, did you talk to Zuriel yet?" asked Ethan.

"About what?" Jacob replied while continuing to peer over his shoulder at the group of whispering boys.

"About what happened last night…you know, your lion-changing act."

"Oh that…yeah, I told him about it earlier this morning."

"And?" pressed Kairo as if he were struggling to extract a tooth from Jacob's mouth.

"And we went back to the Crescent Scar for another try with the Blackstone," said Jacob.

"AND?" Kairo, Leos and Ethan inquired in unison.

"And nothing," answered Jacob, trying not to sound as downbeat as he felt. "The same thing happened as yesterday morning; the Blackstone circled me a bunch of times and then cast itself in the same spot as before."

"Weird," muttered Kairo. "What did Zuriel say to explain what we all saw happen then?"

"Not much," said Jacob. "Just that we'd have to keep trying until the Blackstone finally sensed my Grace."

~   ~   ~

It was an impressive thing to look up and behold when Jacob and the other Shrikes found themselves at the foot of the mountain where the waterfall rained down; even frighteningly so. The power from the thunderous cataract was so tremendous it made the ground tremble noticeably beneath their feet, and the rumbling roar which came from deep within the watery curtain drowned out all other sound. A cloud of mist billowed forth at the base of the cliff like a thin marine fog clinging to the shoreline, bathing everything in a surreal haze. Through the cool, gray wetness the boys passed when they had finished marveling at this marvel of nature and continued on to a stone bridge leading the way across the River.

Max could see Jacob was distracted by something behind him as he kept peering back over his shoulder. It was only when Max followed the direction of Jacob's gaze that he noticed a group of boys walking not too far behind them trading discreet whispers amongst themselves. It was obvious it was becoming a growing source of annoyance to Jacob.

"Do yourself a favor and ignore them," said Max. "They're just being a bunch of gossipy shielas flapping their gums over the Furphy of the day."

"Say what again? Ethan inquired like someone thrown a calculous problem when trying to decode some of Max's down-home expressions.

"I think he said they're just a bunch of Chatty Cathys who have nothing better to do than whisper nonsense about other people," answered Kairo.

"I'd just like to know what their problem is with me?" grumbled Jacob.

"You're the new kid. They're just curious," said Leos who was walking on the other side of Jacob.

"New? I showed up here a few days after the rest of you; a week tops. How am I new?"

"It's not when you showed up, but who you showed up with," said Max.

"Gotham? What's he got to do with anything?"

"For starters, he's a Fallen. There's always been a strange mythical fascination surrounding them, and most of us have never met one face to face."

"Never trust a Fallen! That's what I remember being told growing up," said Leos. "They're good-for-nothing traitors to the Light."

"You have to expect it's going to cause some tongues to wag wondering how it is you came to be brought to Eden by one," said Max.

"I already explained it to you. Anyone who wishes to make more of it than what it is can do so…to my face!" Jacob exclaimed angrily before turning on Leos with a defensive snarl. "As for being a traitor, Gotham explained to me how it is he came to be marked and it was anything but traitorous on his part."

"And you believed him?" replied Leos with a chortle of skepticism.

Before Jacob could open his mouth to answer, Ethan, who was walking ahead of the trio with Kairo glanced back over his shoulder. "I think it might be a good idea if you told him the rest."

"Quiet you!" Max snapped. "Now's not the time."

"Tell me what?" Jacob inquired.

"He's going to hear about it eventually," said Ethan. "I think it would be better he heard it from one of us."

Jacob watched an uneasy exchange of glances suddenly being traded amongst his friends, which only stirred an uncomfortable feeling inside himself.

"What is it?"

"It's about the last time Gotham was here in Eden," Max began to explain with some reluctance while making sure to keep his voice low should any uninvited ears attempt to eavesdrop on the conversation. "It was way back before any of us were born; much less an idea. He brought his own son here."

"Yeah I know…David…so?"

"Then you know what happened to David?"

Jacob nodded. "Unfortunately, he died."

"I'll say it was unfortunate," said Max. "But do you know how he died?"

Jacob was quiet for a moment. The only thing he ever heard about it came from his grandmother right before he left Cain's Corner, and then in only the vague and nebulous terms of a "dark plague." Jacob had assumed David had the ill fortune of an untimely illness or some unfortunate accident, though the unanswered question had always lingered in the back of his mind, a question he never seemed able to bring up to Gotham.

"He was killed," Leos exclaimed abruptly, bringing a shocked look to Jacob.

"Killed? You mean by a Fury?"

It made sense. After all, if there was anything denoting a dark plague, it would be the Furies.

"Guess again," answered Leos. "Try skewered at the end of a sword by his own father, the Fallen Gotham."

Jacob's feet came to an abrupt halt.

"I don't believe you," he said with a mix of horror and disgust on his face; disgust that his so-called friends could make up such a vicious untruth. "It's a filthy lie!"

As he stood angrily staring them down with his fists clenched ready to fight he saw the sincerity frozen in the eyes looking back at him in such a melancholy manner from having to reveal something so ugly, and he knew they were telling him the truth. Or at least what they believed to be the truth, whatever the reason.

"Do you hear how sick and insane that sounds to even suggest?" asked Jacob. "First of all, why would he even do something like that?"

"What reason could any father have to justify killing their own son?" said Kairo.

"It's one of the great mysteries Nephilim have debated in Havenhid since it happened," said Ethan.

Max stepped forward and gave Jacob's shoulder a comforting squeeze.

"For all we know, it may not even be true," he said, though with not much conviction. "We're just sharing with you what's long been passed around as truth. Even the Guides have never spoken about it— at least outside themselves."

A hush followed, suddenly, when the whispering group of boys who had been walking behind caught up to them. They lagged at first in passing as if to catch a morsel of what looked to be a heated discussion taking place. The cool unwelcoming glares which turned on them in unison and silently dared them to linger one minute more instantly quickened their steps.

"So that's what all the whispering is about," muttered Jacob as he watched them hurry on up ahead with the rest of the group.

"For once, Ethan was right. We figured if you didn't know you'd want to before hearing it from someone else," said Max. "Havenhid has a way of revealing all things you wish would remain secret. Or so we've been told."

They continued on with the weight of the revelation hanging over Jacob like a dark storm cloud. No one spoke a word the rest of the way.

~   ~   ~

Just as they reached the top of a grassy slope further on and wondered how much farther they would have to walk, they came upon a large open clearing. In the center of the clearing was a large, round structure of stone.

"Is that it?" someone asked.

"What else could it be?"

"I guess we'll find out."

Even though it was the first time any of the boys had laid eyes on Lions Bite, it was clear from the awestruck looks on their faces it was not what they had been expecting, or maybe even imagined. At first glance—and even after studying it awhile—it appeared as an ancient ruin; the forgotten remnants of a long-lost civilization which the wear of time had neither the strength or will to erase from existence. Truth be told, how exactly Lions Bite came to be held more mystery to the approaching band of boys than the rise of Stonehenge or the pyramids of Egypt. It looked to be something that had always been in existence, the product of nature's hand rather than that of man or, more likely, angel.

As the boys made their way closer, the structure became more impressive and awesome in its size. The towering walls were formed by numerous massive slabs of uncut stone standing uniformly at a severe slant like a ring of giant dominoes in simultaneous mid-fall yet stopping short of coming into contact with the stone slab it leaned towards. There was no sign of craftsmanship from a single chisel or piece of machinery, and it was clear its construction was not guided by the logic of modern architecture or even basic physics. It made walking between the columns an unnerving experience, at best. Not only could one not escape feeling instantly diminutive and insignificant, each towering slab of rock stirred an uneasy questioning of whether it would choose at that untimely moment when walking by it to finish its crushing fall to the ground.

Clinging, flowering vines snaked their way in great numbers across the stone furry with jade-colored moss. Their vibrant blossoms filled the air with succulently sweet and pleasant fragrances inviting the sniffing noses through two more rings of stone slanting opposite the other within the outer wall. The curious formation led the way to a large oval-shaped open space paved in green grass. It felt to the boys as if they had stepped into the middle of a large arena like those which had once served as ancient racetracks for thundering chariot races, or bloody playgrounds for sword-wielding gladiators to entertain the Roman masses.

As the Nephilim circled around looking for some sign of how this peculiar place ended up with the name it was given, they each felt very much the eery emptiness surrounding them. They were not alone, however. Damiel, in fact, had been patiently awaiting the group. Out of sight, he stood quietly watching high atop one of the stone columns. It was only when he spread wide his wings and leapt forward into the air did the boys catch sight of his presence, but only in the telling shadow revealed by the sun burning high above as it glided across the arena floor. By then it was too late. In a flash of lightning-quick movements, the boys were stunned by a series of striking blows. It knocked them clean off their feet, one by one, and when they glanced around looking somewhat dazed at what had attacked them from out of the blue they found Damiel standing in the middle of the fallen group with his right foot resting on the chest of one of the boys firmly pinning him to the ground.

"An entire class of Nephilim wiped out in the time it takes to blink without so much as breaking a sweat," Damiel remarked with casual observation before removing his foot from the boy struggling beneath him. "I see I have much work ahead of me."

~ ~ ~

He took a spot in the center in the arena and, with a discerning eye, watched as the group climbed back to its feet.

"Lesson number one," he barked. "Never let down your guard! Like a bird perched on a fence you risk the shredding from a cat's claws if you relax any one of your gifted senses for even a moment. As Nephilim, you will find the civilian world when you return to it a much darker and crueller place than you remember leaving. That is only because you will begin to see things of which before you were blind. From this moment forward, everything your eyes fall upon around you must be viewed first as a threat. I am a threat, the trees are a threat, the very stones of this arena surrounding you are a threat."

Damiel watched as the gazes shifted questionably to the massive slabs of rock. They were listening.

"Lesson number two," he then continued. "You have all failed lesson number one! But do not fret. I am here to ensure it does not again happen. It is my job to see to it that when the day comes for you to leave the jaws of Lions Bite for the last time, it will not be as the boys who first entered it, but as the fighting warriors you are destined to become. Of that, I assure you."

Not that any of the boys were in need of assurances. If anyone was up to the task of such a proclamation, it was Damiel. To be anywhere near where his shadow happened to rest was to witness firsthand the power and might of Heaven's arsenal. Towering in size and sculpted with strength, there was no question how it was he became known as the Angel of the Sword; but he was far from impregnable, and the scars which marked him were not carried on his flesh but treaded the golden pools of his eyes in the form of ghostly reflections from countless wars and battles both celestial and earth-grounded. It was the one thing which brought to his otherwise youthful face a deep well of age whose hand reached far past the accumulation of time recorded in years. Jacob was not alone in pondering what untold tales could be dredged from such a well-lived vessel.

"I hear we'll be learning how to fight with swords," said one of the boys, stirring a chattering of excitement from the others.

The eagerness brimming noticeably from the Nephilim standing before him made Damiel smile. "In due time. For now, you cannot expect to feast on solids when you have yet to teethe."

If there was any confusion as to what Damiel meant—and from the looks on the boys' faces there undoubtedly was—an explanation in the making arrived when the angel led the group out of the arena and into the thick of the nearby Forest.

"Here's where you'll cut your first tooth," he said once they were amongst the towering trees. "Don't expect it to be pleasant."

Whatever "it" referred to was quickly introduced to the group of Shrikes. For the next several days the woods adjacent Lions Bite became a place of basic training for the Nephilim. There Damiel put his students through the paces, running them hard and relentlessly for great distances that seemed to never have an ending point. For many of the boys, it was a shock to the system trying to keep up, but their pleas for rest fell on unsympathetic ears. Damiel proved himself in short order to be nothing less than a militant taskmaster, drilling hard his unseasoned platoons through the woods which he had fashioned into a punishing obstacle course. Strained, cursing cries echoed loudly from the thicket silencing even the birds watching curiously from their perches high up in the trees as the Nephilim were pushed to their physical limits.

Like many their age, the boys were deceptively soft and out of shape despite whatever athletic appearance they revealed outwardly to the rest of the world. Their bodies cramped and screamed in pain, the result of stagnant, untapped movement of muscle suddenly given a rude and unwelcome jolt to awaken. It was the will and perseverance of the fatigued boys, however, that became the focus of Damiel's strenuous conditioning, and it wasn't long before the cobwebs were dusted away and the torturous exertions became less painful to endure. Little by little, day by day, the grueling regimen became less toilsome. The cramps faded. Bodies no longer doubled over in their dire need for breath, and in some cases the need to vomit. All the while, sweat continued to bleed from pores, soaking its way through T-shirts and leaving a hard-earned sheen on straining bodies performing what would soon be demonstrated in unison as unimaginable feats.

For Jacob, it wasn't like before he came to Eden when sporadic moments of self-discovery revealed he could do things other boys could not. Suddenly, what was once thought humanely impossible was now possible, without question or skepticism. What was happening was real. It was as if he had found a footing that had long been elusive to his feet. And with Damiel's taxing guidance, Jacob found himself racing with great speed across terrain not meant for humankind to tread upon even under the most careful of circumstances. He along with the other Shrikes began to move with an unusual grace through the Forest in a range of movements that as far as they knew belonged exclusively to the Forest creatures who lived there. The swiftness with which they ran, the ease with which they scaled trees and the distance they managed to leap from ever-growing heights, even the way their eyes viewed things; it was as if the Forest itself had somehow spawned a new species of human.

In truth there was nothing new about their species. Theirs was a lineage which reached back to the earliest times of creation long shrugged off as nothing more than a mythical blemish in the footnotes of human existence. Each had been given birth to and handed swaddled into their mothers' arms only a stretch of memory ago. Now, as they stood on the cusp of manhood, the panting sounds of labor once more echoed from deep inside Eden's forests. It was here in Eden's care, in a world hidden within a world, where they would truly be born. And like an expectant father wearing a trail into the floor beneath his feet, Damiel watched with growing pride as the band of halflings, with each passing day, began to come into their own until one day a look of satisfaction slowly emerged from behind his often-stony expression in the form of a smug smile, and he exclaimed with confidence, "Now you're ready to learn how to fight!"

~ ~ ~

While Damiel would spend the coming days, weeks and months strengthening the Nephilim' bodies and fighting capabilities, just as Zuriel continued to work patiently in helping unlock the secrets of and wielding the Graces given them, the task of sharpening the boys' minds was left in Thaniel's hands. And rightly so.

All the Guides held rein to a vast wealth of knowledge, but one only had to speak a short amount of time with Thaniel to realize his intellect stretched far beyond the normal boundaries, even amongst angels. And like most top minds of the flesh-and-blood variety where intelligence is known to separate, and even isolate one—in some ways, cruelly—from their peers, there was something oddly unique about Thaniel that made him seem somewhat out of place amongst the other Guides.

It wasn't the fact he was slightly less in stature than the other

Guides, or that he was the only one amongst them who kept his loosely coiled blond locks trimmed short. What left him mildly askew from his winged brethren was far more subtle than anything his physicality made evident. It could be seen in his face; or rather not seen. His notable beauty and youthfulness flourished in great abundance like a flowering vine. And like a vine blotting from view the wall to which it clings, the hard, sometimes even cold veneer shared amongst the other angels, if even but a glimmer, was absent Thaniel. Where the other Guides, just as youthful and beautiful in their own right, were equal parts rose and thorn, Thaniel seemed to encompass only the brightness of a newly budding flower, untouched by the ravages of an aged war against unimaginable dark enemies.

It was such a presence the boys found waiting outside the Library's massive wooden arched doors the first day the Shrikes were to begin their instruction—or Study as it became more commonly known to them. Despite a night of rest in which they slept as soundly as if death itself had taken them on a short excursion, the approaching group of boys was a familiar sight to Thaniel, who watched with some hilarity as their lumbered steps and pained looks straining their faces spoke of the toll their introduction to Lions Bite the day before had left on their now sore, stiff bodies.

"I won't pretend being cooped up in a library surrounded by books and hearing the drone of my voice as I lecture compares much with the more rough and tumble activities you've partaken in at Lions Bite, or the fanciful lessons you've been introduced to at the Crescent Scar," said Thaniel while slowly and purposefully scanning the worn, haggard looks staring blankly back at him. "Although I think it's safe to assume from the looks on each of your faces you might actually welcome the seats waiting for you inside and whatever temporary respite they might provide for your obvious aches and pains. Damiel never was one to wade his way into the water so much as to dive in head first; both in being and in his teaching methods. Thankfully, I can assume he left untaxed for me the one body part I will require from each of you today: your brain."

Thaniel then turned and led the way inside the Library, and the Nephilim slowly filed in behind him with the resistant gaits of inmates forced to follow the warden to their waiting cells. Their dour looks, however, weren't long-lasting. They had managed less than a dozen steps inside when there came from the boys a succession of astonished gasps and whispered mutterings of awe. Thaniel didn't need to glance back over his shoulder to know the unenthusiastic scowls the boys carried with them had instantly receded from their faces and been replaced with dumbstruck wonder just as it happened to all Nephilim who stepped foot inside the Library for the first time. That was because the Library was unlike any other seen before in all the world over.

It consisted of one single, large room, long and narrow in shape and grand in its space. Spiral staircases at each end sprouted from the floor leading the way upward to numerous balconies and landings circling the perimeter of the Library's countless upper floors. Like everything else at Havenhid, the Library was a living creation; its architecture the result of an elaborate and completely inexplicable coming together of arborescent limbs and boughs from the trees inside which it resided. Yet as impressive as it all was, it wasn't the binding and braiding and weaving together of the branches which came to shape such a colossal structure that held the boys' awe, but the walls themselves. They were stuffed with books—far too many to even begin counting— and the eyes marveling at the sight followed these book-filled walls upward where they seemed to stretch beyond any ending within sight from where the boys stood staring with their mouths unhinged.

"How many do you think there are?" questioned Jacob quietly in disbelief while his nose took note of the pungent scent of musky, aged paper in the air, and he couldn't help wondering if this was the place all ancient books went when they died.

"Hundreds," answered Ethan equally transfixed.

"Take a math class," Kairo sniped. "We're talking thousands. Tens of thousands!"

"Anyone care to venture a bet it's in the millions?" challenged Max.

Millions. The idea, itself, was mind-boggling. Especially to Ethan who before wouldn't have believed there were even that many different books in existence, much less a single place with enough shelf space to house them all. Browsing a row of books cramming a nearby wall, he gently fingered the noticeable age which frayed some of the bindings. The spines of many of the books held no markings or words of any kind. Yet one thing was clear just by looking at them; the books filling the shelves were not like the ones at the public library back home. Here, there was no place for fluff or light-hearted fare; no tales of wizards or vampires or fellowships of any kind. One did not need to crack open a book at random to know the pages inside held the kind of writings capable of only one thing—making the brain swell and ache from the heft of the meanings weighting each string of words which filled them.

"Weird isn't it?" Ethan muttered aloud, though more to himself than to anyone within earshot.

"What's that?" asked Jacob as he wandered nearby.

"That something like this would exist here of all places."

Jacob wasn't sure what Ethan meant at first. Sure the Library was an awesome, spectacular sight, but, after growing accustomed to Eden and seeing all they had seen, such grand spectacles weren't all that unusual anymore.

"So many books," said Ethan, looking upward in a straining effort to find an end to the book-filled walls surrounding them. "And I bet you anything not a 'Harry Potter' or 'Twilight' among them."

"That's what has you stupefied?" said Leos with a chuckle. "The fact there doesn't seem to be a teen fiction section?"

Ethan ignored the sarcastic quip. "Don't you find it just a bit strange that there's this library filled with what looks to be every single important book known to man smack dab in Eden? And yet the first two people to ever live here were thrown out of the Garden as punishment because the fruit they ate from the Tree of Life filled their head with knowledge."

The question passed without remark amongst the boys. Not because it was ignored as many of Ethan's inane comments tended to be. Indeed, quite the opposite. For the first time, Ethan had managed to stump everyone with a legitimate and thought-provoking puzzler.

"An astute observation Mr. Richert. Already you are showing you just might possess the perceptive intellect required to do well in the lessons taught here," Thaniel, who was standing nearby listening to the conversations being bandied about by the group of boys, was heard to say.

Ethan couldn't help but shoot a smug look of validation at his roommates, particularly Leos.

"However, I must correct you on one point," Thaniel was quick to add. "Neither Adam nor Eve were banished from Eden because a sense of awareness and reasoning was visited upon them. Rather it was due to their disobeying the sole directive placed on them from the very beginning not to eat of the fruit of the Tree. That willful action led to their downfall, not the gift of knowledge. And before you question me further, no, your ears did not mishear my words. The breadth of knowledge is and always has been God's gift to every thinking creature. Despite a long-held belief by many that God denied his first human creations the ability of rational thinking to ensure they remain less than he, I can assure you nothing is further from the truth. Like all things, it was out of a sense of love that a blank void was created which knowledge could not penetrate. Because with knowledge comes a sense of right and wrong. And the shadow of sin has an encroaching habit to lay in wait where thoughts, however pure or innocent, tend to flourish."

"So you're saying," began Jacob as he along with the others pondered what Thaniel had told them, "it was out of protection that man was first denied 'the breadth of knowledge,' as you call it."

"That is correct."

"Then forgive me if this comes across as a stupid question, but why if knowledge leads to sin are we standing in a place filled with books to fill our brains even more than they are?"

It was with a sense of relief that Jacob saw a somewhat kindly expression in Thaniel's face when the angel looked to him and not in the noticeably contemptible manner the other Guides—most notably Zuriel and Eksel—had when holding the boy in the crosshairs of their gaze.

"There are no stupid questions here, just as there are no stupid answers," said Thaniel with a pleasant, tight-lipped smile. It pleased him to know his students' minds were already turning like the gears of a clock in an eager curiosity to dissect and even challenge his own words. And yet instead of offering an answer to Jacob's probing question, Thaniel suddenly turned and instructed the group to walk with him.

~ ~ ~

The boys followed, trailing behind in a tight cluster. The patter of their footsteps across the unique parquet-like floor, like the drumming of a slow rain beating heavily against a rooftop, echoed off the silence hanging over them. They crossed the very center of the Library where surprisingly—or maybe not so surprisingly—they came upon a large tree. In fact, it was a wayward bough which had long ago broken ranks from the Library's massive architecture of branches and come up through the floor where it took permanent root, as well as the shape of a large tree, Thaniel explained. Beneath its cover of lush leaves and blossoming flowers was a raised, circular platform, and residing upon the platform equidistance across from one another were four very large books. They stood no less than four feet in height and rested on sturdy wood easels.

"Whoa, you gotta come see this," a boy named Koji called out to the other boys after straying from the group to investigate the scratching sound of writing coming from the books.

The others looked to Thaniel and when it was clear he would not squelch their curiosity, they bolted in unison to the platform where Koji was standing. It didn't take long to see what had wowed their classmate once they had jockeyed for position close around where Koji stood.

"Check it out…it's writing itself!" Koji exclaimed while pointing to the book in front of him.

It would have been easy to laugh off such a ridiculous claim. Easy, that is, if it weren't immediately proven to be true. Sure enough, right before their eyes, the boys watched incredulously as words handwritten in black ink bled onto the blank page letter by letter as though written by some invisible pen. They watched without so much as a murmur to one another and before long their collective look of disbelief faded under the weight of frowns as they began reading in earnest the magically appearing words.

"What's it writing?" asked a ruddy-cheeked boy named Roderick, but whom the other boys favored calling Red due to his shocking red mop of curly hair.

"It's almost like those news scroll thingys you see crawling along the bottom of the TV screen on cable news channels. What are they called?" asked Ethan as he strenuously pondered his own question.

"I think they're called those news scroll thingys you see crawling along the bottom of the TV screen on cable news channels," answered

Leos dryly before giving Ethan's ear a teasing, yet stinging flick with his finger.

All four books, in fact, were furiously recording in the same fashion what appeared to be random incidents from all across the world—not Eden's world, but their own mortal world. And yet there didn't seem to be any rhyme or reason as to why the various events were being noted. Some detailed horrible, heart-wrenching crimes like one such entry revealing a school shooting where nearly two dozen high school students were mowed down in a hail of bullets by one of their classmates. Several entries noted the inhumane retaliation by hostile governments against its own people in countries caught up in the uncompromising grips of insurgency and war. Other writings revealed accidents and disasters, both natural and man-made, as well as unspeakable brutality against creatures of the earth such as elephants slaughtered by the herds just to relieve them of their ivory tusks, and frightened dogs being abused in the most cruelest of ways by those who betrayed the strongest bond of loyalty to exist between man and animal.

Not everything being scribed onto the pages of the books, however, was dark and despairing to read. There were also numerous, uplifting inscriptions about selfless acts of generosity and bravery. Such as the fifteen-year-old who braved a sheet of thin ice to save a boy who had fallen through from drowning. Or the man who gave up his entire savings to an elderly woman who had lost everything she owned in a fire. Yet for every uplifting entry there seemed to be three or more that were anything but. Jacob realized this as his eyes followed the latest words suddenly becoming visible on the page which told of Muslim residents in a town called Al Nazla marking Christian homes and shops with red graffiti in a concerted effort to help aid an Islamic terrorist group in their jihadi mission in slaughtering all non-Muslims.

"Al Nazla. That's near where my family lives."

Jacob glanced over his left shoulder in the direction of the soft-spoken utterance and saw it came from a boy named Karim standing beside him. The worry in his voice matched that reflected in his almond eyes which scanned the words several more times before looking urgently to Thaniel for answers.

"They are known as Witnesses," explained Thaniel from where he remained standing outside the perimeter of the platform. "Each book as you can see by the writings is focused on one of the four corners of the world. Their task, from which there is no rest, is simply to make a record of those incidents as they occur, both the good and the bad, that end up shaping the history of man."

"Mostly bad from what I've read so far," whispered Kairo into Ethan's ear which did not escape Thaniel's own keen hearing.

"Man, sadly, has often made it quite difficult in determining whether he is hero or villain in his own story," he said. "I can attest to many a time I've stood here gripped by the unpleasantries of anguish with tears spilling down my face—both from anger as well as sorrow—for the things I've read."

The angel grew quiet for a moment while staring reflectively at one of the books in a way that reminded Jacob of how his grandmother sometimes became in the rare times she spoke about the war.

"That as it may be," said Thaniel, suddenly snapping out of his pensive pause, "it is as complete a testimonial of mankind's existence as there ever will be."

"Then what we read on these pages is true?" asked Karim with a noted anxiousness.

"You need not worry, Karim," answered Thaniel in a tone most soothing. "Your father is a fierce protector. He will not let any harm come to your mother."

Jacob heard Karim exhale a sigh of relief and felt his body relax from the tense grip that had momentarily taken hold of him.

"What happens when the books run out of pages to write on?" came another question.

"So far the Witnesses have recorded thousands of years of history," answered Thaniel. "But as you all know, every book has an ending. The last page—when it comes—will mark the final day of mankind, or as it is better known: Judgment Day. The books will close and man's testimony will have been told in full."

It wasn't exactly an uplifting explanation, and almost immediately upon hearing it there was a collective shift in the huddled boys' gazes to spy how many pages still remained empty. Much to their relief, each of the four books looked to be only at the halfway mark, yet at the same time it proved somewhat bothersome—unsettling, even—to know that the inevitable final pages lurked between the bound covers.

"Come now, you will have plenty of time to revisit these books and peruse their pages if you so wish at a later time," said Thaniel after he had allowed the boys some time to mingle amongst the books and learn the happenings beyond Eden's reach. "Your seats and the day's lesson, for which we are already late, await you."

~　~　~

Curious to see what other secrets might reside inside the Library, the boys filed their way off the platform with a touch more eagerness in their step and followed Thaniel to a nearby swath of six long tables arranged in two rows of three. After the Nephilim had found their seats, the Library once again fell silent from the scuffling of feet and sliding of chairs.

"Now then," began Thaniel with a clearing of his throat while leisurely pacing his way around the tables. "Damiel would tell you the most crucial thing you will learn here in Eden is the art of combat and the skill with which you wield a sword. Zuriel would argue it is the proficiency in which you come to hone the Grace with which you have been gifted. With all respect to my brothers, they are wrong.

"Knowledge—" his voice sent the word upward to echo in the vast recesses of the Library before falling back to a softer register, "knowledge is where victory against all things dark and unseemly is bred. Undoubtedly, there will come a time when each of you will find yourselves forced to face down unimaginable dark forces. Trust when I tell you, all your fighting strengths and swords and Graces alone will be as powerful against these forces as grains of sand caught up in the torrents of a churning ocean tide. That is unless you come armed with the one weapon only the educated mind has the ability to brandish. No matter the passion with which you might be driven, you cannot expect to go up against an enemy this teethed with venom and wrath and expect to win without knowing not only everything about that which you are fighting against, but also what it is you are fighting for. It is the shrewd who exercise a good measure of prudence in ensuring one's head is as equally filled as one's heart, if not more. For it is its mastery of cunningness which makes the Darkness so deadly, and why man has for so long found himself on the losing end of the war being waged for his soul."

Thaniel didn't need to glance down at the Nephilim he strolled amongst to know their eyes were following him with rapt attentiveness as they listened.

"So I ask you," he continued, "if indeed the first residents of Eden were denied access into the vault of knowledge in order to protect them from sin, why then do you suppose I, an angel, stand here touting knowledge in a room filled with knowledge as far as the eye can see, as Mr. Parrish so shrewdly pointed out earlier?"

The sound of his name made Jacob sit up straighter in his seat and for some reason he felt a sudden rush of heat flood his face.

"For simply the same reason: protection," said Thaniel, supplying the answer to his own question. "Just as knowledge leads to the swamp lands where sin resides, so too can it offer protection in the same way a sturdy shield or breastplate deflects the sharpened point of a spear or trident aimed at the flesh. Here, you will hammer out your own armor with these books to guide you by learning everything there is to know, within permitted limits, about the history of the world, not as you and the rest of mankind have come to know it, but as it really is."

All eyes suddenly turned to the immense book-filled walls surrounding the boys, and immediately Ethan raised his hand.

"There's no numbers on any of these books," he noted when Thaniel glanced over and nodded to the boy to speak.

"Should there be?" Thaniel, looking somewhat confused, replied.

"Well, so, how does anyone know what books are where without a card catalog?" the puzzled boy inquired.

"What do you think this is, brainiac, the local public library?" Leos jumped in before Thaniel could answer. "Next thing you'll be asking is where the librarian is."

He then glanced around along with the others in the advent he might have overlooked some winged, pinched-looking figure sitting nearby with a finger poised to the lips ready to hush them; but as expected there was none to be seen.

"Alright then, *brainiac,*" Ethan shot back sarcastically, "maybe you can explain how anyone's supposed to find whatever book they're looking for in here without it taking at least fifty years to do so."

Leos opened his mouth to shoot back a response but it was Thaniel's voice which came forth.

"Perhaps, I could answer that question, if I may." Gazes shifted in unison to the angel. "Would you believe me if I told you I knew by heart every book that resides inside this Library as well as its exact location on the shelf upon which it resides?"

It was a fantastic boast, one which would be met with skepticism had it been voiced by someone else. Coming from Thaniel, it was somehow believable.

"You'll find this Library as you wander through it in the coming weeks to be not as big as it first appears," said Thaniel. "True there are far more books housed here than all the libraries built by man should you put them together. But books are nothing more than an extension of thoughts. Physical thoughts, but thoughts none the less."

He paused for a moment as he looked out at the faces staring back at him, each one carrying a nearly identical crinkle in the space between the eyebrows right above the nose created by the struggle to make sense of his words.

"How might I explain this so it makes sense to you?" Thaniel pondered out loud. "Each of you carry inside your brains vast memories, all of which are stored away separately in certain places just like these books. When a time comes where you choose to revisit one of those memories, somehow you manage to know exactly where in your brain it is and instantly it is there for you. That is all this Library is—a giant brain—and all the books you see are individual memories."

"So you're saying it's possible for each of us to somehow memorize where every book is in this Library just like you?" asked Jacob incredulously.

"I'm saying," answered Thaniel with a smile, "the idea you see now as an insurmountable task is really not so complicated. But I'll leave it to each of you to discover on your own in the coming months whether or not I am full of hot air or not."

"Can I ask a dumb question?" asked Leos.

"Better than anyone here," Ethan jabbed jokingly under his breath.

"Touché, mate, touché" said Max with an approving wink which made Ethan's proud grin beam even wider.

"Go ahead with your question," urged Thaniel, nudging Leos' fixed glare away from Ethan.

"Just, uh, how many books are there in here anyway?" asked Leos. The sheer volume had left an impression on all the boys, but none more than Leos.

"You know, I can't say I've ever really counted them before," answered Thaniel. And while no one outwardly contested his claim, none of the boys really believed the angel's answer.

"Besides," Thaniel quickly added as if recognizing the stares looking back at him shared the same suspicions, "I doubt any of you would believe me if I were tell you. Now, if there are no further questions, I suggest we get busy."

And with that, large, identical hefty books—one for each boy—dropped out of nowhere from the upper reaches of the Library. They landed in synchronized form on the tables with a thunderous clamor that made each boy jump with unexpected shock.

"We'll start with chapter one," said Thaniel, making no attempt to hide the thin smirk formed by his mouth as the Nephilim worked their bugged eyes back into their sockets.

CHAPTER TWENTY-THREE

Nov. 20 (I think)

Today at breakfast, Anahel came into the Hall and instructed all of us—Shrikes, Harriers and Ospreys—to head over to Lions Bite as one group after we had finished eating. He didn't say anything further as to why which left us whispering amongst ourselves as we finished eating what might be awaiting us there.

In our eagerness to find out, we made it to Lions Bite a bit earlier than usual which didn't seem to catch Damiel off guard. He was standing in the center of the arena, and behind him came blinding bursts of a painfully bright light as though something was reflecting the morning sunlight back at us. As we crossed the arena and made our way toward Damiel we finally were able to see they were swords. Dozens of them impaled in the ground and lined up in perfectly formed rows like cemetery markers of fallen warriors.

All of us exploded with excitement at the exact same time and took off in a mad dash to claim our weapon. None of the swords were the same and, surprisingly, there was no scrimmage between anyone over any particular one. We each seemed to go straight toward the one we ended up claiming, with no fight or quarrel. The one I grabbed seemed to be made specifically for my grip and surprisingly light for what I first anticipated.

Damiel stood by quietly sharing in our enthusiasm as he allowed us to goof off like a crew of pirates run amok. When he finally managed to quiet us all down, he spoke to us about how proud he was of our progress. But, he was quick to emphasize, we still had a lot more to learn, which all us were more than eager to begin right then and there. Damiel had other ideas and asked which of us wanted to give our new-found swords a try.

You mean on each other? Ethan asked. But we already knew that's what Damiel meant. Only problem was this was the first time most of us had ever seen a sword up close much less held one. Aside from the few minutes of foolishly mimicking what we had each seen in movies, none of us had a clue about fighting with a sword. But Damiel was insistent telling us sword-fighting was instinctual. Then, for some reason, he looked to me and asked, "How about you, Jacob?" Not wanting to be the first to openly make a fool of myself in front of the other guys, I felt my chest tighten instantly. What did I know about fighting with a sword? Damiel, however, seemed to ignore my hesitation and coaxed me forward. Then, if that weren't enough, he told me to choose my opponent from amongst the other guys.

I stood there studying the dozens of faces staring back at me. Max would have been the perfect pick. Being as we are friends, it would have been a much more relaxed and even fun challenge. It even looked to me as though he was readying himself to be chosen. Yet for some reason beyond my comprehension my eyes kept shifting to where Creed Maggert was standing glaring back at me as he's had a habit of doing since the day we first laid eyes on one another. It was like déjà vu to when Coach Mercer gave me the same instruction of choosing my opponent during wrestling tryouts and I chose Yul Dane. In many ways, Creed reminds me of Yul. They both seem to be cut from the same cloth—arrogant, conceited blowhards in desperate need of being cut down to size. Maybe that's why to the surprise of everyone else—myself included—my finger aimed itself in Creed's direction. Not that I was confident I was the one capable of cutting Creed down to size, but at least I was armed with a weapon to attempt a try.

"Now this is gonna be a good show!" I heard Max mutter to the other guys standing around him. Even Damiel looked to be somewhat impressed by my obviously bold choice. And while I tried to give forth an air of confidence, I couldn't help but second-guess what I was sure to be pure

stupidity on my part when I watched Creed step forward with his chest puffed out and sword gripped tight in his hand. Damiel proceeded to tell us the ground rules, but I was too busy concentrating on keeping up a brave face to the hate-filled stare leering down at me to listen. Then before I knew it, or was even ready for it, the fight was on. I braced myself for the first swing of Creed's sword, but instead he caught me off guard with a hard and fast kick to my torso. It sent me flying back several feet through the air and onto the ground. I heard a roar of cheers rise up and knew instantly I was not the fan favorite being rooted for by most of the other guys. I also knew, glancing back at Creed and the smug look pasted on his face, I was going against someone who had no intention of fighting fairly. Still, I managed to get back on my feet while doing the best I could to hide from everyone else the fact I felt like I had just been struck by a speeding train.

When our swords finally met for the first time, the ricochet of the blow was like a direct hit of high voltage electricity to my hands. Still, I kept swinging away and, with each swing and blow, I slowly came to know how best to hold and wield this weapon I was blindly attempting to use. Every chance he had, however—and there were plenty—Creed made it a point of reminding me this was not some friendly lesson but an unfriendly fight by delivering numerous unsuspecting kicks and punches my way and hitting his mark nearly every time. I found myself growing more and more frustrated. Between trying to focus on what I'd already learned in the past weeks and hearing Damiel call out where I was making my mistakes, I could feel the anger inside me beginning to boil. The only thing that seemed to help me through the obvious thrashing I was suffering was hearing the small band of cheers being shouted out in my favor with Max leading the chorus with his humorous Aussie euphemisms which, for the first time thanks to the painful blows raining down on me, didn't have me on the ground laughing uncontrollably.

It was only when I was pretty sure I would be the one who would be nursing the stinging wound of defeat that night and not Creed, as I had fantasized, that something switched. I went for one last swing at Creed with my sword, and while our blades were locked together he swung his arm at me and nailed me square in the face with his elbow. I actually saw the pain in a firework-like burst in front of my eyes. Then my tongue caught the familiar taste of pennies in my mouth, and when I caught a smirking look of contempt staring back at me, as if to thank me for foolishly allowing him the pure enjoyment of pounding on me, and in such a public way to add to my discomfort, something inside me snapped. My arms, which by now were burning like fire and felt like cooked noodles, exploded with movement sending blow after blow in Creed's direction. I found myself wondering if I was actually wielding the sword, or had the sword somehow come to life and was wielding itself as I desperately tried to hold on to it for dear life.

I suddenly felt a certain sense of invincibility as I found myself matching Creed blow for blow, kick for kick, fist for fist. Whatever awkward and downright pitiful start I had in this match had somehow passed, and the smug enjoyment that had been plastered on Creed's face quickly changed to surprise as I came at him with all the speed and gravity-defying movements I had sweated away learning along with the others in the Forest while Damiel barked in our ears. This was fighting of a whole new order. The kind I witnessed when Gotham and the Powers tangled with the savage band of Infectors just outside Eden's gate over the waters of the Van Gölü. I felt like I was in the middle of some Jet Li, "Matrix" or some other insane 3D action flick come to life. The awesome spectacle of impossible movements, speed, and brute force Creed and I unleashed on one another defied anything and everything reality had before this moment made me think was not possible.

More importantly, the cheers coming from my fellow Nephilim— except for a noted few loyal to Creed—took a noticeable shift in my favor. Especially when Creed, who was becoming visibly more frustrated by my sudden ability to deflect his hate-focused blows while suffering a few of my own to his face, took a final dirty swing at me with his sword. I saw the burst of sunlight caught in the mirror-like sheen of his sword as it came my way and I jumped clearing both the sweeping blade and Creed's head in two somersaults worthy of an Olympic gold medal. I landed behind Creed before he could even turn himself around to face me, and when he did I delivered a breath-stealing kick to his chest—the same he dealt me at the beginning of our duel. It sent him flying backward a good, satisfying distance and, when it was clear he wasn't getting back up as he writhed about trying to catch the breath that had been knocked from him, a great cheer of victory erupted for me.

It was a good feeling. The best I've had here so far. And while the pats on the back I received from my fellow Edenites was enjoyable, the real prize—for me at least—was when I glanced over at Damiel and saw by the look on his face that he was pleasantly impressed. It was faint, but trust me it was there. Creed, on the other hand, was quite the opposite. I don't think I've seen quite as murderous a look on anyone's face before than the one I saw on his when I looked over and caught him glaring in my direction from where he remained on the ground.

I guess it's fair to assume that if he didn't despise me before, he most certainly does now.

~ ~ ~

The snake eagle soared weightlessly across the cloudless sky when suddenly it swooped sharply downward toward the Forest below before regaining its graceful glide. With the wind ruffling the feathers of its outstretched wings, the eagle sailed low over the dense canopy of forest trees. Just ahead came a break in the endless blanket of boughs and leaves where suddenly there could be heard growing louder the clanging of metal against metal along with the raucous clamor of boys engaged in competition.

Flying over the clearing, the eagle turned a rapt eye to the towering slabs of stone that was Lions Bite and saw several pairs of Nephilim with their swords in hand vigorously sparring with one another. Even from high up in the air it was quite apparent Damiel's training in such a short amount of time was showing impressive results. Nowhere was it more markedly so than with Jacob, who was seen in the middle of Lions Bite sparring with none other than Damiel himself.

Their blades rang with a high-pitched peal each time they crossed, and every now and then the force of the blows gave way to a burst of sparks. If Jacob felt the strain of going up against Damiel's intimidating prowess and muscle, he didn't show it. Despite the sweat trickling down his sun-beaten face, a fierce determination stayed locked in his eyes and clenched tight in his jaw. It was the kind of spirited display that proved impressive to Damiel, but not as much as the competitive push back the boy showed. It was more than clear the training at Lions Bite agreed with Jacob. He took to the sword with a striking ease and skill Damiel had rarely before witnessed.

Before long, the other Nephilim had abandoned their own matches and formed a cheering line around Damiel and Jacob. Then, like the other duels previously shared between the two, Damiel revealed a victorious move that in lightning speed separated Jacob from his sword and sent him crashing down on the ground flat on his back. Looking up, Jacob found Damiel standing over him with the point of his sword pressed uncomfortably against his neck as a reminder to him there was much he was still in need of learning.

The other boys were dismissed for a short break and, as they ran off, Damiel planted the blade of his sword into the earth and took a seat on the ground beside Jacob with a heavy sigh. "You surprise me, Fledgling. There have not been many Nephilim who have shown either the will or fortitude to take me on with such vigor. You are a natural with the sword."

"I've also become a natural at ending up on my back," noted Jacob bitterly. While trying to steady his exhaustive breaths, his gaze turned skyward where it caught sight of the lone snake eagle slowly circling about the wide stretch of blue overhead.

"Don't let it get you down," said Damiel. " If it makes you feel any better, far greater than you have found themselves in the same position."

"Gee, thanks."

"Remember, you're a newbie to the sword," said Damiel. "That you are able to fend off an angel as well as you have shown, not to mention one proven to be as great a warrior as I, is commendable and a promising testament.

Jacob gave Damiel a mocking glance. "Your humility is truly uplifting."

"Humility, you will find, has no place on a battlefield," replied Damiel with a wink. "Look at it this way, one day you may tire of having your back kiss repeatedly the ground and in your resolve find a way of leaving the stain of dirt on mine."

The idea proved an appealing one to Jacob. Rolling back onto his shoulders, he returned himself to his feet with the graceful ease of a gymnast. Then grabbing up his sword from off the ground he flashed a mischievous glint at the angel. "One day might be today," he said, beckoning Damiel to pick up his sword for another rematch.

"You are a competitive one, I'll give you that." said Damiel with a hearty chuckle as he, too, rose up on his feet. "Well, that's good. It'll make you a strong and worthy candidate for Illumination."

A quizzical look slowly came to Jacob.

"What is that—Illumination?" he asked, lowering his sword. "I heard Anahel mention it in the Hall during the welcoming dinner."

"Illumination marks the next and much more intense stage of your training you and the rest of your band of Fledglings will eventually be graduating to after your first year at Havenhid. It is marked by a daylong competition held here at Lions Bite," explained Damiel while swinging fancily his sword as he dueled the open air about him. "Fathers come to observe what their sons have so far learned and watch them compete against one another. More importantly they stand with their sons as they make their allegiance to the Light official. I guess you can call it a sort of baptismal celebration. It's probably the one time I've seen angels willfully reduce themselves into carrying on like civilians in their boasting and cheering on of their sons from the seats of this arena. Quite the spectacle, really."

Damiel then glanced over at Jacob who had become suddenly quiet and stopped swinging his sword.

"What is it?" he asked, noticing a sullen look in Jacob's downcast eyes. "Illumination is something most Fledglings look forward to with great excitement next to getting their wings. You look as if I've ripped yours right off your back."

"No…it sounds like fun," said Jacob through a forced smile. "Now that I know what it is, I'm looking forward to it."

Jacob's put-on enthusiasm didn't fool Damiel.

"Yes, I can see that clearly," remarked the angel.

"I just hope I'll be able to participate," said Jacob.

"Why wouldn't you?" Damiel, cocking his head ever so slightly, asked with curious puzzlement. "From what I've been observing so far, I'd argue you might end up being the one to beat."

"You know, it being a whole father-son thing and all and me not having one—a father that is. One that I know of, at least."

Now it was Damiel's turn to grow sullen, and he cursed himself silently for speaking of the father-son event in such a casually off-handed manner.

"I'm sorry Jacob, I didn't mean—" began Damiel, whose ease with apologies was awkward at best. "I suspect it's a difficult thing, not knowing one's own father."

Jacob didn't agree nor disagree. "It's just weird. I was okay growing up thinking he was dead—at least, that's what my mom told me," he explained. "But now…suddenly knowing out of the blue he's actually alive somewhere—it's a strange feeling. Not to mention the fact he's an angel to boot."

Jacob looked off to the sound of laughing coming from the far end of the arena where the other Shrikes were joking around and engaging in adolescent horseplay.

"Am I the only one?" asked Jacob.

"The only one what?" replied Damiel.

"The only Nephilim who doesn't know who his father is?"

The angel's silence came as no surprise to Jacob, and yet it somehow was more comforting than hearing what he already knew to be the answer.

"I wish I could I tell you who your father is," offered Damiel while hating himself for knowing the boy would hear the meaning of his deceptive words differently than he meant them.

Stalwart as he was, Damiel, for the first time, felt a pang of empathy for Jacob. Much as he would have liked to deny it, he had found himself with each passing day taking a rather surprise liking to the boy in a way the angel least expected. And in that liking the bonds of a genuine fondness had taken root and strengthened in the weeks since Jacob's arrival to Eden. The last thing Damiel wanted was to see Jacob pained over something he had no control over or say. Yet he knew the secret of Jacob's coming to be would eventually bring just that—pain. And in vast, copious amounts.

"Do you have any…you know…Nephilim of your own?" Jacob's question seemed to catch Damiel off-guard.

"I did…once," said Damiel, though he seemed hesitant to answer.

The solemn tone heard in the angel's voice was instantly recognizable to Jacob who immediately wished he had refrained from asking the question.

"It's okay, really," said Damiel, feigning a weak smile that was in no way comforting. "You will find any angel who has known the joy of fatherhood has more often than not come to know one of the rare things we have found we share with mortal men—the unexpected and deep-running pain that comes when one loses a child, whether it be by the inevitable reach of time or tragedy. In my case, it was the latter."

"What happened to him?" asked Jacob, unable to tamp down his brimming curiosity.

"Furies…Furies ended him," answered Damiel, practically spitting the hatred suddenly pooling on his tongue. "He was a fighter, that one; as skillful as I've ever seen a Nephilim with a sword in hand. And why shouldn't he have been, with me as both his father and teacher? But as it were, it just wasn't enough."

Jacob saw the grip Damiel had on his sword had tightened, and his arm had flexed itself noticeably, as though the angel was itching to make use of his weapon against this enemy he spoke of with such venom in his voice.

"Now maybe you understand a little better, in those exhausted moments you curse me under your breath for being the taskmaster I am, why it is I drive each of you Fledglings into the ground as hard as I do. It's to ensure each of you are one lesson better suited to defend yourselves than my son was," Damiel spoke with a hiss through clenched teeth. "If there's one thing I learned that terrible day, it's that one can never underestimate the ruthless savagery that bends our enemy, nor can we assume we are sufficient enough in our skills for the moment we eventually face down one another. I may have lost my son to this dark enemy, but I long ago vowed it would be over my own dead body that they reap even one of my brothers' after I've schooled them. And mark my words, boy, a day of reckoning is coming when the debt of my loss, as well as my brothers', is settled once and for all, and on that day I promise you there will be blood!"

Jacob didn't need to look any further than the fiery glint in Damiel's eyes to know without doubt the angel meant what he said. They carried the same cutting gleam found in the blade of his sword. And never before in his life did Jacob feel in better hands than at that moment.

~ ~ ~

The ruckus of spirited competition could be heard coming from Lions Bite until mid-afternoon when the sound of a trumpet made itself heard in the distance, bringing to an end the day's training. Tired, but looking less and less haggard than they did in the days when they first started going to Lions Bite, the boys started their way back to Havenhid. As it usually happened when they neared the River, Jacob suddenly stopped and looked to the section of the Forest residing east of where the water flowed. Only this day, it was the sound of Damiel's voice lingering inside his head lamenting over his son earlier in the afternoon that made Jacob pause.

"What is it?" asked Max.

"You ever gone to see the Tree?" inquired Jacob, referring to the most marked and sacred thing in Eden.

"Nah," answered Max with a simple shake of his head while staring off at the curtain of dense woods which held firmly Jacob's gaze with the knowing the thing of which they spoke resided somewhere within its boundaries.

"How come?" asked Jacob.

"Don't know," answered Max with a shrug. "Probably the same reason you don't see many Japanese tourists visiting Pearl Harbor. It's just a reminder of a big mistake that was made, you know?"

It was a simple explanation that somehow made perfect sense to Jacob.

"You coming?" asked Max, motioning with a nod of his head toward the path awaiting them leading the way in the opposite direction. There was something wanting to lead Jacob towards the woods instead; he could almost feel it tugging at him.

"Go ahead, I'll catch up with you in a bit," said Jacob.

"Alright," Max hummed suspiciously, and had he not been in hurry to get back to Havenhid to wash up and feed his grumbling stomach, he most certainly would have pressed Jacob about what was rattling inside his brain. "Don't be too late. You know the food goes fast with these vultures."

Jacob watched as Max ran off to catch up with the others who had made it quite a distance ahead of him. Once Max had fallen from sight behind a grassy slope, Jacob turned back to the Forest and made his way in its direction, slowly at first and then in an easy run which became more and more swift. His feet, as if moving of their own accord, led him through the woods, thin at first with trees but becoming more dense the deeper into it he went. Above him could be heard a great many voices coming from vireos and thrushes as well as wagtails and pipits. Their distinctive calls and warbles filled the air of their wooded haunt in a sweeping unified chorus punctuating their curiosity as they followed Jacob's movements from their perches high in the trees.

Jacob soon came upon a pathway, one that cut a curving swath straight ahead through the trees. He was about to take to it when he was startled by the sudden appearance of a figure dropping down from somewhere above to block his way. His instinct, sharpened through weeks of training with Damiel, had him reaching for his sword. Much to his surprise, however, the figure he saw at the end of his brandished blade was an angel. Or so Jacob suspected by the massive pair of gray plumed wings seen sprouted from the figure's back that had guided him to a soft, yet firm landing on the forest floor.

"Here, here, you won't be needing that!" said the angel, pushing aside the sword pointed in his direction. "What has sent you racing through these woods like a hare through the reeds of a warm meadow in pursuit of a prospective mate?" His voice, deep and honeyed, was pleasant. And his face, while kind and inviting in its youthfulness, held the promise of unmasking an intimidating fierceness when warranted.

"You're an angel," noted Jacob as though it was the first time he'd ever laid eyes on a winged being.

"You were expecting a wood nymph?" replied the stranger.

"No…I wasn't really expecting anybody…that is, I'm looking for the spot where the Tree of Life grows," Jacob, still a bit startled, replied. "I'm pretty sure it's somewhere in this direction. Although—" he glanced around confusingly at the large number of trees surrounding him, "now that I think about it, I'm not so certain I'd know the Tree of Life from any other tree."

There must have been thousands upon thousands of trees in the woods. For all Jacob knew, he already passed it without even knowing it.

"It's quite doubtful," said the angel. "You will soon discover that when you look upon the Tree of Life, there is no confusing it with any other."

"Then you know where I could find it." It wasn't until Jacob finished uttering the sentence that he realized the foolishness of his inquiry..

"I should very well hope so. There doesn't exist an inch of these woods—or all of Eden for that matter—that I do not know intimately. But before I point the way to you, tell me. Fledgling, what is it that has sent you in such a fevered pace in search of the Tree?"

"It's not really the Tree really I'm looking for, but another angel," said Jacob.

"You must mean Gothamel."

"That's right, how did you know?"

"Who but he has spent so much time occupying its shade these days?" said the angel. "Most every hour of each day passed since he first arrived back in Eden he has spent there. Many a night as well with only the moon and the sea of stars flickering in the sky to light his perpetual vigil. It's a solemn sight, if I do say so myself. Having never sired any offspring myself, I nonetheless recognize the pain he suffers from having to bury his own and embrace tighter the grace that my own heart has not been pierced by such a particularly cruel thorn." As he spoke, the angel's eyes, piercing in their pools of molten gold, seemed to drift off in a thought-filled instant before refocusing themselves and gazing newly upon the boy's face.

"You must be the one they call Jacob; the one brought here by Gothamel."

Jacob nodded with some reluctance.

"Yes, of course you are. Now that I look upon you I clearly can see that to be the case."

Here it comes, thought Jacob, recognizing the glimmer of keen intrigue in the angel's eyes. He then waited for the friendliness in the angel's face to fade and quickly be replaced with one of recoiling disapproval, just as he had witnessed with each of the Guides. No such look revealed itself. In fact, much to Jacob's surprise, the angel's smile broadened.

"Well then, fancy I should come across you this way. I've heard much of your arrival and stay so far in Eden and have been eager to see who has been the cause of so much tongue-wagging amongst my brothers."

"I think it has something to do with my face. Couldn't tell you what, but it doesn't seem to be a pleasant sight for some of the others," said Jacob.

"Your face? What of it? Two eyes, a nose and a mouth. Same as every other creature walking around on two legs, that is if God smiled kindly upon you," answered the angel.

There came a shrill echo from some unseen animal veiled somewhere within the thicket of the surrounding woods whose piercing cry Jacob didn't recognize.

"I'm not trespassing or anything like that, I hope," said Jacob. "Anahel said we were free to go anywhere in Eden except a couple places he noted. But I also know the Tree is considered a sacred spot."

"The most sacred spot in all of Eden, without argue. But as long as the intention in one's heart is pure and the path beneath his feet is righted, makes no mind to me your visit," the angel said before his gaze shifted to the pathway ahead. "Speaking of which, your feet have led you in the right direction. The tree you seek resides a short distance down this path. To reach it one just has to follow it until there is no more path left to follow. Come, I shall walk with you and see you the way if you should care the company."

While an unexplained urgency had carried Jacob wind-like to this section of the Forest he had never before visited, the curiosity stoked by his new-found companion helped settle him into the leisurely pace he took to the path alongside the mysterious angel.

"So, are you a Guide as well, er—?"

"The name is Haniel. And no I'm not a Guide, except at this particular moment it would appear," the angel replied as the two strode slowly through delicate slats of sunlight sneaking its way down through the boughs of the trees.

"How is it none of us have never seen you before until today?"

"I serve as Guardian of the Tree," said Haniel, "and as such my time is spent roaming the halls forged by the land rather than those of Havenhid. My presence tends to go unnoticed; unless, of course, one is compelled to pay a visit to this end of the Garden and crosses my path as you have."

"Guardian of the Tree? Why would a tree be in need of a guardian? What, do you fear someone might plot to uproot and make off with it? Or perhaps carve their initials into the trunk?" Jacob remarked with a light laugh.

"I've no doubt you've already come to learn a great many things in your time spent here as you become enlightened about the Nephilim ways. But as your joking nature reveals, you are still green, Fledgling; as green as the fern you see grouped alongside this path we walk," said Haniel with a grin. "The time has not been that far removed when a very real evil took shape in this Garden and its coils found its way into the branches of the Tree. Unfortunately for you, and most of mankind, that dark trespass has become nothing more than a story from an old book, even as its lingering presence stalks you, slithering in the company of your shadow and the shadow of all mortal man, scheming to finish that which it began right here in this Garden those many eons ago."

A couple of trogons perched nearby on the low-reaching branches of a flowering pineapple guava tree offered a high-pitched shriek of greeting as the two passed by before returning to grooming their brightly colored blue-violet, green and red plumes.

"I'm not sure I know what you mean. Finish what?" asked Jacob.

"That which left its eternal stain on man and cast him from this paradise, of course," answered Haniel. "You cannot see it, but it scars you as visibly as the marks seared onto the temples of the Fallen; the mark of sin which came to you with the first bite taken by the Lady Eve of the fruit grown by the Tree. By it came man's fall from grace, and it is the Darkness' sole aim and intention that by it man will ultimately be fully engulfed and perish from existence."

Jacob couldn't help but feel a chill run through him, not so much from fear but the sudden realization he was treading in the exact same spot where the evil of which Haniel referred had once lurked in all its labyrinthine deceit. The angel had been right; Eden and its history continued to exist in Jacob's eyes and mind as nothing more than a tale from the Bible, a make-believe fable of sorts, even as his own existence was embraced in the reality of its lush, paradise-painted lands, a reality he could see, smell and feel. And it was then the Garden came to look different in his eyes and he began seeing it not only for the paradise it truly was, but what it had once been.

"This might sound like a stupid question," Jacob began as an unwelcoming thought suddenly visited his head, "but how do you know the Darkness isn't lurking somewhere in the Garden now—you know, another snake?"

"That's why there's a Guardian of the Tree," answered Haniel with a smile creeping its way onto his face that told Jacob, while his question might not have been stupid, it was naively amusing. "Not that I have much to guard against. The Darkness has about as much chance of setting hoof in these parts as man has in one day being gifted these lands as a vacation destination."

Gold sparkles reflected within Haniel's eyes like light bouncing off the facets of a diamond as they then turned forward to the pathway ahead of them where a parting in the trees revealed a sun-filled clearing.

"Go ahead now: what, and whom you seek you will find right through there," instructed Haniel with a nod of his head, signaling he was about to part company with the boy.

"It was good to meet you, Haniel," said Jacob.

"And I you, Fledgling."

"Hopefully, I'll see you around again sometime."

"It's a most certain prospect, especially now that you know where to find me," said Haniel with a friendly nod. Then as Jacob continued down the path, the angel called to him with a stern warning: "Be sure to steer clear of the Immortalis. Even I would have difficulty holding back the Cherub and his wrath from you should your feet cross the blood-red blossoms."

Jacob gave one last look over his shoulder but the path behind him was clear and held no sign of Haniel. He had forgotten about the Immortalis—and the Cherub, for that matter. Not that he would know a Cherub from a pinecone. Yet the multiple warnings first sounded to all the Nephilim by Anahel in the Hall of Light the night he arrived in Eden made it sound dire enough, and that was enough for him to make extra mindful his steps

~ ~ ~ .

The path led Jacob out of the shade of the trees where it abruptly ended, just as Haniel said it would. There, blinking in the bright sunlight with a cool gentle wind tickling his face teasingly, Jacob caught his breath at the vision awaiting him; for that's what it was, a vision of beauty more exquisite than any Eden had yet revealed to his eyes. It unfolded itself in a spacious, yet quaint circular clearing of green, and resplendent in a rainbow of fragrant flowering plants and shrubs caught in the first breaths of blooming.

Immediately Jacob caught sight of it.

Straight onward in the center of the clearing, rooted atop a lazy slope of ground covered in green grass was the Tree he thought only existed in the biblical words of the Good Book. It looked not so much different than any other tree Jacob had seen in Eden, and yet at the same time it looked like none he'd ever before laid eyes upon. Unlike the towering arboreal behemoths Jacob had walked amongst in the surrounding forests, the Tree instantly called into question its age by its less than mammoth stature. Yet amongst the other trees that stood surrounding it from a distance, it had a regal presence, like that of an ancient tribal leader, and in the full light of the sun, it gave off a gauzy radiance which surrounded the Tree in a halo of gold.

For some time Jacob stood in quiet awe, hesitant that his feet were worthy to pass beyond the edge of the path into the serene beauty before him. Eventually, the wonder in which he became lost urged him forward turning him slowly in circles as he walked. The sweet aroma of fresh grass was carried in pleasing wafts to fill his nose by the breeze. A vein stretching from the River somewhere far off in the unseen distance formed a nearby babbling stream where the playful plopping of fish jumping about could be heard. A shadow skimming across the ground drew Jacob's gaze upward to catch sight of a brightly colored bird of paradise gliding gracefully overhead like a showgirl adorned in a headdress and trailing tail of exotic feathers. All these wondrous simple things existing before Jacob's eyes, filled with the same life force that filled his lungs and pumped his heart. Yet he knew he was strolling through a timeless place unmarked by age or season, no matter how many times the sun rose in the east and set in the west. What became "In the beginning" would remain unchanged "In the end"—if in fact an end even existed for a place such as this. And in that moment of thinking it, Jacob suddenly grew sullen at the prospect that such beauty and peace could ever be swallowed up by such an unkind thing as the end.

~ ~ ~

"What is it you're doing here?"

The sound of Gotham's voice jarred Jacob abruptly from his drifting thoughts. Spinning around, he found the angel seated beneath the Tree's wide-stretching branches. It was clear from the agitated look on the angel's face that Jacob's unannounced appearance had proven to be unexpected and unwelcome.

"The Tree," blurted Jacob, pointing up to the branches. "I figured being here in Eden and not paying a visit to the Tree of Life would be like…like…going to France and not seeing the Eiffel Tower."

"That's all well and good. However, the light tells me you should be heading back to Havenhid from Lions Bite," noted Gotham after a quick glance upward at the sun.

"I thought I'd take the scenic way back," said Jacob.

It was then he noticed resting at the foot of the slope where Gotham was seated was a large rectangular-shaped block of white stone draped in spindly ropes of a leafy green vine constellated with small, white star-shaped flowers. At first, Jacob thought it to be a monument of some sort. He quickly became wiser when he recognized the way Gotham seemed to be keeping company with it that the stone was actually a sarcophagus.

"Your son?" he asked with reluctance.

Gotham didn't answer, nor did he need to; the forlorn look deep-set in his face spoke as clearly as his words ever could.

There was no writing of any kind to be found on the burial vault, only a few intricate carvings etched in the stone. The most notable were two reliefs of large size seen behind the strands of clinging vine on the side of the sarcophagus facing the boy; one was of a lamb lying in one direction, the other a lion lying the opposite way, both stretched out in their repose at the base of the stone. Jacob moved in to get a closer look when he stopped suddenly. Glancing down he saw his foot was nudging a clump of the unmistakable Immortalis sprouting in patches across the grass-covered ground all around the area where the sarcophagus and tree resided like some decorative border, and Jacob knew the beautiful blooms, while enticing to admiring eyes, were equally just as repellant to anyone whose veins coursed with mortal blood wishing to step any closer to the Tree.

"I'd stay firm where you are now, if I were you," warned Gotham. "Should you hold any curiosity for the Cherub, you are a mere half step away from satisfying it. But trust me when I tell you, it's an invitation you do not want to extend. And I for one have no interest this day in incurring a beating while attempting to fend it off you over a careless misstep."

The angel's cautionary words were all that was needed to guide Jacob two full steps backward. Then, just to play it safe, he sat himself down fast on the ground thinking no movement was the best way to avoid any possible missteps in this place where the surrounding wonder offered a great chance for such missteps.

~ ~ ~

Jacob quietly looked on at the Tree standing just a short distance away from him, studying the curves and crooks of its boughs sighing softly. He noticed the delicate veins running through the rustling leaves of the Tree were golden in color, like the veins of precious gold mined from rock found deep in the bowels of mountains in the outside world. They shined a precious brightness in the sunlight and reflected a gold brilliance which created the halo around the Tree. Yet dazzling as the leaves were, it was what he didn't see nestled amongst them that had Jacob's eyes searching deeper within the foliage.

"I don't see them," he said.

"See what?" asked Gotham.

"The apples."

Gotham gave a questionable glance Jacob's way and only when he saw where the boy's attention was affixed did he understand the remark.

"No, I don't suppose you would at that. Not now, or any time before," said Gotham. "Your mind is a field well-tilled with fables in which many saplings have taken root, I see. Apples!" He chuckled ever so slightly. "The fruit to which you are inferring that used to hang from these branches in healthy abundance was a sweet, fleshy fruit much like a pear called a conscius. I say used to because the Tree has not borne a single conscius since the day the hand of woman guided by temptation picked that which she was told not to and took a bite of it."

As he sat listening, Jacob couldn't help but feel somewhat remedial for not only thinking apples grew on the Tree, but voicing it out loud with such naive authority. And yet what else was he supposed to think when everything he knew about Eve showed her holding an apple? Besides, who ever heard of a conscius before?

"It was by that act of defiance that soon after the Tree of Life became anything but," continued Gotham. "It quickly browned and withered, much like the conscius which shed themselves from the branches to shrivel and rot on the ground. Hundreds of years—far too many to count—stretched into thousands. The Tree stood lifeless here, denuded of leaves, barren of fruit, much like it had been struck by the mark of an angel fallen, only the scar was left upon Eden itself. A lasting testament of man's willful disobedience. That is, until the day my son was entombed here, at its feet, as another marker of death to blot this garden of life. For whatever reason, of which I have none to offer, the phantom hand that for so long strangled the Tree fell dormant and life returned to it as quickly and quietly as it was snuffed in a burst of green and gold leaves unfurling themselves from deep within the bark where they had long slept—or so Anahel informed me shortly upon my return following my long absence with you in tow."

Gotham grew quiet, and in his pause it was clear to see the profoundness of the Tree's presence came with a bitter anguish.

"Strange, isn't it, just how cruel a shape irony can take," he said softly. "I'd like to believe—or perhaps hope is the better word—that maybe the Tree's miraculous reawakening was a parting gift from David; an amends of sorts. Life for life."

Jacob looked away to where death remained undisturbed; the stone sarcophagus awkwardly juxtaposed in a place where life flourished with such overwhelming force. Strangely, he felt a sadness, nowhere near as wrenching as what he felt sitting beside his mother's casket on the day of her funeral, but a sadness nonetheless. It was an odd thing, to feel a semblance of grief for someone he knew nothing of outside an aged, black and white photograph. And in that grief he found himself curiously wanting to know more about the boy and how he came to be placed young and still beneath the heavy stone slab.

"What was he like, if you don't mind me asking?" Jacob found himself wondering aloud without really meaning to.

"Like?" The question seemed to catch Gotham off guard, and for a long-drawn-out moment it was as if all language had suddenly somehow slipped from comprehension before Gotham's tongue finally found the sound of his voice. "Your grandmother would often insist he was a lot like me. Not so much in looks—though it was clear to anyone who looked upon him that he came to be from my loins—but in spirit. I used to say he was like a bridled stallion, constantly fighting the lead to get at the world as swiftly as his feet would take him. He was endowed with a competitive nature oftentimes fierce, at times untamable. But at the center of what calm he did possess resided a truly gentle and uplifting soul, glimpses of which showed itself in his disarming smile.

"A beautiful boy, he was!" Gotham was suddenly seen grinning faintly. " 'Boy' I call him, when I can hear his voice in the breeze angrily insisting he was a young man, and not even a young one at that despite his age. But beautiful he was. Of that I wholly credit your grandmother, for who else could birth a child with hair the color of the sun and eyes that of the deepest most peaceful part of the ocean, and yet which held the flame of a deep-set fire in its pools?"

The angel's words came in the same way a paintbrush lends color to a blank canvas, giving shape to a portrait of a son who would forever remain the jewel in his father's eye. As he spoke, Gotham's face seemed to brighten and a glimmer sprang from deep within his eyes as if a vision of his son had materialized before him. And for that, Jacob couldn't help but feel a tinge of jealousy rise up inside himself. What, he wondered, must it feel like to be thought of and adored in such a way by one's father? Yet despite his envy, it proved a striking thing to hear this winged warrior whose intimidating fierceness he'd witnessed firsthand in the beheading of Infectors speak in such tender tones. Realizing, himself, he had inadvertently allowed this vulnerable side to slip into view, Gotham quickly pulled back the curtain and the light that had momentarily filled his face quickly faded.

"Listen to me, going on in such a foolishly doting way," he quickly quipped in an almost self-admonishing way. "I suppose all fathers look upon their children with untainted adoration. Certainly, I've shown myself to be no different. Even now."

"So, how many children have you had?" asked Jacob.

"Only David," answered Gotham, his mouth slanting to a coy smile when he caught Jacob's response. "You find that difficult to believe I see."

"A bit, yeah. Especially considering how long you've been, you know… alive."

"You mean aimlessly wandering the world, don't you?" asked Gotham. "What can I say? The existence I've chosen while under the reign of my fall has been largely a solitary one. Uncoupled and uncomplicated."

"Not to mention lonely," added Jacob, sounding a bit bemused. "Look, I don't want to stroke your ego or anything, trust me on that, but you look like you would have women swarming over you and you've been running around on Earth since like what…the Old Testament times? That's an awful lot of swarming. And you're talking about uncoupled and uncomplicated. You mean to tell me in all that time you never fell in love?"

"Love?" Gotham seemed to ponder for a moment the word and all its inflections, both good and bad, all at the same time. "We cannot allow ourselves to be caught up in such frivolity as love—at least in the way you mean it. To do so would betray the one who remains deserving of our full devotion."

"You mean God?"

"Who else?" replied Gotham.

"But you're a Fallen," Jacob reminded Gotham in an almost apologetic voice. "What difference would it make?"

"What difference, indeed. But some loyalties are hard to sever, even amongst the Fallen," said Gotham. "That doesn't mean we are not besot by the same temptations that have long plagued mankind. Truth be told, I've faced such weakness on more than one occasion and my resolve against bearing the fruit of such temptation has been bent by many a woman locked forever in my memory whose beautiful faces and feminine charms fill a wide sea of the countless generations I've passed through."

"And my grandmother?" prodded Jacob.

"Ava was the one woman to whom I would finally relinquish my resistance and succumb." Yet there was no sound of defeat in Gotham's reply, only unashamed surrender.

"She told me you saved her from the concentration camp she was kept prisoner."

"Saved? No," said Gotham, shaking his head in disagreement. "I may have delivered her from that Hell on earth that took root within the perimeter fence of Treblinka, but she…she saved herself—not to mention many others—with a dim light of hope that refused to go out. I can still see her as clearly as the day I stepped foot in the putrid muck of that horror, where all around me was desolate and hopeless. All, that is, except for the sound of her voice. It came to me in a sound I thought only existed in the far reaches of Heaven and led me to a frail figure of a girl crumpled at the foot of death, yet managed the strength to hold it at bay…all with a sound befitting a wounded sparrow, and battle cry of a trumpet, all at the same time.

"It wasn't until several more years passed that the voice which had so moved me would find me again as I strolled a Parisian street one night. It led me inside a nearby opera house. There I saw her, the girl I had scooped up from the gnarled reach of despair, only now she was a young woman, beautiful and once more filled with life, illuminated in an aurora of firelight burning at the foot of a stage before a crowd of people as equally enthralled as I was. Never a more lovely sight had I seen before or since. I stood there in the wings completely captivated; transfixed by her singing, enslaved to her beauty, and defenseless to the shackles I had long managed to avoid as they fit themselves around my wrists and ankles then and there without so much as a struggle from myself."

The angel suddenly became aware his memory of the moment was voicing itself with the same impassioned flourish that came when he spoke of his son. It made him instantly tighten his lips, much to Jacob's chagrin. If anything, the boy enjoyed seeing Gotham slip somewhat free from the hard-edged demeanor he cinched himself into like some impregnable piece of armor.

"And so the two of you ended up falling in love and having a child," said Jacob.

"No…at least not for some time, mind you," Gotham replied shooting the boy a reluctant look. "My desire not to sire a child was not immediately swayed by your grandmother, despite my feelings for her to the contrary. In my eyes, such a union benefitted neither angel or mortal and was best avoided for the good of both despite Heaven's change of heart on the matter. Neither did I look with judgment upon those of my brothers who did not share my view—and many there have been as the growing brood of Nephilim to this day shows."

"But eventually—"

"As I've told you, we are not immune to temptation," said Gotham. "And whatever favorable purpose I could never fathom coming about from the union of angels and women and begetting from such unions that which was neither fully angelic nor fully mortal vanished the moment I gazed for the first time into my son's face when he was placed in my arms shortly after taking his first breaths."

Gotham's resolve was again weakened by the surfacing of his memories. Only this time he no longer cared what softness it brought to his face. Or who witnessed it.

"I had a son, and nothing brought me as much joy and pride as he," he said. "Especially when the time came for me to bring him here to Eden to learn that which all Nephilim must when the age calls. And yet nothing could have prepared me for the news which came the day he was sent off to the Crescent Scar to learn his Grace with the rest. It would have been less shocking to me, as well as my brothers, had the ground itself opened up and swallowed all of Eden whole than to learn David was anything but a normal Nephilim."

An anxious and bewildered look settled itself upon Jacob who became as still as a stone statue listening to Gotham.

"Normal Nephilim?" he muttered with confusion. "What was wrong with him?"

Gotham glanced over at the boy out of the corner of his eye.

"Your grandmother didn't tell you?"

"I told you," Jacob replied with a testy urgency to hear the rest of the story he had long wondered about, "she didn't tell me anything. It seemed to upset her too much."

Gotham nodded his head as if in agreement and Jacob began to fear the angel might think better of finishing his story.

"You remember when we were at Akdamar Island and the blackened fresco detailing a certain Apocrypha?" continued Gotham much to Jacob's relief.

Jacob knew instantly what Gotham was referring to and nodded.

"Johiel said it had to do with a final Fall," answered Jacob, "A Nephilim known as the Light Bearer is promised to bring angel and man together to form an army that would deliver a fatal blow to the Darkness and forge the path that would help bring about its eventual end."

"That is correct," said Gotham. "What Johiel didn't tell you was that the Light Bearer would be revealed as the Nephilim who carried with him all seven Graces held by angels."

"But…Zuriel said a Nephilim could only have two, maybe three Graces tops. And never the Seventh Grace," argued Jacob. "In fact, the Crescent Scar doesn't even have a spot marking the Seventh Grace."

"No, it doesn't," said Gotham. "Which is why it proved so shocking when it came to be David's turn to stand in the curve of the Crescent Scar."

At first Jacob didn't quite understand what Gotham was saying. And then the angel narrowed his gaze squarely on the boy.

"The Blackstone revealed him to hold all seven Graces," said Gotham. "You see, my son came to be the Light Bearer."

~ ~ ~

The revelation hit Jacob like a flash of lightning lashing out from the gloom of a dark storm cloud, and for a moment it was as if the power of speech had been paralyzed from him.

"I see you are shocked. But no more so than I was," said Gotham. "To say I was humbled to my core that my son—begot by one so marked with Heaven's disdain—was chosen to be the vessel carrying the covenant of a prophesy long awaited…"

He paused, fighting to still the tremble visible in his lip. "For the first time since my banishment, it was if Heaven had at long last smiled down on me and, in an act of mercy, granted me a sliver of forgiveness I had long sought."

A dark shadow was quick in returning to Gotham's face.

"Or so I was led to believe."

CHAPTER TWENTY-FOUR

"How did he die?"

Sitting with the stone tomb just a rock's throw away, it seemed to Jacob a natural—necessary, even—question to voice and one which he had long been anxious, and reticent, to learn the answer. Yet his tongue couldn't seem to find a delicate way in which to ask it. The more likely reason, though he was reluctant to admit it to himself, was the fear of what the answer might be.

"I would have thought the answer to your question would have been made known to you by now," remarked Gotham, as if he had overheard Jacob's debating thoughts.

"I told you, my grandmother didn't care to talk about it," said Jacob.

"I'm not talking about your grandmother," said Gotham.

When Jacob hesitated in speaking further on the matter, the angel turned a penetrating glare on him. "Come now, Jacob, you've been here long enough to know the Garden is seeded with the rumors of which I speak. You've no doubt heard by now some of the stories, of which there is an abundance, regarding David. The halls of Havenhid are never silenced of the echoes of tales told in whispers behind closed doors, whether they be true or not."

"There've been a few, I guess, I've overheard now and then," answered Jacob.

Of course, he knew precisely what Gotham was referring to; tales long-shared by generations of Nephilim about the secrets of Eden, the angels who resided there, and one another. They seemed to have a life of their own, moving from room to room and passed mouth to ear like so many tidbits of gossip in an assembly line of hushed secrecy, especially at night right before the lights were turned out. And as Gotham noted, both truth and untruth rested in each whisper. Yet no stories, as Jacob would come to discover, became more lore-shaped in their telling like those surrounding Gotham's son, particularly that of his fall from grace and ultimate demise.

"Tell me, what is it you've heard?" asked Gotham, but saw Jacob was reticent to do so. "Not to worry, for I doubt there is anything you can say about my son that hasn't already fallen on my ears."

"If that's the case, then there really isn't any reason for me to say the rumors out loud. And even if you hadn't heard them, I'd rather not be made to repeat them. Not here," said Jacob.

He was thinking, of course, of the time the first whispers concerning Gotham's son found his ears during that first long walk so many weeks earlier to Lions Bite when Max, Leos, Kairo and Ethan voiced the shocking allegation of filicide. It wouldn't be the last time Jacob would overhear such rumblings over the coming weeks, and even though he refused to believe something so monstrous, he himself couldn't help but wonder now and again, what if the rumors were actually true?

"You worry you'll offend me, and more importantly the memory of my son in this his resting place. For that, I appreciate your respect." Gotham's face cracked with a show of unexpected gratitude and he rose to his feet. "But I shall share with you, anyhow, what brought David to this crypt as cold and still as the stone from which it was made."

"You really don't have to," said Jacob somewhat nervously. "Besides, I don't see how it's any of my business."

Truly, he meant it. Yet at the same time he couldn't deny the need he felt in wanting to know what had happened to this boy who in reality, strangely enough, was his own flesh and blood uncle.

"It's important to me that any untruths you may hold regarding my son be unbent," said Gotham. "It may eventually prove of some importance to you as well one day."

He descended the slope of grass leaving the shade of the Tree for the bright sunlight. Coming to a bare patch of ground near where Jacob was seated, he stopped. His right hand reached under and behind his left arm and drew forth his sword from the plumes of his outstretched wing. The blade caught the light of the sun's blinding presence in a brilliant flash before Gotham lowered it to the ground and without explanation began carefully etching the soft earth with the sword's sharp point. Jacob leaned his body forward to get a better look at what the angel was doing, all the while mindful not to stretch himself too close to the Immortalis blooming with their radiant warning in scarlet hues just an arm's reach away.

When Gotham had finished, he took a step back and looked down upon his scrawling like an artist admiring the canvas of a finished work.

"Whoa…how the heck did you do that?" exclaimed Jacob who quickly became visibly enthralled by the sight. "It's a sword."

And, indeed, it was; but not one formed from what began as scratches in the dirt; for the moment Gotham brought the end of the last line he drew with that of the first, the crude image took the shape of what looked to be an actual physical weapon resting upon the ground as real as the sword which had drawn it.

"Not just any sword," corrected Gotham. "Does it look familiar to you?"

Jacob shook his head. "Should it?"

If anything, he found the sword to be most unfamiliar; both beautiful and intriguingly strange to the eyes at the same time. The blade was long and shined a bright silver, untarnished and gleaming like a viper's fang wet with venom, and promising a far deadlier bite to anyone whose flesh met its razor-sharp bite. Yet curiously forged within the center of the blade and buttressed against the hilt of the sword was an altogether different weapon. It was shaped like a spearhead, and unlike the main body of the sword which framed it, the metal from which it was made was dark and weathered with both great age and untold battles. A gold sheath bound the spearhead, and it was embossed with several gold crosses at its base.

"I definitely would have remembered a sword like this had I ever seen it before," Jacob remarked emphatically. "It's so unusual…like a sword within a sword. Who does it belong to?"

"The ages have seen it fall into the possession of many except the one true hand destined to clasp it," the angel replied.

Jacob's brow suddenly furrowed and his gaze shifted from the sword to Gotham with a troubled seriousness. "Is this what killed your son?"

Gotham stared raptly at the boy, yet Jacob was lost to his sight. He didn't answer.

Turning his back, Gotham cast his gaze past the Tree to the nearby mountains stretching toward the blue sea of sky.

"The sword has been known throughout history by many names: The Holy Lance; Spear of Longinus; Lancea et clavus Domini," he said. "Most, however, would come to know it as the Spear of Destiny."

~ ~ ~

DEEESSSSSSSSSSTINYYY!

The word seemed to come up and around Jacob like a breath of wind carrying the voice that had whispered the same echo to him in countless dreams. It brought an immediate chill to his skin.

"The Spear of Destiny—I've heard that name before. I think I saw something about it on the History Channel or somewhere," the boy muttered while searching his thoughts, yet choosing not to reveal the phantom voice heard in his dreams. "That's the spear that was used to pierce the side of Jesus, wasn't it?"

"Then came the soldiers, and broke the legs of the first, and of the other which was crucified with him. But when they came to Jesus, and saw that he was dead already, they broke not his legs: But one of the soldiers opened his side with a lance, and forthwith came there out blood and water. And he who saw it has borne witness, and his witness is true: and he knoweth that he saith true, that ye might believe."

Gotham recited the words of the apostle John with a serene grace as if they were his own.

"Born of the sacrifice of Christ, the spear is a weapon of immense divine power, one by which God binds the world he created with the celestial," continued Gotham, in his own words, following a short pause. "Whoever claims it holds the fate of the world, and all who dwell in it, in his hands be he good or evil. I'm sure I don't have to tell you it is a long and storied history of those who have attempted to hold reign over such power, however briefly the spear resided in their grasp.

"The soldier who pierced Jesus' side carried the spear with him the rest of his days and witnessed its power only once when it pierced through the shroud of darkness blindness would eventually bring him. With his death, the spear passed quietly into the world and into the legend awaiting it. Many would spend their years obsessively seeking it out, yet only a few would bear witness to its existence: St. Morris, Charlemagne, Constantine the Great, to name a few. Marked men you could call them, though not near the way I and other Fallen have come to be scarred. By them, and through the power wielded by the spear, dark armies were cut down, hollow religions were driven underground, and a holy empire was birthed. Yet each who would come to possess the spear knew intuitively they were merely guardians of the divine weapon, momentary protectors chosen to help guide it to the one in whose hand it was ultimately destined. And they were not alone in that realization."

Gotham lowered himself in a squat next to the sword and leveled onto Jacob a look of upmost seriousness.

"From the moment the spear pierced the side of Christ, a darkness has closely shadowed its existence," he said in a low tone, as if what he was sharing was something he wished not to be overheard, even by the nearby trees or creatures residing within and amongst them. "Most cunning and wretched, it has grown more incensed with rage with each passing of the spear. It knows the destiny awaiting it—a destiny aimed at piercing the heart of the Darkness in which all damnation dwells— and has tirelessly schemed to turn the spear from its path."

A puzzled look came to Jacob. "So why doesn't it just take possession of the spear itself?"

From the slight grin which found its way to Gotham's mouth, Jacob knew he had asked another naive question.

"You would think it would be that easy, wouldn't you? But such things rarely are. One cannot just seize the Spear of Destiny, at least not outright. Not the Darkness, nor mortal, or even angel," answered Gotham. He could see by the look settled in the boy's face more explaining was necessary. "You see, the spear can only be possessed in one of two ways: the first being that the owner of the spear must willfully relinquish his claim to it to another."

"And the second way?" inquired Jacob impatiently.

"Death," replied Gotham simply. "At the moment the life of the one who holds the spear ends, naturally or otherwise, the spear falls back freely to the world for any to claim who wish it. Should anyone attempt to acquire it by force, thievery, or any other ill-gotten manner, their life will be snuffed out the instant they take it in their grasp."

The feathers of Gotham's wings rustled in the gentle breeze as he stood back up and took in a deep breath.

"Luckily for all, the spear has remained relatively protected from the Darkness' reach. But that hasn't always been the case," he continued, sounding somewhat grim in his even grimmer faraway stare. "It came close to succeeding in its mission when the spear nearly fell into the clutches of Napoleon Bonaparte before being miraculously spirited away to safety. Unfortunately, that wouldn't be the case when the Third Reich invaded Austria. By then the spear had fallen out of existence, and out of memory to most of the world whose belief in such things had rapidly fallen to the wind like leaves shed from a wintering tree. That is until a man by the name of Adolph Hitler—a vessel for the Darkness, if ever there was one—uncovered the spear long ago released by death and left to hibernate amongst a horde of ancient relics pillaged from Austria. With the Spear of Destiny in Hitler's hands, the Darkness staked its victory with a vengeance and an unimaginable evil was unleashed and reared itself upon the face of the earth with unspeakable cruelty."

As the angel spoke, Jacob couldn't help but recall learning of the war during history class and seeing the nightmarish images of Jews perishing in concentration camps. The sight of their lifeless, starved bodies in countless piles like so many stacks of cord wood waiting to be disposed had seemed so unreal to him and so far removed from any kind of reality imaginable. Even though she was not Jewish, fate had arranged his grandmother to come and know intimately those horrors. And even though she rarely unburdened herself to speak about what no living person should ever be made to witness, the crude mark of numbers etched on her aged skin yet looking as eerily fresh as the day it was tattooed onto her alabaster hide was all the testament needed. Jacob thought of his grandmother as he sat looking at the sword on the ground and a chill ran through him as he realized the evil it could turn in the wrong hands.

"A lot of good the spear did Hitler," said Jacob. "He ended up both defeated and dead."

"True," agreed Gotham. "But only after he foolishly and unknowingly gave up the spear in the fevered hours before his demise."

"That makes no sense. Who would he give it to?"

"Me," answered Gotham.

~ ~ ~

Jacob shot the angel an incredulous look held firmly in the arch of his brow. "Okay, now you're losing me. Why in the world would Hitler—knowing he had the one weapon which would allow him to conquer the world—turn around and hand it over to you…an angel?"

The angel flashed the boy a wily smile.

"He didn't hand it over to an angel. He handed it over to an SS officer," said Gotham. "And even then he didn't know he was actually handing it over."

Confused, Jacob could only stare blankly at Gotham and hope some sort of clarity would soon follow.

"I came to realize the Darkness had finally seized the spear; for nothing else could have given rise to such horror unfolded by that war," explained Gotham. "And I knew it was only going get worse—much worse—if the spear remained in its possession. So I set out in search for it. To my luck, Hitler, thinking he was keeping it safe, had the spear sealed up in a bunker deep beneath Nuremberg, yet not realizing that by doing so he had robbed himself of its very power. A weapon allowed to stray too far from its owner's reach is as dangerous as a defanged lion.

But just to ensure that was the case, I went to him disguised as one of his own as the allies drew near. With the sound of bombs laying to waste his crumbling empire growing ever nearer, I presented him papers allowing for the bunker to be emptied and its contents moved to a more secure place. By signing them, he inadvertently handed over possession of the spear to me. I managed to get to it shortly before the allies and in its place substituted a replica now housed in Vienna which, to this day, is believed to be the true Spear of Destiny."

"So this is it, and you've had it ever since." Jacob shifted his gaze back to the sword dazzling in the sunlight as it rested upon the ground.

"What you see isn't real. Only a mirage," said Gotham. "But yes, it is now under my watch."

For Jacob, the angel's words brought a reassuring comfort.

"This is way more interesting than anything my history teacher Mr. Larson taught back in Cain's Corner," he said. "Although I still don't get what the sword has to do with your son."

Gotham was at first quiet. It was as if he was suddenly reluctant to finish the story he started out telling. Again, he lowered himself down onto his haunches near the sword he claimed to be an illusion yet looked anything but.

"I told you of the Darkness' unrelenting pursuit of the spear. Well, it did not end when it came into my hands," he began. "It is prophesied that the Light Bearer will play a most important role leading to the Final Fall against the Darkness by delivering to it a mortal wound with the light of Destiny emblazon over his head like a torch. So when David's fate was revealed by the Blackstone at the Crescent Scar, the Darkness saw its fate coming ever so frighteningly nearer, and it turned its reptilian eyes on my son knowing its best and only hope was to twist him in ways it had so often done to man."

"What would make it think it could turn your own son against you?" asked Jacob.

"You have much still to learn about the ways of the Darkness, Fledgling," answered Gotham. "David was a strong and uncompromising force of nature, which I claim responsibility with both pride and some degree of humility. He also showed himself to be a trusting soul, far too much for his own good. In that way, he mirrored his mother. In her, it was an endearing trait; in David, it proved a fatal kink in his armor; one the Darkness quickly saw as a burrow into which to worm itself."

"But how?" asked Jacob. None of this was making sense to him. "The Infectors, not to mention the mere thought of Furies, were unsettling enough for me to ever want to know what else makes up the Darkness. I definitely couldn't imagine ever being swayed by it."

Gotham held the boy's gaze as he muttered those last few words while quietly contemplating the dire, prophetic nature of such a simple statement, one to which Jacob, of all people, was innocently oblivious to, even as he spoke it.

"So you're now convinced, as happy as I am to hear you say it. But the Darkness, as you imagine it to be, rarely reveals itself as the monstrous presence it is, but rather that which it is not," explained Gotham ominously. "Such is how it came to David, in the way that it does what it does so effectively well with its hallmark cunningness and excruciating patience. It was then I made my gravest mistake. Not my first, mind you, but without argue my worst.

"It happened shortly after David's destiny was revealed at Crescent Scar when the White Circle formally declared him to be the Light Bearer. I fetched the Spear of Destiny from where I had long ago stashed it for safekeeping until this moment, and removed it from the swaddling of cloth in which it was wrapped. That night with the flicker of fire licking at my skin, I forged a sword of great strength and married it with the power of the spear, and the Spear of Destiny became the Sword of Destiny you see here at my feet.

"The next day, when David was celebrated before all Eden, I came forward with the sword, only now it was wrapped in a fine linen. Unbeknownst to me that David's will had already been bent, I revealed to him my gift. And as I handed it to him, I noticed for the first time a strange look in his eyes, one I had never before seen. I can't explain it, but it filled me with a strange sense of dread I've rarely come to know. But this was our Light Bearer and, more importantly, my son. I knew him body and soul, or so I thought. The Dark forces, however, are shrewd in their wicked doings, and even those of us who have seen right to its very heart occasionally fall blind to its clandestine ways. And so I stupidly ignored that which whispered caution in my ear. In doing so, I completed the spear's destiny by placing it, and all its power, into David's hands. It was a moment long awaited by many, but no more so than by the Darkness."

It was impossible to ignore the burden of regret which visibly weighed heavy on Gotham, and it was clear to Jacob the angel carried a great guilt that he had failed his son. Just how deep that guilt ran, however, he could not even begin to know.

~　~　~

"You said the sword is now under your watch," said Jacob. "But you also said one could only come to possess it if it is handed over willingly, or by death."

His eyes then shifted to the stone burial vault draped in fragrant flowering vines and an uncomfortable gnawing feeling made itself felt suddenly in the pit of his stomach.

"The same day I gave David the sword, I discovered that which I feared," continued Gotham. "I spied him stealing into the forbidden

Northern Lands and, of course, I followed him. What business he had venturing there, I could not imagine. The Barrens is a deceiving place where, beneath its frozen beauty, the fires of the Underneath are encased in an icy tundra found at the foot of ten thousand treacherous mountains. To step one foot within its boundaries would be to invite a most unpleasant fate. Yet there I found him, standing alone in the middle of a vast, lonely stretch of snow and ice beneath a blanket of vapor and steam floating in the air like the breath of some great, unseen sleeping dragon spilling out from its cavern within the nearby mountains, and it carried with it the unmistakable, sickening stench of sulphur. He was alone and motionless, staring out further northward. I was about to call to him from where I stood looking down from the precipice of a nearby cliff. Then, to my horror, I saw him."

Jacob waited in anticipation for Gotham to say who it was, but a cautious look suddenly came to the angel that made him tighten his lips.

"Who was it?" Jacob pressed eagerly.

"Samael."

Gotham eyed the boy curiously but could see the name meant nothing to Jacob. Thaniel obviously had not yet begun to school the Fledglings on the history of the Darkness. More importantly, none of the other Guides had let slip or maliciously revealed the one damning revelation regarding Samael that Gotham had demanded be kept from Jacob ears. And so the angel, with firm lip and even more firmly mindful of his words, carefully explained to the boy who Samael was.

"My heart quickened in my chest at the sudden sight of him," continued Gotham. "As I told you before, the Darkness doesn't often reveal itself as it is to those it sets its sights on. Neither did Samael show himself to David as he really is but the mighty angel he once was—a striking figure of youth and beauty and power—before Heaven cast him into the Pit. The only thing he couldn't disguise, however, were his eyes; they were dark, void of the fire that had once lit them and as frigid as the ice beneath his feet. And his mouth carried a sinister crook which could not be hidden. But the eyes…"

Gotham paused, as if remembering in vivid clarity the sight of his nemesis and a growing anger lit the burners housed in his own pupils.

"I knew the second I saw him his purpose. It revealed itself in those cold, dead eyes. They came to life; not the kind of life you would imagine, but a stirring of deep-seated evil. It came not just at the sight of my son, but what he held plainly in sight in his hand: the Sword of Destiny of which I had willingly placed there. And when I saw David take the first step toward Samael, it was nothing short of cataclysmic. I made my presence known with a cry that would rival thunder capable of drawing down the snow and ice clinging to the mountains in a rumbling avalanche. To say Samael was most displeased to see me would put it mildly. He in return could see the biting cold had no effect on the burning hate I turned on him.

" 'Stay far from my son,' I warned him.

" 'Your son came to me, freely I might add, not me to him,' Samael replied with a smirking sneer.

"Why didn't I just cut him down right then and there, you might be wondering. Believe me, never was I visited by such an overwhelming desire. But I was in the Northern Lands, not our fair Eden, and to do so would have unleashed all of the Underneath itself, and even I am no match against such a force alone. So, instead, I turned to David, for his safety was most crucial to me, and I beckoned him to my side, but he resisted me. There was a look of defiance in his eyes. More unsettling to me, however, was an undeniable disdain he directed my way. It was then clear to me the dark spell he was under, and it drew his feet closer to Samael one step at a time no matter what I said to him. It was only when I finally drew my sword that he stopped, and in that moment a look of surprise came to him.

" 'I cannot let you do it, David,' I warned him sternly. 'Can't you see what is happening here? He has warped your thinking in order to get Destiny. Once he has it, your blood will be the first he draws with it.' Of course I wasn't lying to him. I did not need to read Samael's thoughts to know his plan, and a perfect one it was at that: not just to finally take possession of Destiny, but smite as well the one who had been promised to place the Darkness under foot.

" 'Look where you are. Come back home with me, back to Eden,' I pleaded holding out my hand for him take. 'You are a good boy. More importantly, you are my son, my pride and my immense joy, of whom I love very much.'

"And for a brief passing moment, David seemed to hear me and take my words for what they were. But Samael in seeing this began to move his evil lips and from them came whispers my ears could not make out, and the dark invisible hand that had taken hold of my son tightened its grip. Then, in a voice which has come to haunt me these long years, David cursed me and rebuked me both as angel and the father I was." Gotham's look became long and weary, as though the voice he spoke of was even then continuing its taunting refrain. "It was then—right then at that very moment—I understood the brevity of my own sin which had come to mark me and cast me in free fall from Heaven's bosom, and I was ashamed. For what father wants to ever feel the barb of a son's disdain? Trust me when I tell you there is no greater wound."

For a moment, it looked to Jacob as though Gotham wouldn't— couldn't, even—go on with his story. It quickly became apparent in the visible way the angel pushed to steel himself that he refused to find himself cowering in the shadow of this stalking pain.

"Even as David leveled his hateful words at me, I could see the anguish in his face. He was wrestling against this thing that had taken him, trying to fight it, but it was moving him closer to Samael's side. 'Don't you make me do it,' I cried out angrily. My words were not to

David, but to my own father who I knew was watching. The hilt of my sword was wet with the sweat from the palm of my hand, and as my grip tightened around it I thought of Abraham and how God tested him by asking for the sacrifice of his son Isaac. Was this such a test now being laid before me, I wondered? Was I being asked to make the ultimate sacrifice? And I recalled at that moment the anguish the sword I clutched imprinted on the faces of so many mothers whose Nephilim sons I left still and bloodied in their arms when my place was still in Heaven, and as their pain pierced my heart I again sent my cry to Heaven above, only this time in the most pleading of ways, 'Don't make me do it.' "

Jacob listened in complete stillness, too taken with the angel's words to even breathe. All around him became quiet, as if the animals themselves whose sounds had echoed lively through the Garden had stopped to listen to the story Gotham was telling.

After a long pause, Gotham continued. "I knew the moment I stepped forward and swung my sword that my plea had been ignored, and the mercy shown Abraham would not be extended to me." Surprisingly, as Gotham spoke, there was no welling of tears or trembling of his lip; just a blank, far-off stare that held the quiet torment of reliving such a memory every moment of every day.

"Sacrifice? There exists no word to even begin to describe what it means for a father to extinguish the life of his own son, even for the good of the One greater than I. But there it was, for however you wish to deem it, lying limp and emptied of breath in my arms. Never had blood flowed so bright as it did, seeping its way across the cold whiteness of the ice."

It was true.

The rumors bandied about Havenhid were true, and even though Jacob had heard it spoken from Gotham's own lips as if reciting a confession inside a church confessional, he had great difficulty believing his own ears. When Gotham had finished, a breeze stirred and blew its way across the grass toward where Jacob sat and swept from sight the mirage of the sword upon the ground in the same way an ocean wave washes away any trace of a sand castle left in its path on a beach. It then rose up and rustled through the trees, as well as the Garden surrounding them, awakening once more the sounds of life.

~　~　~

"The only thing my grandmother ever said was that the Darkness had killed her son," whispered Jacob after a while.

Gotham seemed to respond squeamishly to the boy's words. "And why wouldn't she believe such a thing?" he said. "Do you really think a cowardly, vile act as killing one's own son wouldn't be followed by an even more cowardly act of lying about it?"

The contempt Gotham felt for himself was as obvious as the sun's blinding presence in the sky lighting the day; he was mired in it. The sight of it left Jacob feeling weighted with a great and painful sadness, and a part of him wanted to lunge forward and embrace Gotham with a tight, comforting hug; be damned the Immortalis blossoms and the Cherub it threatened to bring out from whatever place it lay hidden; but he knew the angel wouldn't tolerate for even a brief second any such sympathy to be had for him.

Instead, Jacob sat for what seemed like a long time just looking at the sarcophagus where Gotham's immense heartache had been entombed for all eternity and he couldn't help but wonder; wonder how it was a boy came to be buried like a king when his last act of life not only was a betrayal to his father, but Eden itself. How did such a betrayal manage to bring in return a final resting place in the Garden's most revered spot and not even bring cause for the Immortalis to uproot themselves from the ground in rage? Yet curious as Jacob was, he couldn't summon himself enough courage to ask.

"Why the lion and the lamb?" he asked instead, breaking the awkward silence with a nod to the two lifelike carvings embossed in the stone of the sarcophagus. The figures of the two animals, full-sized and shown lying in repose had caught Jacob's attention the moment he saw them peering out from behind the ivy.

"Beautiful, are they not?" asked Gotham catching a glimmer of recognition in the boy's eyes.

"It reminds me of a story my mother used to tell me when I was younger. About how one day the lion and the lamb would lie down beside one another and what had made them enemies would be forgotten."

"And in the space resting between them would reside the dawn of everlasting peace," said Gotham. "They also serve as a reminder of something I tried to instill in David from the time he was a young boy."

"Which was?"

"By claw and fang, the lion owns a dominion most prized; yet its the humble steps of the lamb which lead to a far greater treasure."

Jacob was given only a brief moment to ponder the angel's words when there came the familiar, far-off blare of a trumpet sounding its call. Jacob glanced upward at the sky and was surprised to see the approaching twilight beginning to show itself in the way the day's fading reaches of sunlight bathed everything all around in brilliant gold

"Guess I'm late for dinner," said Jacob. "Anahel talks about the other Guides, but he's definitely the most anal about tardiness."

Gotham's gaze followed the boy as he rose to his feet. "So are you going to tell me what really brought you here today?" he asked.

Jacob opened his mouth to answer before hesitating. Truth was he had no idea what drew him there with such driven curiosity.

"I told you; I wanted to see the Tree," he said giving an acknowledging nod to the Bible's most arboreal legend whose gold-trimmed leaves glistened like sequins even in the weakening sunlight. "And now I have."

Jacob's half-hearted grin drew a questioning look from Gotham, but before he could be prodded any further he quickly scampered off. When he reached the curtain of trees at the edge of the clearing he glanced over his shoulder and watched as Gotham returned to the perpetual vigil he held beside his son.

~ ~ ~

Later that same night, long after the Nephilim had turned in, including Jacob, who after a fitful stretch of tossing and turning in his bed and staring blankly at the black emptiness hovering above him could no longer fight off the hand of sleep that placed itself over his eyes. Anahel retired to his own chambers and immediately sensed a presence waiting inside for him. Looking to the open terrace, he found a darkened figure standing with its back to him. He did not ask who it was. There was no need to hear a voice, nor see the face for Anahel to know it was Gotham, though he thought it curious to find the angel unannounced in his chambers at such an hour.

He took the book tucked beneath his left arm which he had fetched earlier in the evening from the Library for a little night reading and quietly set it on a nearby table. Then, instead of bringing light to his room, which was already awash in the silver blue of the moon-lit night, he made his way to the balcony where a cool, caressing breeze made his long tresses dance and the weightless fabric of his open shirt billow.

"You always did hold the best view of Eden, even when wrapped in the thin veils of night," remarked Gotham in his soft but deep voice when he felt Anahel join him at the rail of the terrace.

Anahel stood quiet for a minute or two and looked out over the Garden and he could not deny what Gotham said was true. The night seemed to douse everything from the grassy open spaces and patches of forests nearby to the towering, serrated cliffs of the congregating mountains surrounding the Garden in a dreamlike state of periwinkle-colored surrealism. In the distance, the thundering falls, roaring yet immensely soothing, appeared as fluorescent liquified diamonds spilling down the face of the mountain to the valley floor where the River slithered peacefully, twinkling and glistening brightly with the reflection of the giant waxing orb of the moon branding its watery hide.

"Something tells me it was not the view that brought you here to my chambers at this hour," noted Anahel.

Gotham revealed a slight smile. "You were always a perceptive one, Anahel. So I'm sure it will come as no surprise when I tell you I am leaving Eden."

If Anahel was surprised by the pronouncement, he didn't show it. Rather, he seemed to expect it from the deep breath he took as he continued to stare off into the distance.

"So where to this time, Gothamel?" he asked. "Does there even exist a corner of the world to which you have not already fled in your fruitless attempt to outrun your own existence?"

There was an unmistakable edge of hardened annoyance in Anahel's cool tone which caught Gotham off guard.

"I've never fled from anything in my life, Anahel. You more than anyone should know better than to say such a thing to me."

"What would you call it, then?" countered Anahel.

Gotham stood silent for a moment before answering with a quiet resignation: "You know why I can't bring myself to stay here any longer than I already have."

"What I know is that many months ago you surfaced here, suddenly, without word or announcement, after vanishing from all sight for near fifty years, with a Nephilim in tow. Not just any Nephilim, mind you, but Samael's son. *His son*, Gothamel," Anahel stressed with a whispery hiss as if at that exact moment he had realized the gravity of his own words. "Against my better judgment, and because of my fondness for you, I made a decision that not only puts Eden in a most perilous situation but has cast me once again in a questionable light with some of my brothers."

It was not without some weight of guilt that Gotham took notice of the position he had forced Anahel to take.

"You must know, Anahel, how much I appreciate everything you have done in my name, both with my own son and now with Jacob," he said. "You have shown me a loyalty where none is required to exist, and it will not be forgotten. But with all due respect, surely you would have assumed my time spent here would be brief. At least long enough to see that the boy has settled in and taken to his training without any problems, and already I've stayed longer than what should have been expected."

Anahel glowered suddenly at Gotham. "What I assumed is that you would live up to the responsibility you chose to take up whether willingly or otherwise."

"What do you mean by that?" questioned Gotham, his voice rising in anger. "I've done what I promised to do, and that was bring the boy here to Eden to learn who he is and ensure a barrier of safety between him and the Dark Shadow that will surely stalk his every waking moment like some unrelenting nightmare."

"And you see yourself free of your duty by simply acting as chaperone through the Gate?" Anahel barked just as loudly. "Well then, if you would be so kind to allow me before you take your leave of us the chance to throw forth a feast in celebration for what you have shown to be a true, unfettered act of selflessness."

The dripping sarcasm drew a narrowing of Gotham's brow.

"What more would you have me do?"

"Something…anything," cried Anahel who remained riled. "Help mentor the boy in his training. Nurture him. Surely you can spare him one ounce of the attention you have chosen instead to dedicate to your daily vigil of pity at the foot of the Tree of Life."

Anahel's cutting remark took Gotham aback.

"Is that how you see me?" asked the angel, sounding slightly wounded.

Anahel wavered briefly, and in that moment he questioned whether he should have kept his cruel tongue firmly behind his teeth.

"There comes a time," he continued in more gentle voice, "when one who mourns must decide to rein in their sorrow or continue their drift on the waters of perpetual wallowing."

A cold look came to Gotham's eyes. "I wouldn't expect you to understand; you who's never experienced the bond of having a son."

"It's true, I have as yet never sired a child," said Anahel, turning away from the beauty of Eden to circle slowly around the wide-open terrace. "But lest you forget, I was also there that fateful day and saw you carrying your son lifeless in your arms toward Havenhid from the Barrens where he last took breath. I cared for your son as much as if he were my own, and I tell you I needn't have known then the bonds of bearing such fruit to share the tears streaming from your face or feel the angst that pierced your heart that woeful day."

"And you think it's the same thing?" bellowed Gotham with a sneer while wrestling the memory of the moment of which Anahel spoke.

Anahel shook his head meekly. "Don't misunderstand me, I'm not competing for what is your rightful pain."

"Yet you want to chastise me for it."

"The manner in which death comes is often times unpleasant. Horrific, even. Cemeteries are full of little boys and little girls who have met an untimely demise. Have you lived so long amongst civilians that you've come to welcome death with the same black shroud they have long chosen to bestow upon it? Death did not destroy David, only the clay vessel which housed him. What you mourn is the remnants of a cocoon, while turning a blind eye to the butterfly that has emerged from inside it." Anahel came before Gotham but his gaze was aligned with the star-studded heavens draped in blackness above them. Yet somehow it appeared to bask his face in a soft light. "Life does not pass unto death, it is death which passes unto life."

Gotham stood staring hard and stone-like at Anahel revealing not so much as a crack to his hardened demeanor.

"Do you hear your words, even as you speak them?" he seethed barely above a whisper.

"You above all cannot deny what I speak is true."

"And you think it lends me comfort?" Gotham growled.

There remained a disconnected look in Anahel's eyes which prevented him to see how deep Gotham's pent-up angst had taken root. And so Gotham craned himself forward until his face, fixed and intense with emotion, was just inches from Anahel's and with his right hand he swept back the wandering strands of his long locks away from his forehead to reveal the jagged-telling mark of the skeletal star scarring his temple.

"Look upon me and pontificate to me now, if you so dare, about the beauty of death," challenged Gotham. "This mark which has shackled me to a desolate existence amongst men with its unbreakable curse has stolen any such beauty from my vision. Even when the last of mortals are gone, I will remain; tethered to a malediction that will long outlast my own immortality where the only door left open to me to walk through—the one that has left me to flee, as you so called it, to every corner of the world to escape its threshold—is that leading to the company of my Fallen brethren in the Underneath."

Gotham looked away suddenly, casting his eyes back towards the waterfalls to keep Anahel from witnessing the gripping pain he was unable to stifle from surfacing. Well acquainted with Gotham's great pride, Anahel left the angel's side with some reluctance and retreated to a seat behind a large ornate desk.

"A mortal life passes so quickly," Gotham's voice continued softly, "and I knew I only had a brief period of time with David. He couldn't even allow me that. Not only did he take him, he ensured I be the one to deliver him in the cruelest of manners."

There was no confusion to Anahel as he listened who the "he" which Gotham referred was, and his heart, which swelled with sorrow at the sound of pain quivering subtly in the angel's voice, sank. And when Gotham looked once more to him with eyes wet with an anguish he'd never know, Anahel turned his attention to a particular book residing amongst many on the desk before him; not because he couldn't bear the obvious pain revealed by Gotham, but because his thoughts turned to the ratted edges of paper seen sticking out from where they had been tucked away inside the book for a good many years.

Might this be the moment? Anahel wondered in silent pondering.

"What you choose to see as perpetual wallowing, Anahel," continued Gotham, "is a father keeping company the only way he knows how with a son who has passed through a door where all souls are reunited, yet a door nonetheless eternally locked to me. The cocoon of bone and dust resting inside a stone vault is all that's been left to me."

It was with those words Gotham spied a sympathetic look of understanding pass across Anahel's face. And again Anahel mindfully turned his gaze downward to eye the loose pages peeking out from the innards of the book and, as inconspicuously as he could, he grabbed hold of a corner between thumb and forefinger and slowly began to slide them out into the open.

~ ~ ~

"Now I'm just tired," said Gotham. "Tired of the sorrow which has been welded into the bars of my prison, not to mention the guilt that has become my jailer."

The words froze Anahel. For it was the first time he had ever come to witness the once great angel seemingly surrender to the grip of defeat.

"Don't misunderstand my words, I'm not looking for pity," Gotham remarked quickly before Anahel could extend to him any. "Just a semblance of understanding of why I must go."

And it was with more than a semblance of understanding that Anahel's fingers paused for a long-drawn-out moment before reversing course and sliding the papers out of sight back inside the hidden confines of the book. He looked to Gotham and, with some reluctance, nodded his blessing. "When will you leave?"

"This minute, before the day has yet to arise."

"And where will you go?"

"As you quipped earlier, I'm not sure there's a corner of the earth my feet have not already left their mark. Which footsteps I choose to retrace, I do not know."

Anahel rose from behind his desk and came around to Gotham where the two embraced each other warmly.

"What of the boy?" inquired Anahel as he walked Gotham to the door. "You will be saying goodbye to him before you leave, won't you?"

"I think it would be best if you said it for me," answered Gotham.

Anahel chose not to argue the point, though the look of his disapproval could not be ignored.

"And what shall you have me tell him?" asked the angel. "He's become quite fond of you, as I'm sure you're well aware. I'm fairly certain he will be most heartbroken by your unexpected parting."

Gotham stood silent in the open doorway for a moment or two. It was evident he had hoped to have escaped Eden without having to lend a thought in regards to Jacob.

"Tell him…," began Gotham before pausing. "Tell him I wish him luck."

And before Anahel could say anything further, Gotham quickly closed the door behind him.

CHAPTER TWENTY-FIVE

Time has a way of not existing here in Eden. It's the weirdest thing. When I first arrived here, it was autumn. At least it was outside of Eden. Here the trees don't change color or lose their leaves. The only sign of winter to be seen is the snow covering the mountains of the Northern Lands. Although it did snow the one time in Eden—on Christmas. But only because Anahel made it do so as a gift to all us (along with turning a large forest tree growing nearby into a magnificent Christmas tree decorated by the presence of thousands of blinking lightning bugs) to help ease the homesickness some of us felt with not being home for the holidays.

Other than that, there are no seasons in Eden. Only the most perfect spring day, every single day. Not that I'm complaining. In fact it's incredible. After a while, though, it does rob you of a sense of time. I honestly couldn't tell you what day of the week it is, or day of the month for that matter, which is why I don't even bother dating my journal entries anymore. Because in Eden there is no time. Only day and night.

That's why it was kind of surprising to hear today marks the one hundredth day we've now been here in Eden. And the only reason we know that is because Anahel told us so when he announced to us at dinner that all of us—Ospreys, Harriers and Shrikes—would be going to Broken Earth in the morning. Of course he didn't need to say any more for us to know what that meant. It has been such a long wait, many of us had begun to wonder if the day would ever come when we would finally get the chance to learn to fly. Now it seemed the wait was over. And yet despite the excitement, I couldn't help but feel a sense of unease about it. The most obvious concern for me was simple: Where's our wings? The protrusions on our backs are still there, even more noticeably so since being in Eden. And yet, as far as I know, no one had sprouted so much as a feather, much less wings, the entire time we've been here. I also have come to trust Anahel, and if he says we are finally ready for the challenge then I have to believe he knows what he's saying, despite how it looks to anyone with two good eyes.

Early this morning, we all set out northward toward the roar of the waterfalls where the mountains loom highest. At the foot of the mountains we came to a narrow passage which wound its way up the side of the steep, gray cliffs and our feet eagerly took to it. It was a steep climb; full of twists and bends. Slabs of rockformed shallow steps to what seemed an unending stairway. It snaked its way around the outer rim of the mountain, and at times the passage would turn into the mountain itself where cut arches led the way through stretches of dark tunnels before emerging into the sunlight again. With every step, the Garden below us fell further and further away, and soon we were high enough where the wider lands of Eden came into view. I wasn't the only one instantly taken with the beautiful sight. I was, however, the first to demonstrate the danger from becoming too captivated by the sight when my feet tripped upon one of the steps and I suddenly found myself stumbling toward the edge of the narrow pathway. In that moment, the beauty of Eden was stolen from me and replaced with an ugly, deadly drop suddenly unfolding itself from the mountain's sheer cliffs from which I could not keep myself from teetering toward. Just as my eyes widened in terror to my fate, a hand reached out and clasped me firmly by the arm keeping me from what I was certain to be my final swan dive.

With my heart pounding like a tribal drum in my chest, I turned and found Max had been my savior. "Thanks, I owe you one," I managed to gasp more out of embarrassment than fear.

"Looks like this day didn't come too soon for you, eh mate?" he replied back with a teasing smirk.

On and on we climbed until some wondered out loud in tiresome grumbles whether the stairs would outlast the mountain. Even with all of Damiel's training, the mountain path was a taxing workout, and just when we had ventured far higher than the waterfalls that spilled from dizzying heights and the enthusiasm with which we had greeted the passage at the foot of the mountain had begun to wane noticeably in us, the strain of the ascent burning in my legs began to ease. The steps became shallower and gradually leveled out and receded into the smoothness of the surrounding rock. With what appeared to be the top of the mountain in eyesight, we trudged over one final hump when much to our relief we found there was no more rock for us to climb.

We stood proud with the conquering feeling of the mountain beneath their feet. Looking out in quiet awe at the immense vista encircling us, I'm sure each one of us felt we were standing on the very top of the world. To the south, Eden stretched as far as the eye could see in all her green open plains, vast forests and far-reaching River. To the north, mountains reaching higher than the one we stood upon filled the foreseeable distance. Their shoulders were white with snow and the towering peaks were veiled by misty clouds clinging tight to them. These made up the Northern Lands, or Barrens as they are better known, and it was the first time any of us had gotten an up-close glimpse of this place which was strictly forbidden to us. And yet there was nothing—at least at first sight—that would indicate why such a place was off limits. But all of us knew.

However, it was what resided most noticeably between Eden and the snow- dressed mountains to the north that quickly grabbed hold of our attention: a massive gorge, like none I had ever seen. It looked to be a giant crack; a place where the world seemingly had inexplicably split in two. And it quickly became apparent Broken Earth was not just a name for this place. Proving more puzzling was the sight of two angels none of us had ever seen before perched on the end of separate outcrops of rock stretching several feet out over the gorge. And standing between them at the edge of the drop-off with his back to the ravine was Eksel. His face was expressionless, I would even argue unfriendly, as his keen, brooding eyes slowly took into account all of us grouped before him.

"So you wish to learn to fly, do you?" he asked in that way of his that wasn't so much an honest question as a contempt-filled comment. We were united in our boisterous cheer, and for the first time ever I saw a smile find Eksel's face, though in reality I believe it was more of a sneer.

"Many of you will rethink your eagerness when you see the path required for you to take in order to share the domain owned by the birds," he said.

He then turned his sneer to the gorge behind him and said, "Behold that path!"

The ravine was so threatening that some of the guys inched their way closer to the cliff's edge with timid, cautious steps. Even I, who never before was bothered by heights, was greeted by a queasy feeling churning inside my stomach when I stretched my neck as far forward as possible in an attempt to see what lay inside the ominous black hole and how deep it went.

Eksel then asked which of us was brave enough to go first. By the confused looks on our faces, it was safe to bet none of us knew what exactly he meant. Go first? First where?

"Down there, naturally," Eksel said, motioning down into the gnawing pit which was filled by a blanket of clouds that—thankfully or not (I'm still not decided)—shrouded from sight a clear view of what made up the bottom or how far down it resided.

What's down there? we asked.

If you're lucky to find them, your wings, Eksel told us.

To everyone's surprise (though not mine), the wait for a volunteer was short- lived when Creed pushed his way forward in his usual brutish manner to where Eksel was standing. Naturally he made a big show of his so-called "bravery" which at first take seemed to impress Eksel, who directed the rest of us to clear some space.

"So?" Creed asked as if waiting for further instruction. "What do I got to do?" "Jump, of course" Eksel replied simply with a touch of a dare in his voice.

Creed looked down into the ravine one more time. If he had any trepidation of following through with such a direction, he didn't show it outwardly.

"And if I may," Eksel was quick to add. "You might want to remove your shirt."

Creed quickly stripped off the T-shirt he wore and blindly tossed it aside into the face of one of the boys standing nearby. I immediately took note of his naked upper back where two unnatural, yet familiar protrusions beneath the skin distended from behind each shoulder. Unless he was going to glide on the air by flapping his arms, I didn't see how this challenge was even possible. Creed then positioned himself a running start between himself and the gorge and vigorously rubbed his hands together. If anyone held doubts he would muster the courage to follow through, it evaporated when he suddenly charged forward with all his might. When his feet reached the edge of the cliff, they pushed off the rock mightily as if it were a diving board and with his arms stretched out wide he jumped head-first into the long fall awaiting him.

I wasn't looking at anyone else, but I guarantee all our eyes grew as big as headlights as we watched him sink like a stone down into the gullet of the ravine. Nothing seemed to happen at first in his swift and frightful descent, and when he disappeared into the dense blanket of white clouds there came from those of us peering over the side of the ledge a collective gasp. A long, bated silence followed and with each second that ticked past a growing look of horror found our faces. Even mine. True I hate Creed— with a passion—but even I wouldn't wish him the bone-crushing, body-mangling death like the one I was certain we were witnessing. Only when it seemed Creed's fate had been sealed by such a horrible end did Eksel look up from the gorge and nod to one of the angels standing attentively nearby.

Instantly, the angel dove off his perch and sailed with great speed down into the depths of the ravine where he too slipped from sight into the clouds. His vanishing act, however, was brief and, when he reappeared, Creed, much to everyone's surprise and relief (including my own, which I readily admit) was seen dangling from his arms like a rag doll.

Except for the shell-shock look branded on his face and noticeable quivering of his legs when the angel returned the secure feeling of the mountain to his feet, Creed seemed unharmed by the experience. Giving a confused glance over his shoulder, he looked to Eksel. "No wings."

"No," Eksel echoed, though with little surprise in his voice, "no wings."

He then turned to the rest of us. "All of you over the course of the last several weeks have been hard at work honing the gifts given you as well as strengthening yourselves both body and mind. But all your training, important and vital as it is, will serve you no purpose here today. Broken Earth exists for two purposes: as the place where clouds come to rest and, more importantly, where blind faith is put to the test," he said. "You all carry the stirrings of wings on your back, that is most obvious, but, as Anahel explained to you when you first arrived in Eden, the gift of flight is not wholly given, but earned. The only way a Nephilim can fully come into his wings is by demonstrating the trueness and depth of his faith in the face of the White Mountains where the forbidden Northern Lands lie."

Exactly what kind of faith was he talking about? I wondered to myself. Surely everyone who was standing there at that moment had faith. Even Creed. How could any one of us be standing in the presence of angels on a mountain overlooking Eden and not have faith? Or was there more to it that we just weren't seeing?

"If you have to ask in such uncertain a manner then my guess is your back will remain bare to see another day," Eksel remarked as if he had been listening in on my thoughts, or those of any of the boys who most likely were mulling the exact same thing I was. "The faith of which I speak," he continued, "will take you without hesitation full speed into the treacherous

unknown you see before you and accept gladly whatever fate he chooses for you.”

Of course we all knew the "he" Eksel was referring to, and I suddenly got an even more queasy feeling being on that mountain. Eksel then introduced us to the two angels who had remained inconspicuously quiet on their perches. Their names were Acruxel and Betryel, and they were there, Eksel explained, to ensure that Broken Earth does not become home to broken bodies. And if any two angels looked up to the task of diving after wingless Nephilim who didn't meet the faith bar and hauling them out of the jaws of death one after the other all afternoon, it was these two. But Eksel was quick to scrub the look of relief he saw on our faces and warned us not to rest in the false comfort our guaranteed safety gave us. The courage gained from knowing one is safe from the clutches of death does not true faith make, he told us.

He then asked for the next volunteer. Without missing a beat, Max quickly threw off his shirt and thrust it into my hands. "Wish me luck, mate," he said.

The others cleared the way for a straight run between where Max positioned himself and the cliff's edge. Eksel barely finished telling him to proceed when he was ready when Max barreled full speed toward the gorge and hurled himself into the vast openness awaiting him without so much as a second thought. As he dropped from view in the same way Creed did, we all rushed cautiously to the ledge of the ravine and watched as he fell to the blanket of clouds below and disappeared into the white shroud. Just when it seemed his fate had mirrored Creed's and Eksel was about to send one of the angels down to fetch him, there came a flash of bluish light deep inside the churning vapor like a belch of lightning. Eksel halted the angel named Acruxel who was about to leap from his perch and we all watched and waited with growing anxiousness. Then suddenly came the surprising sight of Max emerging from the clouds into which he had been swallowed. He was being lifted by a pair of wings suddenly rooted to his back. That is, what appeared to be wings. Only they looked nothing like wings—or at least the kind of wings normally seen on the backs of angels. They had a ghostly quality to them, as if they were only an illusion of wings.

"That's right, buggers, check me out," Max called out to us with smug excitement. "I'm flying."

I'm not sure the ungraceful way he fluttered about would constitute flying, but it was definitely the opposite of falling. With his wings flapping furiously in a clumsy cadence, Max darted about the sky in awkward, jerking movements. The strain upon him was evident as he struggled to climb upward and make his way to the cliff where the rest of us looked on with idle curiosity. In many ways, it was like witnessing a newborn calf teetering on wobbly legs while trying to take its first steps. Yet eventually Max managed to navigate his way successfully. His sense of accomplishment, however, was quickly doused by the sounds of snickering coming from some of the other guys.

"What in the world is this?" asked Creed's friend Giff in his snobby, English accent that made me want to strangle him with his own tongue. His face was screwed up in a look of disgust as he strained to get a closer look at Max's back. "You call these wings?"

Max turned his head in an attempt to look past his shoulder. As he did he stretched wide his newfound appendages and saw instantly what had captured so intently the puzzlement of those gathered around him. They were smaller than expected. Most noticeably, there were no plumes, no feathers. Just two capes of skin that had somehow formed themselves to the once protruding nubs on his back. And while they were shaped like wings, they were translucent, like those of a dragonfly or the body of newly hatched fish whose very insides can be observed through its transparent hide. So delicate and unreal looking they were, no one dared to touch them. Even Max appeared surprised such wimpy things could have carried the weight of his body out of the ravine.

"You look like some kind of pixie!" mocked Creed with a sneer.

The snide remark drew a chorus of laughter from the other boys that instantly flushed Max's face, but only for a moment. I could see he was getting mad as a cut snake (to borrow one of his often-used Aussie phrases). "How'd you like to be dropped on your backside by this pixie, no-hoper?" he replied in his no- nonsense way of his, taking a threatening step toward Creed before a sharp reprimand from Eksel kept him in his place.

It didn't stop me from spouting out my own two cents. "At least he made it back with wings and didn't need to be rescued," I said, earning a "For reals" from Ethan who at the same time focused as intimidating a look as his young, puppy dog face could muster at Creed.

Creed and I glared at one another in a way that silently spoke of our immense dislike for one another before he turned back to Max. "If looking like Tinkerbell is the result, I'm glad I failed," he said with a smirk that drew Max another step closer.

"Enough!" Eksel barked. "If fighting's your preference, I suggest the two of you take yourself from this mountain and get your fill at Lions Bite."

He waited, but no one moved. "Very well," he grumbled before turning his gaze to Max and asking him how his wings felt.

Great, Max answered while moving his wings up and down behind him. It was clear, however, something was bothering him about them.

"You're worried you look like a pixie as Creed so mocked you," Eksel said.

I have to say it was the first time knowing him that I saw Max looking anything less than fully confident.

"What's with these bodgie wings? They don't look anything like yours, or my fathers," he said. It was a question we were all asking quietly to ourselves. Eksel told Max not to worry (actually his response was to fret not) and assured Max his wings would grow into him as he would grow into them. Even in the first few hours, he said, Max would begin to see a noticeable change, and by weeks-end the wings which Creed mocked him for

will be ones he himself covets. That seemed to relieve not only Max but the rest of us who weren't all that eager in sharing such a delicate look.

With the concerns over wings now settled, Eksel asked for another volunteer. Before anyone could step forward, I was startled to hear Eksel call out my name, and I knew emphatically I had not raised my hand. I looked to see his unfriendly eyes firmly on me and I instantly began to sweat, not out of fear of him but because I knew what was coming when he instructed me to step forward. Never before had my feet approached the edge of a cliff, no matte ho high or perilous, with any hesitation or with such wary steps as they did then. Truth be told, this should have been a piece a cake for someone like me. After all, Ty introduced me to BASE jumping just as he had Bungee jumping off the Darren's Creek Bridge, and I can't count the number of times the two of us willingly leapt off the highest peak at Penuel Point when we were looking to get our adrenaline fix back home, and every time it had been nothing short of awesome. Then of course, I had a chute strapped to my back which may have had something to do with my courage. Broken Earth was different, chute or no chute, and as my toes touched the edge I looked straight down the sheer rock beneath my feet into the cloud-filled gully and I was suddenly met by that rush. Only this time it was not precipitant to the frisson of the waiting free-fall. Rather it was fueled by an inexplicable fear; a fear completely unknown to me, and yet at the same time intimately familiar.

"Sometime today would be good, Mr. Parrish," I heard Eksel remark impatiently from somewhere over my left shoulder. Then I felt Max's hand on my shoulder.

"Go on," he said giving me an encouraging nudge. "It's a piece of piss" (Whatever that meant).

I looked to Acruxel, then to Betryel, and found both angels standing at their posts patiently waiting for the plunge that would determine whether eitherwould be making another journey down into the unseen depths of the ravine to retrieve yet another Nephilim who had shown himself weak of faith. Thing is I knew I believed in God. It was the fact I had a while back lost faith in him that was the problem, and somehow, I figured that earned me a sure-fire ticket straight to the bottom of the ravine before me. And while both angels looked superior in power and capable of wrangling every last boy to safety should they decide to jump in unison, for some strange, unknown reason their presence offered me no comfort.

Eksel's voice was at me again, only this time it was joined by the other guys. The knot in my stomach tightened. I took a step away from the ledge, and then a good dozen more. I think everyone thought I was giving myself a running start, but the truth was I was backing away out of fear. My feet were begging to haul my butt down the mountain and back to the safety of Havenhid. I think the only one who could see my dilemma was Max, and usually he could shoot me the right look to give me the needed strength lost to me at the moment. Yet even he couldn't break through the paralysis that had gripped me. It was only when I caught sight of Creed and his smirking face did I realize fear or no fear, faith or no faith, there was no way I couldn't not jump or I'd never hear the end of it. And there was no way I was about to give him that satisfaction. So I took in a deep breath, clenched my jaw until I was certain I would drive my molars back into my gums and charged.

I don't remember my feet leaving the mountain. Or even the first few seconds of the fall that followed. The only thought I was left with was "You idiot…you forgot to take off your shirt." But by then it was like I was suddenly wiped out of existence. The world was enveloped in a misty dense grayness and I knew I had slipped into the veil of the waiting clouds. Nothing was happening; nothing except constant falling. I wanted to reach around and feel my back for the wings I hoped would miraculously sprout from it, but the intense drag wouldn't allow any such movement. Not that it mattered. I already had failed, that much I knew. The wings wouldn't be showing themselves, of that I was certain, and all I had left was the hope that Acruxel or Betryel had already made their jump and were rushing their way toward me before I hit the bottom and shattered into a gazillion pulverized pieces. However, the hand I waited for to grab hold of me never came. Where were they? I looked above me but all around was thick clouds. I began to panic. I knew Eksel didn't care for me (he made that clear the night I arrived at Havenhid). Yet whatever his reasons, which were lost on me, did he actually dislike me enough to let me fall to my death?

Just when I resigned myself to the inevitable and braced myself for the coming end I felt something grab hold of me and my fall was suddenly yanked to a stop before eventually reversing course. I was being lifted upward, and the sound of flapping wings was music to my ears, even though they weren't my own. Still, I was more than a little pissed for having to wait so long for a rescue and was ready to let it be known, but I knew better to wait for such an outburst until my feet had the mountain safely under them. It was only when I came out of the cloud blanket that I saw my rescuer wasn't Acruxel or Betryel, but Damiel. And his eyes were flaming with anger. So much so that I didn't even dare ask him what he was doing at Broken Earth.

What happened next is a blur. Damiel brought me back to the mountain ledge where the others were standing with shocked looks on their faces and cast me aside like a bag of potatoes leaving me to roll across the ground. Then the moment his feet touched the ground they were walking briskly toward Eksel and the next thing I knew there was a punch and Eksel was sent skidding across the ground. A commotion ensued ending with Acruxel and Betryel jumping in to hold back Eksel as he and Damiel traded heated accusations. It ended abruptly as it started when Damiel told Eksel, "Pull another stunt like that again, Eksel, and mark my words I'll see to it your days as Guide in Eden comes to an end faster than it takes a rock cast into this gorge to reach the bottom!" And off he went.

I remained on the ground completely confused over what had happened. It was only later on our way back down the mountain at the end of the day that I found out. Max told me that during my jump, when it was clear I wasn't going to be returning on my own, Betryel was about to fly down after me when Eksel motioned him to remain standing where he was.

The other guys were starting to panic and urging Eksel to do something but he ignored them. Even Max finally was ready to take the leap after me with the hope he could muster enough strength from his fragile-looking wings to carry the two of us back to safety, but Eksel yelled at him to stay put. That was when Damiel appeared out of nowhere. Only no one knew at first it was him because he was flying so fast.

Even as I write this, I can't imagine what would make Eksel do such a thing. It's no secret he's not my biggest fan (why, I have no idea). But he is an angel. I'm hoping it's as I heard him arguing with Damiel after being punched—that he was giving me every last possible moment to prove myself, which I assume meant getting my wings. After all, who knows Broken Earth and how long a Nephilim has to fall until he runs out of open air separating him from the ground below better than Eksel? Then again, I can't seem to forget the cold glare he sent my way after Damiel threatened him and stormed away from Broken Earth.

One thing's for sure—to hell with wings; it'll be a long time before I make another jump off Broken Earth anytime soon, if ever. I can promise you that!

CHAPTER TWENTY-SIX

Jacob was deep into his sleep and dreaming, that much he remembered. Of what exactly he was dreaming was lost to him instantly like a puff of smoke when his eyes suddenly opened to find Max leaning over him and shaking him awake.

"Come on, get up Sleeping Beauty."

"What is it…?" asked Jacob groggily. The last thing he remembered before dozing off was lying on his bed writing in his journal, which remained opened on his lap.

"Get dressed. I want to show you something," whispered Max.

Jacob shifted the slits formed by his tired eyes to the nearby window. No longer having to rely on a clock or watch, he had come to learn how to tell the hour of both day and night by reading the sky.

"It's the middle of the night," he said with a groan before dropping his head heavily back into the softness of his pillow. "The only thing I'm interested in seeing is the inside of my eyelids."

He rolled over and attempted to doze once more into unconsciousness when the snugness of the blankets he had pulled back over his shoulders were cruelly yanked off him.

"I promise you, you'll want to see this," prodded Max in an urgent whisper.

When it was clear to Jacob sleep would be deprived him until he had gone to see whatever "this" was, he forced himself up with a grunt of annoyance. Lying quietly on the floor near the foot of Jacob's bed, Mist watched intently as Jacob fumbled for his clothes and sluggishly got dressed.

"Aren't you going to wake them up as well?" whispered Jacob, motioning to the still lumps in the other three beds belonging to Ethan, Leos and Kairo who continued to fill the room with their chorus of snores and the whistling of their nasal breathing.

"Trust me, it's better we do this without an entourage," said Max.

They slipped out of the room then tiptoed their way along the winding of corridors and down the steep staircase where every creak pressed from a step beneath their feet sounded like a scream let loose to rattle the peaceful hour.

"So, what is it that's so important it required you dragging me out of bed in the middle of the night?" asked Jacob once they were outside standing beneath the trees where Havenhid resided like a lumbering body wrapped snug in a bedding of leaves. Max answered only by putting a finger to his lips. Then, with a mischievous grin, he darted off into the night forcing Jacob to follow after him knowing that at any moment their punishable escapade could be inadvertently discovered by one of the Guides stealing a glance from one of Havenhid's many windows and terraces while wandering about in their perpetual awakened state.

~ ~ ~

The night offered little cover with the presence of the moon parked full and immense in the sky above like some neighboring planet making an uncomfortably close pass. It bathed the Garden in an almost florescent silver and blue iridescence. So bright was it that Max and Jacob were trailed by shadows of themselves scampering along the ground after them as they tramped over the cobbled slabs of stone paving the bridge arching over the River near the falls. Once they had crossed the River, Max led the way swiftly along a curving path. For a good long distance they ran, even when they were certain they were out of range of even the Guides' all-seeing eyes. And even then they raced on deeper into the night toward the furthest north-easterly pocket of the Garden valley until they reached a waiting open stretch of grass where the looming presence of Lions Bite could be seen curled up beneath the moon in the distance.

Once Lions Bite was behind them, they quickly found themselves approaching a bank of towering trees forming the leading edge of what looked to be a deep wood. When Max started toward it Jacob was quick to grab him by the shoulder.

"What do you think you're doing? You can't go in there."

"What's got you suddenly looking like a stunned mullet," said Max without any show of concern.

"It's the Silent Forest."

"So?"

His friend's nonchalant disregard made Jacob's brow crinkle in a show of growing puzzlement. "So? You know we're not allowed to step foot inside there."

"When did you suddenly become a momma's boy when it comes to rules?" asked Max which Jacob clearly didn't like. "Besides, who's gonna know?"

"I'm not sure I want to take the chance in finding out."

"If I didn't know better, I'd swear you were packin' darkies," said Max.

"Of course not," Jacob shot back, though not completely sure what "packin' darkies" entailed exactly. "But I think it's safe to assume when an angel specifically states something is forbidden then most likely there's a good reason for it."

"True. But there is forbidden and then there's *forbidden*," said Max with a cunning wink. "Aren't you the least bit curious to find out which, too?"

"Too? You mean you've already been in there?" asked Jacob.

Max's sly grin which held untold mischief widened. "And boy am I glad I did."

At those words, Jacob's eyes shifted past Max to the unwelcoming darkness gathered deep within the trees. Then, as he saw how Jacob's curiosity was slowly getting the best of him, Max cajoled his friend forward and the two slipped inside the forest.

~   ~   ~

What was it that led to the Silent Forest being deemed off limits as ardently as it had been since the days when the first Nephilim were brought through Eden's gates was not immediately apparent, at least at first glance. Walking deeper into its presence, Jacob found it to be no different than any of the other forests shading untold miles of Eden's reaches. The trees stood like giants with ropes of vine dangling from towering branches and winding tightly around wide, twisting trunks which carried the furry scruff of greening moss. The bough-like roots holding firm their stance snaked along the top of the damp ground where feathery ferns, night-blooming succulents and other low plants both exotic and not congregated. What light from the moon managed to pierce its way through the thick forest canopy came down in soft silvery shafts to marble the darkness below. The moon itself, however, or the star-dotted sky for that matter, was blotted from sight behind a thick tangle of branches and leaves high overhead.

"Do you hear that?" asked Max, suddenly.

Jacob paused and listened. "I don't hear anything."

"Indeed," replied Max with a cryptic smile. "What would you expect in a place called the Silent Forest?"

Jacob turned his focus from what his eyes could see to what his ears could hear. Only there was nothing to be heard; not a night owl calling out from its perch or the smallest of nocturnal woodland creatures foraging along the ground. Even the trees were deathly still without so much as a gentle breeze to creak their branches or rustle their leaves. Where the rest of Eden was filled with the sounds of life, this forest was completely devoid of it.

And that in itself was eerily unsettling to Jacob.

"I think we better turn back," he suggested. The silence was so deafening, even his whisper sounded like he was speaking at the top of his lungs.

"Don't tell me you're getting ready to drop eggs," said Max.

"Drop eggs?"

"Turn chicken."

"I'm not turning chicken," Jacob shot back defensively. "I just have a bad feeling about this place."

"I did, too, when I first nosed around here. Trust me, it'll pass."

Against his better judgment, Jacob followed Max onward accompanied with an unrelenting gnawing feeling of what might lie ahead of them as well as the repercussions that awaited them should one of the Guides catch wind of their outing.

Soon they came upon a small clearing, and within the clearing resided a pool of mirror-smooth water. It was then Max placed a hand to Jacob's chest to keep him from continuing on while at the same time bringing a finger to his lips. As quietly as they could, they moved with soft steps around the clearing while staying within the company of the trees encircling it. Halfway around, they came upon the hollowed remains of one of the wooded giants that had long ago fallen and come to rest upon the forest floor, and they crouched down behind it.

"We won't be seen from here," said Max, peering over the top of the massive hull.

"Seen by who?" whispered Jacob, sounding more uncomfortable by the mysteriousness that had led him into the woods. "There's nobody here."

Max seemed to ignore Jacob. Instead, his eyes intently scoured the pool which could be seen through a parting in the trees. Back and forth they shifted from one end of the pool to the other with a growing eagerness.

"I don't see her," he muttered.

"See who?" asked Jacob with growing impatience.

"The lady in the water."

Lady in the water?

Jacob followed Max's gaze with his own and through the dimly lit blue-tinted darkness of the night he saw nothing. Not even the subtlest of ripples cast upon the pool's dark water to indicate the presence of fish nipping at the surface from below. Everything around them was deathly quiet and it was joined by an even more deathly stillness. To Jacob, there was nothing peaceful about this silence. In fact, it proved to be more and more uncomfortable the longer he sat in the forest; as if the quiet itself was an unseen entity moving stealthy about the two boys and moving in ever so closer.

However long they stayed bent down behind the trunk of the felled tree, it felt to Jacob to be much longer, and just when he had lost patience with staying one minute longer and was about to open his mouth to tell Max so, there came from the pool a splashing sound. The gazes of both boys shot back to the pool, and as before they saw nothing at first. Even the water remained completely calm and undisturbed despite the continuing sounds of movement heard to be swishing about somewhere within it.

"It's the lady," replied Max. His eyes frantically began searching all about the pool.

"What lady?"

"I told you—the lady in the water."

They soon saw a figure emerging from the far end of the dark basin where the pool met a yawning cavern of rock. Sure enough, it was a woman just as Max had insistently claimed, but not just any ordinary woman. Of that, there was no question. To begin with, she came out of the water completely dry without even a drop of water left glistening on her skin. It also appeared she wasn't wearing any clothing. And yet her nudity was completely covered by her Rapunzel-like tresses which were the color of the deepest hour of night and draped themselves across her body like some elegant gown.

It was neither the woman's lack of wetness or the glimpses of flesh bared by her exotic, unconventional attire that made Jacob's eyes grow wide and cease blinking at the sight. It was her beauty; breathtakingly astonishing, even from a distance, while both delicate and grave at the same time. She looked almost to be an apparition; her white, alabaster skin radiated under the sparse moonlight and proved a stark contrast against her raven hair and eyes as dark as the pool from which she emerged.

"She's beautiful!" gushed Jacob with a sigh.

"Yeah, she is," said Max equally transfixed.

"But who is she?"

"Isn't it obvious? What other earthly thing could she be but an angel?" It was clear from the dreamy look on his face Max was taken with the woman.

"Out here, wandering around the middle of the forest at night?" asked Jacob.

"Have you forgotten? They don't sleep," said Max. "And in case you haven't noticed, Eden doesn't have much of a nightlife. What else do they have to do but roam around or go for a midnight swim while the rest of us saw logs in bed?"

"I don't see any wings."

"That's what you're looking for? Wings?" asked Max. "Besides, how can you tell what's beneath all that hair?"

However, a troubled look came over Jacob. "I don't know. Something's not right. There's something strange about this place. I can feel it," he said. "Anyways, when's the last time you saw a female angel?"

Max thought about it. "I haven't, now that you mention it." he replied.

"Neither have I."

They continued to watch the strange woman as she leisurely combed her fingers through her hair while sitting on a rock swirling her feet around in the water.

"I say we go ask her," suggested Max and immediately started to rise to his feet when Jacob grabbed hold of his arm.

"You can't go out there."

"Why not?"

"For one thing, if she is an angel, don't you think she's going to tell Anahel we were out here?"

"And if she's not an angel?" Max countered.

Despite his resistance, Jacob couldn't deny he held as much curiosity about the woman as Max, so much so that it almost was worth whatever punishment they faced for breaking Anahel's strict order where the Silent Forest was concerned. So it was against his better judgment, not just for the trouble he could be walking into but the unsettling feeling he had, both about the pool and the woman lurking strangely in it which stirred noticeably in the pit of his stomach, that he slowly rose to follow his friend.

~ ~ ~

"You should know I don't much care for unannounced visits," the woman was suddenly heard to casually remark.

Max and Jacob quickly ducked again out of sight again behind the cover of the felled tree. For what seemed a long while, the boys made not one sound. Not even so much as an exhale of breath.

"She talking to us?" whispered Max, finally.

"Who else?" answered Jacob.

"Why don't you go see?"

"You were the one so keen on meeting her. Why don't you?" argued Jacob.

Both, however, held firm to their crouched positions. After a long pause of quiet, they both snuck another glance over the top of the tree trunk.

"Well?" the woman called out. "Are you just going to stay there hidden in the shadows?"

Both Jacob and Max traded a hesitant look with one another while feeling the urgent tribal beats beginning to play inside their chests. They each motioned to the other to step out from behind their hiding place and speak to the lady, now that she knew they were there. Since it was Max's idea to go snooping inside the Forest in the first place, he finally acquiesced. Just as he began to rise to his feet, the two boys saw to their surprise it wasn't them to which the woman was speaking, but another strange, unknown figure. It emerged stealthy from the darkness congregating amongst the trees, cloaked in a long, dark gray cape with a hood draped over its head to conceal whoever, or whatever, it was. Max quickly ducked back out of sight.

"Who's that, now?" asked Jacob.

"Did you see me go over and exchange introductions?" answered Max.

Then in unison, their heads slowly rose from behind the trunk so they could peer out at the lady and the newly arrived cloaked figure.

"I was beginning to think that maybe I had managed to somehow take leave of your mind," the lady commented coyly as the figure approached the water's edge.

"Take leave? Yours is a presence not readily forgotten since the day you came to lend the single solitary heartbeat heard inside the folds of this mute woodland." The voice was instantly familiar, even before the figure reached up to draw back the hood from its head.

"It's Thaniel," Jacob gasped with surprise at the unexpected sight when both boys finally saw who it was hidden within the cloak's velvety folds..

"What's he doing here?"

For a moment both boys worried the angel had caught sight of the two of them stealing into the night from Havenhid and decided to take after them. It quickly became apparent, much to their relief, that Thaniel was unaware of their presence and had come to the Silent Forest for other reasons.

"Now that you've decided to compliment me with your presence the question that remains is whether your visit will serve to please or displease me." The lady's eyes left the shimmering mane that was her hair which she continued to groom and fixed themselves keenly on the figure. "Judging by the sight of your empty hands I fear the probability lies in the latter."

"I can't help but detect a distinct note of perturbation in your voice, even more so than usual" said Thaniel as he shrugged the cape he wore from his shoulders and let it fall to the ground at his feet.

"Did you come expecting, instead, that I would fill your ears with a lilting song of gratitude?" replied the woman in a most wilting manner.

"Gratitude, if I may be so candid with my words, has never been your strong suit." Thaniel's thin lips took the shape of a condescending smile as he spoke. "Neither has the virtue of patience. But I think you would find it would benefit you at this time."

"Patience." The woman seemed to ponder the sound of the word as if it was the first time it had come to meet her ears. "Then you have answered my question. This visit will not end pleasantly."

If Thaniel was at all troubled by the ominous way with which the lady spoke, he did not show it. Still, he bowed his head as though hesitant to reveal whatever it was that had brought him to this mysterious place.

"Gothamel has gone," he finally blurted.

"Gone? You mean, he's left Eden?" gasped the lady with horrified surprise. "When?"

"Several weeks now."

A flash of anger passed across the lady's face at the same time a wounded look of sadness came to settle upon Jacob's. He had done his best to try and put Gotham out of his thoughts since learning about his abrupt departure from Anahel. Yet the feeling of dejection the news left him proved a difficult thing to shake. After all, he had come to form a strong bond with the angel—something he hadn't expected. And he had begun to think Gotham had come to feel at least somewhat the same toward him. Why would he suddenly up and leave? And more importantly, how could he do so without so much as saying goodbye?

"Weeks? And you've waited until just this moment to tell me this news?" bellowed the lady. "More importantly, how could you allow such a thing, after all these years waiting for his return?"

Her anguish at the news echoed in the emptiness of all other sound blanketing the Forest.

"He had already long taken leave for the Gate when I learned of his departure. Not that I could have stopped him had I the chance," answered Thaniel.

The more he spoke the further agitated the lady seemed to become. Rising to her feet, she paced about angrily along the rocks though her movements appeared somewhat stilted, as if she were corralled within some invisible pen that kept her from straying too far towards the water's edge.

"Then the purpose in your coming here this night is to inform me you have utterly failed in your promise," the lady hissed.

The cool assertion brought an arrogant smile to Thaniel's face. "When have you known me to fail in anything I've set out to do?"

"If not failure, then what?"

"I told you in the beginning this would be no easy task," said Thaniel in an attempt to sooth the lady. "Truth be told, I do not believe Gothamel even had Destiny in his possession when he surprised us all with his return to Eden.

DEESSSSSSTINYYYYYY…

The mention of the name was the only thing to break through the mournful fog that had suddenly settled itself upon Jacob.

"You sound as if what you say is welcoming news," said the woman. "For all we know he could have destroyed it."

"Destroy?" Thaniel echoed with a lilting laugh. "No…a fool Gothamel is not, even if such a thing were possible, which of course it is not.

"No, if I know Gothamel—and, indeed, I do, probably better so than he knows his own self—I assure you he has it safe and secure, but hidden away out of sight; his sight to be more precise."

The lady seemed to grow somewhat calmer as curiosity slowly took over in place of her anger. "What do you mean his sight?"

"Destiny serves as a bitter, painful memory of the fate it brought to his son, the blade of which continues to stab at his guilt," explained Thaniel. "If I were to make an educated guess, I would say he has buried it somewhere deep and remote in the bowels of the earth to help rid himself of that memory which holds both his failure and his loss, yet close enough should he ever find himself in dire need to retrieve it. If not to extol his vengeance against the Darkness, then to brandish it on himself."

"Brandish it on himself?" the lady remarked with a tilt of her head. "What absurd nonsense is it that you're attempting to feed my ears?"

"I speak metaphorically," said Thaniel. "You do know what a metaphor is, do you not?"

Beautiful as the lady was, it could not camouflage the ugly look of loathing which momentarily spoiled her loveliness and sent daggers across the water straight toward Thaniel, who could not help but grin in return.

"Naturally, I don't mean he would literally turn the blade on himself. But, nonetheless, I do speak of a sort of self-mutilation," continued Thaniel. "Guilt is a curious thing, especially when it wounds one so deeply as it has Gothamel. Sometimes it gains such a strong hold that one doesn't feel worthy enough to be granted relief from its pain. If anything, it's the wallowing in pain that allows the sufferer to survive the burden of such guilt. A sort of self-flagellation, if you will. What better instrument to keep alive and fresh such a painful and dark memory imprisoning him than the physical presence of the very thing that led to the demise of his son…in this case the sword?"

"Sounds like an affliction suffered by mortals," remarked the woman with a dismissive sneer, though it was difficult to determine whether the affliction itself or the mention of mortals had left the bad taste in her mouth.

"For the most part, it is," said Thaniel. "But it is not one angels are immune to, Fallen or not."

Jacob and Max kept themselves hidden behind the shield of the felled tree with just the tops of their heads and unblinking eyes visible as they peered over the top of the trunk, eavesdropping on the conversation of which proved difficult to make any sense.

"Do you know what they are talking about?" whispered Max.

Jacob was too caught up in his own thoughts to answer at first.

"Something about Gotham's son."

Max continued to think out loud. "Whose destiny do they keep referring to?"

"I don't think they mean destiny as in fate, but rather a name," answered Jacob.

"Name for what?"

"A sword," Jacob replied quietly as he thought back to the last time he saw Gotham at the foot of the Tree of Life and the mirage of the Sword of Destiny the angel had unveiled from a scrawling in the dirt. And he found himself growing more and more befuddled as he and Max listened in on the curious conversation taking place between Thaniel and the even curiouser woman in the water.

~ ~ ~

The lady continued in her pacing about the rocks while mulling over what Thaniel had shared with her.

"Buried. Somewhere. Anywhere!" she muttered to herself before turning her attention back to the angel. "Your words offer anything but encouragement. Am I now to somehow hold out hope that you will uncover this elusive hiding place?" she asked with great suspect.

"Gothamel had not gotten too far a head start when I learned of his leaving that I was able to send Betryel to follow after him," said Thaniel.

"And what makes you so certain he will lead the way to the sword so easily?"

"One thing you can always count on with a dog when it buries its prize bone," said Thaniel, "it always digs it up now and then to make sure it's still where it has left it."

"The dog being Gothamel?"

"Both are equally loyal and just as predictable."

"I hope for your sake, Thaniel, you are able to deliver on your promise in short order," said the lady coolly. "There is only so much patience one can wring from the well. When it runs dry, as I assure you it slowly is, all that remains is an unquenchable anger. Of course you know it's not mine of which I speak; neither the patience, nor anger. And with each day that passes, the more difficult it becomes for me to quiet his grumbling. I trust I need not remind you the unpleasantness held in the coils of his rage."

"Who is she talking about? Whose rage?" Max whispered to Jacob as the two listened intently.

Thaniel, who showed no pause to what could only be construed as a menacing warning, said simply, "I ask you again, when have you known me to fail in anything I've set out to do?"

Yet the smile fixed with such assuredness on Thaniel's face gradually began to fade, as though he suddenly sensed something not right in the air.

For a while the lady stared out across the dark still water to where Thaniel stood on the opposite side of the pool. Her beauty was as frozen as sculpted marble but one could see a frenzy of thoughts swirled about behind her mask or porcelain flesh.

"It's a funny thing about this Forest," the lady began again. "The piercing quiet which surrounds it sometimes allows for the faintest whispers from even the furthest corners of Eden to tickle the ears."

"Is that a fact? Thaniel murmured in response as he continued to search suspiciously the surrounding woods as though his own lobes had been grazed by such a whisper.

"I understand Gothamel was not alone upon his unexpected return to Eden," the woman with her dark eyes firmly fixed on the angel said.

"And who exactly would Gothamel have trailing after him to Havenhid?" questioned Thaniel though somewhat preoccupied.

"A boy…a Nephilim boy to be precise; one who is the same age as was his son when he last stepped foot upon Eden's shores," the lady answered, and when Thaniel wasn't immediate with his response she pressed all the more urgently, "Well…is it true?"

"She's asking about you," Max whispered the obvious before he was quickly hushed by Jacob.

Just then, Thaniel spun quickly around and the boys ducked from sight only a split second before his gaze fell on the hollowed trunk behind which they hid.

"What is it?" they heard the lady ask.

Jacob's heart was pounding so hard and loud inside his chest he was sure the angel could hear it. "Now what?"

"I say we make a run for it."

"Are you crazy? He'll see us for sure."

Then came the sound of heavy footsteps fast approaching and panic set in.

"He's coming this way," said Jacob.

"Quick, lay yourself on the ground!" ordered Max.

"What good's that going to do?"

"Do you want to get caught? Just do it" Max barked impatiently while forcing his friend down onto the damp earth. "Now, don't move a muscle…and definitely don't take what I'm about to do the wrong way."

No sooner had Jacob stretched out flat on his back on the ground did Max throw the full weight of himself down on top of him painfully knocking the wind from his chest. Jacob fought to keep silent the sharp, uncomfortable groan struggling to escape him, but it was quickly forgotten when he finally managed to pry open his eyes and found himself staring not at Max as he expected, but through a thick covering of what appeared to be fern leaves surrounding him. Only he remembered the ground around the felled tree to be bare.

"Keep still," he heard not only the whisper of Max's voice but the feel of his breath against his face as though his mouth was just inches away, "and don't say a word!"

Then came a heavy booted foot as it came to rest on top the tree trunk. Jacob froze, allowing himself not even to breathe through his nostrils. A moment later Thaniel slowly came into view as he leaned himself forward to peer over the top of the trunk. There was an expectant look fixed upon his face, as if he was certain he would find something that shouldn't be lurking on the other side of the tree. It was quickly replaced by questionable surprise, however, when instead he found nothing but a thick patch of fern nestled close to the trunk. Jacob followed Thaniel's gaze with his own as it raked itself across the fern. He dared not make even the tiniest movement, scared that even the slightest tremble would cause the delicate fern leaves to quiver. For the briefest of moments the angel's eyes met his own and he couldn't help but catch sharply his breath. He quickly realized, however, he was completely shielded from sight beneath the shroud of fern.

Thaniel then stared out into the darkness held by the distance of woods and only when he was certain there was no one else besides himself paying a visit to the company of trees did he finally retreat back to the pool. Once Thaniel had gone, Jacob released a breath of relief and noticed the many fern leaves blanketing himself begin to shrink and recoil. It was like watching the life cycle of the plants captured by a time-lapse camera only in reverse. The feathery leaves and thin stems curled inward and disappeared back into arms and legs and fingers and shoulders from which they sprouted until Max could once more be seen stretched across Jacob.

"Bloody ripper!" exclaimed Max with a victorious grin as he rolled himself off his friend much to the relief of Jacob. "Never imagined the ability to mimic plants would ever come in handy. Guess I was wrong."

They gave a fleeting glance back over toward the pool where they saw Thaniel had returned. Instead of testing their luck any further by continuing with their spying, they carefully and quietly as they could retreated into the darkness. Only when they emerged safely from the trees and felt they had escaped the Forest's reach did they allow themselves to breathe easy and even celebrate in muffled giggles how two Fledglings had managed to put one over on someone with eagle-eyed brilliance like Thaniel, and right under his nose at that.

Yet despite being "happy as a box o' birds," as Max put it, they quickly made a pact with one another to keep their covert outing absolute secret. Not even Leos, Kairo and Ethan could ever hear about what they had been up to while they slept knowing all it would take would be one loose tongue to land them both in hot water. Once they had made their agreement binding with a handshake, they took off again into the night, allowing whatever adrenaline remained flowing through their veins to carry them back to Havenhid.

CHAPTER TWENTY-SEVEN

It didn't take long before the first cracks in the pact Jacob and Max had made to keep secret their excursion into the Silent Forest began to appear. Jacob started feeling a gnawing at the pit of his stomach during Study the next day. Thaniel was at the front of the class lecturing; the topic of which Jacob had fallen deaf to as he found his attention becoming more and more fixed on Max who was seated off to the left one table in front of him. Max's eyes were fixed firmly ahead, but it was clear to Jacob just by looking at him that his thoughts were no more focused on what Thaniel was saying than his own.

I'm going to ask him about the Forest, Max's voice suddenly echoed inside Jacob's head. The new telepathic way of communicating with one another without having to actually use one's mouth was one of the more useful things Zuriel had taught them.

Are you crazy? Jacob answered back while keeping his eyes directed forward like everyone else around him. *You'll get us into trouble.*

Chill, mate…I can be discreet about it.

How do you discreetly ask about something inside the Silent Forest we're not even supposed to know exists? Besides, did you forget the promise we made? Just leave it be!

You've got to be just as curious about what we saw as I am, Max argued back.

Even though their back and forth came with not one utterance, it quickly became apparent their ping-ponging of thoughts were just as disruptive as if they had been whispering out loud to one another under their breaths when Thaniel suddenly stopped in the middle of a sentence, looked to Max and asked with pointed irritation, "Curious about what?"

Jacob felt the blood drain from his face, especially when he could practically see the gears of Max's brain churning away like the innards of a clock. He wanted to scream into Max's head to keep quiet, but he dared not risk Thaniel overhearing any more trading of thoughts between the two of them. All he could do was sit back in his chair, cross his fingers and hope Max was smart enough to bite down on his tongue, and hard.

"Come now, Mr. Kelly, what apparently is so pressing a question to distract you from my lesson?"

"I was just wondering…," Max began slowly.

Jacob felt his blood pump itself faster through his veins. "Yes? What is it you're wondering?" said Thaniel.

"I was just wondering…are there any…female angels?"

There came a hushed snickering from the other boys seated around, except from Jacob who held his breath while almost reluctantly glancing back at Thaniel to see his response. The angel stood quiet for a moment with a perplexed look which Jacob had a hard time determining whether it indicated Thaniel was preparing to scold Max for interrupting his lecture with such a randomly ridiculous question, or whether he was crafting an answer for said random question.

"The topic of today's lesson, Mr. Kelly, is the philosophical lessons of the emperor Marcus Aurelius," said Thaniel finally, "not the gender of angels."

It appeared to be the end of the discussion, and Jacob took a breath of relief.

Yet no sooner had he exhaled than Max's voice sounded itself again.

"It's just, I was sitting here looking around and suddenly realized that all of us here are…well, you know…men…"

"Boys," Thaniel quickly corrected, "is the word I think you meant to use."

There came more giggles, causing Max's face to flush briefly.

"My point is, I don't ever recall seeing or knowing an angel or Nephilim that wasn't a…male."

"And why, may I ask, do you find yourself preoccupied with the curiosities of sex? Are you suddenly in the market for a prom date?"

Thaniel's off-handed crack drew even more snickers from the other boys.

"Just curious, that's all, like any bloke," said Max.

At first Jacob wasn't sure what to make of the grin that slowly appeared on Thaniel's face.

"A teenaged boy whether he be a Nephilim or a plain old mortal child is still just a teenaged boy, isn't he?" asked Thaniel, and yet it was clear he wasn't posing a question in need of an answer. "I'll be happy to discuss the matter with you after class, Mr. Kelly. For now, however, I'd really like to get back to the lesson at hand. Unless, of course, you have any other urgent inquisitions."

Max gave as subtle a glance as he could back over his right shoulder at Jacob who took the moment to mouth as clearly and succinctly as he could back to Max to *SHUT! UP!*

"I will take that as a no," said Thaniel much to Jacob's relief when Max begrudgingly sank quietly down into his seat. "Now then…"

It wasn't that Jacob didn't share Max's hungry quest to figure out the mystery surrounding the Silent Forest. Truth was he had a hard enough time trying to concentrate on much else than the lady in the water, and it was only when his body slumped down into his seat and he looked upward toward the Library's surrounding walls of books while silently muttering a prayer of thanks that Max had finally managed to seal his lips that Jacob realized the answers to the questions he was ping-ponging about inside his head were most likely right in front of him. Or rather above him.

~ ~ ~

Jacob had planned on going on his fact-finding mission alone later that same night after everyone had fallen asleep. It was well past midnight when he quietly tip-toed his way past his snoring roommates only to find Mist fast at his heels and threatening to blow his cover with a well-timed bark should he think twice of not allowing her to tag along on his secretive outing. Together they made their way through the quiet that had settled itself throughout Havenhid, but just as Jacob descended the stairway leading to the foyer and rounded the corner leading to the main corridor he nearly came out of his skin when he ran face-first into Max who casually stepped into his path from out of nowhere.

"Jeez…you just about gave me a heart attack! And how did you even do that?" Jacob, who could have sworn he saw Max sawing log with the rest of his roommates as he snuck out of his room, screeched breathlessly.

"Bloody oath, you're a genius! Why didn't I think of that?" Max replied, ignoring his friend's inquiry into his Houdini trick.

"Think about what?"

"The Library," answered Max. "That's where you're going, isn't it? To see if it has anything on the Silent Forest?"

"Will you not do that?" Jacob huffed with exasperation.

"Do what?"

"Read my thoughts. It's creepy enough when the Guides do it."

"Then you should train yourself better in blocking what goes on in that melon of yours," Max whispered in reply. "I can't believe it didn't dawn on me, myself. It's so simple. What do you think you're going to find?"

"I have no idea," said Jacob. "There's something about it. I need to know why it's forbidden. And who that lady is."

"You know, we'd probably have the answer now if you would have just let me prod Thaniel about it a little more during Study today like I wanted."

"And risk him discovering we broke the cardinal rule about setting foot in the Forest? You haven't exactly mastered the art of blocking your own thoughts, mate."

Max didn't attempt to argue Jacob's point. "And you think the Library is going to have the answers?"

"Why not? There's like a gazillion books there, and Thaniel said they hold a record of everything in existence. There's got to be at least one that holds a clue."

Jacob then suggested Max head back upstairs before the two of them got caught wandering around at such a late hour, but Max insisted on going along.

"You said it yourself. There's a gazillion books in the Library. You think you're going to find what you're searching for on your own? You'd have better luck trying to spot a black cat in a coal cellar," said Max.

Jacob couldn't argue such logic. In fact, he welcomed Max's company and help. If anything, it was his fault for dragging him into the Forest in the first place and opening this mysterious can of worms. It was only fair he had someone to share in all the yawning he would surely find himself dealing with during Zuriel's class at the Crescent Scar in the morning.

~   ~   ~

Like the rest of Havenhid, The Library was noticeably quiet in its vast emptiness. The light was dim, giving the cavernous room an almost somber feel. Eerie even. The only sound to be heard was the scratching of writing coming from the Witnesses as they tirelessly continued to record the ongoing history of all existence. For some time, Jacob and Max stood in the center of the circle formed by the four books and perused the events as the words miraculously inked themselves to the thick parchment pages.

There came a brief moment Jacob wished one of the books offered some news from home. Even if it was just a sentence or two telling how his grandmother was faring alone. And maybe a few words on Ty and Wray. Especially Wray. Yet he knew the chances were next to nil for such a thing when an entire world full of happenings was being archived before his eyes. Max, too, had a similar quiet look of longing on his face as he stared down at the pages and Jacob wondered what news his friend wished would somehow catch his skimming eye at that precise moment, though he didn't ask.

"Weird, isn't it, seeing it all being written down like this?" said Max. "Growing up you'd always hear jokes about some great book somewhere up in the sky keeping tabs on all the things people did. Now, here it is. Only there's bloody four of them!"

Almost simultaneously their attention then turned to the endless number of books lining the walls in all directions around them and stretching upwards for countless stories. Or at least farther than the eye could see. Jacob remembered when he first stepped foot in the Library and thinking it would take someone a good full lifetime, and then some, to read even a fraction of the books lining the walls. Even one of immortal ilk, with endless years at his disposal, would find it a breathtaking challenge to consume so much knowledge, he imagined.

And even if one managed to read his way from one end of the Library to the other, he debated whether any one brain, mortal or immortal, could feasibly attempt to store so much information without at some point imploding on itself. If anything, it made his head hurt just thinking about such a prospect.

Jacob and Max both looked to each other, their faces mirroring the same pained expression brought about by the shared realization of the needle they sought in the massive haystack before them.

"Where do we even begin?" asked Max. "It's not like there's any kind of card catalogue we can go to and look up 'Silent Forest'."

"Well," began Jacob, as his eyes wandered upward along the many, many floors circling the Library overhead, "if I remember right, there was a whole section of books about Eden I came across a while back as I was nosing around somewhere around the forty-fifth—no, forty-seventh floor."

Unlike the other Nephilim who much preferred the excitement of learning how to use their Graces or maneuver a sword to the stuffiness of the Library, Jacob, oddly enough, had come to favor the time spent in the massive hall of knowledge, though he made sure to keep such nerd-like tendencies to himself. While the other boys couldn't wait to bolt from their seats the moment they were dismissed from Study, Jacob would more often than not linger behind and wander about browsing the endless shelves crammed with books. There was so much to learn, and all of it surprisingly interesting to him, and he found the more time he spent there, the more he was able to slowly memorize exactly the spot in the Library certain books he wished to revisit were kept, just as Thaniel had said would eventually happen much to everyone's disbelief.

"Forty-seventh, huh?" groaned Max, squinting as he looked upwards at the great distance awaiting them before turning back to Jacob. "You wanna race?"

The challenge caught Jacob by surprise.

"Race? In here?" he replied as though the thought itself was sacrilegious.

"That's right," said Max with a sly grin. He then quickly stepped his way to the other side of the Library where a spiral staircase identical to the one a few feet away from Jacob stood. "How 'bout it? Straight up. Winner gets served breakfast in bed for a week."

Jacob gave it a quick thought then confidently took his mark at the other staircase. "You're on!"

He readied a foot on the first step of the staircase and the second Max reached the end of a whispered countdown from five, Jacob set off in a mad dash up the spiral path in front of him. To anyone watching, Jacob would have appeared as nothing more than a blur of motion as he raced at an unnatural speed up the staircase. Within moments he had reached the forty-seventh story of the Library and barely out of breath. Surprisingly, however, Max was already there waiting for him sitting casually and relaxed on the railing of the balcony overlooking the rest of the Library. It was only when Jacob noticed Max was without his shirt that he realized he'd been duped.

"You believe this, Mist?" mumbled Jacob to his wolf companion who had made the long dash in just as equal a blur. "We've been outfoxed by a dirty cheater."

Mist let loose a round of barks in Max's direction in agreement.

"The bet was who could get here first, not how," said Max, with a cunning turn of his shoulder to offer a peek of his wings which by now were nothing like the delicate things he first showed off at Broken Earth many weeks earlier. Since then, he'd been relentlessly prodding Jacob to make another attempt to get his own wings, but without success.

"Yeah, well, your stomach's in for a rude awakening if you still expect to see me playing butler in the morning," said Jacob.

"Dirty welcher!" grumbled Max.

~ ~ ~

With no plan of action of how to proceed except to just dive into the task at hand, the boys wandered off in different directions and began scouting through the endless rows of books lining the shelves. As Jacob stopped to skim through several of the bound volumes, he found he had indeed been correct about the location of the section of books dedicated to an eclectic and fascinating array of varied subjects on Eden. Everything from the different geographical spots to the different animal species and vegetation was documented. More than once, Jacob had to force himself with measurable regret to stop reading from whatever book or another had managed to engross him in order to refocus his concentration on the task at hand: finding something—anything—on the Silent Forest. Yet strangely there was nothing to be found.

After what seemed a good hour or so had passed with no luck, frustration began to set in as well as fatigue. Jacob had finished scouring the floor from one end to the other before climbing the stairs to the next. There he made his way along another balcony landing gently dragging his finger across the rows of spines lining the shelves. His nagging curiosity about the Silent Forest had begun to wane. The books were all beginning to look the same and the sound of Mist's claws tapping against the floor as she followed alongside was like a metronome slowly making the lids to his eyes heavier with every tick. Suddenly, his feet came to an abrupt halt at the same time his finger came to rest on a particular book. It was almost as though the book was covered in super glue and dried instantly to the tip of his finger to keep him from continuing on in his search.

Jacob slid the book out from its place on the shelf. The worn binding revealed its obvious antiquity and Jacob was careful opening it. The first thing it revealed to him was a painting depicting Jesus hanging on the cross while a Roman soldier was shown running the point of his spear into his side. As he turned the page, Jacob's eyes grew larger.

"It's the Sword of Destiny. Just like Gotham showed me that day beneath the Tree of Life," Jacob mumbled quietly to himself.

He began thumbing his way through the yellowing pages and familiar names long engraved in history jumped out at him: Saint Morris, Constantine, Charlemagne. Hitler.

"It's all about the history of the sword. Before it became a sword, that is," muttered Jacob to Mist, who sat watching attentively at his feet. "What are the chances I'd stumble across this without even looking?"

Then he remembered something Thaniel had once said about the books; how sometimes a particular book might find its way into a person's hand, even when the person wasn't looking for it. Which left Jacob wondering if this was one of those incidences, or just a spooky coincidence. He closed the book, but instead of returning it back to its place on the shelf, he tucked it protectively under his arm to take with him for a closer read later when he heard a whispering of voices. He moved to the edge of the landing and glanced over the wood-braided railing. Immediately, he was struck by how high up above the Library's main floor he found himself; much higher than the flights of stairs he felt he had climbed. The whispers came again, only this time swirling from somewhere higher above him.

"Is that you, Max?"

There was no answer at first to the echo of his voice as it rang through the cavernous room.

"Max…?"

"Up here," came Max's voice finally, though distant-sounding, from some unseen place higher above. "You gotta come check this out."

Maybe he found a book on the Silent Forest, Jacob thought as he took to the spiral staircase once again, but with each passing floor there was no sign of Max. So on and on Jacob climbed, higher and higher, floor after floor, and then many more floors after, until finally he caught sight of his friend.

"Any luck?" asked Jacob. However, he quickly fell silent when he saw he was standing on an open landing where Max stood motionless with an astonished look on his face. And when Jacob followed the direction of Max's stupefied gaze he quickly understood the reason.

~ ~ ~

Hovering high above, the convergence of numerous tree limbs had come together and entwined themselves to form a magnificent domed ceiling. Shafts of bluish, silvery light spilled down through three large oval openings in the dome revealing the moonlit night on the other side and illuminated the highest section of Library to where no spiral staircase extended its reach to the waiting balconies. There, many more books were housed. Only these were far more ancient-looking than any of the others found in the Library. And not just books. There was also entire sections of wall housing thousands upon thousands of papyrus scrolls rolled up tightly and stacked one atop another.

Far more curious, however, was the presence of three large birds. They were raptorial in appearance, yet unlike any species Jacob had ever laid eyes upon. Each was perched on the ledge of one of the openings in the dome, and with their necks craned downward and their fierce-shaped eyes instantly fixed on the two boys, they appeared to be anything but friendly.

"What do you make of them?" asked Max.

"I haven't a clue. And I'm not sure I want to find out," answered Jacob, narrowing his gaze on the birds. "They almost look as if they are guarding something."

"What's to guard? Some old, dusty books?" replied Max with a half-hearted chuckle.

Jacob didn't find it humorous. It was the first time any animal in Eden, no matter how ferocious looking, gave him any pause since he crossed the path of Mist's wolf pack. There was something about these birds he found to be extremely—

"Intimidating, aren't they?"

The sound of Thaniel's voice startled the boys, both of whom quickly spun around to find the angel lingering quietly at the edge of the balcony.

"You're quite right to be leery of them," he said. "If there's one thing a Greffier takes seriously, it's making sure no one trespasses where they shouldn't."

"Greffier?" inquired Max.

Thaniel emerged into the light and brushed slowly past the two boys while keeping his gaze on the large predator birds lurking above.

"Keepers of the record. You might even think of them as the watchdogs of this noble institution—or watch birds as it would be in this case," he said. "As you can see the upper most portion of this Library is cut off from the rest and inaccessible. The Greffiers' duty is to ensure this restricted area remains undisturbed and to protect what is housed on these shelves."

Jacob glanced around and saw Thaniel was right. There wasn't a single staircase he could see leading any higher than the landing where they stood .

"I know what you're thinking," said Thaniel. "What's to stop anyone with a good strong set of wings like young Max here from just flying on up?"

In fact, the thought had not yet crossed either Jacob or Max's mind. Even as Max, who remained bare-chested with his shirt draped over his shoulder, absent-mindedly flexed slightly his own wings.

"The answer," continued Thaniel, "is nothing. But only if that someone is immune to the pain that comes when a fury of razor-sharp talons carves flesh into ribbons."

It was hard to determine if the angel's words were meant as a harmless observance or a warning. Jacob and Max took them as both.

"So, what exactly are they protecting? All I see are a bunch of old dusty scrolls and books," said Max.

Thaniel smiled. "I suppose you would. But I ask you, if the shelves you see were filled with gold bullion and priceless gems would you leave them unguarded?"

Max, who was always at the ready with an answer, seemed somewhat baffled by the question.

"I would think by now you would have come to realize knowledge is just as equal a treasure, if not more," said Thaniel. "For with knowledge comes boundless power, and the old dusty scrolls and books, as you so call them, contain wells of knowledge only a noted few have ever been privileged to ingest. Even I cannot tell you what untold secrets they hold, and the Greffiers will ensure that remains the case. The more pressing question is why do I find the two of you wandering the stacks at this hour of night when you should be in your room asleep in bed?"

Thaniel then spied the book tucked under Jacob's arm. He reached for it, but instead of taking hold of it the angel's fingers only grazed the leather binding and immediately it was as if he had been jolted by some unseen thing.

"An intriguing choice for reading," said Thaniel, his eyes boring themselves into Jacob's. "I don't recall the Sword of Destiny coming up for discussion during Study."

"Gotham told me about it awhile back just before he left," answered Jacob.

"Did he?"

"It was a bit strange. Earlier tonight when I was browsing through some of the books I happened to stumble across it somehow. It was almost like you described on the first day of Study—how books you seek will sometimes find their way into your hand by just thinking about them. Only I wasn't thinking about the Sword of Destiny. At least, I don't think I was…"

Jacob's voice trailed off and he suddenly felt overcome by a slight nervousness when he realized a strange look in Thaniel's gaze as it remained fixed on him. At first he thought maybe he had unknowingly taken from the shelves one of the books considered restricted, even though the birds above didn't seem to mind his having it in his possession.

"It's okay that I take this to read, isn't it?" asked Jacob while nervously eyeing the birds staring down at him from above and not wanting for anything to accidentally be the cause of their leaving their roost with their gleaming talons aimed at him.

"Of course. After all, that's why they're here," answered Thaniel.

"Truth of the matter is, we were here looking for a book about the Silent Forest," Max blurted out suddenly, and he quickly found it to be his turn to feel the weight of Thaniel's fixed stare.

"What more do you possibly need to know about the Silent Forest other than it's forbidden?"

"You would think that, wouldn't you?" answered Max. "Thing is, when I learn something is forbidden, it tends to make me curious about the reason why. It's a little quirk of mine."

The angel cocked his head and stood quiet for some time while studying him, leaving Max to wonder if maybe he had made a mistake opening his mouth. Had Thaniel managed to sneak a confessing glimpse from the thoughts he consciously fought to keep hidden?

"I wonder," Thaniel finally spoke, "if maybe we are responsible for inadvertently stoking these strange quirks, as you Mr. Kelly have so uniquely deemed them. I've often felt the stern warning that greets each brood of Nephilim who pass through Eden's Gate to steer clear of the Silent Forest only leads to—pondering. The Forest, after all, rests in the furthest corner of the Garden. Hardly a place where boys such as yourself would be prone to wander should no mention be made of it in the first place."

"I certainly wouldn't," said Jacob. "There's something creepy about it. Something dark, even in the sunlight.

"Egg dropper," Max chided jokingly under his breath while giving Jacob a ribbing poke to his side.

"Even the name—Silent Forest—does nothing but stir unwanted curiosity. A dangerous trait to possess if ever there was one, especially if one finds he is not in full control of it, wouldn't you agree, Mr. Kelly?" asked Thaniel.

Max was quick to nod in agreement to which Thaniel smiled.

"Now the two of you are standing before me with a look in your eyes as if you are waiting for me to regale you with some tale of unseen monsters or untold curses," said the angel. "I have no such tale to tell. Disappointing as it may or may not be, there is nothing sinister lurking within the wooded boundaries of the Forest except that which your wandering minds have managed to conjure up."

A look of both disappointment and relief passed visibly across both Jacob and Max's faces, but also confusion.

"Then why is Anahel so adamant that we stay out of the Forest?" asked Max.

"Anahel, I'm afraid to say, tends to make much when there isn't much to be made," said Thaniel. Without saying another word, he then went to the winding stairway and was about to take to the steps when Jacob's voice stopped him.

"Then you're saying the Silent Forest isn't dangerous?"

Thaniel stood quiet for a moment and without so much as a glance over his shoulder he answered simply, "No, that is not what I'm saying. Not in the least."

~   ~   ~

Jacob and Max both struggled to keep pace with Thaniel's feet as they followed him single-file down the narrow, spiraling steps. Both wrestled the same thoughts: what did Thaniel mean when he inferred the Silent Forest was dangerous after he clearly stated nothing sinister lurked inside it? And what of the lady in the water? He made no mention of her. And while they both longed to ask about who she was, they bit their tongue just short of the point of bleeding knowing any such inquisition would be equivalent to admitting they had broken the rule of stepping foot in the forbidden woods.

They walked in silence a good portion of the way down the stairs, making the long descent seem all the longer. After a while, the continuous coiling path became dizzying to follow, particularly with so many thoughts niggling at the brain.

"I suspect I don't stand much chance of soon being rid of the feel of your breath on the back of my neck until I have silenced your idle curiosity on this matter, am I correct?" Thaniel inquired finally with some semblance of annoyance when they had reached the halfway mark of the staircase. "Very well then, let me be as terse as I can on the matter. There is located somewhere inside the Silent Forest a Through."

Jacob and Max's expression mirrored one another's in an almost identical manner of puzzlement. "What's a Through?" they asked in unison.

"A Through is a doorway; a gate, if you will," answered Thaniel. "You passed through one when you were brought here to Eden. There are several more of these gates in various places outside the realm of the Garden. Because water is the one shared thing most living creatures pass through on their journey into life, so, too, are where most of these Throughs reside. In the case of the Silent Forest, its particular Through rests in a pool hidden amongst the trees."

"Where do they lead…these Throughs?" Jacob asked with growing interest.

At first Thaniel didn't respond, as if he himself wasn't sure the answer. Or possibly it was a reluctance to reveal it for worry of stoking even further the boys' needling curiosity. Finally, he said, "The Heavens."

Jacob and Max looked taken aback, as if the answer exceeded the wildest guess either may have been contemplating.

"Did you say Heavens plural? As in more than one?" asked Max.

"Of course. Just as a house has many rooms inside it, why would you think Heaven to be any different?"

Thaniel's face softened and an even more youthful glow seemed to wash over him as he continued down the steps. A semblance of enjoyment crooked the corners of his mouth as it became clear, without needing to lay eyes on the boys, the overflow of imaginings flooding their skulls.

"I can only imagine the thoughts erupting inside your heads. Like a pair of dormant volcanos suddenly awakened," he remarked. "Perhaps it would have been better leaving the two of you to believe some dark force was at work instead."

Jacob wasn't listening. He was too busy thinking back to the underwater passage seeped in impenetrable darkness deep beneath the surface of the Van Gölü through which Gotham guided him so many months earlier, and the welcoming brightness of light that eventually revealed itself. He remembered how it reminded him of stories he heard told by people claiming near death experiences. Then, suddenly, he grew even more pensive.

"If this is true, how come you inferred that there was something dangerous about the Silent Forest?" he asked once they reached the main floor of the Library. "How can a Through leading to Heaven, any heaven, be dangerous? Or did I mishear you?"

Thaniel spun around and settled his gaze on Jacob. His eyes glittered with specks of glowing amber swirling about like embers cast from a wildfire into a dark smokey sky.

"You are nothing if not bright, Mr. Parrish. It's no wonder you fare as well as you do in Study," answered Thaniel. "The danger lies in the fact that a Through offers only one direction of passage to anyone with mortal blood flowing though his veins."

"Meaning?" pressed Max.

"Meaning what goes in can't come back out, including Nephilim," Jacob cut in before Thaniel could answer.

"Wait a minute…maybe I'm not the full quid, but that doesn't make sense. You said the Gate to Eden is a Through, and we're still able to return to the outside world," said a confused Max before a vague look of panic quickly lit up his eyes. "Aren't we?"

"Not on your own," answered Thaniel. "Not without an angel leading the way. You can try if you wish, but you wouldn't get very far and the end result I can assure you would be tragic. Only with the guidance of an angel can you pass into a Through in both directions.

And then only a noted few allows such journeys; the Gate into Eden being one of them."

"And the one in the Silent Forest?" inquired Jacob.

Before Thaniel could answer, Max's growing impatience forced him to abruptly interrupt.

"I don't get this. Instead of creating all this mystery why didn't Anahel just come out and warn the lot of us, 'Steer clear of the Throughs. They'll swallow you whole and you'll never get out!' I suspect that would do the trick."

"That so?" said Thaniel, raising his eyebrows with intrigue. "Well then, let's give it a try now, shall we? Boys, steer clear of the Throughs. They'll swallow you whole and you'll never get out!"

Just as he suspected, such funning only brought the opposite of quieting the boys until an exasperated Thaniel finally raised his hands in front of himself as if ready to bat away a couple of pesky mosquitos buzzing incessantly around his head.

"It's enough I've entertained you in your late-night sleuthing to warrant from Anahel the fierce scolding that no doubt should be held in reserve for the two of you," he said. "I don't think I care to incur the wrath of my brothers for your nodding off in class tomorrow."

Then before either boy could utter another word, he suggested firmly they return to their room and retire for the night while ushering them in the direction of the Library door. Whether they knew it was fruitless to prod Thaniel any further, or they found themselves wrestling with the heaviness of the late hour, Max and Jacob made no argument and went along their way down the dimly lit corridor. Just as they reached the staircase leading to the dormitory where the other Nephilim were fast asleep, Jacob stopped suddenly and told Max to go on ahead with Mist, and Max, seeing that something weighed heavy on his friend's mind, restrained himself from prying further.

~ ~ ~

When Jacob returned to the Library, he found Thaniel standing in the center of the room, his back turned while staring upward at the vast stretch of space hanging over him seemingly lost in thought. At first, Jacob thought the angel was praying and not wanting to disturb him any further was about to tip toe his way back out the door when Thaniel's voice stopped him.

"I thought there might be something more occupying your mind, tonight." Thaniel then turned around to face the boy and revealed a knowing look of understanding in his faint smile. "Something that hasn't to do with the Silent Forest, I assume."

Jacob nodded and Thaniel motioned to him with his hand to take a seat at one of the wooden tables before sinking into the chair across from him.

"Now then, how may I help ease your mind, if I am able to at all?" asked Thaniel. There was a deep-seated kindness Jacob found in Thaniel's eyes. Much like Johiel's. They had a way of drawing him in and putting him at ease whenever they came to rest on him unlike the other Guides. Not that the other Guides lacked kindness in their eyes (except maybe Eksel). but theirs was dominated by a piercing intensity which proved intimidating, to put it modestly. To stare into the cauldrons of molten gold which gave shape to their irises was to never lose sight of the fearsome warriors they were. Yet golden as his eyes were, Thaniel, somehow, managed to be free of such reflections. As a result, Jacob found himself at ease in the angel's company, and in that ease he came to like and trust Thaniel as much as he admired him for seemingly knowing everything there was to know. And Jacob knew if anyone could help quiet the nagging voices inside his head, it was Thaniel.

"Can an angel who has fallen ever have the mark on their head removed?" asked Jacob.

The question brought a crinkle to the space just above the bridge of Thaniel's nose. "I'm not sure I understand fully the question. The scar is permanent if that is what you're asking."

Jacob took a labored breath as though struggling to transfer the thoughts swarming his head to his voice. "But if a Fallen was sorry and expressed regret for whatever it was he did to earn that scar, he could be forgiven, couldn't he?"

Thaniel suddenly straightened himself in his chair. "Ah, now I see! You have been pondering the mystery of redemption."

Mystery?

Up until he came to Eden, Jacob thought when it came to redemption it was all pretty much cut and dry.

"When I was around eight or nine," recalled Jacob, staring down at the reflections caught in the polished wood surface of the table, "there was a comic book I saw at the store that I really wanted, but I didn't have any money. And I didn't want to ask my mom because, well, she wasn't really in good health at the time and I knew things were tight. So, I took the comic book and stuck it under my shirt and into the waistband of my pants without anyone seeing, even though I heard voices whispering in my ear telling me what I was doing was wrong. I don't think I ever managed to read past a couple pages of that stupid comic because every time I did I kept hearing in my head Sister Marie Theresa's voice scolding me in that terrifying way she had that my soul would be damned because of the sin I had committed. It got to where I couldn't sleep at night because every time I closed my eyes I saw myself burning in a fiery pit. I was sure I was going to Hell…er, rather, the Underneath.

"Then came the first time I ever went to confession," continued Jacob as Thaniel wholly listened. "Going into a small dark room and saying out loud your sins to a faceless silhouette peering through a screened window, it was the scariest single thing I'd ever known, not to mention shameful. Then the priest would do something I found to be remarkable. He would mutter three words: 'You are forgiven.' And just like that I once again felt…clean. It was almost like magic. And I knew from then on out no matter what awful thing I did, no matter what terrible sin I committed, all I had to do was go into that tiny, closet-like confessional and poof. Just like that, you were given a do-over all in exchange for saying three Our Fathers and ten Hail Marys."

"And now you wonder if somewhere there exists a confessional where the Fallen can go to be granted absolution," said Thaniel.

"Is there?" It was not so much a question as a hopeful utterance. "I can't help but replay in my mind the story Gotham told me about what happened to his son."

Thaniel pursed his lips and bowed his head slightly. "Yes, it was a very tragic thing to have happened. But forgive me, you've lost me with what this has to do with your question of redemption. Gothamel's Fall did not come from the killing of his son."

"I know that…that's not what I mean," said Jacob.

Thaniel studied carefully Jacob's face and a look of clarity slowly came to him.

"You see David's death as Gothamel's three Our Fathers and ten Hail Marys," said Thaniel.

"Isn't it?" asked Jacob. "I mean, Gotham was faced with the decision to allow the Sword of Destiny to fall into the hands of the Darkness or kill his own son. *His own son, Thaniel.*"

Jacob spoke as if the words alone could not justly describe the gravity of the choice of which he spoke of without a hammer to drive them with a firm blow into the ears listening. Yet he mindfully kept his voice from being carried by the echoes surrounding the Library any further than the table where he sat.

"How is it Gotham can consciously make such a sacrifice in the name of Eden—and, frankly, beyond—and still be made to carry this curse that has left him an outcast?"

"Be careful, Jacob," Thaniel was quick to caution. "Do not mistake the noble action taken by Gothamel—no matter how teethed in pain and loss it inarguably was—as a display of his willful penance."

Jacob sat quietly for a moment while staring blankly at the angel from his seat across the table.

"You're saying killing his only child on behalf of his own father was for nothing?" asked Jacob softly while trying to hide the tremble of frustration in his voice.

"What I'm saying is Gothamel's decision to do what needed to be done to keep the Sword from being possessed by a force which would have undoubtedly wielded great harm and destruction upon countless souls with it does not take the place of atonement for his sins."

"Atonement? What sins did he commit that were so damning? Expressing anger over being forced to do something so incredibly horrible? For cursing Heaven after being made to commit what was itself arguably a sin?" asked Jacob with hushed passion. "I could live my life a thousand times over and it would only be a fraction of time Gotham has been punished because of these so-called sins."

"I would caution you to be careful in your assessment of what you don't fully understand, Jacob," said Thaniel in a stern yet sympathetic manner. "It is obvious you have come to care a great deal for Gothamel, and I think it would gladden his heart if he were here to see you coming to his defense as you have. However, you are looking at his plight through the eyes of someone residing in mortal skin. It is not for neither you or I to say what Gothamel's sins may or may not be. Or that which should be his penance. But know the laws of good and evil which govern angels are not the same as those which govern man. What I can tell you is we are all held accountable—mortal and angel together— differently from one another."

~ ~ ~

This revelation concerning the laws of good and evil, as Thaniel deemed it, seemed to especially grab hold of Jacob's attention. "What do you mean differently?"

Thaniel leaned himself across the table as if he didn't want what he was about to say to drift any further than the two of them, even though they were the only souls in the Library.

"Whether justly or unjustly, God holds all who teeter upon the righteous path to a different standard," he whispered. "A moment of weakness visited upon one bathed in the grace of the Light is seen as worse than untold atrocities committed by a man infected with a dark soul. The same is true of angels. Where one can lead a rebellion against his Creator, it's the one framed in the light of God's smile who entertains the disloyal thought, however fleeting it may be, that draws tears from Heaven, as well as its harshest ire."

"But…that's not fair," balked Jacob.

"What exactly do you find to be unfair?" asked Thaniel. "That the breadth of one's sins is measured by a different yardstick than others? Or that the punishments Heaven chooses to dole out is based on favor, or lack of?"

"Both," insisted Jacob. "They're both not fair."

"Yet there it is, unfair or not. And just as the scorn of sin is different for every man, so too is the road to redemption," continued Thaniel. "In Heaven, Gothamel was held in favor worthy of all our envy. But enjoying the view from such a high pedestal meant the footing beneath his boots could be loosened by a sin that wouldn't necessarily cause any other angel to lose his own balance. Yet lose his balance he did, and the star which shined brightest was unhinged instantly from the sky. I don't have to tell you when one falls from such stately heights, the return climb upward is expected to be an insuperable toil, if not impossible."

A glum, defeated look came over Jacob as he listened to Thaniel. "I thought God was supposed to be all about love and forgiveness."

"Don't believe differently, for he is, in more ways than you can imagine. To be forgiven, however, one must seek forgiveness," replied Thaniel. "Unfortunately, the fate of my Fallen brethren forever resides in the Underneath. It is not that they refuse to do penance. It's that repentance does not exist within them. It was overcome and drowned long ago in the murk of the Darkness they chose to dwell within. And without repentance there is no chance for salvation."

Jacob felt a slight lump rise in his throat hearing those words and it caused a flash of anger to spike inside himself.

"Then if what you say is true," he said, "Gotham sacrificed his son for nothing."

Thaniel lowered his head in an effort to catch Jacob's sinking gaze with his own. "Do you honestly think Gothamel drew his sword on his only son with the intention his action might win him renewed favor with Heaven?"

The question seemed to leave Jacob all the more befuddled.

"Why else do such a thing then?"

"If that is what you believe, then your true knowledge of him is as thin as the haze of light burning above out heads," said Thaniel. "Gothamel's actions that day, if anything, revealed the true convictions of his soul, and that is one untainted by reward. More importantly, he remains untwisted by the far- reaching embrace of the Darkness despite the unbridled anger sparked by the sting of Heaven's rejection festering and curing inside him day in and day out through all these endless centuries. Whatever saving grace he might still cling to, it is that."

Jacob wasn't fully certain what Thaniel was attempting to convey to him, but his face softened at the sound of his words.

"And now I think we've done enough talking for one night, don't you?" said Thaniel, straightening up and sitting back in his chair.

Jacob felt somewhat numb as he got to his feet while smiling his thanks to the angel for lending his ear and sorting words of wisdom. Then as he turned to make his way toward the Library entrance, Thaniel's voice stopped him once again.

"You're forgetting something, aren't you?" asked the angel.

Jacob glanced back to see he had left behind the book about the Sword of Destiny he had found earlier; or rather that which had found him. Thaniel slid the book across the table toward him, but when Jacob when to pick it up, the angel's hand remained firmly on the book.

"The Sword of Destiny," said Thaniel, his voice laced with a notable inquisitiveness. "It holds quite a tale. Do you know much about it?"

"Only what Gotham's told me," answered Jacob with a shrug.

"And what, exactly, has he told you?"

"Bits and pieces…enough to intrigue me to know more about it, and tonight out of the clear blue I stumbled across this book."

"Well, you won't find a more complete accounting than what's held in these pages." Thaniel's eyes remained fixed on the book whose cover the angel continued to slowly trace with his finger. "Of course seeing the sword up close and personal is an entirely different experience altogether. Pity you were denied the privilege of such a thrill."

"But I have seen it," answered Jacob, bringing a gleaming spark to Thaniel's face.

"That is…well…sort of," said Jacob. "Gotham drew it on the ground next to the Tree of Life as he told me about it. It looked real enough…for something that wasn't, that is."

"I see," said the angel in a somewhat disappointed tone. "Then you have no idea if he brought it with him when the two of you came to Eden, do you?"

"Not that I know of," said Jacob, shrugging again. "Why do you want to know?"

"No reason, really. I guess, like you, I fancy its mystery. It's one thing to hear about something so mired in legend, it's quite another to see it firsthand and feel the proof of its existence in one's own hands."

There was something Jacob found strangely odd in the way Thaniel questioned him about the sword. However, the aging hour of the night was finally beginning to wear on Jacob's tired eyes and making them heavier with each passing minute he stood in the lulling quiet of the Library, even as his thoughts returned to the mysterious lady in the water he and Max had spied on Thaniel speaking to the previous night inside the Silent Forest. Who was she? And for what reason were they talking so secretly about the Sword of Destiny? He wanted to ask Thaniel. And perhaps he would have if the angel didn't suddenly turn his golden-tinged attention upon him and, handing the boy his book, sent him on his way with a, "Now then, off to bed with you."

CHAPTER TWENTY-EIGHT

The Call of the Champions

When the morning of Illumination finally arrived, Damiel found Jacob alone in his room staring out his window with Mist at rest on the floor by his feet.

The cool breeze wafting through the open pane carried with it the enthusiastic sounds of the celebration coming from the Garden grounds below. Whether by willful choice or because he was too lost in his own thoughts, Jacob took no notice of Damiel when he crossed the room to stand at the other side of the window to share in the view.

"They've just about all arrived," said Damiel to no reply as he peered at the boy from out of the corner of his eye. There was no need for him to question the forlorn look Jacob carried on him, or the reason for it. Outside, the sky stretching to the south was dotted with the approach of angels who came swooping down by the dozens to join where the other Nephilim boys were gathered along the tranquil River bank eager to greet the one they called "father."

Quietly, Jacob sat observing the happy embraces taking place with an especially keen eye, as though he were studying something foreign and unfamiliar to him, and for the most part it was. The loving tousling of hair. The showing off of new wings with pride. And especially the shared characteristics, both physical and not, that seemed to join the classmates he had come to know over the past many months together with an older version of themselves like two puzzle pieces. For Jacob, it was a strange and unique thing to watch. Whatever he expected, it certainly wasn't seeing angels appear so...well, fatherly. Every once in a while as he looked on unobtrusively from his spot at the window, a reunion would crack the solemn look on his face with a smile; like when Ethan was seen showing off his Grace to his father by changing form into a chubby but cute pot-bellied pig, whose high-pitched squeal rang out loudly to mark the successful transformation. It was, however, a lonesome, empty kind of a smile; one that seemed to only accentuate a deep longing held in a most noticeable way in his eyes.

"We should probably go down. The competition will be starting soon," said Damiel.

Jacob seemed unenthusiastic by the suggestion.

"If it's all the same to you, I'm going to pass."

Damiel continued to stare on ahead and shook his head disappointingly. "Do this often, do you?"

"Do what?"

"Hole yourself up and spend the day feeling sorry for yourself," said Damiel. "If so, then I have sorely overestimated the kind of Nephilim I believed you to be."

"Who says I'm feeling sorry for myself?" replied Jacob, shooting the angel a defiant glare.

"What, then, would you call sitting in your room with a face so long your chin is practically resting on the floor?"

"You wouldn't understand."

"No, of course not," said Damiel. "Why don't you try explaining it to me, anyway."

Jacob drew back from the window, unable to watch or hear any more or the cheerfulness taking place outside.

"Look, I've done this more times than I care to count," he said. "Every year of school was filled with these same father-son events, and every year I'd watch the teachers scramble to find someone to pair me up with just so I wouldn't be left out. A husband, a boyfriend, another teacher. One time, it was old Mr. Grimley, the school maintenance man, who looked to be more like my grandfather than father. It became a game to other kids. 'Who's gonna get picked to be Jacob Parrish's dad this time around.' It got to the point where I felt like a charity case, so much so that any time one of these events came up at school, I faked being sick. See, for me, it was better to be left out than to hear the whispering and snickering behind my back. I was okay with not belonging and being made to feel like an outcast. It was something I made peace with."

Damiel's face softened as he listened to the boy.

"If that's true, then tell me," said Damiel, "why is it I've come to find you alone up here with your befriended wolf?"

"To be made to feel like an outcast back home is one thing," explained Jacob, after a long-drawn-out silence. "I'm just not sure I'm ready to feel like one here."

Damiel gave a reluctant nod of understanding.

"It's a difficult thing to bear, I can imagine. Like a ship set adrift without a rudder to help steer it through rough seas. I trust during your first days here you have felt the sting of my own indifference, intentional or not, and for that I'm sorry," said Damiel. "But listen to me when I tell you the start of Illumination is too important a day to observe from a bedroom window. True, fathers have come to witness this marked moment, but today is about Nephilim, and Nephilim alone. Do not let discomfort keep you from taking your rightful part in this occasion. If the label of outcast awaits you, I say out loud: So be it! Wear it with pride and refuse to let it keep you from holding your head held high, for it will only make you that much stronger. Goodness knows you will come to face far worse things in the coming years than the absence of inclusion."

It was hard to ignore Damiel's words which he spoke with both an uplifting fervor and a pointed firmness. It was equally difficult to act on them as far as Jacob was concerned. Still, if there was one thing Jacob did not want to show himself to be in front of the one who for the past many months had trained him to wield a sword and become a warrior, it was the image of a boy reduced to cowering from judging eyes and gossipy tongues. And the only thing left for him to do was to buck up and accept Damiel's offer to walk him down to where the gathering was taking place.

~ ~ ~

Once outside, Mist darted from Jacob's side and rushed to the River's edge. Tail wagging, she began yelping high-pitched cries of excitement while fixing her piercing white eyes onto the sky where the last of the angels could be seen soaring in their approach to the Garden. The crowd of winged men and their winged offspring felt much larger to Jacob being in the middle of it than it did looking down from his bedroom window, and he did his best to make his way through the gathering with a confident posture and self-assured steps, though it helped to have Damiel at his side and the feel of his guiding hand on his shoulder offering a reassuring squeeze now and then. Yet, try as he might, he couldn't ignore the feel of eyes already beginning to shift his way.

"Jacob!" a voice called out.

Jacob turned to see Max making his way toward him.

"I've been looking everywhere for you," said Max visibly cheery. "Where you've been hiding yourself?

"I haven't been hiding," answered Jacob somewhat testily.

"Easy there, mate, just a figure of speech—nothing to get your knickers in a twist," said Max before introducing his friend to the imposing figure accompanying him. "Just wanted you to meet my father. This is Gradiel."

Jacob looked up to find a pair of brilliant gold eyes bearing down on him from behind a face he couldn't imagine to be more intimidating had he found himself standing in the shadow of the statue of the sphinx for the first time.

"Hello," said Jacob, while extending his hand to the towering figure who ignored the gesture. Not in a cruel or unfriendly way, but ignored it just the same.

Gradiel.

Jacob's mind feverishly worked to recall the name from the endless ranks of angel names he and the other Nephilim had been tasked by Thaniel to both study and commit to memory. Thankfully, it came to him in short time.

"Gradiel…it means 'might of God,' doesn't it?" asked Jacob.

"You've obviously been paying attention during Study," answered the angel, though looking none that impressed.

Jacob immediately took note to himself of how well the name suited his friend's father. Like the other angels gathered about, Gradiel was of great stature attesting to even greater physical strength. To stand in the shadow of such an intimidating presence was, to say the very least, unnerving.

"Maximilian here has told me a great deal about you," said Gradiel.

Jacob looked immediately to Max and grinned coyly.

Maximilian? Well…pardon me for suddenly feeling grossly underdressed for this formal introduction. So, is there a title that goes with that name…like Count?"

Jacob's telepathic teasing instantly wiped the cheeriness from Max's expression.

Tell one person about this and you'll be down for the count! replied Max silently while his unmoving lips pressed tightly together to keep from reprimanding his father for his slip of the tongue.

"I understand the two of you have come to form the bonds of a close friendship," remarked Gradiel, in a rather cool manner.

"He's alright," replied Jacob, giving Max a joking nudge.

"Yes…that he is," Gradiel grumbled without so much as cracking the slightest of smiles. "I must say I was surprised to find out you have come to share a room together. When I left him at Havenhid I remember there to be only three other roommates."

"I was a little late in getting here. But Anahel managed to find an extra bed in Max's—that is Maximilian's room," replied Jacob. His sarcastic quip, much to his delight, only seemed to make Max's lips press themselves even tighter together.

"So I understand." Gradiel's eyes, swirling with the life of a boundless age that defied the youthfulness held in his face, then shifted to Damiel, who stood quietly nearby. "Perhaps I might have a word with you in private."

There was a grated seriousness in Gradiel's voice and Jacob and Max watched with some semblance of shared curiosity as the two angels excused themselves to huddle together a short distance away.

"I don't think your father cares too much for me," remarked Jacob to Max.

"The sun's baking your head. What would make you say that? He just met you," replied Max.

Then why, Jacob thought to himself, was Max's father being most insistent Damiel move his son to another room? And as quickly as possible.

"I will not have my son colluding with that boy."

One thing about Nephilim ears, there isn't much they don't hear. Particularly when it comes to conversations they may inconspicuously choose to focus themselves to eavesdrop upon.

"Come on, let's go find the others," said Max, referring to Ethan, Leos and Kairo, who were somewhere in the growing crush of mingling bodies. "And while we're at it, we'll find you some shade."

Just as they turned to wade further into the crowd, who should they spy coming straight toward them but Creed in all of his ever-present, marked smugness. It wasn't the sight of their unfriendly rival, however, that halted the boy's mid-step, but that of the imposing figure accompanying him. Jacob knew it was Creed's father even before Max whispered it in his ear. At first sight, the Archangel Sandel was nothing what Jacob had pictured in his mind, not that he had spent a lot of time imagining Creed's father. For starters, he was a vision of white, Sandel was; colorless, pure, bright white, from his long, straight mane of hair to his clothes, except for the black boots he wore on his feet. It was as close to an image of an angel Jacob had carried around in his mind before Gotham set him straight on the reality of what real angels were like. However, as Creed and his father made their way closer, Jacob quickly saw there was a disquieting and forbidding air surrounding Sandel that all his whiteness couldn't hide. Even his skin was a pale alabaster, like a corpse's, which Jacob thought most appropriate.

As one of the twelve Angels of Plague, Sandel held a centuries-old reputation steeped in apocalyptic tales which the Nephilim boys were well versed in, thanks to Thaniel's instruction during Study. The image of white that he was, ironically, was in many ways more fearsome than if he appeared in a dark cloak and carrying a scythe. It was a whiteness as cold as it was revealing. One could almost catch the sorted stench of despair, disease and anguish clinging to Sandel's clothing like the stink of stale cigarette smoke. After hearing some of the reputed stories about Sandel, Jacob couldn't help but wonder whether the archangel might better be suited for horns and a pitchfork. It was only when Sandel stood looking down at him did Jacob spot the horns. They were kept in the pupils of his eyes which held the archangel's icy, cool gaze that slowly looked him over in a most disapproving way. The pitchfork? Well, that was quickly revealed the moment Sandel opened his mouth to speak.

~   ~   ~

"You must be the one I've been hearing so much about," said Sandel, without so much as an introduction. His voice was as cold as his stare which was devoid of the golden warmth Jacob had grown familiar to seeing in other angels eyes and, instead, held the appearance of two colorless icebergs adrift on a dark, black sea.

"I can't imagine you hearing anything about me. And the name is Jacob." This time, Jacob didn't bother with the courtesy of a handshake as he had with Max's father.

"Jacob. I once knew of a Jacob long ago," recalled Sandel. "He came to wrestle with one of my brothers and would not give up until he received Heaven's blessing."

"My mother used to tell me the story," said Jacob. "It's why I was given the name I was."

"Yes, well, I wouldn't crow about such a thing if I were you. The name, after all, means the supplanter, or taking what belongs to someone else. Then again it's no secret that Jacob had his deceitful ways, which is why God ended up changing his name," remarked Sandel.

"I don't know about any of that," Jacob replied. "I just know that Jacob was determined to get God's blessing at the end of that wrestling match, and he did. Personally. That's why my mom liked the name, and it's why I do as well."

"Of course it is," the white angel grumbled in response.

Jacob found there was an unsettling, almost hypnotic way Sandel's eyes were fixed on him.

"I couldn't believe it when I first heard the news, but now that I lay eyes on you…yes…I see undoubtedly it's true," said Sandel.

"What's true?" asked Jacob, who was fast finding himself losing patience with the judgmental gazes that seemed to accompany each new angel he came to meet.

"Why your existence, naturally," said Sandel matter-of-factly. "I'm rather quite intrigued—flummoxed, really—as to how someone of your, well—should we say breeding, for lack of a better word—came to be in as ironic a place as Eden?"

Breeding? Jacob almost felt the urge to dig into his ear with his finger to check if his hearing was being impaired by some ear wax in need of removal. Did this angel—and an archangel, at that—actually just make a nasty dig at his expense for being without a father? Thankfully, he had Max at his side who inquisitively sensed Jacob's blood begin to simmer and quickly stepped in before the barb quickly beginning to form on the end of his friend's tongue could be launched in retort.

"Through the Gate, of course, like everyone else. If you're looking to thank someone for his fine presence here, that would be Gotham. He obviously thought Jacob here was the perfect breed for Eden, and I couldn't agree more," said Max, whose pointedly snarky tone in the face of an intimidating figure such as Sandel brought a gleeful grin to Jacob.

"Couldn't you, though?" said Sandel, his right eyebrow arching high upon his forehead as though an exclamation point to his dour demeanor. "And just where is Gothamel, may I ask? I've looked, but I don't seem to see him anywhere."

He's off enjoying an afternoon of collecting puppies and placing them into sacks and then throwing them into the River to drown, is what Jacob wanted to tell the high-and-mighty angel whose voice held a dripping disdain when uttering Gotham's name. Just as Jacob's mouth began to part he felt a firm hand on his shoulder, and when he looked to see who it belonged to, he found Damiel suddenly at his side.

"Gothamel parted Eden some time ago. Exactly why I couldn't tell you, any more as to point you in the direction of his destination," said Damiel.

"Left Eden?" said Sandel. "Well, I can't say I'm surprised. To be in such a beautiful place and constantly reminded of the utter failure that was your own son would be a bit much to withstand for any angel, even a Fallen, I imagine. Tragic, really."

Yet, there was no sympathy in the archangel's voice. If anything, a morbid glee. It inflamed Jacob, and any intimidation he felt from the angel vanished, if just for that moment.

"Probably ran off to drown his sorrows with the other Fallen scum, which is where he belongs," Creed piped in with his eyes full of nastiness locked on Jacob and a cruel curl forming at the corners of his thin-lipped mouth.

Jacob had more than once contemplated on the almost poetic way in which nature worked where the existence of Creed was concerned. For where else could someone as malicious and thoroughly unpleasant a boy come from other than the loins of an Angel of Plague?

"Now, now son. Let us not be overtly nasty," said Sandel. "Not to say Gothamel has ever been known to be select in his company. At least not since his banishment. Why should he start now?"

The smugness was obviously a family trait passed on from father to son, amongst other noticeable, lesser traits. It was nearly tangible in how it dripped with such viscosity from both tongues.

"Besides, it is not Gothamel alone who is befitting a showing of scorn," continued Sandel, speaking pointedly to Damiel. "If anyone's deserving of admonishment it's you and your wayward band of Guides. You befouled Eden the moment you made the decision to allow undesirables to step foot in Havenhid, beginning with Gothamel and his treasonous son. Rest assure, I will make my displeasure about it known to Anahel this day."

He looked down the end of his nose at Jacob and there was no misunderstanding to whom he was referring when he mentioned "undesirables" with such venomous contempt. Had Damiel's hand not instinctively tightened its brace on his shoulder, Jacob likely would have befouled Eden right then and there with a choice of a Grade A rebuke directed straight at the arrogant archangel and happily take whatever wrathful punishment Heaven might send his way in the form of lightning.

"Be thankful there are children around, or I would tell you, Sandel, exactly what you could do with your displeasure," said Damiel in a voice that dared from Sandel the slightest retort in return. "It's the same thing I told Gradiel, and what I will tell any one of our other brothers who feel the same way. If, however, you'd like to discuss it now in private I'd be more than willing to oblige you."

The two stared daggers at one another. Yet fierce an angel as Sandel was in his own right, he was also familiar enough with the unyielding look in Damiel's eyes to decline the invitation extended to him.

"Now's not the time. But mark my words, Damiel, this conversation is not ended," hissed Sandel. He then nudged his son while turning a withering look on Jacob. "Come, Creed, you have a competition to win. And win it you shall!"

"The last time I saw a mouth like that, it had a hook in it," remarked Max as he and Jacob watched father and son continue on deeper into the surrounding crowd.

"If that's a sample of Heaven's welcoming committee, I could see the Underneath becoming a destination resort...like Hawaii," said Jacob.

"Don't judge him too harshly," said Damiel. "His duty far too often takes him into the underbelly of darkness, and such work has a tendency to stay on a person, like soot to a chimney sweep. His beliefs, while sometimes harsh and abrasive, come from an honest place."

There was a sound of compassion in Damiel's voice, as well as a tinge of sadness. It kept Jacob from saying anything further about Sandel. That and the long swell of a trumpet suddenly sounding loud its call across the Garden from Lions Bite.

~ ~ ~

Anahel was found standing in the center of Lions Bite when the gathering of boys and their fathers streamed into the arena. An electricity of excitement was alive in the air, especially for the young boys who, before this moment, had only heard stories about one of the most important days in the life of a Nephilim just coming of age. When everyone had finally found themselves a place to sit and the murmur of excitement had been quieted somewhat, Anahel's voice took command of Lions Bite.

"I welcome you, my brothers, to your home away from home," he began to a warm reception. "Illumination, as you all well know, is a day rooted in tradition; a tradition celebrated since the voices of the first Nephilim could be heard across Eden's once silenced lands. It is a day where a continuing generation of our fair Fledglings puts on display the education they have so far learned during their stay here. More importantly, it is time when fathers and their sons come together and stand as one in their shared service.

"The earth upon which Lions Bite stands has been watered by the sweat and toil of many a Nephilim boy, and it will be so again today. Illumination is not just a day marked by competition, but nonetheless the awaiting contests is where we choose to begin such a day. And as I can readily recognize in the many of the anxious looks staring back at me, it no doubt is the reason they wish for me to wind down my speech so they can eagerly get to it—and so we shall," said Anahel with a smile. "Today, all of you Fledglings will be competing in a number of contests, not in groups of Harriers or Ospreys or Shrikes, but as individuals."

The boys smiled their unanimous approval upon hearing the first guideline of the competition.

"You will each compete against one another in a number of contests," explained Anahel. "Each contest has been carefully conceived to allow you to demonstrate all the skills you have been taught by the Guides over the course of your stay here in Eden. Utilize them well, or you may find yourselves quickly defeated and eliminated from the competition. Those who prove victorious will continue to move forward to more difficult challenges until we have a final five. Those five Fledglings will earn their spot in the final, and I dare say the most difficult of challenges: the hunt for the elusive Illume."

The boys exchanged amongst themselves a coo of excitement upon hearing the final contest.

"Now then, does everyone understand and, more importantly, are you ready?" asked Anahel.

Not surprisingly there came in return a roar of approval from the now fidgeting group of boys. And with that a giant cauldron in the center of the stone-pillared arena was lit with a burning white flame, and the Illumination was officially begun.

~ ~ ~

The competition proved itself to be everything a Nephilim boy had heard about growing up, and more. For Jacob, it was like the Olympic Games on steroids. Except instead of being proficient in one sport, he found himself competing in a long steady string of events. And just as Anahel had explained, each challenge required the boys to use the skills they had honed under the Guides' guidance in order to stay in the game. To show off their strength, they competed against one another in a number of expected physical contests such as wrestling matches and sword duels, as well as those that were more out of the ordinary.

One such match, called "Sheer Will," proved particularly combative, and equally taxing. It involved a long rope of Herrinsu vine which, while infamously imperishable, ironically. could be harvested from the Forest by the simple act of plucking it from the soil at the root and going about the task of uncoiling it from whatever tree the delicate-looking, clinging stem had snaked. Each end of the vine was secured to the back of a pair of harnesses worn by the two opponents facing against the other. At the sound of the horn, the two competitors raced full-speed toward an obstacle of half a dozen poles positioned before each. They would weave their way through as fast as they could with the slack of vine trailing behind until they reached the last pole upon where the runners would make a hard U-turn and then a dead sprint back to the starting point, each boy racing the other to hit the waiting bell and sound their victory. However, reaching the bell proved itself to be a challenge quite worthy of the calibre of skills and strength one needed if they wished to shine at Illumination. For just as the two opponents— more often than not neck and neck with one another— could see their victory within their reach the slack of the Herrinsu vine would come to an abrupt and jarring end causing them to be yanked sharply backward from off their feet and sent sprawling onto the ground. It was then that it was quickly understood why the competition was given the name it was, as it took every ounce of brawn and grit within each boy as they clawed and strained inch by inch while face down in the dirt against each other, and the merciless, unyielding vine to which they were tethered, to graze with their fingers the bell gleaming in the sun.

Achievement throughout the day's festivities, however, wasn't gained solely by muscle. Equally as trying were the number of mental challenges designed to test the wealth of information and critical thinking Thaniel had drilled into the Fledglings heads, as well as those centered around the various Graces each boy had come to hone with growing adeptness thanks to Zuriel's stringent instruction. The competitive zeal the teens brought to each of the events was fierce, if not good-natured; Jacob, himself, could not deny the spirited pull Illumination had on him, even as he remained self-conscious about his ability to perform well despite his athletic tendencies. Mostly, it had to do with the fact he still had not obtained his wings. In fact, he was the only one amongst the group of boys whose back was still bare while everyone else, over the course of the past several weeks (and for a handful of others, months), had earned theirs. Even Creed, who had failed miserably that first day at Broken Earth, was proudly sporting a pair. Of course, it didn't help matters that Jacob had steadfastly refused any repeat attempt to coax out what remained hidden in the confines of his back. With the harrowing effects of his last leap still fresh in his mind—not to mention insides—and the fact he didn't trust Eksel any further than he could throw him, the closest he managed to muster the courage to take the plunge was to watch the others do what kept his feet frozen to the ledge of Broken Earth.

Then there was the fact he still remained Graceless, a point made clear every time he went to the Crescent Scar where Zuriel would attempt another reading by the Blackstone, despite Jacob's inexplicable ability at Cloaking, which by now he had mastered, and quite well at that. Yet, somehow, the mystery surrounding his Graceless self grew all the more curiouser when it came time for him to compete in "The

Underground." The challenge called on each contestant to descend a hidden passageway of stairs leading into the subterranean darkness beneath the arena floor. There, they were met by a maze involving a litany of obstacles of both inanimate as well as living (in some instances unwelcoming) things. The only way to successfully maneuver one's way through the maze, which mysteriously transformed and conformed itself to each challenger, was through the solving of various puzzles, riddles and questions posted along the way, or the successful utilization of the Grace or Graces one had at his disposal. Only by the reappearance of a contestant emerging through a second hidden passageway at the opposite end of the arena was victory in the challenge determined.

After successfully solving a couple of cerebrally taxing puzzles and answering correctly three questions that put his philosophical prowess through the paces, Jacob found himself at the halfway point of the intricate maze where he came upon an obstacle—a solid wall of hard earth—blocking his way. With no sign of a puzzle, riddle or stumper in sight that called upon his mental agility to open some hidden door and win him passage though the impregnable wall impeding him from advancing further, he realized the test before him rested in his ability to successfully make use of one of the two main things he was sorely lacking when he came to participate in Illumination: one of the blasted Graces.

At least, technically.

Sure, the Blackstone had continued to deem him as Graceless as a ballerina with two left feet attached backwards at the ankles, to borrow a pun from Max. However, Jacob had also learned quite by accident the night he helped coach Ethan in exercising his own Grace of Cloaking that he somehow, inexplicably, also had the ability to change shape. Seeing it was the only card in his deck with which he had to play, Jacob studied the wall before deciding his best course of action was to change himself into a squirrel or badger and burrow his way through the earthen barrier. Just as the pupils of his eyes were about to reflect the critter he focused his transformation on, he heard a faint voice. It came from an ant, and being as it was so tiny and the surroundings so dark, it took Jacob a minute or two before he spied the minuscule insect perched upon the end of his sneaker. The ant offered its services to help, and Jacob who was stunned by the fact he was having a conversation with the insect asked as inoffensively as he could what possible assistance the tiny creature could give.

"Not much, if it were just me," said the ant. "But I am not alone."

In an instant, the ground, walls and ceiling of the underground cavern was moving with a massive swarm of ants. They descended upon the wall and in a matter of seconds the fortified barrier of earth disintegrated. The swarm of ants then disappeared as quickly as they came, and as Jacob saw the passage leading to his victory now unobstructed in front of him he could help but mull silently whether he had just taken part in a bit of unsportsmanlike cheating.

"Not when the removal of the obstacle is dependent upon a Grace," came the ant's voice again, as if it could hear Jacob's thoughts. "And not when the competitor standing before it has the gift to call out to those who can hear his Whisper."

Whisper…

Could it possibly be, Jacob found himself wondering, that he had yet another undetected Grace lurking inside him unbeknownst himself, or Zuriel and, more importantly, the Blackstone? Intriguing a thought as it was, he quickly laughed off such a notion. He did, however, emerge from "The Underground" with an extra spring in his step when he was greeted with cheers as he stepped back into the sunlight radiating Lions Bite. For the rest of the day, Jacob proved himself a worthy competitor during Illumination and, despite lacking the two important tools needed to compete, he managed with the athleticism and sheer determination at hand to emerge victorious time and time again against those he went up against who came armed with a full tool belt.

And so, after a grueling demonstration of strength and, as Anahel promised, a great amount of sweat, the day of games wound itself down to the next to last competition, and no one was more surprised than Jacob to find himself among the last seven Nephilim still standing. Nothing, however, could have prepared him for the next event awaiting him which would decide which five boys would go on to compete in the hunt for the Illume, even when he spied seven angels rolling into the arena the means to which the final contestants would battle it out over a coveted victory.

In something straight out of "Ben-Hur," seven chariots were lined up at the far end of the arena; only there were no horses attached to them. It wasn't until the seven boys were directed to their assigned chariot did it become clear they would be the horses running the race. As Jacob stood while one of the angels fitted him with a harness around his mid-section that secured him to his chariot, he looked to his competition. To his right, he was happy to see Max was in the running.

"Is this a ripper or what?" exclaimed his amped-up friend.

Jacob wasn't certain whether "ripper" meant good or bad, but judging from the way Max was beaming as he was being strapped into his leather harness attached to his chariot like a stallion on two legs he assumed his friend was stoked for the challenge. Looking to his left, Jacob was equally unhappy to see Creed's sweaty face. Yet, as physically exhausted as Jacob was at that moment, having his nemesis right beside him might be exactly what he needed to push himself to get to the finish line in the same way a mechanical rabbit drives speed out of greyhound at the racetrack.

When all seven boys were finally bridled to their chariots, the race began. Immediately, in the first step he took, Jacob knew this race would be the most strenuous to his muscles and taxing to his drive than any of the previous contests he had competed in that day. The weight of the chariot provided a constant drag and proved unrelenting to the increasing burn flaming up inside his legs. Nine times around the arena, the race called for, but it might as well have been nine hundred times around. The arena carried the clamor of cheers coming from the angels watching with enthusiasm from the sidelines, but the only sound to meet Jacob's ears was the pounding of feet against the ground and the grinding of the chariots' wheels mixed with the strained, snorting grunts coming from the boys as they fought for the lead with the weight of their load wrestling them like a dropped anchor. Now and again, in a bit of nasty maneuvering, chariots sideswiped one another and testosterone-fueled bodies rammed and elbowed each other in an effort to win ground. Creed, especially, focused such dirty tricks on Jacob, but Jacob managed to fight off his aggressive plays and keep himself and his chariot from veering off course, or worse. When the chariots finally entered the final stretch accompanied by a cloud of kicked-up dust, it was clear by all watching, victory would be determined by a nose, or a chest, as all seven Nephilim made their dash toward the finish line.

~ ~ ~

When the dust from the chariot race had finally settled and the runners had been given a moment to catch their breath, quench their thirst and cool their sweating selves with a splash of water, Anahel came forward and gave an approving nod to the competitors gathered in the center of the arena looking famished and exhausted.

"You have all shown yourself worthy of the angel blood flowing through your veins, and a testament to the teachings and wisdom bestowed upon you by the Guides of Eden. You each serve your father's name with honor and I have no doubt they stand here today as proud of what you have accomplished already in your short time here as I am," he said. "That said, there are five among you who have shown yourself today to be most impressive. And as such, you will move on to compete against one another in the final competition of the day: the hunt and capture of the Illume."

A grumbling of excitement swirled about the expectant seven Nephilim anxiously awaiting to hear who amongst them had emerged victorious in the too-close-to-call chariot race and would move on to compete in the most prestigious event of the Illumination.

"When I say your name, please step forward."

Anahel stared out at the young faces whose eyes were intently fixed on him, and in his pause he could both hear and see the growing restlessness rising both from the boys as well as their fathers seated nearby as the silence became almost too unbearable a suffering for them. Finally, his lips parted, and the powerful tenor of his voice sounded with the first name.

"Creed, son of Sandel."

The announcement was by no means a surprise revelation to either the other Nephilim or Creed himself. With an entitled swagger, he made his way toward Anahel shoving aside his fellow competitors who stood in the way of his rightful path. He then turned to bask in the adulatory applause which was led by his father standing proud at his seat like a preening albino peacock.

When the roar died down and his voice could be heard once more, Anahel continued. "Issac, son of Bariel. Michael, son of Irel. Maximilian, son of Gradiel."

The three came forward beaming proudly while receiving congratulatory pats on their backs from the other boys who seemed pleased with the choices, even if it meant not hearing their own names called. Only Creed didn't seem particularly thrilled when he found himself suddenly being forced to share the spotlight.

"And finally, the fifth Nephilim who will compete in the final competition will be...," began Anahel, his gaze making its way through the faces of the other boys before coming to rest on Jacob. "Jacob, son of…"

The happy glint in his eyes dimmed as he abruptly drew silent when he realized the announcement he was in the midst of making allowed no way for it to be concluded, and his face suddenly became grievous. The brief moment of joy that visited Jacob also dissipated when he knew instantly the reason Anahel's tongue had become twisted into silence. Embarrassment swept over him as he felt every eye fall upon him, and just when he wished with everything he had that the earth beneath his feet would show mercy upon him by performing the simple act of opening up and swallowing him whole, there came a neigh of a horse. It was quickly accompanied by a familiar, if not unexpected voice.

"Ward of Gothamel."

The collective attention of everyone gathered at Lions Bite turned in unison to the western end of the arena where to everyone's surprise Gotham emerged from the shadows of the towering stone walls. No one, however, looked to be more in shock at the angel's reappearance than Jacob. The arena became silent except for the chattering of birds chirping loudly with excitement from the trees of the nearby Forest as Gotham came forward. Only he was not alone. With him was a magnificent white stallion which he led with a garland of ivy noosed loosely around its neck. The Nephilim cleared a path as Gotham made his way with the horse to where Jacob stood.

"I say ward because it is the role that has been left me," said Gotham to the boy, but with a voice intended to reach every ear in the arena. "But make no mistake, I would be more than proud to call him son."

The angel's words stirred a buzz of whispers, but it was Jacob who was found to be most taken aback. He knew Gotham well enough to know he was not prone to saccharine-laced sentiments, and even as the angel spoke them his steely composure was broken only barely by the faintest of smiles.

"How long have you been here?" asked Jacob.

"Long enough to be impressed by your performance today," answered Gotham. "It reminded me of when David competed here so many years ago. His name, too, was among the five read by Anahel then." Gotham's eyes remained fixed on Jacob, but they were focused on the memory of which he spoke. "Illumination was a day of great importance to him, as it is to all Fledglings, as I'm sure it is to you. And while I'm not your father, I couldn't, therefore, let you spend it without someone at your side.

"Besides," he quickly added in an effort to steer clear of making the moment more sentimental than it needed to be when he saw a pleasing smile come to Jacob's face, "I certainly couldn't let you attempt this competition without some kind of fighting chance."

He then reached out and offered up the rope of ivy in his hand and the horse to which it was attached. Visibly surprised, Jacob took the lead and as he did the stallion stepped toward him and took in the scent of the boy's hand .

"It's one of the Snowdrifts, isn't it?" asked Jacob, though he already knew just by looking at the magnificent animal. Its hide and mane was whiter than any color white Jacob had ever seen—blindly so. And like snow it shined and glittered under the bright sunlight as if the horse had been dusted with tiny grains of crystal.

"He'll carry you today and any time you call for him from this day forward," said Gotham. Jacob stared deep into the steed's dark yet kind eyes, and he knew what the angel said was true.

~ ~ ~

"I object!" a voice suddenly bellowed from the arena seats. Jacob looked to find Sandel on his feet in protest. "This is a contest between Nephilim, and Nephilim alone. Your attempt to aid this one with a horse is nothing short of cheating."

The outburst didn't seem to surprise Gotham. In fact, from the look on his face, it was as if he expected it.

"The boy, as you can see Sandel, has yet to come into his wings while the others have," replied Gotham coolly without so much as a glance over his shoulder at the angel. "You know as well as I he doesn't stand a chance in the competition with just the aid of his own feet. Do you think that fair?"

"Rules are rules," countered Sandel. "I think everyone here would agree with me that the boy has had the same opportunity as the others to earn his wings. Should they be put at a disadvantage because one amongst them has proven himself inadequate?"

The disdainful tone with which Sandel spoke made Gotham turn a fierce, challenging eye on him. "I hear only yourself making issue of this. Could it perhaps be because you lack confidence in your own son's ability to match wing with hoof?"

The cutting assertion muted Sandel's tongue momentarily, and in the awkward pause that followed Anahel took the opportunity to keep the disruption from escalating as the two angels glowered at one another.

"I see nothing unfair or underhanded with Jacob riding the animal in this contest if he so chooses," said Anahel. "You know as well as anyone here, Sandel, that without wings the boy will still be at a considerable disadvantage. A capable Nephilim can more than easily outmaneuver a horse, even a Snowdrift. But, seeing as how you have raised the objection concerning fairness, I would be more than happy to ensure that you, and everyone present in this arena, find satisfaction that an even playing field has been set in place by making horses available to any of the other four competitors, should they so choose."

Creed was quick to respond first to the offer before his father could open his mouth.

"I can assure you, I won't be needing any horse," he said snidely before leveling a smirking scowl at Jacob.

The other three boys also declined with a simple nod of their head.

"Very well. Then the matter is settled and we can now move on to the contest," said Anahel with a thankful sigh. Clearly bristling from the outcome, Sandel reluctantly sank back into his seat while continuing to stare daggers in Gotham's direction.

"Make no mistake, the task before you will not be an easy one, wings or not," continued Anahel, speaking to the five he had earlier named to compete in the contest. "Unlike the other animals of Eden, the Illume is an elusive creature who lives a nearly mythological existence out of sight from both Nephilim and angel alike. This day is the one time of the year that the Illume emerges from hiding deep inside the corner of forest touched by the looming shadow of the western peaks. It is there that what may be the most beautiful bird ever hatched into creation ventures out for a brief period in a futile search of a mate. I say futile because there has only ever been one Illume in existence."

"How will we know what it looks like or where to look for it?" asked Issac, curiously.

"There will be no mistaking the Illume the moment you lay eyes upon it, though it will likely be the unique clicking sound it makes that will first alert you to its presence.

"Be mindful; you will only have a short amount of time in order to prove yourself victorious in the task before you," continued Anahel. "The Illume's beauty is quite striking, but never is it more stunning than when witnessed in the presence of the moon whose light causes the Illume's plumes to radiate with a striking shimmer as though it were powdered with star dust. So luminous it is that when the light of day retires so, too, will the Illume; driven back to whatever dark, secreted place it conceals itself to douse its resplendent beauty in the desire of keeping its existence invisible to all to attempt to search it out."

It was then that Creed let out an impatient huff. "It's a little bird. How hard can it be to catch?" he muttered under his breath, though not low enough to escape Anahel's ears.

"Well then, if it sounds like a walk in the park, by all means it must be," said the angel in a subtly ominous tone while turning a quieting glare onto Creed. "You'd be wise, Mr. Maggert, if you're serious to win this challenge, not to underestimate the Illume. Some of the most beautiful creatures ever to exist have proven themselves to be the most indomitable…and dangerous."

He was speaking, of course, of the Illume, but his words at the same time could easily have been a wink and nod at his own existence as well as the other angels filling the arena, something that was not lost on the other boys.

Anahel then proceeded to pass out a black sack to each boy, who looked them over with notable confusion. They were large sacks made of soft fabric, much too large for just a bird.

"The Illume will give up quite a fight, of that you should prepare yourself," said Anahel. "To quiet the fight, you will need to get the sack over its head and cover its eyes."

Again the boys looked with some bewilderment at the sacks which looked like they could each hold a hundred birds much less serve as a hood for the head of one. In their increasing eagerness to get the final contest underway, however, they simply tucked their sacks away and prepared themselves for the competition to finally begin.

"There's just one more thing," said Anahel, addressing the five boys in a firm tone. "Be cautious in your quest. No matter the circumstance, no injury or harm must come to the Illume in your pursuit of it. Should one of you prove victorious in this task, the creature must be returned back to the Forest later this very night precisely as it was before you gave chase after it."

He then instructed the contestants to prepare themselves.

"I don't stand a snowball's chance in hell winning this thing, do I?" Jacob asked Gotham as he climbed onto the Snowdrift's back.

Gotham noticed Jacob's gaze was on his four challengers who were seen quickly stripping off their shirts. What he eyed were the wings stretching themselves into view, the sight of which brought a noticeable longing to the boy, not to mention embarrassment as a reminder of the one thing he lacked to make him fully a Nephilim like the others.

"Keep thinking like that and you'll quickly learn prophesies have a way of being self-fulfilling," said Gotham. "It won't be wings alone that guide the victor, but rather a keenness of both mind and eye as well as a courageous and tenacious spirit, both of which you have already proven to possess in great measure."

The angel's confidence in him likely would have proven more reassuring to Jacob had he not been preoccupied with other thoughts swirling around inside his head.

"So, how long do you plan to stick around this time?" Jacob asked suddenly out of the blue with a bitterness in his voice that made clear his lingering resentment of the angel's earlier abandonment had not completely dissipated.

"Long enough to fully enjoy the look on Sandel's face when you return the winner," answered Gotham, flashing a grin both enthusiastic and mischievous before quickly adding with a seriousness devoid of any smile, "and then for some time after, if there are no objections."

The answer was obviously good news to the boy's ears.

Then while stroking the neck of the horse, Gotham leaned in closer to ensure his words would not be in earshot of Jacob's rivals. "A couple pieces of advice," he began. "Unlike most birds, the Illume can't see what's approaching it from directly behind."

"That's good to know. And the second?" asked Jacob.

"The key to ensuring a win is to not treat this is as a hunt. If you want the bee to come to you, all you need is a little pollen."

Before Jacob could ask the angel to expound on what he meant, Anahel called the five boys together.

"It is quite possible none of you will succeed in this task before you," said Anahel. "That as it may be, you each have until the sound of the trumpet rings out, at which time you must return immediately for the oath ceremony. For the one amongst you with whom fortune finds favor, your trophy will be in knowing your distinguished feat is a victory shared by a prestigious few. Now then, are you ready?"

The answer came in the deeply focused looks that fixed themselves with an intense seriousness on each of the boys faces as their bodies tensed themselves into position in preparation of springing forth into action. Jacob glanced over one last time at the other four boys. Only Max looked back and gave him a friendly nod of luck and Jacob happily returned the gesture. When the word—sounding like a thunderous gunshot—finally echoed through the arena, there came a furious storm of beating wings and stomping hooves which whipped up the earth in a whirlwind of dust. As the cloud thinned, Jacob could be seen drilling across the Garden upon his blinding white steed with the same vengeance his winged rivals took to the sky.

CHAPTER TWENTY-NINE

THE SHRIKE AND THE HARRIER

The race soon reached the open lands of Eden, and as the Snowdrift took to the vast grasslands in full gallop, the speed with which it traveled caught Jacob by surprise. He could feel the intimidating power of the animal churn between his legs like an unbridled storm and it took all of his strength just to hold himself to the horse's broad back and not be thrown to the wind like a fuzzy seed released from a dandelion. It made him recall the first time he watched a herd of the majestic beasts the day he first arrived in Eden and how they appeared as a blinding snowstorm sweeping across the land befitting the moniker bestowed upon them. Anahel had remarked it would be a challenge for a horse to keep pace with a Nephilim with wings, but that was not the case with the Snowdrift. It trailed only slightly the shadows moving across the ground from the four winged boys soaring high above, and the hot breaths coming from the steed's flaring nostrils kept beat with its pounding hooves in a fierce determination to pull ahead.

Then, in the closing distance, as the trees forming the part of the Forest resting at the foot of the mountain range running along the western edge of Eden grew nearer, the shadows moving along the ground suddenly parted. Jacob trained his eyes to the sky and saw his competition veer off in four different directions and disappear over the treetops. Only it wasn't the sight of his fellow classmates his eyes found themselves focused upon, but that of a lone snake eagle, the familiar majestic bird whose presence he often caught drifting on the higher elevations of sky directly above wherever he was. It began to feel to Jacob as if the eagle was stalking him, trailing his every movement no matter where in Eden he went.

Soon after he reached the first trees shaping the edge of the Forest, Jacob dismounted from the Snowdrift and left it to graze happily on the sweet, lush grass. Then with the black sack given to him by Anahel tucked in the waistband of his jeans, he glanced again skyward to catch the eagle as it sailed ahead over the Forest and disappeared out of sight before Jacob, himself, hurried on foot into the cluster of trees. He had only gone a short distance when he was suddenly struck by the breadth of the challenge before him. The Forest was an immense and far-reaching place, and as he looked at the towering trees green with moss and dripping with vines all about him for as far as the eye could see— even the sharp eye of a Nephilim—Jacob realized he had a better chance of finding a needle in a haystack.

He also knew giving up was no option, especially for him. There was no challenge he had greater desire for winning than this one. Maybe it was because at no other time had he felt more of a need to prove himself. Particularly to the fathers who had come to Eden to lend support to their sons. There was no mistaking their contempt for him from the moment they laid eyes on him. He could feel it in the cold reception he received whenever he was offered an introduction to one of them. Even those who managed to extend a warm greeting could not hide the disdainful look held in their eyes. It was clear they viewed him as beneath them, and the more he thought about it the angrier he became. And it was through that anger he was determined more than ever to be the one to seal for himself the prestigious accomplishment of bringing the Illume back to Havenhid.

Jacob made his way deeper into the thick of trees. How long he was mired in what was seeming to be more and more a fruitless search he did not know before he began to wonder if the others were having any luck on their own separate quests. As he strained his ears to pick up some telling sign from them in the distance, there came a strange noise he had never before heard from inside the Forest. It was a subtle and easily ignorable clicking sound, like that made by a tongue to the roof of one's mouth. Could it be what he was hearing, he wondered, was the sound Anahel described back at Lions Bite—the actual sound of the Illume? It drew his gaze upward to the trees towering over him. There the clicking seemed to bounce about to different places, yet he couldn't see anything lurking in the branches fanned out above him.

Then suddenly Jacob's eyes caught sight of something taking to the air. It swooped down toward him at a great speed accompanied by a high-pitched shrill. A blur of blue and white, it buzzed past and disappeared into the thicket before Jacob could get a good look at the creature. Jacob immediately took off in pursuit of it, following the unusual shrieking that echoed itself through the Forest. He hadn't gone far when he heard the trickling sound of water. It led him to a small babbling stream which he crept up upon as quietly as his steps allowed. Crouching down, Jacob carefully peered through the patches of fern and reeds he found cover behind and was treated to the most surprising and unexpected of sights.

Just a short distance away was a small pool formed by the stream, and standing at the water's edge was a bird of great beauty. It was about the size of a quail and colored the most magnificent shades of blue Jacob had ever seen. Its tail was a train of white that would make any bride-to-be in search of a wedding gown green with envy, and from its head sprouted a headdress of white lush plumes from which a solitary blue feather grew. So bright and richly colored was the bird that it carried an iridescent glow to it that at first Jacob thought he was imagining.

"Hello," Jacob whispered to himself when he realized the bird could be no other creature than the coveted prize he had been sent in search of. "So, you're the Illume."

Afraid to make so much as the slightest movement that might spook the bird, Jacob stayed frozen in his place for some time and just watched the creature as he pondered his next move. The Illume in turn seemed too preoccupied to have any notion of Jacob's presence. Cocking its head from side to side, it stared curiously into the water of the pool next to which it stood. As Jacob watched it, he realized the Illume was transfixed on its own image reflected on the water's smooth, mirror-like surface and he recalled what Anahel said earlier about it being the one day the Illume ventured out in search of a mate.

"You think you've found yourself a possible friend, don't you?" whispered Jacob as he watched the Illume poke at the watery image now and then with its beak only to be met by ripples.

Slowly, Jacob reached for the sack tucked in the waistband of his jeans only to freeze suddenly when the Illume raised its head in alarm. Instead of turning an eye his way, the bird gave a spooked glance over its shoulder and furiously began pumping its wings just as Creed came sweeping out of nowhere to pounce upon it like a springing cat. The Illume, however, proved itself far speedier and eked a razor-thin escape.

Visibly frustrated, Creed glanced toward where Jacob remained peering out from behind the fern.

"Stay put, Parrish, I'll take it from here," he said with a contemptuous sneer as the two boys glared at one another before he flexed his wings and took off after the Illume.

"I bet you will," muttered Jacob as he jumped to his feet and tore off in a run after him.

While Jacob may have lacked wings, he definitely was not deficient in speed. And it was with tremendous swiftness he made off after Creed all the while looking skyward where flashes of sunlight revealed the furious chase taking place in the crotchet of branches stretching high overhead. The Illume's shrieking cry rang out bringing Jacob to a standstill.

"You're not allowed to harm it!" Jacob shouted angrily as pieces of tree rained down around him from above. His eyes scoured the treetops, but while a terrible ruckus roared through the Forest, neither the Illume or Creed could be found. Growing more and more frustrated in his inability to intervene, Jacob made a dart for, and scurried up, one of the trees with the agile gait of a squirrel. He had made his way halfway up the massive trunk when suddenly the Illume came into sight in a desperate dive toward the Forest floor at breakneck speed. Creed was fast on its trailing tail and there was a mad, intense gleam in his eyes.

Jacob readied himself, and the moment the chase rushed past him in a frenzied blur he threw himself from the tree and dove onto Creed's back. Caught by surprise, Creed attempted to buck Jacob off by swaying his body sharply from side to side like a ship tossed about in the grip of a storm-churned sea. Jacob held tight by utilizing one of his wresting moves and putting Creed in a choke hold. Creed struggled to gain the needed movement of his wings under Jacob's weight to keep from losing air and barely managed to muster enough glide to slow the ground that was rising fast to greet them.

At the very last second, the Illume veered away sharply leaving the two Nephilim to the unpleasant landing awaiting them. They hit the ground with a cringe-sounding thud and, like a pair of dice rolled across a craps table, were bounced in two separate directions amid a chorus of jolting grunts and painful groans.

Creed was quick in his return to his feet, though somewhat unsteadily, with anger fuming in his eyes and fists clenched tightly. "Tell me, Parrish, just how stupid are you?" he seethed.

Jacob sat up and with the same dizzying look marring his focus he seemed to pose the same question to himself as he looked up with some amazement at the distance the two had fallen.

"What can I say?" Jacob managed in reply as he, too, got to his feet, though with some amount of effort. "We're competing in the same contest. You didn't think I was just going to stand by and watch you walk out of here with the prize without a fight, did you?"

"You honestly think you have a chance against me?" hissed Creed both incredulously and with an undeniable arrogance.

"I think I got a one-in-four chance. Not too bad of odds."

"There's five of us competing, moron."

"Yeah, well, I really don't count you as much of an obstacle as I do the others."

A look of hate concentrated itself in Creed's glaring gaze.

"That so?" he said, flexing his chest and stepping uncomfortably into Jacob's space.

"That's so," said Jacob coolly with an unflinching confidence. The two stood nose to nose, their silent, hard gazes boring deeply into one another that spoke without words of their intense dislike for one another. Then Creed did something he never did before in his short life; he was the first to take a step back. Just as he turned his back to Jacob, his right wing flared suddenly outward. It struck Jacob on his left side with enough tremendous force to knock him off his feet and send him hurtling several yards through the air. His body slammed hard against a nearby tree igniting an explosion of intense pain inside him that sent him crumpling to the ground.

"Let that be a lesson to you, Parrish," said Creed. "Stay out of my way, or next time I won't be as gentle."

And while the ground at that moment felt just fine to Jacob as he fought to still the pain throbbing its way through him, he wasn't about to obey an order to heel. Especially, from Creed.

"Anahel really had you pegged right off the bat, I see," remarked Creed with a sneering chuckle. "You really are a shrike, aren't you?"

"You obviously don't know a whole lot about birds, do you? Especially, shrikes," said Jacob as he found his feet again.

"Of course I do. They're loser birds. Songbirds."

"It's true, they do make a pretty sound," said Jacob. "Were you also aware they're referred to as 'butcherbirds'? That's because they're known to impale their prey on thorns and barbed-wire fences. So I'm not so sure a shrike is the bird you want to be messing with."

The smile on Creed's face dried up as quickly as a pool of water in a scorching desert.

"Well, I'm one hundred percent sure a shrike doesn't want to have anything to do with a harrier. I can promise you that," said Creed referring to both the bird and the name of the group of Nephilim he himself had been placed by Anahel.

"What exactly is your problem, Creed?" Jacob called out just as Creed was about to resume his hunt for the Illume.

"I thought I just made it clear to you," answered Creed. "Or did you hit that tree just a little too hard?"

"No...I mean, what's your problem with me...in general?" said Jacob as he struggled to both catch his breath and hide any sign of distress from his face courtesy of Creed's painful blow. "You've hated me since the first day I came to Havenhid. Why? What did I ever do to you?"

"Ah, what's the matter? Your feelings get hurt?" said Creed feigning weeping. "Why can't you just accept the fact I don't like you? Not one little bit."

"Trust me, Creed, the feelings entirely mutual. I'm just curious, that's all."

"No one embarrasses me," answered Creed finally. "Least of all you."

"Excuse me?"

"Back at Lions Bite...the day we were given our swords."

Even with the daze of being slammed into a tree lingering, Jacob knew immediately to what Creed was referring. After all, the day he chose Creed to face off with their newly gifted swords at Lions Bite and come out the victor wasn't something that was easily forgotten. What sweetened the memory even more was knowing now how it continued to remain an emblematic festering thorn he had unwittingly impaled Creed upon.

"That's it?" said Jacob. "You've been p.o.'d at me just because I happened to get the best of you in a sword duel?"

Being reminded of it in such a cavalier manner wasn't something Creed took to kindly.

"Don't flatter yourself, Parrish. Everyone has a lucky day. But I wouldn't count on luck smiling down on you twice should we ever throw down for reals," Creed groused. "I mean, look at you. You're wingless. You're without a Grace. You're a total embarrassment and a pathetic excuse to a real Nephilim like myself."

As much as he tried to hide it, the barb stung Jacob. "I'm as much a Nephilim as you, or anyone else at Havenhid."

"If by Nephilim you mean a Weed, then by all means, yes, you are. In spades."

Now it was Jacob's turn to feel his nose suddenly out of joint. "What did you say?" he asked, as if daring Creed to repeat himself. "You deaf? I called you a Weed," Creed spat back.

If there was one thing a Nephilim took offense to being called, as Jacob had quickly come to learn, it was a Weed. The derogatory remark was the ultimate insult a Nephilim could hurl at one of their own. In one biting syllable, it cruelly and pointedly was used to label those looked upon as beneath the others. Outcasts. Pariahs. Their sin? Simply being the sons of angels who carried the mark of the Fallen.

"You want to know why I dislike you so much? That's the real reason," said Creed. "You're a defect. An undesirable. A spawn of a damned castaway."

"You know as well as everyone else Gotham's not my father," said Jacob. Not that he would be embarrassed or ashamed if anyone thought such a thing, least of all Creed.

"Who said I was talking about Gotham?" said Creed. "Oh, it was a real touching display back at Lions Bite earlier when Gotham made a big show of returning to Eden to proclaim his father-like devotion to you. Truth is he's nothing but a Fallen standing in for a further Fallen."

"I'll give you to the count of three to take back your filthy lie, Maggert," Jacob threatened with a deepening scowl.

"I'm only a liar if what I say is untrue." A slow-cooked, almost grotesque look of glee unfolded itself across Creed's face like a picnic blanket being spread across summer-warmed grass. "Fact is, my father told me."

"Your father?" echoed Jacob in confused disbelief.

"That's right. After I accidentally happened to overhear him talking about it to a group of other angels. Although, he made me promise I would keep it to myself and make sure it didn't get spread around Havenhid." Then with a tight smile and roll of the eyes he gave a most unapologetic, "Oops!"

Jacob began to feel the muscles in his body begin to tighten in a most uncomfortable way.

"Unfortunately, he caught me eavesdropping before I could learn who exactly this low-life Fallen of a father of yours is and was told to mind my business when I asked," Creed continued in his jabbering. "But I can assure you I plan to make it my mission to find out."

"I don't believe a word you're saying!" Jacob spat with increased disdain.

"You don't have to believe me. Just go ahead and ask my father. Better yet, ask Anahel; he knows the truth. In fact, I dare you!"

If Creed was indeed lying, he certainly was enjoying the yarn he was spinning, pausing to lick his lips like a lion right before indulging in its kill.

"It's not all that surprising a revelation, really," he continued with his dangling taunts. "I knew the first time I laid on you that you were the byproduct of questionable breeding. What surprised me was how bottom-rung you really are."

"You're lying!" Jacob repeated. The Forest began to spin counterclockwise around Jacob as Creed's voice took on an echo inside his head as if it was coming from deep inside some mountain cavern.

"Didn't you ever think it was strange that you were the only one in the history of Nephilim not to know who his father was?" pressed Creed with unrelenting vigor. "Angels aren't the same as regular men. They don't have their sons on a whim, or even accidentally. And they certainly don't abandon them like some derelict dad up to his elbows in child support payments."

The more Creed spoke, the more contemptible a glare he drew from Jacob. And from within his eyes came flecks of flame as they watched Creed beam with sheer delight at his growing expense.

"I guess that would explain how it is you came to be in Gotham's care," said Creed. "Then again, Fallen always look out for Weeds, even when it's not their own."

Jacob had enough. The piano wire he felt being pulled tighter and tighter somewhere deep within himself finally snapped.

"YOU'RE A FILTHY LIAR!" he cried out angrily.

Before he was conscious to the fact his feet were moving, he was already upon Creed. Only this time it wasn't Jacob who went careening through the air and slammed mightily into a tree but Creed.

"You want to take your anger out on someone, I suggest you take it out on Gotham," snarled Creed angrily, trying to shake off the painful impact of Jacob's starburst-inducing punch. "He's the one who made Anahel and the other Guides promise to keep the truth about who your father is a secret."

Jacob could feel another tremor rumble through him signaling another violent eruption of his rage was imminent. Fists clenched, he stepped toward Creed who wasn't about to take another right hook to the face without a fight and quickly got to his feet.

"Face it, Parrish, you're an orphan of the Darkness. You don't belong in Eden, but the Underneath," Creed spit venomously. "Take my advice. Make good of that present of a horse Gotham got you and have it carry you south to the Dilmum Sea where the Gate is. You've got no one here who cares enough to see you win today. Certainly not a father as important as mine. A true angel."

"The only place I'll be riding the Snowdrift today will be back to Havenhid," said Jacob in as cool a manner as his anger allowed him. "Unfortunately for your true angel of a father, he'll have to face what I am sure will be the inexcusable embarrassment of seeing a defect and undesirable in possession of the Illume, not his son."

A grim shadow washed away Creed's smirk.

"I'm warning you, Parrish," he seethed, "if you know what's good for you, you'll stay out of my way. There's only going to be one Nephilim who leaves his mark on Eden today, and that Nephilim is going to me."

"Maybe," replied Jacob with matter-of-fact simplicity. "Maybe not."

Creed took a threatening step toward Jacob, and Jacob happily braced himself for another physical clash, only this time he had no intention of being on the losing end of any more punches—or wings—thrown his way. Just then the now familiar shrill of the Illume rang out in the distance grabbing both boy's attention.

~ ~ ~

"I'm not playing, Parrish," Creed warned again. "Be smart for a change and remember what I said. Stay out of my way."

He then began beating his wings and in a flash flew off in the direction of the elusive bird's call. Jacob, however, remained put, frozen by the scathing revelation left to echo in his ears as he watched Creed slip from sight into the depths of the Forest.

Orphan of the Darkness.

The phrase kept repeating itself over and over inside his head. So much so that he didn't hear—or chose to ignore—a rustling of movement coming from the tree heights above him moments before Max came swooping suddenly down from out of nowhere.

"Like leading a flaming galah to sand and convincing him its water," he said with a mischievous grin while giving Jacob a firm pat on the back as he strode by him.

"I really don't need you to run interference for me," Jacob snapped irritably when he realized his friend had cleverly feigned the fake bird call while quietly perched in the trees above sending Creed off on a wild goose chase. Or this case a wild Illume chase.

"You ain't gotta remind me, mate, I know you're fit as a Mallee bull. But you ain't gonna get too far in the contest wasting time playing paddy cake with that one," said Max. He then looked off in the direction of the Forest into which he had seen Creed disappear. "Not a bad imitation of the Illume, though, if I do say so myself?"

The pleased look on his face was a far cry from the sullen expression he spied glancing back at Jacob.

"What is it? You look like you've seen a ghost in a marble orchard."

It was then Jacob felt a surge of panic rush through him. Did Max know? Of course not—at least Jacob didn't think so. No way Max would continue acting like nothing was amiss while being in the know of some fantastic rumor like the one Creed had unleashed just moments ago, especially when that rumor concerned Max's best friend. That would all change now, wouldn't it? The friendship, that is. If anything, this would instantly make him the enemy in his friend's eyes—in the eyes of everyone at Havenhid, in fact—faster than Max could mutter "Crikey Moses!" If not enemy, what else could someone revealed to be the son of a Fallen—a Weed—be looked upon as? Certainly not friend. Not any longer.

"Let's go before Creed has another go at the Illume," said Jacob.

Max grabbed hold of him as he attempted to brush past.

"Cool your heels a sec!" said Max. "Now, something's eating at you—and pretty good from the crazy look in your eyes—and I want to know what it is."

"I don't want to talk about," argued Jacob irritably. "Not now, at least."

"Might as well spill it," pressed Max. "Otherwise you know I'll rifle through your mind just like I do your drawers when I'm in need of some clean socks and find out for myself."

It was the rare moment Jacob resented the powers afforded Nephilim. This was one of those moments. At least now, however, he knew why his socks had a habit of disappearing on him.

"Creed just told me he knows who my father is," blurted Jacob suddenly. If he was going to remove the bandage, he was going to do it quickly rather than suffer a slow pull.

"Crikey Moses!" replied Max, just as Jacob predicted he would. "Well, that's a good thing, isn't it?" Max's brief smile was quick to fade. "Isn't it?"

"He said it's a Fallen," answered Jacob with a meek voice.

Max's first response was to retreat from Jacob a step. A grave look surfaced in his face and for a moment Jacob wondered whether a renewed round of fisticuffs was about to take place then and there.

"You sure 'bout this?" asked Max finally.

"Creed all but dared me to ask his father about it," replied Jacob. "He said Gotham's known the whole time and made the Guides promise to keep it quiet."

Max took silent for a moment or two looking as grim as one could possibly look when he suddenly cracked a smile and let loose a whopper of a whooping chuckle. "And you believed him?"

It wasn't quite the response Jacob expected from Max.

"What do you mean do I believe him?" asked Jacob. "Why would he lie about something like that?"

"For starters, he's a putrescent mass of walking toad vomit," said Max, a colorful statement of character if ever there was one, and one Jacob couldn't argue against. "Don't you think it's a bit odd he drops this bombshell on you out here in the middle of the Forest? Why not before the competition. Why not scream it from the middle of the arena so everyone knows? Let's face it, mate, 'ol toad vomit can't stand the sight of you. And you know as well as I do if what he said was true he'd make sure to get the most mileage he could out of such a disgusting and damaging rumor."

Jacob thought about it for a moment, and to his surprise it made sense. "You really think?"

"Let me ask you...do you really think Gotham—or Anahel, for that matter—would keep something as important as who your father is from you...no matter who it might be?" asked Max. "Better yet, you really think the son of a Fallen would be allowed into Eden, that is besides Gotham's, which of itself was quite a miracle?"

Much to his reassurance, Jacob found he couldn't argue against the questions Max was posing. Of course Gotham wouldn't deceive him in such an unforgivable way, and no way would Anahel, or Johiel for that matter, have allowed a Weed to pass through Eden's Gate. And as Jacob came to realize this, he found himself taking his first easy breath since Creed stole it from him. With it came a soothing calm, which began to trickle up around him as if he was slowly being immersed in a vat of liquid relief. The comforting feeling lasted as briefly as it arrived when it was quickly replaced by a sudden resurgence of anger.

"Why would Creed mess with my mind like that?" he found himself asking once again.

"You have to ask…he's the north end of a south-bound camel; a canker sore that won't go away. More likely he's scraping the muck to throw you off your game in this last competition. Looks like he did a pretty good job, too, if you ask me."

Max's reply at once served to add fuel to an already burning fire igniting inside Jacob; the flames from which could be seen swirling inside Jacob's brooding eyes.

"When I find him…"

"A word of advice," offered Max. "You don't put a wank stain like Creed in his place by swapping haymakers. You do it by hitting him where it hurts—his ego."

"Any suggestions on how I go about doing that in short order?"

"For starters, we can make sure he doesn't get a hold of that Illume."

Easier said than done, Jacob thought to himself.

"Man, I can't stand that guy," he muttered while staring off into the Forest.

Max came up behind him and gave Jacob's shoulder a strong but friendly squeeze.

"Well, if it's any comfort to you, my guess is he's not too fond of you either," said Max. "A waste, really, if you ask me. Here Anahel should have just sent the two of you out here alone to fight it out and see which one came back with the other stuffed in this black sack instead of chasing some old bird."

Whether it was imagining such a thing or hearing it through Max's thick Australian accent was enough to crack Jacob's furrowing frown, and the two boys were soon sharing a hearty laugh over the idea.

"So where's Michael and Isaac?" asked Jacob.

"Scouring the trees closest to the mountain cliffs last I saw," said Max, motioning to the West with a nod of his head. "Looks like you're the only one of us who's had any luck spotting the Illume so far. Gorgeous bird from what I saw of it. Too bad Creed had to ruin your chance of catching it. Goodness only knows where it's flown off to now. The Forest's a big place. We could spend an entire day looking and not come close to finding it again, never mind in the short amount of time we have left."

Jacob had an idea it might not be as impossible a task as Max made it out to be. "I have a hunch it hasn't gone far. Care to come see if I'm right?"

Max arched an eyebrow while tilting his head with curiosity. "You want to share with me where you think it's gone? Have you forgotten we're in competition against one another?"

"Gotham told me before the contest the secret to catching the Illume is to not hunt it. After seeing it in action I see he's right," said Jacob. "I think I have an idea on how to catch it. But it requires the help of another person. Especially someone with your undeniable gift of bird-calling. You game?"

Max gave Jacob a half-cocked look. "And what do we do if we catch it?"

"What do you mean?"

"Who gets the credit?"

"Seeing as we're working as a team, it only makes sense that we share it equally," answered Jacob. "Of course, that would also mean you most likely would receive an equal share of hatred and disdain from Creed that he has so far reserved solely for me when he comes up empty-handed."

From the smile that slowly stretched itself across his face, the last point seemed to be the selling point for Max. "Partners it is then, mate!"

They clasp hands to seal their pact before Jacob led the way through the Forest toward the gentle sound of the gurgling stream.

~ ~ ~

Jacob and Max kept themselves crouched low, wading quietly through the cover of fern and lilies of the valleys and sweet after deaths, which gave the air all around a sweet vanilla scent. Sure enough, just beyond the brush, the exotic creature had returned to the spot upon the boulder near the stream where Jacob had gotten his first look of the bird up close. If the Illume had been left skittish or frightened by the harrowing chase through the treetops only a short time ago, it didn't show it. Instead, it stood staring into the water with visible fascination, just as before, tilting its head from one side to the other in a curious manner.

"What's it doing?" whispered Max.

"I'm not sure, but I think it's fallen in love," answered Jacob.

An incredulous look came over Max. "In love? With what, a trout?"

"Don't you remember what Anahel said back at the arena? Today is the day the Illume comes out in search of a mate. Only thing is, there are no other Illumes. Just this one."

"Yeah, so?"

"Are you blind? Obviously it sees itself in the water. Only it has no idea it's staring at its own reflection. It thinks it's finally found another Illume after all this time," said Jacob. "And from the looks of it, I think it's quite taken with itself."

"And I thought I was narcissistic," remarked Max. He watched quietly as the Illume poked at the water with its beak when its pleading calls went unanswered. "Can't help but feel a little sorry for the bugger. Nothing should have to spend life all alone."

"Maybe it doesn't have to," muttered Jacob.

"What are you talking about?"

"A way to catch the Illume and bring it back to Havenhid," Jacob replied. "But it's going to require from you more than just copying a bird call."

At first, Max wasn't following what Jacob was saying, but then he caught the devious gleam in Jacob's eyes when they shifted his way and he quickly realized Jacob's plan. "You're joking right?"

"And make it good," said Jacob, with a teasing wink. "We'll only have a short amount of time before the others hear and head this way."

Before Max could object, Jacob slunk off through the thicket. He crawled around along the ground on his belly until he was positioned a short distance downstream behind the bird and waited. At first nothing happened. The Illume continued to be spellbound by the floating reflection. And then, just when Jacob began to feel the growing twinges of impatience, there came a series of quivering chirps. The Illume appeared to be taken by surprise by the sound and, for the first time, its eyes left the water and directed themselves to the bushes where the familiar call came. Again came a morse code of chirps, and this time the Illume answered with a welcoming, yet questioning, reply. It then craned its neck forward with curiosity when there came a rustling sound followed by visible movement from inside the bushes where Max had remained hidden. What emerged from within the brush, however, was not Max—at least not in his normal everyday human skin—but another Illume.

The seemingly coy and unresponsive reflection in the water was quickly forgotten by its owner who became immediately taken with Max's mimicry. Finally, the Illume had found that which it had searched the Forest through and through, year after year, without success. And in its happiness, the Illume released a chorus of high-pitched shrieks and loud pinging clicking to echo through the trees. Jacob knew it was only a matter of time before they reached the ears of Creed and the other boys he was competing against, and so with his sack in hand, he crept forward. His hands and feet made not a sound in their stealthy movements across the ground, but Max was doing such a good job enticing the mating dance now being performed by the Illume that Jacob wondered whether the effort he was putting into sneaking up on the bird was even necessary.

Closer and closer he moved in until he managed to be just a few short feet from the feathery prize. Then, just as he was about to pounce on the Illume and scoop it into his waiting sack, Isaac came swooping down from out of nowhere and dove onto Max. The attack startled the Illume. It quickly spun its head around and, when it saw Jacob sneaking up from behind, it parted wide its beak and let loose an angry shrill of a scream. Jacob knew at that moment he had lost his one sure chance, but nonetheless he lunged forward with the empty possibility luck might somehow guide the bird into his sack. As expected, the Illume bolted from reach and briskly disappeared into the cover of the trees leaving Jacob splashing about face-down in the stream.

"I got it," Isaac cried out victoriously while continuing to wrestle his sack over his struggling capture.

"Congratulations, Isaac," Jacob sputtered sourly. "You've managed to catch Max."

Isaac appeared dumbfounded at first until he looked down and saw there was nothing bird-like about the flailing arms and kicking legs he was in the midst of wrestling.

"What's this?" he begged incredulously while revealing what at first looked to be a bowling ball stuffed inside his sack only to come nose to nose with Max's scowling face and not the Illume he swore he dive-bombed.

"You arse burp!" scolded Max.

"But I saw it…it was the Illume," Isaac vigorously defended himself when it suddenly dawned on him he wasn't hallucinating and that Max, in fact, was the Illume. "Why would you trick me like that?"

"I wasn't trying to trick you, Einstein."

Somewhere hiding amongst the trees, the squawking of the one true Illume reverberated loudly. Sure enough, its cries found Creed, who Jacob spied sailing past overhead in quick pursuit.

"Let's go…hurry," barked Jacob, jumping to his feet. He tore his way across the Forest floor at a blinding pace in the direction of the bird's echoing shrieks, while Max and Isaac shadowed him from above.

~ ~ ~

"Comin' yer way," Jacob suddenly heard Max call down to him.

However, the warning came too late. The Illume buzzed past him in a fluttering blur before he could even think of making a catch for it. And coming straight toward him hot on the bird's tail was not only Creed, but now Michael, who had honed in on the commotion and joined in the chase. So swiftly they flew that Jacob barely managed to clear himself from out of their flight path, but not quick enough to escape the reach of Creed's foot, which purposely managed to clip him in the chest with a painful kick in passing, sending him to the ground.

The ruckus from the brawl that followed decimated fully whatever semblance of peace resided within the Forest. Now there were five Nephilim in fiery pursuit of the Illume which eventually took refuge in the foliage of a Guelder-rose shrub where Jacob and Max followed after it. With their sacks in hand they were about to close in on the Illume when Creed, Michael and Isaac found them.

"Time to end this silly game," announced Creed.

He strode forward revealing in his flexing of muscle his every intention of taking custody of the bird no matter who attempted to stand in his way. Both Jacob and Max immediately accepted the challenge.

"No way, it's ours!" Jacob stated forcefully.

"Until it's bagged, it's nobody's," replied Creed.

"Then considered it bagged!" countered Max, firming an unintimidated stance between the brush where the Illume remained in hiding and Creed. "And not by you, Maggert."

Creed's face tightened with disdain and he gave Max a forceful shove out of his way. If, however, he thought Max was a pushover like most other boys he crossed paths with, he had another thing coming.

"You'd do your health good keeping your paws off me, I can tell ya that," said Max with a tell-tale gleam in his eyes which conveyed in no uncertain terms the message that he was not one to shy away from a fight. "You see, unlike the rest of these blokes I don't give two blind mullets who your father is. You want to have a blue, then give it a burl. Fair warning, though: I'll do better than making you kiss a tree like my mate Jacob did with you a little bit ago, I'll put you clean through it!"

Creed didn't look put-off by Max's even-tempered threat. In fact, he seemed eager to wager a bet against it, and Max was more than willing to prove he meant what he said. Yet before either could take the first swing, an ear-piercing cry came from the Illume. Only it was like no other sound any of the boys had heard come from the bird in their fruitless pursuit of the creature. There was an oddly unpleasant weight to it. And at first the group of boys questioned if the sound came from the Illume, or something entirely different hidden inside the bush.

Then the shrub began to shake violently and its branches snapped and cracked like kindling before falling still again. An eery silence followed and a guarded curiosity shared by the boys made them lean in for a closer look when suddenly the massive head of a fiendish beast revealed itself in an unsuspecting lunge from the foliage of the bush and let loose an even deeper bone-chilling roar. In an instant, the bush was reduced to an explosion of leaves and twigs left to scatter on the ground and in its place was a horrid creature of incredible size—nothing like the charming, delicate bird seen preening in front of its reflection earlier by the stream—with the body of what appeared to be that of a dragon fitted with the tail of a scorpion. And when the beast unfurled and began beating with tremendous, furious strength what looked to be a pair of giant, leathery wings better suited for a tremendously over-sized bat, the color drained from Max's face, and with a disbelieving look settling in his eyes he managed to find his tongue to mutter quietly to himself, "Stone the crows!"

CHAPTER THIRTY

BAGGING A BEAST

"What the heck is that thing?" shrieked Michael.

"Believe it or not, I think it's the Illume," answered Jacob who eyed the familiar headdress adorning the front of the hideous creature's head. Only instead of a crown of delicate white feathers encircling a larger dazzling blue one, they were razor-sharp spikes encircling a single threatening horn.

The boys looked at the oversized sacks clutched in their hands, then at each other and from the same confused look they exchanged it was clear they shared the same thought: Even if they managed to sew all five sacks together to make one giant sack, it still wouldn't be enough to contain even half the creature. They had little time to ponder such things, however, as the beast began to advance on them. Suddenly, the thing they had chased after so fervently through the Forest sent them slowly retreating away from it in unison, even Creed, though he managed to regain the courage to steel himself by the eighth step when he remembered he was not completely helpless.

"Creed's got a sword!" Isaac pointed out to everyone, when Creed drew his weapon.

"And I'll bet right about now you wish you brought yours," Creed remarked smugly.

"You dirty cheat! You know swords aren't allowed in this competition," charged Max.

Creed appeared flattered by the accusation. "You call it cheating, I call it playing it smart. If you want to have a go at that thing with your bare hands choirboy, by all means have at it, and we'll see where your honesty—not to mention stupidity—lands you."

The Illume, however, did not take kindly to the sight of the sword. It drew back its head and let loose a screeching cry that made the trees tremble and the ground quiver. And when Creed answered the cry by raising his sword and taking the first couple steps toward it, the Illume narrowed its reptilian-like eyes on the boy and dug its claws into the earth. Arching its back, the Illume opened its mouth to reveal an igneous glow deep in its gullet before it breathed forth an incinerating inferno of blue fire. Creed, having the quick reflexes he had, managed to dive out of the way just in time to escape being grilled alive by the fireball as it roared past him and consumed fully a grouping of dogwood saplings.

"If you got any ideas on where to go from here, mate, now would be the time to voice them," Max said to Jacob as the two looked on and watched the young trees burn.

"I just need to somehow get on its back and get this sack over its head," said Jacob.

"Oh, is that all?" replied Max sarcastically. "And how do you suppose you're going to accomplish that minor task?"

"Gotham said the only way to come up on the Illume is from behind. That's its blind spot. But I'm going to need you to distract it."

"I've got a better idea. How 'bout you keep from being turned into a charbroiled kabob and I'll risk venturing into the blind spot?"

"I would if I had wings to protect me," answered Jacob, to which Max muttered "Curses!" under his breath knowing he couldn't argue the point further.

The others watched curiously as Max made his way willingly in front of the Illume. The beast lunged several times at him. Each time, the blue horn protruding from its head was thrust ever closer in his direction, and each time Max managed to dodge its pointed aim until the Illume gave up in frustration and finally unleashed its fire. Unable to escape the fireball in time, Max brought his right wing in front of him like a shield to protect himself from the full intensity of the flames that engulfed him with a fiery fury. The impact left his wing smoldering, yet singed not a single plume, which only made the Illume screech louder with rage.

It proved to be a difficult and exhausting dance for Max, dodging the combination of fire and tusk looking to impale him, but he continued as best he could all the while keeping an eye on Jacob, who slunk back unnoticed behind the beast. The Illume's own keen eyes, however, caught Max's drifting gaze and just when Jacob was about to make his move, the creature spun its head around and spied the Nephilim attempting to sneak up on it. It bellowed loudly and drew back its tail. Jacob dove to the ground as the deadly tail made a dangerous swipe at him and slammed into a nearby tree severely splintering the trunk with the might of its blow. Jacob had barely managed to catch his breath when the Illume's tail came at him again, only this time it was the six-foot venomous stinger which took aim.

The other Nephilim watched in horror as a furious blur of blows rained down on Jacob one after the other. Each one narrowly missed Jacob, who writhed frantically about on the ground like an unearthed earthworm. Never before had the nimbleness of his reflexes been put to the test than at that moment, and through all the rolling and tucking and dodging and scrambling he did in his desperate turn to steer clear of the stinger, Jacob couldn't help but wonder was all this really happening as he was seeing it? Was the beautifully delicate bird he first saw by the stream and this hideous fire-breathing beast actually one and the same?

And how, he wondered, could Anahel and the other Guides have sent the five of them out in pursuit of something as dangerous and deadly as they now found themselves facing? Especially without any warning to prepare their naïve selves for what awaited them in the Forest?

Such thoughts, themselves, proved dangerous as the final jab by the Illume narrowly missed Jacob's skull. And as Jacob looked out of the corner of his wide-fixed eyes at the savage stinger impaled fully into the ground where he had a second ago laid exposed, his jaw tightened with anger when he realized he had narrowly avoided his end.

~ ~ ~

It's now or never, thought Jacob, refusing to become skewered by this hellish, unrelenting monster. He quickly leapt to his feet and was about to make a running jump at the creature when the tail dislodged itself from the dirt. This time, however, it did not miss its mark as it whipped itself toward Jacob. The glancing blow it leveled delivered an unwelcome flash of pain while sending Jacob sailing through the air. The hull of a nearby giant tree which abruptly ended Jacob's brief moment of flight caused an altogether different, and arguably worse, suffering.

What happened next was lost in a hazy blur. As Jacob fought to recover from having the breath instantly and completely swiped from his body while writhing about on all fours at the tree's roots, he heard the Illume's cry pierce the Forest. Then came the loud pronounced beating of leathery, webbed wings followed by several pairs of feet running and more wings—softer Nephilim wings.

"You okay, Jacob?"

It was Max's voice. And even if he wasn't sure, Jacob could see the familiar sneakered feet standing next to him. He managed to look up and sure enough it was his friend and partner in this most unpleasant hunt helping him to get to his feet.

"It's flown off," said Max, pointing off into the distance. "Creed, Michael and Isaac have gone after it. We've got to get it in gear if we want to catch up. No way am I losing to one of them after all this."

Jacob nodded and motioned for him to go on ahead. "I'm right behind you."

"Come on, hurry!"

As Max took to the air and disappeared into the trees, Jacob forced himself to his legs. He remained somewhat dazed, but it would take more than a blow from the Illume's tail to sideline him. Focusing on the direction Max had flown off, he knew he was going to require more than the speed he could muster from his feet to get back into the game. So he whispered for his horse and amazingly the Snowdrift emerged from the Forest behind him as if by magic.

"I'm counting on you," Jacob spoke quietly into the horse's ear once he had mounted its back. As if to answer, the horse bolted forward with a force that nearly sent Jacob backward and once more to the ground. Yet Jacob managed to hold tight and, in that instance, he was met with a spellbinding intensity rivaling any amusement park thrill ride as the Snowdrift lived up to its name by maneuvering its way through an obstacle of trees with near-miss swiftness and precision. At times it felt to Jacob as if he was astride a squall whose power he could feel surging between his legs was both unnerving and exhilarating at the same time.

In a matter of moments, Max and the others were in eyesight, and ahead of them steaming through the Forest like a rabid banshee was the Illume. Jacob gently nudged the Snowdrift with his knees and, remarkably, the freight train made of flesh of bone upon which he rode went faster still. The horse nudged its way ahead of the flying teens one by one until Jacob found himself neck and neck with Creed, who scowled at the sight.

Through the trees, Jacob could make out the silhouette of a looming mountain fading against the twilight sky. The light from the sun was nearly extinguished and soon the sound of the trumpet would send forth a wail beckoning their return to Havenhid and, more importantly, the end of the hunt of which no one yet could claim victory.

The boys closed in on the Illume, even as it did its best to lose its pursuers by swerving and weaving a difficult trail to follow through the Forest. If that wasn't difficult enough, Creed, unable to muster the sizable lead in front of Jacob he would have liked, turned to his book of dirty play by dive bombing his competitor in an attempt to knock him off his steed. Where the Illume proved masterful at navigating the unseen twists and turns of the Forest before it was too late, the Snowdrift was unmatched. And with a little mindful jockeying, it led Creed straight into the path of low wayward branch and stilled him instantly— and from an onlooker's point of view, painfully—from the chase.

~ ~ ~

They emerged from the thick of the Forest and found themselves nearing the foot of a great mountain. It was shaped by steep, jagged grey cliffs which held the black shadowy openings of many caverns and caves high up where the Illume was believed to live. Jacob knew at any moment the creature would turn skyward to retreat into the safety of whichever crevice it called home and once there it would be impossible to capture.

With the Snowdrift still in fierce pursuit, Jacob rose up to stand on the horse's back and steadied himself with several deep breaths. Then, when he was certain the distance between the Illume and himself could not possibly be closed any further, Jacob clenched his jaw and made a blind leap at the beast. It was an astounding jump; one that could only be managed by someone with angel blood pumping through his veins coupled with an unbridled determination to see through this feat. In an instant, the course-haired hide of the Snowdrift beneath Jacob was replaced by the hard, rough scales of the Illume. Upon feeling the unwelcome rider on its back, the creature immediately took to the ground. There it bucked and lunged and jerked like a rodeo bull in an attempt to rid itself of the strong hold Jacob had on it. It howled with anger, beat its wings and sent a plume of billowing flames into the darkening sky. Jacob was unmovable. Like a tick attached to a dog, he held tight. Nothing was going to kick him free until he got his bag secured over the beast's head.

Then Jacob spied once more the infernal tail. It was whipping about wildly in the air behind him, and the stinger was moving uncomfortably closer. Jacob couldn't help but wonder if the Illume would actually risk stabbing itself in a blind, desperate attempt to stick him. Luckily, he didn't have to wait and find out, for Max suddenly swooped down and to Jacob's shock threw himself onto the tail and buckled in for what he knew would be a wildly unpleasant ride.

"Get going, QUICK!" Max cried out as the tail immediately flailed about with violent jerks in every direction in an attempt to flick him free.

As fast as he could scramble, Jacob scaled the Illume's back toward its head. The creature screamed, threw more fire and whipped its head in the same manner as its tail. It was all Jacob could do to not be flung free and still make a grab for his sack. Somehow he managed, and in that moment he threw all caution to the wind and worked the black sack over the top of the Illume's head. He struggled with every bit of strength he had to maneuver it over the eyes which blazed with a burning anger, and yet the moment those hate-filled eyes were covered by the velvety blackness of the sack the bottom fell out from under Jacob. He hit the ground, and when he looked about frantically for the creature it was nowhere to be seen.

Vanished.

Disappeared.

All in an instant.

Glancing over his shoulder, he saw Max also sprawled out face-down on the ground. The tail he had been hugging for dear life had also dematerialized. Jacob then looked to the black bag grasped in the tight clutches of his fingers and he could see it was not empty. Climbing to his knees with his face dripping with sweat and smudged with dirt and soot, he held up the sack while cautiously keeping it at an arm's length distance. It bulged and squirmed with some living thing and at first he questioned what it could possibly be, though he dared not peek inside to find out. And then, from inside he heard a familiar quiet clucking coo.

It was the Illume.

~ ~ ~

Upon their return to Havenhid, none of the five shell-shocked boys carried the expected glee of victory as they stood beneath the great arched doorway leading to the Hall of the Light where they found their classmates and fathers gathered beneath a constellation of soft firelight patiently awaiting the group's return.

"There you are. Come forward, if you will," Anahel's voice echoed enthusiastically through the great Hall at the sight of the returning competitors.

Looking haggard and worn from a long day that had tasked in good measure their endurance and strength both physically and mentally, the five boys made their way with unhurried and somewhat pained steps down an aisle formed by a gradual parting of the way by those assembled in the Hall. Jacob gave a casual glance around, his face dirt-smudged and singed from the Illume's fiery breath, and through the sea of expectant faces he passed he found the welcoming sight of Gotham standing amongst them. Gotham offered a faint smile and nod and it pleased Jacob to see the angel had stayed true to his word and awaited his return. Standing at the front of the room was Anahel looking august and noble as ever in white. He was flanked from behind by the Guides: Zuriel and Thaniel on one side and Eksel and Damiel on the other.

"I'm unsure whether the notable lack of excitement exuding from each of you means you were unsuccessful in your quest, or that you have surrendered yourselves to the clutches of fatigue," Anahel, motioning the boys forward to line themselves before him, wondered aloud. "Have all of you returned to Havenhid with empty sacks? Or does one amongst you carry inside it the Illume?"

No one answered at first, and then Jacob stepped forward. "One does," he replied.

He held out his black sack which squirmed about in his grip and Anahel, who had secretly hoped for the revealed outcome, did the best he could to keep the corners of his mouth from curling upward in a pleased manner as he took the sack from Jacob. What followed next was a collective holding of breath by Jacob and the other four boys when Anahel gently reached inside the sack and removed from it a furious fluttering of wings. Yet upon looking into the face of the angel in whose grip it was held and the intense look coming from the golden eyes greeting it, the Illume instantly grew calm and settled.

"A rare pearl hidden inside the lustered shell that is Eden, if ever there was one," Anahel voiced softly. "I can recall the small number of times I have been gifted to look upon the beauty of this creature, and it gives me great pleasure to do so once more."

He then held his hand up so all the eyes straining for a glimpse of the mythic bird could see it. Beneath the moonlit-filled night filtering down through the canopy of branches that shaped the ceiling which on this night remained unfolded to the darkness outside, the Illume's feathers gleamed with the sheen of a rippling iridescence bringing forth a wave of admiring coos from those who looked upon it. All, that is, except Jacob, Max, Creed, Issac and Michael who still carried with them the fresh memory of the fire-breathing beast that somehow resided within the deceptive hide of the delicate and beautiful creation now before them. Their guarded gazes moved as one, following the Illume sitting tame and without any sign of threat—or ability to breath forth an inferno—on Anahel's hand as it was set on a nearby waiting perch.

"By the looks of you, I take it the quest to capture the Illume was not as easy a task as you presumed it would be," said Anahel, turning his attention back to the boys, and more precisely Creed. "An unusual creature, the Illume. As wondrous as it is inscrutable. And, despite what you might have seen today in your pursuit of it, quite friendly, once it gets to know you. If its existence serves to prove anything, it is that nothing is as it first appears."

"You could bloody well say that again!" Jacob heard Max utter under his breath.

"To you Jacob, I say a job well done," continued Anahel. "By facing the heat of the Illume's breath—without wings, I might add— you have shown a commendable strength of courage that resides inside you."

The angel's encouraging words warmed Jacob, even as he felt Creed's eyes fixed contemptibly on him.

"Thank you," said Jacob. "But I can't take full credit for capturing the Illume."

Anahel turned a quizzical look on the boy. "Oh?"

"Max here is just as responsible, if not more. It was he who faced down the Illume and dodged its flames."

Anahel's gaze fell onto Max. "This is true?"

"You can say I'll never look at snags on the barbie the same way after today, but yes," answered Max. "It was Jacob, though, who actually jumped on the back of the Illume and managed to get the sack over its head. Nearly got turned into a shish kebab for the trouble, I might add."

"I see," said Anahel, his studying gaze shifting between the two boys before him. "This would be the first time I've seen any Fledglings work together instead of fiercely battling one another in pursuit of the Illume. And now, instead of insisting your own rightful claim to the prestigious victory that its capture brings, you choose to argue a case in favor of the other's heroic role."

Anahel stood quietly for a moment staring down at the two boys and before long a smile broke his stoic look. "Suddenly, the stunning presence of the Illume in this great Hall is momentarily dimmed, and rightly so."

He turned his back on the boys and crossed to where the luminous bird rested quietly on its perch. A curious silence settled itself upon the room as Anahel brought a hand to the exotic headdress of feathers sprouting from the Illume's head. Anahel took hold of the vibrant solitary blue feather nestled in the center of the crown of white plumes and gave it a gentle pluck. The Illume squawked calmly but didn't seem to mind surrendering the quill, the end from which held a brilliant blue flame. Anahel then walked the feather with its flaming tip back to where the five boys stood and instructed Max to hold out his right arm with the inside of his wrist turned upward. Max did as he was told. If he was nervous about what was to come next, he did well in veiling it, especially as he watched the fiery feather make its way closer to his exposed skin. Jacob felt his friend standing beside him tense up before quickly relaxing again. Then, with Max making not so much as a whimper, Jacob watched with equal parts curiosity and wonder as the burning tip of the feather inscribed upon his wrist, like a pen to paper, a strange and unusual glyph of angelic letters and symbols.

When he had finished, Anahel turned to Jacob and asked for his arm as well. Jacob clenched hard his teeth and braced himself for the expected pain as the tip of the quill neared his skin, only there was none. Instead of an expected searing heat, the flame that touched his flesh was strangely cold and tingly. And even if there had been pain, it likely would have been easily ignored as Jacob's attention remained fixed solely on the silver dollar-sized marking he watched being etched into his skin as it glowed fiery like hot embers left to smolder amongst the ashes inside a hearth when a fire is left to go out.

"You now join a rare handful of Nephilim who came before and stood where you are now to carry the sigil of the Illume," said Anahel, once he had finished. "Wear it as the prestigious mark of honor it is, though without being too prideful, even as you one day, perhaps, may discover it to be a mark of exemption."

Without expounding upon the meaning of his words, he then turned his sights on the rest of the room.

"To the other Nephilim, I tell you there is at hand for you an even greater honor on this night—far greater than any sigil. It is by no accident or happenstance you find yourself in this heavenly paradise called Eden. You are not just offspring of the angelic order, nor are you mortal gods, winged and bestowed the exceptional power of some mythic entity. Your fathers brought you here for one purpose and one purpose only: to serve as they serve. We—the Guides and myself—have spent the past year readying you for that service. There is still much work to be done."

Anahel's face suddenly took a grim turn, as did his voice. "Now it is time for us to put aside for a moment the exhilaration of today's games. As I made mention at Lions Bite this afternoon, Illumination is more than just a day of competition. It more importantly begins the next stage of your training that, over the next several months, will focus on the true purpose of what has brought you here to Eden, and for which we've gathered together in this illustrious Hall this night."

~ ~ ~

A quiet descended upon the Hall of Light from which a pin could be heard to fall upon the floor. Only, in this case, it wasn't a pin, but a feather—the same feather Anahel had earlier plucked from the Illume which he suddenly released from his hold with a casual yet deliberate toss of his hand. The feather, with the tip of its quill still carrying its blue flame, landed like a dart nearby, embedding itself firmly in the floor. The flame flickered once, twice, then took to the fuel that was the wood flooring created by the limbs of the trees in whose arms the Hall and all of Havenhid was cradled. With ever-widening eyes, Jacob and the other boys watched with growing alarm as the flame became flames and slowly began to spread like a blue oil slick eating its way outward in all directions and leaving in its wake an empty void where the floor seconds earlier had been. The boys' first inclination was to step fast and quick out of the way of the blue fire approaching where they stood before the floor disappeared from under their feet, but Anahel—sensing the Fledglings skittishness—told them in a calm, unalarmed voice to hold still to where they were. Reluctantly, they did as instructed and watched the blue approaching fire without so much as taking a breath as the flames passed beneath their feet, and only when they realized they had escaped both burning to their selves and the imminent fall for which they all braced themselves for when the floor was suddenly no longer beneath them did they signal their immediate relief with one collective sigh.

"The forces of Darkness and man have been entangled in a lengthy and contentious struggle against one another for countless eons," came Anahel's voice once again. "Their mutual hatred, not to mention twisted passion for one another began the day mortal breath made itself heard within the boundaries of this Garden. Together they have weaved a patchwork of history like some unsightly homespun quilt and assembled a most grotesque scrapbook of memories the most dysfunctional family forced to exist under one roof would be hard-pressed to rival in all its mangled and maligned acts."

The off-putting weirdness that came from standing upon nothing was short-lived when the window-like void, which offered the boys a view of the garden grounds beneath them, was suddenly filled with a swirl of color shades and shadowy shapes that gradually came together to form images. Suddenly, it was as if the Nephilim found themselves standing upon a massive television screen as a flash of channels passed beneath their feet. Only the channels were connected to specific moments long past reflecting images of persons and places and events made familiar in history books—dark horrible moments history would likely rather cast from its memory than relive. Instantly, a gloom found its way into the Hall and surrounded the boys as they were reminded of mankind's torrid reign by the images that unfolded themselves in a barrage of unpleasantness: reflections of unspeakable crimes man would mimic with greater flare and design to add to the blood first spilled during Cain and Abel's fatal spat; not to mention resurrected images of death and suffering birthed from the countless unleashed wars, from ancient battles fought with sword and shield to the modern-day conveniences of carrying out wide-spread horror with convenient aplomb through body-stilling chemicals and disintegrating flashes of atomic annihilation.

"Man was certain it had finally defeated its dark enemy in the end days of the second world war, and in many cases he was right to think so," Anahel's voice sounded over the images playing out across the floor of the Hall. "However, the evil which had schemed to bring about so much ruin had simply retreated back into the darkness it knew so well to nurse its wounds, leaving the victors to celebrate their conquest amid the litter of ticker tape parades and plentiful flow of fermented spirits. And when the streets had been swept clean of confetti and the last bottle of champagne had been swilled, and when the memory of the battle just fought had become just that—a memory shrugged off into the hands of history's curators in favor of pursuits of happiness stolen by such a dark chapter—evil finally emerged from its den, like a bear awakening from hibernation to meet the spring. Only this time it did not come with a march of troops or the call to battle blaring from a trumpet; this time, rather, it was on tip-toes, like a cat burglar searching for an unlocked back door through which to enter to commit its next caper. And find it, it did."

Anahel became abruptly quiet, as if his tongue—or will to use it—had suddenly failed him, and the look held in his face suddenly became even heavier than the solemn look caused by the onslaught of disturbing images being regurgitated in the parade of scenes playing out at his feet.

"Even those of us who know intimately the true depths of evil that is the Darkness were caught off guard by where it would wade next," said Anahel when he finally found his voice again. "For the door it chose opened to a vault filled with a far more precious cache of treasure than money or jewels; it in fact led to the one place long shunned, violently even, by the Darkness: the sanctuary of the holy church built by God. There it dwelled not in shadow, but light; not the true Light mind you, but a false light known to often catch the eyes of man; as when a glint of pyrite is spied reflecting beneath the waters of a mountain stream. It dressed itself in the robes and collars of the righteous men of the church like the fabled wolf stepping amongst the sheep and, with its sights aimed at the most vulnerable and precious of the flock, it set about to do to the human soul what the bullets and bombs of war does to flesh."

As Anahel spoke, the images of countless priests and clerics flashed by in an endless parade of faces, none of which held an outward or even noticeable blemish of evil. In fact, they appeared quite pleasant, decent and moral—virtuous even—which made the sight of them all the more uncomfortable to Jacob and the other boys to take in knowing what lurked somewhere beneath the flesh and bone and staring out from behind what appeared to be kind eyes was anything but.

"The collateral damage was immeasurable," continued Anahel. "Mankind has long struggled to build with his faith a solid enough foundation upon which to stand, and slowly and surely the bedrock of this credence began to crumble beneath his feet in light of the unspeakable crimes and scandals perpetrated by these cassocked wolves. Pride, greed and narcissism dug its roots into the rubble like some fast-growing, invasive vine. And when faith was depleted, and the Light nothing more than a dim flicker seen in a dying candle, the Darkness moved in to steal once and for all the victory man had briefly enjoyed over it."

Anahel's voice was suddenly smothered silent by the rumbling of a massive fireball that exploded upwards from within the floor, and for a terrifying moment Jacob and the other boys feared the Hall of Light and all of Havenhid might instantly be incinerated by the inferno. The flames then quickly retreated, and when they did a most unsettling image revealed itself in the shape of the centuries-old Notre-Dame cathedral in Paris being choked by a billowing, unforgiving smoke while a fury of flames worked in concert to overwhelm the celebrated shrine in all its Gothic and stained-glass beauty and bring her to a slow and agonizing end while the whole of the world looked on in horror.

Jacob recalled vividly the day just a few years earlier when the same unsightly scene brought his grandmother to tears as it unfolded as a breaking news alert on TV. The destructive fire had been ruled an unfortunate accident, but the images upon the floor pointedly suggested otherwise as they quickly morphed into the shapes of numerous other houses of worship throughout the world that had been left horribly disfigured through wanton acts of vandalism, looting, and outright desecration.

~ ~ ~

"Alas, my words should carry no surprising revelation when I tell you days much darker than what you've just seen reside before us," said Anahel, sounding glum and disheartened when the ruins of the church faded away. "And it is in preparation of such turbulent and tempestuous times in the dawn of days soon to come that you—and those before you—have come to be gathered here. Let it also be known, in the same way Heaven has been nurturing and growing itself an army in which each of you have lent yourself to its ever-strengthening ranks, so, too, has another army quietly taken shape."

The unnamed army Anahel spoke of revealed itself inside the frame of a lone scene showing a barren swath of desert landscape that slowly unfolded itself upon the floor at the Nephilim' feet where a highly regimented flurry of activity was taking place in the dusty parched heat. Dozens of what at first appeared to be soldiers of some foreign army were seen making their way one by one through a grueling, makeshift military-type obstacle course. Upon closer look, the Nephilim could see these soldiers were not made up of young men, but young boys—far younger, in fact, than even themselves—dressed in a uniform of drab gray and black head coverings. At first, the Nephilim wavered silently on what was more torturous to witness; the sight of the boys looking like melting wax figures as they struggled visibly in the brutal, unforgiving heat beating down on their broiled hides, or that of the much more oppressive-looking men sporting long straggly beards and clad in camouflage lording menacingly over the young waif-like figures.

"Seriously? This is what we've been training to fight? They're a bunch of kids," Creed remarked with a sneering chuckle which instantly garnered a silencing glare from Anahel.

"I seem to recall a similar dismissive snicker when you thought the quest for the Illume involved nothing more than simple task of bagging a bird. Now, here you stand looking somewhat like a serving of baked Alaska," scolded Anahel before widening his gaze to the other boys. "You'd each be foolish to misjudge the severity of the bite your enemy packs in its fangs no matter the repugnant choice of guises in which it has chosen to dress itself on its latest outing. They are but emissaries of the horror to come—the seeds from which a field of unspeakable wickedness has been sown. A caliphate of evil."

The image on the floor morphed again revealing the impressive stone ruins of an ancient Semitic city whose history had touched the pages of the annals of the Assyrian kings. There the boys Anahel had deemed the messengers of horror were seen being led inside the ruins of a once-great amphitheater by their menacing handlers to stand behind a row of men positioned on their knees with their hands tied behind their back. Watching from the audience, more bearded men in fatigues sat as if upon springs, looking like hungry lions awaiting their feeding; and in their midst were several Infectors, lording over the ruins like the unmistakably menacing specters they were. Surprisingly, not a flicker of fear was betrayed by any of the boys while in the presence of the forbidding hovering shapes, including one of the boys who was suddenly ushered forward to stand behind one of the Christian prisoners. The boy, who appeared to be not a day beyond ten years of age, looked straight ahead with a chilling dead-eyed stare as an overly large hunting knife with a blade of serrated teeth was placed in his hand. The black headdress he wore framed a face that was at once as innocent as a lamb's. The eyes, however, told a completely different story, reflecting an icy— lifeless, even—vacancy. They appeared to register nothing, not the threatening Infectors, or even the presence of the man kneeling before him who was forced down onto his stomach at the child's feet. In a frightening instant, one of the Infectors was behind the boy and fed his ear a hissing of whispers which carried an unholy directive.

The Hall of Light became silent as a tomb as the boy removed the headdress from his head before he took hold of the prisoner by the hair and pulled back his head. The Nephilim then watched in growing horror as the boy's head slowly rotated a full one hundred and eighty degrees upon his neck. Far more unsettling than the unnatural twisting of the neck, however, was the unexpected sight of a second face when the back of the boy's head was suddenly and impossibly facing forward; and a nightmarish vision of a face it was. Two orbs of white absent pupils serving as eyes peered balefully from behind a visage that appeared to have been sculpted from black cinders. The ears were shaped like horns, and the grayish gums lined with a threatening grill of sickly teeth, twisted and overgrown, protruded from the confines of a frighteningly grotesque mouth.

Jacob instantly felt Max's whole body tense up standing beside him.

"It's one of them!" he heard Max mutter under his breath in a tone he rarely witnessed come from his friend: fear.

"One of whom?" asked Jacob.

"A Fury," Max replied with a reluctant gasp.

Now it was Jacob who felt the uncomfortable chill move through his body as he finally was given a glimpse of the terrifying terror that until then had only existed in his imaginings of the evil beings he had heard so much about. Even the darkest corner of his mind, however, could not have conjured up the reality he was witnessing unveiled at his feet, and he watched in stunned stillness as the monstrous boy who had revealed his other half to be an even far more unspeakable monster brandished the knife still clutched in his hand which he immediately put to use on the man at his feet without pause or flinch.

The barrage of unsettling images suddenly went dark and vanished from sight, much to thanks of most, if not all of the unnerved Fledglings who had been quietly watching.

"The world has seen evil rise up and take countless shapes, but nothing in its history will have offered preparation for what's to come," came Anahel's voice once more. "Like a worm gnawing its way through an apple, the Darkness won't stop until the spoils of the fruit have been consumed. A great war awaits you, the drumbeat of which has already sounded. It's wrath will bring with it death and misery of a great magnitude never before witnessed. For the multitudes, what remaining threads of hope still clothing mankind will unravel, the last breath of light from the candle of faith will dim, and darkness will fall upon the face of the earth in a way it has never before unfolded itself."

~ ~ ~

"I tell you this now, not to strike fear or despair into you," continued Anahel, "but to impress upon you the importance of this moment. For this night, you are being asked to reconfirm your baptism, not as young mortal men, but as Nephilim. Whether you choose to recite this oath within the four walls of this Hall of Light is solely upon you; not myself, nor your fathers from whom you came to be. You must decide whether to accept fully the place held for you on the front lines of this battle which draws itself ever nearer. But search deep within yourselves in determining your answer, and know that those among you who have been met with a change of heart, you are free to return without shame or judgment to the life you lived before coming here to Eden."

The boys stood expressionless under the weight of silence looming heavy over them following Anahel's words. If the grim reminder of the Darkness and the declaration of war promised by it was meant to cause sway in any of them, they didn't show it. Despite the day filled with good-natured competition and play, each of them knew the true mark of Illumination would unfold itself in the days and months to come. Their training was just the beginning, and even in the levity that came from the newness of their Graces and wings and unusual feats of strengths, the young teenagers never lost focus of why they had been brought to Eden, nor the duty or service expected from each of them. A great army was being formed of which they were each soldiers, and proud to be so.

"For those who have chosen to wade forth into the Illumination awaiting you, I ask you now to come forth so that you may pledge your oath of loyalty and service to the Light," instructed Anahel.

While it did not surprise Anahel to see every last Nephilim in the Hall step forward, it nonetheless filled him with an immeasurable warmth of pride.

"And to my brothers, I ask that you find your rightful spot behind your sons."

For a large portion of the day, Jacob had managed to put out of his mind the uncomfortable insecurities he wrestled with being surrounded by fathers and their sons. Now, suddenly, he found himself facing them once again. To his left, he spied almost timidly out of the corner of his eye Max beaming proudly as Gradiel came up from behind and gave a warm embrace to his son's shoulder with his right hand. So, too, did Creed's father, only it wasn't pride with which Creed beamed but a content-filled mocking sneer which he directed fully toward Jacob. It was then Jacob felt an overwhelming sense of aloneness, and whatever surge of self-worth and inclusion he had managed to feel in the brief moment his wrist was marked by the Illume's feather instantly vanished and was replaced by the more familiar feelings of being inadequate and out of place—enough so that his feet were ready to carry him out of the Hall. Then, suddenly, he felt a hand on his right shoulder. It had in its grip a knowing firmness, as if whoever was attached to it sensed rightly the discomfort that was about to make him bolt. Jacob looked over his shoulder and not surprisingly—or perhaps so—he found Gotham staring down at him with a soothing smile fixed upon his face. Only then did Jacob feel a comfort which had long eluded him settle within himself.

They turned forward and with Anahel leading the cue, the Hall of Light was soon filled with the echoing chorus of the Nephilim as they recited their oath, pledging loudly and wholly their everlasting loyalty and service to the Light. It was an unexpectedly moving experience; far different from saying the Pledge of Allegiance in class or reciting the Boy Scout oath, both of which flashed in Jacob's mind as he enunciated carefully each word as if they were, and would ever be, the most important ever to leave his tongue.

When they had finished, Jacob glanced at his wrist and was struck when he saw there was no sign of the glyph Anahel had branded onto his skin. Frantically, Jacob examined his arm, but it had, inexplicably, vanished without so much as a trace of a scar. Or so he thought until Gotham took hold of his arm and without explanation raised it with the inside of his wrist turned outward so that it came in contact with the moonlight shining down into the Hall. Only then did the sigil magically reappear, illuminated much like the Illume's luminous plumes.

~ ~ ~

The remainder of the night was spent in cheerful celebration. A rich buffet of food and drink filled the tables which the Fledglings unabashedly ate from with gusto to quiet their grumbling, hard-earned appetites. Even the angels, who only nibbled on occasion for the simple enjoyment and pleasure tasteful fare brought rather than necessity, partook in the feast. Music—a sea of strings—came from some unseen source, and its soothing melody moved about the Hall in the same sweeping fashion of a graceful couple waltzing across the floor.

However, the only thing anyone seemed interested in hearing was how Jacob and Max managed to successfully snare the Illume. The other Nephilim crowded themselves around the two boys and they listened intently as Jacob and Max took turns recounting the hunt. It was only when they described how the Illume morphed itself into a monstrous, fire-breathing beast did eyes begin to stray one by one; but then, only to glance across the room with cautious disbelief to where the bird continued to rest on its perch looking beautiful and delicate and graceful, and nothing like the nightmarish creature now being described to them.

One gaze, however, did not stray—from Jacob, anyhow. It belonged to Sandel. He stood by himself in a nearby corner of the room staring ahead at the boy with an intense coldness. Whatever he was thinking, or considering, was interrupted when Anahel came up quietly behind him.

"If I didn't know any better, Sandel, I'd mistake you for someone attending a wake rather than a celebration," said Anahel, to which came no response. Even without looking into the archangel's face, Anahel could see clearly where Sandel's attention was fixed. "I understand from Damiel you are considerably displeased with the boy's presence here in Eden."

"Does it matter either way my feelings?" asked Sandel coolly.

"In regards to me changing my stance on the matter, no, it does not," answered Anahel.

"Then we have nothing further to discuss Anahel, do we?"

"Do not ask me why or how, Sandel, but if this day offers any hints it is that this Fledgling will prove himself to be most remarkable. At least, that is what my instincts tell me. I can't explain it, but already I have found myself to be quite fond and protective of him even as I see his father in his eyes," said Anahel. "Just because something is seeded in darkness does not mean it won't thrive in the light. As the question was once posed to me, so do I now ask you: Don't we at the very least owe him the chance?"

Sandel was quiet for a moment, as though maybe he was considering having a change of heart on the matter. Or so Anahel hoped.

"Well then, Anahel, I leave it to you to see where the boy ends up thriving; in the Light, or the Darkness," said Sandel. "Let us just hope, for all our sakes, that your instincts have sharpened themselves from the last time you flipped such a coin."

As Sandel quickly stormed off, Anahel caught sight of Gotham watching the exchange from across the room.

"What's happened?" Gotham's voice sounded within Anahel's thoughts. Anahel gave a dismissive shake his head in reply. *"Just Sandel being Sandel, that's all."*

At the same time, Jacob was quietly watching Gotham from his own corner of the Hall. Exhilarated as he was, he couldn't keep his thoughts from wandering back to that moment in the Forest when Creed unleashed his bombshell concerning who, or rather what, his father was. And even though he had managed to shrug it all off with Max's help as a hornet's nest of lies unworthy of even Creed Maggert's caliber of nastiness, Jacob couldn't help but replay the unsettling moment over and over again in his head.

"Congratulations, Weed!"

It was Creed's voice suddenly transposed in his thoughts drawing Jacob's gaze to where he spotted his rival leering at him from nearby, his mouth poised in an unsavory grin. Jacob glanced away quickly and caught sight of Gotham huddled on the other side of the Hall with Damiel. *Could it be true?* Jacob found himself wondering. Why else would Creed be taunting him so blatantly?

"You're not actually still thinking about what that gator turd spewed to you earlier, are you?" came a voice suddenly. It was Max, suddenly at his ear.

"Of course not," Jacob lied.

"Cuz if you are, you can just walk yourself over there and ask Gotham point blank and put this whole thing to rest."

Not that Jacob hadn't been wrestling with such a suggestion, but as he stood staring over at Gotham, the more he became convinced Creed was yanking his chain. Gotham may have been a lot of things, but a liar he wasn't. Certainly he wouldn't knowingly deceive the boy over something as monumental as what Creed charged. This, Jacob knew wholeheartedly when Gotham, at that very moment, happened to look over and catch his eye. It was rare to see the angel look so outwardly happy, and more importantly proud. Proud of him.

No way was it true, Jacob thought to himself. No way.

"It's like you said," Jacob told Max. "That gator turd was just trying to throw me off my game, not that it did any good."

"Now that that's settled, maybe you can rejoin the fun," said Max, ruffling his friend's hair playfully. "After all, this is a shared celebration. Show a little happiness, for Pete's sake!"

And indeed Jacob was happy; happier than he could ever remember being before in his life. With smiles beaming, he and Max proudly held out their arms for the other boys yearning to get a glimpse of the prestigious sigil marking the inside of their wrists beneath the light of the moon hanging big and with magical brightness over Havenhid and the whole of Eden. Jacob knew the start of Illumination had been an important stepping stone, for him especially. He had finally managed to do what he had strived for since coming to the Garden, and that was to prove himself. Prove himself to Anahel. Prove himself to Gotham and the Guides. Prove himself to the other Fledglings. Mostly, though, prove himself to himself. And for the first time in the many months that had passed since he first arrived in Eden, he felt like a true Nephilim. Even despite the fact his back still remained absent a pair of wings. More importantly, he felt as though he belonged—belonged in Eden, and belonged amongst this special and unique group of boys.

And for the rest of the night—and for a good many days that were to follow—everything was exceptionally good.

CHAPTER THIRTY-ONE

"In all my many years of instructing Nephilim, I can honestly say I can't recall a more skilled bunch than these. I dare say this may be the finest brood we've yet to turn out."

The proclamation was made one afternoon by Damiel to Gotham as any proud teacher would of his students as the two strolled leisurely alongside the River.

"And in all my years knowing you, I can honestly say I can't begin keeping track of the countless times you've made such a boastful declaration," Gotham responded good-naturedly.

"Ay, but this time I mean it whole-heartedly," said Damiel "They are without exception, these Fledglings, and of tough stock. The ease with which they have taken to the sword, not to mention mirroring the angels' way of fighting when a blade is not in hand, is nothing short of impressive. You will see."

"And Jacob...," inquired Gotham finally, after a moment of pause, "how is he progressing?"

"I was wondering when you were going to get around to asking about him."

"Can you blame my curiosity?"

"Would it surprise you to learn that of all the Fledglings I'm training, he exceeds them all by leaps and bounds?" asked Damiel. "Rest assure when I tell you he displays a strength and speed of ten Nephilim. Even I've found it difficult to fend him off the times we've sparred together, hard as it may be for me to admit. That's why I wanted you to come today to Lions Bite so you can see for yourself."

"And yet, still no wings," muttered Gotham.

"He's not the first to struggle," Damiel offered in a comforting voice. "There have been plenty of other Nephilim who have been slow to come into their own."

"Only he's not like the others, now is he, Damiel?" replied Gotham with a weary sigh. "No...something is amiss, and it's not just the wings. It's been many months now and even the Blackstone is still somehow unable to read his Grace. Can you explain it? Because I am at a loss."

Damiel gave a glance over at Gotham and could see clearly the angel was weighted with worry over the boy. Yet try as he might for a semblance of an easing answer to the question posed to him, Damiel found much to his frustration that all he could offer was a meek, if not defeated, "No, I cannot."

It was then a pair of white-tailed deer frolicking in the grassy openness stretching out into the distance caught the two angels' sights, and they watched as the two graceful creatures bounded and scampered about without care beneath the soothing warmth of the sun.

"As I was leaving Eden," remarked Gotham after a while as they continued on with their stroll, "it was Anahel who, in his pointed way, reminded me of my duty to the boy, whether I chose to recognize it or not, and despite whatever grievances may continue to roil my insides."

"I can't say I could argue with him," said Damiel.

"It's why I chose to return to Eden," said Gotham. "But in seeing through what has been called upon me, I find myself needing to ask something from you; something I'm not sure I have a right to request."

"You can ask from me anything, you know that," replied Damiel.

"I'm glad to hear that, because I need your assurance that you will step in and take my place watching over Jacob should I be unable."

Damiel was visibly caught off guard by the request.

"Unable?" he echoed. "You just got through saying you were ready to embrace your duty to the boy, and now in the same breath it sounds as though you are already planning on taking your leave yet again, but not before entrusting Jacob's welfare into my hands."

"I have already made my promise to the boy, and I now make the same assurance to you that I have no intention of going," said Gotham vehemently. "I also have no idea what bends shape the road that lies ahead of me."

Despite Gotham's assurances, Damiel found the request surprising, to say the least.

"Why me?" he asked finally without giving an answer one way or the other.

"Because I trust you," came the angel's response, which Damiel found strangely flattering to hear knowing Gotham was not the trusting type. "More importantly, Jacob trusts you. And rightly so after coming to his aid at Broken Earth when the expectation of wings—and Eksel's role as teacher and guardian—failed him."

Of course, Damiel knew instantly Gotham was referring to the first day the Fledglings were first brought to Broken Earth when instinct sent him racing down to end Jacob's long fall from the cliff top while Eksel looked on without so much as moving a muscle.

"You've heard."

The fiery gleam in Gotham's eyes served as more than an answer.

"Eksel would be remiss in not thanking wholly our father for my absence that day," said Gotham. "He'd have suffered a fate much more severe than a bruised jaw."

"Hard as he sometimes makes it for us to see, Eksel means well," said Damiel. "We must be mindful his way of seeing things is mostly limited to two colors: black and white. Jacob, unfortunately, is a shade of gray seemingly lost to his color blindness."

"Which is all the more reason I have come here to ask you what I have today," said Gotham as he stood waiting to hear Damiel's reply to his request.

Before Damiel could give his answer one way or the other there came suddenly, in the distance, a desperate wail of a cry carrying Damiel's name. They turned to see Ethan coming up over a slope. He was running with all his might toward them with his sword gripped tight in his hand carrying the blinding glint of the sunlight in its blade.

"What on earth has sent you howling through Eden like some kind of wounded banshee?" asked Damiel with a grin when the boy finally reached them.

Though desperate to answer, Ethan stood stooped over grasping his knees trying to catch his breath from his long, hard run.

"It's Balantine...he's hurt...!" he managed to sputter through his strained gasping.

Gotham immediately eyed the sword clutched in the boy's hand and caught a stain of red on the blade. Grasping Ethan's wrist, he raised the weapon for closer inspection.

"And what exceptional display of skill has colored your blade, Fledgling?" he asked with calm concern.

"Huh?"

"This blood...where did it come from?"

"I'm not sure," answered Ethan. There was an edge of panic in his voice. "We were just messing around...sparring...you know, like Damiel instructed us to do. I don't know...I guess we must have gotten a little carried away. The next thing I knew Balantine cried out in pain and fell to the ground holding his leg. I saw blood...lots of it!"

Ethan barely finished his sentence when Damiel bolted. He was half a dozen steps into a fierce sprint when his form began to change. His body became hunched, bending to all fours so his hands could find the ground and join his feet to speed him in his run. And in a quick instant, he was no longer human, but a cheetah tearing across the grassy turf with wind-like swiftness toward Lions Bite.

"I didn't mean it, I swear!" Ethan exclaimed fervently to Gotham. It was not the time for apologies, and with a loud flap of his mighty wings unfurling themselves, the angel lunged for the sky with a strict directive to Ethan to follow.

~ ~ ~

Damiel reached Lions Bite with extraordinary quickness and as he passed through the large stone markers heading into the arena his form shifted once more to its angelic likeness. Without missing a step, he raced to where a group of Nephilim was seen huddled in a tight circle around a pair of feet donning dusty sneakers sticking out from within the scrum. When they saw Damiel approaching, the boys quickly stepped back to make room revealing Balantine, who was lying motionless on his back on the ground. He was conscious and didn't appear to be in any pain. Kneeling beside him was Jacob, who was applying pressure with blood-soaked hands placed one on top the other to Balantine's upper thigh.

When Jacob looked up and saw Damiel, there was a wide-eyed panicked look in his face. "I didn't know what else to do. It wouldn't stop bleeding. I think he may have cut an artery or something."

Damiel offered Jacob a calming smile while sinking to his knees opposite him, then turned his attention to Balantine who remained surprisingly quiet and calm.

"Now, you know why this place is called Lions Bite," he said. "Don't be afraid. You're not the first Nephilim to shed blood here."

"I'm not afraid," replied Balantine replied calmly. "In fact, I don't feel any pain anymore."

Damiel instructed one of the boys to fetch him some water from the River then gently took hold of Jacob's hands sticky with blood and tried to remove them from the wound, but at first Jacob was reluctant to relinquish his hold.

"It's alright Jacob, I can take it from here," said Damiel reassuringly.

Jacob looked into the angel's face and the smile that was returned gradually filled him with a peaceful ease. He relaxed onto his haunches and as he did Damiel felt the boy's hands slacken and slowly guided them away from Balantine's thigh. When Damiel lowered his gaze to examine the wound, however, a curious look came over him. The jeans Balantine wore were blood-soaked around the upper leg area, and it carried the unmistakable mark of a mishap involving swords in the clean tear without fray several inches wide in the denim.

There was, however, no wound.

Damiel pulled wider the slashed denim opening and searched more closely the flesh of the leg hidden for any sign of injury that would explain the presence of blood. Yet strangely there was no nick, no scratch, not even a bruise. And the kindly look of concern quickly fell away from Damiel's face.

"What is this?" he hissed before casting a suspicious leer upon the group of boys watching quietly and searched their faces for some tell-tale sign of mischief-making. It certainly wouldn't be the first time Nephilim engaged in a good-natured prank to help ward off the tediousness of their training, though no one had yet gathered the nerve to target an angel in order to get a quick laugh. And if indeed this was an attempt at such a prank, the stone-faced expressions staring back at Damiel offered no sign betraying their involvement. If anything, their faces carried the same dumbfounded expression as the angel, even as they strained forward by the neck to gain a peek at Balantine's leg, especially Jacob.

"So, how is it?" asked Balantine impatiently.

"Why not see for yourself?" grumbled Damiel.

Balantine quickly sat up and when he peered inside his lacerated jeans he beamed with delight, and relief, when he saw his leg was wound-free.

"Oh, thank heavens…you healed it!" he exclaimed happily.

"Heaven had nothing to do with it," Thaniel grumbled.

It was then that Gotham and Ethan reached the arena and hurried over to where the group of boys were gathered.

"I see you've made him good as new again," noted Gotham when he glanced at Balantine's leg and saw it was in perfect health.

"There was nothing in need of making good as new again," Damiel stated gruffly which only drew a confused expression from Gotham. Then, raising his hand to his face in order to look closer at the red coloring coating his fingertips, Damiel turned a questioning glare back on the group of boys. "The blood is certainly real enough, though I doubt any of you were dedicated to this bluff enough to have it squeezed from you, and I can only hope for all your sake it wasn't siphoned from some animal in order to harvest your laugh or I assure you the punishment for all of you will be of utmost severity."

"It didn't come from any animal!" said Balantine. "It's my blood. I didn't think it would stop gushing from my leg. I thought I was going to need a transfusion."

His declaration did little to erase the questionable look with which Damiel peered down his nose at the boy, which only seemed to raise the boy's rankle.

"Why are you looking at me like I'm lying. Look, these jeans cost me almost two hundred dollars—which by the way, Richert, you owe me a new pair," barked Balantine when he caught sight of Ethan standing nearby. "Do you really think I would ruin them for some lousy prank?"

"He's telling you the truth," Jacob intervened. "I saw the cut myself."

"Really?" replied Damiel dryly. "And how do you explain the fact that this cut is suddenly gone without any intervention from myself or Gotham? Have you got an angel stashed somewhere in your pocket? Or perhaps you've suddenly been gifted with the power to heal?"

The words, laced in sarcasm, barely passed Damiel's lips when his face suddenly darkened and, in a brief glimpse, Jacob saw a direful shadow pass across the angel's golden eyes before they turned away and settled on Gotham, who was held captive by the same stricken look. A hushed silence fell over the arena except for the chattering of birds fluttering about. Gotham stepped forward past Ethan and, in concert with Damiel, leveled his gaze at Balantine's leg and then back to where Jacob remained kneeling

"Perhaps, you should tell us what occurred here," said Gotham in a tone equally cautious as it was guarded.

"I'll tell you what happened," Balantine interjected before Jacob could utter a word in response to Gotham's inquiry. In a flash, Balantine was up on his feet demonstrating fully that whatever injury he claimed his leg suffered was no more. As he began reciting how he and Ethan had engaged in a friendly match of crossing swords, one couldn't help but compare the two boys standing in close proximity of each other and wonder how Ethan, who was noticeably shorter and somewhat slighter than the more athletically apt Balantine had ended up being the one with blood on his sword and showing no signs he had even been in a duel, friendly or not.

"Before I knew it," continued Balantine while focusing Ethan in his sights, "I was in a scene from 'The Empire Strikes Back' with Luke Skywalker here jumping and bouncing all around me in all these elaborate moves while swinging his sword—I'm sorry...I mean light saber."

The chorus of chuckles that came from the other boys gathered around only made the look on Ethan's face turn more sour.

"All I could do was stand here and watch the show this idiot was putting on when in the middle of one of his Jedi spams his blade caught my leg," Balantine explained.

"Accidentally," added Ethan fervently.

"Accidental or not, you still sliced my leg open! Not to mention ruined my favorite pair of jeans."

"Alright already, enough about the jeans you big baby!" balked Ethan. "I'll replace them with a new pair...Jesus."

He immediately felt the fire of Damiel's gaze turn itself on him at the sound of a name he knew better than to utter in such a flippantly vain way and offered a quick "Sorry."

"I thought I had made it clear what takes place within the walls of Lions Bite is not a game," Damiel reprimanded not just Ethan, but all the boys.

Gotham's attention, however, remained unwavering on Jacob. "And now I want you to tell me precisely what happened once you saw Balantine had been injured."

Jacob was silent at first, unnerved by the sea of inquisitive eyes suddenly cast upon him, most notably those of the two angels.

"I saw Ethan's sword strike Balantine's thigh, and even before I heard Balantine cry out in pain I knew he had been badly hurt," said Jacob. "We all rushed over to him. He was on the ground clutching his leg, so we couldn't see the cut at first. But we could see the blood. It seemed to be coming out in buckets and it was seeping between his fingers and running down his leg."

"Go on," prodded Damiel.

"No one seemed to know what to do, so I went to his side. I learned enough about first aid in school to know I needed to apply pressure to the leg in order to stop the bleeding. Before I did that, I grabbed my water bottle and I had Balantine remove his hands so I could wash away the blood and clean the area as much as possible."

"It burned like crazy at first," Balantine jumped in. "Like someone had placed a hot poker against my leg."

"That's when I could see how deep the wound to his leg was," continued Jacob. "I tore the bottom half of my T-shirt to tie around his leg as a sort of tourniquet, and once that was in place I quickly washed my hands and placed them one on top the other over the wound to keep the pressure applied."

"And then what?" pressed Gotham. Jacob hesitated answering at first as he became more uncomfortable with the gruff way in which he was being questioned. He was beginning to feel as if he'd done something wrong, committed some kind of crime, though he couldn't for the life of him figure out how helping a fellow classmate who had been injured could necessitate such a reaction.

"What happened then?" Gotham repeated curtly.

"Nothing!" answered Jacob. "I yelled for Ethan to go find Damiel and he ran off."

"And that was it? You didn't do anything else?" Damiel, whose demeanor was much calmer and more collected, though a dire urgency could be seen clearly upon his face, asked.

"No! I just knelt here and pressed hard against Balantine's leg. I could feel the wound pulsating against the palm of my hands as it forced up more blood. All I was focused on was wishing the bleeding would stop. That's it."

"Is the account he's told us true?" Gotham asked the other boys who were grouped tightly together in a circle around him. And in unison they nodded their heads.

"What...you think I'm lying?" said Jacob, sounding offended as he slowly felt himself becoming angry.

Damiel again knelt down and turned his attention to Balantine's leg. Pulling back the flap of denim where the jeans had been cleanly sliced open, he gently he ran his forefinger across the exposed patch of smooth pale skin and his brow crinkled in a show of puzzling curiosity when his eyes could find no sign of injury other than the red tint of dried encrusted blood. He turned and looked over his shoulder at Gotham. "What do you think?"

Gotham stood silent for a moment before he turned the fiery orbs which illuminated his gaze once more in Jacob's direction. As he did, Jacob felt a chill run through him. He had never felt fear of Gotham, nor had the angel ever given him a reason to fear him. Suddenly, however, Gotham was upon him.

"Come with me!" said Gotham.

~ ~ ~

Grabbing hold of the boy by the back of the neck, Gotham lifted him up with such force Jacob felt both his feet briefly leave the ground. He found himself tripping and stumbling awkwardly as his legs struggled to keep up with Gotham's swift pace as he was guided roughly out of Lions Bite. Once they were far beyond the earshot of the others, Gotham released his hold and Jacob felt his legs give way from underneath him sending him sprawling face forward across the grass-covered earth.

"Why did you not tell me you had this ability?" barked Gotham angrily.

"What's wrong with you? And could you be a little rougher next time?" snapped Jacob, rising onto his knees and brushing his front of the dried debris clinging to him.

"I asked you a question: Why did you choose to keep this from me? Speak!" The angels' voice rang out like a clap of thunder sending several startled birds scattering from their resting places high above in the nearby tree tops.

"Keep what from you? I have no idea what you're even yelling about."

"HEALING BALANTINE!

Jacob would have been taken back by such an exclamation had he not found it so preposterous.

"Excuse me?" Jacob, unable to keep from chortling at the preposterousness of such an idea, said.. "You think I healed Balantine?"

The angel stood silent, and his eyes alive with disbelief were fixed on the boy in such a way that Jacob began feeling uncomfortable, as if he suddenly found himself in the presence of a hulking cop accusing him of shoplifting from the neighborhood convenience store.

"Look, if anything healed his leg it was the water I poured on it from my bottle, which I filled from the River like I do every morning," said Jacob. "You heard Balantine say it himself; he felt a burning sensation when I doused his cut with the water."

"Water from the River does have healing powers, it's true," said Gotham. "But what undid the wound set into Balantine's leg by Ethan's sword could come only from someone with the true gift of healing."

Jacob felt tiny droplets of sweat break out across his brow, and he had no idea why suddenly he found his nerves roused in a discomforting way.

"I don't know what you want me to say," he said. "But I have no idea what happened back there with Balantine, or how it happened."

"You're lying to me," said Gotham. His booming voice had retreated to a calm tenor, yet strangely it was somehow more threatening to Jacob than the roar that sent the birds fleeing. "On Akdamar Island when I overheard you share with Johiel the story of when your friend Christopher was killed, there was something you said which struck me as curious. I asked you about it later as we were rowing across the Van Gölü to the island inhabited by the Powers; you said you had to be held back from going to your friend as he lay dead in the middle of the roadway after being struck by a truck. 'I can save him, I can save him' you said you cried out. I asked you what you had meant and I sensed then the answer you gave was not the truth. So now I ask you again, what did you mean?"

"The same as I told you before," answered Jacob. "It was nothing...just a stupid reaction from a hysterical kid. I'm sure a lot of people in the same situation would yell out the same thing."

"No...they wouldn't!" said Gotham emphatically with a dismissive shake of his head. "Not unless they truly knew they could. And you knew, didn't you?"

"Knew what?" Jacob all but screamed in his growing agitation.

"Knew you could save him, just as you had cried out you could."

"I'm telling you I didn't. It's just..."

There was suddenly a wavering uncertainty in Jacob's unwavering defiance.

"Just what?" inquired Gotham.

"Forget it, you won't believe me anyway."

"Try me."

At first Jacob was hesitant to speak.

"There was a time when I was young—maybe eight or nine. I could..." began Jacob.

"Could what?"

"Make bugs come back to life," Jacob finally offered with noticeable reluctance.

"Bugs?"

"I was out in the garden with my mother and came across a butterfly on the ground, a really beautiful butterfly," said Jacob. "I had never seen one quite like it before. It was deep blue and black with touches of bright yellow. I found it dead on the ground among the flowers...at least I thought it was dead. It had already started to wither, and holes had begun to eat their way through its delicate wings. But I sat there and just gently stroked it wishing it would somehow come back to life and fly away. Then, to my amazement, I saw the holes in the wings slowly begin to close and before I knew it, it was perched in the palm of my hand full of life again."

Jacob looked to the angel with the same unsettling expression staring back at him.

"After that, I found whenever I came across a dead bee out in the yard or a fly lying shriveled on a window sill, I could stir it back to life by just touching it with my finger and concentrating on it to move."

"Was that the only time?" asked Gotham in a quiet tone as though what they were speaking was secret in nature.

"Yes," answered Jacob. "I mean no...that is, I'm not really sure now that I think about it."

"Tell me," instructed the angel.

"A few days before coming here I was riding with my friend Wray."

"Go on."

"We hit this dog by accident...or rather Wray hit it," said Jacob. "I was sure we had killed it...I dunno, it wasn't moving. But then as I was petting it while Wray went to grab a blanket from her Jeep, I noticed the veins in my hands and arms—"

He stopped suddenly, as if suddenly afraid to say another word, especially when he noticed Gotham's expression growing more severe.

"I felt the dog stir...its eyes opened. Suddenly it got up and went on its way like nothing had happened..."

His voice trailed off as he stood thinking back to that day in the roadway before his thoughts shifted to the image of Balantine writhing on the ground in agony. It was almost exactly the same; two living things seriously injured one minute, and then perfectly fine the next after he.... It was then his gaze turned ever so slowly—almost fearfully—downward to look at his hands.

"This is ridiculous," he muttered to himself, as though to quiet his own uneasy suspicions he felt beginning to awaken. "Nephilim don't have the power to heal. Zuriel told us so the first day we went to the Crescent Scar. It's the one Grace we can't possess."

"Zuriel would be right. Yet here you are recounting to me the extraordinary feat of awaking butterflies and dogs from death's slumber," said Gotham.

The angel began briskly pacing back and forth, his heavy steps wearing into the grass-covered plain the makings of a faint path from which his feet left when he suddenly veered to stand looming over the boy once more.

"What made you not think to inform me of any of this when you had the opportunity?" The angel's voice once more roared making Jacob shrink back before mustering a courage to lean forward into it.

"Inform you of what? I didn't even think much of it. I just thought it was all...I dunno...a weird coincidence," answered Jacob.

"Bringing forth life where it had been snuffed out, and you shrug it off as a weird coincidence? Is it possible your mortal mind can really be that dense?" Gotham bellowed incredulously.

Jacob was now feeling his own anger rising up. He had more than put up with being physically dragged by the neck across Lions Bite and interrogated like some defendant squirming on a witness stand, but to be made to feel as though he had committed some grave, unforgivable sin, especially one he did not consciously know he had committed—and worse, one he obviously didn't even have control over—had pushed him to his limit.

"Maybe it is," Jacob hollered back. "Maybe I thought it was all part of this mysterious package called a Nephilim that suddenly out of the blue was dumped on my shoulders—literally—with no instruction manual. Maybe, if it was such an important thing, you should have asked me instead of leaving me to try and figure it out blindly on my own as I have everything else for the last sixteen years of my life."

Gotham was stunned into silence, whether by the words the boy spoke or the ferocious veracity with which he spit them forth, it was unknown. Whichever it was, it made the angel lower his head with weighted remorse close to Jacob's until their temples were pressed together.

"I'm sorry," whispered Gotham with a soothing tongue. Jacob felt the angel's hand once again clasping the back of his neck, only this time in a gentle manner.

"I'm sorry," he repeated, and the anger that had taken hold of Jacob slowly began to recede by both the comforting nature of the apology and the tender stroking across the back of his head.

"You have no idea what any of this means," Jacob heard Gotham say to him before the angel pulled back from his embrace and gazed down at him. "Do you?"

"Not the slightest," answered Jacob. "And seeing how it's made you react I'm thinking I want to keep it that way."

Gotham straightened himself and smiled knowingly while giving an affectionate tousle to the boy's hair.

"Come!" he suddenly instructed.

"Where are we going?" Jacob asked.

"To see the one person who must not only be informed with what's happened," said Gotham, "but who can hopefully help shed light on the bountiful questions to which we need definite answers."

~ ~ ~

The person of whom Gotham spoke, of course, was Anahel.

For many hours they remained in quiet counsel with him inside his chambers before the other four Guides—Zuriel, Damiel, Eksel and Thaniel—were summoned. There they remained in seclusion until the last remnants of day gave way to night, and the light seen shining from his balcony held steady its fiery glow long past the deepest hour of the night. And even when the sky began to lighten to make way for a new day and send the darkness into retreat, the movement of shadows could still be seen stirring about and mingling inside. More than once did the bellowing of arguing voices disturb the peaceful calm that had settled itself upon the Garden.

Only when the sun finally breached the crest of mountains extending like an outstretched arm in the east did Anahel step alone outside onto his balcony. Looking to the direction of the approaching dawn, his face, illuminated by the soft golden rays of the waking sun, appeared worn and weary as rarely seen amongst angels. A piercing shriek echoed in the distance and almost immediately five falcons came into sight gliding majestically against the lavender-colored skies. They swooped down one by one to land on the rail of the balcony where Anahel stood.

It was there they received their instructions from the angel, coming to them like a whispering breeze whipping its way along a mountain pass. Then, when he had finished, Anahel gave a wave of his hand and the birds once more took reign of the sky, and with the gravest of looks etched in his visage he watched as the falcons departed in five separate directions to deliver the most urgent of messages.

COMING SOON

Tales of the Nephilim Brotherhood:
Book Two

The Seventh Grace